I, TARGET

The Complete Series

BRUCE ROUSSEAU

Dark Teal Press

ISBN-10: 1505499909
ISBN-13: 978-1505499902

Acknowledgments

Heartfelt thanks to Sammye Johnson, David Rousseau, Susan Barker, Marti West, and Donald Bosart for their generous and supportive contributions.

Special thanks to my beloved Carol for believing in my crazy story ideas, and especially for wanting this one to be written down for others to enjoy.

To Carol
who transforms me

Table of Contents

I, TARGET
PART 1

1.1 It Must Be Said

This is my story and it begins straight-up with my death.

Yeah, truly.

My name is Marko Noviño Santana. To my mother, I am Marko Mijo. To my father, I never even existed.

I speak neither Serbian like my father, nor Spanish like my mother. But I ask that you do not blindly label me Euro-Latino. I am intensely American. Some might say I am the American dream: hard working, pragmatic, and something of a cultural mongrel. But just like the American dream, I am a work in progress. I live awash in blockbuster films, FPS games, epic game music, major league football, and even some playoff hoops. I am as all-American as any other white guy—with a permanent tan. And a somewhat hot-blooded nature.

I am Texas born, an awkward high school graduate, and an ingenious college dropout. But at 22, I am not stupid. I am genius—admittedly unpolished. I am as sharp as they come and often just as blunt.

I drive a taxi. I make my own way in life. You could say I have pride. Lots of it. It comes with the perma-tan.

As you hear my story, I ask you not to judge me for what I have done or what I have become. Only that you walk in my footsteps—for a life or two. Judge me then—not before.

As I live my lives, so I tell them.

And so it begins.

* * *

It was a humid Friday night in Austin, Texas. Overcast with some light drizzle, but still hot enough to remind you today had been near 100. You have to understand, it was only the first week in May, but full-blown summer officially starts here in late April. March is the bastard child of a globally screwed winter and the lobster-pot hell we call summer.

Like most Friday nights, I was trying to make the most of my cramped orangey-yellow office. The taxi.

It was 10:40 p.m., just about when Austin's airport rolls up its only sidewalk. The late night flights were dwindling down. So after dropping off my fare at the Driskill downtown, I started to cruise South Congress Avenue, as well as the downtown hotels, nightclub hot spots, and outlying bars and strip clubs.

Just so you know, airport fares are always predictable. Folks from the Midwest don't notice the high humidity, and the hot nights makes them think Texas is some sort of tropical paradise, which it ain't. Folks from California step off the plane and instantly know they're not gonna like it here. Folks from New York? They know they won't like it here even before they board the damn jet at JFK or LaGuardia.

Welcome to Austin, y'all. Enjoy the live music. Respect the dancers. Don't forget to tip your waitstaff.

Nightclubs, bars, wall-to-wall bands, gentleman's clubs. All do a booming business. Hard to believe the Texas Legislature only meets a few months every other year.

Lady travelers are what I call standard tippers. Pretty much 15% regardless of how helpful or rude I am. Yeah, I've tried it both ways. As for helpful tips on the local nightlife, only one out of a hundred ladies are ready to cruise. Sadly, I have to tell them the nearest hunk show is two hundred miles up the road in big D. Hey, lady traveler, I'm available. Not interested? Then we have a wide selection of drunk frats on 6th street. Just make sure to get your kicks before they barf some slightly used brews into your lap. Don't blame me, lady from Cincinnati. You should have taken my fine brown American ass when you had the chance.

Yeah, working alone can make you a little off-center. I guess truckers know what I'm talking about. I can't say I've ever met one, but every one of those guys must be felony-grade unstable. Especially if they spend much time tuned in to the tunnel-vision drivel being served up on talk-radio.

Anyway, the guys I pick up at the airport are a different matter. Suits get the lowdown based on my feel-out patter. Players are divided into two groups: rural johns and city jackasses. However, I do offer a select few the opportunity to get setup with some trusted ladies I know pretty well, but can't afford. But most suits get my casual warnings about undercover vice cops and the overcrowded jail conveniently located on 8th. One way or another, suits always leave the cab feeling like we've bonded and my advice was golden. And no matter how many drinks they've had on layovers and in their roomy business-class seats, they always seem to remember it's not their money—but it *is* their money if they don't get a receipt.

But the non-suits get the boring local weather report, and I set my tip expectations low enough not to be pissed. But I always wind up pissed by the male non-suits. Those guys are nothing more than a pile of disappointment stinking up the back of my cab.

Like I said, welcome to Austin. Don't let the sultry clime lead you to crime—unless you've got a local guide for the ride.

I made that up. Nobody says that in Texas.

Inside my taxi there's no big Latino cross hanging on the rearview and no bobblehead gang whatsit doing its thing on my dash. But under my seat I do keep a very sweet little .40 cal Glock with nine rounds in the clip and one in the chamber—all waxed hollow points for our mutual pleasure. And yes, I have a concealed carry permit. Welcome to the lone star state, stranger.

Okay, I've been driving way too long. A year and a half is too long for anyone. It gets to you. It turns your mind to mush. I used to have more ambition. Two semesters in college—assorted majors. It was a real hope for my mother that I could make it to a better life. She's big on respect. She always insisted I have it—respect from others as well as respect for myself.

But these days, it's drive as much as I can stand, play video games, drink too much, and try to do the right thing by my girlfriend. That's Marie Turner. Don't let the last name fool you. She's a mongrel like me, but reversed. White on the outside, seriously brown on the inside.

I know when Marie is disappointed with me. She doesn't hold

back. She's just that type. But I also know when she loves me. Sometimes I know I'm not worth it. But she gives me what I need, and even throws in a swift kick now and then. I deserve that, too. Her amazing love—her harsh words. She tries to make me whole. I can't leave her, and I hope down deep she can't leave me either.

I should probably say I found the taxi job through Marie. And maybe they hired me because I was half Serbian and it was Ethnic Oddities month. But however the hell I got in, I earned it. And I proved it every damn day with persistent hard work—and desperation. Desperation because the world runs on money and there's never enough down here at my level.

My girl was solid. Work was solid. Even if I had to earn both, day by day.

But I didn't know that it would be the night I died. Hell, if I'd known that, I would have gone to church. It's like, wake up people—don't leave the plane without a parachute. You know? Don't die without a priest giving you a big thumbs up.

Well, it couldn't hurt.

The last time I'd seen a priest, he'd given me a pat on the head. I naturally figured that'd hold me until I was an old man. Then I'd give one a call, get blessed and sprinkled in my hospital bed, and I'd be good to go.

But I have to believe that at some level I knew tonight would happen. Nothing good lasts. Nothing steady lasts.

Looking back, I think about that night often. I play it in my head like a broken record. And it always sounds the same. A small mistake. Something I could have prevented—should have prevented. A thing that cut through my life like a swift cruel blade.

So many people hurt by that simple twist in the way things went. So many people dead because of it.

My mother always told me I was special. I never believed it, but down deep I always wanted to. You know? It was comfortable to believe her, to believe I was somehow special. But I always knew it was a lie. Yeah, down deep I knew I was nothing amazing. But I was about to realize I was.

* * *

So I was driving that Friday night. The evening shift was slow. I only caught a few fares. Some shifts were just like that. I bonded with passengers I'd never see again. I flirted with a cute girl from Dallas. Of course I'm always thinking about Marie. Hey, a little flirting in the cab was harmless fun. Besides, I had that Dallas chick laughing and blushing. It made for a fun ride.

That brought me to about 1:45 a.m., maybe about a half hour from knocking off work. Time to head back to the countless bars along 6th street. I was down on South Congress so I made a u-turn to head north. One last pass on South Congress. I kept it slow.

Some light drizzle was hinting at rain. Always good for business.

The bars all close at 2:00 and that can be a great time to pick up fares. Something to look forward to as I headed north to 6th street. So I kept it going even though I was seriously tired and Marie had insisted on dragging me to some little kid's party in the morning. Just so you know, Marie teaches preschool. When I was a kid, teachers never went to student parties. Hell, no. They did their time during the day, wiped a lot of snotty noses, and tried not to yell too much at the little rats. But as sure as darkness follows the light, teachers went screaming into the night looking for something adult. That's how I met Marie. Halloween on 6th street. We were both zombies. Undead. Same cheap costume, too. She staggered toward me. I staggered toward her. She moaned and pawed my crappy costume. I did the same to her. Instant rapport. Who could ask for anything more?

So reading between the lines, it was totally obvious why I had to go to the little kid's party. Marie wanted to see how I'd do around the little monsters. Well, I knew not to punch them out. Other than that, being around them was just plain awkward.

Guys, we know the drill. Mess with their little heads all you want as long as they laugh. But we silently count the minutes. I have to admit some guys seem to enjoy the little trip hazards. But whenever I see that behavior, I shake my head and wonder how messed up that is.

Where was I? Oh yeah, trying to keep my brain alive while I drove my usual late-night route.

Fares were usually decent on scruffy South Congress. Plenty of motels charged by the hour down there. Vice cops were always down there, too. Maybe they brought the rookies for some on-the-job training. It was all just too easy.

Vice always seemed like a weird way to make money. I was pretty sure it suited anyone who liked a good costume party, followed by a cruel twist of fate. I've met lots of people who've bumped into a vice cop on duty. Fortunately, I'd never actually met one. We've got bumper stickers that say, *Keep Austin Weird*. I have no doubt local vice has a lot to choose from when they size up the new recruits to see who'd be a natural for vice detail.

But on South Congress, everyone looks like vice. That night was no different. But it was misting a bit, so maybe the vice squad was off somewhere sipping coffee in their van.

As I was making a slow last pass, two teens in hoodies stepped off the curb and flagged me down. Wrong type for this street. Who wears hoodies on a hot humid night? White guys at that. I'm good with the greasy older guys that reek of bourbon and aftershave. And I love mismatched couples looking for a vacancy sign. They're always happy to see me. Well, I was hoping these teens were just too drunk to walk home.

They weren't.

"Where to?"

"Oh man . . ." The guy who spoke looked around like he might be strung out on flammable products—yeah, since he was three. "Go south. Left on Dead Bluff." The other one laughed like it was an inside joke and turned to look out the window at nothing.

Great. Either the trailer park or the woods. Worst I can say about the trailer park is that I'd get hassled with a lame sob story and stiffed. However, the scruffy woods and drainage ditches were practically made for trouble.

I leaned over to start the meter, but mainly looked them over. As I did that, my left hand pulled the Glock quietly from under my seat. Sometimes you just get a bad feeling about things. It almost never happens. But when you get it, it's up and down your spine. "Got an address?"

"Nah. Just drive."

I ran the windshield wiper a swipe or two to pause and think about it a second. Just long enough to think it was nothing I couldn't handle.

I pulled away from the curb and made a u-turn.

The Glock rode uneasy under my left leg as I got on with the business of driving. I've cleaned blood off the back seat before, but never from one of my bullet holes. Actually, I'd never shot anything but paper targets. But somehow I couldn't stop thinking about a shooting scenario. Probably one of them would pull out a gun and aim it in my direction. Maybe he'd press the cold steel barrel against the side of my neck—nothing like a little emphasis. My Glock would slip quietly into my left hand. I'm not a lefty, but it's the best move from the driver's side. Then I'd turn to politely ask what the fuck. A few seconds would pass while they made their demands—time enough for me to decide their lifespan.

And that's what cabby's think about. We live in our heads. Occupational hazard. There's no escape, but sometimes we share the tedium and dark thoughts with another driver while in a taxi queue.

It's a shitty job and it caters to the antisocial corners we all have in our heads. Mine was well-developed.

"Pull over here, dude."

That snapped me back into the moment. They indicated a convenience mart at a gas station coming up on the right, and I was thinking they weren't going there to buy me a cold one or fill my tank.

I pulled in close to the mart's front doors and unlocked the passenger doors. I had second thoughts about that, but there was no easy call.

"Keep it running." One got out and the other one stayed in the back looking nervous.

Shit.

I casually shifted it into reverse but kept my foot on the brake. I thought that would give me more options.

It's all about actions, isn't it? Words are hollow little things. They're the yacky banter I have with passengers who are too uncomfortable to ride in silence.

So I was back in my head again. If both teens had bailed, then I'd expect to lose the fare. If both had stayed, I'd expect them to demand my cash, or maybe they'd just give me some stupid crap about needing drugs or sympathy.

One in, one out. Worst case, I'm their getaway driver. Then after a short drive I'm a witness they don't need. So now I had a few options. Drive off immediately with my new pal? Easy enough to lock him in. But that just seemed cowardly—not to mention dangerous if he got spooked. Plus a judge might see it as teen-napping. Or I could wait for his buddy to exit the convenience store. Yeah. What then? If he walked calmly back to the cab with a big grin and a 12-pack then we're just one big happy family. But if he ran like he was going to get shot by the clerk—well, that just led me to more nasty options I didn't even want to think about.

Front windshields are surprisingly bullet resistant because they're laminated. Being sloped helps a lot, too. I think I saw that on a Myth Busters rerun. Or maybe I'm dead wrong. But the other windows are easy enough to blow through with the first shot. And the thin metal bodywork is like cardboard—through and through, as they say.

The guy in the back seat opened his door just as his pal burst out of the store, swinging a big chromed revolver at me then back at the store. He fired one cannon blast through the plate glass window about where the cash register was, then he hopped in the back, laughing.

"Drive!" they both yelled, laughing and bouncing around like doped up maniacs.

My Glock was now in my left hand, and I turned to look at them like in a slo-mo bullet-time bad dream, gun held low and hidden from their view. It was aimed toward them, and gave me seconds to decide if I'd blow the hell out of them and my back seat, or save the carnage for down the road.

They suddenly went slack-jawed quiet. They couldn't have seen my gun. One let out an, "Aw, fuck." I turned enough to see the clerk marching up to the glass doors with a double-barrel shotgun rising slowly, his foot rising up to kick the glass door open.

My ears gave me instant pain, confirming a cannon shot fired from the back seat. Muffled sounds of passenger glass spraying outward. The clerk seemed to decide down was better than Clint-Eastwood-upright. A hand reached out of the shattered passenger window and fired three more blasts in quick succession. The convenience mart's doors went wild with crazed glass and jagged gaping holes. In the background, over-priced plastic bottles exploded their carbonated guts out.

I found my foot flying off the brake and my knees approaching my chest as I instinctively wanted to get small. But a half second later I forced it down, mashing my foot onto the gas pedal.

The shop receded in slow motion in front of me. The clerk seemed down—hard to tell. My gun tumbled to the floor as I grabbed the wheel with both hands and turned the cab sharply to keep my passenger from having another clear shot at the clerk. I slammed the brakes, which was good because it sounded like I'd just backed into a dumpster or another car.

Somehow this small parking lot had become a damned obstacle course. Shifting into drive, turning sharply to avoid the gas pumps, I finally got it headed toward the street. I caught a glimpse in the rearview of the clerk lining up his shot. There was traffic coming up from my left.

Then a boom, like thunder straight from hell, but also strangely muffled. Bits of everything hit the windshield in front of me and blew holes through it. And all I knew was that something was very wrong. I wasn't driving right. The dashboard slid past my vision like the world decided to roll over. My sight and hearing squeezed down to shut out the world as everything headed toward cotton-packed numb.

There was a timeless breath of pleasant silence before a muffled impact spun the cab sharply. Bumper cars.

It's not so bad here, I told myself.

A muffled sound. A few more.

I knew I could rest now—with no effort. Nothing hurt. Nothing needed my attention. All quiet. A time to wait.

1.2 Maximum Wrong

Sensory dark.

Then muffled sensations.

Then I was body-slammed into awake.

The first thing I fully remembered was tripping and falling face-down onto a wet sidewalk at night. But it was eerie because it was like I was already halfway down. The streetlights down the block cast long hard shadows as a light mist fell.

I sat up—everything body-awkward.

My hands stung. I must have scuffed them on the sidewalk.

I didn't feel right. Nothing felt right.

I just sat there on the sidewalk, blinking, staring at my hands. They didn't look right. They were stubby things. My fingers looked too short and my hands were puffy. My wrists were thick and hairy. My watch was gone. Stolen after the accident?

How'd I get here?

My clothes were all wrong, too. Nothing I'd ever worn before.

The inside of my mouth tasted bad, like an ashtray. I tried spitting it out. But more than that, the inside of my mouth felt all wrong—especially my teeth. My tongue repeatedly probed a missing tooth, obsessing on it, but it didn't hurt.

I needed more light.

As I stood up it struck me that I was wearing pants and shoes and a jacket that didn't belong to me. How long had it been since the gunshots and the crash? Did I have amnesia until now?

And then I almost fell over again, because standing full upright made the ground too close. *Too close?*

Bad lighting. Bad everything. I felt totally fucked up.

Another stumble and I almost hit the sidewalk again. I was too damn short! It was like I was trapped in a wraparound fun-house mirror, or . . . or maybe on some really weird crazy-shit drugs.

That was it! I was on drugs, which was a relief because it made a lot more sense. I relaxed a bit. It was good to know. Drug induced distortion. Sensory shift.

I stepped all awkward toward the nearest streetlight. I watched my feet take each weird step. Stubby shoes clomped along.

My hands instinctively searched myself, going through my pockets. I pulled out a cell phone. Great, but not mine. Keys. Also not mine. A pocket knife. Not mine, but it looked like a quality little blade. A sales receipt and a lottery stub.

My hands kept searching. There was a wallet tucked in the jacket's inside pocket. It had cash and cards, but it was too dark to see them clearly.

I ran as best I could to the streetlight. Hey, good news. My coordination was getting better. I was getting used to being drugged.

There was a driver's license. *Hugo Martoni*, age 39, whoever the hell that was. How did I get that guy's wallet?

Back to the cell phone, it said *2:19 a.m. Saturday, May 4*. I remembered driving the taxi Friday night. So of course, it was very early Saturday. Damn! Only about twenty minutes after I'd passed out?

I tried to think it through, but the gears were turning so slowly. What the hell was going on? Twenty minutes to get free of the wreck, change clothes, wind up with some guy's wallet—and get mildly high on LSD? Or peyote. Or some equivalent life distorting crap.

My drug of choice was a simple ale—nothing fruity or seasonal. Rum and coke if I could get it. But whatever drug I was on, I was eager to get off it.

As I looked around the mixed residential-commercial neighborhood, it dawned in the back of my mind that what I really wanted was a good mirror. Something flat that wouldn't lie to me. There was a parked car up ahead. That would do.

There were no streetlights near the car, but as I squatted next to the driver's side mirror, I took a cautious look. Some old guy was looking back at me! I stared at him. He stared at me. I touched the mirror like a damn monkey. His finger touched the same damn spot.

I put a hand on the car to steady myself and slowly stood to the sound of buzzing in my head, probably the sound of every neuron firing up at the same time, struggling to make sense of all this.

The only thing that made sense was that I was seriously messed up on mescal. Or something the ambulance guys had given me. Or I was enjoying a trippy coma. Or a trippy death.

Cool?

Not cool.

I needed to check the driver's license again. I held it next to the mirror as I crouched down to compare the images. The old face in the mirror was close enough to the photo on the license.

Standing slowly again, I felt no panic—just an urge to find out what drug I was on and slip it to some of my permanently stupid friends.

A walk seemed like a good idea. The next street light beckoned me.

Along the way, I wiped some drizzle from my face. That stopped me in my tracks. Fat nose, bushy eyebrows, wide cheeks, stubble, puffy ears, and what felt like wrinkles. It was one thing to see their reflection—another thing to feel them on me. It sickened me to know it matched the hairy man-ape I saw in the mirror.

Not good.

At the streetlight I dug through the wallet again. Lots of Hugo Martoni stuff and an employee ID that said he worked for the same convenience store chain that I'd just—

I quickly smelled my wet hands for burned gunpowder. Nothing. But looking again at my hands under the streetlight, my revulsion slapped me again. I was wearing someone else's hands. I had on someone else's face.

Hugo was all over me!

I spit. Someone else's saliva was in my mouth. Well, I guess it was technically his mouth, but that didn't make it taste any better. From the persistent taste in my mouth, it was obvious Hugo was a smoker. Maybe he'd smoked recently.

Addicted to cancer sticks? Not gonna happen, Martoni.

If I took off his shoes, I was sure I'd find his stinking dirty gorilla feet—his gross toenails that needed clipping. I didn't take them off.

If I dropped his pants, I was sure I'd find—

I wasn't going to look at it, or touch it! Ever! If he ever needed to take a leak, the pants would just stay on.

And no way was I ever going to wipe his ass!

I shuddered and it became an uncontrollable convulsion. I dropped his stuff. Hugo Martoni was a vile husk I needed to shake off any way I could.

A wave of nausea and dizziness knocked me down. I found myself sitting in wet grass. His jeans. His butt. Not mine. None of this was mine. *None of it!*

* * *

It was just the drugs screwing me around. Yeah, that was it. I told myself that again and again. Or I was shot in the head and this was the messed up result of my ruptured brain. I hoped the docs could fix it. Hospital anesthesia plus a bullet in the brain equaled this nightmare fueled hallucination.

No. My thinking was too damn clear. No pink bunnies. No visual weirdness, other than some kind of screwed up body-image. I was certain there was a part of the brain devoted to self-image and that's where the shotgun pellets were lodged.

Thinking back, I was probably shot in the back of the head by the clerk with his double-barrel shotgun. That was a jolly image. Buckshot or birdshot? Birdshot through the rear window, maybe through the hoodies, through my headrest, through my skull, and through the front windshield? Not possible. No way.

But buckshot? Now that seemed plausible. Both barrels? Absolutely possible.

A lot of things were possible.

Looking around me, the street at night was absolutely real. All my senses confirmed it. Confirmed it with absolutely no distortion. The night was totally real. I was totally sitting in wet grass.

My only problem was that I was now in Hugo Martoni's disgusting body. Another option? I was dead and this was my hell.

Living small in my killer's gross-out body. A really good definition of hell.

Nah. Too simple. Too weird.

Besides, hell was supposed to be hotter than Texas.

So I picked myself up from the wet grass. Time for a sanity check. I decided to use Hugo Martoni's phone to make a call. His minutes. He owed me. Who to call? Why wake anyone other than my sweetie, Marie?

Perfect. She could call around and see if I was admitted to a hospital. See if I was still alive or not. Man, I wasn't sure how I'd deal with either answer.

That might seem like really messed up logic, but all gamers know, if you're in-game you play the game. When you've stepped into the Unreal Zone, you do as the Unreal Zoners do.

Something like that.

Hell, I wasn't going to just sit here waiting for the sky to open up and a giant brain surgeon to peek in on me.

I dialed Marie's number. It rang.

"What!" She sounded really annoyed.

Yeah it was late, but just wait 'till she heard my story. "Hey, babe. It's me." My voice sounded weird.

"You're drunk. Sober up before you go calling people late at night."

Dial tone. She was gone. I dialed again. Only one ring.

"Look, you!" She was pissed. Pissed, but just warming up. "Leave me the hell alone!"

"It's me, Marko. There's been a wreck."

Marie paused. "Who is this? One of Marko's wasted friends? Take your sick jokes somewhere else."

"There was a shooting . . . and a wreck. I know this sounds really weird, but—"

"What's weird is you and your sick sense of humor. So take your comedy routine somewhere else!" She tossed in a "Sicko" as she fumbled for the hangup button on her cell.

Dial tone. She was gone. I dialed again. It rang. And rang. Then voicemail.

I hung up. What could I say? What could I possibly say? I

sounded like Martoni, I could hear it in my voice. She thought so, too.

Not the reality check I was hoping for.

I should go to her apartment and—

And what? Ring the doorbell? "Hi, I'm Marko, your semi-dead lover. Hey, I know what you're thinking: I look like some hairy old Italian guy. Well it's been a really rough night. Let's curl up in bed and I'll tell you all about it."

That could go really well.

Yeah, right.

Even if she believed me, what would I say then? Maybe something like, "I'm feeling kind of dirty, babe. I really need a shower, except I don't want to touch myself 'cause I weird myself out. So maybe you could just grab the soap and like—"

At that point I stopped my thoughts in their tracks. I needed help. My mental health was not so good.

Yeah, that was a major understatement.

Would my mother or my friends take it any better? No. It wouldn't take much to push them into a 911 call.

Standing there, slowly getting soaked, I felt so completely lost. I felt mugged by the weird night and my internal darkness. But the worst part was I had convinced myself I was in Martoni's body.

I was now the damn clerk who'd shot me.

I debated getting help from the cops. Yeah, maybe they'd understand. They were an understanding group of guys. Oh, yes they were. I could just picture their laughter, getting such a ripe comedy-case on the night shift. Nothing like lots of capital-murder paperwork, punctuated with another zinger about body snatchers.

Which led to the question of where exactly was the real Martoni, anyway. Did he even think about waiting for the cops so he could explain his return fire? This was Texas after all. Even if it wasn't exactly self-defense, it was arguably community defense. Hell, Martoni stopped a freakin' hoodie shooting spree. Given a clear line of fire, plenty of cops would have opened fire on a fleeing vehicle.

It seemed likely that Martoni fled before the police arrived. Right? I looked down at what I was wearing. It looked about right for the clerk's clothes except for the jacket. So Martoni ditched the shotgun, grabbed his jacket, and fled? He ran for a while, then got tired and walked? Maybe he smoked a cigarette to calm down? He finally walked down this street? Headed where?

And out of nowhere I got a glimpse of a small house, chain link fence, tired old mutt with bad breath, and in every room a cluttered mess. Martoni lived there, and he lived alone—if you didn't count the dog.

Codardo! The dog's name was Codardo. It meant fool in Italian. And how did I know that? Martoni's brain? Mental cohabitation?

Holy crap! I must be thinking with his damn brain!

I shuddered. He was in here with me! I could feel it—him in here—with me. Creeping around in the shadows. Like—

Damn. I was back in the mindset that I was Martoni. I hated myself again. Mainly, I really needed to ditch the body I was in.

Then what? Back into my body? Which was where, exactly? At the hospital? Chilling on a cold metal slab in the basement? Waiting for paperwork and a positive ID?

I needed to talk with someone. I needed confirmation. No, make that serious help. Yeah. I needed some serious shit-fixing help. Who from?

There was my mother. Couldn't call her, she'd freak at the weird Martoni voice. Texting was an option, except she couldn't tell a text from a phone burp. Texting Marie was a great idea, except it should come from my phone, not Martoni's.

Where was my phone anyway? I'd watched enough TV to know it was in a property bag hanging next to my toe-tag. Unless I was in a body-bag. The zippers were near the head. That meant the—

Options. I needed options.

I needed a friend. A reliable one who wouldn't freak. I knew reliable ones. And I also knew bongheads who'd actually believe anything. No overlap.

Martoni's dog would sniff me and wag his little butt off. Same for Martoni's friends. I could pass for Martoni anywhere.

Cool.

Semi-cool. I didn't want to be Hugo Martoni.

Martoni's house was just three blocks down, then a right, and five blocks more. How did I know? Again with the Martoni flashes.

I walked slowly on my way to Martoni's house.

Two blocks later I ground to a halt. Wouldn't the cops have a few questions for this Martoni character? They knew where he worked, so they'd know all about him. They'd be knocking on his front door.

I checked the time on his phone. 2:42 a.m. Enough time to look him up and drop by for a chat? Time enough to get a search warrant? How fast do cops work, anyway? They had almost instant transportation on crime shows. No way they could really be that fast.

All the same, I decided to take an indirect route to the house.

So what did I need at Martoni's, anyway? A leg hug and some licks from his dog, Codardo?

Besides that.

Cash? Always good. Guns? No guns. I'd had enough of guns for one night. Phone numbers? I already had plenty of contacts on his cell. Food? Pills? Damn, what if this guy had medical problems I didn't know about?

I had his keys. I wanted to borrow his car. I got the funny impression of an old brown truck. Okay, so he had a truck. My truck now? Yeah, my truck.

Why didn't you take the truck to work, Martoni? You just like walking in the drizzle?

No answers.

A short block later I spotted the tail end of a police car in an alley. I froze.

No reaction from the cop. I was partly obscured by some trashcans, but I turned my head a bit to see if I was silhouetted. Things were dark all around, so I backed slowly out of sight.

If I worked my way closer to Martoni's house, what would I find? An unmarked police car sitting quietly a half-block away? A raid in progress? I didn't give a damn about Martoni. But I found myself thinking about mangy old Codardo, waiting patiently for Martoni to get off work. Poor little guy.

I could almost see Codardo. Scruffy, ugly, and fiercely loyal.

Hell. Why exactly did I care about Martoni's mutt? Was Martoni's brain trying to push me out? All I knew was that I cared about Codardo and wanted him to be okay. Actually, it was a weird and very intense feeling I was having about the dog. Hey, I like dogs and they like me, but it was freaky to feel so attached to one I'd never even seen.

I decided not to think about it anymore. Cops like dogs and I'd just leave it at that. Codardo would be okay. Maybe better off. I reminded myself I was only there for the cash and the truck. Maybe some supplies.

I was sure it wasn't an easy life, being Martoni's dog. I was also sure it wasn't going to be easy for me—being Martoni.

At that point I was determined to like myself, even if I hated my body. Maybe I wasn't the first to have to deal with that. But it was a mini-revelation. Like saying, *I am not my body*. I really hated being Hugo Martoni. He disgusted me. But it seemed like I had no choice.

Play the cards you're dealt, Marko.

1.3 Escape

Hiding under a wet bush in the drizzle, I tried again to imagine what I'd find at Hugo Martoni's house.

I got nothing.

I tried harder. Still blank.

So, what was that about? I'd lost touch with Martoni's memories? Well, screw that. I didn't need Martoni's memories. Or his emotions about the dog. Speaking of the dog, I was now feeling ambivalent about the little guy.

I held still in the bushes while a suspicious dark brown sedan drove by slowly.

That's when it occurred to me that Martoni's truck would be under a corrugated metal roof on the side of the house. A carport. It needed some repair, not to mention some paint. There was paint in the laundry room, and some tools. Everything was a clear mental image. That's where I left the truck . . . where *he* left the truck.

Okay. I tried to picture where the cash would be.

Nothing.

And just like that, it was all blank again.

So I looked down at my hands. I was getting used to the stubby fingers—the heavy wrists—Martoni's hands looked strong. Stronger than my old ones. I could do things with these hands. They'd need to be scrubbed clean. I didn't want to even think about where they'd been.

The cash was in a shoebox in the hall closet. There wasn't much—about $200.

Great. So where exactly was the hall closet? Blank again.

The more I tried to access Martoni's memories, the harder it was. The more I focused on something else, the easier it was. I decided Martoni was more like a subconscious thing. Always there, but nothing I could force to the surface. I felt like the driver, and like

Martoni was a quiet passenger in my back seat. If I tried to strike up a conversation, he'd go quiet on me. If I shut up and drove, he'd get chatty.

So there it was—the perfect analogy. It was a lot like driving my cab, dealing with a self-centered passenger. I knew that game all too well. Drive. Ignore the passenger. Keep it subtle. Let them do the talking. They weren't interested in meaningful dialog with me, so skip the outright questions. Touch on a subject and sit back and let them rant.

Yeah. Martoni's body was my vehicle now. Martoni was just along for the ride. Screw you Martoni—I just figured you out.

So where was I? There'd be an unmarked cop car somewhere on Martoni's street. I was just guessing about that part, but it seemed likely.

Sneaking up to the truck seemed doable, but driving off with it was going to be difficult. What could go wrong with that? A chase resulting in me behind bars? Seriously bad. Followed by a trial and Martoni convicted of a crime I didn't commit? Killing myself? The current me, Hugo Martoni, convicted of killing the original me, Marko Santana?

Harsh. Not to mention seriously twisted.

Why was I so obsessed with going to Martoni's place, anyway? All I had to do was go to my apartment. Brilliant!

All I could say was: Martoni's ideas sucked.

Note to self: Don't let Martoni drive. He'd lead me right back into his life. I had an image of Martoni as a zombie passenger. Great—a dead semi-controlling zombie passenger riding in my head. Martoni's head. My head! Whatever.

I sure was arguing with myself a lot.

Focus, Marko. Focus.

Okay, what about my apartment? Would the cops be there? Yeah, maybe, if they were looking for my next of kin. But somehow I got the impression they'd skip the legwork and make phone calls instead. That's what I'd do. Call the relatives. Don't tell them Marko was dead. Just let them know it was serious and they'd, uh, need to go to the hospital where his body . . . where he was taken.

How was I going to get into my own apartment? No keys, so

break a window around back? Ground floor made that easy. It would have to be quiet. Food, beer, some cash, a spare set of keys awaited. My ATM card, too. No fighting with Martoni for the PIN number. Nothing wrong with my memories, even with Martoni's head.

Well, my clothes wouldn't fit me. And unfortunately my car was at the taxi yard behind a gate.

Going to Martoni's was a stupid idea, so I set plan B into motion. I moved carefully out of Martoni's neighborhood. Forget Martoni's truck. Grab my stuff and go get my car out of the taxi yard. Leave town. Leave Texas. Martoni's face was too hot for Texas.

Hey, Martoni. Why'd you bolt? Got priors?

No answer from my passenger.

* * *

As soon as I was on South 1st street I walked north. My apartment was about ten miles up the road and several blocks east. I needed a ride. South 1st looks kind of iffy, but it really isn't so bad. Still, I didn't like the idea of sticking my thumb out. What I wanted was a taxi.

The farther north I got, the closer to downtown Austin and the likelihood of finding a cab. And if I got tired of walking in the drizzle I could always use Martoni's cell phone to call a cab. That would be weird. I could ask for Earl. He was cool and kept to himself, which was what I needed.

Walking along, I was mindful of police cars. Chances were good there'd be some.

I looked behind me. A taxi was coming, driving a bit slow. A bit of luck. About time, I'd say. So I turned and flagged him. He saw me right away and started to pull over, moving slow.

The headlights were in my eyes and I was sure he was sizing me up: a wet little Italian man in a black leather jacket that wasn't meant to be worn in the rain. And I was dirty. As a driver, I'd be considering if it was worth it to wipe off the back seat after a mess got in.

I guess he decided it was worth the risk and the mess, because he pulled to a stop and waited for me to get in.

I bent over to open the back door, and to see who was driving. Earl looked back at me, his wide black face looking a bit skeptical about what he saw.

That really unnerved me. I'd thought about calling the company and asking for Earl, and now here he was.

Damn! That's the kind of crap-coincidence you get in dreams. Was I dreaming? Or maybe it was fate messing with my mind—what little I had left—what little I could call my own.

I slid in and pulled the door closed. Good old Earl. Quiet. Not stupid. Kept to himself, unless the subject turned to sports, then he'd get loud and animated. Seemed fond of the Lakers for some crazy reason.

"Where to?" He sounded cautious.

I couldn't help but wonder if he kept a gun handy.

"Uh," I thought better of being dropped off at my apartment. The neighborhood would be close enough. "51st and—" No, I should get my car first. The fewer taxi rides, the better. "Make that Bluff Bend Drive and Collinwood." There were some apartments there. Not mine. "I'll give you directions," I added.

He shot me a look in the rearview. "I know where it is."

Of course he knew where it was. Only a couple blocks from the taxi lot. But that look—it said quite clearly that he was suspicious about me. Yeah, I felt the same way about passengers who seemed to be pulling destinations out of their butt.

He drove. I dripped on his back seat. I liked Earl, so I tried to keep the puddle small.

He glanced at me a couple times.

I made something up. "Car trouble." That would explain why some guy was walking in the rain late at night.

Earl gave me a longer glance in the mirror, but kept quiet. I'd do the same. Let the wackos do the talking.

As we drove I wanted to tell him about the hoodies, the shotgun blast, the crash, and winding up inside Hugo Martoni's body. I wanted to say Marko Santana died tonight, but was reborn—just not in a good way. I wanted Earl to go to Marie and tell her how much I loved her, but there were events outside my control. She'd cry her beautiful brown eyes out. Earl would tough it out—be a rock for her as she cried. I wanted it to be just like in the movies.

Hell, I just wanted to wake up in the hospital with my head wrapped up. I wanted Marie to be there and tell me I was going to be okay, even if it was a lie.

I wanted my own damn life back.

We pulled up in front of the apartment manager's office. I was tempted to pull out one of Martoni's credit cards. He owed me. But I didn't want a trail for the cops. The less information people had about Martoni's movements, the safer I felt.

I handed over some of Martoni's cash, including a good sized tip. "Sorry about the mess in the back."

He noticed the tip and almost smiled. "It cleans up."

I was sorry to watch him drive off. I really needed a friend.

* * *

A few minutes later I was outside the chain link fence surrounding the taxi lot, staring in. Getting through the security fence and out with my car would be a problem. But a bigger problem was that I didn't see my car in its usual spot. Not good.

I walked along the fence trying to remember if I'd parked it somewhere else. And there it was, parked on the street with several other cars.

That made no sense. Sure, I sometimes parked on the street. But I hadn't done that in weeks. I would have remembered that.

Earl had arrived when I'd really needed a cab. Now my car had moved to the street when I'd really needed it. Reality wasn't doing its usual thing.

Or maybe it was just my memory that wasn't doing its usual thing. Or maybe reality was somehow intertwined with memory?

I walked slowly to my car, sensing it was a trap. Everything about tonight was beginning to feel well laid out. Too planned to be trusted.

Paranoia. Lovely clusters of shadowy paranoia tinted everything.

Yeah, the way things were going, adding paranoia to my mental mood felt about right.

I pulled out my car keys. They were all wrong.

Oh yeah. I should have gone home first to get my keys.

Oh yeah. Martoni's brain had somehow persuaded me that I already had the keys.

Well, crap.

Martoni and I were headed for a fight.

* * *

After walking south about a mile, I crossed under the freeway and found a small hotel. Standing in their parking lot, I pulled out my Martoni-phone and called a different taxi company for a ride. Easy for a driver to find. Less suspicious than being picked up in an unusual place. Ten minutes later I was dripping on another cabby's back seat.

He tried to chat me up. I wasn't in the mood. Not a fun ride for either of us. Not to mention it burned through the last of Martoni's cash.

As I walked around to the rear of my apartment building, it was just me and the local loudmouth tomcat—the one I often wanted to hit with a shoe when I got in late after my usual night shift. He was gray with an oddly wide head and a scrawny-fat body. Pretty much what you get when you're a well fed stray with a bad attitude.

He watched me as I approached my bedroom window.

I scowled at him. He stared back at me like this was his own personal window.

I used Martoni's useless keys to help pry out the screen.

Using the leather jacket, I muffled a blow to the glass. It cracked but that was about it. Double paned glass. I used the key to quietly remove some of the broken outer pane, then smacked the window a couple times to get the inside pane to break.

A sheet of glass fell inside, bounced off a nightstand, and tinkled as it settled on the carpeted floor. From where I was standing it was seriously loud. Neighbors were probably calling the cops. Time was rapidly slipping away.

The damn cat just stared at me like I was doing the right thing. Yeah, this was cool for him to watch. Some shady Italian guy breaking into Marko's place. Cat justice.

I reached in, flipped the latch, slid the window open with as little blood and new broken glass as possible, pulled the drapes aside, and squirmed in without knocking too many things over. Looking back there was a bit of blood on the broken glass. Martoni's blood, not mine. They'd blame him. No time to wipe it off. No reason to.

Like it or not, Martoni's crimes would only multiply with everything I did.

As fast as I could, I grabbed my spare keys, some cash, a credit card I was trying not to use, and a duffel bag. Into the bag went socks, underwear, an old Beretta 9mm with ammo, lots of assorted food, and some basic tools I might need later.

I tossed the tools out because I remembered I had tools in my car and the bag was getting really heavy.

In the bathroom I took care of my small cut and added the usual travel items to the bag. Looking at myself in the mirror was a taste of hell to come. The toothbrush gave me pause, too. Brushing Martoni's teeth—not looking forward to it. And, yeah, I added a fresh roll of toilet paper to my bag. Not a good day. Worse days ahead.

I would have loved to have put on something clean and dry, but my clothes didn't fit my new body and I was eager to get out of there. But I did dump the soggy leather jacket and grabbed a windbreaker, plus a small umbrella.

One last glance around. Time to get the hell out.

Marie's photo caught my eye. Damn! I wanted it. So I took it. They'd really think Martoni was some sick bastard.

The front door was within reach. But I was forgetting something. My brain yelled, *Go*, but my feet refused.

Something for mom and Marie.

I grabbed some paper and a pen. Separate goodbye letters? No time. One for both of them? Too weird because how did I know I was leaving. Not to mention I never wrote letters. They'd think it was from Martoni and it would make their skin crawl.

Not a letter, then. A simple note to myself. A to-do list. Perfect. So I wrote:

-Get the left rear tire checked, valve stem probably leaks
-Find a better life than driving a cab at night, Marie deserves it
-Visit mom more often, take her to dinner
-Tell Marie I love her. When's the last time I did that?
-Same for mom
-Save some money for a vacation
-Stop buying booze and games and pay off the damn Visa bill
-Iron a shirt or two
-Stop being so selfish, life isn't about me, it's about how I treat
  others
-Go to church once in a while

I crossed the last one out and added:

-No need to go to church, God's everywhere if he's anywhere
-Find out if God hates me. If so, just deal with it
-Love while I still can, life's too damn short to screw it all up
-Buy some multivitamins

Good enough. I placed my to-do list on my dresser and walked out the front door. No need to lock it. The only real thing of value in my apartment was my to-do list.

Five blocks later—no sirens. I was kicking myself for not taking longer. I was starting to think of things I'd forgotten to bring. I was wishing I'd done a better job with the to-do list.

* * *

Blowing Martoni's cash on taxi rides was one thing. But for some reason, my hard earned cash was completely different. So I walked the five miles back to the taxi yard.

As I got to my car, morning was about to raise its dangerous head, so I made it quick.

Mexico was out. Louisiana and Oklahoma were hundreds of miles away. New Mexico was even farther. But I liked the idea of hanging out on some beach in Southern California, so west it was.

I needed highway 290, which was south a few miles. I stopped at an all-night quickie mart to use my ATM card and grab as much cash as possible. $500 seemed to be my bank's limit for one day so that's what I got. Anyway, $500 just about tapped out my account.

What the cops got was a video of Martoni pulling up in Marko's car, standing at the ATM pulling out Marko's money, and flipping the finger at the extra ATM fees. And this was on I-35 south of the apartment break-in and the car theft so they probably thought I was aiming for sunny Mexico.

While I was still at the ATM I asked Martoni for the PIN number to his credit card. He was mute on the subject, so I hauled his sorry ass back to my car and we drove off in silence.

* * *

Highway 290 got me to I-10 west. I was a bit surprised by the 80 mph speed limit on I-10. I like *yee-haw* as much as the next guy, but mainly I hoped the tires would survive. Three hours out of Austin I pulled over in Junction to get gas and empty Martoni's bladder. It went as expected, gross-out factor and all.

Next on my list was to snag someone's license plate. In Texas you're required to have them front and back, but somehow local law enforcement had bigger fish to fry. So it seemed that plenty of cars had no front plates. And that's what I wanted. Take both of mine off and borrow someone's front plate for my rear. They wouldn't get pulled over for a missing front plate and neither would I.

The old guys said Texas used to put its registration and inspection stickers on the rear plates, but the stickers were getting stolen (at least that's what people said when they were pulled over because they hadn't renewed them), so we switched to stickers obstructing the driver's front windshield. Now front and back plates were identical.

Ideal for borrowing plates.

I was driving a silver Civic, so that's what I wanted as a donor. I drove around looking for the local Walmart, but somehow Junction didn't seem to rate one. Several hotels and other parking lots, though. I found a silver Civic, even close enough in age.

I unscrewed their bolts and grabbed the plate. I drove off to a private spot to do the swap. Both of mine wound up in a dumpster and the new one was on the rear. Unlikely the owner would see their front plate missing anytime soon. And even then, maybe they'd just think it fell off. If they did report it stolen, would the cops put out an APB on a silver Civic with those plates around Junction? It seemed to me they'd just pull over the poor donor, then give up and find something else to do.

The duffel bag wound up in the trunk and my old Beretta handgun made itself comfortable in the glove compartment.

No breakfast in Junction. I needed distance between myself and Austin.

1.4 Are We There Yet?

I found out there's nothing between Junction and Fort Stockton. But between Fort Stockton and El Paso there's even less.

So about forty minutes past Fort Stockton I was having deep regrets about not stopping there for lunch. I'd survived my own death and was coping heroically in Hugo Martoni's body. I deserved a treat. A sit-down meal at one of Fort Stockton's finer establishments was in order.

I did a u-turn and spent the whole forty minute return trip telling myself that I didn't deserve it and reassuring myself that I did deserve it.

Fort Stockton's finest was apparently Jolly Bob's diner. After circling the diner and seeing no kid-friendly playground, I decided I could eat there in relative peace, bathed in whatever relaxing '80s tunes they pumped in to keep their diners happy.

I parked a block away on a side street just in case, and made sure everything was tucked away in the trunk or the glove compartment.

A short walk and I was standing in front of Jolly Bob's staring at a newspaper stand. Martoni's mug wasn't on the top half of the front page. I would have bought a copy, but I didn't have any quarters. Maybe on the way out I'd get one and see if I needed to swing by a costume shop.

Inside I was greeted and offered a seat on a barstool, but I was feeling expansive so I asked for a cushy booth.

With a menu in my hands and a whole pot of coffee on my table, I felt a bit like a king. A tired king, but still really good.

I ordered eggs and Texas toast. Hash browns, too. The sausage looked irresistible. Hand squeezed orange juice. A side order of steak fries. Blueberry pancakes—better make that just a short stack. Ham! Yes, but stick it in a farmer's omelette.

As the waitress was turning to go, I added a side order of biscuits and gravy.

That's when Martoni requested a trip to the toilet.

I was tempted to say no. I really was.

I was because it was suddenly clear that he was driving this entire pit stop. I was exhausted from events and lack of sleep, and apparently I'd let my guard down. He was hungry and this was his idea of a royal banquet. Hugo's usual lunch and dinner probably involved whatever wasn't selling well at his gas station and needed to be put down.

Apparently saying "*no*" to his toilet needs wasn't an option. So I yielded to his disgusting urges and trudged along to Jolly Bob's men's room.

Martoni gave me his memories, if I didn't try too hard to get them. And Martoni gave me his basic urges, something I never asked for. The rest of Martoni's brain seemed to be all mine. And for better or worse, I was now in charge of his bodily upkeep.

As I sat in the men's room, I resolved to put some fresh cantaloupe and steamed broccoli into my new furry little Italian body. Martoni would just have to suck it down.

*   *   *

Lunch was big and admittedly really good. I had forgotten how delicious grease could be. Then Martoni piped up that he wanted cherry cobbler a la mode. It sounded good to me too, but I put my foot down. No dessert for us.

The to-go bag was big, but this was a cash deal and I wasn't about to waste food. Martoni approved of the takeout, too. It always made me nervous when I agreed with him. So yeah, now that I thought about it, a big bag of leftovers would stink up the car. He didn't care.

So we agreed to never agree. That logic bothered me a bit as I got up and walked over to the checkout counter.

At my request, my change at the cash register included a small stack of quarters. Just outside I fed the newspaper stand and pulled out a Fort Stockton paper. Good—the last one. I flipped through a few pages. No Martoni. All good.

Walking through the parking lot, I was again worried about my sanity. Fatigue and a seriously ripe Italian stranger wrapped intimately around me were more draining than anything I'd ever experienced before. But the possibility of jail-time was a powerful motivator, so I kept moving.

As I stepped across the parking lot some white guy with a backpack jumped to his feet, pushed his hoodie back, and homed in on me. Early to late twenties, hard to tell. Dirty long hair, might have been off-blond. Thin. Tall. No, not tall, just taller than Martoni. Damn, I used to be taller and thinner.

"Hey," he said as he eyed my big to-go bag.

I kept walking and gave him a disapproving look, hoping he'd veer off. Besides there was something not right about him. Seriously white for someone who hangs out in a parking lot in West Texas, like an Anglo with a sunscreen addiction.

He moved closer. "Any chance you could give me a lift?"

Yeah, right. "No."

He followed me—keeping to the side and one step back. Puppy position.

He piped up again. "Heading east?"

"No."

"Good. I've got friends in New Mexico."

I said nothing as I walked down the side street to my car.

"Albuquerque?"

"I'm not going that way."

"That's fine. I just need a lift as far as you care to take me. I'll buy the gas."

I stopped, worried that if I jumped into my car and locked the doors he'd kick me a new dent. "Look. I don't need gas and I sure as hell don't need a new passenger. I've got one too many as it is."

He looked at my empty car, obviously wondering what passenger I was talking about.

"I'm good company," he said. "I won't talk unless you're in the mood for it. And I'm really hungry. But I'm no freeloader. I pay my own way. I could buy your leftovers from you. Beats having them go bad in the car. And like I said, I'll spring for gas, too."

We stared at each other. Martoni probably looked rougher than he did so maybe he was the one taking the chance. What could go wrong? Law of averages said I was clear for the rest of today. Law of averages said that, not me.

"Look," he dug into his pocket, "here's . . . here's sixty bucks for gas, right up front. Take it."

He held out three twenties. I considered it. Cash was what I needed most.

What can I say. I was tired and I took it. Or maybe Martoni took it because his job was collecting money for gas. Either way, my hand reached out and took the cash.

"Here." I held out the bag of rapidly degrading leftovers. "Just don't cause me any problems. I've had the worst day possible so it's no problem for me to toss your ass out, even in the desert. *Capisce?*"

"Thanks, man!"

"With the rattlesnakes." I don't know why I added that.

* * *

The next thirty minutes were punctuated with the sounds of my leftovers being methodically devoured. He was occupied and I was happy not to have to carry on the usual mindless conversation with someone I didn't care about.

He didn't ask my name, I didn't ask his. We both seemed to be avoiding that subject.

Things were going better than expected. He was occupied. Martoni seemed totally quiet, maybe even napping. Traffic was very light and miles of nothing rolled by, almost with optimism, putting distance between me and the worst day of my life.

I casually moved the newspaper behind my seat in case my face was in there somewhere. You know, Martoni's face. I supposed it was our face now.

My hitchhiker did a respectable job of disappearing the food. The bag of crumbs and sticky bits was tossed into the back. He turned to me, expectantly. Very expectantly.

He just stared at me.

If he were a dog, and he wasn't that far removed from one, his look could have meant devotion. Or the need for more food. Or—

He pointed out the window. "Do you know where we are?"

I glanced at him. There was absolutely nothing out there. But his tone of voice was almost metaphysical. Like there really was something important there. I was about to say, "We're on I-10 headed west. Where the hell do you think we are?" when I recognized the spot. It was exactly where I'd made the u-turn to head back to Fort Stockton for lunch.

Yet another déjà vu from hell.

"You know this spot?" he asked.

"No." I wasn't about to admit I did.

"Alien country."

Like that was supposed to mean something? Illegal aliens? Mexicans weren't stupid. He who gets out of the car in West Texas, dies in West Texas. Besides, I knew enough to keep my mouth shut in the presence of mental instability. Cab drivers learn that one fast.

"Area 51," he continued. "You know . . . Nevada . . . alien spaceships . . . government denial?"

"We're not in Nevada." I was ready to pull over and boot him out the door.

"This is Area 71."

No fooling? "Yeah?"

"Yeah. Area 51 was shut down years ago because of sightseers. So they moved the ops to Area 52."

I nodded, looking for a place to pull over. "Makes sense."

"But that would've been too obvious, so they put the UFO program in rotation. Like a shell game. You know?"

I nodded, but I was thinking about what belonged in shells: nuts. I could tell Martoni was awake because I just wanted a smoke. Forget it, Martoni. Maybe your body's addicted to nicotine, but I was stronger than that.

"So this is Area 71," he continued.

"Wow. I guess there must be 70 others."

"Actually, 113. But 71 is one of the better ones."

"Why's that?" I asked, but immediately regretted it. Well it was my own damn fault. I invited his insanity to be shared with me. And he obliged.

"You see, 71 and 113 are special number," he asserted. "They are both Eisenstein primes. 71 is also part of a Brown number. There are only three number pairs that are Brown numbers."

And just like that I lost consciousness.

The miles rolled by as I heard about tracking devices hidden in paper money. About the Pentagon blowing itself up on 911 because they were a bunch of wannabes. About how the U.N. wanted to take over Texas—just Texas. About how Wyoming's House Bill 85 secretly passed and they now have a fully operational stealth aircraft carrier named the USS Casper parked behind an island in Yellowstone Lake that is suspiciously fuzzy on Google maps.

But that one really shook me up because did that mean Wyoming's legislature only had 84 other bills in its entire history of government? Or did they recycle numbers when they got to 99, like in a fast food restaurant?

My head spun.

And my passenger went mercilessly on and on and on. Looping on government black ops, and pharmaceuticals, and taxes, and fluorine, his parents, Vegas showgirls, and lots of things beyond our knowledge or power to control.

But somehow *he* had knowledge. *He* had knowledge of all those things.

And more importantly—control.

Even over his parents, which had to be a flat out lie.

Somehow the miles of flat endless brain numbing West Texas highway went by like sandpaper scraping endlessly through the unsettled cavities of my desperate day.

I so wanted to kill him.

* * *

I think he picked up on that because after a long while he stopped his rant and stared at me. Again just like a dog. My mantra of *death to this nameless one*, stopped too as I glanced over at him.

He graced me with his thoughts, "I can drive if you want."

"No!" I screamed in my mind. *"No, this is my damn car and you will not be damn driving it!"* And it screamed in my head loud enough that I knew he must of heard.

But he stared at me. Expectantly. A confused puppy. Slight head tilt.

"No," I said calmly enough. "I'm good." But I wasn't good. I was nowhere near good. I had lost everything I'd loved. From my deliciously sexy Latin perma-tan to my deliciously loving Marie. I was so totally screwed. I wanted nothing more than to punch the gas and drive headlong across the median into an oncoming 18-wheeler.

That's when things went sideways—he opened the glove compartment. "Let's see where we are," he said as if *where we were* hadn't started his whole mental upchuck.

Naturally, he pulled out my gun.

"Put that back," I said with a slight edge to my voice, trying to keep the tone serious but non-confrontational.

He looked it over. Flipped off the safety. "Beretta 92fs. Something of a classic." He racked the slide.

"Put the damn gun back!"

He rolled down his window and aimed it at nothing, because that's all there was.

I pulled over. Hard. More than a bit annoyed.

A surreal cloud of drab orange dust blew over the car as it skidded to a stop.

"I said, put the damn gun back."

He tilted his head, seemingly surprised at my overreaction. "Sure thing." He decocked it like he was born with a 92fs in his hand, then he slowly put it back. He looked at me as he closed the glove compartment door. "No need to be alarmed. I just wanted to compare it to mine." And before I could think much about anything he pulled a short .38 revolver out of his backpack.

"Mine's not nearly as nice," he said, turning the cylinder as he pointed it at my head.

I could see tips of bright brass aimed at me. No doubt that was his point—showing me a full load.

"Take the next side road," he said.

"Then what?" Dumb question, but I asked anyway.

"Then you'll get to keep that kneecap." He aimed his .38 at my knee.

I had half a mind to tell him it was Martoni's kneecap, not mine. Mine was in a morgue somewhere in Austin—not improving with age.

I scanned the road up ahead. No side road.

He caught my drift. "Whatever's next," he nodded up the road, "you take it."

I checked for oncoming traffic in my rearview. I thought about distracting him, then moving fast enough to start a fight over the gun. He wasn't as beefy as Martoni. I was betting Martoni had some motor skills left.

He backed the gun away from me.

Was I really that readable?

I drove. He wanted a carjacking? Fine. Martoni and I were both seriously pissed. Martoni and I weren't your usual victim.

* * *

Eventually there was a side road. A dirt road going nowhere. I turned onto it. My little Civic wasn't too happy about it.

A minute later he said, "Stop here. Leave it running. Now get out."

"Leaving me here to die?"

"There's traffic back on the freeway, dude. You'll be just fine."

I mulled it over as I slowly got out. He got out, too. We circled the car, keeping it between us.

I had so little. A duffel bag and a car. Now he was taking that. More than that, he was tossing a wanted man into the callous hands of fate. A fate who no longer loved me, or even pretended to.

I stood by the passenger door as he got in the driver's side. I opened the passenger door, but didn't step in. He pointed his gun at me.

He waved the gun at me. "It's not worth it."

I might have agreed. But he didn't know me. Hell, he had no clue what I was about. Or what I'd been through. Or what I had become.

Martoni had an urge, and it was what I wanted, too. I leaned in the passenger's side. "At least give me a chance to explain my side of things."

The car was in park. The hitchhiker needed one hand for the gun and one to shift. He reached his left hand over to put it in gear.

"That's what I'm talking about," I said as I nodded to indicate something behind him. He didn't fall for it, so I lunged for the gun. Chances were good he wouldn't pull the trigger.

He did.

One loud blast to my chest—right of center. Weird. I felt it stab me like a hot poker, but it didn't stagger me. He looked shocked so I lunged again. Two quick ones to my chest and one for good measure pushed me back.

I remember falling back, thudding onto the hot dirt. *Not too graceful, Marko*—a stupid thing to think as I lay there staring up at the sky. I coughed. My lungs were slowly filling. Lots of pain, oddly nothing I couldn't handle, but I was intensely uncomfortable as I slowly drowned on my own blood.

A few minutes later, I was still hanging on. I could see the car hadn't moved. Apparently the hitchhiker was okay with watching me die. Not a show you get every day.

There was a lot of ringing in my ears. I coughed again. Death seemed to take its sweet time getting around to me. I wondered if I would die this time. I coughed and blood splashed my face. Death would be a relief from this bloody pool I was creating.

The desert was very pleasant in late afternoon. I was relaxing into it. My eyes might have been partly closed, but the desert colors were keen in my mind. The dust had a smell to it that I'd never noticed before. Cactus held their juicy life well, better than people. Rabbits had been here, somehow I could sense it. The desert was everywhere alive and fresh, vivid, enhanced. It was like my brain was spiking all the colors and smells—amping everything up, even as my body shut down.

Nice. All nice.

The light shifted brighter, then dimmed. Normal dark.

Super comfortable.

1.5 The Road To Hell Isn't Paved

I gulped for air. Air free from blood. I pulled it into my lungs—so sweet. A deep breath. I opened my eyes, but it seemed like they were already open.

My vision cleared. Focused.

There was blood in my car, passenger side. I felt dizzy as I tried to clear my thoughts. Yes, it was my car. I had a gun in my hand. Not my hand.

I checked the mirror. Oh, God. A wrong reflection again.

There was something outside, beyond the open passenger door. I leaned closer for a better look. It was Martoni. I felt sad to lose him. Sure, I hated his sorry hide, and I hated what he did to my taxi last night—and to me.

But he didn't deserve this. Not like this.

His face wore a distant expression, streaked with red. His chest was splashed with slowly spreading blood, soaking into his shirt. No dignity in the way he was splayed out on his back.

I put the gun down and stepped out of the car. I was thinner. Taller. Younger, mid-twenties. As I walked around the car I adapted to the change quickly. Better than last time. Maybe because the nameless hitchhiker was closer in age and body-shape to the original me.

Martoni lay there so quietly. I'd never seen anyone freshly dead before. There was a single gurgle, so I waited. After several minutes—I don't know, maybe waiting for Martoni to reclaim his body—I silently said whatever goodbyes I had in me. I picked through his pockets to get my stuff, then turned and walked around to the driver's seat.

The motor was running. Gas being wasted. But I felt refreshed. Not by the killing—by the Nameless One's body. Martoni and I worked nights. Nameless apparently didn't.

As I got in the car, I felt that it was poetic how the dusty road was thirsty for Martoni's blood. Kind of sick, even for me.

Oh, great. A new passenger. Hello, Nameless.

The blood in the car was a problem. Not much of it, but it would be hard to explain. So I got a rag out of the trunk, got it wet with some bottled water I was saving, and I scrubbed the blood off the plastic interior.

Not bad. Martoni's bloodstains weren't really noticeable. I'd do a better job when I had more resources.

I wanted to toss the revolver. They could easily trace it to this murder. I started to wipe it down, but there could be partial prints on the ammo. What a hassle. So I tucked it in the glove compartment with my old Beretta. It looked like I was starting a gun collection.

I tossed the bloody rag out the window and made a u-turn. Before I made it back to the highway I stopped the car, pulled the battery from Martoni's phone, and threw it as far as I could into the desert. It was just too risky to hang on to it. Besides, Nameless had an expensive new phone. Very cool.

Heading west on the highway, I tried to not think about anything. Maybe I was getting numb. Maybe it was all just too much to process. On the other hand, someone was drooling over Las Vegas showgirls. Nameless? Martoni? Me?

Hey, we were headed that way anyway. Maybe Las Vegas was on the way to the beach in California?

Okay, so thoughts of well endowed leggy pretty-much-nude dancer babes filled our thoughts. Better than focusing all day on the slow trucks ahead or the dead bodies behind us.

* * *

Three hours later I was past El Paso and coming into Las Cruces, New Mexico. Las Cruces looked like a good place to stop for the night. A nice little town. What I needed was a seedy motel that would take cash with no questions asked.

The sun was going down fast.

After spending endless hours driving all over town, finding only nice motels that certainly had clean sheets and hot water and cold AC, I wound up parked in front of a scruffy local bar around 8 p.m.

I sat in the car a few minutes trying to decide if booze was what I really needed. No doubt I wanted it. But with two killers riding shotgun in my mind, alcohol might not be the best thing.

Four Harleys in the parking lot were testimony to the fun that waited inside. Was I being facetious, or was one of my passengers comfortable with bikers? Or afraid of bikers? It was getting hard to know my own mind.

So what would happen inside? I'd belly up to the bar and order New Mexico's finest—on tap. They'd eye me like a damn fool stranger. Yeah. Then I'd lay it on them that I was the Nameless One. They'd let the outlaw name sink in a moment, then go back to playing pool. I'd get my space to belt a few back, just me in the private company of my two inner killers.

It sounded good. And unlikely.

I dug through Nameless One's backpack for his CV.

Clothes, toiletries, two tubes of SPF 100 sunblock, a map of Florida, a partial box of ammo, and a healthy stack of cash wrapped in aluminum foil. Just about what I expected. Plus several wallets— four from guys, two from women. Judging by the photos on the driver's licenses, none of these wallets were his. Plenty of credit cards and family photos. Nameless didn't seem to mind hanging onto evidence.

Hey, Nameless One. Not so smart for a serial killer.

It crossed my mind he was a serial mugger, not a serial killer. He'd only killed me, and besides, it was my own damn fault for lunging for the gun. Well, that's what Nameless seemed to think about it. Personally, I wasn't so sure.

But if all those people were still alive, they deserved to get their wallets back. Maybe the Las Cruces cops had a night deposit slot? I was oddly chipper.

Yes, and speaking of dark humor, Nameless had about a dozen comics at the bottom of his backpack. None I'd ever heard of before. Superheroes with major psychological problems. Sick stuff. Well drawn, especially the hot babes in bondage. Nothing wrong with that. But these were seriously on the sick side. Flipping through them (yes, I flipped through them), it was kind of hard to even tell if the heroes were good or bad. Everyone in those comics looked like they deserved to be in a high security nut house.

Speaking of deserving a nut house, I check the mirror to make sure my long dirty hair was kind of straight and made sure my new face looked old enough to not get carded. I asked my passengers their opinion. Silence. They never talked directly to me, but there was a consensus that I should get in there and start drinking.

All they ever gave me were their memories and urges. Maybe not in that order.

Come to think of it, real passengers were a lot like that.

I put Nameless One's backpack in the trunk with my duffel bag and locked the car. I double-checked that it was locked. Nameless should have known better than to try and take everything I had. I do have a protective streak. I, meaning Marko. I doubt the other guys cared.

Inside it was exactly like I'd imagined. Dingy brown, punctuated with beer ads in bright neon colors. Some Harley posters were on the walls to let bikers know they were welcome here. Posters of babes on bikes. ZZ Top types on bikes.

Some locals sat at a table. Four bikers at another. Two just-got-out types at the bar. A pool table sat idle toward the back. No women—a crying shame. Note to self: Find out where biker babes go at night.

All eyes were on me. They caught me standing at the entrance daydreaming about their women.

I had a teacher once tell me that if I got nervous in front of a crowd then I should just imagine them all naked.

Oh yeah? I wasn't going there.

I walked in tall, knowing that not a one of them could top my day. Each of them were probably thinking they were the toughest creature on the planet. But, I thought as I glanced around, had any one of them died today? No? Shot repeatedly and died twice?

I didn't think so. Pack of thick-necked wusses.

There was no doubt who was the biggest badass in the bar. No doubt in any of my minds. *Hooyah!* My guys were behind me one hundred percent.

As I found a stool at the bar, my head was spinning again. Maybe I didn't even need a drink. Behind the bar, six beer taps said it all. Two labels were well advertised, both were for sissies. The rest I didn't recognize.

I had the bartender's eye (everyone's, actually) as I sat ramrod-straight and ordered up. "What's good?"

Laughter erupted. Big hands slapped tables and rough voices laughed again.

It could have gone better.

"It's all good here, son," the bartender said with a grin.

Son? I felt dangerously close to getting carded. I nodded at the taps. "I'll have a Dog's Head." Whatever the hell that was.

The bartender hesitated and I could feel the carding coming.

"I suppose you'll want to start a tab."

"Sure."

"I take cash."

Okay. I dug into my pocket and pulled out a twenty. It disappeared quickly and was replaced with a foamy Dog's Head. They were all still looking at me so I held it up, cut myself off from offering a toast, and started in on a long first chug.

After that, I turned away to settle into my drinking. A minute later they'd all lost interest in me.

But several minutes later, as I was relaxing into my second beer, I had the undeniable feeling I was invincible. It was a revelation. I was immortal. No one could kill me. It had been proven twice in the last 24 hours. No, closer to 18 hours.

Exactly how immortal was I? That was a good question. What happened if I jumped off a cliff? Would I become the cliff? Not likely. Not good, even if it was likely. What if I had a heart attack? Maybe I wasn't as immortal as I'd hoped.

Clearly I could take my killer's body. That sounded simple enough. I glanced around the bar. I could provoke one of those beefy bikers into killing me, then too bad sucker because now I've got your machismo-ass life. It occurred to me, that life might be pretty gross. For starters, bikers were probably into body sweat.

Bugs in their teeth. Loose stones from dump trucks in their face. Broken bones. Oily rags. Weathered skin.

It also occurred to me that if I provoked one he'd probably break my jaw and leave it at that.

I turned back to my drink.

My immortality wasn't ideal. Actually, it was very problematic. I was always going to look like a murderer. My multiple personality disorder was likely to worsen. Avoiding jail and death row would be a constant struggle. Actually, death row was a way out. Somebody had to inject me, right? Or open the trap door, or turn up the voltage, or whatever. Then as the guard or the doctor who'd killed me, I could waltz right out. A free man for life. Not a murderer.

Cool.

Until I got too old, then I'd find someone else to kill me.

After setting another twenty bucks on the bar, the bartender allowed me a third beer. How much were beers here, anyway?

If I played my cards right I could easily live hundreds or thousands of years. I could be anyone—anyone tough enough to pull the trigger and kill me. I could be really handsome and cool, too. Maybe I could find Johnny Depp and get into a duel with him.

Hell, I could even be Penélope Cruz.

Not a good idea. But I got the impression Nameless liked it.

Urges.

Speaking of urges, I stepped away from the bar to find the little biker's room. Easy to find. I followed my nose. Hey, first time to take a leak with this body! No unexpected surprises, I hoped. None found.

Relief came in many forms.

Getting dark. Time to find a bed. And dinner.

I chugged the last of my beer and closed out my tab. The bartender seemed happy enough, but I can honestly say I didn't bond with any of the guys there.

So sad. I just wanted to fit in. I'm sure they saw me as a wimp. Well, someday I might be wearing one of their skins. That would have made a good conversation starter.

As I turned toward the door, I bumped into a biker just stepping in. Man, he was solid.

"Watch it," he said, pushing me off and looking me over.

I stuck out my chest. "Make my day, roadwipe. Kill me. I'd like that. Just kill me now. And be quick about it."

He looked at his buddies for some sort of explanation, but they just laughed.

"Damn," he said as he walked over to his buddies. He knew he'd just missed tonight's entertainment.

I staggered out of the bar. Nameless was obviously a wimpy drinker. Martoni and I were made of tougher stuff.

I was hungry, but decided to conserve my cash and eat what I'd grabbed back at my apartment in Austin. Sitting in the trunk wasn't making it any fresher.

* * *

It took a lot more searching to find a seedy motel. Las Cruces was way too clean. I made a mental note to be more selective about the towns I stayed in.

I finally found a good rundown motel. Cash was accepted. But the clerk thought it was a problem that I wouldn't show any ID. I solved it with a story about a crazy wife and a shy mistress. Unfortunately, that led to paying more cash for double occupancy, plus a large deposit on any pay-per-porn I might consume. Then I jotted down a wild guess at my stolen license plate number in the allotted space on the intake form, and left the rest blank. And just like that, we were good.

I had some trouble getting into my room with the keycard and the fussy lock, but I was eventually inside with my duffel bag and the backpack I'd inherited from Nameless.

The car was locked. Motel door locked. Curtains pulled closed. Guns stowed strategically. Loud neighbors were up to something I didn't want to hear. TV on. AC on. I started the hot water in the shower. Stripped and took a good look in the mirror. Not my thing, but I had to know what I was dealing with. After all, it wasn't like I'd ever get my own body back. Love the one you're with. Right guys?

Yeah, I was back to weirding myself out.

As I stepped into the shower with the body of Nameless, I actually felt sorry I'd never had the chance to clean up Martoni before he died. At the very least, he deserved that. And a smoke, which sounded seriously wrong in the shower.

A smoke? It crossed my mind Martoni was definitely still with me. Welcome to our first communal shower, Martoni. Close your eyes and pass the soap.

* * *

I gave the beers a lot of credit for getting me through my first shower as non-Marko. Alcohol was a wonderful thing. Easily forgotten when it wears off.

In bed, I pushed stale food into Nameless's mouth, checked out his cool cell phone, and channel-surfed as I thought about my future. It was a serious problem, but it was also an opportunity. What kind of opportunity? The guys were silent. There was no answer from me either.

I think I fell asleep watching an infomercial about a great new dog handle. Carry your mutt anywhere. Martoni liked it.

Somehow Nameless had found the comics channel on his own and nudged me awake. I was soon engrossed in an old rerun of the short-lived TV show, *The Tick*. But it was the Batmanuel character I was watching most. Batmanuel was me, only with better dialog. A Latino superhero who was making a difference in the world. I could be Batmanuel, only not just on TV. I could use my superpowers to ... to ... to do something more important than drive around on the run and live in shabby motels.

I had it in me to make a difference. Yes I did!

I would be the *Killer of Killers*. I'd be known as *The KoK*. No need to hide behind a mask, because every new kill was a fresh mask. But no tights. I'd wear regular clothes. The perfect disguise because my face would be whatever it was that day.

Okay, I had to admit being called *The KoK* was problematic. I'd be the *Murderer of Murderers*. *MoM?*

It needed some work.

A superhero would need a super girlfriend. A different breed of woman. Nameless and Martoni urged me to head to Vegas and seek out showgirls. Preferably all of them. Mega-super girlfriends—seriously enhanced. It's what we deserved, because we were a lot more than one guy. We were Mega Mind. Nameless indicated that name was already taken. Okay then, we were Multi-Mind. Invincible. Uber cool. And synergistically sexy. Whatever that meant. Together we would right all wrongs. Together we would be super smart, super sexy, and super powerful.

Actually super sexy sounded best. But how? We were such a long way from any super ability. Frankly, even normal abilities seemed like a challenge. Too many opinions. Too few solutions.

So we focused on visions of headlining with topless super Vegas babes. We'd invite some schmuck from the audience to kill us. We'd take over his body, then get ravaged by Vegas babes. The crowd would go wild—except his wife. We'd up our fees, work our way up the Vegas venues, ramp up the hotties. Total sweetness! The best of all earthly endeavors.

With great multi-brainpower, comes great need for sleep.

I passed out.

1.6 With Good Intentions

In the morning I decided the Nameless One was out of touch with the reality of our situation. I tossed his disturbingly interesting comics into the trash. I abandoned his crazy ideas of becoming a superhero. Sorry, Nameless, I'm onto your game.

Honestly, Nameless, I watched your TV show and I still had no clue who *The Tick* was. As far as I could tell, he was just some big blue tick with twitchy antennae. Stay out of my head, Nameless.

Yes, I remembered it was originally Nameless's head. But it was mine now.

Okay, the Vegas showgirl fantasies could stay—I was good with that. But the superhero crap had to go. I was no superhero—just some guy lucky to be alive, lucky to be walking around in other people's bodies.

And sorry, Martoni, not getting a dog. Not even getting a dog handle.

As I packed up my stuff in the motel room, I thought about *my* goals—*Marko Santana's* goals.

The cops were looking for Nameless, but it seemed likely it was only for armed robbery. Well, I got the impression Nameless thought his crimes were modest, not a murder spree. All he cared about was the cash and collecting interesting IDs. As for Martoni, whether his crime was manslaughter or justifiable homicide, it didn't matter. Hugo Martoni was simply a body to be found. His case would soon be closed.

For me to continue being the Nameless One was a disaster in the making. With absolutely zero ID for my new face, it made nearly everything impossible. I had no clue who Nameless was—who I was now supposed to be. I supposed I could tell everyone I had amnesia and had lost all my identification and somehow wound up driving a dead guy's car. Not to mention I was packing a wad of cash that was best kept in aluminum foil.

Yeah, right.

Now what? Well, for today I'd grab some New Mexico license plates, but it was only a matter of time before I got pulled over and locked up. Of course, I could resist arrest, wave one of my guns in the cop's face, and with luck the cop would kill me outright.

Actually, that scenario had a lot of appeal. In a cop's body, I'd be completely free. No criminal charges, solid ID, a small but tangible bank account, and all the rest that goes with life as an underpaid cop. Then I'd say I was traumatized by the shooting, leave the force, and I'd get my own semi-normal life back—even if I wasn't legally Marko again. At least as a legit guy, I could even try to get back with Marie. Long odds, but I liked to think Marie loved me for who I was down deep. I was still me, despite my newly acquired ex-cop body.

The downside of that scenario? The cop would be an innocent man, forced to be a passenger in his own brain. And if he had a family, domestic life would get messy fast. A lot of innocent people would get hurt. Him, his wife, his kids, his friends, and assorted relatives. What could I possibly say to his wife and kids? *Sorry, ma'am, but I don't love you no more. You're better off looking for a new hubby, anyway. Bye, kids, I don't love you guys no more, neither. What'd you say, ma'am? Alimony? Ha! You know there ain't no alimony in Texas. Oops, we're in New Mexico. Child support, too? Aw, damn!*

Okay, maybe not like that. But those were the salient points.

Wait. I didn't know what salient meant. I assumed one of my passengers did. My vocabulary was improving. Cool.

I checked out of the motel, fought like hell trying to get my unused porn deposit back, and wound up in the car driving around but not sure which way I was going.

Life's often a sucky parable of itself. We check in, we check out—with a hell of a lot of *lost* in-between.

While I mulled things over, I picked up an new set of New Mexico license plates and ditched the old Texas ones. Not ideal because New Mexico puts their stickers on the license plates and Texas puts them in the window. It was a messy combination that could get me pulled over. Why don't they give you helpful plate-swapping tips on crime shows?

But nothing seemed to help my state of mind, or my indecision. Breakfast was unimportant, so I skipped it. I sensed some annoyance from Martoni on that score.

Nameless was sullen, too. His dream of superpower had finally come true, except I'd just dropped Kryptonite in his spandex panties and kicked him to the curb. Not to mention his erotic-hero comics (first editions, I'm sure) which were now languishing in the motel room's trashcan and fair game for some soon-to-be-shocked motel maid. I had the vague impression Nameless was planning revenge against me in the form of diarrhea. His body, his rules, he seemed to say.

None of that mattered to me.

The original Marko Santana was far better than anything I had become. The original boring unremarkable Marko Santana was now my dream life. Steady job. Knockout girlfriend. Real friends who took me just like I was.

And my future?

Yeah, future. That said it all. Marko had a future in every sense of the word. And whatever that future was, it was a hell of a lot more promising than what I had now.

So screw this life. I would have traded anything in heaven or earth to just be me again. Me! Marko Santana! Less than perfect, and far less than I could have been if I had applied myself.

This life sucked.

I was a dead guy walking. A pathetic body-snatcher. Nothing more, nothing less. I was a damned fool, doomed to roam the earth in search of a future, feeding on one hapless soul after another. I was just some pathetic little bardo that God had kicked to the curb in a fit of merciless justice.

I would have said something on my behalf, but God knew what I deserved. There was just no arguing with the Universe Slinger. Bottom line? I was just some schmuck who was good at getting killed.

So what then? If I wasn't a superhero, maybe I was tailor-made to be a super villain?

Hey. If the spandex fits, wear it.

Fine. That's what the universe wanted? Then that's me. But where was the devil when I needed him? Someone to guide me along the path of evil. I was a natural reborn killer. That was obvious. I was the anti-man. Maybe Satan wanted me to find him on his own turf? Under a rock? Area 71?

Or maybe I just needed a really good therapist. One who understood emerging death-suckers.

Wait. *Bardo?* Did I just think that word—use it in my brain speech? Who the hell even knew that word? Nameless, of course— the frickin' bardo expert among us.

When I finally pulled myself out of my self-pity, I found myself driving on the highway headed east. Back to Austin—back to Marie.

Hell, it looked like I'd already crossed the border back into Texas. In fact I'd zipped right through El Paso without noticing.

It was like some part of my mind had made a decision and forgotten to tell me about it. Yes, I was clearly heading back to Marie.

The sun was in my eyes. It was like an omen that a bright future lay ahead. I was a different man, wanting desperately to be me again. I wanted to wipe the tears from Marie's eyes and tell her that I loved her—tell her I wasn't dead, although it might seem totally like it. Somehow I'd make that happen. I was determined to try. If we broke up it would be her decision, not mine.

She could be difficult at times. Hell, I was no picnic. But I'd try my best to explain things. She'd eventually understand. But if she didn't, then I wouldn't give up. She'd come around. Yes. Eventually she would. Or?

Or she wouldn't.

Was I being unrealistic?

That thought was swept from my mind as I found myself approaching a border patrol checkpoint. Aw, shit. No way out. I was stuck in line behind a dozen other cars. I had no ID, stolen plates, a murdered guy's car (my car), assorted guns, dried blood on the passenger's side, no plausible stories about what I was doing. Hell, I was a rolling disaster.

As I inched up to the border agents it crossed my mind to jump out of the car with my hands up and explain everything until they decided I was delirious from the heat and needed a complementary bottle of spring water. I guess that was my idea. Or I should drive like a bat out of hell and outrun their little fleet of cruisers and SUVs—Martoni's idea. Or just be the cool super-dude I was—Nameless's idea.

I went with Nameless, kept my sunglasses on, and decided sweating was normal in the West Texas heat.

When it was my turn, the dog sniffed the car, the guy in lite commando gear glanced at me and in my car, then waved me on.

What? Not even a question about my nationality?

Being white had its moments. Viva los blancos!

The desert rolled slowly by. The miles seemed endless. Somebody was depressed again. We looked around at each other. It was me.

Martoni, Nameless, and me, all driving along I-10. Three loners in a car, a silver Civic with plates du jour, looking exactly like anyone else on the road. No one suspected we were the three seeds of the coming apocalypse.

No one suspected the state of my mental health.

Anyone who's driven in West Texas knows that mental state, too. Welcome to West Texas, y'all. Enjoy the lack of scenery. Respect the rattlers. Don't forget to pack a survival kit.

Friends don't let friends drive alone in West Texas. Mine sure didn't.

* * *

We stopped in Van Horn for gas with maybe 500 miles to go until we reached Austin. Nameless was still buying. We all went to the restroom while Nameless took a leak. Martoni and I stared at the lame graffiti on the restroom wall while Nameless repeated the mental message that he was just a mugger, not a killer. Whatever. Give it a rest, dude.

Then back in the car and more endless miles. The road ahead was filled with mirages. I could only hope that getting back with Marie wasn't also a mirage.

We stopped in Fort Stockton for fresh license plates and lunch. I'd promised Martoni we'd eat at Jolly Bob's again, but there were police cars outside and hungry cops doing God knows what inside. So we settled for Amy Lou's Pie Barn. Despite the disturbing barn motif, the food looked and smelled good. I had a Clucky Burger with fresh strawberries and dipping yogurt, plus mixed veggies on the side. I was careful to isolate the lima beans. I let Martoni have his chicken fried cheese sticks. Nameless craved the waitress's rear end, but I held him back. Actually, we all wanted the waitress's rear end. It was that good.

One horny guy is a problem in search of a solution. Three horny guys in the same body is pure murder. We all wanted the same thing, but we refused to share. Sucks to be us.

As it turned out, we all saved room for dessert—I mean food wise, because she wasn't that interested in our multipronged sexual advances. We compromised and ordered the trucker-approved top-heavy-load Amy Lou cherry pie à la mode. Every bit as good as its name.

We looked for Amy Lou while we were there, but never saw her. But we knew just what she looked like because of the life-size replica sitting on a bale of hay next to the cash register. People think Texas is a serious place until they walk into a massive convenience store like Buc-ee's. But instead of Buc-ee's jumbo beaver, Amy Lou's had an anatomically exaggerated Amy Lou—plastic farm girl cleavage at its finest. We were excited because she looked animatronic and we wanted to see her in operation. Sadly, she was on the fritz. Such is life. The best in artificial womanhood often looks stunning, but falls short of man's expectations.

After the pie barn experience, it was obvious that cash was dwindling meal by meal, gas tank by gas tank. So Nameless urged me to use one of his recently acquired ATM cards. I wasn't happy about the morality of it. Hell, he'd already robbed those people, so why keep it going? Nameless seemed good with his face on the ATM's security video, but we needed his face relatively unused, so I vetoed the withdrawal.

That's when I happened to see a mailbox, so I ditched all the stolen cards and wallets. Kept the cash, of course. I bet postmen see a lot of weird shit—and love it.

Dinner in Junction was a drive-thru burger and a coke.

Then I did a smart thing. I disassembled Nameless's cool smart phone and tossed it into a dumpster. Man, that was hard to do, but I couldn't afford for the cops tracking me with it.

Then I bought a prepaid burner phone and a car charger. Super important. Anyone who'd ever watched any spy movie knew just how important a burner phone was. I almost bought two.

Okay. I'll admit it. I went back into the store and bought another one—just in case. One black, one white to keep things straight. Black ops. White ops. Seemed logical.

* * *

We arrived in Austin Sunday night around 9:30 p.m. and pulled over in a parking lot somewhere. I picked up the freshly charged white burner phone to call Marie.

What to say?

Sunday night, so my mother was surely aware of my death very early Saturday, and she would have called Marie. They probably would have gotten together last night for a good cry.

What else would they know? Martoni was wanted by the cops for questioning. My apartment had been broken into. Some valuables were apparently stolen. My car was missing.

It wasn't looking good for Martoni.

Oddly, he let me know he was happy being with me. I didn't have the heart to tell him there wasn't much of him left.

For the call to Marie, I thought about trying to be Marko again. Yeah, right. We all knew how well that went last time. Besides, she'd want to see me. Very problematic.

Then how?

I felt like I needed to be close, but not in a freaky kind of way. Something natural. Consoling. Like one of Marko's friends. That could work. And the truth could come out later.

I was about to dial. Which friend was I? Some guy called Nameless One? I'd need a name. Something cool like Marko Santana, but not suspicious. Mark was good. Mark Santa. Too weird. Mark Montana? Too big. Inigo Montoya from the movie *Princess Bride*? Marie loved that movie. Inigo Montoya was a really cool name, too. And it was a Latino name. Indigo Santa? No way. Mark Montoya? Perfect. She'd have good thoughts about me if I were Mark Montoya.

I tapped in her number. It rang.

"Hello?" She sounded really sad.

"Hi. Is this Marie Turner?"

No answer, but someone in the background wanted to know who was calling.

"My name is Mark," I said. "I was a friend of Marko's."

"Mark who?"

"Montoya. Marko and I played a lot of online games together. You know, *Zombie Apocalypse Now, One and Dead, Aliens Must Die.* Stuff like that." What to say? I knew an awful lot about Marko. I kept going, "Look, I'm really sorry. He talked about you a lot. We talked about a lot of things. And . . . I know he really loved you. I think he felt bad that he didn't tell you that as often as he wanted. Anyway . . ." There was muffled talking in the background. "Anyway, I'm sorry. If there's a funeral," duh, of course there'd be a funeral, "uh, I'd really like to attend."

There was a slight pause on her end. "Of course," she said. More talking in the background. I think Marie was starting to cry.

"This is Marko's mother, Reya. We're still making arrangements. Can I call you back?"

"Yes, absolutely."

"I'm sorry. I didn't get your name."

"Mark—" I almost said Marko! "Mark Montoya."

"And your number?"

Damn. I didn't remember my white ops phone number! It was in the car somewhere. "Uh, you've got it. It's in your call log."

Silence. Mom didn't know much about cell phones.

"Sorry," I tried to cover, "I switched to a new phone carrier. I don't have my new number memorized yet. But I can call you right back with it."

"Okay. But you said it's in a log?"

"Yes, on Marie's phone. She knows how to get it off her phone."

"Okay then. I'm sorry you lost your friend, Mr. Montoya."

"And I'm so sorry for your loss, Mrs. Santana. He was so young. It's a terrible tragedy, especially for you and Marie. He spoke of y'all often."

"Really?"

Another dangerous turn. "Yes. But you know how guys are. We'll talk to each other about feelings, but often not to the ones we love." So much BS. I was digging myself a major hole.

"Yes." She paused to think about that. "We'll be in touch and see you at the funeral."

"If there's anything I can do to help, just let me know. I'm serious about that. Marko—" I almost said Mark. "He was a really great friend. Maybe I could say a few words at the funeral and, uh, be a pallbearer or something. Anything to help his family . . . anything. Just let me know."

"I will. Some of his friends at the taxi company offered to be pallbearers, too. He had a lot of friends. Well . . ." She trailed off into awkward silence.

At this point I wanted nothing more than to say, "*And tell Marie I love her so very much.*" But I could only stumble through some words. "You are both in my prayers." I never prayed, but it seemed like the thing to say to mom.

"And you're in ours. Goodbye, Mark."

"Goodbye, Mrs. Santana."

It was both goodbye and hello. The words were lies and heartfelt truths. I could comfort my loved ones with words, but they could also cause immense suffering.

The future was a minefield.

1.7 Going Under

I slept in the car that Sunday night with the doors locked. Austin was hot and muggy but I kept the windows open just an inch. I didn't need to meet another Nameless One looking to cash out a victim.

Sleep was fitful that night. Weird dreams. Horrible brain sucking dreams. Shit that would wake a man in a cold sweat and fill him with dread. Normally, dreams like that would creep me out, but lately my nightmares were nothing worse than my reality.

As I tried to go back to sleep, I worried that I had changed somehow. Yeah, the skin was new, but somehow *I* was different. A part of me thought Marko Santana was just some naive kid. Well, I wasn't. Or was I? Or maybe I'd matured a bit—not a bad thing. But it also occurred to me I had become a mental conglomerate. I used to like my thoughts. Now I wasn't so sure.

On a more positive note, I felt more connected to Nameless. Made sense—I was using his brain. So maybe the older passengers, like Martoni, would eventually get pushed from the back seat to the trunk? More like baggage than passenger? We all had baggage. Easy to forget baggage.

A couple hours later I woke up to the sound of Monday morning traffic. The sun was almost up.

The car smelled like I needed a shower.

I really needed a better place to stay. And I needed mother to call me and let me know when my funeral would be. Maybe I should call again? Maybe not.

I picked up the Monday morning newspaper to see if Marko was listed. Nothing in obits. I guess they were waiting until they knew the funeral details. Nothing about the holdup and shooting at the convenience store. Yesterday's news.

I knew where a library was. I hadn't been in one since I was a kid, but I wanted to read yesterday's newspaper. Weird how I had to make sure I was really dead. Maybe I had simply skipped out of the morgue and was walking around messed up on formaldehyde. Yeah, I was on formaldehyde and driving around Texas just fine, so that meant I wasn't far from detox and recovery.

Wishful thinking at its finest.

When I arrived at the library, it didn't surprise me that the parking lot was empty. No one reads anymore. I sure didn't. The Monday hours said they opened at 10. Two and a half hours to kill before I could read about my own death. So I headed to Town Lake to think. It was a beautiful morning for it. It was early and still cool and the grass still thought it had a future, so I settled down in it, dappled with shade from a nearby tree, and watched the puffy little clouds drift by.

Yes, I knew it was now called Lady Bird Lake, but I couldn't get used to it. I'm sure Lady Bird Johnson was a real hoot. I'd seen her briefly when I was a kid. Getting out of a black Lincoln with two suits that had to be Secret Service.

Besides renaming the lake, they renamed 1st Street. They renamed 19th Street. Austin politicians had money to rename stuff but not to improve the horrible traffic?

The lake was actually just a part of the Colorado River, except it was really the Lower Colorado River and in no way connected to the real Colorado River. And rumor had it that in the 1800s the governors of Texas and Colorado were playing poker and the Colorado governor bet Pikes Peak and lost. I don't know why we haven't gone over to collect. Heaven knows Texas could use a real mountain.

Funny how one thought leads to another.

I must of dozed off in the grass running taxi driver trivia through my head and reinforcing my hatred of politicians. A bit ironic because those same crappy politicians built this beautiful jogging trail along Town Lake.

When I woke up I was in full sun. I got a bit worried that I'd burned Nameless. He was a lot more blanco than Martoni or me. Back at the car I checked in a mirror and he was turning pinko blanco. Sorry, Nameless. I'll try to take better care of your shameless husk.

I still had more than an hour to kill so I picked up some sun screen, bought new clothes, and got a much-needed haircut. I looked much better now. Fresh cooked migas from a taco truck really topped off my mood.

A little later I walked into the library, not sure what to expect. I was surprised to see metal detectors. Banks don't need metal detectors but libraries do? I walked through and smiled at the cute girl at the desk, hoping she'd let me browse the stacks without a library card.

She looked me over and perked up. "Can I help you?"

"Uh, I just need to check the weekend newspapers."

"You'll find them over there to your left."

"Thanks." Easy peasy. She looked really cute peeking over glasses she probably didn't need, so I naturally felt disappointed she didn't give me a pat-down. We all were. Cute librarians should give pat-downs. More guys would read.

Saturday's paper was easy to find. Hey, my shootout was on page eight. Disappointing journalism. Not even a single photo of the carnage. Crime never sleeps. Reporters do.

I read the sad news. Taxi driver dead on arrival at the hospital. That would be me—and my only ambulance ride. Too bad I had no memory of it. Name withheld pending notification of kin. Passengers unharmed. That figured. Passengers arrested. Good. Throw the book at 'em. Let their crappy parents sort it out. Store clerk, Hugo Martoni, had felony priors. Fled the scene. No shit.

What felonies? You know, don't you, Hugo? No answer.

So that was it? Six paragraphs of journalistic fluff. It was my life, damn it. I deserved more meat on the page. I was Marko Noviño Santana! I had a life. I had a future.

I started to rip out the article for a scrap book I didn't yet have, but librarian girl was circling behind me. I smiled at her. I hoped Nameless had a decent smile. "Can I make a copy?"

"Sure." She seemed happy to talk with me. "There's a copy machine right there."

Yes, there was. I walked over and noticed the big warning sign about copying copyrighted material. Homeland Security was probably monitoring the copier. Well, there were CCTV camera bumps nearby. Only 50 cents was needed to do the deed and make me a felon.

I pulled out a dollar bill. "Can I get change?"

"Sure." She took it with a big smile, swirled her summer skirt when she turned, and made a very sexy trip to her desk. She made a point of bending over to get into a drawer, her gorgeous ass wiggling nicely in my direction as she rummaged around for my quarters. She glanced back at me to make sure I was watching her enticing librarian assets. Yup, I sure was. She smiled. Then she came back with my quarters. She placed them in my hand. Skin touched skin. I believe it met the one-second rule. She was flirting. Not too subtlety.

I smiled and said, "Thanks." That seemed to cover all of my thoughts.

As I was making my illegal copy, she moved closer. "I see you got some sun."

"Yeah, I woke up early so I hung out on Town Lake."

"Lady Bird Lake." She said it with a playful cock of an eyebrow and a dangerous curl of her lip, almost like she was using a light touch with her riding crop. Message received. Message understood. You sexy dominatrix. Me Cro-Magnon man-fodder.

Not my preference, but it had possibilities.

"Right." I imagined correcting people was an occupational hazard for librarians. I had my own occupational hazards, like offering hot passengers my fine brown ass—now disgustingly blanco. But I never followed through. It was just talk. I never cheated on Marie.

But was it cheating if I went after the librarian's skirt? Legally I was the Nameless One. Marko was legally dead, but I still had designs on Marie.

Legally I could screw around all I wanted. My only obstacles were mental.

I decided right then to screw what the law allowed. I was Marko! And damn it, I was going to keep being Marko! Like I said, Marie still had first crack at the new me.

"Thanks," I said as I walked out, head held high, ever the proud fool.

In the parking lot the guys were clearly pissed at me. Suck it up, guys. I'm driving this life.

That's when I turned around and marched right back into the library. I had forgotten to check the obits in Sunday's paper.

I walked in. "I seem to have missed Sunday's paper."

She perked up again. "We keep those on that table."

She started to get up, but I waved her off. "I've got it. Thanks."

I started leafing through Sunday's massive pile of ads. Obits, obits, obits. Where were the damn obits? Hidden on an obscure page, of course. Only two dead. And one was me! I felt proud until I read it more closely: *Marco Santana.* They'd screwed up my name in my one and only obit! Obit reporters must be the same ones who handled the classifieds.

The funeral was tomorrow at noon. Mother's Catholic church. The article had some good stuff about me. I hoped people would show up.

I firmly believed funerals were for the living. The dead had moved on. For the living, it was a time to celebrate a life, and to grieve the loss. I'd sure as hell be at my funeral—body and soul. Martoni and Nameless would be there, too. So yes, I was a plus two.

Why hadn't Marie called me back?

I made a copy of my obit and walked out.

* * *

I'd need a suit. Something in black. I found a discount store and bought black jeans and a charcoal striped dress shirt. No tie. The suit jackets were priced crazy at $400. Even the sports jackets were pushing $200. In the afternoon I found a store with red dots and acceptable prices. I picked up an off-black jacket on clearance for $99, but with an extra 40% off. Woo-hoo!

I hated shopping.

More than that, I hated not having money. My burn rate was frightening. I vowed to someday have money. Lots of it. Rob from the 1%—keep some for myself. Batman had an unfair advantage: he was born loaded. Well, he pretty much needed it for his gear.

Lunch and dinner consisted of a big bag of greasy chips and a box of lifeless granola bars.

Tonight I'd break into some evil millionaire's mansion, wave a gun at him, and try my best to get shot dead. I had two guns so it occurred to me I could offer him one, if his wasn't handy.

A handsome millionaire. Marie would really like that.

But not a married guy. The last thing I needed was a messy divorce haggling with her lawyers over my newly acquired millions.

I was watching joggers along Town Lake when the White Ops phone rang. It was mom. I was so happy she remembered me.

But I was cool. "This is Mark."

"Hello. This is Mrs. Santana. I have information about the funeral . . . if you're still interested."

"Thank you for getting back to me, Mrs. Santana. I found Marko's obituary in the paper, but I want to make sure it's still okay for me to come." Mom didn't know what Nameless looked like. I'd be there regardless of what she said.

"Well, of course. We want all his friends to be there."

"His friends from the taxi company will be there, I hope."

"Yes, they have a special place at the services. They'll be the pallbearers."

I wanted to be a pallbearer. "I'd like to be one of the pallbearers, if that's possible."

"Well, we really have all we need."

"I could be an usher."

"Yes, but the taxi drivers have shown such loyalty. They insisted on helping out with pretty much everything. Almost like the police, if you know what I mean."

Drivers were nothing like the police. Drivers were pretty competitive when it came to catching fares. But a death in the line of duty—yes, I could see solidarity. Strong solidarity. All cab drivers shared the same risks on the streets. It kind of choked me up thinking about drivers from lots of companies turning out for one of their own.

We picked up all kinds of people in all kinds of conditions. Drunks, and people who'd been in wrecks, and single pregnant women who needed quick transportation. We'd show up at night for domestic disputes. Cops would tell the drunk SOBs they could either ride with us somewhere or get cuffed and booked downtown for failure to disengage from a fight. We usually got those guys and I have to think the cops knew what they were handing us. A shit-faced guy ragging on his wife the whole way and even more pissed that he had to pay for the ride.

I liked to think cops had our back. I liked to think a few might show up for a cabbie who was blown away while trying to make an honest living on the street.

I had mixed feelings about cops. I'd seen too many of them pissed at the world and not afraid to pass their bad day along to anyone they met.

But I also respected them. I'm not sure why, but I did. Maybe because they dealt with shit all day long. I vowed to go to the next funeral of an officer downed in the line of duty. They should know cabbies cared, too. Hell, we both drove the streets and dealt with some people we'd rather not meet.

Mainly I hoped I'd never have a cop riding in my head.

"Hello?" Mom asked. She was wondering if I'd hung up.

"Sorry. I've been kind of lost in thought these days."

"I understand. Are you doing okay?"

"Would it be possible for me to say a few words at the cere-mony?"

She was quiet. "Well, I suppose. But we have others saying words for the ceremony. Maybe just a few words would be okay."

"Thank you, Mrs. Santana."

"And you said your name was Mark . . ."

"Montoya."

"I'll see what I can do."

I wanted to tell her I was still alive. Maybe I'd get the chance later. "You're in my prayers." That's all I knew to say.

* * *

That night I bought a cold six-pack and went downtown to park and drink in the car.

An hour later I was in my scruffy Nameless One clothes checking out alleys. I needed a place to stay. So it made sense that if I was now homeless, I should find out all the tricks the homeless guys knew.

It didn't take long to get tired of hearing, "Can you spare seventy-five cents for some food?" I guess I didn't look homeless enough. But I knew full-well food was routinely handed out to the homeless at charity kitchens, but you had to listen to the sermon first. Or homeless guys like me could knock on the back door of almost any restaurant and maybe get some of the fancy stuff. Restaurants generate a ton of waste they can't sell. No, what the beggars really needed was money for booze, smokes, and drugs.

I tried to keep my street-wise education short and sweet. Five minutes into it I thought I knew all about it.

But the most annoying come-on line was, "Say, do you mind if I ask you a question?" That was my cue to walk away quickly and not look back. It may have seemed like an innocent question, but it was the opening hook to a long and determined interrogation designed to wear people down into opening up their wallet.

I tried asking about homeless shelters—something for the night. "Hey, guys. I'm homeless, too. Where's the nearest shelter?" But they all said I couldn't get in. There was a daily lottery for beds, and I'd already missed out on my chance to win. But they also seemed upbeat, because it promised to be a warm dry night. The consensus was: I should just curl up in an alley somewhere where I wouldn't get run over. But hide your stuff first.

Women and children had other options. Homeless men were as low as you could go, 'cause we were all wife-beaters and thieving liars. It felt like we were simply branded based on gender.

Okay. Good to know. I decided to treat these guys a little better. Except for the ones who'd ask for a few quarters, then throw them back at you because they really wanted bills.

Mental health in the big city? Good if you can find it.

Next to the fancy Paramount theater, was the plain-Jane State, the rarely used theater. So I checked out the alley behind the theaters. Might be something interesting there.

There wasn't.

Dumpsters. Heating grates. Utility meters. Loose trash. But no guys claiming the good spots. Not yet. I guess it was still too early for beddy-bye. It seemed like we were supposed to beg at night while people were in the streets, then camp out later.

I found a nice grate behind the State Theater. Hey, early birds get the best spot. By nice grate, I mean moderately clean with no bad smells coming out of it. I tried to get comfortable on it, but sleeping in the cramped Civic was looking way better.

I pulled on the grate and found I could get in. Not that I wanted in, but Nameless had an urge to explore. So I peered into the dark below and decided it was only about a seven foot drop. I climbed in but hung onto the lip of the opening. My feet dangled. It was deeper than I'd thought. And no surprise, I lost my grip.

No sprained ankles.

I looked up at the open grate. Not good. Homeless guys would be piling in fast.

The space under the grate was dimly lit from the alley but looked to be a storage area, mostly for junk. Wooden crates, broken tables, miscellaneous broken items that looked like sad old stage lights. Also buckets, a mop, and a ladder.

The ladder was heavily splattered with paint and had a broken rung, but it worked fine so I quickly placed the grate back where it belonged.

I poked around in the dark, feeling a bit like the masked guy in Phantom of the Opera.

No light switch. No flashlight. Not much light coming in from the alley above.

I used one of my cell phones as a weak flashlight.

There were some drain holes in the floor I almost tripped over, three big exhaust vents, lots of paint cans, and some metal cabinets with more paint supplies. Nothing of use. Best of all, there were two doors. One was locked. The other was locked but not closed all the way.

Using the light from my cell phone I peered inside. There was a long hallway with flat scenery things leaning against both sides.

I found a light switch and the florescent lights flickered on. I closed the door behind me so no light would entice anyone who might wander into the alley.

This was cool.

The hallway led to what looked like a low place under the stage—a wide five foot high area with large wooden struts and beams. Looking up, there was a trap door, heavy timbers kept it closed. An elephant couldn't break through it. No orchestra pit that I could see.

Then another hallway with lots of rooms on both sides. Some were being used for storage. Some were obviously dressing rooms. Two were just empty, two were restrooms, and two were packed with clothes on racks. Costumes. Mostly ordinary clothes like you'd find in any Goodwill. But there were also some uniforms and hats and plastic swords and tunics and feather boas and all kinds of stuff like you'd see on stage. Very few shoes, mostly long boots like the French Foreign Legion might wear, and some fancy women's shoes. No socks or underwear.

There was a rickety set of wooden stairs going up. But the hallway kept going, with some branching.

The place was a maze. Costumes, furniture, restrooms, and even a shower. I was in hog heaven.

With more searching I came across boxes of bottled water, soft drinks, a few opened bottles of wine, a mostly empty fridge, and a triple-padlocked liquor cabinet.

Fabric, sewing machines, tools, lumber, assorted supplies, and on and on it went. Home Depot meets Goodwill meets Phantom of the Opera.

I had found my paradise.

Under what I guessed was the lobby, I found a little practice stage with a little curtain and microphones. Another small refrigerator. Another locked liquor cabinet. Another hallway with dressing rooms, restrooms, a workshop, and furniture storage rooms.

Another wooden stairway led up, and there in the basement was a real elevator. I wanted to ride it, but I was afraid there'd be a night watchman hanging out somewhere.

With the underground part mostly explored, I backtracked. There was a lunchroom I'd missed—nothing fresh to eat. Then I arrived at a flight of wooden stairs to the side of the stage. I decided to go up, very quietly. That led to a hallway with doors that opened along one side of the theater. I took the first one and peeked out. I was very close to the stage. There were two green emergency EXIT lights on the back wall, left and right. One over my head and one on the other side of the stage. The theater had a simple slanted floor leading up to the back where I was sure the lobby was and the street-level entrance.

The stage was high and wide. No orchestra pit. No box seats. One balcony in the back. It was a simple long rectangular theater, probably better for movies and music than anything else. The Paramount was ornate with lots of box seats and balconies. This was obviously the State Theater.

Cool.

Most importantly, no night watchman. And apparently, no motion detectors.

From the looks of it, it had been recently decorated. Maybe not the abandoned theater I was hoping for. The old State Theater had become modern.

Not cool.

There'd be concerts and movies and shows and crap. Too many people. Not exactly the Fortress of Solitude I needed. Not the Batcave. Not a good hideout.

Still, it was an interesting place to explore. And I could sleep here tonight, assuming I didn't trip any burglar alarms.

I regretted leaving my stuff in the trunk of the Civic, especially the food and the two remaining cold ones.

There were drinks in the liquor cabinet. Easy to break in for refreshments. But if this was going to be my new home, I needed to keep a low profile.

I walked up the theater ramp to the big doors at the back and peeked out into the lobby. Nothing fancy, but I could see lots of light flooding in through big glass doors and windows. People walked along the street. The lobby wasn't private enough for me. Off to the side was the elevator. And over the street-doors were little boxes that were probably motion detectors. Okay, so the lobby was off-limits.

But no little blinking red lights in the audience area or under the theater so apparently the motion detectors were only for the glass doors facing the street.

It looked like the elevator went up a couple levels. Balcony and what? Offices, maybe? More storage?

I decided to check out the stage.

It was cool. I resisted the urge to twirl around and sing *The hills are alive with the sound of Marko's brain sharing*.

Backstage was good, too. Ropes along a side wall going up really high. A large back door, big enough to load sets from the alley, and it had an alarm on it. A regular back door also wired to an alarm. A large locked cage with lights and sound gear. Two changing rooms. And a tiny office with a padlocked door that wasn't locked. Inside the office was a desk facing one wall, filing cabinets, and what I guessed were the usual stage manager trappings. But a wooden box on one wall caught my eye. Inside I found keys. Lots of keys. All on nails and nicely labeled. Jackpot. I took one of each, thinking that in the morning I'd get copies made and put the originals back.

The alarms would be a problem, but at least the door under the alley grate didn't seem to have an alarm on it. That's when I noticed the alarm code stuck to the inside of the key cabinet.

My new Phantom Driver lair was starting to shape up.

* * *

As Omni-God pushed the Adam and Eve units out the spaceship door, out onto the harsh new world, he said with a twisted grin, "You will have great power in this world, and also great weakness. Know that you will be judged by your deeds, as well as your inactions. And lo, just to keep you on your toes, the hard things shall be easy and the easy things shall be hard. Now make me proud, or die trying." And with a cruel chuckle he slammed the spaceship door and prepped for liftoff.

Adam and Eve knew they were in some really deep shit because there were snakes and dinosaurs everywhere. So they ran like hell, screaming naked into the night.

Survival came first. Creating Cain and Able came a day or two later. And after having enjoyed the fruit of each other's loins, they prayed that Omni-God on high wouldn't return. Sin was truly better than anything! But he did beam down when it was least convenient, as gods always seem to do, and beat on them as if he were their drunk pa, angry at what he'd created and determined to beat the living crap out of everything in sight.

There followed plagues, and earthquakes, and floods, and pestilence. Blood oozed out of many wrong places and all was screwed to the max.

In time, Omni-God grew bored with the machinations of man, so he moved on to seed other worlds. Man was left to his own self-destruction. Earth was soon drenched in the unending war of good versus evil, for every man possessed both. And both good and evil wore raiments of the righteous.

But as the millennia passed, the teeming metropolis of Dystopia One rose up from the imperfect hand of man and gave refuge to troubled masses, as well as great heroes and even greater villains.

So began the saga of Dystopia One. The saga of those who cowered in shadow, and of those who gained twisted-tech mutant super abilities.

With humility comes humanity. But with awesome power comes awesome destruction.

Okay, so I'd already put the theater manager's keys to good use and helped myself to some straight shots of rum. Some trash-comic from Nameless was running wild and free through my head, and I was powerless to stop the sick drivel that spewed into my mind.

I ate some stale chips, took a shower, set the alarm on my black ops phone, then curled up on a prop couch—safe in my new Phantom of the Theater digs. Not safe from Nameless One's incessant fantasies.

He liked *Phantom Driver*. PD for short.

I liked PD too—for Psycho Dystopia.

1.8 Bury Me Deep

Tuesday morning came early with the burner phone's alarm clock. The State Theater was looking less like a cool hideout and more like a trap.

The rum was returned to its liquor cabinet, now locked again. All evidence of my night under the State was cleaned up and removed. Most of it, anyway. Nameless was safely back in the passenger seat. At the rear exit door of the theater I disabled the alarm on the keypad, opened the door, reset the alarm (I thought I had 30 seconds), exited carefully, and made sure it was locked behind me.

Back at my Civic, I felt lucky it wasn't broken into or ticketed. I'd need a better place to park the bat mobile. I drove to a quiet spot and got dressed in black for my funeral.

As much as I was looking forward to my funeral that afternoon, I needed to write some words. So I drove to Magnolia Cafe to get a comfort-breakfast amidst my fellow fringe Austinites. And of course, to write myself a wickedly edgy eulogy.

Life just doesn't get any weirder than that.

Breakfast was exactly what I needed. The words weren't coming, but I was already looking forward to my first planned death—or kill, depending on your point of view. Who would it be? A handsome millionaire for Marie? Or someone more villainous for a true serial hero? I already had some ideas, but it had to be someone who needed killing.

For starters, I had to be the aggressor. That was the easy part. Nameless would be all up in someone's face, throwing death threats at them and waving a loaded gun.

But finding the right bad guy to kill me required some research. And then there was always the chance he'd just wound me and I'd wind up in a prison hospital bed. I needed to be killed outright so I could make a nice clean jump.

I glanced down at the doodles I was drawing and was surprised to see words.

Marko deserved to die. Help me! I'm trapped in my own body.

Nice eulogy, Nameless. Too bad I won't be saying those words.

* * *

After breakfast, I found a hardware store and got some of the theater keys copied. The rest were non-standard, so I risked a visit to a locksmith. They looked closely at the keys, then at me—like I'd just stolen the keys, which I had, which didn't help me look any calmer about the transaction. But I guess locksmiths always looked like that. They accepted my cash, always good, I got my keys, and I was out of there.

I had some time before my funeral, so went down to Town Lake to think things over. I needed help. Nameless seemed to be pushing for a sidekick. Why? Because all heroes needed someone to trust and make gadgets. I'd already ruled out all of my friends—some too straight-laced to believe my crazy new reality—some too off-center to be trusted.

But it occurred to me I didn't have to divulge my whole death-leaping situation. Somehow it felt like I'd won the lottery, but to play it safe, I wanted as few people as possible to know.

Okay. So what if I pretended to be dead, but told my sidekick that my spirit channeled itself through assorted hosts? I could call up my sidekick, go into a psychic trance, and convince him I was a spirit who needed a worldly helper. That might work. Then whenever I needed some help, my trusty sidekick would deliver.

Or maybe I just needed someone to talk to.

Jason might do. Nineteen, not too attached to reality, and probably someone who'd enjoy following weird instructions, especially if some cash landed in his pocket.

But what I really needed was someone really smart who wouldn't be tempted to peek behind the curtain.

Raj was the smartest guy I knew. He could sound like a guy from New York, or London, or from the back streets of India. He was a software guru and he was doing something secretive with stock market numbers that made my head spin. But I was thinking Raj might be too smart because he could probably hack my burner phone, then somehow turn me into *his* sidekick.

So Jason it was.

I thought I'd start him off with a text from my black ops burner phone.

Me: *Jason, dude. It's Marko.*

A few minutes later, Jason replied: *No way!*

Me: *Way! I found a connection.*

Jason: *No way. U lie*

Me: *Look, if you want your Zombie Pirates on Mars game back you'll deal with it. I'm dead, but I found this connection.*

There was another pause. Jason: *Who the hell R U?*

Me: *Marko Noviño Santana. I could use your help.*

Jason: *No way. UR middle names Novino?*

Me: *That's me. Ask Marie. Ask my mom.*

Jason: *Whats my middle name?*

Me: *How the hell should I know?*

Jason: *If U R ded Ud know*

Me: *The dead don't know everything.*

Jason: *Total BS. Real ded know*

Me: *Real dead know squat. Don't believe the lies. Dead people aren't as cool as we'd hoped.*

Jason: *U R bringing me down*

Me: *You broke your elbow trying to ride a horse. You dig redheads. You almost asked Julie to her prom. You got a tat on your left ankle. It's me.*

Jason: *Yeah? If U R ded, tell me something I don't know*

This was so much harder than I thought it would be.

Me: *I'll pay you for your help. You don't want my money?*

Jason: *I want $ but U R ded. Ded dont have $*

Me: *I'm working through a psychic.*

Jason paused, then responded: *LMAO, just use the psychic. Live Marko was smarter than ded Marko. U R 2 dum 2 B Marko*

Me: *Last chance, Jason.*

Jason: *Drop ded! ROTFLMFAO! U R some psychic con man. Take UR con job 2 hell LOL LOL LMAO Drop ded psychic con man*

Why would anyone need a sidekick?

* * *

I arrived at my funeral early. I wanted to help, but mostly I wanted to see Marie and my mother.

As I was driving to the parking lot behind the church, it occurred to me I shouldn't park my Civic there. Even if it had different plates, it had Marko's unique dents and scratches, not to mention the sticker for the taxi yard. So I parked a few blocks away.

Walking to the church, I could already tell it was going to be another really hot day. The usual puffy cotton ball clouds drifted by, keeping whatever water and coolness they had inside them. Considering the cloud balls, the forecast should have been for scattered shade.

The closer I got to the church, the more nervous I got. What if someone recognized me? A stupid thought, but I just couldn't shake it. I was comfortable in Nameless's body, and without a mirror I was easily thinking of myself as everyday Marko.

The church parking lot was already half-full. Maybe my funeral was up against bingo in the basement? I could just imagine the muffled screams of joy coming from down below as the poor priest tried to send my soul upward. Not that I knew much about Catholic funerals, or even whether they tolerated bingo.

But there was a hearse. A nice one. Clean and black and fairly new. I wondered where they'd take my body. I liked the idea of cremation. No need to take up real estate. But mom was more the traditional type.

Open casket? Might be too messy for that. But I was still morbidly curious about my body. There still a lot of unanswered questions about what happened that night. Or maybe I was just hoping my death in the taxi wasn't as pointless as it seemed.

Walking around to the church's front doors was a surprise. Lots of guys from the cab company were already there. And a couple cops. A nice touch, assuming they weren't just hired for funeral crowd control.

As I walked slowly up the steps, I was feeling very self-conscious again. I glanced at my hands to make sure I was still wearing Nameless. It would be classic Twilight Zone for me to suddenly be in my Marko body again. I was dizzy enough without thinking of that scenario.

The priest was standing in the doorway, waiting to greet mourners. Farther in, I could see Hakeem and Earl. I had to hold myself back from going up to them and saying hi.

I had expected to have fun at my funeral, not faint from confusion.

The priest would be easy to deal with. Friends and family would be another matter.

He reached out his hand. "I'm Father Dunley. Welcome." He shook my hand with both of his. There was compassion in his voice. There was a lot of sincerity about him.

"I'm Mark Montoya. A friend of Marko's."

"Yes. I'm so glad you're here. Please accept my sincere condolences on your loss. So very tragic." He ended the long handshake. It wasn't clammy or weird, just concerned and welcoming. He reached into his pocket and pulled out some notes. "I see you offered to give a short eulogy. Would you still like to do that?"

No, because I was feeling massively weirded out and wanted nothing more than to just sit and watch. "Yes."

"Good. Good. I understand you and Marko were into games together."

"Yeah. Uh," I was tempted to rattle off my favorite blood drenched first-person shooters, "computer games."

He smiled. Maybe he knew the violent nature of most games. "I understand they're very popular."

Being a priest had to be rough. The poor guy was probably not allowed to kill, even in a game. As an in-game priest, he'd be splattered by aliens in the first few seconds. Unable to pull the trigger. Unable to defend himself against their semi-inexplicable hatred of humans.

I really liked this guy, even if he was a holier-than-me priest. So I was tempted to say it was harsh that he wasn't allowed to have sex.

Well, sex with women, anyway. Oh man, that would have been a seriously bad thing to say. Mainly I just wanted to sneak an Xbox into his house and a passionate woman into his bed.

Bad thoughts. Evil thoughts. No real Catholic would ever have those thoughts. Would they? And if they did, then what? They'd have to go to confessional and tell the priest they'd sinned because they wanted him to get laid. Or maybe Catholics had even worse thoughts about sex and their priests.

All weird. All bad.

"Thank you," I said, not knowing what I was thanking him for. Mainly, I was just trying to end the conversation—and my twisted train of thought.

"Please sit near the front," he said. "I'll call your name when it's time for you to share your thoughts about Marko."

No. I wanted to sit in the back and watch everyone. "Sure."

I walked in and was greeted by my friends and fellow workers. Greeted like I was a stranger. A stranger with an unknown connection to Marko.

As I walked into the cathedral it just all opened up around me. The high ceiling. The stained glass. Echoes. Rows and rows of pews. Organ music droned quietly in the background. And the heavy smell of those damn flowers they always used at funerals. White lilies? The musky smell of death and Catholic greenhouses overwhelmed everything. Constantly reminding everyone that the dead were here.

And there, front and center, was my casket.

Way too expensive. Mother didn't have that kind of money. A horrible waste.

And the fucking lid was open.

Holy crap. I must be in one piece.

Damned embalmers. Sticking bits of my shattered head back together—with super glue, and chewing gum, and who knew what sorts of evil crap and magic.

I was too far back to see myself. I didn't want to see myself. But I had to. Morbid curiosity doesn't serve any purpose. Or does it?

Then I realized some guy was shaking my hand. I turned to look at him. My uncle. Didn't like him. Never would.

So who made him an usher?

He was mumbling something about me. Me, Marko? Or me, Mark Montoya, the intruder from another dimension?

It didn't matter. I dropped his sweaty hand, and said, "Thank you," then took a few steps down the center aisle.

I paused, remembering to cross myself. Was it left to right? Right to left? I'm not sure I ever knew.

Then I remembered the holy water, but I was already past it. It didn't matter. I had recently slapped death in the face, twice, with no ill effects. I didn't see how a little holy water would change things. Or more likely, it would melt me. Best to avoid it.

I sensed my uncle still behind me. His family evil was a poorly kept secret. So I walked farther down the aisle.

My spidey senses said he was now hanging back. Good.

Mom and Marie were standing near the second row. Both in black. Talking with people in a short line. Maybe somehow this day was my fault. I didn't know what to think—except that I really craved a smoke.

Thanks, Martoni. It was good to know he was feeling something approaching desperation and panic. Maybe some of my anxiety was due to Martoni being dragged into a church to view the innocent young man he'd just blown away a few days ago.

I smiled a bit, knowing he was about to meet the grieving family. Maybe I'd finally get an apology from him. Remotely possible at best.

Yeah, whatever remorse I felt was just my own.

I walked slowly down the aisle noticing many familiar faces. There were lots of mother's friends and relatives. Same for Marie. Yesterday when I wondered if folks would turn out for my funeral, it never occurred to me that just about everybody would be here to support my family. This was so much about mom and Marie and their loss, and so little about me. I was dead and gone, with so little left behind. It was hard to believe I amounted to so little. If I had it all to do over again . . .

Odd that no one gave me much notice. Wasn't I the guest of honor? No. I was an unknown. Someone that supposedly knew Marko. Maybe I should leave. Maybe I didn't really belong here.

Dead and gone, but still hanging around. Like the last guest at a party who didn't know enough to leave.

Unwanted guest or not, I was determined to see mom and Marie again. So I sucked up my doubts and kept inching toward them in the reception line.

Then it occurred to me that mom and Marie were about to hug my killer, Martoni, now my passenger. I hesitated. But I reminded myself I was in the body of Nameless. Nameless killed Martoni. So yeah, I was good with them giving Nameless a hug.

Nameless seemed good with hugging my girlfriend, too.

Life, or whatever the hell I had, was complicated.

As I got closer to mother and Marie, people stepped away. My turn.

"Mrs. Santana," I said to her, then to Marie, "Ms. Turner. I'm Mark Montoya, a close friend of Marko's. Please accept my deep appreciation of your loss." I kicked myself for saying something that lame.

"Yes," mom said. "We spoke on the phone. Thank you for coming."

"I wouldn't—" I stopped myself from saying, *"I wouldn't have missed it for the world."*

I guess they thought I got choked up.

I kept going. "We played a lot of games together—shared a lot of laughs. Good times. It's hard to believe he's gone."

"It's hard for us, too," mom said.

"If there's anything I can do," I said, "please don't think twice about asking. He shared a lot with me. Photos of you and Marie. I know he had a lot of plans . . . things he wanted to do and share with Marie. He loved you both. Maybe more than he ever said. We shared a lot. Marko was like a brother from another . . . portal." I couldn't believe how much I was screwing this up. "Portal . . . like in online gaming. Anyway, I just wanted you to know that I share your loss. More than you know."

Before they could respond I reached out to give my mother a hug goodbye. She accepted my gesture and hugged me back. Somehow she seemed smaller. I was her only child. She'd never remarried. I couldn't imagine how dark this day was for her.

Hugging Marie was much worse. It was a non-hug. It was a cold and vacant thing. Not even a pale shadow of our hugs when I was whole.

I don't know why I expected her to sense my inner spark. My soul was still here—so close and in her arms. But she obviously felt no connection. How much of me did she really love? How much was love for the body, the face, the familiar person I once was?

As I stepped back, it struck me that Marie had basically projected her love on a 3D canvas. The canvas was Marko. A human canvas that reflected, and became, and animated the love she gave it. Mirrored her love in such a responsive way. And now that canvas was gone.

I turned away, unable to look at her disappointment—her disappointment that I was now dead. But mostly the love that had left her—the love that had delivered her to this dark day, so cold and empty.

Where the hell had that come from? I shook my head in disbelief that I'd had such thoughts. I was practical, Nameless was a dreamer, and Martoni was . . . just a Martoni.

In front of me was my casket. People stepped away. My turn.

I stepped up and looked in. I didn't want to see it, but I wanted Martoni to get an eye-full. This is what happens when you put fools behind the trigger.

There was Marko looking all waxy and stiff. My head was miraculously in one piece. Not that I looked at it closely. Hey, I was wearing a suit I'd never seen before. Hopefully they'd be able to return it after the ceremony. I didn't seem to be stinking anything up. Hell, the damn lilies overpowered everything.

If Hugo Martoni had any remorse, I sure couldn't find it. If anything, I supposed he blamed me. Typical.

Time to find a spot and sit through the priest's boring speech about how we seem to die but aren't really dead. Amusing concept. I was tempted to give the speech myself. Yeah, that would have popped open a few eyes.

Look Ma! It's me, your little Marko Mijo. I'm alive and I don't need my stinkin' body. Bless me Father for I have killed the son of a bitch that blasted me with buckshot. Then I took control of his body, then with the help of Nameless, I ditched that bloody body in the desert. I'm sure buzzards had a field day with it.

So you're absolutely right, Padre. I've survived my death, almost like you said I did. Only catch is, I didn't quite make it to heaven. Or hell. I'm stuck right here with y'all.

And surprise, surprise, I've died twice and I've come here to my own funeral to spread the good word. The gospel according to Marko. Say hallelujah everybody! Shoot me once, shoot me twice. It just don't matter, so keep it coming. It's made me the man I am today. So load 'em up and keep on shooting, brother. Praise the Lord and pass the ammunition.

Crap! I might have zoned out.

"Mr. Montoya, would you like to say a few words?" Father Dunley was looking expectantly in my direction.

All eyes turned to me.

Why was I first to give a eulogy?

I got up reluctantly and walked to the microphone. Which speech was I going to give? The lame one I'd written down? Or God's own truth that I was still kicking?

I glanced over at my casket—at my original body. There was a time for lame speeches, and a time for plain honest truth. I wanted neither. So I just started talking.

"Hello. I'm Mark Montoya. I've done a lot of soul searching the last few days. I'll admit I often felt lost and alone. Marko and I were like brothers. I never thought we'd be separated like this. Honestly, it's been hard for me to move forward.

"I've thought about him constantly. I've searched for all that I knew about him, hoping to keep him alive inside me.

"But as well as I knew him, I know now there was so much more to Marko.

"We were brothers—brothers in arms. Online gaming. FPS, uh, that's a style of play called first-person shooter. We were Rogue Squad in the Call of Heroes game-world.

"That might not sound like much to you. But I had Marko's back, and he had mine. And yeah, it wasn't Afghanistan or anything you might appreciate. But at times, it felt about as real.

"If you've never been immersed in a game like that, I can never fully explain it to you. But we suffered together. We died together. And we tasted victory together. It was a world we always tackled as a team. We figured it out. We assessed the risks. We made our plans. Always together. Always. We were a team and focused on our goals for more hours every week than I care to admit.

"I don't care if you're building a home, planning a business, or raising kids. If you're with someone, it's an experience you share. It's a facet of your life that comes alive and binds you to your partner.

"It's no different in-game. It's a shared struggle. It's shared victory and shared defeat.

"And what would life be without a thing shared? A life alone is cold and harsh. I guess he got his fill of that driving nights in his taxi. I guess that's why we buddied up online and kept our camaraderie going over the years. And I know that's why he sought out a wonderful woman like Marie. Someone to share love with. Someone to experience life with.

"As much as I miss my buddy, I know he misses his Marie a thousand times more.

"So yeah, Marko Santana was my online brother in arms. I'll admit, I saw more of his avatar than his earthly form.

"But In a very real sense, you're looking at my avatar right now. I exist beyond this guy you're looking at giving a speech. There is so much more to me than meets the eye, so much more to all of us. The same was certainly true for Marko. He may have lost his avatar, but he's still going. It's obvious to me there's more to life than meets the eye. And I feel certain good ol' Marko is still with us, only in a different form. Maybe not in a form the good Father expects. Maybe not like any one of us expects.

"Well . . . Marko was close to me. And in a very real sense, he still is."

I looked around for the first time. My words were lame, wasted on people who would never understand. I could see it in their blank expressions.

Someone coughed so I returned to my seat.

All those people were still in the dark. What happened to me deserved to be told. It was unfair that the truth was still under wraps. But worse than that, it was a truth no one really wanted to hear.

The other eulogies were better. They were funny. They were touching. I would have laughed. I would have cried. But the only one responsible for these people's loss was me. I should have told them what really happened. That I wasn't really dead, I was still here, in the flesh, just not the right flesh. That would have really blown the priest's mind.

Yes, I was a freak of nature. Yes, they'd probably study me, probe me, electrocute me, dissect me. I had a gift. But like it or not, I stood alone.

Nameless wanted me to use my gift to fight crime, superhero style. It made a certain kind of sense. A natural way to take out killers of all sorts. I could walk into gang territory, start pushing them around until someone killed me. Then do it again and again until they were wiped out. The ones who wouldn't kill would survive. Sort of like a kinder, gentler law of the jungle.

I could disguise myself, walk into a rough bar, and find someone to take a hit on me. They'd kill me. I'd take their body and do it again and again.

It seemed like there was a lot of ways to eliminate killers. When one city ran out, I'd move on to the next one.

Kind of a grim way to tour the U. S.

All superheroes had super villains to play with. But all I'd ever get were the dregs of society. And I'd wind up wearing them.

Bummer.

Martoni wanted me to smoke. Not gonna happen.

Mother wanted me buried. That's what I got.

1. 9 A New Day Loomed

After I was buried I spent the rest of the day doing mindless things. Buying the cheapest food at the grocery store. Walking around in a mall. Watching joggers around Town Lake. Everywhere I went, people were alive. Doing things. Living their life like that's all they really needed to do.

My life was ripped out from under me and turned into a shell game. It resembled little more than a slo-mo train wreck wiping out everything I came in contact with.

Marie was very distant and wanted nothing to do with me. Understandable, but contagiously depressing.

Friends and family treated me like a complete stranger, because I was.

For the next several days I wandered aimlessly. Each night I returned to my hideout under the State Theater, shamelessly drank their booze, and slept it off with fitful dreams filled with blood soaked solutions.

To top it off, my cash was nearly exhausted. I seemed doomed to a life of begging on the street or a life of crime. My bright future was reduced to a pinhole of hope vanishing into the distance.

Man, was I depressed.

I was like a frog in hot water, hating it but determined to tough it out as the temperature slowly became lethal.

Great. I was about to be boiled by my own inaction.

I needed a door to open, a window, anything. So I did what any superhero would do when the chances of survival go to zero. I picked up the black ops phone and I tapped in Rema's number.

Last week when I went looking for a sidekick, I'd looked only to my friends. Sad to say, none were sidekick material. But Marie had friends, and one was a force to be feared. Rema was the queen of I'll-kick-your-ass-till-it-screams-for-mercy-like-it-ain't-never-screamed-before. Rema was a savvy self-taught business woman who owned a bunch of daycare centers. Marie had worked for her and always spoke highly of her, mainly saying how tough and no-nonsense she was. I'd only met Rema once or twice, but frankly she scared the hell out of me.

Yeah, that's exactly what I needed.

Did I mention she was black? If you ever met her in an online FPS game she'd be the one packing the BFG with a trail of smoldering aliens behind her.

Her phone rang. She picked up.

"Whoever you are, I ain't got time for none of your whiny-ass sales shit, so tear up this number up and forget you ever called me 'cause if you don't, you're gonna wish you'd died and gone straight to hell. Have a blessed day."

Dial tone.

Man, she could talk fast.

I was determined, even if it was bad timing for her.

I called again. She picked up.

"Fool! Didn't I just tell you I ain't got time for this shit? So leave me the hell alone or I swear I'll track you down and put my foot where it don't belong and where God never intended. You know what I'm talkin' 'bout? Now do yourself a favor and walk away while you're still able."

Dial tone.

I called again. She picked up.

"Look, I've been real nice with you so far, but it sure does appear you need to be reeducated about the meanin' of what walk away really means. I only hope you've been in the navy 'cause what I'm about to lay on you ain't real lady like, but you brought this on your own fool self, so don't say I didn't give you fair warnin', sucker."

"Rema—"

"Don't you Rema me—"

"I need your help."

"Ain't nobody that doesn't need my help. Now tell me what you're sellin' so I can tell you what's gonna happen with it, and it ain't gonna be what you're thinkin' neither 'cause it's gonna be sooo much worse than anythin' you could ever imagine. Well?"

"I'm a clairvoyant and I've been in contact with Marko Santana. He has a message for Marie."

"Is that the best you could do? 'Cause, sucker, you just opened up a great big bag o' nasty snakes that's gonna make you sorry you ever darkened my day." She paused. "That's all you got to say?"

"Marko loves her."

"That's all you got? Hell, boy, you ain't much of a clairvoyant, are you?"

"He left a to-do list on his dresser. He wants to know if she got it."

"Did he now? What to-do list are you talkin' 'bout? Laundry and such?"

"Yes, but also important things like taking his mother to dinner and telling Marie he loves her more often and, uh, saving money for a vacation."

"Is that what he wrote? 'Cause you know I ain't buyin' this shit."

"Marko also said he needs your help."

"My help? My help?"

"Your help."

"Why would Marko need my help? Lord, he's done dead and buried. Ain't nothin' I can do for him now."

"Well, he could use some cash."

"Christ all mighty! You're even dumber than you sound. What do you take me for, some kind o' brainless fool? I tell you what you do, sucker, you bend way over and—"

"Marko said he felt bad when he accidentally broke that ceramic cat you had in the front room. He was going to replace it, but . . . that kind of fell through a crack."

"That cat didn't fall through no damn crack."

"Right. It fell behind the bookshelf and broke."

"How'd you know that? Only way you'd know that would be if you broke it."

"You were in the kitchen with Marie and another lady. Marko was checking out your books and he accidentally bumped the cat figurine. He would have pulled out the broken pieces, but they were too hard to reach."

"Marko should have told me. Why didn't he do that?"

"He was afraid of you."

"That's bullshit! Ain't nothin' scary about me 'cept my mouth. I ain't never killed no one yet and I ain't never done half the things I threatened to, neither. I thought Marko had more balls than to cover up a thing like that."

"He wasn't perfect."

"Damn straight. None of us are perfect. Now tell me why a dead man needs cash, anyway. And I'm warnin' you, this had better be good, 'cause if it ain't, I've got half a mind to visit every clairvoyant in the county and when I find the one with your damn fool voice I'm gonna beat the psychic crap out of you and stuff it into your lame-ass crystal ball as a reminder to all the other fools who think they know somethin' when they know absolutely nothin' about the crap comin' out o' their faces."

Now what? Try the truth? "I'm Marko."

"Hallelujah! Now we're gettin' somewhere. You gonna stick with that or you gonna decide I'm Marko?"

"I'm Marko. You'll know that when you meet me."

"Meet you? Why the hell would I do that? Oh yeah. So you can take my money. You're 'bout the dumbest joker I've ever talked to, and that's sayin' a lot. You've been real funny and all, but I got better things to do than listen to your mouth—"

"Here's the deal. We meet. If you believe I'm Marko, you help me. Otherwise you kick my ass."

"I ain't your fool. 'Cause I know you'd just pull a gun on me and take my money. They talk about lyin' fools like you on TV every night. So you can just take your—"

"Bring your gun."

"Gun? What gun? Hell, I got so many I'd hardly know which one to bring."

"You hate guns. The only gun you've got is the one you took away from your nephew Deshawn last winter. Probably saved his life."

"How'd you know that? You spying on me?"

"Marie told me."

"She did, did she?"

"Rema, we only met a few times. But you're bigger than life and

Marie talks about you a lot. You're also scary as hell, which is exactly why I need you."

"So now you want my scary shit, too? Listen loser, if you're gonna make shit up you need to get your story straight, 'cause nothin' you've said makes me wanna trust you."

"Meet me someplace public where you'll feel safe. Barton Creek Mall."

"Hell, no. I ain't driving that far. And I ain't meeting you at no damn mall, neither. That's where people get kidnapped."

"Fine. You pick the spot."

"You wanna meet me, then we can do it at the police station at 8th and I-35. I'm sure you know all 'bout that place."

"The police station?"

"That's what I thought."

"Okay. Don't forget to bring your gun, Rema. I'll meet you outside the main entrance, seven p.m. this evening. Don't bring cash."

She seemed to be thinking about it. "I'll bring my boots, 'cause you know your ass is gonna get kicked somethin' fierce."

"Bring Jackson."

"Jackson? Jackson who?"

"Jackson your neighbor across the street. The one Marie said you had the hots for. That's what Jackson."

"Marie's got some explainin' to do."

"See you there."

"Wait. How'll I recognize you? And don't tell me you done dug yourself out o' the grave just 'cause you need to talk with me. I ain't talkin' with no maggoty undead, even if you were rubbin' up against Marie only last week."

"I look nondescript. But I'll recognize you. I'll recognize Jackson too, because of the secret photo you snapped on your cell phone and texted to Marie."

"Damn!"

"You think that's creepy, Rema? Just wait until you hear the story I've got to tell you. And don't bring Marie. We can drag her into this later, if it seems right."

I hung up quickly so Rema couldn't change her mind. Besides, this was a good excuse for her to get to know Jackson better. She'd jump at that.

* * *

I went to the police station early. Near the main entrance there was a little brick planter area with a couple flagpoles in it. It looked uncomfortable so I just sat on the steps.

Rema and Jackson were right on time. They eyed me as they approached. I tried to look nonthreatening.

"Hey, Rema."

"So you're the sucker who thinks he's Marko. I think you should know, you don't look nothin' like him. And while you're gettin' used to that fact, you might also notice I'm wearin' my boots." She showed them off. "Take a good look. They ain't new enough for me to worry none 'bout gettin' them dirty kickin' your lyin' ass up and down the street. So let's have your lame-ass story, sucker."

"My words are only for you."

She glanced over at Jackson. "He stays."

"He can stand out of earshot."

Rema thought about that. "Okay. But just so you know, he can run a damn sight faster than you. So don't be thinkin' 'bout doing nothin' stupid. O' course, this whole thing is stupid. You should know that by now."

I spent the next 20 minutes explaining what had happened to me. Rema wasn't buying it and kept showing me her boots. "See them boots? Are you lookin' at these? 'Cause they're ready to climb your ass, up and down."

Finally, I was at the end of my rope. "Without cash, you leave me with no other option than to get killed by some scumbag and take over his life and his money. Fine. When that happens I'll contact you again, we'll have this discussion again, and you'll know for a fact that I can jump into a new body. Cash or no cash, I need someone I can talk to—someone I can trust."

"If you can do what you say you can, you don't need no sidekick. Do I look like a damn sidekick to you? And in case you hadn't noticed, you're white. Seriously white. And I'm not. See the difference? So there ain't no way I'm gonna be a sidekick to no damn white boy with mental problems. I sure as heaven above don't know what you were thinkin'. Sidekick? Now, if you need a frontkick or a backkick, then I'm there with what you need. Oh yeah. But sidekick? Uh-uh. Your side ain't where I'll be kickin' you, sucker."

"You still don't get it, Rema. If I keep jumping, I'll need a place to stash my money. Someplace better than a hole in the ground. You take your cut, and—"

"What cut?"

"Uh, how about twenty percent? That seems fair."

"Hold on. You say you wanna kill people for their bodies, take all their money and shit, and then make me hold on to it? You must think I'm some kind of stupid, 'cause I ain't doin' that. Uh-uh, no way, no how. Hell, you don't need no sidekick, you need a bagman. Well I ain't holdin' your bag, mister whoever you are. In fact, I've got half a mind to march right in that door over there and turn your sorry ass over to the police, 'cause you are a menace to society if ever I saw one. Know what that means? It means you ain't no damn superhero. You ain't no kind o' hero. You're just scum walkin' 'round with a messed up head."

"It was good seeing you again, Rema. Sorry about the cat figurine."

"Whatever." She tossed a hand in the air and started walking away. "I ain't even wastin' my boot on you, 'cause you're one sick puppy."

Superman walked alone. I guessed I could too.

* * *

The next few days were spent scoping out super villains I could jump into. Texas had plenty of them. Trouble was, they didn't wave death rays around or stage gutsy jewelry heists at VIP parties. Instead, they hosted the VIP parties, they already had the jewelry, and they kept their death rays tucked discreetly in their pants.

Every superhero I could think of had faced super villains that were over the top and easy to spot—no doubt who was who. Give me a twisted joker with messed up lipstick any day. But this was no easy 22 page comic book. My villains were entrenched within the system. Hell, they were the system. Finding them would be the hard part because they'd carefully blended into society. Toasting them would be the easy part.

I was sorry for Nameless. My reality was the exact opposite of any comic book he'd ever drooled over, or any X-Avenger movie he'd watched slack-jawed in the dark. And I was especially sorry for him because moving forward required Nameless to die.

With the last of our cash, I bought him a stack of seriously trashy comics featuring roller derby babes in chains, and some even better comics with super PMSy babes bursting out of their clothes like the Hulk and killing everything in sight.

Sorry, Nameless. I couldn't find the really bad ones.

So I filled Nameless with quality chocolate. I got him drunk on raspberry champagne. I did what I could for the poor bastard, even though he'd pumped my last body full of lead.

He knew this day was coming. We all did.

It was time for Nameless to die.

I, TARGET
PART 2

2.1 Darkness

Having died twice, I was on a roll. Those deaths weren't planned, but the next one would have to be. Today would be seriously interesting, and seriously deadly. Today I'd execute my first planned body-snatch.

So cool.

Now it was time for me to take control of my life, no matter how weird that life had become.

A few weeks ago Martoni got trigger happy with his shotgun. He blew away my body—I got his. That was some crazy shit, but it was real. Then some nameless hitchhiker got in a fight with me and filled Martoni's body full of holes. Same unreal thing happened to me, I got Nameless's body.

After that, I spent a lot of days and nights thinking about those two events. The result was full of assumptions, but it seemed to say I couldn't be killed.

Awesome if I could keep it going—jumping into the bodies of my killers.

Not so awesome if I screwed it up.

They say the devil is in the details. Well, that's exactly where he lived. So that's where I needed to play it safe. Getting shot was safe. Sounds weird but that's what it boiled down to. Any other way of getting killed, like being stabbed, poisoned, or run over by a bus seemed likely to work, but iffy. Untested. But it seemed reasonable that it was the killing that mattered, not the weapon. If my consciousness could jump no matter how I was killed, then I had a lot of options. But there were an awful lot of ways to die. Way too many to count.

So that brought me to a really big question. Was I immortal if I played my cards right?

Okay, so if I was killed by someone, then it was pretty obvious I had a new body to call my own. But what if there wasn't a killer? What if I went swimming alone and drowned? No obvious place to jump—no body to take over. Maybe I'd jump into the nearest bystander 300 yards away? Besides being unfair to the poor guy, it just seemed random.

What if I died of a heart attack? Same question, same unlikely chance I'd relocate into someone else's skin.

What if I died from disease? Germs killed me. Would I become a bunch of germs? How would I even think in a brainless germ body? Nah. I'd be dead.

Suicide? Dead again.

Accident, natural causes, and suicide. They all left me stranded without a killer's body—left me dead.

The only safe path was to be killed by someone. Not just wounded or maimed or crippled for life, but killed outright. That led me to wonder if there was a time limit. Like if I were mortally wounded by someone and I died several months later. Would that count as being killed? Would I eventually get my killer's body?

What if I was accidentally killed by somebody? Like if I wasn't paying attention and stepped in front of a bus? Or like I decided to sleep in a dumpster and it got scooped up, dumped into a trash truck, and then I was squashed in its dark reeking bowels. Crap, that would suck. But would I jump into the bus driver or the trash guy?

Would getting accidentally killed by someone allow me to jump?

Martoni wasn't really trying to kill me, so maybe that counted as an accidental homicide? But a double-barrel shotgun blast into a moving vehicle wasn't exactly an innocent act.

Same for Nameless? We fought over his revolver and it went off. Accidentally? Maybe. The first shot caught us both by surprise, and it was off-center so I might have survived. The other shots were anything but accidental. Nameless clearly put me down.

It was obvious I'd been given a gift. I had all the makings of the ultimate vigilante superhero. I could walk up to any dirtbag, get killed, and walk away laughing through his damn mouth. But I could also screw it up and wind up going through life tied to a feeding tube—or just plain dead if I misjudged the damn details of jumping.

Play the cards you're dealt. They say that a lot. Even my mother says that. Seemed like pretty obvious advice to me. But my cards included this frickin' joker called The Body Snatcher. If the history of the world was any indication, no one had ever held that card before. So how the hell should I play it?

Yeah, what do you do if you're the first guy to ever get the *Get Out of Death, Free* card?

Use it or lose it? I'd already used it twice. It seemed limitless, assuming I was smart enough to keep it going.

That led me to my first planned death. No, my first planned body snatch.

* * *

Mount Bonnell provides a breathtaking view of the downtown Austin skyline and the Lake Austin waterway. Down below there were high-end waterfront homes. Okay, so they weren't homes, they were estates. They were right at the water line and immediately below Mount Bonnell. But like most Texas mountains, Mount Bonnell was little more than wishful thinking, rising less than 300 feet above the water.

Visitors wanting a better view from the top often ignored the warning signs, trekked through a few yards of brush, and wound up going over the cliff. If they were lucky they'd get hung up on a scruffy little tree and have to be rescued by the Austin Fire Department. The others simply finished the roughly 25 story fall.

That's where my first target lived. In a mansion just below the cliffs of Mount Bonnell. Prime real estate located right on the water. Most estates even included private boat houses. Austin living at its finest—if you didn't mind the occasional dead tourist in the back yard.

So there I was, sitting in my old Honda Civic several blocks from my target, soaking up another hot summer night, listening to the crickets. A few blocks away was a private road with a guard house and some underpaid security guy checking cars. Seemed silly because anyone could come up in a boat and step into any millionaire's backyard.

I checked the time again. It was getting close to 11 p.m. Time to drop in on my target, the disgusting Billy Bob Wyville. He was fat, around 60, and ugly as a junkyard dog. The kind of man who goes through the meat-grinder of life and comes out looking like shit but laughing and smelling like serious money. That was Billy Bob. Genetically wired to claw his way up the world of vice.

Actually, that was just a wild-ass guess on my part.

What I really knew surfing the web in a library was that he owned at least three strip clubs, a repo company, a few bounty hunter outfits, two roofing companies, and a string of pawn shops that were willing to buy your worthless gold. None of that justified taking his body. But the part that bugged me was that he'd dodged racketeering charges and was pals with politicians—both sides of the aisle.

If there was anything I hated more than politicians, it was the slime who pulled their strings.

Politicians will tell you they're in charge. Don't believe a word of it. They're all easy pickings for a slap on the back and a sweet deal under the table. Nothing corrupts a politician faster than lakeside barbecue parties, bloated contracts for their relatives, and some high-dollar skirt on the side.

Cutting off the toxic deals at the source seemed like a valuable public service.

Not exactly superhero stuff, but it was a start. Besides, Billy Bob Wyville was as good as I could come up with on short notice. I'd start by taking him out of the picture and siphoning off his liquid assets. His scummy influence drops off the political scene, I get some much needed cash. Win-win, I'd say.

For phase two of my plan, I'd hop into a handsome low-level slimebag so I wouldn't have to stay trapped in Billy Bob's sweaty old body.

Then with Billy Bob's money and handsome slimebag's looks I'd make another pass at Marie. If she didn't like the new me, I'd do the whole damn thing again.

I decided that would be my version of the Texas two-step. Go for the money, go for the looks. Then maybe kick back for a while and enjoy life.

Brilliant.

If I could get good at my two-step, maybe I wouldn't even need a sidekick.

I had it all worked out. At least the big pieces.

I checked the time. Time to get killed. Killed? Actually, I needed to start thinking of it as a body update. Body swap? Brain jump? Something like that. Something less scary than getting killed.

I sat in the car, unable to get out. Getting blown away hurts like hell. Okay, the first time was painless. The second one was a slow blood-gurgling death. Having been shot, I can easily say it was like nothing I ever wanted to do again. If you've been shot a few times, you know exactly what feelings I was going through.

Then there was the total disgust of being planted inside an ugly old troll of a man. Billy Bob Wyville. Wonderful Southern name. Just thinking about it sent chills up and down my spine.

Lastly, there was the certainty that Billy Bob would be in my head—my new passenger. Maybe forever. There was no telling what kind of nasty memories and urges that used douche kit had inside him.

Did I really want to do this?

Hell, no!

Okay, sure. What's the worst that could happen?

As my hand touched the car door to get out, Nameless pushed some of his thoughts to me. I was expecting this, after all, Nameless was about to lose his original body. Martoni and I knew how traumatic that was. Nameless was bound to be frightened.

But what Nameless whispered in my mind shocked me. There were no actual words between us, but the concepts flowed somehow with Nameless's thoughts alternating with mine. It went something like this:

Thank you, Marko.

What?

There was no response because it was a question. Right, no questions. So I put together a thought like: I don't know why

Nameless would be thanking me.

This is what I always wanted.

To die? I mean, I'm surprised you'd want to die.

To be someone else.

Why? Man, it was hard to avoid questions. Well, I couldn't imagine why Nameless would want to be someone else.

Orphan baby. Unwanted.

Sorry, man.

Adopted. Renamed.

Yeah? Okay.

Unloved. Returned.

Oh, crap. That really sucks.

Adopted. Renamed. Returned many times. Never good enough.

Shit!

Others had a permanent self. Never me. Others had identity. Family. Never me.

Those IDs and photos you kept . . .

Fantasy family.

Got it. But you robbed them.

They seemed like family. I wanted them.

Yeah, right. I suppose you killed them. Some of them, anyway.

Only you. Brother.

Brothers? That surprised me, but it didn't seem too far off the mark, considering our brain-sharing situation. It now seemed like Nameless didn't mind losing his body.

Always wanted to be super.

I'm not super. None of us—

We're super. Together. Synergy.

That was debatable.

We're family. Permanent family. Invincible. Super.

Nameless seemed to step back at that point, a big grin on his virtual face. He wanted this body update, even if I was reluctant to get the job done. Getting blown away would make Nameless a happy guy, it'd give him another identity, add another soul to the big happy family I was building in my mental back seat.

Now I knew that Nameless never had much of an identity, and what he did have was forced onto him. No wonder he never gave me his name. For him, names were temporary crap, labels he could never trust to stick. No wonder he lived in a fantasy world, robbing people so he could fondle their identities.

Hell, Nameless wasn't the only one with identity issues. I was seriously on that path.

Back to the bloody business at hand. I checked myself in the Civic's rearview mirror. Nameless was physically smiling, happy with the course of things. As for me, it felt kind of sick to see him in the mirror that way, controlling my face—his face, like he was still alive, which I guess he was.

Nameless was in his original body and still controlling it a bit, so did that make him more alive than me?

Some things were better left unthought.

Enough of this crap. I was stalling.

When I opened the car door, the adrenalin kicked in quickly. My heart was already racing. If things went south, I didn't even want to think about it. Feeding tube, poop bag permanently stapled to a new gut-port, lifelong pain, crap like that. But if things went well, my evening would be filled with blood squirting out of me, searing pain, and my soul barfing and screaming as it landed in good ol' Billy Bob Wyville's bag of bile he called a body.

Fun times ahead.

I grabbed my stuff and stepped out of the car, locked it, and moved quietly into the upscale residential night.

I walked.

Slowly.

I knew Billy Bob's mansion was on Waters Edge road. Surf the web enough and you'll realize the Internet's just one big invasion of privacy. Web maps showed that Billy Bob had a private boat house and a useless decorative fence. More importantly, I was really counting on him having an expensive alarm system. My plan was super simple. Break in through a window, make a hell of a racket, confront Billy Bob in his jammies, wave Nameless's .38 revolver in Billy Bob's face while threatening to kill him, and get myself killed in the process.

Hey, I even brought my Beretta 9mm just in case Billy Bob needed a gun. But if Wyville was the man I thought he was, he'd sleep with something fully loaded under his pillow.

It all played out so nice and neat in my mind. Nameless's body would get blown to bits. I'd take over Billy Bob's revolting body. Then, as the new Billy Bob, I'd call the cops to report a break-in. They'd haul away the body of a nameless drifter. It was all about as easy peasy as it could get.

Well, it looked good on paper. The only way it could go wrong is if Billy Bob put me in a wheelchair for life. I reminded myself to be super threatening, but not enough to give the old guy a heart attack.

About a block away from the neighborhood's guardhouse, I stashed a bunch of my stuff under a hedge—keys, money, cell phones, everything I'd need if the jump wasn't quick. Last thing I needed was another DOA ambulance ride and my stuff pulled from Nameless's pockets and impounded in the city morgue.

Getting around the guardhouse on foot was easy. So much for neighborhood security.

When I got close to Billy Bob's house, I stashed a first aid kit in case my new body got scratched in the heat of battle. Okay, maybe not the smartest precaution, but I imagined a scenario where I'd need to suture myself up. Hell, guys always sutured themselves up in the movies. How hard could it be?

Walking up to Billy Bob's dark mansion, I could sense Nameless was on edge, maybe kissing his ass goodbye. But mainly I hoped he wasn't changing his mind—that mental bit he had left. We all needed money and this was the best way to get it. Besides, Martoni and I had already paid our dues.

Actually, all three of us were ready to throw up in the bushes.

There's a first time for everything. This was my first time to intentionally get killed. If the joker was in my hand, it was worthless if I didn't use it.

I repeatedly tried to psyche myself up, but it was hard. I guess most of us have an aversion to being ripped up by hot bullets. I certainly did.

I chanted *not my body* a few times, but I still wanted to hurl. This was really going to hurt.

Around back of Wyville's house, lights were on in a few

windows. I picked a dark window because I wanted to get all the way in before confronting Billy Bob. I wanted him to see me up close and personal, face to face, not laughing his ass off as I struggled to climb through a broken window.

Things were looking up because there was a big sliding glass door on his back patio. Cool. I picked up a big pot with a little tree in it and heaved it into Billy Bob's house. Glass shattered beautifully. Nice and loud. No backing out now. I raced in to find the ugly sucker.

It was a big house. I ran up the back stairs. He sure didn't seem to be up there. Not even under the beds or in the closets. I didn't hear any alarms, but maybe it was silent. I hadn't had a lot of experience with mansions. Maybe silent alarms were normal.

Damn! What if he wasn't home?

I kept searching.

Finally I found the bastard downstairs sitting calmly behind his desk. I couldn't see his hands. I hoped each one held a machine gun pistol. I didn't know if the Israelis still made Uzis, but that's what I hoped he was holding. One in each hand. Each with massive clips.

Hell, it was Texas. There's a license for anything.

I approached him so he could get a clear shot, filling me with 40 or 50 quick rounds of jacketed lead.

Billy Bob was wearing a Florida souvenir t-shirt with big grinning alligators on it. It said, "Whatever visits Florida, gets eaten in Florida." Not what I expected.

He was so damn calm, just looking at me. He had a cocky devil smile like he handled break-ins every night. "I know you?"

Crap. I didn't need a damn conversation. So I waved my gun at him and made up something. "You fucker! You screwed my sister."

"Hell, boy. I screwed a lot of sisters. Which convent did she go to?"

Billy Bob was a damn comedian! I tried going all hysterical. "I'm going to kill you right now, motherfucker!"

"Fair enough, but first I want you to do something for me."

What? He was an eel. Enough talk! I fired a round that splintered the top of his desk, but off to the side. I didn't want my future body damaged.

Billy Bob started laughing.

He was insane. Or maybe he just needed my spare gun. I reached behind me to pull out my Beretta, thinking I'd toss it to him and get this kill underway.

That's when something smashed into the back of my head. I lost all eyesight. It was followed by the vague sensation of me bouncing off the carpet.

*   *   *

It was damn cold.

It was totally dark. Or else my eyes were ripped out. A definite possibility because of the way my head felt. Actually it felt like my head had been torn off and dropped down a dark elevator shaft. About once every heartbeat it bounced off a wall of the shaft. My body was numb, but my skull was going wham, wham, wham in absolute darkness.

That made no sense.

It felt like I was lying down, but it was hard to tell. I was dizzy, but there was definitely something hard against my back. I tried to sit up but I was caught in something. It felt like I was stretched out and my ankles were tied to something and my neck was tied to something else, and—aw, shit, I couldn't move my arms or my hands or my legs.

When I struggled to get free, there was the sound of plastic.

Strung out on the floor? Wrapped in plastic?

Alive?

Damn, it was cold. I was shivering.

I was stretched out and wrapped up tight like a piece of damn meat.

On the floor. In a pitch black locker? A meat locker? But damn cold like a freezer? There was the sound of a fan or a small motor.

My head throbbed. My heart raced. And somehow it just kept getting colder and colder.

I struggled hard to get free. I kicked and screamed and flailed in every direction.

Hang on, what the hell was I doing that for? I should just relax and let this kill happen. After all, that's why I had confronted Billy Bob Wyville. To get killed. And now it was happening. So relax and enjoy it, Marko. That's what the guys seemed to be saying over and over. *Relax and enjoy it.* Enjoy this nice claustrophobically strung-out damn-slow freezing death. Relax and enjoy it.

Like fucking hell! I struggled again. Wildly.

That went on until the pressure in my head threatened to make me pass out.

I wished it had. I waited in total darkness. Shivered.

What the hell had happened?

Billy Bob had been sitting behind his desk grinning and jerking me around, but his words were nothing but a pile of pure stupid crap. He ignored my threats. I could have killed him. I should have killed him. Screw the plan. I should have robbed the place for whatever I could've found and gotten the hell out.

Now I was going to die and Billy Bob wasn't going to be my killer. No, Billy Bob was laughing his ass off because he sat there in his Florida-friendly t-shirt waiting for the cops. The silent alarm. Cops had knocked me out with a nightstick and hauled me away to—

No. Cops don't toss people in the freezer. Do they? Not usually. No, this was somebody else's handiwork. Some hired lowlife that Billy Bob kept around to take out the trash.

And whoever that was, I was about to get his body.

Assuming he'd let me die.

Assuming I'd eventually die, because lying there shivering my ass off was a slow way to go.

I used to think bleeding out in the West Texas desert was slow, but this? This was a claustrophobic nightmare.

I tried again to relax and let the cold seep into my body. Struggling only warmed me up and made dying take longer.

So I waited, shivering convulsively—violently at times.

Whoever I eventually jumped into, when I finally took over his body I'd shove his hand into a garbage disposal to get even. I'd take a pair of pliers to him and—

And what? Feel all the pain? Mess up my new body? Yeah, while he watched grinning from my back seat.

That thought sickened me about as much as being Billy Bob long enough to siphon off his money. Every time I was killed by scum, I'd have to live with them watching me from the back of my mind. Maybe for the rest of my life. And there was nothing I could ever do to hurt them. Not without hurting myself in the process.

Martoni and Nameless were relatively harmless. At least they weren't evil. I had a bad feeling about the bottom dweller that had clubbed me and wrapped me up to freeze to death.

Maybe I had shitty passengers now, but it could be worse. Hell, it was about to be a lot worse.

I struggled again. There was still a chance I could get free and walk away with little more than frostbite and a three-alarm concussion. Then I'd be free to do what I should have done from the start. Just shoot the bastards.

Find a bastard. Shoot a bastard. Whack-a-mole.

Yeah. I could do that, right? I mean I'd never killed someone before. What if there was some nasty flip-side to the joker card? What if I couldn't kill someone without really bad things happening to me? What if they got my body and I jumped into their freshly dead corpse?

Funny how I'd rationalized how bad Billy Bob was and how he needed to be killed for the public good. Like I knew what he deserved. Funny now that I'd stop at nothing to take the bastard out because I had just cause to bring him down. Then it occurred to me how easy that would be. His lowlife bodyguard had killed me, so I'd get the bodyguard's body. I'd just walk up to Billy Bob, say "howdy boss" and slap him on the back. Then I'd give him a few new holes where he needed them most.

Man, I was pissed! We all were. And payback was gonna be easy.

A while later I stopped shivering. Not a good sign. Or maybe it was. I was relaxing. The cold didn't sting anymore. It actually felt warm—like alcohol warm. Almost cozy and comfortable.

Okay. So I'm not getting free.

This was going to be another death for me. An unknown killer was out there. Somehow I'd make the jump. I hoped distance wouldn't be a problem. Then I'd figure out what to do with his sorry ass. I already knew what to do with Billy Bob Wyville's.

I waited for the jump. It wouldn't be long. How many jumps would this one make? Three. Third death. Third jump. Three charming passengers would be in my head. Four lives counting my original Marko life.

Move over Martoni and Nameless. You're about to get a fellow traveler—a real killer this time. An unknown body awaited us. Third strange body. I should be getting used to this. Yeah, nothing to get grossed out about.

Things were calm now. The pain in my skull was leaving me. Nice. This jump wasn't so bad. Mostly it was claustrophobic. The cold was completely gone.

I decided to take a nap. It'd been a long day.

2.2 Clubbed

Warm. Loud. Soft. I was slammed into the complete opposite sensations of my death.

What had been bitterly cold and hard was now somehow warm and soft and inviting.

What had been quiet was now loud. Pulsing music with an insistent rock beat. My head wasn't throbbing, the music was.

But what had been dark and claustrophobic, still was.

Something was happening. Happening to me.

That something was a woman. A woman who apparently had her bare boobs firmly shoved against my face. Nice big ones at that, judging by the facial sensation I was getting and my need for air. It felt like she was gyrating slowly to the loud rock music. I caught intermittent glimpses of a dark nightclub, alternating with intermittent gulps of air.

I was sitting. Yes, and she was straddling me, giving my face a thorough boobjob. More specifically, she was yakking away with someone while simultaneously giving me a face massage like I'd never forget.

What the hell had happened?

I died. I jumped. And now I was being absentmindedly suffocated by her.

I hoped it was a *her*.

My left hand held something. I guessed it was her ass. I squeezed. It sure felt like a nice female ass. She took that as a request to push herself a little closer—a little harder into me. Not what I wanted, given my oxygen level.

My right hand held a cold wet hard cylinder. I assumed it was a cold drink in a glass. I could hit her in the head with it, or better yet pour it down her back.

Air! I needed air!

Nameless and Martoni were still chanting *relax and enjoy it*. But there was someone new in the back seat. Someone dangerous and very quiet. Someone surprised to be out of the driver's seat. I'd deal with him later.

I tried to talk but between the loud music and her omnipresent breasts, it was futile. I tried turning my head to the right, but that was even worse. To the left was bad. Tilting my head down was better for breathing, but that put my eyes in full dark. Tilting up really blocked my breathing, just another trade-off.

So around and around I went with my head, seeking a way out. She seemed to think that's what I wanted, so stopped talking and grabbed my hair from behind to help gyrate my head around and around in big sensual circles between and over her breasts, helping me to enjoy her top-heavy wonders to the fullest.

Nameless and Martoni were practically jumping up and down in my new brain's back seat. A couple of thrilled man-apes. Don't get me wrong, I enjoyed it too, but I was the one in charge of breathing.

Mercifully, the music stopped and she pulled my passionately pummeled face away from her chest.

I was saved!

And she was beautiful. Big brown eyes, wavy dark brown hair, dusky complexion, and such a big welcoming smile.

She leaned in quickly and planted a major sloppy tongue-flicking kiss on me.

And I responded, tongue and all.

Hell, yeah. Of course I responded. It was in my DNA to respond. Way down deep in my manly Y chromosome. A sexy young woman does things like that and my brain and body switch to automatic.

My left hand did some testosterone-fueled exploring and discovered she wasn't wearing a g-string, or anything else for that matter.

Toto, we're not in Texas anymore.

She finally disengaged, got to her feet, leaned over, and gave me a little pat on my crotch—which spoke volumes about what was going on in my pants.

"Gotta go, Wolfie," she said. "I'm up after the next one." She pulled on a short silk robe, sat down in a chair at our table next to another stripper I hadn't noticed, and worked on finishing her drink.

I was Wolfie?

Then I got my first real look around.

I was expecting a strip club, but what I got was much hotter than the law allowed. Maybe 100 customers, males and females about evenly mixed. Lots of dancers and staff, also about evenly mixed.

Weird.

Topless waiters and waitresses. Unusual, but they were all looking good. Topless customers—some good, most needed to cover up. Oh, hell—bottomless customers, too.

I brought my highball glass to my lips. I needed it. Scotch on the rocks. Yucky stuff.

Sable (somehow I knew that was her name) slurped the last of her drink, got to her feet, and leaned over me. Her robe opened on its own, but I think she wanted it to. "Jade will keep you company while I'm on stage. So be good, and remember, Wolfie—you like me best." Sable leaned in close to my ear. "Later tonight, I thought maybe you'd like to take Jade and me home with you. And if you're feeling up to it, I thought we'd add a new girl, Foxanna. I know you'd like her."

What was I going to say? *No?* "Sounds good." Actually, it sounded freaking amazing.

She winked. "We'll just keep using Billy Bob's credit card. My usual rate. Times three, of course."

I nodded. Somehow Billy Bob was buying me all kinds of wonderful shit tonight. Cool deal. Lovin' ya now, Billy B.

Sable was still leaning over me. She smiled, looked down at her beautiful breasts hanging down. Somehow my hands were all over them.

Oops! Wasn't me. It could have been Nameless, Martoni, or maybe Wolfie doing the fondling. Probably it was all three of them. I reluctantly let go of her breasts and hoped she wouldn't slap me.

Sable gave me a warm kiss on the lips and walked away. The other dancer at our table got to her feet and strutted slowly closer in her seriously high platform shoes, moving in for the kill. Silk kimono. Oriental features. This would be Jade.

I stood up to go find a mirror, and yes, something between my legs reminded me I was having a wonderful time.

Looking down at Jade I began to take stock of my new body. It was definitely big, muscular, and ... well ... big in all the best places.

"No," Jade said, putting a small hand on my wide chest. "You sit now." And with slight constant pressure, I sat.

The next pulsing track was already in progress. Jade was slowly peeling off her green silk kimono for me.

But at this point I was desperate to find out who I was. "Sorry," I said, holding up my hand. Besides, I really had to take a leak.

She paused, a bit surprised.

"Nature calls," I said.

"Oh, baby, it call me all fucking night long." And she continued with her slow strip, occasionally whipping me with her long black hair. "Relax. Enjoy. This nature call for you, sugar." She turned to show me her ass and wiggle it for me. "Your cock be very happy. I make it do tricks. You see."

"I really have to pee."

She stopped and put her hands on her hips. "*Now* you have to pee? *Now? Really?*" She cocked her head. "You can not wait for beauty about to be revealed in front of your beastly eyes?"

Huh? Well, my beastly eyes were definitely primed. I shrugged. She put her hips back in gear—slow gyrations.

Jade continued to slowly remove what little she had on. I smiled. She smiled.

A minute later she was down to nothing but her shoes and was still going. She seemed to pick up on my squirming because she suddenly threw her hands up in the air. "You win. Ta da! Short show."

I grinned, appreciating Jade in her all-together amazing body.

"Okay, big boy. You go now. But you come back fast so I can show you secret oriental feast of flesh. You like it. I hungry."

"Sounds good." It really did.

She scooped up her kimono while I got to my feet, looking around the elaborate club for the men's room.

"Hey. You better not be looking for other girls. I spank your big bad Wolfie ass. Maybe you like that? You very bad man. Go pee now or Sable and me maybe drag you on stage. Maybe you like that, too? Uh-huh. I think you like that very much. Move it now, cowboy. No detour." She shot a finger to the far wall. An animated neon sign in hot pink demonstrated a penis pissing.

Got it.

As I walked past her, she swatted my ass. That made her crack up laughing.

"I whip your ass now." She laughed. "You lick mine later. Uh-huh. Go now. Pee good. Pee fast. Wash hands too, bad boy."

Threading my way through tables and topless waitresses with cocktail trays and dancers doing skintastic things with each other and clothing strewn everywhere and male strippers acting like human popsicle sticks and—

Yeah. It was really slow getting through all that.

So much to see. My greedy eyes reached out, almost like they could touch it—pull it all in.

Then I saw the main stage. It was like a well rehearsed carnival of foreplay and Kama Sutra positions. A mix of really fit guys and seductive girls. The Roman costumes were elaborate and the sex was simulated, or maybe it wasn't. It was hard to tell because I kept tripping over semi-naked people.

I'd start to apologize to the people I'd stepped on or knocked over, but after they looked me up and down they'd invite me to join whatever mini-orgy they had going.

Thanks. But no thanks.

Somebody, maybe it was Nameless or even Martoni, was yelling wildly for me to strip. Or maybe it was assorted people around me. In all that noise it was hard to tell who-all was wanting my bod.

But with all those invites, it occurred to me I might be handsome. Hey, I really needed a mirror.

As I finally made it to the men's room I walked in and almost made a u-turn. Either there were women in the men's room or the other way around.

Both genders were here, both apparently using the facilities. Urinals were here, too. Cool. I must be in the right place. Nothing says men's room like a wall of urinals.

Everyone seemed normal. Pretty much fully dressed and going about their business. No dancers or staff, just us plain-Jane customers. A good place to relax from the pulsing heat outside.

I did get some looks.

But more importantly, there were great big glorious mirrors over the sinks.

As I stepped into view, I was alarmed. Nobody I'd ever seen before. Wolfie looked to be in his late twenties. Tall and well built. Broad shoulders, narrow waist and hips, arms and legs like I'd always wanted. Not muscle-bound like steroid freaks, but he clearly knew the inside of a gym. But that face! Damn! It was a face to make the girls scream.

Thank you, Jesus!

Oh yeah! It looked like I was something of a cultured beast. I was a body born to wear Armani. I was James Bond bolted onto Wolverine. I was—

Damn, I was hot!

Even the hair. That made me a little misty. The finishing touch—perfect.

I started to wash my hands, just so I could stare at myself longer. Holy crap. I was in love with myself.

Who looks this good? No one looks this good. Except the male dancers. Guys in catalogs. A few actors. Okay, maybe a lot of guys. But damn, I looked fine. I could hardly wait to strip and see the whole package. I couldn't believe I actually thought that, but I did. The girls were going to go ape-shit over this steaming hot all-beef entrée.

So why'd the strippers want money to enjoy Wolfie in private? That seemed cheeky. I was ready to read Wolfie the riot act, but the girls were only using Billy Bob's money. Okay. I was cool with that. But the jury was still out on Wolfie's IQ.

After washing my hands a couple times, I walked over to a urinal, away from the other guys, and unzipped. Let's just say, it was easy to find and hard to get out. Pissing with it was an eye opener. Using it for its main purpose was going to be jaw dropping.

Before I'd even started, a woman came up right behind me. I clenched and glanced her way. Maybe in her mid-thirties, maybe a bit older. No surprise. I was now a woman magnet. She was probably admiring my Armani butt. Cool. I relaxed and started doing my business.

Then she was close behind me, pressing herself into me. Reaching around, she grabbed my new all-purpose tool. Weird, but okay. I told myself to relax. She just wanted to help me pee. No problem. It was probably fun for her. I went hands-free and gave her complete control of my glorious leak. It was exciting for me too, actually. I relaxed a bit more. Balance in all things. Good job, lady, you're doing just fine.

She was watching it now. That was fine, too. Steady as she goes.

Wolfie was a big guy, so he had a lot in his bladder. We kept it going.

Damn, this was fun.

I only hoped she didn't think letting her hold my fire hose was an invitation to dinner or anything.

Things got quiet. I looked down. She started shaking it. That's good. Get those last few pesky drops.

We were all done.

No, she was squeezing it now.

That's really nice, lady. Enjoy it, but we're done here.

She switched to stroking it and of course it got happy.

Okay, lady, whose body was this anyway? I'd had this body, oh, maybe 15 or 20 minutes and already others wanted to play with it. Let me check myself out first, okay? At least find out my new name.

She wasn't stopping and I wasn't screaming foul, so we were coming to two obvious scenarios. One: I'd turn around and watch as she got on her knees to suck it silly. Judging by the other women watching us, that could have started a dangerous stampede of kneeling. Two: I'd try to wrestle it away from her without rupturing anything.

Decisions, decisions.

Well, I just stood there with her behind me doing her thing, stroking me in front with one hand and groping my rear end with her other hand. I was happy just to stand there thinking about my options.

Just as I was about to make the call, some older guy walked over to her, pulled her head back by her hair, and stuck his tongue down her throat. She didn't let go of my handle, so we became a very awkward threesome—a sixsome if you count my passengers. It then occurred to me that he was probably her husband. Awkward. Seriously awkward. More awkward than I liked. Both his hands were free, so he started using them on her. She moaned, I suppose because she had my biggie *and* her handy hubby. So with her distracted, I twisted away from her clutches and moved swiftly into an empty stall, closed the door quickly, and slid the latch to the safety position.

Enough privacy for me to ease my new power-tool back into my pants, very carefully zip up, and check out Wolfie's wallet.

The driver's license said, *Waldo Zander Payne*, age 31. I didn't recognize the address. Unusual—I've driven most of Austin. Probably a short street.

So Wolfie was actually Waldo? Great. He couldn't afford a name change? If my name were Waldo I'd switch to Wolfie any day. Unfortunately, I was now legally a Waldo.

In his wallet I also found credit cards, cash, a couple gold VIP cards for normal strip clubs I recognized, and a blushing-purple card for a place called The Zesty Gecko. I was thinking that'd be this place. The club's color scheme seemed to match the card. Then I saw a black VIP card for The Hungry Hole. Okay. And another one for The Tantric Trance. Yeah. All good places I was sure.

Long fingernails were tapping and scraping on my stall door. It wouldn't have surprised me to see middle aged women sliding under the door soon. Note to self: Wolfie had a way of turning women into zombies. Dangerous stuff. I was a seriously potent aphrodisiac.

So cool.

Nameless and Martoni high-fived.

Keys, cell phone, comb, and some business cards. Several business cards from women and a few with *Wolf Payne, Bodyguard to the Stars* on it. No address or phone number on his business card, no website, just a weird hologram barcode thing. As if people could figure that out.

So I was known as Wolf. Wolf Payne. It had a certain ring to it.

And I was a bodyguard to the stars. A bodyguard that only computer geeks with anti-hologram glasses could contact.

Sweet.

Wolf Payne. Wolfie to my friends. Waldo to my mother.

Got it.

Cougar hands were reaching over the stall door, trying to get to the latch. This restroom was rapidly becoming a dangerous place.

I exited the stall forcefully and walked briskly out, glancing at myself in the mirror as I went by. Looking good, Wolf. I reentered the relative safety of the private sex club. What was it called again? The Breasty Gecko? Close enough.

I scanned for the exit. None sighted. So I walked around the perimeter.

But this time I kept moving so I wouldn't get groped, grabbed, pulled down, and forced into having sex with just anybody. I had some fleeting notion of what attractive women must deal with on a daily basis. Avoid eye contact and keep moving at all times. People were such animals.

Oh, yes they were.

The dancers and waitstaff I could deal with, and enjoy. Yeah, I could enjoy them a lot. But the club members were nothing but libidos without borders. Hell, I wouldn't be surprised if Libidos Without Borders was a real organization devoted to spreading free love and STDs around the world.

Interesting—Sable was on stage now. Her carnal skit looked like an Aztec sacrifice with her being carried on high to the altar, and she was the center of attraction. Wow. She was really getting into it. Fake struggling, but very sexy. The gyrating girls beating out primitive rhythms on their drums weren't bad either. Sable moaned and writhed wonderfully as they placed her on the altar, flat on her back. Such a sexy sacrifice. Her skimpy outfit was stripped away by the priestly hunks surrounding her. The sound of Velcro was a bit unprofessional, but the crowd wasn't complaining. Then, no surprise, she was getting fucked from every angle by her fellow Aztec dancers. And from every angle, it wasn't simulated sex.

But I will say she seemed to be really enjoying it. More power to you, Sable. Go girl, go!

As for me? I had paused to watch Sable get it and give it. Hands were now on me, pulling at my clothes. Multigendered hands. Club members—the unwashed masses. I was practically running for the exit now in sight.

The Zesty Fucko was a totally great place to visit. Yeah, but cages for the customers would have made the place even better. Nameless and Martoni had both been well behaved, happy, drooling boys—even downright dumbstruck. Wolf Payne was in his element. Yeah, Wolf, you badass. You rule!

I stifled a howl.

* * *

I soon realized the Zesty Gecko was in the basement of a downtown Austin office building I'd never noticed. From the outside it looked almost abandoned, but under construction. A victim of painfully slow renovation? Maybe they wanted it that way?

I walked around for a while pressing the Cadillac-branded remote on Wolf's keychain. He seemed to want to walk in the direction of a nearby parking garage, but he wasn't more helpful. Eventually I found it on level two in a reserved space—a new black Escalade SUV. Appropriate.

Personally I would have put Wolf in an Aston Martin for that James Bond touch of sophistication. But for hauling dead bodies around, an Escalade made good sense.

I copied the home address from his driver's license into the navigation screen and a map popped up. Great. Wolf lived in the same general neighborhood as Billy Bob Wyville. Of course they knew each other. So Wolf had beaned me and tossed my unconscious body into the deep freeze for the kill.

While I drove, I tried to imagine being Wolf Payne. Was I married? Who else lived at his house? I was learning to casually think about a wife and roommates without actually asking Wolf any questions. The answers were subtle, but seemed reliable. No wife. Lived alone. Liked it that way. Women were too easy to be conquests. They were accessories. They looked good on him.

Huh?

Seven or eight were favorites. They liked it rough.

Okay. More information than I needed, but I drove letting Wolf be himself. There came a point where I felt natural and relaxed with his hands on the wheel. We didn't need the GPS, he knew the way. He seemed perfectly capable of driving. So I let him. He was good with it, so was I. Very weird to let a passenger drive, but I showed him some trust and he liked that. He reached into the center console and pulled out a black Rolex with platinum trim. You go, dude!

Instead of asking where Nameless's body was, I tried to casually wonder where it was.

Freezer.

Yeah. Where was the freezer? No answer because it was a direct question. Even vaguely thinking about the freezer didn't pull up anything useful.

Wolf drove into a steamy night filled with promise.

*　*　*

Wolf's house was upscale and tucked away on a hillside overlooking the water. I pulled the SUV into a big empty 3-car garage. Immaculate. Even the garage's walls and cement slab were painted. Wolf was one sick dude. As I parked, I noted a covered motorcycle off to the side. I quickly closed the garage door, even though it was just me coming home.

The door to the house had a security keypad next to it. That was a problem. He should have had a retinal scan. So I shut out all thoughts, except *Wolf, you're home*. His hand moved to the keypad. I looked but tried to be casual about it. He tapped in 3 6 2 4 3 6. I figured out which key on the keychain to use and we were in. 36, 24, 36? Really? This guy so needed my help.

I flipped on a few lights and was shocked at how clean and neat everything was. It was hard to believe a man lived alone here. There was something definitely wrong with Mr. Bodyguard to the Stars. Every room was like something out of *Modern Homes and Men* magazine. Modern kitchen with lots of rock treatment. Inviting living room with manly browns and tans, leather, touches of cut crystal, indirect lighting—all open and Zen. The living room opened out to a very private pool but still with a great view. Themed bedrooms like steampunk bondage and steamy Bora Bora lagoon, but like no one ever slept there. Everywhere else was manly, modern, and classy—without the slightest hint of tech. No wonder the strippers were hot to come over.

Even the inside of the fridge was showroom ready. I grabbed a Belgian monk beer I'd never heard of and continued my tour.

Cool workout room. Wolf seemed keen to work up a sweat right then. Apparently he really enjoyed pumping iron and doing cardio. Damn, if I looked as good as Wolf I'd keep it looking sharp, too.

Hell, I was exactly that good looking!

Wolf seemed to be giving me a tour so I drank his fine beer and watched as we walked along. A locked gun room, like a walk-in closet. Inside, I saw three high powered rifles, lots of handguns in assorted sizes, and lots of knives—mostly black. No assault rifles or shotguns. Drawers full of ammo and silencers. Not silencers, Wolf had the word *suppressors* in mind. Wolf opened a rosewood box slowly. His pride and joy? A .22 semiautomatic with a silencer. Sorry, Wolf. You're right, it's a suppressor. All custom made. Special ammo. Nice and quiet for up-close wet work.

We locked everything up and continued the tour. A closet full of designer shirts and suits. Actually, I was wrong about Armani because most of his suits were custom tailored from London and Hong Kong. And I'd never seen so many men's shoes in one place— even in the men's department. Wolf was a very twisted man.

It occurred to me that all of his money was tied up in super expensive suits and shoes. I'd have trouble getting any cash out of the guy.

We were wrapping up the tour, but I was stalled in the master bath admiring myself in the mirror. I really had to stop doing that.

But reflecting on the house, not my new bod, the poor guy seemed anal retentive. Everything was just too damned neat. Underneath all the spit and polish there lurked a maladjusted soul—and bad parenting.

Or maybe it wasn't like that. With great taste comes great maid service?

I wondered what his maids were like. French maids all in a row? We all smiled. Easy to imagine sexy maids in the house with feather dusters and seriously short skirts, all in a row, bending over to dust something. Bending over for Wolfie. No, bending over for me. Panties pulled down. Wiggling their curvy bottoms expectantly. So inviting.

Damn, I just couldn't stop thinking about women. Maybe it was Wolf's hormones. Maybe it was just me and the other guys, because Wolf only seemed amused. Watching us. Not hormonal.

His digs were cool, but I still wondered what warehouse held the freezer with my last body. Wolf started walking back to the garage. Okay. Another drive. Lead the way, Mr. Payne.

In the garage we veered to one side. A double-door I hadn't noticed. I unlocked it and stepped into a small room. I was expecting a riding lawn mower, but there was a small commercial walk-in freezer. Padlocked. I unlocked it, knowing what was inside.

Yes, there was poor Nameless. Chilled to death, stretched out, and wrapped in plastic. I noted the thermostat was set a hair above freezing. So frozen stiffs were harder to move?

Speaking of moving. What were we going to do with the body? No answer. I shut the freezer door.

So what was my agenda for tonight? Go get my old dirty Civic? Park it in Payne's pristine garage? Retrieve the meager treasures I'd stashed in the bushes? Finish my deadly business with good ol' Billy Bob? Like I wanted to take over his body now? Like hell, I did.

Besides, Billy Bob seemed to be buying me all kinds of cool stuff. Cool house, manly Rolex, and all the steamy sex clubs I could handle. And all I had to do was kill now and then.

Seemed like a good deal to me. Well, most guys would have jumped at it. Why should I be a snob about killing strangers?

Too much shit to think about.

But what I really wanted was to grab another beer and head outside to enjoy Wolf's hot tub. I hadn't seen it, but a guy like this would certainly have one. I pictured it in my mind.

We locked up the freezer and walked back through the house. We stepped outside and of course it was right where it should be, off to the side of the pool. So I uncovered it and turned it on.

While it warmed up, I went back inside to shed my clothes, grab a towel, and gather up a cooler with some ice and beers.

Okay, so I peeked at my new nudie self in the mirror and it was even better than expected. It occurred to me that Wolf was totally vain. Made sense, because I was sliding down that slippery slope myself.

Back outside, the water was still a bit cool. So I sat on the edge of the hot tub and opened a cold one. It was hard not to notice I had great abs. And my chest was shockingly hairless. Should I have expected anything different? No. Wolf was inclined to get waxed. He probably had women come over all the time to wax and peel him, front and back, top to bottom. Man, that had to hurt.

The water was finally warm enough so I slipped off the edge, down into the bubbles. The jets felt great. Wolf indicated they felt even better after a workout. I could see he was going to nag me about everything. Great, my new passenger was a perfectionist and a backseat driver.

I took the cap off another Belgian beer. Those monks sure knew what they were doing. Wolf seemed annoyed that we were skipping a workout and drinking so many calories.

The vegetables and protein shakes were for me? The beer was for company? Not anymore, Wolf.

The hot tub felt empty. It lacked something curvy to arouse my enjoyment of the night. Sable sounded perfect.

Just great. I was in my head arguing with Wolf about his nutrient regimen while I lusted for the kind of company that lacked a Y chromosome. Not that I knew what a chromosome was, but Wolf did. And he craved some double X chromosome, too. Triple X if he could get it.

Oh yeah. Alcohol did tend to leave me at the mercy of my passengers.

Note to self: Even the best hot tub is boring without women.

A handsome hunk like me all alone. Seemed like a waste of perfectly good beefcake. Besides being kind of lonely. I had the brilliant idea of just giving Marie a call. She could pop over and we'd make it a very sexy night in the tub while enjoying some champagne and the great view.

The good life.

Sable could come over, too. One for Wolfie and one for me. Seemed only fair.

Except Marie wasn't the type to get naked in throbbing hydro jets with just any ol' Wolfie. Women were strange that way. Love, relationship, trust, security—who knew what else? All that stuff took time. Way too much time. Life was short. Why not skip to the good part?

I had obviously skipped to the good part.

All by myself.

Okay, so Marie wouldn't come over. Fine. She'd never know what she was missing.

I thought again about inviting a couple of Wolfie's hot babes over to share the champagne and the view. One for him and one for me. I was pretty sure he'd share. I was also sure his kind of woman would happily skip to the good parts with me. After all, not all women needed dinner and a movie. So it was settled. Wolfie had a little black book full of lusty young accessories. Somewhere. And we'd all enjoy the company. Someone to laugh at Marko's jokes. Someone to bounce around in the hot tub with Wolfie and let him know how virile he was.

Wait. Maybe we should swap dates.

Man, I was already driving myself bat-shit crazy.

There was more to life than sex. Right? There had to be. There was survival. That was important. Sometimes.

How could Wolf be so sexed-up and not appreciate women? It made no sense. Women weren't accessories. They weren't things. They weren't even conquests, although I did understand that one. No. Women were the main reason to live. It didn't matter if you wanted a lover, a conquest, or lust from afar—it was all about women. Hell, without them, all the guys in Austin would just throw themselves off of Mount Bonnell.

Okay, some wouldn't. They had another agenda, but I understood what I was saying to myself.

I drank alone in my fine new skin, enjoyed the view, soaked up the warm summer night. Mainly, I bummed myself out.

It was time to stop feeling sad for Marko. His days were over. I was a patchwork in progress. That's where I needed to focus. On progress.

If I wanted to stay Wolf, I needed to act like Wolf. I needed to know everything he knew. Having him ride all passive in the back seat of my mind just wasn't going to cut it.

Mainly I needed to convince Billy Bob Wyville that I was the same ol' Wolf Payne that he knew and trusted.

Not good odds. At best, Billy Bob would think I was acting weird and fire me. At worst, he'd hire a hitman named Max Hurt to fill my new designer shoes. Then Max would dump my dead ass out in the hill country as buzzard feast.

Okay. Killing me would just keep me going—as Max Hurt. Better the handsome devil you know, than the one you don't. So there it was. I was damn well keeping Wolf's hide wrapped firmly around me.

What I really needed was a video of Wolf so I could learn his style, his mannerisms, his speech pattern. I needed video of him playing golf, laughing it up with the boys, giving a speech at a wedding. Other people might videotape Wolf, but it seemed unlikely he'd record himself. But maybe he would, being super vain and all. Maybe a little video in the bedroom? Seemed unlikely since he could get all the live porn he wanted—no need to watch it.

Unless he was so vain he'd want to watch himself in action? Nah.

Wolf got out of the hot tub and headed straight for the game room. A wall slid open to reveal a big screen TV and a big stash of USB drives. What? Like I wanted to watch myself, I mean Wolf, having sex with assorted women?

No way.

Wolf had the TV on and the show going before I knew what he was doing.

You're a sick man, Mr. Wolf.

So Wolf and Nameless and Martoni and I all sat on the couch watching Wolf perform with one young beauty after another. Sometimes two or more at the same time. All babes, no guys, never any guys. I was relieved.

Wolf seemed kind of rough with the women. Lots of ass slapping and forced entry. He really seemed to like it when they objected to his physical roughness. But mainly he liked to have them all over him, fawning over him while he was spread-eagle on the bed. He seemed to make a point of smiling at the hidden camera while they sucked and kissed and rubbed up against every inch of him. He knew he'd be watching the disk later. He knew this was all about him.

He even winked at the camera once or twice. What a bastard.

Still, the women were amazing. Drop-dead gorgeous. I always wondered what stunningly beautiful women did for sex when they weren't with me—not that they'd ever been with me—but now I knew. Handsome guys and beautiful women—it was a match made in heaven. But for the rest of us, it was a fantasy we wished for often in our dreams.

Not just often—nightly.

The scene ended and now Wolfie was jumping into bed with three new stellar examples of womanhood. That made me depressed since I'd never even had a threesome, but I remembered I was now wearing Wolf's bod so there was some hope for me yet.

Nameless wanted popcorn. Wolf and I just wanted to focus on his Wolfie moves and the way he spoke. He spoke more than I ever did in the bedroom. I guess some women liked it verbal. Martoni and Nameless focused only on the hot babes. Something for everyone.

It was educational.

It was sick.

But we learned a lot.

Really, we did.

Above all, it was a wonderful way to end the day. We were all welcome in Wolf's home. Especially because we all wanted to be him.

And we were.

2.3 Loose Ends

All four of us woke up in Wolf's big wonderful bed. It was a really decadent morning because we slept until almost 10 a.m. Of course, it would have been better if one of us were female.

Personally, I was just happy to use a real bed. Sleeping on props under the State Theater was the pits.

Wolf took a dignified leak while Martoni demanded a bountiful breakfast of bacon and eggs. Nameless wanted to invite someone curvy over to try out the pool. I just wanted enough coffee to regain control of my new brain and put a lid on the guys.

Survival first. Bacon and pool sex could wait.

I started looking for boxer shorts, but Wolf grabbed a pair of workout shorts. Fine. I usually liked an over-sized t-shirt in the morning. Wolf liked his bare chest in the breeze. Fine.

In the kitchen, Wolf wanted a protein shake for breakfast. I wanted coffee. We took turns. We had both. Martoni and Nameless felt pushed aside. Besides, Wolf didn't have any bacon strips or Commander Crunch cereal.

After a liquid breakfast, Wolf headed down the hall to hit the gym. Damn, it was my body now. I didn't need him being this active inside my head. It was almost like he was riding shotgun instead of sitting quietly in the back seat.

Fine. He could work out while I planned our day.

He went right into his morning routine. Okay with me, it gave Wolf things to focus on, like proportion, strength, definition, reps, sets. Whatever. I was never that motivated to pump iron and squeal with the agony of victory.

There was pain. Wolf eagerly soaked it up. The rest of us were spared.

It was like something had surfaced when watching his home-made porn last night. Uh, no, I was referring to how Wolf surfaced and how he was now a lot more real than my other passengers had ever been. Why was that? I'd spent a lot more time with Nameless. Specifically, hours driving around West Texas before he shot me. Why was Wolf way more real in my head? Was he just that forceful? Or was it because I secretly wanted to be him?

Possibly both.

Wolf moved to a different workout station to do some military press sets. I moved on to more important matters. Nameless's chilled corpse was a major problem, mainly because it was still here. Wolf brushed it off as no big deal. We'd handle it tonight.

Okay. Whatever. Billy Bob was a problem, mainly because he wasn't dead and might sniff out the Marko in me. Wolf assured me we could play that game. I was skeptical about that one. Billy Bob might talk like a hayseed, but he was definitely cool under fire and probably suspicious to the core.

So what about my Civic and my stuff in the bushes? What about my stuff still under the State Theater? What about getting Rema to help me, sidekick style?

Sidekick style? Was that a sexual slip? Wolf stopped pumping and the guys all looked at me—figuratively you know, because they didn't have eyes. I happened to notice Wolf was staring at me in the workout mirrors.

So freaky. He was using my new eyes.

Where was I?

No. I wasn't interested in Rema. Not romantically. Just in a normal platonic sidekicky kind of way. Besides, she was way too scary. Seriously, if I made a play for her, she'd probably crush my orbs on the second date. Yeah, no exaggeration. So I naturally had a lot of respect for her new guy, Jackson. He was either a fool, or he had a lot more courage than I'd ever have. I liked strong women, but not too strong. Marie was about as strong as I could handle. Of course, sometimes Marie was too much—in my face about stuff that didn't really matter. Actually—

Damn. Why was I talking to myself about Marie? I already knew all about her.

Wolf smirked, thinking I didn't know jack about women. He went back to pumping weights.

What? What don't I know about women?

Wolf was silent, making me breathe hard, keeping my newly acquired muscles in excellent shape.

Screw Wolf. I'd start by getting my Civic and my stuff from under the bushes. I was in control here.

That's about all the thinking I could do with Wolf hogging the attention and the blood flow. Wolf was a real animal with the weights and the cardio machines. The guys spent a good hour rooting Wolf on as he kicked the gym's butt.

Mainly, I was in the mood to brood.

*   *   *

It wasn't far to where I'd left the Civic—maybe eight blocks from Wolf's house, so we walked. No—*I* walked. From *my* house.

Crap. The Civic was gone. It was dark when I'd parked it so maybe I was just turned around. But no, it was gone. Someone didn't like a working man's car parked in an upscale neighborhood so they had it towed away?

If Billy Bob had wanted it found and removed, he'd have gotten me to do it. Wolf was his cleaner. I knew that much.

That was the end of the Civic. It still had the VIN number so it would be instantly traced to Marko Santana. I was sad about that because it was one of the few things I'd managed to hang on to from my original life.

I looked over my shoulder for cops, but didn't see any. Maybe they thought it was stolen for a joy ride and abandoned here? Unlikely since its owner was killed and his killer disappeared.

Damn! The Civic had Martoni's prints all over it. Hell, Nameless had his all over it, too. Good thing Wolf hadn't touched it.

And if the cops were any good, they'd find traces of Martoni's blood on the passenger's side.

Who knew if Martoni's buzzard-stripped bones had been found yet? It seemed unlikely Martoni had dental records so maybe the bones would be hard to trace. With luck, Nameless's prints weren't in anyone's database. Even if they were, Nameless was just a drifter—now well chilled. I had confidence that Wolf would do his job and disappear the body.

Cool that Wolf could make bodies disappear and hot babes appear out of thin air.

That's when I noticed I wasn't wearing anything but sandals and workout shorts. I'd always hated guys strutting around the city shirtless, maybe because they either looked like cocky SOBs or because they should seriously cover the blubber. Considering my situation, maybe it was time to ditch some of my normal-guy hang-ups.

I grabbed my keys, burner phones, and cash from under the bushes and jogged back to the house, head held high. But I needed to keep a close eye on Wolf. The guy was an exhibitionist.

* * *

Back at Wolf's den, I checked his cell phone. It was still morning, but there were several missed calls, voice mails, and text messages. One voicemail was from Jade: *Bad boy. You die soon. Not too late to get spanked instead. Call me.* A text was from Billy Bob. It only said thanks and that the money had been wire transferred.

Cool. I just got paid for killing myself. That was a first. I tried to get into Wolf's online bank account to see how much money I'd just made, but Wolf wasn't typing in the password for me.

Something was up. Wolf had needs. Lots of needs. Needs that weren't being met.

Okay. Make Wolf happy.

We put the covers back on the bed and fluffed up the pillows. Wolf was still all stony silent.

We cleaned up the kitchen and wiped off the gym equipment. No improvement.

We turned off the hot tub (oops) and covered it. Nada, but I'd be pissed about that, too.

Then we gave Wolf a nice shower. It felt really good, but it also felt really disturbing. Nameless had a rather unremarkable bod, so giving him a shower was easy enough to forget. But soaping up Steve Stunning was more weirdly erotic than I'd imagined. None of us were into guys, but Wolf's body was so hard and smooth and well defined and hairless. Actually he was hard and sculpted all over, making his shape difficult to ignore. If I focused on my hands, I got grossed out. If I focused on my chest being soaped, it felt great. Either way, Wolf liked every minute of it. The rest of us were glad when it was over.

Note to self: Hire a beautician-maid to wax and soap Wolf. We'd all like that. Win-win.

Anyway, Wolf still seemed to have major unmet needs. I scanned his cell phone's contact list. Almost all women. No surprise. The guy had social obligations. The rest of us were comfortable being on our own—some would call us loners. Wolf was a loner too, but he was also a social animal. Wolf needed his social meat.

I selected a horny woman at random based on recent unanswered flirting I found in his text messages. Destiny sounded good.

It rang. Wolf needed meat. Wolf got meat.

"Hi, Wolfie!" Destiny was really excited.

I tried to sound smooth and upscale-dangerous like the real Wolf Payne. "Look, I know this is short notice, but are you available for lunch?"

"Yeah!"

"Great. Antonio's okay?" I didn't know Antonio's but it seemed like the right thing to say.

"Sure. I love Italian. What's the occasion?"

Lunch was an occasion for them? Oops. Not a regular girlfriend. So what occasion was this, anyway? "Hole in one." Did the guy even play golf?

"Ooo, Wolfie. I like the sound of that."

"Meet you there at noon."

"You can pick me up if you want, Wolfie."

That didn't sound wise. "It's been a really busy day. Sorry, but we'll just have to meet at the restaurant. You can still make lunch?"

"Well . . ." Her gears were turning. "Sure. I'll be there."

"Ciao." A weird thing for me to say. Maybe that's what James Bond would say?

"Ciao, baby!"

We hung up. There, now. Is Wolfie happy now?

I suggested Antonio's because he had it in his phone's list of favorite hot spots. I had no clue where it was. I dialed them.

"Antonio's."

"Yes, I need to make a reservation for lunch, 12 o'clock, for two."

"Your name?"

"Wolf Payne."

"Oh, Mr. Payne! Of course we'll have your table ready."

"Thank you."

"Shall I have some chilled champagne waiting for you?"

Champagne for lunch? Well, maybe Destiny would like some. "Sounds good."

"We'll see you at noon."

I had no clue what Destiny looked like. Wolf didn't put little pictures on any of his contacts. How would I recognize her? Maybe she was one of the girls in last night's video love fest? If so, I doubted I'd recognize her with her clothes on.

We did more cleaning around the house for Wolf's appeasement.

It was getting late. Time to go. Destiny awaited.

* * *

I selected Antonio's on the Escalade's GPS and we were off.

As I pulled into the parking lot at Antonio's I could see it was an Italian-Mediterranean kind of restaurant. In other words, it looked like they served really expensive spaghetti. As we walked in, we were immediately greeted by an attractive blond in a wonderfully short skirt.

"Wolfie!" She immediately planted a brief but passionate kiss on all four of us.

We smiled. "Destiny."

She got a funny look on her face. "Tracy, remember?" She glanced around like she was embarrassed.

"Right." Who the hell was Tracy? Destiny was going to be pissed if I sat down with this one.

The maître d' spotted me and came over to greet us. "Ah, Mr. Payne. Welcome. I have a splendid table ready for you and the beautiful young lady."

We followed him upstairs, which was odd since the restaurant was clearly on the ground floor. But upstairs was a cozy little space with panoramic windows giving us a good view of the hill country. The space only had four tables, all were empty. It looked like we might have the floor all to ourselves. A secluded dining spot with a good view. A nice place for private parties.

The champagne was chilled and ready by our table. We were seated, offered menus, and served champagne.

"It's a special occasion," Tracy said to no one, almost making it a question.

The head waiter smiled broadly. "Oh really?"

"Yes." She raised her glass. "Hole in one!"

"Outstanding!" He nodded to both of us, not quite sure who was the golfer. "Quite an accomplishment, I'm sure. I'll give you a moment to look over the menu. The Lobster Tortuga is quite good today."

When he left, Tracy gave me a pained smile. "Wolfie. Destiny is my stage name, you remember that. Please call me Tracy outside the club."

I gave her a Wolfie grin like I'd seen on the videos. "Of course, babe. Just flirting a bit." Great. She was another stripper. Didn't this guy have any regular female friends?

"I like it when you flirt, Wolfie." She started rubbing her foot on my leg. Normally, I'd like that, but lately a lot of women seemed happy to invite themselves right into my space.

Time to relax, Marko. I acted casual about the activities happening under the table. "How've you been?"

"Really good. And yourself?"

"Never better." That was mostly true.

She leaned closer. Her eyes flashed. "So tell me all about your hole in one."

Huh? I adjusted my forks. "Not much to say. It just went in."

"Just slipped straight into the hole?"

Where else would it go? "Yes."

"I'll bet that was satisfying."

"Very."

"Did it go in really slowly, or did it just attack the hole?"

Hell if I knew. "Slowly. Moderately slowly."

"I like it nice and slow. Did you watch it go in?"

"Yes." It was pretty obvious where she was taking this so I tried throwing cold water on the subject. "It was raining at the time."

"So it was nice and wet as it went in. Delicious." She licked her lips.

"There was lightning, too."

"Really? I like it when lightning strikes when I least expect it. But I also like it when I'm really eager for it to strike. You know, when you're all wet and bothered and you're just hoping it's a big strong bolt. Makes me wet just thinking about it."

I adjusted the napkin in my lap. "Golf can do that."

"Yes. Especially the way you play it. I'm hoping you'll play with me someday, Wolfie."

Wolfie never played with her? "Yes, well—"

She grabbed one of my hands and began light strokes. "I've heard good things about your balls. I hear they go really far."

"Well—"

"A girl likes it when they hold up with a lot of vigorous use. I'd like to hold your bag sometime, if you'd let me. And I'd absolutely love to handle your titanium shaft. I hear you really know how to use it on the back nine. So few men do, you know."

"I wear cleats, too."

She neatly snorted her champagne. "Oh my god, I love cleats! More men should wear them. The traction feels so amazing, don't you think?"

"Uh—"

"Especially when it's all wet. Cleats are the best. Little bumpy cleats. Manly cleats. Men need their traction, especially when it's all slippery and wet and delicious." She leaned even closer. "Wolfie, tell me honestly, do you mind the rough? Not a lot, I mean not a jungle or anything. Just a little rough, you know, by the hole. Not really a hazard or anything. I could mow it down if you object to it."

I stalled, pouring us more champagne, which was probably a bad idea. "Well, it's never really bothered me. I just play through it."

"Wow! I know some men mind. Honestly, I don't know why it bothers some guys. It's good to know you're open—you know, to what a real woman is like. I'm sure you're excellent, not just near the hole, but all over the course. It's really about the whole course, you know? Not just the holes. Don't get me wrong, I love it when guys play all the holes, but there's just so much more, don't you think? I love it when a man shows mastery over the course. I mean, with some men I have to practically stick a red flag in the hole and wave it around because they seems so lost. Know what I mean? Then there are the guys that lose it after just a few minutes on the course. They're barely on the green and they have to find their cart and head back to the bar. Then I have to finish playing alone. That really sucks. On my scorecard they get a big fat zero, or maybe it's a mulligan, you know, whatever it's called. But I know you're not like that. Do you keep a scorecard?"

I hoped Wolfie was getting what he wanted. As for me, the endless ditsy banter had me ready to shoot myself.

The waiter arrived just in time with water and iced tea. "May I take your order now?"

Destiny laughed. "Oh my god. I completely forgot to look at the menu. Can you just give me a few more minutes?"

"Certainly."

I wanted to grab the waiter forcefully and keep him at the table. I caught his eye to stop him. "How are the appetizers? Anything you'd care to recommend?"

"They're all good, but the chef tells me the oysters are most excellent today."

Destiny squealed at me. "Oh my god! I love oysters! The way they slide down your throat. I love to swallow. Oh, it's just . . . so . . . sensual." She slid her hand down her throat and down her chest and between her breasts, pulling some fabric down to show off her cleavage. "Oysters are so oral, don't you think?"

The waiter sprouted an enormous grin. "Absolutely. They slide wonderfully. Not my style exactly, but I get that from the ladies when they swallow. I get that all the time." Okay, he obviously wanted to flirt along with us.

Destiny looked at him with annoyance. "Fresh oysters, and a few more minutes to look over the menu."

His smile diminished. "I'm afraid they're fried."

"Then never mind. Sautéed mushrooms?"

"We have those."

"Fine. We'll have that." She dismissed him with a wave and made a show of squinting at her menu.

After he left, she kept sorting through the menu and said in a low tone, "Love the view. Adore the company. Not too fond of the service."

I nodded. "Good service is hard to find."

She looked me in the eye and cocked an eyebrow. "Sometimes, Wolfie, it's right in front of you."

I smiled. I also braced myself for a long hour of salacious banter. And I wondered where my weird new words were coming from. Apparently having passengers upped my IQ.

* * *

Almost two hours later, Destiny was out of her shoes and rubbing her foot up against my crotch in the restaurant, more desperate than ever to get laid by Wolfie. The champagne and a bottle of something white from Napa Valley had loosened my grip on the steering wheel and given Wolf-man all the control he needed to drive Destiny into a titillated frenzy.

My only rest from her incessant flirting, lip licking, and tongue flicking came whenever Destiny needed to go freshen up. Poor girl, she was doing that quite often.

At one point I had half a mind to take her desperate ass home and put her out of her misery. Something any gentleman would be willing to do.

But Wolf wanted none of that. I could tell he was looking for the exit. He'd gotten the sexual adoration he wanted, so his ego was comfortably re-engorged. It was time to dump her and go.

For Wolf this was all some kind of ego game. Leading her on with no intention of giving her any satisfaction. Lying to her with every word and gesture. I understood playing hard to get, but Wolf mainly enjoyed stroking his own ego with women's feelings.

Wolf had a mean streak in him five miles wide. I should have seen it sooner. After all, he killed me without mercy. I got the feeling we were all meat to the Wolf-man. Something I needed to always remember.

But at least Wolf was happy now that his ego was puffed up by her desperate flirting. Now I had a chance to get his stinking bank passwords out of him. *Here Wolfie, Wolfie. Take the nice bait. I scratched your back, now you scratch mine.*

It felt like it was time to go and I was sober enough to drive, so we all got up to leave. But before we made it across the room, Destiny pulled me into her for a no-nonsense kiss. She also took my hand and put it up her short skirt.

She was pantyless, as nature intended, and it was all right there for me—right at hand. Message received.

"Tonight?" she whispered.

Wolf indicated to me that the body of Nameless was ripe for disposal, so tonight was out. As for Destiny, Wolf only wanted to dump her. Leading her on was his ego stroking foreplay, dumping her was his climax. Wolf might have been vicious with Billy Bob's visitors, but he was downright cruel with the young ladies.

Time for me to show Mr. Payne who was driving this life. I stopped thinking of her as ditsy Destiny, this was Tracy. I held Tracy in my arms. "Not tonight." I pulled her tight. "Now." I pushed her back, back toward the small unisex restroom on this floor. I pushed her in and closed the door.

Her eyes were wide. I guess she hadn't seen this coming. I picked her up and set her on the marble counter by the sink. She was light as a feather. Or rather, the muscles I now wore were better than I'd imagined.

She spread her legs. I moved between them, planting passionate kisses on her neck and lips as she struggled with the buttons on my shirt.

As I shed my shirt, she quickly had my belt undone and my slacks unzipped. They fell down to my ankles. I had to admire that skill. She then slipped her hands down along my hips, pushing my boxers slowly down, savoring the view, feeling the curves on my rear. My boxers were hung on something in front of me—to be expected. She teased them down until they slid down my legs. She was pleased at what she'd uncovered. Hell, I was pleased, too. Wolf had some nice equipment. I reached over and pulled her summer top down. No bra to mess with. Cool.

We stroked and pawed each other for a while, getting into the thrill, anticipating the heady joyride ahead. I loved the way she alternated between submission and passion.

But through all of this, Wolf was in a state of disgust. Save it for the good ones, he insisted. Destiny was just some entry-level stripper, not worthy of Wolf Payne's sexual prowess. This was lowering his standards. This was debasing him. This was trashing his ego and risking his image.

Fuck you, Waldo. Tracy wasn't your toy. She had feelings. She had self-esteem, even though her self-esteem needed to be upped. She was very pretty and now that she was talking less, she was amazingly sexy. Tracy was a very passionate young woman, not a jaded stripper to be paid and played.

So I slipped Wolf's most selfish part into her, slowly, deliberately, and I did that with full eye-to-eye contact because I wanted her to know this was all for her pleasure. I made it sensual, and passionate, and I put some heart into it—into her. I didn't know this Tracy person and I didn't love her, but I gave her everything she wanted and I gave it to her exactly like she wanted. Slow when she wanted it slow. Fast when she craved it. I made it all about her and she responded overwhelmingly, again and again. For me, I can honestly say it was the best sex I'd ever had—by a really wide margin—even before we were halfway into it.

Thirty minutes later I decided to show her I just couldn't stand it and needed to lose control. It was a very conscious decision. Amazing to me that I could do that—keep it going when I wanted, let it go when I wanted. Who knew self-control was so liberating?

As Tracy and I put ourselves back together, it was clear that Wolf was the only selfish bitch in the room. The rest of us were adults, willing to put ourselves openly on the line for our partner's pleasure. We gave ourselves completely to the other person, and yes, we also enjoyed every second of what we received.

* * *

As we casually walked hand in hand down the stairs into the main restaurant, Tracy gave my hand a squeeze, then released me. There was a little bounce to her step, a little sway to her hips. Confidence radiated as she walked out of the restaurant. I hung back enjoying the view.

She never looked back. She was perfection.

So there I stood, feeling great about her. I had been worried that she had bonded to me or something and that I'd have to eventually push her away. But, no. She was the strong one, and that really surprised me.

Maybe she knew what Wolf was really like—all ego and bad news. Or maybe she only wanted another notch on her Gucci belt. But maybe she also felt some of Marko inside her when we'd finally collided with all that passion. Mainly, I hoped she had sensed some of my heart.

Who knows?

Wolf loved to dominate. There was no vulnerable side to him, and that meant his heart was hidden. Or it never existed.

Although I never really considered myself Latino, there's one thing I admired about that culture. They seemed to do absolutely everything with heart. That was true whether it was dancing at a wedding or something that involved hot revenge and bloodshed. Everything was served with heart—and heat. When I was Marko Santana I looked the part, but I naively acted more Serbian, like my father. Too often cold—distant. Not that I knew him. Not that I even knew what it meant to be Serbian. Hell, for all I knew they had a hot streak running through their icy veins. Or maybe it was the other way around.

If I had it to do over again, if I had my fine brown skin back, I'd set aside some of that pride, the need to be more American than the Anglos, and I'd wear a little Latino attitude. Hell, the Anglos and Latinos were all just European immigrants—brothers more than they knew, more than they were willing to admit.

A lot of things were sinking in. Post sex revelations? It felt like Marie was drifting even further from me. Had I just cheated on her? Maybe. Maybe not. Was sex after death cheating? In my heart I still loved Marie. I knew I always would. But the physical part of our relationship seemed to be over—lost in my messed-up gunned-down past. How would I feel if Marie had a new boyfriend? Would I be pissed? Maybe I'd be really happy for her. I liked to think so. She deserved the best and frankly that wasn't me anymore. Right now I wasn't sure what the hell I was, what I was becoming.

Strange to feel so lost exactly when I had so much future ahead of me.

Tracy was happy—happy with me and what we'd just shared. Was I happy, too? That was a question I'd never really asked myself before. Not directly. I felt lost, no doubt about that, but damn straight I was happy. I guess Tracy and I both had a bit of a glow going.

Somehow I'd been distracted and forgotten to pay the bill, so I handed my Billy Bob credit card to the head waiter.

He took the card and grinned. Something about his eyes. Did he know? "I trust you enjoyed your meal, Mr. Payne."

"It was very good."

But dessert was amazing. Hot and savory, with a side of savage.

Best lunch ever!

2.4 Poof

I spent the afternoon in Wolf's pool. *My* pool. I couldn't swim, but Wolf sure could. I knew I inherited each host's memories and urges. Now I understood I could also pick up on their skills. What skills did Martoni and Nameless have? Probably none I'd need. Wolf Payne, on the other hand, seemed loaded with possibility. Judging by the crotch rocket in his garage, I bet Wolf knew how to ride a motorcycle—something I knew nothing about. Maybe he'd show off his riding skills someday. Yeah, Wolf's hindbrain had potential. Not that I knew what a hindbrain was, but it seemed certain I had a big one now, getting bigger all the time, packed full of passenger skills.

We enjoyed the ride through the pool as Wolf did his laps. Why was he so driven? Why couldn't he just bob around like most people?

Wolf wanted me to know that giving Destiny those orgasms was due to his amazing skills. I reminded him her name was Tracy and those were entirely my skills, from my hindbrain.

As he swam laps, he thought I was a fool. I thought he was a son of a bitch. I actually told him so. We really didn't like each other.

I wondered why anyone needed a pool this close to the Lake Austin waterway. He indicated I didn't understand. Well, I didn't.

Every now and then, I'd get him out of the pool to see if we could access any of his online bank accounts. But being pissed at each other didn't help his memory any.

I was also expecting a call or text from Billy Bob about work. It seemed like there should be a meeting or an assignment. Something. After all, Payne worked for the guy, so why wasn't I out there guarding Billy Bob's body? Or making sure his sliding glass doors were fixed right? Or threatening someone unless they paid extortion money? Or using those expensive sniper rifles? Or whatever the hell Payne did to justify his high-end cleaner status.

Nothing from Wolf or from Billy Bob.

Not a single request for muscle. Not a clue how to log into my new bank accounts. There were messages from several more women wanting Wolfie's personal touch. None were from Tracy. Good. I hoped she had enough sense to stay the hell away from us—all of us. We were four losers sharing the same magnificent body. Make that three and a half losers—I wasn't completely inept.

Note to self: Find out what *inept* actually meant.

* * *

I stayed in the house and away from Wolf's women. He was in the mood to lure and dump. I wasn't quite ready to offer my sexy bod to another young lady. Wolf said I was. I said I wasn't. Maybe he was right, it was his body and all. Well, it didn't matter because we stayed in for the rest of the day.

We watched some painfully slow golf on TV. Then I flipped the channel and caught a couple innings of baseball. You know a sport's in trouble when the only excitement is watching players spit and chew, then grab their crotch to check and see if the steroids had finally killed their manly parts. We had a healthy but sullen dinner, and we routinely marched into the game room to try and get banking passwords out of him.

Around 10:30 that night, Wolf got to his feet and started walking. It surprised me but I let him go do whatever he wanted. If he headed back to his damn gym room I could always put on the brakes. Or maybe I'd just let him work us into a euphoric state of healthy exhaustion.

Instead, he went into the bedroom and got dressed. Unusual behavior. He had a tendency to peel off whatever I put on him. I thought maybe he was headed to another lust club, but he was underdressed in old jeans and a black turtleneck. Who wears turtlenecks in Texas? Rich oddballs in Dallas? Nah. When you cross the border into Texas you'll see a big sign that says *Don't Mess With Texas*, and a smaller one that says *No Turtlenecks*.

Wolf pushed aside a nightstand and used his thumb print to

open up a small wall safe. Jackpot! He pulled out a fat envelope and closed the safe before I could check out the goodies inside.

I love me some biometric security. His safe was combination free, easy for me to get into later.

In the garage he headed to the freezer room. Good. Time to dump Nameless's body somewhere. I was guessing a long ride to the buzzard zone. Payne pulled the body out of the freezer and switched it off. So that's why it took so long for me to die. The freezer was normally off. Wolf was concerned about his carbon footprint?

Good to know.

We dragged Nameless's cold body into the garage as easy as could be. We set out a big roll of plastic on the immaculate garage floor and proceeded to roll him up like a big tuna. Then we picked him up and placed him effortlessly in the back of the Escalade.

Note to self: Take good care of Wolf's back and knees. The man was a muscular god, but lifting dead weight was part of his job description.

So far so good.

Wolf wanted me to shut up.

Hey. I hadn't said anything.

We let Wolf drive. *I* let Wolf drive. I was in charge—just giving him some slack, that's all. The other guys wondered how I liked living small in the back seat. I would've slugged them if I could've.

Thirty minutes later we wound up in front of a dark warehouse. Wolf opened a big vehicle doorway by pushing a button on a remote. We drove into an empty warehouse space. Wolf transferred the body to a white panel van and we drove off in that. Twenty minutes later we arrived behind a big mortuary. Picking up a casket in the dead of night? Then what? To a cemetery for some moonlight digging and an unofficial burial?

Wolf pulled a ski mask out of the van's glove compartment, put it on, backed the van close to the delivery door, and stepped out. I made mental notes of all this as he pressed a buzzer next to the door. I eyed the security camera. Ski mask and a van that would be hard to trace? Good. Apparently black-market caskets required serious precautions. We waited.

The service door opened and a little guy in a white lab coat opened the door. He scowled. "You're late."

I waited for Wolf to say something.

Nothing. What was I expecting? Wolf could swim, work out, drive, and toss dead bodies around, but he couldn't put two words together?

The little guy was getting nervous.

I came up with something that sounded Wolfish. "We're fine."

Behind the guy was a stainless steel gurney with lots of steel rollers built into the top and a body-size cardboard box resting on the gurney. All this secrecy to buy a three dollar cardboard casket? The little guy opened it. Empty.

I got the impression we were dropping Nameless's body off. Good deal. I didn't feel like digging a big hole in the dark.

Wolf opened the back of the van and picked up Nameless. He plopped him into the cardboard box. What next?

Wolf closed up the van and headed to the driver's seat. Cool. We were done here.

No. He pulled a fat envelope out of the center console, the same envelope he'd gotten from the biometric safe. He headed back. We all went inside. Payoff time.

The little mortician held out his hand. "This had better be the new price." Wolf forked it over. The little guy started counting out what looked like a big stack of hundreds. He finished. "You're short."

Wolf quickly grabbed him by the neck with one hand and pinned him against a wall. I had to admire Wolf's way with little morticians.

What? My turn to speak again? "No. *You're* short." Lame, but I was looking down at the little guy. Wolf squeezed the mortician's neck. It was a good grip. Sweet. Funny how I could feel his neck compressing in my hand.

He started to speak. "You said—" He struggled with both hands to loosen the grip. "You knew the price was going up. Twelve grand. You agreed."

Obviously Wolf was not good with the price hike. My turn again. "Not tonight." Lame, or not lame?

"Fine." We let go of the little guy. He rubbed his neck. His color changed from red to salmon-white. "Next time," he croaked. "Get it right next time." We all pushed boxed Nameless down a hall and through some swinging double doors. There was a big square furnace. We pushed the gurney up to the furnace door. Cremation! So very cool.

The little guy pushed a button to get the burners going.

Jerry. His name was Jerry.

Thanks, Wolf. Next time tell me sooner.

Jerry stared at me, obviously nervous, wanting me to leave.

I wanted to say *I'll be back*, just like Arnold Schwarzenegger. Instead I said, "I'll just wait." Not my best line, but it made Jerry nervous.

After an awkward few minutes, Jerry opened the furnace door and pushed the cardboard box in along the rollers. It went in easily, a perfect fit. The motorized door closed. So long, Nameless. A fitting way to leave. You were so very anonymous, even in death. No headstone. No little plaque. No name, no body, no trace. You were superhero cool, dude.

Cremation was a great way to eliminate messy evidence. I couldn't see cops getting DNA out of carbon and calcium dust. As if I knew anything about it.

Wolf was still hanging around making Jerry nervous. Maybe the idea was to make Jerry think he was next.

"Hasta la vista, baby," I said to Jerry in my best attempt at a Schwarzenegger accent.

He flinched.

Excellent.

I turned to leave. That didn't seem to be what Wolf wanted. Maybe he thought a price hike was cause for execution. Mainly, I was ready for a cold one.

* * *

Back at Wolf's I opened another cold monk beer. We needed to get more. I wasn't sure where to get them, but I definitely wanted more.

I used my thumb to open the biometric safe to check out Wolf's goodies. Loads of cash. Tons. Twenty thousand at least. I could see how Wolf needed lots. He had a pretty high burn rate. In the safe he had a heavily used passport. An unopened Rolex. In case his got scratched? You had to love this guy. Two minty tennis bracelets packed with diamonds. Not Wolf's style, so maybe they were enticements if a reluctant lady ever came along. Seemed unlikely. Meaningless documents. And of course, a small semiautomatic handgun, safety off. Sig Sauer. Pretty little thing.

The phone rang. That freaked me. Normally everything went straight to voicemail. Hot tub time with someone special? Perfect timing.

I picked it up. "Hello."

"Well? What've you got?"

Shit. It sounded like Billy Bob. What did I have? An open safe. A beer in my hand. Maybe he was talking about disappearing the body? That sounded about right. "No problems. It all went smoothly."

"The hell it did. You said you'd call back with an ID on that clown."

Uh. He wanted an ID for Nameless? "He didn't have any."

"You expect me to believe that? Did he have a face? Did he have fingers? You should have run him down by now."

Huh? Wolf knew cops who'd run finger prints on the side? I guessed so. "No match."

"*No match?*" Billy Bob's voice was practically screeching. "Fuck! How's that supposed to make me feel? Some yahoo comes out of nowhere and does a crap-ass job of taking me out? I need information, not excuses. I need to know where the hell he came from—who set him up. Somebody who couldn't afford a decent hitter? That's nobody I know. What about a car?"

"They towed away a Civic." I almost blabbed about who owned the Civic. "It was several blocks away. But the owner was killed about two weeks ago."

"Okay. Keep talking."

I needed to keep the info to a minimum. "He's no match for the guy who broke into your place."

"Yeah? So what the hell are you telling me?"

"The car that was abandoned in your neighborhood was just a coincidence. No connection."

Billy Bob tried to laugh but it sounded more like a hacking cough. "No fucking connection? That's what you gotta say? Payne, every goddamn thing is connected. We're all connected. Every damn piece of crap in the world is connected. Don't forget, Payne, my ass is directly connected to your damn bank account. You hear me? We're all connected. It's a proven fact. We got, at most, what? Six separations between anybody. Who's that fucking actor I'm thinking of?"

"Kevin Bacon."

"Yeah, Kevin fucking Bacon. He proved it. He proved every goddamn thread between somebody and anybody. Now you get your lame ass out of bed and get me a goddamn connection. You get a connection between me and that piece of shit that messed up my place."

"I'm on it."

"Oh yeah? The hell you are. You're acting really strange, Payne. Did you get yourself messed up on steroids or something?"

"No, sir."

"What the hell did you just call me?"

"I'll take care of it."

"Look, Payne, you're not the only one who can clean up a mess. You keep this bullshit up and I'll have Doc take your ass clean out of the game. You hear me? I need to see some goddamn results. Now!"

Billy Bob hung up.

That went really well. Not.

All I needed was a name for Nameless. A name that would tie into Billy Bob's paranoia. This could work out really well if I played it right. I could finger one of Billy Bob's sleazebag friends as the guy who took out the contract. Good. Billy Bob would have that sleazebag toasted, so scratch one sleazebag. Then I'd give the cops an anonymous tip that it was Billy Bob who put out the hit on the sleazebag. A good way to drop two really nasty guys.

Only one problem with that—I'd be the guy doing the hit for

Billy Bob. When the cops picked up Billy Bob, he could drag me down with him.

Problematic.

Wolf seemed to enjoy watching me squirm.

So who was this Doc character, anyway? Doc sounded more dangerous than Wolf. I got the feeling Wolf would enjoy having this Doc guy drop me off at the mortuary. I took out Wolf a few days ago, now Wolf thought it was my turn to die. Wolf laughed. Payback's a bitch.

Wolf still had no clue what jumping was about. Not surprising, considering how much of his brain I now owned. But Wolf's stubborn little mental zone had become a constant thorn in my side.

So I stepped into the gym, whipped off my shirt, and flexed Wolf's muscles in front of his floor-length mirror.

Listen up, Wolf. If Doc cleans my clock, you lose this bod. Take a good long look in the mirror, Wolfie, because when this rock hard bod dies, you can kiss all your hard work goodbye. This handsome guy you see here will be going all moldy in the grave or toasted to a delightful carbon gray in the oven. Hell, Jerry might even barbecue you for free.

Look at it, Waldo Payne! Look at it!

We all looked at it.

And what the hell do you think happens to me? Marko? You think I'll die? Really? You think Doc can kill me? Because I'll just jump into Doc and screw with him.

So think about it long and hard, Waldo. Either you bust your balls to help me, or this amazing babe magnet dies. I thumped his chest for emphasis. Yeah, and whatever brain you have left dies, too.

The last part was a lie. He was already a permanent member of my back seat club, but I tried not to think too loudly about that.

To burn it home, I struck a pose in the mirror. Then another pose. I stripped off the rest of his clothes, full buff nude, and kept it going. Pretty soon, Wolf was doing the posing on his own.

I thought I detected a teardrop forming.

* * *

I needed cooperation. I got cooperation. I was learning the power of leverage. Hell, I was even beginning to think I was born to play hardball with professional killers like Wolf and Doc. They could kill me all they wanted, but I'd just keep coming back for more.

And in the middle of all this infighting, it was becoming increasingly obvious that none of us was happier than Nameless. He thought we'd made it into the superhero big leagues. We were Batman handsome. We were Superman indestructible. And we didn't even have to buy tights or worry about unsightly runs.

I cautioned that we weren't exactly Tony Stark rich. And we certainly weren't Brainiac smart. Nameless thought Brainiac was a bad example because he was a super villain.

Oh yeah? Who cares? And why were all the smart ones evil scientists, anyway?

This was real life. I was a cutting edge crime stopper. I ate hit men for breakfast.

As for Billy Bob, he was just a bump in the road. I was unstoppable.

* * *

I let Wolf work out again in the gym, this time in the buff. After all, his self-image was my leverage. We rooted Wolfie on for an inspired two hour session. After that, we needed a shower big time. It was really late, but Wolf knew Sable was getting off work. Perfect. I needed Wolf to feel totally attached to his body. A power workout followed by power sex would really show him what he had to lose if he didn't cooperate with me. We made the bat-call. Sable responded like the cat woman she was.

Sable came over quickly, without Jade. Thank you, Sable. She ran Billy Bob's credit card through her smart phone swipe thing gizmo. Very professional. All good. She seemed to know where everything was in Wolf's house. She helped herself to some sort of mixed drink. I didn't ask. It was clear that she was one of Wolf's few regulars.

I hoped she would really power into Wolf. I needn't have worried.

Sable pushed us into the shower and soaped us like we'd never been soaped before. I can't begin to describe how beautiful she was or how primal and wildly erotic that shower was.

Women seem to have erogenous zones hidden all over their bodies. Men had all their zones concentrated in one obvious spot. Sable worked Wolf's spot with zeal and determination. We worked all her spots with equal enthusiasm, and a manly sense of exploration. Things got kind of rough. Very physical. Basically we attacked each other. Hell, we were really lucky the glass sides in the shower didn't shatter.

Some things are better left unsaid, but I will say my hands were puckered from a full hour in the shower.

Kudos to Wolfie's deluxe hot water heater for holding up. But mainly, Sable was my new love.

Complete and total bliss was had by all. Even Sable was grinning ear to ear. Wolfie's bod just had that effect on women.

The guys all gave heartfelt thanks to Uncle Billy Bob. He was a total dirtbag, but his money brought us a soapy angel from heaven that night.

Of course, we all wanted Sable to stay the night, but her services were very high-dollar. Ouch. I had no idea fun could get that expensive. Oh, what the hell. Billy Bob should absolutely buy us an overnight with her.

We drank, we discussed it, we paid, she stayed. And I damn well got Billy Bob's money's worth in bed, too. We reenacted my near boob-induced suffocation. We all got a good laugh out of that. I reciprocated sex-induced suffocation on her with something substantial I had going between my legs. That just seemed fair. Hey, I almost suffocated, Sable almost suffocated. We had a great time.

Who knew sex could be that much fun?

I was rapidly understanding why Sable was one of Wolfie's few favorites. One of the few women that he was happy to share his horse with. Sable could do no wrong with it. In fact, she could do whatever the hell she wanted with it, And she did.

Believe it or not, we actually spent a few hours sleeping that night.

Sable got up early in the morning and didn't stay for breakfast. So sad she had to leave so soon. Tip time. No problem because money was no object. We were very generous with Billy Bob's money, but holy crap, Sable's tip was more than I made driving a taxi for a whole month. Well deserved. Man, was it well deserved.

After she was gone, we went back to bed and slept all morning long. I tried not to dream of STDs. I was sure all her sex partners were vetted by the CDC. Hey, I was pretty sure all the Zesty Gecko employees had hourly blood tests.

Right?

2.5 Shifting Gears

When we woke up again it was already afternoon. There was no denying we'd become sex addicts. Which probably sounds like a good thing until you are one, then you realize just how much of life is going by without you. Moderation is a good thing, right?

Right, guys?

Right?

No answer.

I pulled myself out of bed. Nameless and Martoni begged me to seek out more women from Wolf's amazing list. But at least Wolf now seemed to understand what he had to lose.

Yesterday we'd had sex with two amazingly hotties. Today? I could sense Nameless and Martoni drooling as they waited for me to line up today's activities.

Well, guys, the agenda for today was to make Billy Bob happy with me and avoid anything in a skirt, and especially anything out of a skirt. This was serious and we needed to focus on survival.

We cleaned up the place. Made coffee. Ate a healthy breakfast of soylent whey and fiber nuggets. I guess it was technically lunch. Wolf also got in some painful exercise.

All was good. Okay, maybe just a teeny bit grumpy at the thought of a day without skirt.

We switched off the bedroom video recorder. How did that thing get turned on? No problem. I'd erase it later.

We sat down at the computer. Wolf selected a bank website. He logged in, paid some bills, and let me poke around. The balance was a little over $45,000. Very nice. Unfortunately the website password was obscured by a bunch of fat dots. Wolf clicked the Log Off button before I could figure out how to make a withdrawal. I knew where he kept his checkbooks so I could always write myself a check, assuming I could find and fake his signature.

Wolf switched to private browsing mode and typed in the URL for a crappy looking blog website. The last blog entry was four years old. He typed in some password obscured stuff. It popped up a phone number and some kind of coded number. He used his cell phone to text the secret code to the phone number on the screen.

What was that all about?

Next he went to an online grocery store and ordered a bunch of healthy stuff. No beer. Nothing good. Not even the fresh chocolate cream stuffed donuts they had on sale.

Then Wolf went for a quick swim.

I felt like a prisoner.

Thirty minutes later we were out of the pool. The doorbell rang and a guy held out a clipboard for us to sign. No words were said. Wolf signed. The guy went back to his pickup truck and returned with a big paper shopping bag from Marty's Meats. Freshly killed protein?

Wolf took the bag inside and tossed it on the living room floor. Okay. Wolf likes his meat raw and on a nice bamboo hardwood floor? A very weird guy.

I walked over to the paper bag and opened it. There was a canvas bag inside. Unexpected. I unzipped the canvas bag and looked down on bundles of cash. All one hundred dollar bills. All with bank straps that said $10,000. Eighteen bundles. $180,000.

Holy crap.

Was it for me? A peace offering? Hand delivered from some underworld bank's fake blog website?

Or was it for a hit? I had the impression Billy Bob preferred wire transfers for services rendered. So maybe a hit contracted from some third party?

Or maybe Marty's Meats just coughed up some extortion money? That was a lot of money, especially for a place called Marty's Meats.

So I assumed it was for me, probably ordered up from that weird web transaction earlier. A wonderful peace offering. Thanks, Wolf.

We trotted into the bedroom to stash it but it was too much for Wolf's little wall safe, considering the cash, jewelry, and other stuff already in it. So I dropped the meat bag in Wolf's gun room. Seemed appropriate.

Wolf and I were now cooperating. The four of us were like one big happy family stuffed inconveniently into one body. Maybe we were dysfunctional, but hell, all families were messed up if you looked closely enough. Gimme a hug guys. Virtual hug. Air hug.

That thought creeped me out a bit.

Which reminded me of Uncle Billy Bob. I needed a name for Nameless. A name that wouldn't match anybody real. It was easy enough to search the web for weird unused names. After all, I didn't want someone with a face to pop up—the face wouldn't match Nameless's and I'd be accused of being incompetent again.

The unused name was the easy part. The hard part was Billy Bob's obsession with a connection—a connection between Nameless and the guy who ordered the hit. What sort of connection would satisfy Billy Bob's need for an important, but bungled hit? A corporation was being squeezed so they ordered the hit? Too dull. A politically motivated hit? Yes. I'd come up with some kind of political motive behind the hit, a connection to make even Kevin Bacon proud.

So which sleazebag politician did I want to finger? There were so many wonderful choices.

Or I could finger Doc, whoever the hell he was. Apparently Billy Bob used Doc to keep guys like Wolf in line. Even cleaners like Wolf needed enforcers? Hey, Wolf didn't need boundaries because I already had him on a leash.

So blaming things on Doc was an option, but it would be hard to not finger a nice juicy politician.

The doorbell rang. Damn.

It was just someone delivering the groceries Wolf had ordered online. At least I thought they were groceries. Wolf insisted I check before bringing them into the house. I did. Groceries. I gave the guy a reasonable tip and put the food away.

Then Wolf's cell phone rang. Damn. I needed time to plan, not answer bells. Caller ID said it was Billy Bob. I was set to give him a made up name for the hit man, but the political connection was something I was still working on. I needed more time.

"Hello."

"Payne, it seems you and I need to have ourselves a little face to face. So get your ass over here. Now."

He hung up.

We got dressed. I grabbed the keys but paused to think about it. There was a chance Billy Bob would kill me. Not what I wanted, but I could deal with it. I ran that scenario in my mind. If Wolf was killed, I'd need to get back into his house and gather up the valuables. No problem if I planned ahead and tucked the door key under a bush. I already knew Wolf's goofy security code to the house.

Note to self: Always be prepared to die. Wait. Not die, just lose your body.

Wolf thought I was nuts, but I hid the house key under one of his bushes.

We drove to Billy Bob's.

The neighborhood security guy recognized Wolf's face and we were in. I parked the Escalade and rang Billy Bob's doorbell. Some muscular guy I didn't recognize opened the door. Wolf tightened up big-time. Was this Doc? He was shorter and older than I expected, but he looked like he could take care of himself. Judging by his scars, he liked to mix it up. Judging by Wolf's lack of scars, he liked to skip to the kill shot. If I were a big feral wolf comfortable with bringing down elk and wild boar, this guy with a buzz cut seemed like a tight muscled pit bull raised only for fighting. A bloody matchup to be sure.

This was Doc. Thanks, Wolf. Good to know.

We're both good with the kill. Okay, thanks, Wolf.

Don't get in my way. Got it, Wolf.

Wolf was ready to take the driver's seat if events needed his services. Fine with me. I wasn't about to tangle with Doc. If things went south, I'd let Wolf run free and do whatever he wanted to Doc and Billy Bob. If somehow Wolf lost a battle to the death, I'd make the jump and take Wolf's skills with me. We made a good team.

But why wait for a fight to start? Wolf's hackles were already up and his reflexes were on a hair trigger, so I let him take the wheel. This was a tactical situation, so better him than me. Wolf could do the walking, I'd do the talking.

Wolf let Doc lead the way down the hall. That seemed to make Doc uncomfortable. Good.

Billy Bob was waiting in his office. He looked casual sitting behind his desk, wearing a dull green jungle-camo-Hawaiian kind of shirt. Good to know old guys from Florida wore more than gator tees.

"Payne. Good of you to be here on such short notice. Have a seat." He waved to a chair front and center, an unlit cigar in one hand did the pointing.

I sat. Doc stood directly behind me and close. Not a good position to act as Billy Bob's body guard, but good for snapping my neck. Or trying to. I wondered if Wolf could take him if our meeting turned into a life or death dogfight. Wolf grinned, baring his fangs inside my mind. Impressive.

I wondered if it was a good idea to let Doc have a superior position behind us. Wolf thought it was an advantage. Let your opponent focus on a single point of attack. Look weak, be ready.

Okay. Wolf was cocky. I was cocky. Wolf left the talking to me, I left the fighting to him. The buddy system. Wolf pack.

I'd never seen Wolf take anyone apart. Seemed like a good day to sit back and see what the beast could do.

Oops. Billy Bob's nice big desk still had my bullet trail gouged into its top.

Billy Bob caught my gaze. "I got me a new desk. On order. Better than this one. Funny how things work out. I'm sure you'd agree, Payne. Care for something fine from Havana?"

"I don't smoke."

"Of course you don't. Would have been rude not to offer." He lit the end of his cigar while rolling it in his mouth and puffing. "You probably think we're here to talk about the attempt on my life the other night."

"Yes. I've—"

"Relax, Payne. I'm taking you off that one." He puffed. "It occurs to me that you need a vacation from my services. Contrary to my better judgment, this won't be an irreversible vacation. I trust you appreciate my outlook on things."

I didn't.

"So here's what you do, Payne. You take yourself over to the Plaid Cactus tonight. My treat, son. Relax while you're there. Get your head together. Think about your situation. You know, get your damn priorities straight. Whatever the hell it is you need to do. Take a month if you need it. Then get your ass back in the game. Now get."

I got up.

"One more thing, boy. While you're on this little vacation of yours, don't even think about using my credit cards or any of my accounts. Don't run anymore damn tabs in my name, none of that crap. When you return, and one way or another you *will* return, then we'll talk about easing you back into the business, and if that's even possible."

I waited for more.

"That's all I gotta say."

* * *

It was a short drive back to Wolf's place. As I recovered the house key from under the bush and stepped inside, it was clear we were all pissed. We were worried. Mainly, we were in uncharted waters.

Wolf indicated that Billy Bob had always been happy with his services. And now that I was driving, everything was screwed up.

Huh? I hadn't done anything. I let Wolf do his job and scrub Nameless clean off the planet. We were on-call, right? All systems nominal. Whatever nominal meant.

What it meant was that Nameless was still feeding me his retro NASA words and wanted me to know he was still in my head despite being scrubbed off the planet.

Yeah, scrubbed off was harsh. Sorry, Nameless.

Well, exactly who was alive and who was dead here was a complicated subject. I was on the verge of arguing about it with all the guys mano a mano a mano a mano, but my head was seriously spinning.

I sat down on the couch to clear my thoughts and get a grip.

Okay, Marko. Take a deep breath. Think slowly and calmly.

Okay.

It should be pretty clear to all the guys that they needed me to keep it going, crappy job or not. Yeah, so my body was a loaner and technically I was only alive-ish. The guys still needed me to keep this ball rolling, otherwise we'd all be dead. Permanently. All of us.

I sat there letting that sink into our brain. No matter how many of us there were, or whose body we had today, this was my show. So give me a break and cut me some slack, guys. Or better yet, stop riding my ass and give me some serious cooperation.

They could either help me, or I'd pull this rolling wreck over to the curb and figure out how to just walk away.

A moment later, something shifted in the back of my head. The guys all had my back. If I got depressed they'd all cheer me up, crack jokes as best they could, whatever it took. They were now my suicide prevention squad.

Same thing if I put myself at risk for a natural death, like a heart attack. The guys would cheer when I ate my veggies and boo when I opted for a greasy burger. My survival was their survival.

Same for doing anything dangerous. Like climbing up a tree with revved-up chainsaws in each hand or stepping out of a slippery bathtub.

Basically, my guys were now acting like a multi-headed live-in mom. Eat your lima beans, Marko. Get off that ladder, Marko. Drink lots of water. Put that beer down. Don't take candy from strangers.

Right. Like I needed that? Somehow the need for cooperation had become a chorus of nannies.

So I walked into Wolf's garage and pulled the tarp off his motorcycle.

A big Suzuki with a fat rear tire. A lot heavier than I expected. Carbon black? I guess that was cool. No helmet? Not cool, Wolf. No keys?

Wolf walked over to a cabinet. Inside were some leather jackets, special sunglasses, keys, boots, gloves. In the bottom of the cabinet was a black helmet. I reached for it, but Wolf didn't want it. For special jobs only. Besides it was too hot.

Screw you. I put the helmet on. I suited up as we had a

nonverbal 4-way argument about the helmet. There had to be a better way to control my mental passengers. This was just nuts.

I opened the garage door and sat on the motorcycle, engine off. I had no clue how this thing worked. None of us did except Wolf.

We just sat there.

Fine. I took off the helmet and tossed it.

Wolf did something with his feet. His right hand moved to the throttle and a red button while his left hand turned the key.

The big engine between our legs started. Wolf revved it. The tach needle swung up and engine-scream echoed in the garage. A shiver went through the guys. Good stuff. Loud stuff. Manly stuff.

All pretense about being nurturing and motherly left our testosterone enriched brain cells.

I'll admit I was a bit worried about getting my legs burned on the engine, and the thing was really heavy so tipping over was all too easy.

Wolf just smirked. He did something with his foot and hand and we rolled out of the garage. He touched a remote in the jacket and the garage door closed behind us.

Maybe this was a bad idea. Wolf could swim on his own. Wolf could pump iron on his own. Hell, he could even drive his SUV on his own in dangerous traffic. This ride was probably safe enough, as long as I didn't have to do anything. But that's what worried me.

He revved the engine again. It seemed like the whole neighborhood knew whenever he went for a ride.

As we rode into the street, Wolf leaned forward slightly and accelerated hard, bringing the front wheel off the road. Oh, shit! We were doing a wheelie. Wolf was showing off, making us all feel like pansies in his head.

He braked for a stop sign but rolled right through it, turned, and began working his way through the hills and past greenbelts.

It was a hot day but the breeze cooled us nicely. Wolf seemed to have no trouble leaning his motorcycle into the turns. The bike was now alive. It seemed almost weightless when it had speed.

Wolf took us west, along winding hill country roads, past rivers and greenbelts, whizzing past slow cars on blind curves, down steep hills at high speed, pressed into the seat at river bottom, then flying up the next hill to another blind curve.

There were other bikers out here, mostly on Harleys. I thought they'd wave as they often did to other bikers, but I supposed we looked like speed freaks on a damn rice burner. Not their type. And to us, they were just obstacles like everything else on the road, following the rules.

We came up to a quarter mile of straight road with no traffic on it. Wolf opened it up without hesitation. I glanced down at 170 mph. Cool, but damn I looked up to see the end of the straightaway rushing up to greet us. Three of us were watching our lives come to another quick end, while the only guy with his original body smirked and made a breathtaking turn, just barely keeping it on the road. Lanes be damned, we needed the whole damn road.

About a half hour into the ride we passed two young guys on their hot motorcycles. We looked like a challenge, so they took off after us. I was tempted to remind Wolf that if we flew off the road we'd all be perma-dead. But this didn't seem like a good time to start a fight with him.

It looked like Wolf was baiting the other riders, letting them get close behind us. He glanced back at them, as if to say *don't try this at home*, and hit the throttle. We flew ahead, came to a sharp right turn with an unexpected pickup truck moving slow and blocking our lane. And just like the other times, we kept our speed and switched to the oncoming lane. I really wanted to close my eyes, but that wasn't such a good idea.

Just as I was about to tell Wolf to cool it, we passed a squad car waiting for speeders, his radar gun poking out his window. He was a blur as we passed, but it seemed like his mouth was hanging open. I caught a glimpse in the mirror of gravel spraying out from under his tires as he tried to get the cruiser onto pavement. But then the other two guys passed him, slowed rapidly, then changed their minds and decided to outrun him just like we were doing.

The chase was on. Great fun unless someone died. I can't say I was thrilled at the thought I'd been given the gift of eternal life, only to have it ended by a stupid accident.

I told Wolf to pull over and take the ticket. Billy Bob would pay it or bribe a judge to dismiss it. But Wolf was enjoying the wind in his muzzle. If I tried to take over the bike we'd fly off the road for sure. At the speeds we were going, it was no time for me to learn how to drive the damn thing.

So on we flew, around other cars and scaring the shit out of oncoming vehicles—and me.

Just when I thought we'd gotten away with it, Wolf slammed the brakes at the top of a rise. Up ahead, two cruisers had completely blocked the road. Lights flashing, sirens off, and the two cops looking fairly excited behind their wall of steel. We double backed and Wolf laid into the throttle. What? We were now going head to head with the other bikers and the squad car behind them?

I was just about convinced Wolf had a death wish when he suddenly slowed and tucked the motorcycle into a private side road leading up a hill to someone's house.

A moment later the two hotshots whizzed past, followed a few seconds later by the cop coming into view, lights and siren going, rear tires chirping and smoking as he rounded a corner. None of us expected to see him that soon. The guy must have been massively pissed, pushing his cruiser to the limit, just trying to stay in the game with fast bikes. Or maybe hill country cops knew something I didn't about cop tires and cop shocks and throwing a cruiser into the turns. Either way, it was thrilling to watch him use the brake, throttle, and steering wheel, matching his memory of the road to what the squad car would allow.

He disappeared around a turn.

Wolf pulled out of our spot and we headed back to the house. I got the impression Wolf was pissed he didn't get to dismember Doc and Billy Bob earlier today. He wanted me to know what he was capable of, the skills and killing power he had inside him. Well, he'd just given me a glimpse of his abilities with today's high-speed chase. He had a strong urge to show me even more.

So what was I to Wolf anyway? Just some joker temporarily in the driver's seat. This was his body, his mind. He had the connections, the skills, the looks, the women, the money. I had none of those. So Wolf wanted to know what I brought to the table. He thought I was nothing, nothing except the joker in his hand that would allow him to survive being killed. According to Wolf, that was my only value. I was merely a card he could play if the chips were down.

Wolf liked having me in his hand and I should understand that's exactly the way it was between us. Wolf wanted me to know the damn joker doesn't tell the player what to do. The joker doesn't drive, Wolf does. Just like he was doing now with the motorcycle.

Wolf felt he had all the cards and I was just one of them. So I should get the hell out of his frontal lobes and find a small quiet corner in Wolf's hindbrain. This was Wolf's body and his damn brain, and I was just some kind of thought-sucking parasite trying to control him.

I sat quietly letting Wolf operate the bike through the hills and back into Austin. There was a time for battle, and a time to shut up and put some slack on the leash. So I let Wolf ride in the driver's seat. The other guys looked puzzled, like: *Why hadn't they thought of this before? Just give Marko the boot. After all, he was just a mental parasite.*

It wasn't easy sitting quietly with mutiny swirling all around.

Note to self: Relax. The frontal lobes would always be mine, whatever the hell they were. Even if lobes weren't important, this was all out turf war. This was a brain-grab that had to be settled. Not now, but soon—and decisively.

* * *

When we got home, I calmly eased back into my mental driver's seat. No need for confrontation. Wolf was always mine to control, mine to unleash. Same with the other guys, although it never seemed useful to unleash them. When would I ever do that? Oh, I might let Nameless run wild in Vegas or at a crazy convention like Comic-Con or Porn-Con. That might be fun. But why would I ever unleash Martoni? Who knew if either of those guys had any cool skills like Wolf?

I always had as much control as I wanted, something I kept forgetting. I really must remember that.

No important messages on the phones. Well, Sable did text me a happy face.

Wolf swam quietly in the pool and the rest of us cleaned up the house. Not at the same time, of course.

For dinner we ate the usual Wolf chow. Salad on a plate and protein in a glass. For dessert we had chocolate fiber biscuits. Yum. I could have ditched Wolf's miserable diet, but I kind of liked the way it looked on us.

But we were still out of monk beer. Which reminded me about the unlimited drinks we had waiting for us at some bar that Billy Bob recommended. Our last perk from our disgruntled employer.

I asked Wolf if he wanted Billy Bob back again as his boss. Wolf shrugged. Obviously the perks were good and Wolf liked getting physical for a living. But it was clear to all of us that Billy Bob's days were numbered.

What did Billy Bob say? We'd come back one way or another, then he'd decide what would happened to us.

Yeah? Good luck with that, old man.

* * *

Since my future was clouding up, I decided this would be an ideal time to visit Rema, Marie's boot-happy friend. Besides, it would be fun to show off my new bod. Maybe Rema would see the error of her ways and agree to be my sidekick. More than ever, I needed a friend, one who'd help out with my new financial situation. And maybe help me kick some butt.

Okay, so maybe I was being naive, but Rema lived on the rough side of I-35, and she owned and managed multiple daycare centers, so naturally I figured she could handle druggies, gang bangers, pedophiles, zoning politics, anal bankers, and a pack of multiracial teachers who loved to micromanage little monsters, not to mention handling the little monsters themselves—and their parents.

How many cops had all those skills? None. How many FBI agents knew how to give three-year-olds an *accidental* bloody nose to get them to stop tormenting Zelda? Not a one. And how many Navy SEAL Delta Team 6 guys could adequately prep a poopy ADHD toddler for the Texas public school system? I rest my case.

So I stuffed some starter cash into a small paper bag and headed to Rema's house. One hundred thousand dollars seemed like a good amount. No woman I knew could resist a handsome guy bearing lots of cash.

As I pulled up in front of Rema's pert little yellow house I noted the time, a little after 7 p.m. There was just her car in the driveway, no obvious visitors, so it seemed safe to proceed.

I grabbed the money, stepped out of the big black Escalade, opened the little gate on her chain-link fence, walked up the sidewalk, onto the porch, and rang the bell.

As I stood there, bag in hand, I could see Rema checking me out through the beveled glass in her front door. Finally she opened the door a few inches.

"Whatever you're selling, I don't want it. And whatever you want, I don't have it. And whatever you were thinkin', it was probably the biggest mistake any fool wearing New York clothes ever made. So just march yourself right back to your pimp mobile and take your sales pitch somewhere else. But if you really wanna do folks a favor you could take yourself three doors down to the ugly little old fool that lives there and tell him where he can shove his yappy little mutt. Have a blessed day and kindly shut the damn gate."

Rema slammed the door, but she was still talking to me. "Go on. Get your butt off o' my porch and don't stop until I can't see you no more. Don't just stand there pretendin' you didn't hear me, sucker, when we both know good and well you hear me just fine. Now get, and don't ever think about comin' back here. Do you hear me? But of course if there's somethin' wrong with your ears, I just happen to have a pair of knitting needles I could use to clean 'em out for you."

"Rema, it's me. Marko."

"The hell you say! Marko ain't never looked like that, even in his wildest dreams, 'cause you look a damn site better than he ever did. Not that he was ugly, but he did have that Mexican thing going on all over him, if you know what I mean, and I'm sure you do. So get while you're still able, 'cause I've had enough of fools thinkin' they were Marko."

"I told you I'd come back. This is my new body."

"Well, you've done real good with it, I'll give you that. But just like I told that other white guy, you ain't Marko—no way, no how. See, Marko was what we call Mexican. At least he looked that way, even if he didn't exactly act the part. But look at you standin' there so big and full o' yourself. Hell, you're just some big New Yorker with a halfway decent tan and great shoes. Speakin' 'bout shoes, did the last guy ever mention my boots?"

"I still need a sidekick to hold onto my cash."

"Cash? What cash?"

I pulled out a $10,000 bundle of hundreds and held it up to the beveled glass.

She opened the door a crack. "Damn. Lemme see that." The bundle disappeared and the door slammed shut in my face.

"Sweet mother of God! Heavens above, wait 'til Maxine gets a load o' this. Holy mother of pearl!" Rema started pacing back and forth, mumbling to herself.

Back at the door, she inspected me again through the glass with big eyes. "I suppose you expect me to believe this here's real, 'cause what I'm holding is obviously counterfeit, but I expect you already knew that."

"It's real."

"And I'm supposed to believe that? Just like I'm supposed to believe you're some kinda dead Marko, risen fresh from the grave, looking all kinds of pretty, like some kinda movie star in those fancy clothes? Is that what you think I'm thinkin'? 'Cause I'm not thinkin' that. Uh-uh. No one in their right mind would ever believe you're Marko. Next time send over a skinny young Mexican and I might believe it. Now get."

"What about my money."

"What money? This? I'm savin' this for the police. The law's gonna have some fun with you, sucker. All I need now is your photo ID and your license plate number. Then you'll be doin' 20 to life busting rocks in the heat. Just be glad this ain't Arizona. Now get, before the cops roll up and play that In-A-Gadda-Da-Vida drum solo on your fool head with their nightsticks—a tune I'm thinkin' 'bout in my head right now."

"Just hold all of it until I get back. Take 20% off the top like I said last time."

"How much are we talkin' 'bout?"

"A hundred grand. You keep twenty."

"Really?"

"Yeah. Really. Can we talk about this inside?"

"Here it comes. I suppose you want to sit right down and have me serve you some fresh-made lemonade and sugar cookies while we check out your little bag o' trouble? For all I know you got a gun in the sack and you're just lookin' to do some shit to get yourself on the nightly news."

"Here." I turned the bag upside down. Nine bundles tumbled out onto Rema's porch.

She opened the door several inches. "Don't be doin' that! Not in my neighborhood." She started grabbing money and pulling it inside. "People got big mouths 'round here. Last thing I need them to see is some big white fool dumping cash at my feet. Lord only knows the evil thoughts that'd fly into their heads."

I pushed the door open a bit more. "So let's talk. Or I could go door to door telling your neighbors to watch out for thieves because I just unloaded a hundred grand on you."

Rema stood up and looked me in the eye.

"Honest, Rema, I just want to talk." I raised my hands. "Does it look like I've got a gun on me?"

"Don't stand there like that!" Rema opened the door. "Put your damn fool hands down."

"So pat me down, Rema."

"Like hell I will. Get your white butt in here."

I stepped in. She picked up the last two bundles on the porch and closed the door.

I started to sit in a nice padded recliner.

"Not there! Sit on the couch."

"I sat there last time."

"Last time? What last time? You ain't never had a last time."

"When I was Marko."

"Oh yeah, right." She settled into her recliner while keeping a suspicious eye trained on me. "Now I suppose you've got your little scam speech all ready to go." She pulled out some yarn from a knitting basket next to her and began stuffing the cash into the bottom of the basket. "Don't mind me. Just say what you came to say and I'll make sure you find the door."

"Knitting?"

"And you thought I was joking about the knitting needles."

"No one knits in Texas."

"Why the hell not?"

"It's too damn hot to wear sweaters."

"Now you're startin' to sound like Marko. He thought he knew everything, too."

Huh? "Really?"

"Uh-huh. He knew all about everythin'. To hear him talk, he practically invented computer games—and women. But what he knew about women, shoot, you could easily fit it into a coin purse. Not to speak ill of the dead or anythin', just that he was kinda annoyin' to be around. You know?"

People thought I was annoying? "I saw you at my funeral, but you seemed distant."

"We're back to that again? Look, whoever you are, you weren't at Marko's funeral. But your con-artist friend was there, lyin' through his teeth 'bout how he played battleship or some kinda war game with Marko. You and that other Marko wannabe ought to be ashamed o' yourself. So now I suppose you're gonna tell me what I already know 'bout—a broken ceramic cat, 'bout Jackson."

"How is Jackson?"

"What do you mean, how is Jackson? You know damn well how Jackson is."

Rema sounded bent out of shape. More bent than usual. Maybe there was a problem with Jackson? "What's up with Jackson?"

"You know damn well, what's up with Jackson. You and that other guy been spyin' on me. Don't deny it. God don't like lyin' and neither do I."

"Sounds like you broke up with him."

"Is that what it sounds like? Is that what you think?"

"I'm not spying on you. Look, if you broke up, I'm sorry. There are lots of guys out there. You got a lot going for you, Rema."

"What I got is a stack of money with Benjamins facing the wrong way and a damn fool in my living room. Or maybe I'm supposed to believe you just popped out of the grave like some modern day Jesus and decided to park your unholy butt right here on my couch, and hand me a stack of badly printed money like I was born in another country or somethin'. Just look at you, smilin' all cocky like you were God's gift to women, which you ain't, by the way, even if you do look like it. Know what I'm sayin'?"

Smiling? I wasn't smiling. I put my hand to my face. Someone was using it without permission. I wiped the grin off. "No ma'am."

"Then what? What'd you expect me to think?"

"I need a sidekick because I could lose my body at any time."

"Lose your body? No foolin'?"

"Yeah."

"So your tellin' me you keep losin' your body, like you just walked off one sunny day and left it somewhere? I suppose you just looked down at yourself one day and noticed it was all gone and everythin'. Then you said somethin' like, 'Damn! Where'd my body go? I lost it again.' Well, what about your mind? Ever think of checkin' for that? 'Cause what I'm talkin' to is all kinda messed up and not really here. Know what I'm sayin'?"

"I'm Marko. I'll always be Marko."

"Uh-huh. I heard that before. Personally, I think you lost your mind a long time ago and if I were you I'd go out looking' for it right now. Hell, you might even find it, and if you do, just pick it up, dust it off, and screw it back on, 'cause from where I'm sittin' you got the body, it's what goes inside that's missing."

"Really? Because right now I have four minds inside this body."

"Four? Now we're talkin'. That sounds real good and all. But you know what I'd do? I'd make a sign and wear it just to let folks know what's going on inside you. That's what I'd do. Hell, you should walk around downtown with that sign. You know what I'm sayin'? Plenty of folks over there are having the same damn problem with their heads. Lots o' folks downtown have too many minds. That's a proven fact. Trust me when I say that, 'cause I've met more than my fair share. That's for damn sure. Listen here, Marko, I just know you'd make a lot of friends with that sign around your neck, downtown, right now. You need some cardboard and a crayon? 'Cause I can get that for you. You could have it say somethin' like:

Help. Four minds. One Body. Need money for drugs!"

"This is exactly why I need you."

"Why?"

"Because you know how to handle people."

"People? I ain't handlin' no people. Especially whatever people you think you got crawlin' 'round inside you. So you just keep your nasty little people where they belong." She looked at my crotch. "And don't be playin' with them neither."

I glanced down at my hands, afraid one of my passengers was getting weird on me. My hands were still where I'd left them, in a safe position.

Rema pointed at me. "Uh-huh. You know what I'm talkin' 'bout, don't you? I know where you're little friends live and I've got a pair of pinking shears that say they'd be sorry if they ever came out. So don't even think about sharing them with me. Now get out while you still can, 'cause you're one sick puppy."

"Remember? That's what you said to me before."

"That don't mean nothin'. I say that all the time."

"You see it don't you? I'm the same crazy guy you met in front of the police station a few weeks ago. I'm the same Marko."

She shook her head. "What I see is an epidemic of fools."

"And when I come back again in another body?"

"Bring cash. Lots of it. Just drop it off and go."

"What's it going to take to convince you?"

"Convince me? Convince me of what? That you're good at stealin' money and bodies? That you're Marko deep down inside you?"

"Yes."

"Then do a miracle."

I pointed at Wolf's body. "This is a miracle."

"This ain't no miracle. This is a gang of white guys workin' up a con on a sweet little old woman."

"You're not old."

"The hell I'm not. Try being over 50 some time."

"I might just do that. Next body."

"Good." She nodded her approval. "You do that. And since you're comin' back however you please, make it a black man around my age and handsome. At least you got that part right. But not too old. Not 60. Don't you dare do that to me. And bring lots more money 'cause I have a really good imagination. Now get. Come back when you're good and ready. And don't be sayin' you're Marko neither, 'cause that part is too damn weird for words. Go on."

"That's the miracle you want?"

"Somethin' wrong with it?"

I stood up. "So you're good with it, holding eighty thousand for me and keeping the rest?"

"I'm still thinkin' about it. Where'd you get it, anyway?"

"It's not drug money if that's what you're getting at." I patted my chest. "This guy had it. Before that, Billy Bob Wyville had it."

Rema let out a shriek. "*Wyville?*"

"Sounds like you've heard of him."

"I—" Rema seem to be choking on her words. "You're givin' me money from *Wyville?*"

I didn't know black folks could change color. Actually, I was a bit worried Rema was having a heart attack or was about to attack me. "No. I kind of took it from him—indirectly."

That didn't seem to calm her down any. "You stole money from *Wyville?*"

Crap. Was she a friend of Billy Bob's? Or did she hate the man? "I didn't really steal it. It's complicated. Let's just say he doesn't have it anymore and we do. Is that a problem?"

"You—" She struggled to catch her breath. "You're tellin' me this is blood money? Because if that's what this is, you can take this damn money out o' my house! Right now!" Rema began yanking yarn and knitting stuff out of her bag, throwing it in an effort to get to the cash. "Here!" She threw a few bundles of cash at me—hard. "Take your damn money and get the hell out o' my house!" She hit me with more money.

"It's not blood money."

She stood there breathing out fire. From the look in her eyes she was ready to hurl me through the nearest window. From the set of her shoulders and her balled up fists, she was dead set on going flat out into me. I glanced around. Wolf, or no Wolf, this was going to involve a lot of breakage. "*Well?*"

It seemed like she had a problem with Billy Bob, so I tried the truth. "I took Wyville's money. I'm taking all I can get, but not for doing his dirty work." I thumped my chest again. "The last guy, the one I'm wearing right here, he did all kinds of shit for Wyville. But not me. I'm Marko and I'm bleeding Wyville of cash, then I'm taking a wrecking ball to his organization. And it's possible I might take Billy Bob and his crew apart myself."

"The hell you say." Rema cocked her head, looking at me more closely. "Pardon my street language, but you're one messed up motherfucker. You know that?"

"I know that. I need your help. Actually, no, I don't need anything. I'd really appreciate your help, but if I have to take care of every damn thing myself then that's exactly what I'll do."

"And you think you can just get up in Wyville's face and walk away smellin' like a rose?"

"Rema, you still have no idea what I am. So in plain English, I'm the biggest badass motherfucker you've ever met."

She stared at me. "You're up there. But I will say you're the most messed up white guy I've seen all day." She frowned at me. "You think that's funny?"

I put my hand to Wolf's face and found a twisted smile. Nameless or Martoni.

She noticed my surprise, being caught with another unexpected smile. She shook a finger at me. "You need to get some control o' yourself, boy. You can't be goin' around doin' stuff you ain't aware of. Know what I mean?"

"Like I said, four minds, one body."

"Whatever."

"So are you willing to help me?"

"If you're fool enough to mess with Wyville, then who am I to cause you problems? Besides, you won't last long. Somebody needs to do what's right with this money, so I guess that'd be me. But I ain't no damn sidekick."

"Financial manager."

"I'll think about it. You know Wyville's gonna kill you."

"I can survive death."

"Here we go again."

"Maybe we need a secret phrase. You know, when I knock on your door and you think I'm someone else."

"We don't need no damn secret phrase. If another crazy fool knocks on my door, we'll do this same dance again."

"Great." I walked to the door. "What if I come back in Billy Bob's body."

"Then I'll call some guys I don't ever want to see in my neighborhood and they'll take you away."

"Always a pleasure, Rema." I held out my hand.

"I ain't shakin' that thing. In fact, when you leave I'm puttin' hand sanitizer and bleach on everything you touched 'cause what you've got is like I've seen in the movies where everybody gets infected and dies, only what you've got is worse." She opened the door.

"You know, this went a lot better than I imagined. Introductory deal—take fifty thousand. Put it to good use."

"Don't be tellin' me what to do with it. Besides, there's a really good chance you'll be dead and it'll all be mine."

"Later." I stepped out onto her porch and headed to my car.

"Good luck with those mental problems. I hear Catholics are good with exorcisms. Close the damn gate."

Every superhero with mental issues deserved a sidekick with massive trust issues.

The guys all piled into the Escalade, I checked the mirror for a smile, and we drove off.

2.6 In A Bar, Darkly

That night, Wolf filled me in as we walked from a downtown parking garage to the bar. The Plaid Cactus was where Billy Bob sometimes met to discreetly discuss shady deals with assorted politicians and other infamous characters. Billy Bob typically did his business in a quiet rear booth while Wolf posted himself at the bar looking all brooding and ominous in a tight muscle-highlighting black dress shirt and faded black jeans. Anyone heading to the rear only had to walk near Wolf to pick up on his *not that way* body language. Even drunks made a u-turn when Wolf swiveled in his bar stool and locked eyes on his target.

Besides all that, the Plaid Cactus was small, not well known, and for some reason it provided Wolf with a way to get out in public, free from the usual onslaught of random sexual advances. It was a good place for Wolf to be recognized by staff, and still left alone by patrons and staff alike.

Anyway, that's what Wolf thought I should know about the Plaid Cactus. Thanks, Wolf.

He also thought Billy Bob was a part-owner, so that's why Wolf's drinks were always free.

All I knew was we were out of beer at home and this was a reasonable way to start my forced vacation. Billy Bob Wyville could go hang himself, or you know, I could help him with that.

As I walked solo into the bar I was immediately recognized and offered Billy Bob's private booth. I guessed that's where Wolf went when not on guard duty. Not many customers, so I opted for a quiet spot at the bar. Just what I wanted.

"Hey, Wolf." The bartender hustled over like we were pals. He seemed to sense I was off duty and approachable this evening. He held up a bottle and seemed to be showing off some dust on it. "Look here what I've picked up, laddie. She's a real beaut'. A new single malt from Islay. An' would ya look at that, twenty years in the barrel, if it were a day. Unopened, just waitin' for ya, Wolf."

The bartender had a really lousy Scottish-Irish accent. Irritating. And he was offering me Scotch. More of Wolf's drool. I ordered something more to my liking. "Rum and coke."

"Ya must be pullin' ma leg, lad. This here's a finely aged single malt. She'll not be gettin' any better than this."

I half expected him to tell me the warp engines wouldn't hold. Give the accent a rest, Scotty. I leaned toward him and looked assertive. "I'm in the mood for something new."

He looked worried, like Wolf was high-end bad news and now Wolf was getting unpredictable. "Aye, an' yo're sure 'bout that?"

"Right. Your best rum and coke."

"Well, as a matter o' fact I do have an aged rum that's totally special. But it'd be a real tragedy to mix it with coke. It's a real straight up rum, if ya know what I mean. I guarantee you'd like it. Or o'er the rocks, if you've a mind to have it that way."

"Rum. Rocks. Coke."

"Hey, if Wolf wants it that way, Wolf gets it that way. Just so ya know, I try never to serve ma customers corn syrup. Pure swill. So I always keep chilled bottles o' cola with sugar cane. That's the stuff. Much better for ya. And FYI, this isn't your Mexican Coke. Sure an' it says sugar right on the bottle, but a man just canna trust their labels. Know what I mean?"

I didn't. But he was trying hard, so I made it a point to actually taste what I drank here.

He flashed labels and set it up nice and neat in front of me.

All I can say is it went down way too smooth and went well with the bowl of mixed nuts he fronted for me. I liked this place. Wolf should come here more often. Well, we all should. We were four guys sitting at the bar together. A motley brotherhood. Subtly synergistic. Unconventionally erudite. Whatever the hell that meant.

Somebody was providing me with new words. I felt like I had the world's first synergistic brain. I'd have to look synergistic up, but I was pretty sure I'd used it right.

Or maybe it was the rum and coke talking. I knew the penalty for drinking—group banter, losing control to the dead in my head.

Looking around, the lighting was colorful but subdued. No garish neon ads. In fact, no ads anywhere.

Garish? What straight guy says *garish* in Texas? Me. I guessed I was the first.

I relaxed.

The music was soft jazz, but without being atonal and without the aimless tangential improvisation.

Who thinks like this? Wolf? The rest of us were cultural neophytes.

Regardless of the weird words, the Plaid Cactus was a very cool bar. The bartender was watching out for me, and nobody was hassling me. Staff knew my name. They gave me space to relax and enjoy the environment, to feel at home here. Maybe I wasn't feeling Plaid, but I sure was feeling all succulent inside me.

Succulent? What the hell. That can't be right. My passengers were really razzing my thoughts. Thanks guys.

Even though I was liking this place, I'm not sure they would have let me in before, as Marko. But it sure was good now. For better or worse, the right connections made all the difference in life. Wolf had those connections, even if it was through Billy Bob.

Billy Bob was a bitter taste. Better to enjoy the space my head was in and grok this place.

Grok? Thanks, Nameless. I know that one came from you.

But no good time goes unspoiled. I was only halfway through my first drink when a tubby middle-aged guy in a Mississippi white suit pulled up a barstool right next to me, invading my space. Some people just don't wait for an invite. It occurred to me I could say the word and have him bounced. Thanks, Wolf. Good to know.

The creepy guy looked me over.

I glanced back at him, maybe with a bit of *buzz off* to my body language. The guy had an umbrella drink which didn't exactly put me in my comfort zone.

Guys don't let guys order umbrella drinks. An unwritten rule. A rule well enforced. Obviously this guy was solo—hitting a bar without his drink enforcer.

He just stared at me, long and hard. Maybe with a grin or a

smirk. I wasn't about to give him my attention and figure out what his face was saying. Best to ignore fools.

He leaned back a bit, took a deep breath, and I knew he was about to give me his best let's-be-pals line. He took a sip of his drink, then said. "Wolf."

Great. Someone who knows Wolf. Wolf was supposed to tip me off, but didn't. Cooperate, Wolf. Who was this guy? No answer.

I looked the guy over more closely. Pudgy. Around 40 or 45. White lightweight suit with the sleeves pushed up. Pushed up sleeves was the gay influence, rolled up sleeves meant straight. Pale peach shirt. Weird fluffy pink necktie. Well-dressed if you liked horrible combinations. A gay Southern plantation owner? A reject from a black and white 1940s Bogart movie?

Or maybe just another downtown Austin oddball? That seemed about right. Austin was famous for political comedy at Esther's Follies with its big glass window behind the stage, featuring random people on the street in tutus. What's not to like? The weirder the better. Bring it on, Austin.

Since I hadn't a clue who this Maltese Falcon wannabe was, I kept it brief. "Hey."

Okay, come on Wolf, who the hell is this guy, anyway? Give me a clue.

"We missed you at poker last night." His voice had a feminine lilt to it. Fitting.

Wolf missed poker night? With Truman Capote's unexpected offspring? I nodded to hide my confusion. "It was a busy night." I also wasn't sure who Truman Capote was, but maybe Martoni did.

"I still owe you." He pulled out several one hundred dollar bills. Offered them to me.

I ignored him, focusing instead on my rum and coke, desperate for Wolf to remind me who this clown was. Wolf might have been laughing. Well, someone was laughing in my head and it wasn't me.

The guy quickly pocketed the money and leaned in close. His voice was now husky like a starlet in a black and white movie. "You're marvelous. I want you to know that."

A chill ran up my spine.

Relax. Nothing I couldn't handle. Wolf was a real stud with the ladies. No reason he shouldn't be man-bait, too. This guy was hitting on me, which meant nothing in the Plaid Cactus. That's what Wolf thought. Hollywood actors and D.C. lobbyists dropped in when they were in town. Weird shit went down all the time here. No fuss, no muss.

However, if this had been a place like Oilcan Harry's, I'd be tightening up my chastity belt right about now. I tried to dial in a low Wolf voice. "Not interested. And if I ever was, uh, it's not happening again. Ever."

The guy laughed with his mouth closed. Kind of weird. He looked around and made sure our conversation was private. "Enjoying your new body?"

And just like that, my brain unhinged.

I scrambled to gather my cool. I looked back at him to size him up better. New body? That could mean something else. "Uh, I've always worked out, if that's what you mean."

"No. Are you enjoying being Waldo Zander Payne?"

Not what I wanted to hear. "Do I know you?"

He grinned. "No, but you will. How long have you been Wolf? I'm guessing you stepped into his body two days ago. Right?"

"I—" I turned back to my drink and chugged it.

"The Wolfie is thirsty. Let me buy you another round."

No way. "No."

"Bartender." He waved the bartender over. "Another round for both of us. On me, of course."

Crap! The exit was at least 40 feet away.

He caught me looking at the exit. "What?" He had a mocking tone to his voice. "Special snowflake, you thought you were the only one?"

The bartender heard that.

"Something like that," I said. Was he saying I wasn't the only jumper?

I was pretty sure the bartender now pegged me as gay, too. Or at least bi. Not good for Wolf's rep.

The guy pushed his hot pink umbrella around in his glass. "Aw, it's not all about you, dear boy. There are plenty more where we came from."

We? "What makes you think I'm anything like you?"

"You been giving yourself away. We have ways of spotting each other." He held up two fingers to his eyes, turned his fingers to aim at my eyes, then back to his.

The guy was creeping me out over and over again.

I mulled the whole mess over while the bartender smirked and took his sweet time with the drinks. It wasn't hard to imagine what he was thinking. Two gays meet in a bar. One outs the other. Bartenders must see that happen all the time.

Finally we were served our drinks and got some privacy. I turned to the guy thinking how easy it would be to deck him. He was a walking marshmallow, except he had a dangerous edge to his words. I channeled my best Clint Eastwood death-whisper voice. "I'm more dangerous than you know."

"What's that supposed to mean? You'd kill me? You know what? Go ahead and try, bad boy. I'd just get your Wolfie body. Oh yes I would. You'd lose. Besides, I might like that man-suit you're wearing. Hunk me out? Mmm, I'd like that. Yes. Very much."

I hadn't thought of that. How would I kill a fellow jumper? And if there were two of us that could jump, who knew how many others there were.

"Relax, Wolfie. I'm here to help you. You'd be amazed what I can do for you. So hows about we swap stories? Care to go first?"

"Not really."

"They never do." He finished slurping his umbrella drink and moved on to the fresh one waiting in front of him.

Then his whole body posture changed. Weird, like his backbone unhinged or something. He was now sitting up straight, head held high, proud. He had a hard glint to his eyes. The marshmallow of a man was replaced by a stocky guy, ex-military by the look of him. But his hands hovered over the bar top in an unexpected way, like he was feeling the wood without touching it. "I am currently Jack Peoples, but I was born Jacqua Wapun." His voice was very different—calm, proud, but soft spoken. "That was a very long time ago. Call me Jack or Jacqueline if you like. You should know I was woman before wearing my first man. Pardon me, Wolf, if I make my tale blunt. Some stories run dry with age and I have told mine so many times."

Jack now stared at his reflection in the mirror behind the bar, but it was mostly obscured by fancy vodka bottles. I looked in the mirror to see what he must have seen—a distortion. That distortion seemed to define him perfectly.

His voice changed again—closer to sad reflection, softer, younger, much younger. "I was born Native American. Sioux. We lived on land you now call eastern Minnesota, a land of many lakes and rivers. My time was the 1800s. Your Civil War had just started. There was hope among my people that the white man's evil would consume him—the white snake eating its own tail. So many of you being slaughtered in battle. Some dared believe the white man would leave our world. But it was also the early time of trouble and battle between your people and mine. The white man's blood thirst was everywhere.

"So it came to a day when I was a girl in my 15th summer. With my brother's pony I was alone in a meadow by a cool stream. After enjoying the cold clear waters, I lay in the early green of the grass watching the white clouds that passed in the deep blue above."

Jack paused a moment, still staring at his partial reflection in the mirror. "As I napped I was caught by a dirty band of cavalry soldiers. They raped me there." His hands over the bar curled into fists. "I clearly recall all four of them. You would, too. After they had earned my hatred of them, they squabbled. I stood bloodied and bare. I yelled at them—gave them my anger—my wrath. But they stood there in the green grass and yellow flowers, squabbling with each other like bad children. They were men without spirits, blind to nature all around them, blind to my spirit and my rage. That's when one of them turned, pulled his pistol from its pouch, and shot me in the chest. Hot metal seared its way into my troubled heart. They stood there in silence, watching as I fell to my knees. Why they turned to killing me, I will never know. Maybe because it was such an easy cruelty. Why silence me for a deed they could never be hung for?"

Jack turned to me. The pain drained away from his voice. It hardened. "And I died there in the grass. No need to explain what that felt like. You've had your own death. Perhaps many."

He frowned and pushed away his umbrella drink like it now disgusted him. His gaze returned to the mirror—his distortion.

"I found I had become that which I hated most. I was the soulless white man. And worse, I was the soldier who had shot me. Somehow I was in his body, looking out his empty spiritless eyes. After a moment of stunned revulsion, I turned and shot a soldier. I had never shot a gun, but the skill of it came natural to me. Then I aimed and shot another as he stared at me with disbelief. I remember his face clearly, so white and frightened. But before I could turn again, the last soldier shot me in the back. My death was a slow death and he knelt over the new soldier skin I wore. He said words to me because he thought I was his friend. Or maybe because his pale spirit was troubled by all the death in that early summer meadow. His words were both strange and familiar. I recognized the sound of his pain.

"But he had no words for my torn girl body. I was as nothing to him. Yet, he seemed to have some small spirit. At least he cared for his fallen brothers. A small thing. But still a thing.

"Blood was then in my lungs. In my throat. It was a slow, hard path to that death. A death I was forced to walk. But the path to that death ended as he slung my new soldier body over a brown horse whose eyes were bright and wide with fear. Then my spirit was free again. Free to walk the path between all people.

"So as my spirit walked into him, the last man's body was mine. I used his body. I hated it, and I used it. I was now the last soldier. The last man standing in that field of grass and flowers.

"How could I return my young woman's body to the village? It seemed a path I could not take—not in the white skin of a soldier. A husk named Samuel—that's what his pale spirit whispered to me. So I buried my young woman self under a small rock cairn. I chanted the words so the spirits would hear my song of pain, hear of my rebirth—my spirit walk, and bring me peace.

"But peace never came."

Jack turned to me, maybe expecting some shock. Maybe expecting some words from me. But I held my tongue—still stunned that I'd never imagined there'd be others. Of course, there'd be others. Why should I be the only one?

Jack shrugged at my silence and turned to watch his reflection through the bottles. "Sometimes the pain returns. My hatred of soldiers—of men. Samuel taught me the ways of the white man, and their tongue. I soon found the white man's war. I joined the North. The Union. I was led to a battle where I slaughtered men in gray coats. It was slow and hard work, but it hardened my spirit. And their blood was spilled in the grass. I killed as many as I could until I myself was killed. Then my spirit walked from Samuel to one who wore gray. So I killed many in coats dyed blue.

"Each of my deaths was easy because it was rewarded with a spirit walk to my new body. Killing white soldiers was easy. The color of their coats mattered not to me.

"Your Civil War ended. Many years passed. My spirit walks became rare, but I was always careful to preserve each host's money. Another war called me to Europe. I took a suitable body, a civilian. It was easy to get caught in crossfire, so I did. And I died, and I was a soldier again. My taste for blood returned. I fought awhile with my comrades against enemy soldiers. Then I stood up or charged the enemy and embraced my fate. My spirit made the leap to their side and I gunned them down until they were forced to take the life of their friend. Then I turned on them again with my new body. Again and again I did this, until they were destroyed. Then, as the last enemy combatant, I charged my original friends to be killed and become one of them. Sometimes it stopped there. Sometimes the hate ended only after they were also decimated and once again I became the last one alive in battle. I cannot describe how wonderful that silence is—when so many white men are dead around me—when I stand alone, and the only sound in the world is the wind and the crows."

Jack pulled the umbrella drink close. "A dozen men dead, spread around me in a single battle, a killing arena. A hundred men dead. Sometimes more. The numbers were never important. It was only the act of revenge that had any meaning. That would calm me for some time, until another war, and another blood-thirst against soldiers. Any soldiers."

Jack stared at his umbrella drink. Pulled it to him. Now he

appeared more like the girl, Jacqueline, looking for vengeance that she could never quench. An eternal victim of man's violence—and her own.

I started to say something, but the words were too jagged and unhelpful.

"Your turn, sir." Jack's voice was calm, and I could clearly hear the young woman in him.

"Why haven't you jumped into a woman? Uh, I mean—"

"I have. Twice." Jack-Jacqueline took a sip of his drink. "But the time was never right." He looked me up and down and smiled at what he saw. His voice shifted to a shy teenage girl flirting openly. "I always liked your form, Wolfie—never your spirit. But now that you've changed . . . perhaps this time I will choose a woman's form. One to please you. We will see what pleasure it may bring us."

Whoa! I wasn't exactly ready to hear that. This guy who just met me was already offering to get a sex change and get it on with me. Admittedly, his voice did sound almost like a girl's. But at the same time it occurred to me he'd killed and been killed more times than I cared to know. I thought it was rough with three passengers, but Jack or Jacqueline must be lugging around a whole mess of blood-drenched baggage. Hundreds? Thousands? Shit. That can't be good for one's mental health. Is this what I had to look forward to?

Jack smiled. "How many have you been?" He seemed to be slipping back to his original voice. It was still a weird mix. He slumped more, too. Personalities melting, swirling around in an unsavory stew of a human.

How many had I been? I didn't feel like saying much. "I'm on my third. Not counting the original me."

"What was your original name?"

Wait. He knew I was a jumper but he didn't know my past? The less I told him, the better. "Maybe later."

"Fine. I'll call you Wolf. I'm with many others who can walk their spirits across death. It's an organization you'll need for support. I can guide you. I can show you the ropes."

"Like what?"

"Like how to manage your spirit walks. How to get bank accounts, credit cards, anything you want."

"I've already got those."

"But can you keep those?"

Good point.

He tapped my arm. "And I can help you make the world a better place. But to do that, you'll need to learn the rules."

"What rules?"

"An example? Do you know how spirit walkers reproduce?"

"Uh . . . yeah. Sex."

"If I became a woman again and you and I had sex, we wouldn't have a spirit walker. It's not genetic, Wolf. It's a facet of your spirit, not your body."

Sex with him was a bad thought. I was back to thinking of Jack as a grotesque guy with a very twisted head. Well you know, that's exactly what I was looking at.

He grinned at me, not like a person, but like a thing with a human facade. "You have a lot to learn." He said it like a killing machine that knew how to prepare wolf stew.

* * *

We moved to the private booth at the back of the Plaid Cactus. I was on my third rum and coke but wired with confusion and fear.

Note to self: Never drink again. Crazy batshit always happens and it just gets worse and worse.

The Jack-Jacqueline character was relaxed and in his element, except for the booth which was clearly too tight for him. He wedged himself in and proceeded to push the table my direction. Great.

He started the conversation. "You're probably wondering how I found you." He sounded business-like.

Good topic. "Yeah."

"Billy Bob Wyville. I've done some business with Mr. Wyville. You might say he works for me. He's not a spirit walker. But whatever you're planning with him, you should know that Billy Bob is off limits. He's my normal. A very useful one."

"Normal?"

"Not like us. A normal is a run of the mill mortal. People like you and me, we're rarer than one in a million."

Good to know, but that didn't answer how he figured me out. "How'd you know I was a jumper?"

"You're a spirit walker. Calling yourself a jumper demeans you. Jumper sounds very roaring twenties to my ears. Flappers. Jump seats. Jumpers."

I thought he had it all wrong. "Spirit walker sounds like something Yoda would say in Star Wars: *Spirit walker, I am. Kill me, then dead you be.*"

"You're amusing. You lack culture. You're new."

I thought this he-she was amusing, too. "So how'd you find out I was a spirit walker?"

"As I said, Billy Bob has been useful. When you've lived as long as I have, you learn the rules, and use them well. You also cultivate normal spirits. Some normals are good for watching, kind of like embedded spies or roving scouts. Some are good for doing things. Billy Bob's a doer. But I keep him closely watched because of his value. His whole crew is closely watched, too."

Great. Wolf was part of Billy Bob's crew. Wolf was always under surveillance. When's the last time Wolf swept his house for bugs?

Jack saw the alarm on my face, nodded, and continued. "There was an intruder at the Wyville home a few days ago. Wolf did his job. Nothing unusual. But then Wolf changed. Seriously changed. You've already learned how difficult it is to fit into a host's life. Well, Wolf bolted from his favorite sex club. Not the Wolf I know. Wolf's hot tub wasn't filled with eager young pussies quivering with anticipation. And Wolf seemed different to Billy Bob. But the most telling sign was when Wolf emptied a secret bank account. You might remember taking delivery on $180,000 in petty cash. So I asked Billy Bob to send you here. I've observed Wolf but never met him. A test was needed, so I arranged our little meeting tonight. You thought you should know me, know about the poker game we never had. Wolf knew my lies but you were confused. Then I played the Spirit Walker card and you took it. So there it is. You aren't Waldo Payne, Billy Bob's main wet worker and all around egotistical pretty boy. You my friend, are a spirit walker—just as plain as day."

Yeah. What could I say?

Jack shook his head. "You can't imagine how shocked and surprised I was. There are so few of us, we just don't pop up that often."

"How many are there?"

"In the whole world? No one knows. Most die of natural causes and are never discovered. In North America, only 61 are currently known to exist. Yes, you made it 61. The numbers in Europe and Asia are higher. Much higher." Jack's voice had switched to a gleeful whisper. "High murder rates bring out a few. U. S. and Mexico reveal one every few years. Canada not so many. But major wars are a pure delight. The Great War was a godsend, what you now call World War I. But so many millions were slaughtered in World War II—so many new ones discovered. You know, Wolf, war is a lot like Christmas—opening bright new packages near a raging fire in the hearth. Each new spirit walker is carefully held, appraised for its value, encouraged, polished, brought into the fold. I myself head the North American syndicate. A small but potent group of spirit walkers."

Jack waited, but I kept my mouth shut. "As our newest member, I'm sure you have questions."

Questions? Hell, I just wanted to exit the twilight zone. "Syndicate?"

"We work together, helping each other. Learning more about the ways our spirits can walk—and don't walk. We conserve the monetary assets we gain from each new host. We provide shelter and documents to help those of us who are hunted by the police. As you know, each new skin we wear is that of a killer—in the eyes of the law, anyway. But we're merely the innocent victim in a heinous killer's body. So we extract those who become incarcerated. And most importantly, we provide the rules for you to stay alive in this world."

"Because I can die."

"Because you can die all too easily, dear boy."

"Like how?"

"Answers come with commitment. I need to know, will you join us, or stand against us?"

Huh? Couldn't I just be myself? A Wolfie kind of superhero? I could tell Nameless was stunned. We were being drafted into something and it didn't smell like the League of Coolness. "There's a lot I don't know."

"So true, but I've already said more than I should. Answers come with commitment, Wolf-taker. I need your decision and I need it now."

Or else what? Jack would pull out a gun and shoot me. We both knew that wouldn't work. But it didn't take a genius to see that Jack-Jacqueline the Ripper could shred me to ribbons as long as he avoided the kill. His syndicate could kill my loved ones with no consequences. And God only knew what else.

He nodded, watching me closely. "I see some consideration on your face. Good to know your little gears are grinding away. I will tell you one more thing about me. I am very big on using the carrot. The stick only yields temporary results. I'm sure you know that. Besides, it nurtures hostility. I see in you a lot of potential, Wolfie. Expect some wonderful carrots, boy."

I felt like his new pony.

I'd have to find a way to ditch this clown. But for now? "Okay. I'm in." Did I have to sign in blood?

"You just made a very wise decision."

Yeah. I was still in one piece. Maybe the carrots would be cool. More likely, I'd learn what I could and leave this clown by the side of the road, eating my dust.

He held out a finger. "Rule one." Good, Jack was starting in on the jumper rules. "Never let anyone know your spirit can walk through death."

That made sense. It explained why I'd never heard about jumpers before. Top secret stuff. I could do that. Fight Club. Rule one. Never talk about Fight Club.

Oops! Rema kind of knew everything. No big deal. She didn't believe a word of what I'd said. Right?

Jack added more to rule one. "And if a normal does find out that you're a spirit walker, they will be terminated. You will be ended, too."

Not good. Harsh, even by Fight Club standards. "Rule two?"

"Rule two can wait."

"Anything else?"

"Billy Bob doesn't know spirit walking exists. None of my normals do. Rule one always applies. When you're advanced enough to have your own normals, they must never learn what we're about. As for you, there are a lot of roles in the syndicate. We'll just have to see where you fit in. But for now, you've grabbed a great big beautiful skin. It should come in very handy." His eyes were all over me.

Okay, it was actually worse than that. The guy was practically drooling when he talked about my new skin. Not a pretty thing for me to watch him do. I could see how girls would get creeped out by some guys. Well, maybe a lot of guys.

Do I get a carrot now? "Tell me about those carrots?"

Jack ducked my question and babbled on about how I was going to be thrilled with my new role in the syndicate. But he never said what that role would be. He droned on, saying that people in the syndicate worked together to shape the world and help humanity. We were the good guys. Cool. We were like undercover gods. Uber cool. We had responsibility to make things better, even if we had to die repeatedly to make it happen. Ouch. He pretty much said we were bad-ass Marines, Black Ops Rangers, Navy Seals, Jack Bauer, and Bruce Wayne all rolled into one. We gave everything to the team, and we kept on giving, death after death.

Whatever.

There wasn't much I could sink my teeth into, just loads of fuzzy goals and words to make me do anything for the team. Basically, it was the stuff every coach tells you when they don't have a plan.

But there was one thing I could do. Jack said to keep up the Wolf Payne act until he got back to me. So it all boiled down to three things. Keep my mouth shut, don't mess with Billy Bob 'cause Jack had dibs on him, and keep doing my Wolf thing.

I could do that. After all, Jack-Jacqueline and I were like this really cool team. He loved to kill. I was to die for. It doesn't get any better than that.

Soul Suckers unite!

2.7 Stepped In It

Jack-Jacqueline was an experience I couldn't get out of my head that night. We couldn't sleep, so Wolf got in some late night cardio in our home gym. He even pulled out a heavy punching bag. We all watched as Wolf dished out some awesome stuff. Punches, kicks, wicked stuff with his knees and elbows. The man was a dynamo of pain.

After 30 minutes I was exhausted just watching him, but Wolf kept it up for a full hour. So with all those illegal martial arts kill shots, why did he need a room full of guns?

Somebody, maybe it was Martoni, thought Wolf was just showing off. Me? I thought Wolf was totally chafed about Jack, our new Life Coach.

Then I started thinking about limp-wristed Jack who'd personally killed thousands of people, versus hard-as-nails Billy Bob who couldn't seem to do his own wet work. Billy Bob seemed like all bark and no bite. Was Jack all bite and no bark?

The odd couple. And they worked together? I guessed that made sense. Jack might enjoy using a front man like Billy Bob. Was Billy Bob just in it for the carrots? Or did he fear Jack, sensing Jack's casual attitude toward killing?

I also wondered why Wolf had let Billy Bob hold his leash. Wolf let me know he pictured Billy Bob as a side of raw bacon— conveniently on the other end of the leash. Since Billy Bob had kept the good stuff coming, there'd been no reason to fry up the bacon. We all liked that image. Thanks, Wolf. Good to know you weren't someone's pocket puppy.

But frying up Jack was a whole nother deal. If I let Wolf kill Jack, then Jack would simply jump into our body and keep on truckin'. We'd be totally screwed.

We guided Wolf into the shower after the Mixed Martial Arts

workout. But unlike body-pounding MMA, Wolf's moves were geared toward permanent damage and quick death. *One and done* seemed to be his motto when it came to fighting.

It still made us feel weird to shower with the rock hard guy. I really needed to get a body-maid in here. That was something all four of us could totally agree on.

In bed, I was back to worrying about life with Jack. In my head again, I ran through dozens of ways to kill him. Like hiring a hitman, but Jack would simply jump into the hitman. It seemed like there was no way to kill Jack without him just laughing his head off and crushing my balls for the fun of it.

The good news, if there was any, was that I was just as hard to kill. Unless the secret to killing a jumper was buried in Jack's rule 42. Nameless said 42 was the secret to life, the universe, and everything.

I told him to shut up. We needed answers, not sci-fi trivia.

Then there was the whole thing where Jack wanted to become a woman again so we could all do the happy hump together.

The future looked bad. The train was off the tracks. Off the bridge. Diving nose first. Our future was coming up fast at the bottom of the gorge.

* * *

We were having a nightmare about our derailed train running into a giant laughing marshmallow when the doorbell rang.

What the hell.

Okay, so it wasn't that early in the morning—almost 10. Maybe the Avon lady wanted to sell us something.

I opened the door and there she was. A bit young to be an Avon lady because they had to be in their 40s. This one was maybe 19 or 20. She was wide-eyed looking at me. I had my shirt off. Okay. What's not to like?

I was still bleary but willing to start the conversation. "Hey."

"Wolf Payne?"

Uh-oh. Somebody in the back of my head yelled, *body-maid!* Keep it down, guys. Well, there was a Volkswagen Beetle parked in front of the house, so it was remotely possible. Maybe this was a no-hard-feelings gift from Billy Bob? "Yeah, that's me."

"I have something for you."

Body-maid! Body-maid!

She reached into her green messenger bag. Wolf stiffened like this was a hit and we should kill her now or run. I told Wolf that I could survive a hit. Then Wolf thought we—

She pulled out an envelope.

I took it. "Thanks."

She just stood there. Waiting.

Okay, she wants a tip. I started to pat my pockets like I didn't have money on me and that's when I realized I had nothing on me. Not even sandals.

I looked up to see a big grin on her face. I almost put the envelope in front of Wolf's equipment, but you know, what the hell. The damage was done. The last thing I needed to do was squeal and run. Not my style.

I smiled casually, like this happens all the time. "I can get you a tip if you'd like."

"Hey, mister, you've been generous already. But there is something I'd like instead."

Shit. Not here. Give me a break, I just woke up. "What?"

"You could, like, turn around."

Ah! She wanted some Wolfie butt. I started to turn.

"Slower."

Okay. I slowed down.

"Stop. Back a bit."

I craned my head to see if she was recording this with her phone. She wasn't.

"Stop. Can I, like, touch it?"

Huh? Touch my Wolfie butt? This could get out of hand.

Before I could say anything she was touching the Wolfie butt. She wasn't shy about it either. Okay. Fine. Well, she must have spent almost a full minute going over every inch of it. Both hands. Memorizing it, I guess. My rear end wasn't that interesting, just man butt. Woman ass, however, was a thing to hold and enjoy.

She caught me daydreaming about women's asses when she

pinched me—hard. I squealed—accidentally. She ran to her car laughing.

* * *

Safely inside, I opened the envelope. The note said, "Lots to do. Lining up carrots for my new Wolfie. Your place at nine tonight. I'll bring the champagne and your first assignment. I can't tell you how thrilled I am. Jack Peoples."

Carrots—good. Thrilled—not.

I should teach Jack how to text. On the other hand, cute messengers were way better than any text.

Time to stop joking and get prepared, prepared for anything.

Note to self: Wolf's place was probably bugged. Find a spy store and get some good quality bug detectors. Until then, I'd have to watch my words.

Had I used one of Wolf's phones to call or text Rema? I didn't think so. Had I said her name in Wolf's house? Had I used Wolf's computer to look up her address? I didn't think I'd done any of those. But if I had, Jack would use Rule One against us. Rule One Part B: everyone dies if the secret gets out about jumpers.

But if Jack had a GPS tracker on Wolf's SUV, he'd know already. That seemed unlikely because of Jack's friendly attitude toward me.

Or maybe it was Billy Bob who had the place bugged.

Basically, I was rapidly coming to a state of high paranoia.

I spent several hours rummaging through Wolf's place, rounding up survival gear like cash, a couple of guns, and my burner phones. I stuffed them into a new watertight case Wolf had in his gun room. The tags were still on it from a local sports-survival store. Hell, it was Texas. He who gears up last, dies first. Sporting goods was just a code name for prepper supplies.

There wasn't much stored under the State Theater, but it was the wrong time of day to clean it out. So I had to blow off all that stuff.

The things that could identify Marko, but couldn't fit into the case, were tossed into a random dumpster behind a mall.

That afternoon I grabbed a shovel from Wolf's garage and drove off to bury my watertight survival case. I had no clue where I was going, I just drove. It would have been nice to surf some web maps to find prime spots to stash my stuff, but using Wolf's computer was too dangerous. If Billy Bob didn't have it hacked, then Jack had a packet sniffer setup at a junction box by now.

Packet sniffer? Thanks for the cool words, Nameless, but I had no clue what that was. Spy stuff? Then just say spy stuff. Okay?

I wound up parked on some undeveloped land in the hill country west of Austin. After two hundred yards of trudging through oak and cedar and brush and clumps of prickly pear cactus and fire ant mounds, I found a good spot. Good because it was near some power lines I could use as a marker.

So I dug a shallow hole and buried the case. Into the hole went the case containing over $100,000 in cash, guns, burner phones with batteries out, a phone charger, Wolf's new unopened Rolex, the two diamond studded bracelets, and personal items including my one and only photo of Marie.

It was so damn hot, I wished I'd remembered to bring some water. But after a half an hour the job was done. The case was buried. I kicked the loose dirt around and spread some leaves and weeds over the spot. Crappy job. Nature would have to do its part. Then I took a hard look around, memorizing exactly where it was buried as best I could.

There was a power line tower over a ways. Closest one. I marched through the brush hoping I didn't come across a rattlesnake. Scorpions and tarantulas were playthings in this part of Texas. Rattlesnakes were the only things I didn't want to come across. I hoped they had better things to do than come out in this hellish heat.

When I reached the metal tower I looked for its number. Utility companies loved numbers. There it was, stamped on a metal tag. 109774-PE. Writing it down seemed dangerous, especially after losing nearly everything I'd ever owned, so I memorized it. We all memorized it. No way we were going to lose this treasure. I stacked a few rocks near the base, just in case my brain wasn't what it should be.

* * *

Back at Wolf's house we stripped everything off and dove into the pool. God, it was glorious. Probably the closest thing I'd ever had to a religious experience. It's hard to appreciate heaven without an afternoon in hell.

As Wolf did his laps, I couldn't help but worry that Jack was about to mess this all up. Same bad feeling as when I picked up those hoodies in my taxi. When was that? Less than three weeks ago? It seemed like an eternity.

What if Jack came over and I told him to take his syndicate and shove it? What then? They'd come at me with black ops ninja spirit walkers dangling from a stealth chopper? No need for guns because killing me would actually wreck their entire op—I'd jump into them. No, they'd use night-vision goggles, rubber hoses, and big cable ties. No lethal force could work on a jumper. Bag and grab.

And the same twisted jumper logic meant my guns were useless, too. You kill a jumper, you die. Wolf was free to break a lot of jumper bones. But what I really needed was a Taser. Damn. After this meeting with Jack, I'd have to stockpile Tasers.

* * *

After the swim, I got into a bit of a fight with Wolf again. He wanted the place cleaned up. I said it was just Jack dropping by, the last guy in the world I wanted to impress or think I was a good homemaker. Wolf said it didn't matter if anyone came over, the place was still trashed. Looking around, it seemed fine to me.

Martoni said he rarely cleaned his old place. His dog never complained about it. Nameless said being on the road was the good life because he never cleaned anything. To me, it just didn't make sense that a hit man would be a compulsive neat-freak. Wolf indicated he was a cleaner, not a hit man. There was a big difference. Hit men left a big mess. Wolf left no trace. He was far superior.

We argued. Martoni and Nameless even whined about it. Wolf won. No big deal. Choose your battles.

So we all pitched in and cleaned up Wolf's wonderful pad.

That brought us to the end of the afternoon. I was tense about the upcoming meeting with Jack. Someone said sex would calm me down.

Right. Some of my past lives had a one-track mind.

Basically, Nameless and Martoni wanted me to pick up the phone and make it happen. After all, we hadn't had sex all day. It was just making us edgy.

Wolf and I thought that was a bad idea. Wolf wanted the time devoted to threat assessment and contingency plans. He wanted to knock Jack out and take him straight to the mortuary for rush cremation. He'd let the little mortician do the kill in the furnace.

I reminded Wolf that jumpers like Jack loved being killed. Hell, Wolf had killed me and now I was having a ball in his handsome hide. So when that little cremation weasel pushed Jack's unconscious marshmallow body into the incinerator, Jack would simply jump into the little what's-his-name fry guy.

Jerry.

Yeah, okay. Jerry. Jack would inherit Jerry's pyro loving attitude and his weasel body and find a way to come for us.

There was simply no killing a jumper. Jack had all the high cards and we had no choice but to drop our pants, bend way over, smile like we meant it, and say, "Syndicate me."

Wait. Maybe the champagne Jack was bringing over would make getting screwed more bearable.

This was a bad time to be in touch with my inner female—my only X chromosome. Hello X. Let the Y drive. But it was all too obvious, the world loved to screw women. The only defense was to toughen up and screw 'em right back. Right ladies?

Better yet, screw 'em first.

Anyway, that's what I thought all the double-X chromosome chicks would do. Find a way to screw Jack before he screwed us.

Fine. We were going to deal with this head on. Calling dial-a-doll to bounce around with us in the hot tub was just like sticking our head in the sand, wishing the real problem would just disappear. Hell, we hadn't even seen Jack's carrots. Maybe they were primo.

* * *

It was getting dark and I'd run out of ideas. We'd just have to see what Jack had in his massively multifaceted mind. This was a time to do something productive. So with about an hour to kill, I decided to start calling Wolf's contacts to find us a body-maid. Hell, if a weird occupation didn't exist in Austin, it didn't exist in Texas.

Flipping through Wolf's personal contacts, I started by skipping Destiny. She was better off staying the hell away from us.

Then there was Jade. Nope. I didn't feel like getting hair whipped, pussy whipped, or any other kind of whipped.

Well . . . maybe later.

Who's next? Foxanna? Wolf didn't seem to know much about her. And with a name like Foxanna, you know she was messed up trouble. Probably too young, but creative at Scrabble.

Sable again? Maybe. We already knew she was a good shower buddy. Top-heavy was a good thing—a wonderful suffocation hazard. But she was also a little too money oriented. Well, body-maid was a paying gig. I was worried about asking her to soap Wolf *and* clean his house on a regular basis. Maybe that was asking too much. But maybe she knew somebody.

I dialed. It rang.

"Hey, Wolfie. Coming in tonight? I'm not at the club, but I can set you up with some cute friends."

"Uh, I'm probably not going in tonight. I've got a meeting in about an hour. Not sure how long that'll last." I was hoping Jack would just drop off some carrots and keep it short.

"Who is she?"

Even strippers got jealous? "It's just some guy."

"Ooo. Branching out?"

"No. And even if I was, he's not my type. Actually, he's no one's type."

"Does he need an escort?" Sable was looking for clients? Or maybe she was just pimping her friends?

"No, babe. He's not someone I'd ever send your way. I just wanted to let you know I'm in the market for something unusual."

"Sweet. A little something kinky? For you, Wolfie?"

"Maybe. Uh . . ." How to say this? "Uh, I'm looking for a little maid work. You know. Stuff around the house."

"Topless? Nude? Real cleaning or just sex with a feather duster in one hand?"

Huh? You could get maids like that? "Real cleaning. Uh, I'd like her to clean me up, too."

"Wax and shine? Spit polish? Rub-a-dub-dub, three girls in a tub?"

Spit what? "Just soap in the shower, like we did, but with house cleaning. That reminds me, I also need this person to take the, uh, body hair off me. I'm getting a bit furry."

"Bikini wax? Landing strip? Rocket pad? Full Brazilian?"

"Uh, I guess so. But all over."

"Okay. You're talking man wax, bodybuilder smooth."

"Uh, yeah, I guess. Know anyone who can do all that?"

"That's quite a list. You might need a team."

Team? The guys really liked the idea of a team. "I might."

"I'm no good at house cleaning. I can do hair removal, but guy hair is going to take something industrial. Did you lose your esthetician?"

What the hell was that? "Yeah. Lost her."

"That's rough, baby. I'm always happy to do soapy showers with you. Come to think of it, Jade might know about hair removal. If not, I'm sure she'd be happy to pull them out one at a time with her teeth."

Oh, man, I bet she would. "I'll pass on Jade."

"You know, somewhere I've got a phone number for a sexy beautician who could give you the painful full-body waxing you want. But I kind of hesitate to send her your way, because I'm sure you'd like her. Maybe more than me. She's dangerous, and Russian. Just your type—if you survived."

"No one could replace you, babe."

"Say, I do have an opening later. I could come over around midnight. Then you could show me how much you love me, Wolfie. Would midnight work for you?"

"Maybe another night. Mainly I just wanted to call around. You know. See what my options were."

"Baby, don't call anyone else but me. Let me ask some girls I know. You know I'll take good care of you, Wolfie."

"You're the best."

"You know it. Love you, sweetness."

"Love you too, babe."

We hung up.

Love? Did stripper escorts really say that? Was Wolfie in love with Sable? Was that even possible?

Wolf was just relieved I hadn't called her a stripper. Exotic dancer was the right term. The right words were important.

Yup. Wolfie hearts Sable.

* * *

With only a few minutes left before Jack's arrival, we headed into the kitchen for a quick meal. Something better than steamed broccoli and protein powder. An oatmeal survival bar was all I could come up with.

The doorbell rang. Crap.

I checked my teeth in the mirror. Not like I was going to kiss the guy. Although I did expect some kind of weird shit to happen.

The door opened to reveal Jack dressed up in some sort of pinstriped zoot suit. Bright red. No, actually it was flaming blood red with thin white stripes. Long gold chains hanging out of his pockets. White shoes with what I thought were spats. Or maybe the shoes were called spats. Wide brimmed bright red hat with a big pink flamingo feather. Belt way up, high above his marshmallow tummy. And on one hand, a black antique walking cane topped with a claw clutching a crystal skull.

No bodyguards. No limo outside. No nothing. Just Jack in all his weirdness.

"Wolfie!" With only one word, Jack already sounded different—manly, but like something from a Chicago back alley about a hundred years ago. He held out a really big bottle of champagne. I took it. The bottle was sweaty and still cold.

"Come on in, Jack." Maybe he wasn't going by the name Jack tonight?

He came right in. "Nice place you got here. I like it. Very sharp. Suits you, Wolfie. Suits you just fine." He sounded pushy, full of brass, gangster friendly. Not himself. Or even herself.

I needed a bucket for the champagne. Ice! I'd forgotten to get ice. "I'll be right back." I grabbed the champagne stand that I'd seen in the living room.

In the kitchen I started running the ice dispenser in the fridge door. One cup at a time, I dumped it into the champagne stand's bucket thing.

Jack strolled into the kitchen, looking like a puffed up dumpy body wedged into shocking red pinstripes, wild hat still on his head. "What?" His tone was scolding. "No ice?"

"I've got it covered."

"Next time, plan ahead." He slapped me lightly on the side of my face as he walked behind me.

Godfatherly. Like a nightmare father wearing his blood-red let's-all-go-to-hell Sunday suit.

Jack started opening kitchen cabinets. "Glasses?"

"Over there."

He opened the cabinet I was pointing to, then turned to give me a disapproving look. "Champagne glasses, kid. This ain't soda pop we're drinking."

"Uh, I'm not sure."

"Wolf, Wolf, Wolf. You gotta communicate with your host. He's still in your head somewhere. Make it subtle, but always be clear in your mind what you're after."

I already knew that.

"Ah! Here we go." He pulled down two champagne classes. "Good quality. I'm liking your host more and more. He's got good taste." The long tails of Jack's red zoot-suit swished as he walked into the living room. Gotham City would have welcomed him like a Joker from another mother.

I dumped another cup of ice into the bucket.

Everything sucked.

Where was the Sioux Indian? Where was the injured girl? Where was the crowded assembly of soldiers he'd taken as passengers? Where was the Maltese Marshmallow from the bar? What the hell was this guy, anyway?

"Modigliani." Jack was shouting from the living room. "You gotta love that goddamn Modigliani. Died young, like everyone should. But just look at his paintings. All his faces look so dead inside."

I poked the last of the ice around the big bottle. I lugged the awkward silver bucket-on-a-pedestal thing into the living room.

Jack was on the couch flipping through an art book I'd never noticed. "Take a look at this one, Wolf. Or this one here. Look into those dead eyes. It's like they're empty people. Normals, just hoping we'll walk inside them—warm up their souls. Put some pizzazz into their step. Know what I mean?"

"Yeah." But I really didn't.

"Bullshit! Don't bullshit me, Waldo. I can smell it a mile away. I'm being honest with you. You damn well better be honest with me. Know what I'm saying?"

"I don't know much about art."

"That's better. Feels good to be yourself, don't it." He grabbed the champagne bottle and started pulling off the foil. "Your host, he knows art." Jack thumped the book. "You can tell a lot about your host if you pay attention." He removed the wire cage and held the cork down with his thumb. "Hey. Should I shake it up first?"

"No."

"Why the hell not. This ain't your place. Don't let Waldo do your talking. You'd love a good fountain of champagne. Hell, I'd like that, too. So let's let her rip!"

"I live here. Don't trash my place."

"Now we're talking. Respect your host. Respect his body, and his place. That's the least you can do for them."

He started working the cork off.

I was getting pissed with this guy thinking he knew everything. He had no damn clue what Wolf was about. I blurted out, "Wolf doesn't appreciate art."

"Say again?"

"Wolf only keeps art books around to impress the women. Look around. There's no classic art anywhere on the walls. It's modern. It's understated. It's anonymous-man. It's what the interior decorator saw in Wolf when she met him. Then when he fucked her brains out in the hallway, she also learned he was a sexual nonconformist with a strong primitive streak. So she reflected that in the bedrooms."

Jack popped the cork. "Bravo! That's what I wanna hear. You're latching on to your hosts, sucking the essence out of their brains and using it to your advantage." He beamed his yellow teeth at me.

Actually, I'd made most of that up about Wolf.

He filled our glasses and held his up. "To the late Waldo Payne. Hit man. Cleaner. Dumb shit muscle for hire. May you always reap the rewards of his memories and abilities."

I started to drink but he wasn't through.

"And may you enjoy the son of a bitch's body to your complete orgasmic satisfaction."

Orgasmic?

Not something the Godfather would say.

My orgasms? Did guys even have orgasms? If not mine, then who was going to enjoy orgasms with Wolf's body? Jack-Jacqueline? Your Freudian female slip is showing, Jack.

"Cheers!" We clinked. We drank.

Honestly, I can't tell the difference between champagne and carbonated white wine. No one can. Looking at the bottle, I figured it was expensive. Well, the label was 100% in French. Obviously not intended for uncultured American consumption.

After the second glass we were both chugging it.

Jack held up his glass. "To life and death. May the vicious cycle never end."

Woo-hoo! But what was he saying, anyway? Praise the body count and pass the champagne?

It would have been easy to call Jack one sick bastard. But he was far more twisted than that. The clown had walked clean off the edge and was still going. Jack was a one-man three-ring circus. Unpredictable, entertaining, and packed with enough demented clowns to make anyone puke in their empty popcorn bag.

Okay, so there was no easy way to describe him. Look at the red zoot-suit and tell me I'm lying.

Of course, I wasn't a shining symbol of sanity either. But at least I recognized a massive mess when I saw it.

* * *

After a lot of glasses of champagne, he turned the empty bottle upside down in the ice bucket. He pulled out a folder and waved it in front of me.

"Wolf, I'm serious when I say this and I want you to know I've been giving this a lot of thought. I'm sick and tired of wearing skins like this." He slapped his belly.

Tubby skins? Must be hard to find zoot-suits in that size. He had my sympathy.

"Wolfie boy, I've decided it's time to become a woman again. Believe me when I say I've hated every goddamn man I've ever worn. And I've worn a hell of a lot of pricks." His head bobbed up and down like he was remembering each one.

He stopped bobbing and looked me in the eye. "Now don't get me wrong, Wolf. Looking like a man might suit some people, but it doesn't suit me. Not one damn bit. So I'm chucking this stinking hide and trading up. Something classy. Refined. Unmistakably feminine. Something that suits my personality. A skin I can hang on to for a good long while. So that means it's gotta be young, but no brat hide. Know what I mean?"

Unfortunately I did. I nodded.

"Maybe you're wondering why I'm even talking about this with you."

I knew where he was going. He'd thrown it at me the other night in the bar when we'd met.

"I like you, Wolf. You've become a real woman's man. You used to be a damn prick, little more than a bag of sweaty muscles. But since your spirit was replaced, you've improved a lot. You've still got balls, but you don't wear them on your sleeve like that original Waldo did. Now you're just as cute as a button—or at least you're headed that way. That's why I think we can make this work. That's why I'm making you the offer of a lifetime. So here you go, Wolfie."

Jack set the folder on the coffee table and opened it up. Five 8x10 glossy photos—all covert portraits of young women. And five matching full length body shots apparently taken in public places. And one was Sable! Aw, shit!

Jack spread them out so I could get a good look at all of them. "Here we have five pretty candidates that I'm comfortable wearing. Now all you have to do is pick the one you like most. What do you say, Wolf? Who gets the nod?"

Shit! Two dancers Wolf seemed to recognize from another club. Wolf thought one had a little boy. The other two were girls I'd never seen before. And there was our Sable, looking really nice in street clothes.

My body jolted. Wolf was going all ballistic in my head. He wanted to move. Move now. Off the couch. Get the .44 Magnum from the gun room and blow this motherfucker's head clean off.

I wanted that too, but that's not how you dealt with a jumper. And it was worse because Jack headed a syndicate of jumpers. We'd find another way, Wolf. I promise.

Jack was staring at me. "What's wrong?"

"Not her." I pointed to Sable.

"Fine with me." Jack pushed her photos aside. "I only put her in the lineup because I knew the old Wolf had a thing for her. Besides, I know from experience her tits would hurt my back—until I had them cut down to size, that is. So what's it gonna be?"

"One of these has a kid." I touched the two dancers Wolf knew.

Jack waved his hand as if to brush off my concerns. "Not an obstacle. Any family they had would naturally be taken out of the picture."

Taken out? Jack would simply kill off the family? I tried to keep calm. "Yeah, but not these two."

He nodded. "Understandable. You want a fresh start on someone—not a face that could trigger any memory Wolf had. So we're down to two lovelies."

One was a blond, mid-twenties, very pretty but what I'd call a generic beauty—easy to forget. Personally, I preferred a woman with unique beauty. Like a nose that was a bit too long, or maybe some other body part a bit out of proportion. Perfect features just seemed boring to me. Somehow forgettable. The other woman was slightly older, brunette, with thin classy features. A bit too thin for my taste. Women should have curves.

What the hell was I thinking? I wasn't about to pick out a victim for Jack.

"I like watching those gears turn, Wolf." Jack was watching me like a hawk. "Remember, if you don't like the way one feels in your hands, I can always switch skins. Lots to choose from in this world. Mainly, I want you to be happy. You know what I'm saying, Wolfie? I make you happy. You make me happy. Like they say these days—win, win."

No way. I wasn't about to pick one. I needed to focus on how to lobotomize Jack. Kind of messy, but they might have a DIY kit on ebay. The Chinese make everything. Jack just needed a smaller kinder brain. Something to bring a deep chill to his demented ideas.

Jack scooped up all the photos and put them back into the folder. "I understand your dilemma. No need to take this further. I'll take it from here. Mainly, I need to know you're on board with this."

I wasn't. Jack was going to destroy an innocent life, just so he could be pretty. Pretty for my eyes. Damn his eyes.

"Take your time, Wolf. In fact, if you'd like to meet the women first, I think that'd be a swell idea. Get to know them. Fuck them. Make sure everything fits like it should. After all, you're a big one. Then you give the word and I'll take over the one you like best. Sound like a deal?"

Stall. Think of something, Marko. Stall! "Yeah, Jack. And if neither one of these works out for me, you can get more photos."

His face lit up. "That's what I wanna hear." He reached over and put his arm around my neck—real man to man. Real gross. He gave me a wink. "You and me, we're gonna mix a little business with pleasure. Aren't we, Wolfie? Hell yes, we are. It's a damn good way to bond with underlings, don't you think?"

What did I think? Lobotomy kit. Electro shock kit. Something messy from Home Depot's power tool aisle.

* * *

Two hours later, Wolf's flavored brandy was long gone, but Jack was still there, enjoying my company. The only thing left to drink was Wolf's snobby Single Malt Scotch. Jack wasn't happy about that, being a fruity umbrella kind of guy. But he still drank it. Quite a lot of it.

To my credit, I'd stopped drinking after the champagne and switched to water. That probably saved my life because Wolf was on the verge of pushing me aside. He didn't need any damn .44 Magnum, because it would only take a second to break Jack's nose and shove the bits up into his brain, then crush his windpipe, if needed. And that was just for starters. The rest about juggler veins and eyeballs and spinal cords was making me sick because that's what I was forced to deal with in my mind.

Wolf just didn't get it about killing a jumper. But I guess that made sense because I had control of his higher brain functions. Alcohol only sloshed our thinking around and gave Wolf an opening.

Jack was droning on about something meaningless. But maybe I could distract my killer thoughts by trying to focus on what he was saying.

"Another thing, Wolfie. When someone brings over champagne, you gotta have caviar chilled and ready. And keep some white wine chilled, too. Something light, like a Vinho Verde or a Pinot Grigio. Listen to your inner Wolf. At least he had some class. Better yet, spend some time in a woman's skin. Preferably one who's had some upbringing. I would arrange that, but I'm hoping you'll stay Wolf a while longer. That's real important to me, Wolfie boy. Keep the skin." He put his hand on my shoulder. "I'm looking forward to you, boy."

Time to change the subject. "So what are the other rules about spirit walking."

"We're not discussing that shit tonight."

"Then tell me about my assignment for the syndicate." Actually, I was a lot more interested in the carrots.

"Ah! I'm glad you reminded me—your first assignment. It's all arranged, Wolfie. Tomorrow at three p.m. a brand new pearl-white limo will pick you up and take you to the airport. Like I said, it's all arranged. Nothing but the finest for my new man. Oh! You'll be gone a few days so pack accordingly."

Cool. I liked limos. But flying was a royal pain. "Where am I going?" I was hoping for a private island in the Caribbean.

"That's just a detail. The driver will fill you in."

Okay. Deep dark mystery. I stared at Jack hoping he'd throw me something useful.

"Look, Wolfie, here's the deal. My instructions are few in number, but supremely important. One. You will meet a woman named Sonya Clark. Yes you will, and you will do exactly what she says. And I do mean exactly."

"Okay." Was she cute? I could take orders if she was cute.

"And get this straight, Clark is one of us. Everyone else is a damn normal. Got that?"

"Got it."

"That's all there is to it, Wolfie. Follow her instructions and don't screw it up. Do not disappoint me. No matter how fine your ass is, always remember—I have no tolerance for failure."

"Right. What's the carrot?"

"Don't be thinking about any damn carrot. With an attitude like that, you'll be lucky to survive."

I, TARGET
PART 3

3.1 Assignment

B ig day. This was the day of my first assignment for the North American Brain-Walking Syndicate. Or whatever it was called. All I knew was that it was maybe a three day trip, I'd be picked up in a new white limo around three p.m. and taken to the airport, and a woman named Clark was in charge.

Cool.

First time in a limo. This would be my third time to fly.

Hopefully I'd have an aisle seat. And since this was Wolf I was in, I thought an unlimited credit card would be in order. Free in-flight movies. Unlimited pizza at the airport. Free drinks everywhere. Maybe I'd pick up a squishy stuffed animal for Marie.

And Jack was all into Wolf, so there was a good chance I wouldn't have to die on this mission. Hey, I was into Wolf too, but in a normal jumper kind of way.

So let's see. I'd need swimming trunks, sun screen, sunglasses—stuff like that in case I was heading south. But something with long sleeves for the plane in case people all around my seat had their cold air nozzles on full blast. Condoms? Yeah, in case this Clark person was a hottie. I looked all over for rubbers. Damn. Wolf didn't seem to have any. Oh well, Ms. Clark would be on the pill. All the hotties were on the pill. Right?

Note to self: The Multi-Mind is a terrible place to conduct rational thought.

Vasectomy. What's that, Wolf? Now you tell me? Okay. Wolf was shooting blanks.

What about bringing weapons? I thought TSA wouldn't allow guns and commando knives, so no need to worry about any of Wolf's lethal stuff. Jack didn't say this was a hit job. Actually, he didn't say what the hell I'd be doing. I looked for some non-metallic garroting gear because it would be TSA friendly, but Wolf said he could strangle with just about anything handy.

Okay, so maybe poison? Poison was for sissies. Right, Wolf. What about night-vision goggles? Nah. TSA would probably have questions about those. Besides, I suspected Wolf could naturally see in the dark.

Eventually, I had it all laid out on the bed.

Beach gear. Check.

Quart size plastic bag. Check.

Little bottles of stuff to go in the bag. Mostly check.

Long sleeve shirt for the possibly too-cold plane ride. Check.

Assorted clothes. Check.

Fancy suit, just in case we hit the casinos in Monte Carlo. Check.

Wolf's passport. Check.

All I needed now was some luggage. Unchecked.

After a long search, I finally found some luggage in the garage. Who keeps it there? Big check-in bag, or little carry-on bag? Jack was a dick for not telling me where I was going.

Oh well. Little carry-on bag. Unfortunately, the folded up suit and dress shoes took up half the damn bag.

This was exciting. Unfortunately, I had a ton of time before my 3 p.m. limo ride to the airport. So Wolf swam in the pool. Wolf worked out. We scrounged around for lunch. We tried to take a nap. We sat in the hot tub for a while. We cooled off in the shower. I was in the mood to do naked cartwheels around the house, but I didn't know how to do those. None of us did.

Finally the doorbell rang. Right on time. I grabbed my stuff and headed to the front door.

A sexy limo driver? I opened the door.

No. Just some guy in a cap.

He took our small carry-on bag and we hopped into the back of the limo. The guys in my head were totally pumped. Was it primo? Hell, yeah. But looking closer, I saw lots of boring high-end booze and precious little beer that I liked. What? I had to make my own rum and cokes? What the hell was primo about that?

But it was a new limo, and it was freshly waxed and pearl white. Just like Jack said it would be.

Drive on, my good man.

Okay, so I was high as a kite without the aid of any booster booze.

We were off to the airport. My secret assignment was starting, even if I didn't know what it was.

West on 71. I knew the route by heart. Hell, I'd made this trip a thousand times in my taxi. Which airline? I hoped the driver knew, because I didn't have a clue. Wasn't I supposed to have tickets?

When we got to the airport grounds, we made a very wrong turn. Jeeves, the terminals are that way. But I held my tongue because he seemed to know exactly what he was doing.

A minute later we were at some sort of private business jet area. Sweet! Of course the Jumper Syndicate would use private jets. The finest of everything.

But the driver pulled over out in the middle of nowhere. Lots of deluxe little jets all around and we stopped way out here? I got a bad premonition about a shakedown. Taxi drivers know a bad move when they see one. I tried to relax.

He opened the tinted glass partition and offered me a paper bag. "Empty your pockets. Put all of your things in this. Everything."

Huh? My first assignment couldn't start with a robbery. Could it? Do what with my things?

He waved the bag. I took it and started emptying my pockets.

So everything I had on me went into the bag. Okay, I got it. This was just TSA, limo style. "You need my belt?"

"No."

"Shoes?"

"No. Just everything in your pockets. Wallet. Passport. Keys. Cell phone. Whatever you've got. Your watch, too."

"My watch? It's a Rolex."

The driver's eyes widened. "Really?" He seemed to think about it for a few seconds. "In the bag."

Shit.

He continued his demands. "Computer, iPod, anything electronic."

"I don't have anything like that." I felt like I was being robbed blind.

When it was all in the bag, he took it and held out a large sealed envelope. "Take it."

I took it.

He looked annoyed. "Open it."

Okay, okay, I opened it. Inside was someone guy's used wallet and a red passport. Really? That's all? No, in the bottom was a crappy watch with a black leather strap and a plain wedding ring. No way I was going to wear a wedding ring.

No cell phone?

The passport was Canadian and said *Diplomatic Passport Passeport Diplomatique* on the cover. Wow. Inside there was Wolf's picture but it said I was Waldo Jackson. Really? Does my secret undercover name have to be Waldo?

Then it dawned on me I was Waldo, Jack's son. Ha ha. Not funny. Jack was such a little bastard.

At least I could remember my cover name.

I opened the wallet. Good, the credit cards I was hoping for. A few family photos of people I'd never seen. Plus a bunch of U. S. and Canadian dollars. And some euros.

Cool. A Canadian mission. Or a European mission. Either way, I was an untouchable diplomat. Canadian, eh? I'd have to remember to put *eh* at the end of every sentence.

What else do Canadians do? Smoke pot? Chop down trees? Drink beer? Be politically confused? Hey, I could be Canadian.

Eh?

Unfortunately it looked like I didn't need the swimsuit. But I could wind up in Europe, so the James Bond suit for Monte Carlo was a good call on my part.

As the driver was fondling the Rolex from my bag of personal stuff, he turned to me. "Any other identification? In your carry-on? Suit labels? Tattoos? Anything else that could identify you?"

Like he was going to rip off my *I heart Wolfie* tats? Not that Wolf had any. "Uh, there are tags on my carry-on bag." I thought they said Wolf Payne.

"I already switched the luggage tags. Anything else?"

"Nope."

"Then memorize your new identity. You'll need it to survive."

Cool. I opened the passport again and tried to memorize what little it had printed in it. A stamp from Tanzania. Okay, I was a safari guy. A stamp from Rome. Tourist guy. No more stamps.

My driver's license said I was from Ontario. I wasn't exactly sure where that was. Ottawa was in fine print. Ottawa? Some of it was in French. Great. None of us spoke French.

The driver moved the limo close to one of the hangars. He got out and opened my door.

Damn. I'd only had one crummy beer and a bag of chips. So much for the cool limo ride.

The driver pulled my little suitcase out of the trunk and rolled it over to some people standing by what looked like a flight office. I started to walk over to them but they waved me to proceed to a small business jet waiting nearby.

Good. There was a sexy flight attendant waiting for me by the jet's little boarding stairs. She smiled as I walked up to her. "Good morning, Mr. Jackson."

I grinned. It was going to be a good flight. To wherever.

I got on the plane. My bag disappeared with the limo driver.

Hey. No TSA. No ticket. No nothing. Awesome.

Not many seats but they were all empty. They all looked VIP deluxe. Seating was whatever plush leather seat I cared to park my butt in.

I picked one. I parked it. Sweet!

No crap about upright seats, tray tables, oxygen masks, or fighting for the exits in case of emergency. No crap about turning off anything electronic.

Of course, Wolf's cell phone was now in the hot little hands of the limo driver. Not to mention the Rolex. But I still felt like a king.

Two pilots boarded. One gave me a nod.

That seemed to be the extent of the security check. Sadly, no one asked to see my super cool diplomatic passport. Maybe later.

What about all those poor schmucks flying first class in big ugly commercial jets? It dawned on me, those were the corporate wannabes, the corporate losers. The real top dogs on planet Earth flew in private jets. Yes, they did.

That was me.

Top dog.

Jack's bitch.

Who the hell just called me Jack's bitch? Martoni? Nameless? Come on, who was it?

Never mind. There were two flight attendants. Both babes.

I checked them out.

Okay, they were just fashion models or something because they were way too skinny for my taste.

Beautiful, yes. Sexy, no.

Note to self: Tell Jack real men preferred real curves on our women. Greyhounds were sleek and classy, but most guys craved a curvy ass they could hold onto. Jack was so clueless, even if he'd been several hundred men already.

They closed the hatch. I looked around. Just me.

Sweet!

I put my seat belt on, but it seemed like no one was going to ask me to do it. Hell, there weren't any tray tables anywhere. No cold air nozzles. No fat guys hogging my space or farty old geezers or babies bawling their eyes out. This was so alien. This was how God had meant man to fly.

Epic!

We started to taxi. The ladies gave me hot wipie towels. Cool.

They gave me pre-takeoff drinks. They offered champagne, but I asked for rum and coke. Extra rum. They had it. Very cool. Much better than the limo. Limos should all have sexy back seat attendants. Seemed obvious.

Then they gave me weird but yummy appetizers. Cool.

More hot wipies. Cool.

They finally sat down for takeoff.

Actually, I was hoping the model babes would take something off for takeoff. Seemed appropriate for Jumper class. But no clothes were being taken off.

Nope. I was too optimistic. Okay, it was an absolutely lame thought. The rum was potent. I made it a point to keep my clothes on so I wouldn't embarrass myself.

Oh, what the hell. This was Wolf on a solo VIP flight. I had diplomatic immunity. The flight beauties were paid to put up with anything. Weren't they? Maybe not. I decided just to chill and enjoy the service.

What did Jack say? Don't screw up my first assignment. Right. Whatever the hell that assignment was.

Weird tasty snacks.

Drinks.

Weird tasty snacks.

Drinks.

It was a great flight.

Four hours later we were about to land. Damn! I'd just missed my chance to join the mile high club. Lusty thoughts. Too many drinks. I was seriously sloshed. Not good, Marko.

The runway flight models were kinda crafty because they were trying to sober me up before we landed. Easier said than done, ladies.

We landed. My head was still spinning. Whee!

I was a little fuzzy about what happened next. But I was still in my seat and there was an unknown blond now in my face. She had curves. Wonderful curves. The flight attendant of my dreams. Hello, babe. She was bending over to be on my eye level.

Hot legs. Wonderful cleavage. How does cleavage do that, anyway? Her boobies formed a shape I could only call a primal eye magnet. They wanted me.

She put her hand under my chin and directed my gaze up to her face. Good face, beautiful face, natural face, not a model's robot perfect face. She had this little smile that never left her. It looked really good on her. It was a smile I instantly loved. She was a bit too blurry so I tried to focus.

I smiled and offered myself to her as best I could. "Hello."

She had a sweet voice. "Hello there. I'm Sonya Clark. I'm here to help you with your assignment."

Yes, of course. This was the mission's titular Sonya Clark.

Who said titular? Someone knew what that meant. I suspected it wasn't used correctly, but she was titular none the less. Man, I thought I was clever. Whee!

Sonya gave my face a little slap. "Waldo?"

I looked up at her face again. Such a great little perma-smile. Oh those lush kissable lips. They needed kissing. Right now. Then I grabbed some self-control and gazed into her deep brown eyes, yeah, like poets obsess about. I loved those eyes. But I gotta say, those lips—they needed my lips on them so bad.

Wait. What did she call me? Waldo? I was no Waldo. Oh yeah. I remembered the mission briefing. She was a jumper like me and Jack. Hopefully not as weird.

I looked around. We were still on the little VIP jet.

She pulled my face back to her. "Waldo?"

"I prefer Wolf."

"Empty your pockets, Wolf."

"What?" Hell, I'd just done that a few hours ago. I wanted an explanation first.

She started going through my pockets—a real no-nonsense kind of girl. I smiled and let her do just that. It felt really good. She was all leggy, curvy, and stacked and I was whacked and damn it, it just felt good to have her hands deep in my pockets.

She seemed to finish. "Do you know who I am?"

"Yeah. The angel in charge of my assignment. First assignment. You're Clark." I almost called her Titular Clark.

"Call me Sonya. Did Jack fill you in?"

"Screw Jack. I just wanna fill *you* in." Oops. I couldn't believe I'd just said what I really wanted to say. Never do that, Marko. Never.

"You're drunk. You know that?"

"Of course I know that. Why the hell wouldn't I know that? But that doesn't change our relationship, or my desires." I thought that sounded less blunt. Good job, Marko.

Sonya sat her divine curvy ass in a chair. "Look. You've got another flight to catch."

"I do?"

"You need to sober up." She held up some new identification. "You need to take these papers and board a flight to Antwerp."

"What-twerp?"

"Wolf. Look at me. You're in Montreal."

"Canada?"

"That's where we keep it. You need to take this wallet and this passport and get your sorry ass over to another plane waiting to take you to Antwerp."

"Antwerp where?"

"Antwerp, Belgium."

"Fuck. I can't go there."

"Listen to me, Wolf." She leaned closer and slapped my face lightly a few times. She was really good at that. "You're going to Antwerp. You're going to be given a courier case and you're going to bring it back to me, eh? Do you hear me?"

She said *eh*. It was wonderful how she did that. "I hear you, Sonya. My mission is to fetch. I'm the dog. You're the master."

"Yes. And what are you going to do right now?"

"Take the passport. Memorize the new me. Fly somehow to Amsterdam."

"Antwerp."

"Right. Antwerp. Screwy name. In Brussels—"

"Belgium."

"Right. Belgium. Wherever the hell that is."

"Europe."

"Right. Somewhere in deepest darkest Europe—"

"No. It's on the coast, between France and the Netherlands. Many of the people who live there actually call the city Antwerpen."

Antwerpen? "No way."

"Listen to me, Wolf. When you land in Antwerp, you'll stay on the plane for the return flight. You'll only be on the ground long enough for refueling and to take delivery of the courier case. Please remember it's a very valuable case. Are you listening to me?"

"Yeah, babe."

"You will let no one open it. Absolutely no one. You won't open it, either. It must never leave your sight until you see me again. You will give it to no one but me. Is that clear?"

"I'm giving it to you."

"You can remember that?"

"Hell, yes. I'm giving it to you, babe. Believe it or not, thoughts like that come natural to me."

"I'm sure they do."

"You better believe they do, Sonya, babe. Anything for you. You want the case, you get the case. I'll save it all for you. Until we meet again. No one gets it."

The light caught her beautiful eyes. "Then I get it?"

"Yeah. Then you fucking get it. You get everything I've got. Babe, it's all yours. You want it, don't you? Tell me you want it." Man, I really wanted to give it to her.

Sonya looked at me and maybe smiled. It was hard to tell because she always seemed to smile. Mainly, it was hard to tell in my condition. "Baby." Her voice was hotness wrapped in pure sultry. "I want it so bad. I want what you've fucking got." She grabbed my face. I thought she was going to kiss me but she didn't. "You bring it all back to mama. You don't share it with anyone. You hear me? You bring it all back to me and you give me everything you've got."

"Hooyah!" I'm not sure if I said that, but I guess I did.

She spoke like the sexiest blond Marine that ever existed. "So it's just you and me. We've got ourselves a fucking hooyah deal. Right?"

Man, I loved how she talked. I held up my hand. "Fuckin' A." And we high-fived.

Un. Real.

The rest was a bit of a blur. She put her hands in my pockets again. I loved when she did that. This time I suspected she was loading me up with more fake documents. She pulled me to my feet. She was shorter than I thought she'd be. But she was strong, and not too shy about getting physical, either. I was looking down at her hair. It smelled really good. Did I say she was blond? No dark roots. We got off the plane together, and I'll admit I leaned on her. Well, I was tipsy so I leaned on her a lot. Nobody would have blamed me.

Then there was a short car ride. We might have been in the back seat. My head might have been in her lap. Or maybe that was just wishful thinking. Either way, it was like being in heaven. Head down in the car. Head in her sexy lap. Dreamy. Even better than being shot in the head by Martoni.

We got out of the car somehow and she helped me park my butt on another private jet, then she disappeared. Different flight attendants on this small jet. One male. One female. I glanced around to see who else was on this flight. No one. It was another solo flight for me. They reclined my seat and put a soft blankie on me. That's all I remembered.

3.2 Flight

I opened my eyes a crack. Night. Private jet. Cool lighting in the cabin. I guessed we were still over the Atlantic. Same two flight attendants I'd barely noticed when I'd boarded. She was now dozing. He was reading. As I looked around, it seemed like I was still flying solo.

I wanted to hug Jack. I'd never had the VIP treatment before. Of course I still wanted to kill him, but first I'd let him know his assignments were awesome.

Then I'd kill him.

But for now, I mainly needed to take a leak. I looked around, got up, and headed to the rear where it had to be. Yup, the little flier's room. Very fancy. Lots of wood, brass, and mirrors. Ultra clean. The modern amenities took a little time to figure out. This was nothing like cattle-class on a regular airline.

Heading back to my seat, I decided I was hungry. Starving, in fact. It looked like the flight attendants were both off duty, but hell, I was the reason for this whole flight.

The guy seemed to sense what I was thinking and came over. "Can I get you something?"

"Yes. Water. And I seem to be starving."

"No problem. For appetizers, we have calamari in a light cream sauce, oysters Rockefeller, and also—"

"You know, I'm more of a meat and potatoes kind of guy."

"We have a marvelous veal marsala, topped with rosemary remoulade on a bed of jasmine—"

"No veal. I don't eat baby cows that aren't even allowed to move around. Maybe chicken? Grown up chicken? You know, the kind that were treated like VIPs until they had their little heads lopped off." Not a good image. It reminded me of my current situation.

He rubbed his hands together. "Duck a l'Orange. Very tender and—"

"A hamburger? Fish and chips?"

"Dolphinfish?"

"I don't eat dolphins."

"How about some mahi-mahi?"

That sounded Hawaiian. "What's that?"

"Dolphinfish. But it's not dolphin."

This was going nowhere. "What do you guys eat?"

Bingo. I was soon served a wonderful homemade stew. They seemed happy to eat the food I wouldn't touch.

So who was I today? I pulled out my passport expecting to be an Antwerpian kind of guy. No such luck, I was still Canadian. Still a diplomat. But my name was now Jack DeFlame. You're a funny guy, Jack.

Why switch from one Canadian diplomat to another? Why switch planes at all? I decided they must be covering my trail.

It also occurred to me that if they were going to disappear me, this was a good way to do it. But Jack wouldn't do that. No, Jack-Jacqueline lusted after my hot Wolfie bod. I was a keeper. Soon to be his trophy bed bump.

* * *

I must have dozed off because the lady flight attendant was trying to tell me something.

"Mr. DeFlame. Good morning, sir. We'll be landing in a few minutes."

It looked like daylight outside. "What time is it?"

"The local time is 9:30."

Morning already. "We're in Antwerp?"

"Yes. Can I get you anything?"

"Nope. I'm good."

"You have time to use the lavatory before we land."

How did she know? "Thanks."

I used the facilities. Checked myself in the mirror. Not looking my best. Drinking too much was doing bad things to Wolf's hair. His eyes weren't too good, either.

I wandered slowly back to my seat.

Really, what was there to do on the little jet? Eat. Drink. Use the head. Sleep. Repeat. Repeat. Repeat. I'd have to talk with Jack about getting a decent gaming rig setup on his jets. Hell, the thing was probably on autopilot all the time. I bet the pilots would enjoy sitting with me and getting into a little mano a mano gaming action.

As we landed, I tried to remember Sonya's instructions. It was hard. All I could remember was a blond angel who liked to slap me around and stick her hands in my pockets.

Oh yeah. Get a package. Give it to her.

Did I really tell her I wanted to fuck her? No wonder she slapped me around. I had the feeling I'd blown my first mission even before it'd really started. Never send a horny novice jumper out to do a man's job.

Sorry, Sonya. No more booze. Second chance me, okay?

I hoped she would.

We rolled to a stop. They cut the engines. They opened the hatch and the pilots left.

Now what? Sonya had said something like I needed to stay on the plane, or maybe just fly back on it. Mostly, I wanted to get out and stretch my legs.

So I got up and headed to the exit. The flight attendants started looking nervous.

The lady attendant got to her feet. "We're refueling."

"That's okay. I won't smoke." I walked down the short ladder and stepped onto Antwerpian soil. Tarmac. Close enough. My first time in Europe. First time outside the U.S., assuming you didn't count yesterday's drunk stop in Canada. So far, I wasn't exactly representing America very well, or Canada for that matter. Less booze, Marko. Set a good example for the world.

But hell, I was now a diplomat and I suspected they usually went around drunk, like I'd been, just because they could. So maybe I was just playing the part of a diplomat really well.

Behind me, the flight attendants still looked worried.

I gave them a friendly wave. "It's okay. I'm staying by the plane."

I looked around the tarmac. Where was the city? I had a view of the runway, grass, trees around the perimeter, and a small airport terminal building. Antwerp was flat. The city was out there somewhere. Probably very old with lots of cool places to see.

Man, the weather was great. Mostly cloudy and in the low 70s.

Hey. We weren't refueling? Where was the gas truck? There was a black sedan about 100 yards away. Just sitting there. So where was my package?

A white car pulled up close to the plane. Two new pilots got out of the car and paused to talk with the driver. Papers were stamped. Money was passed. Well, I couldn't really see what was going on. All I knew is that I wanted to show my Canadian diplomat passport to someone. Anyone.

I checked it again to see who I was.

A truck pulled up and refueling began. The white car drove off. One pilot glanced at me and boarded while the other one walked around the plane, poked a few spots, then boarded. The black sedan just waited well away from us. I stood there wondering if this was what James Bond did most of the time. Stand around. Look good. Keep an eye out for Octopussy. I could do that.

Refueling was finally wrapping up and the flight attendants were waving for me to get back on the plane.

No package? I wasn't going anywhere without my package.

"Please come aboard, Mr. DeFlame."

No. Maybe I was supposed to walk over to the black sedan and get the package? Sonya said what, exactly?

Sonya said to stay on the plane. So I got back on the plane. They all just stared at me like I was messing things up and they couldn't tell me what to do. Even the pilots were watching me.

Fine.

I took my seat. At least I'd been to Antwerp, near the coast I couldn't see, on the outskirts of Europe I couldn't see.

Out my window I saw the black sedan pull up. Okay, I finally understood. This jet was my multimillion dollar office. They'd come to me. I'd show them my passport and they'd give me the package.

I straightened up. Business-like.

A middle-aged woman in a too-tight gray business suit entered the plane, walked straight over to me, and sat down. Very serious, with a completely no-nonsense attitude. She was carrying an aluminum briefcase. "Good morning, sir."

"Hi."

"I trust you had a pleasant flight."

I nodded.

"Are you right handed or left?"

I had to think about it. I was a rightie. Wolf seemed to be one, too. The other guys? Never mind, I was taking too long to figure it out. "Right." Hey, it's not like I was expecting medical questions.

"Please give me your left arm." She placed a wide strap around my wrist. Kinky. "Is that too tight?"

I used my Antonio Banderas voice. "It's never too tight." I don't know why I said that. What can I say? Wolfie was a beast flirting with the ladies.

She gave me a surprised little smile. Then she attached my wrist strap to a black cable coming out of the briefcase. A little green light on the case blinked a few times.

She leaned closer. "Don't try to open it. Don't take it off. Only give it to your handler."

Handler? Sonya was my handler? I liked the sound of that.

The lady held her hand over a broach she wore and leaned in like she was going to nibble on my ear. Well, okay. Good to know Wolf was still a cougar magnet, even in Europe.

Her lips brushed against my ear. I'll never get tired of having a woman surprise me with intimacy.

"I can tell you're new at this. Only trust your handler. Do whatever she says. Your life depends on it."

My life? Obviously this lady didn't know I was a jumper—unkillable. Probably unkillable. "Okay. Thanks."

"Be safe." She gave my ear a little kiss.

Really? She fell for Wolfie just like that?

As she left the plane she glanced back. I was expecting to see a glint of lust in her eyes. Instead, I saw concern for my safety.

They closed the door and gave me a pre-takeoff hot wipie, along with a croissant and some little cakes. I knew the drill, only this time I decided to stick with rumless coke.

The flight back was all daylight. I assumed we were going back to Montreal. No one ever told me anything.

I was tired, they were tired. New pilots, but no shift change for these flight attendants. Mainly being strapped to an electronic metal briefcase was a pain. Everything from eating to washing my hands was awkward, and I had to keep checking the damn blinking green light every time the case bumped something. They made it look so easy in the movies. But in real life, it was a royal pain.

Let's just say the aluminum case looked new when we took off, and embarrassingly dented by the time we landed.

But there was good news, too. By the time I was supposed to get off the plane I'd really gotten to like the flight attendants. Try spending about 18 hours cooped up in a cramped metal tube crisscrossing the Atlantic with friendly helpful people and you'll know what I mean. The CIA should skip waterboarding and go straight to good times in a partially pressurized cramped metal tube. We're talking vastly improved results. No one's going to give you the time of day if they're surrounded by people they hate. But with one big happy family surrounded by a horribly cold oxygen-deprived environment and a long fall to certain death, the truth flows out like nature intended.

Hell, someone needed to slap those CIA sons of bitches around and clue them in on The Tube. Party with your enemies in The Tube—everyone comes out happy. And well informed.

After we landed, both flight attendants gave me a hug and promised to look me up if they were ever in Austin. Wolf thought that was a bad idea. Screw Wolf. Those attendants were like family now, except I had no way to contact them.

Mainly I was just happy to exit The Tube. My feet touched tarmac. I sucked in fresh Montreal air. At least I thought that's where I was.

A black Mercedes was waiting for me. Nice, but it wasn't the limo I was expecting.

What? No customs agents or pesky forms? No hassle about anything? No luggage? Where was my bag, anyway?

The driver was waving for me, holding the back door open. I

walked over to him. "Hang on. I still need to get my bag."

"There is no need to worry, sir. Your bag is already taken care of." He sounded like he was from India.

"Yeah?"

He held the door impatiently. "Please to get in, sir."

I got in the back, hoping Sonya would be there. She wasn't.

The driver got in and we drove off. But a minute later he pulled over and held out an empty bag. "Most kindly empty your pockets. You should know I will be needing all of your things."

So this was just another ride, another empty bag to fill, another mugging.

I was expecting stuff in return, but I got nothing. "Don't I get some papers? A wallet?"

"You will not be needing such things."

"Yes, I will."

"Do not argue with me. You must also be handing me the briefcase."

What? Only Sonya-babe got my case. "No. I have my orders."

"And I have mine, sir. You are to hand me the briefcase immediately. It has a simple Velcro strap. Undo it now and hand it to me."

"No way."

"Do it now, I say."

"Forget it. Just drive. Sonya gets it, not you."

He laughed like he didn't care if it sounded fake. "You do not understand. There has been a change of plans. Jack is now taking charge of your assignment."

No way. "What assignment?"

"The assignment you are no longer on. Now hand me the case."

Wolf was ready to kill him. All my mental passengers were upset. "I want to talk with Sonya."

"Look around you. Does it look like she is here? She is not. I have already told you Jack is taking over Sonya's part in this matter. Jack is in charge. Do not think Jack will be pleased with you. He will not. Now be removing the strap from your wrist and hand the briefcase to me."

"Fuck you."

"Oh really? You say fuck me? You think that's what will happen when Jack finds out you are the one refusing to cooperate?"

"Just drive. I'll deal with Jack."

The driver let out a loud sigh. "Then I will drive. And the fucking will be entirely on your head."

"Good."

He drove. We were obviously pissed with each other. It was a silent ride.

About five miles later he pulled over by the side of the road. "I wish to apologize to you, kind sir. We got off on a bad foot and for that, I am sorry."

"Okay."

"I have had some trouble at home, you see. I should not let that bother me, but it does. So please, allow me to start over. Welcome to Montreal, sir."

"Thanks."

"I trust your flight was pleasant. Perhaps it was?"

"It was good."

"Most excellent. The weather here was quite good. The humidity was a little high for my taste, but quite good for this time of year. And how was your weather?"

"Good."

"Excellent. I trust the food on your trip was to your liking?"

"It was okay."

"Also excellent. I regret to inform you that Ms. Sonya Clark was called away on most urgent business. However, I am most pleased to tell you that Mr. Jack Peoples is here to take her place as manager of your assignment. So all is going well here."

"What assignment?"

"Your assignment. The one you have just completed."

"And what was that assignment?"

"That is not important to our discussion. But I am telling you a thing most vital, sir. Jack is now giving the orders and we both have ours. Your orders are to hand the briefcase to me. Mine is to take the briefcase and transport you to a certain place for you to wait for further instructions."

"I'm not handing over the briefcase."

"Yes, kind sir, you will please do that now."

"Not gonna happen."

"Ah. If you are thinking you will hand the briefcase to Jack, you should know my assignment is to receive it from you now."

"Screw your assignment. Who am I seeing next?"

"Another driver. After that, I cannot say."

This was going nowhere so I tried another path. "Drive or I'll kill you."

"What?"

I kind of liked how his eyes bugged out. I kept the pressure up. "You heard me. I have a gun."

"No. Impossible. Do not threaten me with weapons you do not have."

He was right. I was fresh out of weapons. Of course I could hit him with the metal case. But I didn't want to dent it up any more than it already was. Besides, it would take a while to kill him with it.

Wolf pushed me aside, slipped off my belt, and quickly pulled it across the driver's neck and pulled hard. It seemed like Wolf wanted me to say something. "Drive."

The driver choked and clawed at the belt. Wolf was comfortable with the driver's panic and the little choking sounds he made. I wasn't, but hey, I let it happen. Wolf knew what he was doing. I'd just have to trust him. Finally, the driver put it in gear, and drove.

Wolf loosened his grip, but kept the belt around the guy's neck for our 20 minute drive.

The driver pulled over. Near an empty field. "You are to walk to that silver car on the other side of the field." He didn't sound so good.

"You're kidding."

"I assure you I am in no position to kid."

"True. But you're in a good position to dump us."

"Us?"

Oops. There was only one of me. Damn, I'd just had a Multi-Mind moment. "Me."

"To be honest about it, sir, I would love to dump you. But protecting the briefcase was my assignment, too. Please go now."

Wolf and I thought about it. "Hand me your keys."

"Why? No, I will not do that."

"Then die here." Wolf pulled on the belt. "Either way, I get the keys."

He handed me the keys, but it was some sort of keyless ignition system because the engine was still running. I scowled and he turned off the engine.

"Smart move." I motioned to the car waiting across the field. "If I like my next ride, I'll leave your keys by the side of the road over there."

I got out. "Pop the trunk. I want my luggage."

"Your luggage is not here."

I fingered the keys and found the right button on the remote. The trunk popped open. It was empty.

I walked to the driver's window and held out Wolf's big muscular hand. "Your cell phone." He wasn't happy but he didn't argue. I pocketed his phone.

Wolf wanted to tie him to the bumper, but I thought we were good here.

I started trudging across the field, threading my belt through the loops. As I got closer to the silver car I could see the windows were rolled down and the driver was a blond woman. Sonya Clark, to be precise.

She had a big grin for me. "Looking good, Mr. Payne."

I got in. "You're looking kind of good yourself."

"Any trouble?"

"Nothing I couldn't handle." I dropped the Indian guy's phone and keys out the window. Sonya drove us to wherever the hell we were going.

3.3 Canada Wet

Sonya drove us through a rural area outside of Montreal, generally heading north. Rolling hills and green meadows. Trees. Flowers. Lakes were everywhere. It was hard to believe they ever had snow here. I'd seen snow only once in Austin. It'd melted by afternoon. Hard to imagine what real snow would be like.

"Is it always this beautiful in Canada?"

Her smile was more like a glow. "Always."

Cool. "When do I get this thing off my wrist?"

"Soon."

"Soon is good. I still seem to be missing my luggage."

"I've been saving it for you."

"That makes two of us."

Sonya tried to hide her smile. "So you remember being drunk."

"I remember the good parts."

"Like what?"

Now it was my turn to hide a smile. "Mostly you. I've been kicking myself for, uh, the way I acted. Maybe some of the things I said. But the damn minibar was wide open. You know? I won't let those little bottles sneak up on me again."

She looked at me. I thought she was going to say something snarky, but she didn't.

We drove along through amazing scenery, up into the green hills, white capped mountains in the distance.

After 15 minutes of riding in silence I thought I should be saying something. I suppose it was nervous passenger syndrome. "So you're a jumper, too."

She frowned, shook her head, and winked. "A subject for another time."

Okay, some things were not good to talk about. Well, Jack sure loved sharing his spirit walking tales. So why was Sonya sending me her serious hush-up body language?

* * *

After a few more miles of country road, we pulled into a kind of estate—ritzy electric gate, hints of a home peeking out through tall bushes, rock walls, and lots of trees. We pulled around a circular gravel driveway and up to an upscale rustic two story house with ivy growing up part of it. Hard to describe, because it seemed almost modern, but still said rustic hideaway.

I got out of the car, still tethered to my metal courier case. "Nice place."

She got out and locked the car. "Thanks."

Apparently my luggage wasn't in the trunk. So she'd kept it while I was jetting to Europe and back? I guess she'd had a good laugh poking through it and finding beachwear. Looking around at the house and the secluded grounds, I was a bit confused. Maybe I was expecting an underground bunker filled with guards and techies. Or maybe I expected—

Hell, I had no idea what I was expecting. "It's your place?"

Her smile faded slightly. "Technically it's Jack's. But I have exclusive use of it. Let's walk around to the back. You'll like the view."

We started walking. "He vacations in Montreal?"

"No. I don't think he vacations anywhere. Jack spends most of his time in D.C., but he's often in your state capitals doing business."

"Like Austin."

"Exactly."

"Montreal's the capital of Canada?"

"Ottawa. It's about a two hour drive from Montreal. We use the Montreal airport because it's bigger."

"Right."

As we rounded the house, I caught sight of a wonderful tree-lined grassy field sloping down to a lake. "Wow!"

"It's a great view, eh?"

I loved when she said *eh*. She couldn't say it often enough for me.

She suddenly pulled me to her. Wow! Pressed close to me, and firmly pulled my head down to her level. She put her lips to my ear. "The whole house is bugged. Don't say anything you don't want Jack to hear."

"Okay." I noticed my arm was around her. She didn't pull away.

"By now, Jack has bugged your house, your car, and everything you own. He might even be watching your friends and family."

I liked our conspiratorial whispers. "Jack doesn't know the original me or any of my past lives."

"Are you sure about that?"

Her warm breath was steaming up my ear—and my libido. "Yes." He'd never figure out who Nameless was, or even track him back to killing Martoni in the desert.

"Then know that Jack is doing everything he can to find out all about you."

"Okay. Why?"

"Leverage." Sonya pushed me away just as firmly as when she pulled me in. It was hard for me to let go of her. She was amazingly holdable.

We continued our walk while I tried not to think about what kind of leverage Jack was after. "It's hard to believe it snows here." Was I repeating myself?

"It snows like crazy. You're here at the best time. Early summer."

We walked up the back steps to a large covered back patio. Tables, chairs, rockers. It seemed ideal for breakfast. Hell, make that lunch and dinner, too.

The view from the patio was fantastic.

She pulled the cover off a plush sofa. "Do you want to sit for a minute, Wolf?"

We sat down. The view was amazing. I kept my eyes on the grass, wildflowers, and the lake, but I wasn't thinking about the landscape.

She watched me for a moment. Maybe deciding something.

"Later we can go for a walk down to the lake if you'd like. But maybe you're tired."

"I slept on the plane."

"That's good. Let's get that thing off your wrist." She reached over and simply removed the Velcro. No alarms went off. Nothing exploded. She noticed my expression. "It has GPS built into it. It knows it's in a safe place." She stood up. "I'll just take this inside. Something to drink?"

"Uh, water."

"Water it is." Sonya went inside the house.

I sat there for a minute, relaxing and spinning at the same time. So this was Canada. My passengers were sure enjoying it. Maybe we should get a place here for the great summers. It sure beat the Texas heat.

After a few minutes, I got up and went inside to see what she was up to.

Just inside, there was a breakfast morning-room kind of space with lots of big windows looking out the back of the house. A few split-level stairs led up to the wide open kitchen—also with a great view.

She turned around and smiled. "Your water, sir."

I took it. The briefcase was gone. "I take it I passed my first assignment."

"Yes. A bit of a rough start, but you passed. I especially like how you handled Vijay." She put a hand on Wolf's big chest.

"The guy from India?"

"That guy. He really loves to jerk recruits' chains. But you passed his test, too."

"He was testing me? The flight attendants? Everybody?"

She nodded. "Wolf, everything we do is tested and evaluated. The syndicate is very careful about the people in their organization. Very careful."

"And if I'd failed?"

"You didn't. And you won't on any of your assignments."

I reminded myself I swam with some pretty big sharks now. "Where am I staying tonight? In Canada, or on a flight back to Texas?"

"I was hoping you'd stay here tonight."

Yes! "Sounds good."

"Would you like the tour?"

"Absolutely."

She held out her hand for me to take it. That's all it took.

* * *

Sonya's house had all the usual rooms. Except one upstairs—a dimly lit Zen torture room. I just stood at the doorway taking it all in.

She caught my confusion. "I do massage."

"Massage?"

"Yes. You know what I'm talking about. Massage table. Candles. Oil. Aromas. Ambient music. Stuff like that."

But I wasn't looking at that stuff. She followed my gaze upward. "Ah. My inversion rack. It's better than an inversion table because I can massage the whole body while you hang there."

Right. I instinctively checked the floor for blood splatters. "Cool. Hey, do you do wax jobs? I mean bikini wax kind of things."

"No. Just massage."

"For people?"

"Of course, for people."

"I mean any people."

"No. I try to keep it to just women. Guys can be total dicks."

I wanted to ask her if she'd oiled up Jack before. But if she had, she was probably forced to do that. Anyway, I was sure she'd find the question really rude.

She pulled me close and whispered, "Not Jack."

How'd she do that? "You know what I'm thinking?"

"Of course I do. All men have the same thoughts."

"Even Jack?" Okay, so I was dragging out the conversation just to be up close and personal with her.

She paused a moment. "Jack's not exactly a man. In fact, whenever Jack gets a new body the first thing he does is castrate himself."

Crap! "No way. He cuts his own balls off?"

"Yes, and he's bloody good at it. He's had a hell of a lot of practice."

"Shit."

"If he does that to himself, imagine what he'd do to others."

Others? Like me? "Jack's seriously messed up."

"He seriously hates men."

"Yeah, but I think Jack likes me." Well, that was my impression.

She shook her head. "Don't count on it."

That was a disturbing thought. Hell, whatever Jack thought about me was disturbing. "So do *you* hate men?"

"Of course. But I make a few exceptions." She bit my ear and pushed me away.

As we left the massage room, it dawned on me why she was so good with her hands. Slapping me. Pushing me. Walking me drunk off a plane. Sonya was a physical girl.

* * *

Back in the kitchen, Sonya opened the fridge. "What does Wolf like to eat?"

Snacks? Or was early dinner a Canadian tradition? I moved in close for another private conversation. Well, you know, I just liked being close. I whispered in her ear, "You should know who I really am—who I was."

"Don't. Don't tell anyone your past. Not even me. I'm serious."

I moved just far enough away to check her eyes. Dead serious. Her mouth still had her perma-smile, but those eyes. Note to self: Sonya speaks with her eyes. Trust them.

I backed away. Changed the subject. "I like being called Wolfie."

"I know you do. I've read your file. But get this straight, Mr. Payne. I'm not even remotely like those other women in your life."

What did I say? Okay, back to dinner time. "I like chicken."

"Wolf likes chicken. We'll cook up some chicken."

"Or salmon."

That seemed to piss her off. "Look, you can't have it both ways. You need to know that about me. Got it?"

Her eyes flashed. Yipe. A sore spot? "Okay. Got it."

Sonya handed me a beer. I stayed out of easy knife reach. We both slowly eased back to our comfort zone.

I set the table and opened a bottle of white wine for her. That's what women drink, right?

We sat, we ate, we drank. We made light conversation. Sonya was a good cook, but a little scary in the kitchen. Prior kitchen trauma? Or was it me saying wrong things like I often did?

The sun was going down so we headed to the back patio to enjoy the early evening. She guided me onto a plush sofa—she was good at guiding. Then she plopped down right up against me and put my arm around her. Unexpected. Very cozy, but I still couldn't tell what was going on with her. One minute she was making advances, the next minute she was pissed with me.

Sonya took a deep breath, then seemed to let it all out like this was an important decision. "Would you like to hear about my past?"

I thought we didn't talk about that, but Jack probably knew about her already. Knew her family. Maybe even held her family hostage in a loose, threatening kind of way. "Yes. I'd like that."

"My original name was Ana Clark. I grew up in Vancouver with my parents and my younger sister, Sonya. I was a physical therapist, 29, taller than Sonya, darker hair, not as pretty—well, not as shapely. My dear little Sonya was finishing her training to be a nurse."

Damn. Ana was now in her sister's body. Not good.

"One night I was driving to my apartment when I was hit by a drunk driver who ran a red light. I don't remember any of it, but it was bad." She stopped for a moment, seemingly lost in a tangle of memories. "His car hit me hard on my driver's side."

Oh fuck. She was t-boned.

"My head was thrown through my side window. My door was crushed. I had major spinal injuries. Broken ribs. A shattered hip. Brain injuries—hemorrhaging. They . . . they drilled a hole in my skull to relieve the pressure. I had lacerations everywhere." Tears were rolling down her cheeks. "They were able to save my legs, but they had to remove my left arm. It was seriously bad. But I didn't know any of that because I was in a coma—a coma I wasn't coming out of.

"My family was there in the hospital, of course. Waiting for me to wake up. I don't know, maybe secretly hoping I wouldn't. I should have died in the crash. I should have, but I fucking didn't. I wish I had. Dear God, I wish I had.

"Sonya didn't work ER or intensive care, but that was her hospital. She worked days on another floor, then sat with me every night, holding my only hand. She slept in the room with me for almost two months, waiting for me to come out of the coma. But I wasn't coming out of it. Never. And even if I did, it would be to live ... piecing the minutes of my life together ... in my shattered body."

Sonya-Ana was quiet for a moment, then took a deep breath and continued. "I have her memories so I know for a fact she sensed what I wanted. Looking back, she was absolutely right. So one night, my dear sweet Sonya quietly hushed my body. It was the blessing I would have wanted if my brain could've had a thought. I love her so much for wanting to end my suffering."

"I'm so sorry for you, Ana. For both of you."

"Please call me Sonya. That's my name now."

"Okay."

"So I moved into her body—an absolutely shocking experience. At first I thought it was temporary, like a little visit with dear Sonya before my passing. We were both in there—in her mind—in her body. But she was so silent.

"Some would say Sonya was an angel, kind enough and strong enough to end my suffering. Others would label her a killer, pure and simple. All I know is that I love her deeply and I hold her close to me. I always will. And for whatever reason I was given her body, it's now mine to protect. And by God, I will protect Sonya. I will not take another body. Never again.

"So I tried to be her, step into her shoes, but I couldn't. Her nursing career was lost. I couldn't fake it. It would have been dangerous to her patients to even try. Not to mention, selfish of me. But my family saw me only as Sonya. They wanted me to continue with nursing, but it was impossible. Sonya's nursing skills were hard to access in my mind. I was afraid I'd accidentally kill someone if I tried to fill her shoes at the hospital.

"As for me, Ana, the physical therapist . . . I now looked like Sonya, so no one would believe I was still certified to do physical therapy. Yes, I still had those skills, but to be recertified would take years. I didn't have the heart to do that all over again. So I fell into massage work. My friends drifted away. I was lost. Lost in my own sweet little sister.

"A few months later, Jack tracked me down. He has people watching for euthanasia, looking for nurses or doctors who abruptly drop their own way of life. I certainly made a sudden change in Sonya's career. Jack knew who I was, who I'd been, and that my spirit could take my killer's body. He threatened to harm my family if I didn't join his syndicate. That's the threat he holds over people. Did he give you the carrot and the stick speech?"

"Yeah." Then I whispered in her ear. "It's okay for him to hear you say that?"

She nodded.

I switched back to my usual voice. "So you moved to Montreal?"

"Jack wanted me in his syndicate. He wanted me here. His threats worked, so now I live in this beautiful house. And because I won't take another body, he's been trying me out in assorted positions."

"Like being a handler for agents in the field."

"Yes. Some agents are easy to work with. Others get drunk right out of the gate and need to be slapped around."

"Like me."

"Yes, like you. However, you did get your panties in a serious twist when Vijay tried to talk you out of the briefcase. You have some skill, Mr. Payne. I don't know which of your hosts brings you that skill or whether you've always had it. It doesn't really matter. What matters is that Vijay is pissed about his neck and I'm very excited to have you."

Huh? "I'm excited to be had."

Her eyes flashed deviously. "You've only begun to be excited, Mr. Payne. Since you're now my new agent, I was thinking we should celebrate by hanging you from my inversion rack. It's good for the body. And it does wonders for the soul."

"Yeah, I don't think so."

"Well, I think so. March, cowboy." She winked like something fun was up. More secret stuff?

She pulled me off the sofa and prodded my butt into the house. Inside, she locked the back door and pulled me close to whisper. "Sorry, Wolf. Getting fucked is part of the assignment."

I couldn't tell if she was kidding or not. "Nah."

"Don't wimp out on me, boy. This is the fucking hooyah deal you made with me on the plane. Remember?"

"Vaguely."

"More importantly, Jack wants me to be your fucking carrot. But it's my choice whether to keep you or pass you to another whoring handler. So I've decided. I'm keeping you whether you like it or not. Now march."

What the . . .

* * *

Upstairs I paused in front of her massage room. Handlers were like prostitutes? They were Jack's carrots? No wonder Sonya was shifting in and out of a bad mood.

I whispered in her ear. "How many agents do you handle?"

"I handle three, all women. Believe it or not, I've passed on all the dickheads Jack sent my way. You seem different, so that makes you the first stud in my stable. Sonya likes your sorry ass and so do I. Good news, Wolf, we're keeping you." She pushed me into the room. "Strip!"

Why were all the jumpers I'd met so weirded out with personality problems? I wasn't like that.

She started lighting candles while I did a slow very unsexy strip. I eyed the rack. "Maybe we can start with a regular massage. You know?"

She cocked her head. "Fine with me." She pointed to the large padded table in the center of the room. "Butt naked. Face down."

Sir, yes sir! Man, she was going all drill-sergeant on me. "My face goes where?"

"Face in the hole."

No way.

Okay, so I did like jumper-girl said. I was butt naked face down with my face wedged in this weird padded hole in the table. I had a good view of the floor. No drool bucket. Nothing good was going to come of this.

She started some music. Really bland airy stuff. Maybe I was supposed to relax? Seemed impossible. She moved my arms and hands by my side. Apparently they weren't supposed to hang off the edge. But my feet were hanging off the edge. Okay. Whatever.

"Relax, Wolf. You're way too tense."

Hell yeah, I was tense. "Okay."

"Don't talk. It spoils the mood."

Sonya had a lot of Red Sonja in her. So who could relax with a hot-tempered barbarian sword master at your back?

She started by touching me in various spots. Nothing sexual, just warm pressure. Weird, but oh well. Spot touch—good.

Then she pulled up a stool, took one of my hands, and started massaging it with warm oil. I could see her legs and a bit of a short silk robe through my padded face hole. Massage wear? Shouldn't I have a towel over my butt or something? Maybe some black rocks arranged like crop circles on my back? Something green like guacamole in my eyes?

It occurred to me, she had two women in her head and I had four guys in mine. That was an awful lot of people in the room. Especially since it was my bare butt in the air. Wolf's butt. I really wanted to join the other guys in the back seat. Well, Sonya was driving everything now. Hey, guys. Who brought the popcorn?

Okay, I might have been feeling a little weirder than Sonya about this.

The hand massage was good. The arm massage was even better. Wolf had a lot of muscles and Sonya seemed to enjoy working them. She did both sides. Then my feet. She certainly had talent at this. From her background in physical therapy, she must have known where everything was and how it worked.

Then she worked her hands up my legs. Wonderful. Relaxing, but not completely. She continued with a butt massage. Oh, wow.

Highly recommended whether you work at a desk all day or not.

Then the back. Oh, yeah. Wonderful. So relaxing. Everything unwinding. Then lots of even pressure on my butt and both hands were doing my shoulders. What the . . . ?

I peeked. She was now sitting on my rear and she was wonderfully naked.

She slapped the back of my head. "Head down. You'll strain your neck."

Hell, yeah. I was happy to strain my neck. She was a goddess, a vision, and I couldn't keep my eyes off of her.

She slapped me again.

Fine. Head in hole.

Note to self: Always remember what you just saw. Sonya sitting on my ass, working it with her crotch. Hands on my shoulders, breasts hanging down so full and wonderful, swinging slowly to the rhythm of her hips.

Now this was awkward. I had a place for my face but my erection was trapped. She seemed to sense what was going on because she shifted her crotch off my hips, reached between my legs, and moved my multipurpose tool up and slightly to one side. Much better. It felt a little clinical, but still a nice relief.

Then she lay down, massaging my back with her breasts. Her hair swished across the back of my neck. Her head was next to mine. She breathed steam into my ear. "Enjoying your carrot?"

"Yeah, I—"

She bit my ear. "I said no talking. Just relax and feel it. Feel me all naked on your back, sliding sensually up and around. Feel my breasts, my legs. Feel my crotch grinding into your tailbone. Feel me stripped down and giving you all my bare-assed pleasure. You like me naked, don't you, Wolfie?"

Wolfie? I bit my tongue. I didn't need another slap on the head or another ear bite.

At that point I might have drooled a bit on the floor.

She gave me a kiss on the cheek—my face cheek. "Good boy, Wolf. You *can* be trained."

Trained? Why, because she said not to talk and I didn't? I huddled together with my guys. Guys, did that make us *trained*?

Hell, no. We could talk any time we felt like it. We just didn't want to. Free will—we still had it.

So we were all good—until she flipped me over.

There was no hiding it. Wolf was undeniably big and eager. Such a showoff.

* * *

I was on my back watching Sonya's bare ass. She was now off me gathering up more warmed up oil. All my guys were trying to climb into the front seat. No way. I might be in the back with them, but it was still my body to drive.

Or something like that.

Then she was spreading around the oil. Feet, legs, private parts (nothing shy about her), multi-pack abs, massive Wolf chest, arms, hands. Good job, Sonya. Towel time?

No. She had a devious grin on her face. And before I could brace myself, she jumped on.

Wow! Seriously wow!

She started sliding around with full body contact. I got the impression I was still out of her. Good. So far this was very professional. Not that I'd ever had a professional massage, but I was kicking myself for not having joined a spa years ago.

Then she started kissing my face passionately. Tonguing me. She reached around and grabbed both of my hands and placed them on her large breasts. I was good with that. It gave them something to do. Unfortunately it had a cruel side effect. Man, I really needed to be inside her.

Who knew Canadians could be so cruel?

She slid her womanhood up and down my hips, sliding up and down against my desperate pile driver.

And like all men faced with the onslaught of a supremely sexy cocktease, I thought about taxes. What were Wolf's taxes like, anyway? There were a lot of unexplainable expenses and income. Didn't banks report transactions over $10,000 to the IRS? Maybe Billy Bob handled Wolf's tax forms. I bet he had a good CPA, too. A guy with thick glasses and—

Sonya grabbed my throat with one hand, I guess she sensed my distraction from her, and she slid her hips down, forcing my shaft inside her.

Finally.

Then she slid up on me and Wolf popped out.

Damn.

That same cruel smile crossed her lips as she slid her pelvis down my stomach and I was in again.

And you know she did that trick over and over.

And over and over.

Somehow Wolf's tax problems were slipping from my crazed mind. My Multi-Mind was right on the edge. Clenching up. And Sonya damn well knew it.

Dozens of thrusts later she stopped, cocked her head to give me a wonderful smile, and jumped off.

Then she spit on my eager man-parts. Whoa! More than a little weird, even by my standards. So was that some kind of Canadian cowgirl compliment? She stepped back and nodded with approval, looking me up and down. "You're a damn fine specimen of manhood, Wolf."

I was a quivering semi-fucked man, is what I was.

"Feel like a shower?" She opened a door I had assumed to be a closet and was gone.

No wonder Canadian guys could survive horrible winters.

* * *

The next room was a bathroom. Antique clawfoot tub. Modern glass shower with a bench and a minibar. Yes, a minibar.

Sonya had the water running and she seemed friendly again. "Come on in, Wolf. Let's get soapy."

Hadn't we just been looking for this kind of friendly soap-happy shower? Yes, but from a regular body-maid, not a sexy jumper.

She bounced over to me. I really loved her bounce. "Watch your step."

Good advice because my feet were oiled.

I stepped carefully into the shower with her holding me steady.

The floor of the shower was textured. It felt good on my feet.

She handed me a bar of soap. "Do me first, please." She held her hands above her head, offering me her whole body.

I didn't need a second invitation. Her breasts were right there, so I started with them. Why not, eh?

Sonya smiled like an angel while I went over every inch of her. As I passed in front of her, she gave me little kisses on the lips. After I'd made a few slow sensual passes over her entire body, I reluctantly started to rinse her off.

She seemed to hold herself out to me. "Feel free to kiss anything that needs kissing."

I did. Well, it all needed kissing.

My turn? Yes, it was. I put my arms up and she went over every muscular inch of me. Just one pass, but it was a seriously good pass.

When she was done and I was rinsed, she pushed me, so I took the hint and sat on the shower bench.

"Shampoo time." She selected a bottle from an assortment. "I like my men to smell like trees."

She moved closer and placed my head between her breasts as she proceeded to wash my hair. Maybe the breast view was supposed to be nothing more than that, but I naturally couldn't resist fondling them. I could easily have done that all day.

"My turn." She selected a bottle for me to use and got on her knees in front of me.

And yes, she immediately began doing what guys really enjoy.

My eyes rolled to the back of my head.

She looked up. "Well?"

"You're totally awesome."

"You're supposed to wash my hair."

Right. She went back to work and I used the shower hose to get her hair good and wet. She gurgled a few times. I guess breathing was an issue, but she didn't bite.

Actually at this point, I was totally hooked. I didn't care what she did with me. I was moving here. Hell, I already had my Canadian passport. What more did I need?

She looked up. I was daydreaming again. I lathered up her hair and she never stopped working me.

Some shampoo got in her face so I hosed it off. She gurgled a bit more, but kept it going for me.

Finally, she was rinsed. She kissed my happy tool and stood up. "Are you sure you're not gay?" She grinned, gave my perma-happy thing a playful swipe, and stepped out of the shower, giving me a good view of her curvy ass in motion. Stunning. I wanted her to get back into the shower just to watch her walk away again. And again.

The guys were seriously impressed with Wolf's stamina. Hell, the man was a walking rod of steel. Okay, so we almost lost it on the massage table, but this was seriously impressive.

As I stepped out of the shower, a fresh towel landed in my face.

She opened a door. "After you dry off, put on the robe over there and meet me downstairs for happy hour."

Didn't we just have happy hour?

* * *

I found Sonya in a matching fluffy robe, curled up on the couch in the living room, sipping a glass of white wine.

She patted the spot next to her. "Sit with me."

I sat.

She waved at a spare glass next to the wine bottle.

What? No beer? No margaritas? "I'm good."

"I thought we'd give your lodgepole a rest. But don't worry, the night's young and we're just getting started."

Sounded good to me. Besides, it *was* throbbing a bit.

She grabbed the lapel on my robe and pulled me slowly to her. "Closer."

I was really starting to love that word. Sonya could say it anytime.

She kissed me lightly. Somehow these kisses were different— something completely new. I gave her the same. I have to believe there was real affection behind those simple kisses. It sure felt like it.

Then she put her lips to my ear. More kisses. A nibble or two. "I'm not your fucking carrot." Her voice was a tender whisper, but still serious.

"I never thought you were."

"Liar."

"Well, I didn't know what you were. It's not like I've ever had a handler before. Jack's a nutcase. I'll admit I like a reward now and then. Who doesn't? But Jack is cruel to use you as a reward." I was talking too much, thinking too much. Yes, Jack was cruel to use Sonya like this, but at the same time, sex with Sonya was better than any reward I could imagine. I needed to change the subject off of us. "Jack's sticks must be like bludgeoning sticks."

"Do you even know what those things are?"

"Yeah, I think Wolf owns a couple."

She stayed close. "How can you stand that killer inside you?"

"He's not so bad. He has skills. Some really good ones. Some I'm sure you already appreciate. And yeah, he's good at killing people. But the other guys in me aren't mean-hearted."

"Stop. Don't tell me anything about them. Nothing about your past. Remember?"

"I remember."

She kissed me again. And again. Gently, then teasingly, then passionately, then openly from the heart.

It struck me like a bolt of lightning that I hoped she wasn't kissing Wolf. I'll admit I looked like Wolf and sounded like Wolf, and I could clearly see how any woman would be attracted to him. But these little kisses were so different. Maybe this was the inner Ana kissing the inner Marko. Maybe like when we'd shed our clothes for sex, except now we'd shed our bodies and this was genuine affection between two souls. That thought really made my head spin—in a good way.

Our souls were kissing each other. Who knew that thought could be so electrifying?

It also struck me that when we were having sex, it didn't bother me that we were *all* there doing it—sharing the amazing experience. Sonya, Ana, Martoni, Nameless, Wolf, and me, all having hot sex together. Six minds, two bodies. Weird, but somehow having us all in it together was fun. Like we were all in the pool splashing around having a blast. Good clean fun.

But the sweet kisses she was giving me now? Completely

different. I wanted those all to myself. The sex I could share with the crowd, no problem. Hell, this wasn't even my body, and Ana wasn't using hers either. But these kisses were from the heart. Private. Just between Ana and me. And that's absolutely how I wanted it. Sonya, Martoni, Nameless, and Wolf should all just disappear for a while. Ana and me, kissing, soul to soul. Possessions, including bodies, be damned.

She pulled away just enough to look into my eyes. She looked different, like she saw a change in me. And yeah, I looked at her the same way. Freaky. Marko just touched Ana. Ana just touched me back.

Just like when I met Marie on Halloween, both of us hidden under body paint and zombie costumes, but somehow our hearts had touched that night. Kindred spirits, ignoring the physical plane. Lust was great, no doubt about it. But that spark—that soul to soul spark—

Ana put her hand to my lips to silence me. Well, I wasn't planning on saying anything. Was I? Or maybe I was, and she could see it coming.

Love, even the early spark of it, gave us power. It also gave us an adverse tactical situation. (Thanks, Wolf, for pitching in.) In other words, it gave Jack massive leverage to manipulate us even more.

Ana and I now had a bridge. A secret bridge. No words needed. Love was a word too dangerous to speak, or otherwise acknowledge. Was it too dangerous to even think about love?

Sonya pulled me in for a little ear nibbling and a private chat. "New subject. What did you think of Jack?"

I didn't want to talk about Jack, but I forced myself. "He's completely off the wall. Every time he talked he kept changing personalities."

"He does that when he's nervous, especially with someone new."

I made Jack nervous? Cool. "Nervous?"

"Yes. And looking at you, I can see why."

I waited for an explanation. Then I filled in the obvious answer. "Because I look like Steve Stunning."

"Half right. You're all hard on the outside, but you're cute and cuddly at your core. Women really get into that combination."

"Like soldiers or bikers, looking tougher than they really are?"

"I suppose, but only if they're just great big teddy bears in disguise."

"So I'm Jack's teddy bear?"

"You are. He hates men. And this body you have," she poked me in the chest, "it's so completely virile. So he hates that part of you. But he started out as a woman, so he also lusts after Wolf's cute butt."

"And my soft inner core?"

"Well, I think it's cute. But to Jack, it's a weakness. It makes you easy to manipulate. He does love to manipulate." She bit my ear gently as if to say she liked a bit of control, too.

"I've noticed."

"Did he tell you about his first time to die?"

"Yes."

"Which story was it?"

Which story? "Uh, he started life as an Indian girl—Native American. I think he said Sioux. Raped by solders more than a hundred years ago."

"He uses that story for special occasions. It's one of his better ones. No one knows which story is true. But judging by the way he acts, I'd guess he started as a crazy bitch who went door to door slaughtering people until she was finally killed."

I nodded. "Sounds about right."

"That's completely made up. I have no idea how old he is or what he did before I met him."

"How many jumpers are there?"

"Jack didn't tell you?"

"He said I made 61. But that was just North America."

Her voice was the barest whisper in my ear. "There are many more. He hasn't found all of us."

Awesome. Long live the free jumpers. "And the ones he found, their families were all held hostage like yours?"

"Some were. But a lot of the recruits really bought into the power trip thing. Did that attract you?"

No, but I remembered that Jack's carrots seemed promising. "No. I do just fine on my own. Nothing worse than some politician wallowing around in a power-trip. But Jack did mumble a bunch of stuff about using our powers to help the world."

"You liked that idea? Us helping the world?"

"Uh. Sure. Why not? It seemed like a plan. I mean, who doesn't want to help people who are under someone's boot. You know? Shit happens. Maybe there was a way for jumpers to cut off some of the shit in this world." That was a weird thing for me to say. It was hard enough making my way through life, much less trying to improve the world. "Uh. How the hell should I know?"

"So you think you're some kind of superhero?"

Hell, yeah. At least I wanted to be one. "Uh, not exactly. I'm still learning the ropes. I'm no one's superhero. I just have this weird gift and I thought I'd use it, you know, to help people." Assuming that was even possible.

"Did Jack mention some of the ways he punishes, like locking you away and cutting your dick off?"

"*What?* Hell, no. Okay, I did kind of read between the lines and figure out that's how you take out a jumper. Stick him in a secret prison until he dies of old age."

"You have a lot to learn. Look up oubliette sometime. There's a rumor Jack had a modified oubliette dungeon built. It's an underground room with only one exit: a hole in the middle of the high ceiling. But the worst part was the deep funnel-shaped hole in the floor of the dungeon. If you fell in that hole you'd be wedged in tight and eventually die. So when Jack found a jumper he didn't like, his goons would lower the man down into the dungeon and cut the rope. They'd drop in food and water every day or two just to keep the jumper alive. It was pitch black in there. If the jumper wandered around and fell into the hole in the floor, he'd die—an accident with no jump. Or if he went mad and deliberately jumped into the hole, it would be a suicide. Also no jump."

"Damn. What if the jumper needed a doctor? Wouldn't denying him something needed for life be like killing him? Then he could jump into someone else. Or if he was driven to suicide, wouldn't that make someone responsible for his death?"

"I'm sure that kind of dungeon had its problems. But we have proof that Jack designed and built more than a dozen different kinds over the years." Sonya squeezed my shoulder. "Just so you know, Jack's afraid of killing anyone because they might be a jumper. He never orders a hit directly, but he uses normals who enjoy killing."

"But he said he killed lots of people. In wars. He loves wars."

"Yes, but he stopped playing in battlefields a long time ago. He probably realized he might kill a jumper someday and lose everything. Or maybe he just got bored with war. No one really knows what goes on in that sick head of his. But these days, Jack absolutely goes out of his way to avoid a direct kill. And he experiments on jumpers, looking for better ways to control them—and ways to kill them without a jump."

"He can actually kill a jumper? Perma-dead?"

"That's just rumor. Let's get back to you. If you were a superhero, what kind would you be?"

"I don't know. Maybe just a regular one."

"What's a regular one?"

"You know, I'd just help people, fight crime, then drink beer and watch a good game on TV. Stuff like that."

"Really?"

"Yeah. It's the American dream."

"Sounds Canadian to me."

"Yeah? I guess it's universal."

"What about leading the other superheroes?"

"That's a desk job. I'm no Professor X."

"Who's Professor X?"

"Beats me. One of my, uh, inner guys knows." Nameless knew. Nameless also thought Professor X had dark mental problems like me. Problems that sometimes came out in comics, not the movies. Hell, it was pretty obvious that most superheroes had serious mental issues, whether it came out or not. Good thing I was nearly normal.

"So you'd only be a little superhero, like Robin?"

Nameless laughed. He seemed to know more about Robin than I wanted to know. "Not little. Mid-level, maybe. Semi-super. You know? Super helpful by day, but able to put my feet up at night."

"That's it?"

"Sure. Bust crime lords during work hours, then chill with my super-babe."

She looked both concerned and hopeful. "You have a super-babe?"

Oh, man, I sure wished. Sonya-Ana was out of my league, but I was thinking she would be a dream come true. "Not yet. A guy can dream, can't he?"

She searched my eyes for a moment. "And that's your dream? Just a mid-level semi-super kind of guy?"

"Yeah, but with a super-babe. Best dream in the whole damn world. What's your dream?"

"It's evolving. I'll keep you posted."

That's all she'd give me? I needed more. "How about a few details."

She shook her head.

Come on, give me something. "Hints?"

"None. So tell me, what did Jack say about your role in the syndicate?"

"Just that he'd figure something out. But the only thing that's clear is that he's got the hots for me."

"You know that's not good."

"You think? Jack wants to become a woman again. Then hump me to death."

"You'd survive that." She seemed confident.

"I doubt it. He brought me pictures of women for me to look at. He asked me to pick his next body."

"Bloody hell!"

"Exactly."

"And you picked one?"

"Hell, no. I'm stalling until I figure a way out of this."

She held me tighter. "You have a plan, don't you?"

"No."

"Jack needs to be stopped."

"Totally. But how?"

We were silent for a long time. We held each other tight and kissed, but it was always colored by the shadow we lived under. Lovers. Compassion. The struggle to find a way to be free.

Sonya got me to sit sideways on the couch, then she sat between my legs with her back to me. I put my arms around her. She leaned back against me. I slipped my hands under her robe, then caressed and held her voluptuous breasts. She was good with it. Yeah, both Sonya and Ana were good with it. I threw in some neck nibbling. I was in newbie superhero heaven.

I had the spark of love with Ana. But all six of us enjoyed everything sexual between Sonya's body and Wolf's. I knew that sounded completely mental, but it was the heaven we were in.

Welcome to Canada, eh.

* * *

Later we turned out the lights and headed upstairs. Her bedroom was in the back of the house and had the same great view of the trees and the lake, except better because the moon was out.

We stripped, because it seemed that's what Canadians do in the summer, and jumped into bed.

Just as I was mulling over Wolf's list of positions for serious intercourse, Sonya spread her legs and announced, "Eat me."

Really? Okay. An appetizer before the *bœuf de résistance*.

As I slid around, Sonya grabbed my gadget. "Tonight's my turn to sing, Wolf. This little guy can fuck me silly in the morning."

Right. House rules. Got it.

I eased into position as the guys in my head went ballistic. They thought it wasn't fair, but actually it was, because she'd gone down on me in the shower—and almost drowned doing it. I hoped I wouldn't drown. She'd get off tonight and I couldn't, but of course I'd already had plenty of opportunity. And on and on it went in my head.

The guys were in a foul mood, but as I got into it, it was just more sexy fun to me. Not that I'd had that much experience in this position. No big deal. Sonya was good with directions, and as an ex-taxi driver I knew how to take directions—and even improve on them.

Wolf started pissing and moaning that Marko didn't have a clue what he was doing. So I told him to shut up. Sonya knew damn well what she liked and I wasn't about to second-guess her. Wolf thought he knew everything. Maybe he knew what a generic woman liked, if there even was such a creature, but Sonya was no generic woman.

Besides, the view from down there was good. Her breasts and torso were shaded and sculpted wonderfully with moonlight.

After a very long time, I could tell Sonya was really enjoying it. Hell, her thighs were threatening to crush my skull. Then the bucking started, which made it hard for me to keep things lined up like she wanted. She reached for the rails in the headboard.

Go, Sonya, go!

Seriously, go! My tongue was about to fall off. Wolf had all these muscles, literally everywhere—everywhere except his tongue. Why the hell didn't he exercise it more? I guess that was now my job.

Sonya screamed. The good scream. The scream that meant we both had some relief. I think some of it was in French.

But she reached down and grabbed my head. "No. Keep going. Slow."

Okay. More. Got it. My tongue could heal in the morning. Onward. Slowly.

"Stop!"

I stopped.

"Don't stop. Lightly. Keep going lightly."

And that's how it went. And each time her tide would rise and she'd be swept off the shore into another orgasm, she'd buck and my head would be squashed between her thighs while she gave me instructions I couldn't hear.

Sonya stopped at three.

Thanks, babe.

Wolf was mortified we weren't jumping on her. I mean, we all looked down at her, and she was like this sweaty exhausted creature who embodied sexy womanhood with every heaving breath, a creature whose loins ached for us to mount her and make it four in a row.

Or maybe we were just projecting.

Yeah. We were.

Sonya wasn't a shy girl. If she wanted something, she pretty much grabbed it and pulled it to her.

So I washed my fatigued face in the bathroom sink. No need to turn on the light. I knew what I'd see in the mirror. Wolf's deadly blue eyes staring straight at me, thinking only about the kill.

Back in bed, I spooned with Sonya, the moonlight washing over both of us. I would have pulled up the sheets, but she didn't even have one. Just this goofy blanket wrapped in a sheet.

Duvet. Thanks, Wolf. I don't care what it's called, it's still a messed up sheet around a blanket.

I held her close as she slept. A Wolf in the moonlight.

* * *

In the morning Sonya was gone. I don't know what I expected. At least I didn't wake up this time with any bad Jack dreams. Jack had become my recurring nightmare bunk-buddy. It was good to finally sleep with no thoughts of him.

I slipped on my robe and peeked around upstairs. All quiet. But there was music coming from downstairs. A smooth jazz saxophone. Something familiar.

Dave Brubeck's *Take Five*. Thanks, Wolf.

Sonya was in the kitchen with her back to me and in the background were the forests of Quebec in all their new summer glory. But the real glory was Sonya, gorgeously stark naked, cutting fruit, moving her hips to the sultry sax and drums. Honestly, some people shouldn't be allowed to wear clothes.

My God, she was born to move that sassy ass of hers around. I watched as the muscles in her back rippled with her every gesture and sway. Cut fruit, a bagel, coffee, something in a frying pan—all part of the dance.

I stood there mesmerized. Slack-jawed.

When the song ended, she waved me over without turning her head. Was I panting that loud?

I moved up behind her, said a soft, "Hey," into her delightfully tousled morning hair. She moved her hips slowly as we touched, pressing into me.

She glanced over her shoulder. "You hot?"

Yeah, baby. Then I noticed she meant my robe. I ditched it.

She smiled, rubbing her fine ass into my crotch. "Hungry?"

"For you."

"Hold that thought, cowboy." She stuffed a plum slice into my mouth.

She reached for a spatula and a plate. "You're just in time." She scooped a few things out of the pan and arranged them on the plate. "I made you something to remind you of Texas."

Cool.

I stared down at three unidentified food items on my plate. I poked at them with my fork. "Taco crepes?"

"You don't like them?"

"They look great."

"They're perfect. Eat while they're hot."

"We usually use tortillas."

"Well, I'm fresh out and I make a mean crepe, so work with me here."

I took a bite. Surprisingly good. "Wow."

"Wow good or wow bad?"

"Wow great."

"Eat up because you have a plane to catch this morning."

"I'd rather stay."

"That's what I want, too. But we don't always get what we want, do we?"

"But we should."

She grabbed Wolf's main attraction. "I promised you some enjoyment this morning." She squeezed it. "Do you feel up to it?"

Hell, yeah! "I'm sure I do."

"I was hoping you would. When you finish eating, join me on the patio." She picked up a folded towel and some shoes and went out to the covered deck.

I probably ate too fast to enjoy anything, washed it down with some orange juice, and headed out to join her.

She stood there watching the small lake in nothing but stiletto heels and an elegant diamond necklace. "Beautiful day."

It certainly was. The grass was all covered in dew. The air was crisp. And Sonya was looking awesome.

She casually grabbed my rod with one hand. "Do you like my costume?"

Not much of a costume—just the way I liked it. "Yeah." She was stroking me, so naturally my poor brain was losing the battle for blood flow.

She fingered her elegant diamond necklace with her free hand. "In case you wondered, it's quite real."

"Cool."

She whispered in my ear. "Your courier case was filled with cut diamonds, worth about 40 million I'd guess. Plus some finished jewelry. The dazzler I'm wearing is worth about one and a half million. Jack won't mind if we use it. Especially if it pleases you. It pleases you, doesn't it?"

I nodded.

"You'll like fucking me in it, won't you?"

I nodded a lot.

Sonya pulled me by my eager handle and I followed her to the table.

"We have a choice of positions. I know what I like, so we'll start there. I hope you'll see the beauty in it, too."

The towel was already spread out on the patio table. She turned to face me and sat on the edge of the table, her back to the view. She pulled my enlarged leash, moving me close to her. "Sorry to do this to you, Tex, but your flight leaves at 11." She set the duration on a kitchen timer and placed it on the table. Then she started oiling up my full-sized game-boy. "Your mission, should you decide to accept it, is to fuck me nonstop for the next 40 minutes. If you want to switch positions that's fine, but there's no stopping. And there's a harsh penalty for scoring the goal early or icing the puck. Get it?"

"Yeah." Not really. This was how Canadians played hockey in the summer? I seriously needed to move here.

When I couldn't get any harder, she reached behind her and pulled out a pair of handcuffs that were tucked under the towel. She held out her hands in front of her. "Put them on me, sweetness. My hands are a little slippery to do it myself. And not too tight, please. But not too loose, either, because I want you to know I'm really bound for you." I cuffed her hands in front of her.

Sonya started massaging my cock with both hands and motioned for a kiss.

I kissed her sensual lips. Our tongues flicked each other playfully.

"Wolf, you're going to fuck me real good, aren't you?"

I nodded. Absolutely!

"Because I want you inside me so bad. Oh God, I want to be fucked so hard by you." She leaned back to lie down on the table. Her beautiful ass was hanging slightly off the edge. She raised her legs high in the air. "Ankle hold. V for Victoria."

Huh? I grabbed her ankles, held her legs straight up, and spread them in the approved Canadian Hockey League *V for Victoria* position. I was sure Victoria must have been some hot little number.

Hey, when in Canada . . .

"One more thing, Wolf. If I scream, you're in too deep. You're a big one and I'm not built like a warrior queen. We'll just see how it goes." Sonya put her cuffed hands over her head, her breasts raised high, a symbol of submission to me. "Saddle up, cowboy. Fuck me like you've never fucked a woman before."

I love a challenge. So I slipped my big greased up Yank into her beautiful wet Canada.

But I took it slow in the beginning. Slow for me, because she was over the top sexy with her hands cuffed, her legs pointing straight into the air, and her curvaceous tits bouncing with every thrust I made.

But also slow because I didn't want Wolf's animal meat to rupture her soft Wolf trap. Sonya seemed to wince when we bumped crotch to crotch, so I used Wolf's quadriceps to keep that last inch from going in. Good for her, and good for me too, because I could still make contact with every stroke and keep her breasts going.

I don't think women quite realize it, but guys like to experience the results of their labors. The slap of flesh against flesh, breasts bouncing back and forth, and the sounds a woman makes when she's being fucked like there's no tomorrow.

After struggling to keep my act together for the first 10 minutes, I relaxed and enjoyed everything about the view of her, and of nature.

No one really knows what thoughts go through women's minds when they're having sex. Okay, *they* do. But men sure as hell don't. On my end it was mostly a balancing act. Don't relax too much, but don't enjoy it so much that I'd reach the point of no return.

I wondered what would happen if the gardeners came by to mow the back yard. Not a good thought. I was kind of busy to be chasing them off the property.

I'd never tried this tabletop-Victoria position before, but instead of distracting myself thinking about taxes, I could enjoy looking around and being one with nature. Sort of like enjoying being the cool animals we all are. I hate to say it, but I felt like the king of the world. Godlike. Well, it wasn't exactly humbling to have the beauty of the universe moaning wonderfully right in front of me.

All my guys were feeling it, too. So big. So in control. I actually worried briefly about our egos, each and every one of us guys. But I knew our egos would eventually deflate. Things always do.

And looking down on amazing Sonya-Ana as she lay there smiling up at me, her eyes wide and bright—I hoped some of this was filling her with happiness, too, because it was 40 minutes of complete ecstasy for me.

Before I knew it, the kitchen timer rattled its little bell.

Damn.

I knew what Sonya wanted. I wanted it, too. I wanted this again for us. But in different positions. I liked variety. Well, the Multi-Mind liked variety. Maybe the Sonya-Ana duo liked variety, too.

So I focused on her and on switching my gears. But I'll have to give her most of the credit. She arched her back, thrusting her breasts up in the air. She moaned like only a woman can. Her hips twisted and seemed to ache for all of me, pulling me into her. And a glorious minute or two later, I was there. And, God, she felt it and writhed on the table before me, losing herself in me, wanting every inch of me with every fiber of Sonya's body and Ana's soul.

A minute of quiet rapture later and we were still there. Sweat glistened all over our bodies, so similar to the early morning dew on the fine summer grass.

* * *

We quickly showered, dressed, and headed out to her car. I put my luggage into the trunk and moved to the passenger side.

Why the rush to leave? Wasn't there another private jet just for me? They could damn well wait for Sonya-Ana and me to give each other a proper goodbye. But it wasn't happening.

Sonya barely looked at me as we drove back to the Montreal airport.

Why couldn't she just drive me back to Austin? A road trip would be perfect, plus I wanted her in Austin.

I guess she could tell I was becoming really gloomy, because she reached out and took my hand, gave it a little squeeze, and placed it on her thigh.

Really nice. But I wanted so much more.

* * *

Arriving at the corporate part of the Montreal airport, Sonya pulled over for some privacy.

I knew the drill. Empty my pockets, get a new identity. Except my pockets were already empty. I turned to her, hoping to see Ana in her eyes, but they seemed focused on business. So I tried to make contact with Ana. "I hope I see you again."

"I hope so, too." She pulled me in for a kiss, but went for my ear instead. "You might not see me again, but you'll see others. Trust your heart. A storm gathers in the dark."

Not what I expected, or wanted. Mainly, I wanted to see a lot more of her.

Sonya-Ana kissed me, at least I thought they both did. Then soft words. "Safe travels, sweetness."

That felt so good—just what I wanted. Only three words? Why so minimal?

She nodded to someone I hadn't noticed. My car door opened.

"Bonjour. Come with me, please." A female flight attendant skillfully extracted me from the car. And just like a paramedic guiding a dazed and confused trauma victim to an ambulance, she guided me to the jet's stairway.

I turned, but Sonya's car was already gone. My luggage was on the tarmac near the jet. Hands guided me up the ladder and on board to my seat. I sat. Papers were handed to me.

I had found love, and lost it. That's all I knew.

Some would say the universe gives you what you deserve. Others would say you only get what you earn. And everyone knows you occasionally get a curveball. Somehow, finding Sonya and losing her felt like all three.

3.4 Home Again

The morning flight back to Austin started out somber. I waved off the usual steamy wipies, cold drinks, and haute cuisine preflight snacks.

I brooded through takeoff as I mulled over Sonya's words. She'd said I might not see her again, but I'd see others. Others? What others? I really didn't want to see *others*. I only knew two jumpers—Sonya and Jack. One was seriously wonderful, the other was seriously mental. Not good odds for a happy meetup with more of my fellow jumpers.

What else did she say? Trust my heart. I preferred to trust my head, but come to think of it, my head was infested.

What else? Something about a storm coming, in the dark. That seemed to trigger Wolf's senses. He was born for dark storms. Personally, I preferred a sunny beach, a reclining chair, a giant shade umbrella, and a bucket of cold ones. Hell, I'd even brought beach wear in my suitcase, wherever the hell that was.

The guys huddled around me and gave me half-baked advice. Trust your gut, not your heart. Make lemonade. Let rain roll off my back. Chin out. Gird your loins, but trust them. Be more than you can be. Don't get cocky.

Whatever. Mainly, it was great they all had my back—my inner back.

About an hour later, I'd worked myself into a nearly normal mood, relatively speaking. Mentally, I was relaxing on the beach. My passengers were relaxing there, too. Except I imagined them at the edge of the tropical jungle behind me, bound and gagged, enjoying life vicariously through my sandy-beach happiness.

Vicariously? Yes, I probably knew that word.

Life was good. Yeah, except for the sucky fringe around it.

No, life was great and I would learn to love skin-hopping.

No, life was absolutely weird and words like *vicariously* were now vicariously in my vocabulary. Yeah, something like that.

As the cabin crew prepped lunch, they said we were over Bowling Green, Ohio. Well, that's what they told me and I had no doubt it was the bowling capital of the world. Pro bowling was one boring strike after another. Date-night bowling was wonderful if you could convince the girl she was on a winning streak. Bowling was invented to make girls scream and laugh and dance, and force guys to lose the game. In other words, guys learned to be vincible.

Vincible? Really? Not in my vocabulary. None of us were even remotely vincible. We were all invincible, which meant we dominated on the bowling alley and never got a second date.

Out the window, it looked more like farmland than bowling greens.

This time the menu was more to my liking. They brought out fried chicken, mashed potatoes, corn, biscuits, and apple cobbler—all topped off by Belgian monk beer.

Funny. I was just in Belgium. If I ever got back to Antwerp, I'd have to find a bar. I bet I'd like the Belgian people, too.

I must have dozed off because I had a massively disturbing dream that I was on the beach, and the wind was starting to pick up and there were storm clouds out at sea. But it was disturbing because I was in Jack's body. Yeah, in Jack's body walking along the beach with the wind in my hair and my feet in the water.

Walking around in Jack was creepy enough, but it was much worse—seriously worse. His private parts were completely chopped off and a light trickle of blood was running down one leg and into the water. There was also a school of hungry sharks following me along the beach, following the blood in the water. I think they were waiting for me to make a mistake and get in deeper so they could rip Jack's body to shreds. Easy to understand—Jack probably had lots of enemies.

Now the bad part of the dream.

Jack and I were sharing his body, but we were both in control. We were in his body as equals. But Jack was not just one guy, he was hundreds of people—people Jack had jumped into, mostly soldiers, people in the business of killing.

It was like I was in a sealed room with one giant boa constrictor named Jack, and also with hundreds of little jumping cobras, coming at me from every direction. They were biting me, injecting poison in me, and wrapping themselves around me, trying to squeeze the life out of me and regain control of Jack's body.

Then I was running to get away. But I couldn't, because the killer snakes were inside my head and I could never truly get away from that. They'd all be swarming inside my head forever. Even if I jumped into another body, they'd still be slithering around inside my mind, attacking me relentlessly.

Escape was impossible. I was perma-screwed.

Then I dreamed that I'd somehow wound up at the top of a really high cliff overlooking the water. Waves crashed on big jagged rocks below. And I knew the only way to get Jack out of my head was to jump off and die. I'd really be dead. Finally dead. Completely dead. Jack and all of his passengers, and even my passengers, would finally be completely dead, too.

All I had to do was jump. We'd all die.

The sharks circled in the water far below the cliff. They wanted me to throw myself off. They were hungry for some fresh dead Jack.

There was no way out for me. It was just the way things were. Death or permanent insanity. Maybe death wasn't so bad.

There had to be another way out.

Looking over the edge, it would be a sure death. So I moved closer to the rim, threatening Jack with our mutual destruction. If he didn't get out of my head, I'd kill us both. It was a good threat—the only real threat I could come up with.

But Jack just laughed. He was insane. Hell, anyone would be with a mind like his. And now our shared mind was exactly like that. Insanity from here on out.

Wind gusted at my back. A few rocks slipped underfoot and tumbled over the edge. Everything seemed to want me to end Jack. *Sucks to be you, Marko. You wanted to be the designated superhero. So here it is. You made this day, so die this day.*

My indecision was ended when the ground crumbled, gave way,

dropped out from under me. We were all falling to our final end. I could see the sharks grinning. Jack snack.

I opened an eye. One of the cute flight attendants was messing with my pants.

"Sorry, sir. Best to have your seat belt on." She buckled me in. "We're coming into Austin. A bit of turbulence."

She was right, we were really bouncing around. Small plane, even if it was a jet. No wonder I'd dreamed the bottom was dropping out from under me.

It was a bad sign—my nightmares and reality were overlapping.

* * *

I arrived home again at Wolf's. Late afternoon, still hot. Scattered storm clouds. Austin needed rain, but in this part of Texas, dark clouds were often just a tease. We were used to brief drizzle that only raised the humidity, as well as flash floods that killed people. Not much in between.

I set the suitcase down in the entryway and looked around at Wolf's empty digs. Sad that Sonya wasn't here with me, but it was good to be back in Wolf's den. A swim was in order. That sounded really good to all of us.

Wolf froze. Muscles tightened hard. I felt a kick of adrenalin, but just enough for Wolf to kill effectively. Something was very wrong. A slight sound? A smell? Something wasn't right.

I let Wolf take complete control. Hell, the dark animal was already in control.

We all listened intently.

Nothing.

Wolf moved silently to the hallway. Something down there? The door to the gun room was open slightly.

Oh, shit.

I turned to Martoni to see if he'd left it open. That's when I noticed we were already in the kitchen. Wolf had a well tooled kitchen knife in his left hand and was quietly pulling a revolver out of a drawer.

In a knife fight, it's as much about the handle as the blade. Grip is everything—Wolf could kill quickly with any blade, but a good handle would make all the difference.

Wow. Good to know. Nice of Wolf to give us killing tips while we nervously ate popcorn in the back of Wolf Theater.

Wolf moved us silently out of the kitchen and approached the hall.

Nameless thought this was going to be a slasher. Martoni wanted Wolf to switch to a pump action shotgun and start blowing big holes in the walls.

I told them both to shut the frack up and let Wolf think. Heaven knows Wolf had precious few brain cells left to call his own. All good ones, I hoped.

He moved quietly down the hall.

At the gun room, it looked like the door was open about six inches. It was hinged to open inward.

Wolf swung his knife hand behind him, but held it close to his body. Odd, but I guess that was a good position if we were attacked from behind. He seemed more concerned about what might be behind the door than what opening the door would reveal.

Personally, I would have put my weight into the door and plowed it open like they did in the movies.

Wolf thought that was a good way to die. Instead, he got low, used a toe to slowly push the door open, and aimed the gun into the opening crack near the hinges.

He indicated the doorway was a tactical choke point, and it focused both sides on a small fight zone. Wonderful, but I didn't care as long as we didn't lose good body parts.

Inside, there was a man bound and gagged on the floor. No one else.

Wolf quickly stepped inside. I screamed it was a trap because the guy who tied the knots was still unaccounted for. Wolf said he already knew that, but the hallway was a damn shooting range so exiting the gun room was not the best move.

We waited.

Another man stepped into the doorway, aiming a black gun at us, but Wolf was already moving low and spinning for a kick.

A stun gun dart and wire flew past my head, followed immediately by Wolf's kick and the muffled crack of the guy's ribs breaking. Air whooshed out his startled throat.

Wolf had landed a dead-on kick to the guy's chest. The intruder was already down and Wolf was on top of him, one knee on his Taser wrist, the other knee pressing on his freshly cracked ribs, our knife to his throat, and our gun aimed down the hall in case someone else wanted some of this action.

Wolf's instinct seemed to involve smashing this guy's head on the floor and continuing with a sweep of the house. I vetoed that. At least I thought I did. It was hard to pry Wolf away from controlling his own body.

We needed answers. Unconscious or dead, this poor sucker couldn't help us.

Wolf reluctantly disarmed him, searched him, and used serious cable ties he had in a drawer in the gun room. After that, Wolf continued with his sweep.

As for me, it was hard to get the sickening muffled sound of snapping ribs out of my head. Hell, we didn't even know if the guy was friend or foe. For all I knew, he could have punctured a lung. He could be bleeding out right now.

Wolf ignored me and continued his search pattern, but it was clear he thought I was a fool. Thoracic trauma was one of his specialties. Besides, anyone in his home was fair game for extermination. Interrogation was for sissies. Survival was all about the kill, not chatting up your prey.

His sweep seemed to include doors and windows. There was no sign of any forced entry.

So where did that leave us? Two guys. It didn't seem like they were pals. Both here at the same time, right when I was due to arrive. Security was bypassed—lock and security code both compromised. And neither seemed to have a firearm.

Back at the gun room, both guys were a bit bug-eyed at the sight of Wolf returning.

I'd seen real cops enough to know you always separate people before getting statements. That was all Wolf needed. He promptly started to drag the guy with the broken ribs into the garage. There was no blood gurgling out of his mouth, so it seemed likely his lungs were still intact.

Wolf started the freezer going, then opened the guy's shirt to check his bone-snapping handiwork. Lots of bruising. Wolf poked around. Lots of stifled screams from the guy, trying to be so tough. But I got the impression the guy would live long enough for a chat, followed by some unpleasant time alone in the freezer.

He looked up at me and finally decided to speak. "I work for Jack, asshole. You're in deep shit."

I wasn't impressed. Easy enough to just keep my mouth shut and let Wolf run his game.

The guy had more to say. "Look, shit head, you had an intruder. I went in and tied him up for Jack. Jack didn't say who lived here or that you were coming home now. So how was I to know?"

"Why the stun gun?"

"Jack's orders. And just so you know, he's going to fry your sorry ass for this."

"If I were you, I'd worry about that freezer over there. Why? Because it's your new home." Without asking, Wolf rolled out a big sheet of plastic on the garage floor, picked him up, and dropped him on the plastic. The guy let out a scream. I guess being dropped on your back with busted ribs will make even the toughest guys scream. Then Wolf rolled him up and took him into the freezer. We hooked his feet and hands into eyelets built into in the freezer floor.

I stood there admiring Wolf's efficient work. Strange to be killing someone just like Wolf had done to me—done to Nameless.

The writing was on the wall for this guy. If it were me, awake on the freezer floor, being methodically executed by Wolf, I'd be begging for a way out. But not this guy. No. He thrashed in his plastic wrapper. "Hey, you dumbfuck. Hey!"

I wanted to say he was just lucky I'd kept my inner Wolf from an early kill. Funny how tough guys get all confused when it's their loser ass strung out on the freezer floor.

We shut the door. It was fine for him to cool off, but if he was a jumper from Jack's syndicate, killing him would be the end of me. I could see how jumpers needed to be cautious about who they killed.

Walking back into the house, Wolf was pissed with me. I understood. Sorry, man. The days of simple kills were probably over for him.

Back in the gun room, I removed the other guy's gag.

"Don't hurt me, dude. Please." Good. This one was a talker. "You're Wolf, right?"

Wolf reached into a gun case and pulled out a long barreled .44 Magnum revolver—a thing of obvious consequence. Very messy. Very loud. Wolf cocked it and aimed it at the poor guy's head. Not looking good for the fool on the floor. But honestly, I wasn't worried Wolf would shoot him. Wolf would rather kill in a hundred ways that didn't involve messing up his immaculate floor.

For some lame reason I tried to channel Clint Eastwood's Dirty Harry. "Do I look like Wolf? Well, do I, punk?"

"Yes! Yes, you look like Wolf. You sound like him, too!"

Huh? This is what Wolf sounded like? Well, all I knew was that he didn't talk like Dirty Harry in his bedroom porn tapes.

We looked down at the guy, sighting along the long barrel. "That's all you've got to say? Because from where I'm standing, you don't look so lucky."

"Sonya sent me."

I lowered Wolf's big revolver. "Go on."

"Jack had you bugged. Sonya wanted me to switch out the bugs for ones that could be looped."

"Looped?"

"Yeah, looped."

Like I knew what that meant. "Who was the other guy?"

"I don't know, man. One of Jack's men. Maybe. Yeah, probably. I guess I tripped something and they sent him to check it out."

Was I buying any of this? I needed more info. "How's Sonya?"

"Oh, man! She's really wonderful."

Oops. There was nothing platonic about the way he said that, so I swung the big revolver back at him.

He let out a shriek. "Dude! Don't kill me! I'm on your side."

Did you have sex with her, punk? Did you fall in love with her, too? There were so many things I wanted to say before I filled him full of big messy holes. "Anything else, punk?"

He stopped wincing and seemed to develop a backbone. His voice was hushed, but strong. "The resistance has started, dude. We're all betting on you."

WTF? "Yeah?" I mean seriously, it was a total WTF moment. Mainly, he was just lucky I didn't accidentally shoot him. I backed my finger off the trigger.

He kept his conspiratorial tone. "Yeah. It's like, *you*, man. Sonya said you were tough enough to pull this off."

I was out of words, so I simply waved the gun for him to continue.

"Step one. Identify the problem. We had that one figured out a long time ago. It's Jack and his crew." He paused, looking for my reaction, but I was still wearing Clint Eastwood's total intimidation on my face. At least I hoped I was.

"Step two. Identify the solution."

"And you think that's me."

"No. Step two is the rest of us. We're the resistance, we're the solution. Dude, you're step three."

Somehow I knew I wasn't going to like step three. I nodded for him to continue.

"Step three. Knight to c7. Fork the king."

"You're not making sense." Although forking the king seemed pretty obvious.

"It's chess. You're a knight, you've already worked your way near the back rank. The king doesn't see you as a threat, but you are. The king's distracted. Actually Jack's distracted because he wants to jump your bones."

Word traveled fast. Too fast. "So who are you?"

"I'm an advanced pawn, too valuable to ignore. I'm just hoping I don't get sacrificed for a damn rook."

"No. Not what I asked. You got a name, punk?"

"Peter."

"Peter what?"

"Less is better. I'm outside Jack's syndicate. Invisible to him."

"Yeah. That's what you thought."

"No optical bugs anywhere. I was able to switch out all the audio bugs. But I might have missed a motion detector."

No shit. "So what does that make Sonya? The queen?"

"Absolutely. She calls the shots. She's got a foot in both camps. She's the only one who does, as far as I know."

"So why are you telling me all this?"

"Really, dude? Like, there's a gun in my face. Actually, Sonya said to trust you with . . . uh . . . almost everything."

Almost? "Why not everything?"

"It's classic security, man. Compartmentalized. *Need To Know* basis. You know? If you get tortured and killed, we survive because you didn't know more than you needed to. Sorry, man. I'm sure you're tougher than that. But it totally works both ways. I know stuff you don't. You might learn something I don't know."

"And you just happened to be here rewiring things when I was due back?"

"We knew exactly when you'd be back. So the plan was like, after I finished my job, I was supposed to stick around. You'd pop in and we'd chat. So if you don't mind." Peter offered his bound hands. "Hands? Feet? I could use a little help here, dude."

"We're chatting just fine."

"We're on the same team, man. So do us both a favor and cut me loose. You know? So like, we can go relax on the couch. Then maybe we could bond over a cold brew, or an energy drink if that's your thing. Just you and me. Killer to geek. You know?"

Yeah, right. Somehow I liked talking with the guy in the freezer better. "I'm gonna go think this over, so just chill. Your little playground buddy's in the freezer right now, and you should know there's room enough for you, too. So understand, I'm giving you some slack here." I walked to the door, decided to keep the .44 Magnum close, but turned to add a word. "A part of me really hates mess. So don't even think about taking a piss on my floor."

I walked down the hall.

"Dude! We're on the same team! Hey, Wolf. Sonya loves you."

That stopped me in my tracks, but Wolf kept right on walking.

In the kitchen, I searched for a beer or even an energy drink. Nada. Wolf wanted a refreshing glass of strawberry flavored protein, but I made us a tall ice water instead.

Out at the pool, we set the drink and the gun in a handy spot, stripped naked, and jumped in. From my point of view, it seemed like if there was trouble headed our way, we'd need clothes. Wolf indicated that clothes wouldn't stop a bullet, so they were pointless in a fight. In fact, if your assailant was shocked to see your big dick flying in the breeze, he might also be surprised by your foot shattering his jaw.

Wolf swam.

Actually, he now seemed to favor the deep end because he knew I gave him less grief there.

Note to self: My passengers could still learn. Damn! That was so *not* good.

* * *

Thirty minutes later, we got out of the pool, picked up the gun, and went out to the garage to check on Jack's man in the small walk-in freezer. Still alive, so I turned it off and decided to leave the freezer door open.

He gave me more lip about how dangerous Jack was, and how I was a screwed asshole, so I shut the freezer door. Judging by the size of the freezer and the fact that carbon dioxide is heavier than air but hot air rises, Wolf thought he'd last another seven or eight hours before he suffocated on his own exhaust fumes.

Good deal.

Back in the gun room, Peter seemed focused on Wolf's feral schlong and his neatly shaved nether region. Actually, we were getting a bit scruffy without a proper wax job.

It seemed like a good idea to see what he had to say. "Time to get more out of you."

Peter looked up at me, rapidly turning white, like he'd just stepped into some kind of badass pink flamingo horror flick.

I got him untied and escorted him to the living room couch. "Tell me what you came to say."

Peter looked really uncomfortable. "Uh." Then he went quiet.

Off to a great start. "If you're expecting a beer, forget it. This is the house of Payne." Ooo. Catchy phrase. Even better because I was still hanging onto the .44 Magnum, which was kinda the elephant in the room—if you didn't count my flagrant manhood.

"Uh." He was grasping for anything.

Uh, what? The poor guy needed some help. "So Sonya sent me her regards."

"Yeah."

"And she had some instructions for me?"

"No."

"I thought you wanted to talk."

"Yeah. But could you, like, put that gun away? And put some clothes on?"

"No."

Peter looked like his head was spinning. I didn't want him to throw up, so I tried again. "What did Sonya say about me?"

"She said you were one big badass motherfucker, but your head was screwed on straight."

"Yeah?"

"Yeah. I'm totally picking up on the badass part, but your head's kinda on sideways. Nothing personal, dude. She also said you were kinda cute."

Kinda cute? I had to admire a woman who had a flair for understatement. "What else?"

"She also said you were really handsome."

Huh? So *really handsome* was one thing and somehow *kinda cute* was something different? I was never going to understand women.

"She said you were tough enough to take out Jack and help us clean out his syndicate."

"So you're a jumper?"

"What's a jumper?"

Crap. I just broke rule #1—again.

Peter's mental light bulb clicked on. "Oh, you mean a head humper. Yeah, well, I've only been killed once. Hey, I wasn't always this skinny. And I never heard it called *jumper* before."

"Head humper? Really?"

"Sure. Spirit walker, brain buddy, life sponge, brain drainer, host toaster—I kinda like that one. Then there's the original name, larva. That's Latin for mask. We call ourselves a lot of things. There's not much consensus on what we are."

Understood. There wasn't much agreement in my head, either, so it was easy to see how a bunch of jumpers would be a serious pack of confusion. "What about the guy that tied you up? Is he a jumper, too?"

"How should I know? I never saw him before. But knowing Jack, he's probably just a normal. Jack likes to use normals for most criminal assignments. Head humpers are just for high-dollar assignments."

"Why?"

"Why? Because it's easy to find normals who'll kill. But most head humpers have figured out that killing is dangerous—you know, because if they killed someone who turned out to be a jumper, they'd lose everything and just be a remnant. You know, a leftover brain bit, a shadow. We all have them inside us. Some are cool. Some suck. But you're cool. Except you've got a problem with clothes. Not that that's a problem, dude. It's just a little odd, you know. Sonya didn't warn me about that part."

Wolf wanted to shoot him. Martoni and Nameless did, too. I reminded them that killing him would just load him into our brain. As the driver. Forever. You just don't kill a jumper and walk away intact.

That shut the guys up.

Peter was watching my face. "You do that thing, you know. Like head humped guys do. I can see it in your eyes. Kinda like you're talking to yourself. Or you're arguing with yourself. So your face goes one way, and then it goes another way. Hey, with the right coaching, you can clear that up—so it doesn't show, I mean."

Peter noticed the gun now pointing at him. "But it's totally cool, man. I mean, it's fun to watch and all. I'm sure it feels good, too. So yeah, like keep it going, dude."

"And you've adjusted to your host?"

"Totally. Except I'm a geek and he's a nerd. So we're different that way."

Great. This guy is the mess you get when you mix a geek and a nerd. I almost asked him what the difference was, but I was so much smarter than that. Instead, I asked something important to me. "What's your relationship to Sonya?"

"Oh wow. I mean, are you asking if we've had sex?"

"Yeah."

"Well, sure. Jack uses her as a kind of . . . uh . . . a reward. You know? I mean, she's a real hottie and all, but, yeah, she was good. Maybe a bit self-centered, unless you like that sort of thing. Not my type. Brenda on the other hand. Wow! Don't even get me started on that hottie."

I wasn't. "So why'd you say Sonya loves me?"

"I could see it in her eyes. It's all in the eyes. You know?"

"She never said it?"

"Dude, she didn't have to. It's all over her, like her body language—hips, hands, everything. Oh, and her mouth. And get this, Sonya's pupils even dilate when she hears your name. So freakin' autonomic. I should turn it into an animated GIF. Like: 'Wolf.' Her eyes dilate. 'Wolf'. Her eyes dilate."

Peter loved to drift off the subject. But that didn't stop me from trying to keep him focused. "You said she's the queen."

"In the North American Underground, she is."

"Who's the king?"

"Some guy. Nobody important. It's a lot like chess. The king is just some wimpy guy with a target on his back. It's all about the queen, man. She drives everything."

"But you said Jack was like a king. Your chess analogy is falling apart."

"Dude, Jack is the king *and* the queen—both combined into one badass piece. Like a king, the game ends when he falls. But like a queen, he's got massive power. My chess analogy is still solid."

Whatever. "What else did Sonya say?"

"That's about it. Just to establish contact. Unhack your place. Uh, there was some concern about Jack's plans for you. Like maybe he was going to pimp you out or something."

"What?"

"You know. Use you as a reward, because some of the female ops prefer guys. Hey, I can totally see that. I mean, just look at you." He looked me up and down, then tried to focus on my eyes. "Not that I'm looking at you, or anything."

Just great. Wolf was meat for hire. But hey, good to know Jack was willing to share.

"Dude, can we get a beer or something?"

"No."

"Seriously?"

I sat there a moment, processing the whole thing. Sonya sent a junior jumper nerd to unhack the house and chat me up. He bungled it and now Jack was on to us. But all this guy could think about were refreshments. "So you blew your assignment and now Jack knows."

"No way. They call me Captain Comms. Jack's in D.C. and his team knows squat about this."

"But his guy knows."

"What guy?"

"The one in the freezer."

"Don't worry about him. That guy's about to be scrubbed. I made the call. The body disposal team will handle it."

Call? What call? Peter the head humper was either tied up or with me the whole time, so when did he have time to make a call? Oh, wait, he's Captain Comms. Whatever the hell that meant. Scrubbed? Wasn't I the expert cleaner here? "Scrubbed?"

"Yeah. Don't ask. I sure don't."

Conversation with Peter was pointless. The guy was a fountain of non-information, a constant stream of chess analogies and geek-speak, so I took a break and went into the bedroom to put on some clothes. When I returned to the living room, he had a big grin on his face.

I wasn't in a mood for more guessing games. "What?"

"Wolf, my team just picked up the guy in the freezer. One less bad guy to worry about." He noticed I still wasn't smiling. "You can thank me later."

Right. Like that was going to happen. And shouldn't he be thanking me?

He stood up. "One more thing. Jack had all your bank accounts drained because you joined his team. But you knew that was coming, right? Jack's syndicate holds onto Wolf's assets as a favor, just in case you get whacked and lose your Wolf Payne identity. You wouldn't want all that money to go to Wolf's relatives or anything. But not to worry—I'll set something up for you on the side."

Peter headed to the front door. "Gotta go. You're all set here." He opened the door and stepped out into the front yard as I followed him to see what he was up to. Then he turned to give me some final advice. "Keep your head in the game, Wolf. We're counting on you. And don't worry about me hooking up with Sonya. I'm locked on to Brenda. But I'll give Sonya a big sloppy kiss for you, man."

He laughed as he ran to a waiting black Tesla and jumped in the passenger's side. The car pulled away smartly with Captain Comms waving at me like a grinning idiot.

Talk about a foul mood—Wolf missed seeing the guy in the freezer removed. Hell, it was *his* kill. Wolf felt like someone had just walked off with his prey. Wolf brings down wild boar. Monkey steals wild boar. Wolf pissed.

As for me, I just wondered why Wolf didn't have his own Tesla.

Another jumper, another weird meeting.

Note to self: All jumpers are messed up mentally. Except me, of course.

Standing in front of the house with a flashy .44 Magnum and no pants seemed problematic, so I went back inside.

So what did Peter say about the house being hacked? Only that his team would be listening in and somehow they'd censor things before Jack's men heard anything they shouldn't.

Great. I was hacked before, and now I was double hacked. Wolf didn't like the world of high tech. Things should always be up close, in person, and very, very physical.

3.5 Strangers In The Dark

The doorbell rang around 6 p.m. That always put us on edge, even if we were expecting somebody.

We walked up to the peephole. Wolf thought that was a good way to get shot. Really? I had the impression Wolf's enemies disappeared fast. Was Doc a threat? Maybe. Doc was an enforcer. Very visceral, but not so calculating. Was Doc out there?

We peeped. Young perky girl about 19. Okay, Avon girl was back. No threat. Down, Wolf. I've got this.

I was wearing a full set of clothes this time, so I opened the door.

She looked me up and down and was instantly disappointed.

I smiled. "I know. You were expecting man-butt."

"I could really use some right about now."

"Yeah? You broke up with your boyfriend?"

"No. He's still cool."

"If you're craving man-butt, he must not be doing his job."

"He does fine. But not all guys have an ass from heaven."

Whatever. I wasn't stripping for her. "Clothes happen. Got something for me?"

"Sure do." She moved closer. "We could step inside, you know."

Nameless and Martoni voted yes. Wolf voted no. I was interested, but didn't want a damn democracy in my head. So I held out my hand and she reached for something in her green messenger bag.

Wolf tensed.

Relax, Wolf. Just another message from Jack. But Wolf was running attack scenarios through his mind. Come to think of it, Martoni was running attack scenarios through his corner of my mind, too. A different kind of attack. Martoni seemed to like them about this age.

That's sick, Martoni. Old guys shouldn't want them 19. But Marko was only 22, so she was firmly in my target zone.

She pulled out an envelope and sniffed it. "This one's scented. Lavender, like my grandmother's bubble bath. You should really try some younger ass, mister."

As she handed it over, I thought I'd set her straight. "Actually it's from a guy named Jack." I might have been smiling.

She took a step back, her face switched from flirt to disgust. "That so blows." She pivoted around and marched back to her VW Beetle mumbling about how all the good ones were gay and how life sucked.

Before she drove off, she rolled down her window and shouted. "You let me grope your ass last time! Eww! Your gay ass! Warn a girl first, jerkwad!"

She drove off leaving me confused. I liked lesbian-chick ass just as much as straight-chick ass. Hey, a beautiful butt was just a beautiful butt. Right? So why did she care where my butt had been?

Back inside, I opened the letter.

"Dear Wolfie. My first prospective female body is ready for you to check out. Meet her tonight at Resort Electra. Nine o'clock sharp. The elevator code for the 17th floor is 1733. Go straight to suite 1717. Her name is Shanna. She seems vivacious, but remember to focus on her body, not her personality. If you pick Shanna, only the body stays the same. Bring roses, thorns on. I hope you like her. If not, there are plenty more for you to sample. I can't tell you how thrilled I am. Jack Peoples."

Oh, great. Jack was thrilled.

I checked Wolf's Rolex. Just enough time to get in a swim, a workout, a shower, and dinner. And maybe some house cleaning. Wolf was high maintenance.

Roses? Where was I going to find roses, anyway? Besides, giving flowers on a first date was a sign of desperation. Sorry, Shanna, no roses for you, and it's just gonna be one date. Then you'll get dumped. Jack will be disappointed, but we'll move on to potential victim number two. Yeah. Shanna would be spared having her body ripped away from her, having to endure eternity in Jack's back seat, and having her immediate family killed. Killed? Like really killed? What did Jack say about messy family members? Taken out? Somehow removed. That didn't sound good.

Nameless insisted we didn't know any of that. Jack was full of hot air. Besides, if we liked vivacious Shanna we should have lots of sex with her before making the call to let Jack know how disappointed we were with Shanna's skills in bed.

I argued back that Jack would be watching and if we showed too much interest in Shanna, it would just put Jack in motion. Then what? I asked Nameless how he'd like having sex with Jack wrapped in Shanna's skin.

No answer.

It seemed like Nameless was focused on the vivacious part and not thinking it through. Thinking it through was my job.

So I stripped, walked out to the pool, and stood at the edge watching the hot afternoon sun make cool ripples on the surface. I wasn't about to jump in because I'd just belly flop and drown. Water and I just didn't get along. Besides, Wolf had precious little body fat to keep him afloat.

I released the steering wheel in my mind, gave Wolf the nod, and he dove in head first like I could never do.

Wolf swam. I rode along. But Nameless and Martoni were like little kids in my head, bugging me to know if we were going to have sex with Shanna, bugging me to know if we were going to have one-and-dump sex with lots of sexy women that Jack was considering wearing. How many would we have? How many? Please tell us. How many?

I told them to shut up.

But it was hard to keep secrets isolated from one part of my brain to another. So they found out it was my fantasy, too. Especially if we could get several in the hot tub at the same time. I suppose that was every man's fantasy. Women fantasized about flowerbeds full of beautiful roses, men fantasized about beds full of beautiful Roses. But not every fantasy made a good reality. Some drool-worthy ideas were best left to the imagination.

Hey. You guys get it, don't you?

They didn't. Even Wolf didn't. They wanted to know who died and made me their bossy parent. Then Wolf started to dog paddle, making lazy circles at the deep end, thinking of himself as a shining example of a fantasy come true. After all, he filled his days with killing and fucking—same as all men wanted. Wolf Payne was the real deal, the ideal man, the whole purpose of the Y chromosome. Fuck all the beautiful hotties. Kill all the male competition. Survival of the fittest Y. Wolf beamed in my head. His Y was fittest. Nameless and Martoni beamed, too. They now shared his Y.

Since I had serious fear of the water and we were at the deep end, I let Wolf express his opinions. Besides, it was clear he wasn't thinking on all burners, because it was kinda hard for Wolfie's superior Y to populate the planet considering his vasectomy.

I invited Nameless to share his thoughts on the subject of sex and murder. He indicated my super jumper skills were number one for him, followed closely by Wolf's super sex. He seemed to glance over at Wolf, then he wanted to add that killing was okay, too, but really it was the jumping sex combo that made him happy.

And Martoni? He hoped Shanna was around 18, give or take a couple years, and a squealer.

Anything else, Martoni? Because he really sounded like a dirty old man.

Martoni thought I didn't understand. He was in and out of jail growing up, mostly in, mostly for minor crimes like armed robbery and tying people up in their homes while he gathered up their stuff and made himself dinner. He indicated he'd missed out on his high school years and still craved cheerleader types.

I was back to thinking we all needed therapy. Finding the right psychiatrist would be a challenge.

Wolf pulled us out of the pool and started doing naked jumping jacks for everyone in the hill country to see. I wasn't entirely cool with that. You know, a man's equipment just doesn't stay still for naked jumping jacks, it kinda waves to the crowd. But Nameless thought it was righteous because the Spartans used to fight naked, and the Olympics started as an all nude male extravaganza. Those were the good old days when men were men, and women packed the arenas.

Whatever. This wasn't Rome. When in Texas, you kept your pants on. Unless of course, you were a politician, then their universal clothing-optional rule applied.

I took the exhibitionists inside the house and headed to the kitchen, but Wolf pulled us down the hall toward the gym. If we were going to have sex with Shanna, then we needed to pump up to look our best. It was all about looking our best.

So Wolf pumped free weights while admiring himself in the mirror. Actually having sex was completely unimportant to him— but giving Shanna an orgasm as soon as she saw us was vital. Wolf pumped it all up in the mirror. The guys couldn't stand it and looked away. I crawled into a hole in my mind and focused on fresh hot pizza. Beer and pizza. Pizza with everything on it, but no pineapple. No fish, or chicken, or peanut butter, or refried beans, or any other weird crap. Beer and pizza should be pure and natural.

Life should be the same way, except it wasn't. We were like breadless pizza in a blender with protein nuggets. Physically stunning—mentally not.

After a long workout, Wolf took his time in a hot shower. Good for the muscles. But without a body-maid, it was bad for my hetero brain. Wolf's body still felt alien to me, showering it was like porn from the wrong side of the tracks.

Would dinner never come?

Yes, it came. But we ate standing up in the buff. And I think Wolf was trying to catch a glimpse of his reflection in the brushed metal refrigerator doors. We ate the usual healthy crap.

Then we brushed Wolf's teeth and combed his hair, still in the buff. I was beginning to wonder how I'd get him into the downtown resort without clothes.

Downtown? Wolf seemed to know that Resort Electra was a private area in the Armadillo Towers. Okay, so was it a nudie kind of place?

No answer.

Driving around Austin naked would be easy. Private parking garage. Quiet elevator to the 17th floor. Knocking on the door to room 1717 naked? Was it too late to get roses? I didn't want the poor girl to faint when she saw us.

I managed to get Wolf into the bedroom and put something nice on him, but frankly it was like dressing a 3-year-old boy. Not that I'd ever dressed one, but I could imagine it. In my case, the left hand wasn't cooperating with the right one. One hand tucked in the shirt while the other pulled it out. When I reached for some socks with the right hand, the left had unzipped us.

It got so bad I wondered if I'd been drinking. I hadn't. So why wasn't I in control?

In the garage I dropped the keys to the SUV. Or maybe it wasn't me who dropped them. What was up with that? Was I worried about having sex? That seemed unlikely. Worried about not having sex? I was pretty sure I could handle that one, too.

I picked up the keys and almost fumbled them again.

Clearly something was wrong.

What if Jack had selected some escaped convict named Shanna? If I were picking a new body, I'd pick a person that deserved to lose their hide. So was Shanna the deadly Shropshire Slasher? Or Shanna the She-Devil? Who? Nameless came up with those names, but wasn't giving any details.

Bottom line: Shanna wouldn't be deadly because Jack wouldn't risk my lovely man-hide.

Good. Shanna was likely just some innocent young woman. Fine with me. I'd introduce myself. We'd chat a bit. Then I'd leave and tell Jack she wasn't my type.

I was worrying for nothing. This was simply a chat or sex kind of date. Either way, it was nothing one of us guys couldn't handle.

* * *

Wolf drove, found a visitor spot in the underground parking garage, and stepped into the elevator. The building looked like a typical high-rise condo. The elevator buttons went up to 22, so why was the 17th floor a resort? Never mind, there weren't any buttons for floors 16, 17, and 18.

Missing floors. Very cool.

I pulled out Jack's letter, found the part about the elevator code, and punched in 1733 on the keypad. That's all it took.

Sweet.

Secret floors, here we come.

We rode the elevator with only silence in my head, but something was wrong. My sense of dread was magnified by the *Girl From Ipanema* playing quietly in the background. Elevator music. Bad things happened in the movies when they played that song in the elevator. What movie was it? It seemed like it was in multiple movies, like a Hollywood thing. At the end of the elevator ride, the doors would suddenly be riddled with hundreds of bullet holes. Shafts of light would illuminate the bloody carnage inside.

Well, that's how that song always ended in the movies.

My spidey senses were tingling. Or maybe it was just Wolf dreading the thought of sharing his body with some young woman who was unvetted.

The elevator doors opened slowly. Nothing happened. All quiet. Dim mood lighting greeted us. Things were pretty dark, but at least no tracer rounds lit up the hallway.

I took a deep breath and tried to ignore my paranoia.

Yeah, all good. So relax, guys. Jack was good with carrots. We were in no danger here. Yeah, Wolfie's manly butt was in good hands—Jack's hands.

Not exactly a good thought.

Stepping into the dimly lit hallway, it was pretty obvious someone had way too much money. Deep cobalt blue carpet. Awesome color. No overhead lighting, just weird artsy wall sconce light things, each one was a unique work of frosted glass swirls. Only the lights near me were on. The hallway went zigzag, sort of like lightning bolts zigzagging left and right into inky cobalt darkness.

No signs. No room numbers. Doors with elaborate frames around them, each one different in bronze or copper plate. Some with rich swirly wood grain, maybe from endangered trees. No room numbers anywhere. Kinda problematic.

I turned left, walked to the nearest door and the number 1709 started to glow blue. Actually the glow was more of a slow pulsing throb. Seriously wicked. I continued walking down the hall and triggered another wall sconce light to slowly illuminate. I stopped, then backed away, and it dimmed slowly as I moved. These weren't cheap motion sensors. No, these were proximity sensors. Deluxe.

The next door's number woke up and pulsed 1711, but this time the color was amber.

A little farther down the hall, lights in the floor woke up to show me a few steps going down. A split level hallway? No way. How the hell did this place get past the fire marshal? Kickbacks?

Then it dawned on me, this is what you get when you fused together Austin's high-tech businesses, its art scene, and our money-drenched Texas politics.

So I walked down the eerie hall, triggering one cool firefly glow after another. Suite 1717 had a deep red throbbing glow.

I touched the white illuminated square buzzer touchpad thingy. I liked that it glowed brighter as my hand approached it. Even the door's touchpad anticipated my arrival. Muffled chimes seeped through the solid mahogany door. Footsteps ran to the door. Someone was eager to meet us.

The guys all smiled.

The big door opened. An attractive blond in her mid-twenties stood before us. She wore a big smile and a curve hugging cocktail or nightclub kind of dress. Cobalt blue. We really liked the color on her. Blond and cobalt blue.

"Hi. You must be Wolf."

"And you must be Shanna."

She looked around. "No flowers?"

"Sorry. None were good enough." A lie, but it sounded good to me. I hoped she'd take it the right way.

She rewarded my naughty self with a warm smile.

Were guys bad for lying to women? Or were we just trained that way because women seemed to like a flattering lie?

She waved us in. "Come in, come in."

We walked in.

The place was nice. Sunken living room, maybe a retro '60s look to it, confused green colors mixed with oranges and tacky golds you don't see except on really old TV shows. Cheesy Greco-Roman vases and artwork, a flat square fireplace, furniture from the Jetsons—all flat on top but curved around the sides. In the back was a big stereo cabinet like I'd seen in old movies. The lid was open and a retro phonograph was scratching its way through some smoky jazz without a melody or even a beat.

She motioned for me to have a seat on one of her curved boxy sofas. I crossed the room, careful not to trip on the sunken part of the floor. I sat where indicated. She sat near me.

What was her name? Shawna? Shanna.

Shanna had a pleasing figure without resorting to exaggerated features that most guys liked these days. Her face was definitely perfect, but forgettable. She also seemed to have a lot of grace about her. Amazing what a little grace can do to get a guy's attention. It occurred to me, Shanna was the generic beauty in Jack's photo lineup, only she was looking a lot more real and a lot less like pretty plastic.

She caught me staring, taking her all in.

Awkward.

What to say? Should I just tell her Jack wants a fuck test? Might be a good conversation starter. I was tempted to just spit it out. Mainly, I wanted to touch my face to see what it was doing.

She touched my arm. "Can I get you something to drink?"

I needed something stronger than alcohol. "I'm good."

"Mind if I drink?"

Better if she did. "Not at all."

She got up and gave me a fine view of her rear as she wiggled over to the drink cart in dangerously high heels. That set up all kinds of erotic thoughts in each of my minds. Good thing women don't have a clue what guys are thinking.

Then she bent over, giving me a show of something we hadn't noticed yet—a wonderful slit skirt that went up the side, all the way up to the middle of her hip. Maybe a little higher. Oh yeah, baby.

Sweet.

She glanced back at me. "You know, Wolf, I can mix something up for you. Rum and coke?"

Alarm bells! Rum and coke? "How'd you know?"

"Jack told me how you like it."

Yeah, right. Uncle Jack knows exactly what I like. Or he thinks he does. "No thanks."

"Nonsense." I could hear the clinking of ice. "I want you to have a good time." She walked back to me with a rum and coke in one hand, a bottle and a corkscrew in the other.

I took my drink, sipped it to be polite, then parked it on the bare coffee table—its poor wood, bleached to the color of light gray ashes, completely robbed of its natural brown color. Strange how I felt connected with the coffee table. I stared at it. The wood and I were both dead and robbed of our natural brown color. What, no coasters for the drinks? The coffee table would suffer without protection.

Was this a premonition? I needed protection? From what?

Shanna was sitting close to me, this time on the other side so her slit skirt opened to me. "Wolfie, would you be a dear and open this for me?"

"Open what?" I might have been confused because I was staring at her sexy skirt. It was kinda open already.

She handed me the chilled bottle of white wine and the corkscrew. Martoni bombarded me with corkscrew jokes. I said none of them. "Sure."

As I screwed my way into her bottle, I tried to be more casual than nervous. Not easily done. "How do you know Jack?"

She put two fingers to my lips. Neurons lit up in my brain—all the ones that reminded me of Sonya Clark, amazing sex in Canada, Jack's bugs everywhere, the need for secrecy, and then back around to sexy physical Sonya. Shanna was nothing like Sonya, but a clump of my brain cells were too primitive to care. Bad clump. Reckless *must-have-sex* clump. That was the clump that kept divorce lawyers in their shiny new German autos.

"Shhh." Shanna's voice was soft. "Let's not talk about him tonight."

Who? Jack? Why not? Let's talk about him all night. Hell, I was trying to stay out of her bedroom, but the force was strong within her, it was. Jack was my Darth Vader. All I had to do was bring him into the conversation and my lightsaber would fizzle back to pocket size. Then Shanna would be spared a Jack attack and I could drive to one of Wolf's private sex clubs and—

And what? Work myself into a frenzy watching dancers wrapped around big poles, then drag my own big pole back to the house and break out Wolf's private bedroom tapes?

Not a bad evening, especially by my old Marko standards.

I poured her a glass of whatever white wine she was drinking.

"Thanks, Wolfie." She put her hand on my muscular leg. Or maybe I wanted it to be Wolf's leg. She gave me a suggestive smile. "I hear you guard bodies."

I nodded. Yeah, and a part of me also enjoyed killing people. Then there was the part of me that was into superhero comics with lots of women in bondage. And of course, I talked incessantly to my motley inner passengers. Not a problem because they're all dead— mostly. So I guess that made me a typical first date. Right? "Guard bodies? You might say that."

She rubbed my leg, but that only reminded me of Sonya. Bad thoughts. Dangerously mingled thoughts. Sonya, good. This one, bad. My neurons were betraying me when I needed them most.

She moved a bare leg out of her slit and pressed it against mine. "Sounds exciting. I'm into excitement."

I was sure she was.

One of her eyebrows was cocked. "I want you to know that."

She reached for me but I leaned forward to get another micro-sip of my drink.

I swallowed hard. "And what do you do?" I wanted to say her name, but I was rapidly losing touch with my smarter brain cells. "I wasn't told much about you."

She gave me a devious little smile. "I'm into acquisitions."

"Oh?"

"Assets. Very firm, tangible assets."

Not going there. "For your clients."

"Yes, but also for myself."

"That's good."

She gave me a knowing look. "I know a firm asset when I feel it."

"Me, too." Lame. What could I say?

"Then feel me." She grabbed my hand and shoved it down the front of her dress.

Uh, okay. Yes. Um, she did have boobs. I gave one a little squeeze. "I feel you." Beyond lame.

"Yes, you do. Do you like them?"

I nodded. I groped. There were two. "Sure. I mean, they're awesome."

"I feel you, too." Her hand was squeezing the force into my lightsaber.

Oh, man.

She jumped up unexpectedly. "Be right back." She dashed into the other room.

Pure relief. I stood up to go. No problem telling Jack this one wasn't my type. Okay, she kinda was, but she was scaring me. Too direct, maybe even pushy. Maybe with a few drinks in her, she'd mellow out and let me lead.

She dashed back into the room with a wooden cigar box. "I've got a secret I'm dying to share with you."

Great, what is it? Shut up, Nameless. "Maybe another time."

"Now, Wolfie, now." She opened the lid, quickly pulled something out, and shot me with a stun gun dart. Every muscle in my body tightened up, a barb was in my chest with a wire leading to her high voltage gun. Electric fire raced through my body. She fired another barb into me and the vibrations and electric jolts were overwhelming. Wolf was clenched but still standing with everything he had. Maybe that's what the Hulk goes through— muscle tension to the max.

She fired again and we collapsed onto the floor, unable to move, an electric buzz vibrating every muscle.

I watched helplessly as she pulled out handcuffs. Serious looking ones with a hinge where the chain usually goes. My hands were cuffed in front.

She pushed the couch out of the way and pulled one of Wolf's legs around. There were two manacles under the couch each with a short chain connected to a ring in the floor. She clamped a manacle onto our right ankle.

Crap!

Wolf struggled and was able to move a bit, but she came at us with a long jolt from a cattle prod and we tightened and burned all over again.

After she had both ankles secured, she produced a syringe.

"Relax, Wolfie. Think of me as your new dominatrix. Jack knows you're full of yourself. Getting submissive for a change would help that male ego of yours. Don't worry, we're just going to have a little red hot sex, then I'll release you unharmed. A little rough stuff never hurt anyone, right Wolfie? Anyway, by the time I'm through with you, you'll be begging for more. So relax while I get things comfy for you."

Like hell.

She stuck me in a vein with the needle, stood up, and pushed one of her high heels into my chest. "Relax."

No way.

A few seconds of something burning through my veins, then I was out.

* * *

I woke up in her living room hanging from the ceiling, naked, with my arms straight up over my head. My feet were chained to the floor with my toes barely touching the ground. A ball-gag was in my mouth. I tried looking up at my hands, but it was difficult with Wolf's big biceps squeezing my head. A chain ran from my handcuffs to a wooden beam overhead. Shanna had pulleys rigged to make it possible for her to hoist Wolf's body into this position. A ladder leaned against one wall. Over in the corner I saw Wolf's designer clothes. Shredded. Near them, a pair of scissors told the story of their destruction.

It was almost funny remembering how worried I was about going on this date naked. Coincidence? Or was I psychic, but in a pathetic kind of way?

Note to self: Worry more. Pay attention to the prickles on the back of my neck. When I used to drive a taxi at night I thought I could sense trouble. Hell, all the guys in me were paranoid. Maybe combined, that gave us a psychic edge.

I heard footsteps behind me.

"Good. You're awake." Arms reached around me from behind and gave me a hug. "You're a real trooper for doing this, Wolfie." Her hand traced down my stomach, down to my only vulnerable spot, now betraying me and becoming my one and only happy spot. "All I need is a little cooperation, Wolfie. I'll play this B&D game with you for a while, then you're free to run wild. You know," she patted my ass, "I was going to tattoo my name and phone number on you, but damn, there's not a single tat or mark on you anywhere."

I mumbled around the ball-gag, something about her being a crazy bitch and how if she were smart she'd get me down. And yeah, I threw in something about her not knowing who the hell she was tangling with. But none of it was intelligible.

"Save it, sugar buns. I was noticing you've got a little blood on you from the stun barbs, but they should heal nicely. I'll put a little antibiotic on it later. Don't forget to remind me."

She slapped my ass really hard. "You like that? I know you do." She slapped my ass a few more times as she played with my unmagic wand. "Having some trouble, sweetness? Here, let the dom-tastic dominatrix take care of it for you."

She moved around me, grinning and rubbing me all over like I was a wonderful side of beef she'd just found in a slaughterhouse. Then she wrapped her mouth around my obvious vulnerability like she knew what she was doing. Unfortunately, she knew.

Wolf screamed in my mind like he was being raped, which he was. But Nameless and Martoni were overjoyed, like everything good in the world was now sucking its way into their unified heart.

She stopped for a moment to strip. "I know guys are visual. This should help get you nice and hard."

Not like I wanted visual stimulus, but she had all the right parts and the guys looked at her with approval as she did a slow turn in front of us. Then she went back to sucking my brains out. Yes, plural.

So how did I feel about this, uh, ultra aggressive foreplay? I really didn't care how I felt about it. With a mind full of conflict, I decided my options were limited until I could get the hell out of this. That was my bottom line. Deal with it. I could always snap her neck later if I wanted to.

I wasn't exactly proud of this, but I did what any guy would have done in this situation—any guy but Wolf, that is. I did my best to enjoy it.

Sure, it was fuckin' *creep-me-out* kind of sex, but to most guys, any sex with a beautiful woman is great sex. Period. Even if it was on her terms.

So it went on like that for maybe 10 minutes. Then she decided it was time again to spank my ass really hard. I shook my head to let her know I didn't like getting hit, but she said she loved doing it and I'd learn to love it.

At that point she pulled over the coffee table, squared it right in front of me, spit on my rooster a few times, then stood on the coffee table, bent over for me, and presented her ass.

It was the finest of asses. It was the cruelest of asses. It was the Yin and Yang of lust and hate. It was sexual confusion incarnate.

She peeked around at me. "You have a preference, Wolfie?"

I mumbled something even I couldn't understand.

She grinned. "Good. I like it both ways, too. We'll start with door number one." She reached around and aimed my game-show contestant at door number one. She was wet. She backed up and I easily slipped in.

"Put your hips into it, Wolfie. Get a nice steady stroke. Oh, God! You're a big one."

I got that a lot.

"Keep it going. Don't worry about me. I like to feel it all the way, going deep, getting serious inside me. God, this feels good! If I get ruptured, I'll just get a new body, so make it good and hard, sugar."

What the hell! She was a jumper. I screamed and thrashed.

"Oh, God! Struggle for me, Wolfie! Get your whole body into it!"

I stopped.

"What? Jack didn't tell you what I was? He likes his little surprises, doesn't he? You thought Sonya was good. Wait until I'm done with you, sailor."

Damn, I was learning to really hate surprises.

She turned to look at me again. She seemed annoyed. "Time for the cattle prod? Keep it going, you motherfucker."

I kept it going. I was learning to hate jumpers. They had such a desperate lack of sanity.

Then she decided to give me more bad news. "Did I mention I was a mother? Honey, you were built for women like me. Now put your back into it. Harder!"

At this point, Wolf and I slipped into the back seat to close our eyes and cover our ears. Extreme trauma. The only cure was *revenge therapy*. I was sure there was such a thing. If not, I'd invent it. But Nameless and Martoni were super happy to carry the ball for the team, thrusting for all they were worth.

It seemed like forever, but what's-her-name finally had an orgasm. That might have involved door number two, not that I was paying attention. Hell, the less I knew, the better.

She beamed, breathing hard. "You are un-fucking-believable. You know that?"

Huh? I only knew that she was mental, and liked sadistic sex. Same thing.

She reached for her cigar box of tricks. "Now I have to give you another injection. Sorry, it'll take me a while to wash you off and get you repositioned for round two. Next up—bull ride! My favorite. Nighty night, Wolfie."

* * *

I woke up lying on my back on a hard narrow bed in another room, but still chained and stretched out. It seemed like a modern version of a medieval rack. Great. Shanna was a jumper who knew about ancient torture devices. And her idea of sex was to attack and dominate—on the first date.

I struggled to get free. It reminded me of Nameless wrapped up and stretched out in Wolf's freezer. Wolf was getting a taste of his own methods, only weirder. Massively weirder.

Looking around, it might have been a bedroom, but without most of the furniture. Assorted shackles and clamps hung on the walls.

What's-her-name walked into the room, still naked. "There you are. Remember me?" She got onto the bed and straddled me, then slapped me in the face in a weird familiar way. Familiar? Where was that from? Sonya on the plane? No, Sonya's slaps were somehow caring, loving. These slaps were . . . *Godfatherly!*

Oh, shit!

"Wolfie, likes his ears bitten, doesn't he?" She bit me. Hard. I was pretty sure there was blood.

I mumbled something around the ball-gag, a look of total horror on my face. She was Jack! I'd had sex with Jack! I'd actually thrusted into him—or her. My head spun. I wanted to hurl, but not with the damn ball in my mouth.

He looked down at me. "Oh. You guessed my little secret. So what do you think of the new me?"

Jack grabbed his boobs and jiggled them for me. "Absolutely sterling, wouldn't you say? Not too big and not too small. And they're not all saggy, so I guess having one kid didn't mess her up that much. But I am a little loose between the legs. Makes me glad a big one like you fell into my lap." He peered closer at me. "Cat got your tongue?"

I was still struggling with the realization I'd just had sex with Jack, the bastard from hell. Yes, he looked totally different. Yes, he was even in a beautiful woman's body. But it was still Jack in there, down deep. I wanted to spit and scream, but the ball-gag was still in the way, so I started convulsing, trying to buck the bastard off me.

Jack just rode on top of me, disappointed I didn't have an erection.

"Save it, Wolf. Wait until you're all dicked up again. Then buck for all you're worth while your delicious rod rides cowboy style inside me, thrashing, bucking, and pounding against my wonderful new parts, sending me into waves of ecstasy."

I stopped thrashing.

The sick clown looked down at me. "You're good with that, right?"

I shook my head, *no. Absolutely, no!*

"You need some water? Those drugs made my cowboy parched?"

I shook my head again.

"Then what?" Jack looked very disappointed. "You're not done for the evening, are you?"

I nodded.

"But we haven't even gotten you off. You know I want it. And my big bad Wolfie really wants it, too. Wants it so bad. Bull ride?"

I shook my head.

"I'll slap you if you want it. You need a whipping, don't you?"

I shook my head.

Jack threw Shanna's arms into the air. "Well, fuck! What the hell am I supposed to do with you now? What's wrong? You don't like this body? It's an excellent body. Fresh. Beautiful. Alive."

Jack stared at me a moment, obviously pissed and confused. "Is it the tits? You need them big? Is that it? You chickenshit. Think about the woman for a change. Big knockers are unnatural. Women were built to carry weight lower down, not way up here. You're a fucking inconsiderate asshole! Typical male. Bunch of demanding little weenies. You know what? You've got serious problems, Payne."

I wasn't the only one.

Jack got off of me and started pacing. "Fuck! You're just another dipshit. I suppose you expect me to run out and get another body, just for you, just because it's all about size. What next, 42 triple D? Massive implants? You want to see me doubled over in pain, is that it?"

He got that last part right.

"Well, screw you!" He pulled an antique knife off a table. "I've got half a mind to neuter you to the bone right here and now, then let you bleed out."

Not good.

Jack paced.

We both knew he couldn't afford to let me bleed to death. That'd mean I'd take over Jack's new body and he'd get bumped to the passenger seat. On the other hand, any man who could castrate himself multiple times had mad surgical skills. Skills I didn't want to experience.

Jack dropped the knife on the floor and moved Shanna close to me. He dug her nails into my scalp. "Maybe I should simply get your brains rearranged. A lobotomy might do you a world of good. Hell, I knew Wolf had serious misogynistic problems, but you?" Jack grabbed my face hard and shouted point-blank at me. "You, inside there, whoever the hell you are—I'm talking to you! I had goddamn fucking hopes for you!"

Then his Shanna face softened. His posture changed. His eyes filled with a brightness I'd never seen in him. He moved even closer, now so very feminine, soft, caring.

He caressed my face with her hands and spoke softly. "Jack, listen to me. Listen. I need you to love me."

WTF. He called *me* Jack?

"Only *you* understand me. Only *you* can make me whole again, keep me alive, save my soul. Jack. Love me. Love me, Jack." He kissed my cheek gently, her lips warm and so feminine, then straightened up.

"Okay, Wolf. If that's what you want, I'll give you one more chance. Just one."

He did a military-perfect about-face and marched out of the room.

Mega-nut.

* * *

Two hours later—no Jack. Why would I even think the most insane person I'd ever met would come back and cut me loose? Why? Because Jack could do anything he wanted to me, anything except kill me.

Leaving me here to die was a kill. Right?

When Wolf left Nameless to die in the freezer, it counted as a kill, so I got Wolf's body. Therefore leaving me here to die from thirst would be a kill and I'd jump into Jack's body. And Jack knew that, so there was no way he'd leave me to die.

Right?

Right?

I spent the next hour repeating that thought over and over. This was not a bad situation. Either Jack would cut me loose or I'd get Jack's body—now Shanna's body.

Yeah. There was no way for Jack to kill me. At least not this way. Maybe Nameless was right and there was a Rule 42—a way to kill jumpers, but this wasn't it. No way.

A few minutes later, Wolf decided I didn't have a plan and

resumed his thrashing. I'll hand it to Wolf, if there was any way to work something loose and escape, he was the one to do it. Having already spent three hours struggling on the rack, Wolf was ready to detach a body part to get free. I guess real wolves do that if they get caught in a trap. As for me, it was way too drastic. I vetoed it, knowing I'd survive this death.

Actually, I completely stopped Wolf from struggling further. His wrists and ankles were already raw and maybe bloody. If we bled out from struggling, that might count as an accident-suicide kind of thing and I'd be dead without a jump. We'd all be dead. Perma-dead.

So I went back to memorizing the ceiling while Wolf tore up my mental back seat. No understatement. The back of my mind was being mauled. I would have said the man was fit to be tied, but since we already were, it wasn't even remotely funny.

Try thinking through a tough situation when your head is full of screaming passengers ripping the ever-loving crap out of the back of your mind. It's not that easy to focus.

The frontal lobes, or whatever the hell I had that my passengers didn't, were awash with brain chemicals that all wanted action—and blood.

Honestly, I was in complete agreement with Wolf. There'd be hell to pay. People would die and I'd be happy to let Wolf do his bloody business, as long as I picked the targets. Jack was at the top of my list, but like it or not, he was a very complicated kill. If there really was a Rule 42, I'd find it, I'd bring Jack down. And whoever was propping up Jack would have a bad day coming. *So say we all.*

Okay. Nameless was channeling Commander Adama. Good. I had no problem pushing Jack and his ilk out the fracking airlock.

Ilk? Another word to look up.

It was hard to not replay tonight's nightmare over and over in my head, but I forced myself to focus on the future. Jack said he'd give me one more chance? A chance to do what? Do the happy hump with him? Go fetch more blood diamonds being channeled through Europe? Find another innocent woman for Jack to infest?

Or maybe Jack was going to pimp me out like Sonya and Peter suggested. Normally, the thought of playing a gigolo would have some appeal. But now, it was really important to know who the hell I was having sex with.

Yeah, that was a weird thought. I was starting to care who was inside the hot babes—who they really were. The old Marko never really cared to look inside the woman—not too much, anyway. The fact that Marie was deeper than just a sexy shell was a lucky break. She was a keeper.

What would she think of me now? She'd run. She should run.

Were sexy women really more than skin deep? Some certainly were.

It occurred to me my thoughts about women might still be kinda superficial. Really? Nah. The guys all thought my head was screwed on straight. Maybe they were right, I was nearing perfection.

I could feel my insanity spreading, so I focused on the ceiling. Nice ceiling. Not much up there.

* * *

I woke up to sounds in the living room. Voices. Women's voices. Maybe two. Neither one sounded like Jack, but his voice was hard to pin down.

They were laughing. Speaking a mix of Spanish and English. Moving furniture. Clinking glasses.

Time to get free. I mumbled though the ball-gag and thrashed around to make some noise.

Two maids peeked in the doorway. "Ay, Dios mio!"

Why so shocked? Maids were like doctors—they'd seen it all. Right? Yeah, so I was butt naked and stretched out on a sweat-soaked padded torture rack. Big deal.

They disappeared around the corner, chattering in rapid fire Spanish.

Hey, come back! The ball-gag wasn't helping me any.

They kept talking. Nothing I could really understand. Well, I'd spent most of my life trying to avoid learning the language, trying to be 100% American. But I caught a few words, like *policía*, *ambulancia*, and *no molestar*. All bad choices. Come back, ladies.

I mumbled using friendly tones, hoping not to frighten them

away. Come back, ladies. Naked racked gringos are friendly. At least this one is. Please.

One walked slowly back into my room, checking me out, nodding almost like she approved of my position. She might have been in her early 40s. She also seemed to have a sense of humor. Her words sounded like: something, something, *grande*.

The other one, cute and in her mid-20s, ran in and tried to pull the older one out of the room. They argued. The younger one avoided looking at me, but the older one couldn't take her eyes off my bare Wolf.

The cute one ran off while the older one continued to admire my bod. Then she began feeling my muscles. Seriously? I felt like a slab of ham at the butcher shop.

The girl ran back in and threw a towel over my privates— actually they were more like publics. She also slapped away the other woman's hands and began scolding her.

They argued. Finally the cute one spoke some English. "Juana wants to know if you have any broken bones. She said she's just checking you for injuries. Look, mister, just tell me if you want to be left alone or not."

I started mumbling, but they were at it again. The older one whipped off my towel, gesturing that she needed to check all of me—especially my public pubic parts.

The cute one screamed and they fought over the towel.

Ladies? Please? Just take this thing out of my mouth.

The fight moved into the living room, leaving me to await their decision. I got the impression this was a serious dilemma for them. Their Prime Directive seemed to be: never mess with the clientele.

A few tense minutes later, they both returned. No towel. Young one focused on my face. Older one focused on my nicely chiseled manscape.

Naturally, the cute one had my attention. Unfortunately, she seemed very businesslike. "Okay, look. Do you want us to release you or not?"

I nodded.

"So what's that mean? You want us to release you?"

I nodded again.

The older one pretended to misunderstand and reached for my manhood. There was more screaming, slapping, and shouting.

With the older one resigned to work with the manacles on my ankles, the cute one had the foresight to remove my ball-gag.

"Thanks."

"I'm sorry about Juana. I hope you won't get her fired."

"No way. The less we say about this, the better."

For a split second I thought she was going to kiss me. Well, there was clearly a light in her eyes. "Thank you. Are you hurt?"

Hurt? Of course, I was hurt. My wrists and ankles felt pretty chewed up. And my ear had been bitten by a rabid gender bender—I might need shots for that. What else? Torn skin from the stun gun barbs. Minor burns from the cattle prod. Needle holes from a few injections. Slap marks. Claw marks. Nothing worth mentioning. "I'm okay."

"You don't look okay. I mean—"

Juana was complaining in Spanish about my feet.

"She says she can't remove the chains because of the padlock."

Great. "There might be a key in the kitchen or maybe in the living room. Look around."

The cute maid told Juana to go look for a key. They argued. Juana finally left the room.

I wiggled my hands. "What about my hands? Can you get them loose?"

She struggled a bit, but quickly gave up. "Sorry, mister. Chains and another padlock."

"What about breaking the bed somehow."

She looked under the rack. "Sorry. That's not going to happen." She looked concerned. "Is there something I can get you?"

A bedpan would be nice. I really had to take a leak. I thought about having her go into the kitchen and get something that she could poke my dick into, but I didn't want to freak her out. "Nah. I'm good."

She nodded. "You might need a doctor to take a look at your wrists."

"Right. It's on my to-do list."

She smiled.

I smiled too, because I noticed her hand was resting on my chest. Reassuring. Comforting. I wanted her hand to stay on me, so I distracted her. "You've had medical training?"

"No. I'm finishing a bachelor's degree at UT in RTF."

"RTF?" Of course, I knew what that was, but I liked her company so I was chatting her up. Or maybe I just liked being around a normal human being.

"Radio, Television, Film."

"Cool. Which one?"

"Not radio. Digital editing."

"I'm impressed." Actually, I was confused. She was now happy to have me fully exposed with her hand resting absentmindedly on my chest. Wasn't she the one who was eager to have my junk covered up? Women were beyond understanding.

Juana shouted something that sounded like failure to find a key, then she walked in on us. The cute one yanked her hand off me and they launched into another argument. No need for a translation.

There was a long minute of shouting, and pointing at my various body parts, and body language that seemed to ask how it was okay for one woman to touch and drool but not for the other, and how things were different, but maybe they weren't so different, but they were.

I tossed out a solution. "Bolt cutters."

They ignored me, so I offered that solution again. "Bolt cutters. You know? Big ones to cut the chains or the padlocks."

The cute one turned to me. "We'll get maintenance up here."

Did I really want maintenance men up here laughing at me and taking pictures? No way. Couldn't the cute one just go get some bolt cutters? "No maintenance men. The fewer who know about this, the better."

"I understand. But we might not be strong enough to use it."

"You are. Trust me."

"Okay. I'll go get it."

"No. Don't leave me here alone with Juana."

She smiled, but Juana seemed indignant—and able to understand English.

"Please hurry." Yeah, because Wolf really needed to raise a leg near a hydrant. "Go."

They scurried off.

Nothing to do but wait. And hope they found the right tool.

* * *

Several minutes later they were back with a serious looking bolt cutter with really long handles. It looked ancient, rusty, and very heavy—the good old stuff.

"Do my hands first."

They struggled to lift it and get the cutter in position. "What do we cut? The handcuffs?"

"No. The chain." I couldn't see where they were cutting, so I curled up my fingers just in case.

After some fussing and complaining, they cut through the chain. My hands were still cuffed together but at least they were free of the chain. Man it felt good to lower my arms.

I grabbed the cutters, stuck one handle under a leg, and used my cuffed hands to manipulate the other handle. Quick and easy, I was completely free from both of my leg irons.

I hopped off the table. "Thanks, ladies. I can see myself out." Still clutching the bolt cutters, I made a beeline to the bathroom.

Ahhhh! All four of us guys felt the relief.

As I came out of the bathroom, it was no surprise they were still standing there. I guess a muscular naked man, handcuffed, and wielding a big rusty tool had some visual appeal.

I nodded to them. "Thanks, ladies. You were great."

They just stood there waiting. Maybe they wanted to watch me cut my handcuffs off?

Yeah, they did.

Fine. I was on display. I'd give them a show. I had mad skills, and I could easily figure this out.

Hey, try using a three foot long bolt cutter with your cuffed hands at the cutting end, but nothing to work the handles and keep them steady.

I had an idea to use the bottom of a door frame to hold one

handle stationary while I leaned into the other handle, but the handles were long and I could see that would be awkward.

So I got on my knees straddling the cutters with one handle resting on the floor between my knees and the other crowding my crotch. Easy to reach out and get one handcuff in the maw, then lean back and sit on the handle to do the cut. Once for the left wrist. Once for the right wrist.

Yeah, a naked guy was using his butt crack to operate bolt cutters. Naturally, they thought that was hilarious. But it worked great.

"Thanks, ladies." They didn't budge. What did it take to get them out of here?

The cute one grinned. "Would you like some clothes?"

Oh, yeah.

I walked into the living room to inspect Jack's handiwork with the scissors. I thought maybe I could salvage something, but my clothes were simply gone. "What happened to my clothes?"

The cute maid produced a trash bag. "I don't think they're usable. You know?"

I pulled out shredded ribbons of designer menswear. My fitted Hong Kong dress shirt. Ouch. The hand-tailored London sports coat with the stuffing everywhere. Damn. Even my belt was in chunks. Hell, I couldn't even find my underwear.

Or maybe I wasn't wearing any. Who knew? Routine things, like eating and dressing, were a team event these days. The perils of a shared brain.

"Your shoes are still good. They're over there."

That's nice. I kept pulling ribbonized clothes out of the bag. Jack really hated my clothes. Or maybe he idly shredded them while he waited for me to wake up.

"If you're looking for your wallet, there wasn't one."

"Keys?"

"No. No keys."

"Cell phone? Watch?"

"Sorry, there was nothing."

Okay. Now what? Toga time with bed sheets? I had scissors, so I might be able to turn a large pillowcase into a shirt. Maybe two big holes would turn another pillowcase into some pants? A strip of cloth to make a belt. Weird, but street legal in Austin. "Yeah. I could really use some clothes."

Juana shook her head and said something in Spanish. The cute one thought that was funny. "We can get you a uniform."

"What kind of uniform?"

Juana held out her skirt and started laughing.

No way. "I'll take a man's uniform."

"That'll take some time. But we have lots of maid outfits. It'd only take a minute to get one. A big one."

Standing there with no good options, all I could think of was how naked I was. This was a massive fail. No superhero or super-villain was ever so exposed. Right, Nameless? No? I didn't think so. Oh, sure, some supers might've had their identities exposed, but never their junk of infinite shame.

Okay, my junk was pretty awesome, and I sure as hell wasn't ashamed of it. But I was still trying to keep it together while aiming Wolf's wonder-tool at two gawking maids—two maids who knew how to make me feel very exposed.

Without keys, I'd need a ride back to Wolf's place. A taxi without cash or credit cards, and me wrapped in a sheet or wearing a dress? Austin was a major college town, so I could easily pass off a maid's dress or a tubular pillowcase or a toga as a frat initiation. Except Wolf was a bit too old to be a pledge.

So assuming I got a ride, then what? I'd have to break into Wolf's house? Hadn't I left keys under a bush somewhere? Seemed like I was always doing that. But not this time. So who else had keys to Wolf's? Billy Bob? Not calling him. Jack? Forget it. Who else? Sable? Maybe. She certainly knew her way around Wolf's, but did she have a key? Seemed unlikely. Wolf wasn't one to violate security by passing out keys. Maybe Peter, except I had no way to contact him.

"So do you want the maid's uniform?"

Huh? No. I wanted man-clothes. On the other hand, the sooner I got out of here, the better, because Jack might return with power tools and a blowtorch to teach my reluctant man-parts who was boss. So, exiting quickly definitely had its advantages.

I needed to make a call. Sable was a good start. I assumed Wolf could somehow remember her number. Or I could call Marie or my mom. Not good choices. What I needed was my sidekick, but I just couldn't remember Rema's phone number. A couple of my passengers really wanted Rema to come over and get a load of my man-parts. There was a chant brewing in the back of my brain: *You got it, you flaunt it.* Maybe that's why so many beautiful women liked to strip for the camera—show off their beautiful parts.

No. Not calling Rema over for this one.

Note to self: Never give your sidekick the visual shock treatment.

I looked around for a phone. Nothing. Who doesn't have a land line? Oh yeah, me. And just about everyone I knew.

"Juana says you'd look good in a dress."

What? No. I saw that movie and it wasn't that good. Okay, the one with Robin Williams was good. The rest were lame.

"I need to borrow a phone."

The cute one quickly handed me her cell phone. I guess naked men were easy to trust.

I checked the time on the phone. 7:30 in the morning. Not the best time to be calling exotic dancers. I thought about Sable and handed the phone to Wolf to do the dialing.

Yeah, the Multi-Mind was a terrible thing, but we each had unique skills and memories.

It was ringing, so I took the phone from Wolf and held it up to my ear. Please pick up, Sable.

"Wolf?"

"Hey, babe."

"This isn't a good time. Are you in trouble?"

"Yeah."

"How bad?"

"I need clothes, transportation, and keys to my house."

"What? What happened to your clothes?"

"Bad things. I need you to come over."

"Now?"

"Yeah. Armadillo Towers. Suite 1717. The elevator code is, uh—"

The cute maid refreshed my memory. "1733."

"Thanks. 1733. Got that?"

"Hang on." Sable set the phone down briefly. "This isn't a good time, Wolfie. Can it wait?"

"Not really. It's life or death here."

Sable was quiet—thinking it over.

"Look, I'm standing here naked in front of two maids. A dangerous crazy guy might come back at any time so I need to move fast."

"You're in your element, Wolf. I don't know why you need my help. Just do what comes natural."

Good advice, but not now. "I need clothes."

"No, you don't. You look great without them. Are they wearing clothes?"

The maids? I looked at them to make sure. "Yes, but—"

"Then you know how to fix that. Why so inhibited?"

Huh? "You don't understand. Forget the clothes. Forget the maids. I need a tactical extraction."

"A what?"

"Just get me out of here."

"Okay, okay. Reinforcements are on the way."

"Thank you."

"You owe me big-time, Wolfie."

"You got it."

"Now relax and enjoy the maids. And don't sweat the crazy guy. You eat bad dudes for breakfast, remember?"

"Right."

"Love you."

What would Wolf say if he had a heart? What would the Tin Man say? "Love you back."

I thought I detected stunned silence as I hung up. What? Wolf never said he loved anyone?

So if Wolf was the Tin Man in need of a heart, then who was I? The Scarecrow looking for a brain to call his own? Or maybe I was Dorothy, just trying to get back home to Marie? Then that made Jack and his crew the Wicked Witch of the West and her gang of flying monkeys?

Or was I something out of another movie? Like some kind of evil Multi-Mind escaping from Arkham Asylum. Walking like a brain-screwed zombie antihero toward Gotham City for a little meet-and-eat.

Hell. Who gives me these ideas? Nameless?

I handed the phone back. "Thanks."

Something had happened to the maids, like I was no longer sexy. Huh? The cute one grabbed a pillow off the couch and slapped it in front of my hips. They turned to leave.

What? They no longer thought I was fun? "Wait."

"We're done here. Your lover can help you."

Really? I said the word *love* on the phone and now they wanted to dump me? One word suddenly made me taboo? "I still need your help. I can't stay in this room." Yeah, because if Jack returned, he'd head straight here.

I stepped out into the hallway and watched as the cute one walked away, triggering mood lighting along her path. Juana hung around just outside the door, keys in her hand, waiting to see if I was through with the room.

"Look, Juana. *Por favor.* Uh . . . I no stay here. *Yo no aquí. Comprendo?*" She gave me a blank expression. I needed to find another suite because crazy Jack might come back here. "Uh, crazy Jack . . . *loco gringo aquí.*"

She nodded.

Good. She was getting it. "Shoes." What was the word for shoes? I pointed to my feet and said, "*Zapatas.*" No, Zapata was a famous Mexican general. "Boots. *Botanas.*" No, that was bananas, or maybe something botanical. "*Momentito.*" I dashed inside and grabbed my shoes.

Back in the hallway, Juana was sporting a big grin.

What? I had shoes and my modesty pillow. "You can lock the door now, please. Lock *la porta, por favor.*"

Her grin grew as she locked the door.

I wanted an empty room with a clear line of sight to this suite. If Jack came calling, I'd just stay hidden. If Sable arrived first, I'd be rescued. A good tactical solution.

"Juana, *por favor*, uh, *uno no occuepoddo roomo.*"

She didn't seem to be getting it, so I used the universal two-finger gesture going from my eyes to suite 1717. I moved down the hall to the next door. *"Aquí occuepoddo?"*

"Ocupado. Ah-ku-pa-doe."

Okay. Whatever. I moved down to the next suite. *"Ocupado?"*

"No."

"Okay. Open *la porta*."

"Es la puerta. Puer-ta. Y no."

No? *"Por favor."*

"No."

"Que paso?"

She grabbed me by the hand and led me a few doors down. "Use this one." She wagged a finger in my face. "But don't make a mess. And don't take anything." She unlocked it.

Good English. I felt like a damn fool.

"Okay. Thanks."

I stepped inside and closed the door behind me. It was dark except for a few dim lights on the far wall. I groped the wall around the door, searching for a light switch. There was none. Probably more of that proximity sensor lighting stuff, so I began walking forward. A fire started in the middle of the living room, but somehow it was about five feet up in the air. Random. Wait, it was a fire in the air surrounded by lots of water on the floor. Now that was cool. Instead of Jack's sunken living room, this place had a small built-in pool with an open gas fireplace in the middle of it. Okay, the fire seemed to be on a rock pedestal. As I stepped closer, hydro jets began to circulate the water in the pool.

Wow. It's a big donut shaped hot tub with a raised fire in the middle of it.

Seriously cool.

I dropped my pillow and shoes. Sable was really gonna love this place. I had to watch the hallway for her, but maybe I had time for a dip. Juana might hate my Spanish, but I sure loved her choice in unoccupied suites. I guess my hotness compensated for my insulting attempts at Spanish.

Note to self: Never underestimate the power of a cute butt.

It occurred to me a lot of women had figured out that one and were using it every day to their advantage. No wonder guys were so controlling. It's all most of us had going for us in the battle of the sexes.

With great hotness, comes great power.

Looking around the room, it was done up in a pretty cool grotto motif. Fake rock walls. Ferns. Fallen log furniture. Wait, the hot tub was supposed to be a lagoon. As I stepped closer to it, a waterfall started on the opposite side. The ceiling had a recessed dome above the lagoon and it was obviously intended to look like the night sky with stars. Like a big starry hole in the rock ceiling. Ferns were hanging down from the rim of the hole and that's where the waterfall was coming from.

I walked around the lagoon, but the waterfall shifted, always staying on the opposite side. Why? So the ladies wouldn't get their hair wet? What if two people got in and moved to opposite sides? What if someone wanted to get under it? I had to admit I really liked the blend of high-tech with the sexy caveman theme park. Maybe Wolf should buy this unit.

Someone was clearly making a ton of money off these condos. Maybe Jack lived in suite 1717, or maybe the whole 17th floor was his playroom. Or maybe he owned the whole damn building. Hell, maybe he had one of these in every state capital. All the better to influence politicians and channel power to his jumper syndicate.

Who said I couldn't admire the handiwork of the man I hated most? Jack was probably smarter than I gave him credit for. Not a good thing, because taking him out would be that much harder. But good to know, with Jack gone there'd be lots of goodies for my fellow jumpers. Goodies for Sonya. Goodies for me, too.

Being under the State Theater was cool, but this sexy grotto was even better. Being an ethnic-oddity taxi driver was cool enough, until I'd become this mental-oddity Wolf jumper thing.

And I used to think Marie was sexy, until I met Sable. But Sable was not in the same league as my Super Sonya.

That made me a little sad.

I guess it was human nature to like something—until you liked something better.

I wasn't bad for moving on. Was I? After all, I was going to make a difference in the jumper world. And maybe even keep them from screwing with normals.

Weird thoughts.

It occurred to me, the North American Syndicate was a dumb name. Too corporate. Too sterile. I was thinking something like Jumper Club. Informal, friendly, but still exclusive, and secret. Like Fight Club.

Oops. How'd I get in the hot lagoon? Judging by my relaxed state of mind, I'd been in it awhile. I should be watching for Sable.

I got out. No handy towels? Who cares? The floor was a waterproof carpet of rubber leaves and rubber bark bits.

Out the door's peephole I could see dim lights at one end of the hallway. Someone had tripped them, but it was impossible to see anyone.

Behind me, the flames had died down when I exited the pool, so it seemed safe to open the door a crack. But still, some light would spill out into the dark hallway. A second later the fire went out. Perfect. I opened the door. Someone was moving around out there. Probably a woman. Sable, or maybe Jack in what's-her-name's body? Sara? Shanna? Yeah, Shanna.

Peering down the hall, this person was small, thin, and had long dark hair. Not Shanna, unless Jack was in a wig and I was confused about Shanna's size. Not Sable either, not with Sable's aggressive bra size. Just another lost condo guest wandering around suite 1717? Yup.

Or maybe she was sent by Jack to unchain me? No, she'd have a key to that suite.

She seemed to be looking my way. "Wolfie?"

Whoever she was, she knew my name. And she saw me. Someone with good eyesight in the dark?

"Wolfie!"

Someone who worked in the dark? With Sable? A stripper? She was running down the hall in spiked heels. Fast.

"You bad boy!"

Crap! It was Jade from the sex club. The sadistic oriental girl who liked to whip me with her long black hair. Sable sent me reinforcements in the form of Jade the Merciless. I almost slammed the door.

Jade was pushing on the other side of the door. "Open up. Don't make me ask for it twice."

What could I do? I opened the door. "Jade. Good to see you."

She came in and closed the door behind her. "You naked. Good. Not need clothes." She tossed a paper bag she was carrying into the room's darkness. That triggered the lagoon fire. "Oh, baby! Hot room." She grabbed my dick and started pulling me. Why do women instinctively pull guys around by their dicks? At what age do they learn that?

"Show me around, bad boy." She pulled me toward the lagoon. "Hot tub, too. Fake rocks. Look! Waterfall. What, no music?"

"I haven't found it yet. Look, I really need to leave."

"Too late now." She kicked off her shoes but stayed in her slinky white dress. "My pussy very happy. More happy soon."

"Sorry."

"Sorry why? You need butt spanked? Oh, baby, look at that butt. It need spanked now." She slapped it hard.

"Ow!" It was still sore from Shanna-Jack's slaps.

"Pain good. You enjoy. I bite dick. Make him happy, too. Man have two heads. Both like to be fat and stupid happy. You see."

"No." I grabbed her by the shoulders.

"Fight game. I like fight game." She grabbed my arms, hooked a leg around one of my legs and pushed me into the lagoon. I surfaced just in time to see her belly-flop onto my face. We both went under. I was lucky she didn't break my neck.

As we thrashed in the hydro-jets she got a nasty hold of my nuts with her mouth. Actually she had somehow sucked one into her mouth and clamped down with her teeth. I stood up in the lagoon with her sharking between my legs. Holy crap! That wasn't even possible. Wolf's balls were pretty big.

Wolf wanted to take over. This was a serious fight. Okay, but don't hurt her.

So we moved a bit lower so her head was just underwater. She'd have to release and come up for air. Right?

Right?

No such luck. Instead, she was giving one of my legs an underwater bear hug, twisting around on me, getting her hips above water. Then a leg shot out of the water and hooked around my neck, followed by her other leg. We fell over with my neck in some kind of leg-lock. Both underwater now. All those lap dances and pole routines at the club had given her legs impressive strength. My head wasn't going anywhere, not without her say-so.

Great. Underwater 69. I grasped for anything. Found the bottom of her dress billowing to the side. Found out she wasn't wearing panties. My back was arched with my face pressed up against her pussy and she was still actively sharking Wolf's vasectomized parts.

I had more air than she did, so I figured I'd outlast her. That's when she stuck a very long fingernail into my bumhole. Wolf should've had a counter-move, but he didn't. Holy crap! Don't they teach this in let's-fight-dirty school?

Apparently they didn't. So I stuck Mr. Index in her matching orifice. She squirmed her hips around, giving me the impression she really liked it. Great.

That's when I discovered she'd spent way too much time with proctologists, because her finger was—

Damn! Forget it. That's it. Game over. Jade won.

I took my finger out and went limp like that was some kind of universal white flag or something. She released me and we surfaced, both gasping for air. Except she was standing over me laughing, her white dress twisted but still clinging to her. "Wolfie." She gasped for another breath. "Wolfie lose to little girl. Big bad man not so tough. Got ass whipped."

First, Jade wasn't looking so little. Second, she was no mere girl. More like a Ninja warrior in a wet fighting suit.

"Jade go for kill." She launched herself at me again, but this time, going for an embrace—aiming for a kiss.

And she kissed like she did everything else, biting my lips, biting my tongue, pulling my hair, pushing me underwater.

* * *

I'd like to say we had sex in the lagoon. But we didn't. I'd like to say it was a loving sensual experience. But it wasn't.

What we did have, was blood in the water. All mine. And there was an insane desire to just consummate it with some simple fucking. Well, that was the desire. All mine.

Apparently, Jade lived for the attack, not the kill. She was all tease and no trophy. And she was ideally suited for her career as a sex entertainer. Honestly, I couldn't imagine anyone having real sex with her.

Ever.

Jade was wonderful. And I needed stitches.

Which reminded me of that weird dream I'd had about walking along the beach, my blood in the water, my private parts doomed, and sharks. Lots of sharks. This was oddly similar, but that dream had been about being in Jack's body.

Too many symbols to sort out.

I was either slightly psychic, or life was over the line weird.

Or both. Yeah, definitely both.

And that brought me to the need for clothes. Jade's were soaked. Mine were somewhere in the paper bag she'd brought.

We both stepped out of Fire Lagoon. Yes, it now had a name.

"You want me naked, bad boy?" She started to pull off her wet clothes.

Yes, but not right now. "No. We need to get out of here."

"Why?"

"It's too dangerous."

"Oh. You say we're too dangerous."

"Yes, that too. But mainly there's a guy, a very dangerous guy. He might be coming back."

"Wolfie afraid?"

"No. Wolfie chooses his battles. He also chooses his battle-ground."

"Wolfie smart man. Not smart with women."

"What?"

"Wolfie lose every time with women."

No. Maybe. I'd have to think about that one.

Jade continued stripping.

I held up my hands for her to stop. "Hey." This was no time for more fight-sex.

"Clothes wet. New car. No drive in wet clothes."

"Then I'll drive."

"Silly man." She pushed me. "Go find towels. And hair dryer."

So I scrounged up some towels in another room, but couldn't find a hair drier. I tossed her a towel, but she was slow to use it. Instead she was modeling herself for me.

"You like?"

I nodded.

"You want?"

I just smiled. Of course, I was attracted to her, only she was all cactus and no gloves.

"You take. Take now, bad boy. I make cock sing and dance."

I'll bet. There was a flash in her eye, maybe because I took a step toward her. Somewhere inside her, a shark named Jaws waited for unsuspecting men.

U-turn. I found the bag she'd brought and began putting on the clothes. They didn't fit very well, but at least I was covered up. "Where'd you get the men's clothes?"

"Guys. They leave clothes all the time."

And they ran naked and bleeding into the night, lucky to have survived Jade's violent passion. "What are you going to wear?"

Jade threw me her towel and swished her hips. "A real lady not need much."

Yeah? I wanted to say, *a real man like it that way*. But I didn't want to encourage her. I shrugged. "Fine with me."

She walked into the jungle hut bedroom and returned wearing an Armadillo Towers bathrobe, complete with an embroidered armadillo standing up and pushing over a high-rise.

We bagged up her wet clothes and strolled arm in arm through the lobby and outside to her car. I told her I needed to get back to my place. She said I'd lost the pool fight, so I was hers for the day. As she drove, she pushed her robe open so I could enjoy the sight of one of her legs.

Yeah, I looked. It's a guy thing. We can't help it.

Then I used the vanity mirror to see if my lips or my ears needed stitches. My wrists and ankles where pretty raw from Shanna-Jack's cuffs and shackles. Mainly, I was happy to have survived the amorous attention of two crazy women.

3.6 East Meets Beast

When we arrived at Jade's, I was surprised to see how normal it was. Just a quiet apartment in the hill country west of Austin. Her new car was a modest Chevy, not a cool new Corvette. Inside her apartment, it was the same quiet way of things—everywhere, nice but simple.

Jade kept flashing her sexy body parts for me, but I decided it was just an occupational habit, not a come-on. Still, I didn't mind appreciating her assets.

So there we were, sitting in her living room, her in a naughty negligee she'd slipped into, me getting weird oriental stuff spread on my wrist abrasions.

"You like?"

"Yes." It felt good. But in the mirror it looked like Wolf had been in a cat fight. "Are you okay?"

"No. Wolfie hurt."

I'd been looking at some pictures on her end table. "Your family?"

"Yes. Family in my bedroom, too."

That sounded weird, but I knew what she meant. More photos. At least that's what I thought she meant. "They live in Austin?"

"No way. The clubs I work at—" She looked a little distant. "My butt only wiggles for strangers, not family."

"You send money home?" I don't know why I said that. I was sure it was true—and rude.

"Sometimes." She switched to putting stuff on my ankles, avoiding eye contact, almost bowing.

I gathered I was embarrassing her, so I switched topics. "That was a nice condo we were in. Kinda weird, though."

"Not condo. Hush house. Syndicate city."

"You've been there before?"

"Not your room. Other rooms. Sand pit room. Mud wrestle room. Vodka ice bar—too cold. Dead animal room. I like your grotto room best."

"Dead animal room?"

She nodded. "Dead animal room."

"Oh. It's a hunting room."

"No. Room for *after* hunting."

"Right." After hunting you get stuffed animals. Trophy kills. "Dead animals on the wall."

"Dead animals everywhere. People, too."

"Dead people?"

She avoided eye contact. "Dead people after hunting."

Gag. Who collects dead people trophies? I didn't want to know, but I could easily guess—Jack or his messed up friends. But I still didn't want to think about it. Sometimes it was best to look away.

"What kind of syndicate?"

She shrugged like she didn't know—or maybe didn't want to know. "Big syndicate. Bad people. Good money."

"You must see a lot of that."

She looked up and frowned, her eyes searching mine.

It seemed like I'd just insulted her. Did I? I certainly didn't mean to judge her. "Sorry."

"You not Wolf."

"Huh?"

She grabbed Wolf's bicep. "This part Wolf." Then she tapped my head. "This part not Wolf. So who?" She tapped my head again. "Who up there? Strange man inside you. New man."

"It's just a head injury. One of the hazards of being a bodyguard."

"BS. Head injury not make you smart. Not make you care. Not make you huggable panda."

"I'm no panda."

"Wolf now sheepdog. Killer now becomes protector. I see you in there. I see you now, nameless one."

Was she looking at Nameless? Impossible. "People change."

"Not that fast. I see you. Ego Wolf gone. Sable said you changed.

She was wrong. Not changed. All different now. You different man inside. You have name?"

This was really creeping me. I put my hand to my face, just to make sure it was acting normal and stood up. "I need to go."

"No, good boy. I save your ass. You belong to me today."

Good boy? I liked it better when she called me bad boy. It was time to go, but of course I still needed transportation to Wolf's and house keys would be nice. Not to mention getting Wolf's SUV still parked under the Armadillo Towers.

"If you leave, I take clothes back now. If you stay, I make breakfast and put you to work."

I thought about it.

"It's your future karma, good boy. Choose wisely."

I let out a long sigh. Well, I still needed her help. "I liked it better when you called me bad boy."

"Good choice, bad boy. Now we feed Wolfie. Maybe you eat, too." She grabbed the condo bathrobe, slipped it on over her negligee, then took my hand and led me into the kitchen.

* * *

Jade fed me and put me to work fixing assorted things around her apartment. I unborked her TV remote control, changed light bulbs, tightened up a leaky hose on her clothes washer, and downloaded some software to get some nasty malware off her computer.

I spent the entire day there, laughing, eating, and trying to help her with things a guy would normally do around the house. I guess sex entertainers had an uneasy relation to men. I could see how getting a boyfriend wouldn't mesh too well with her odd career.

The only weird part was how she treated me—like I was two people. Body by Wolf. Brain by anonymous. It seemed like she knew nothing about jumpers, but there was still a weird familiarity she seemed to have about my situation. Like maybe something from ancient oriental lore. Like they somehow had experience with this.

Western cultures were more likely to drag a priest out for an exorcism. Or get the village together for a good ol' witch burning.

Possession was always evil. If in doubt, kill it.

But maybe in the orient, it was seen differently. Maybe spirit possessions weren't automatically cause to open up the pit of bamboo spikes.

Basically, I was clueless about what Jade was thinking, and I didn't ask. Hey, it's a guy thing. Questions just make us look stupid. Guys are genetically wired to figure things out on our own. When our ancestors went out on the hunt, it was better to shut up and listen. When they got back to the village, the women preferred guys to shut up and listen. Not much had changed in thousands of years.

I had no clue which one in my head had that opinion, but the rest of my passengers listened around the campfire in my mind, and we all grunted our agreement.

After dinner, it got dark.

Okay, I'd had a few drinks. Warm rice wine. Good stuff. I called it *sake* and Jade gently corrected me with a Chinese name I promptly forgot.

I was going to ask her if she had to go to work, but I forgot and she never mentioned work.

We laughed. Jade told me long, boring stories about her relatives. We enjoyed each other's company. We friended without a single mouse click, and amazingly, without sex.

Somehow I made it through a shower, alone, and wound up in a low bed all alone.

* * *

In the morning, I woke up sandwiched between Jade and Sable. All three of us were delightfully naked and close.

No sex, at least none that I could remember, and yes, I'd remember something like that. But as weird as this sounds, it was absolutely wonderful. A bit like waking up cuddled up between two Bengal tigers and not having any missing limbs, or even any shredded flesh.

I just lay there, trying to burn the experience into every brain cell I had. This was the experience I wanted to remember when I was 90, or 290, or however long I lived. As sexist as this sounds, this was absolutely the penultimate goal of every humanoid male since the dawn of time—to be this close to multiple sexy naked women, on good terms, and survive to remember it.

Although I didn't exactly believe in God, I was ready to now. Hallelujah, brother! I was one of maybe only five men in history to ever accomplish this feat, and damn, it felt so freakin' good.

Wolf yawned and said it was no big deal. He'd often had lots of naked women piled all over him in the morning.

Thanks, Wolf. You almost spoiled the moment. So you were one of those five lucky men? Big deal. You were no better than me.

Wolf smirked. He'd done it lots of times. With lots of women. Man sandwich? Two were nothing. Try eight or a dozen, Marko.

Whatever.

I hated him.

3.7 Welcome To Texas

Later that day, Jade dropped me off at Wolf's place. She didn't want to come in. I guess she had things to do.

"Thanks, Jade."

"No problem, Wolfie. Keep your head down and your pants up. Unless you're with me, then I spank your Wolfie ass and kiss your new self."

I was still working on a snappy come-back as she drove off.

Without a key, getting into my own place was my immediate problem. I wracked my memory for a bush with Wolf's key under it, but I seem to have gathered them all up already.

So I needed a window to break. Something out of sight and easily fixed. I started circling the house.

But it was an uneasy feeling. Jack could be anywhere, in anyone. The last thing I needed was another Jack attack. Or maybe Peter was lurking under my bed, spying on me, waiting for me to have sex so he could give me hot tips. Or join in.

I stopped. Was paranoia my friend these days?

Wolf tensed. His feral muzzle sniffed the air. Something in the wind, boy? Great. Just great. Well, whoever the hell it was, I just wanted Wolf to kill him quickly so I could get on with my life.

We moved slowly.

Just kill it, Wolf. Don't sneak up on it, just charge it and kill it. Be quick about it. I had a window to break and beer and pizza to order.

There were voices coming from behind the house. Laughing voices. Women. Maybe in the pool? Wolf relaxed.

What? Just like that, and my inner psychopath relaxed? I was beginning to believe Wolf's killer instincts were no better than the average dog's. Little noises? Bark. Loud happy voices? Wag your tail and see if they had any puppy treats.

As I rounded the house, I caught sight of three people in Wolf's hot tub. *My* hot tub. I instantly recognized the guy, Peter. Captain Comms. The skinny nerd-geek who had no problem inviting himself into my home. Only this time, he was making himself comfortable in my hot tub with two women who had their backs to me.

I marched up, ready to tell him to get the hell out of my unused babe magnet. An odd choice of words, but not for one of my passengers.

Peter caught sight of me. "Wolf! Dude, where've you been?"

His two hot tub chicks turned around. One was a normal looking stranger in her 30s. The other was—

Sonya.

She smiled and waved. I just stood there, coping with a flood of mixed emotions. Confusion, jealousy, anger, hope, and a heart full of love.

Not a good combination. I preferred it when emotions didn't touch. Blends were very confusing, so this hot tub head-trip needed to be sorted out quickly.

Damn. It was now obvious they were all naked. No surprise, nobody I knew wore clothes these days. Jealousy was winning in my head, followed closely by the need to kill Peter for making out with my Sonya-Ana babe combo.

So I thought I'd get the fight started. "Hey." Too weak. I searched my confused mind for stronger words.

Sonya got out and came over to greet me. Man, she looked great, all splashed with water and Texas sun.

"Wolf. We need to talk." She gave me a kiss on the lips. Not a passionate I-missed-you kiss. But not a bad kiss, either. I hated middle ground kisses. Let a guy know where he stands.

Somewhere, there was a hell devoted just for men in love. Yeah, and maybe I was already in it.

But all I could focus on were the beads of water that glistened on her curvaceous body, the constant smile she wore—better than any clothes. She looked gorgeous. Damn, she was several inches too far away. So I pulled her up tight against me. She responded and heaven opened up for me, blowing away sun drenched Texas with a light so bright that everything except Sonya ceased to exist.

A solid minute later, I took the initiative and pried us apart. Mainly because the jealous part of my mind was obsessing on the fact that she was giving Peter an amazing view of her fine ass.

Oh, hell, he'd already seen her entire body naked. Why was I even remotely concerned about it? Why? It was a guy thing. Some guys shared. Most of us didn't. On the other hand, Jade shared me with Sable, so why was this any different? What was mine, was mine, but others should share?

I'd have to think about that later.

"Strip." Sonya was using her sexy voice, the one I couldn't possibly resist. "Join us. We need to talk."

Of course, I started to strip. As I dropped my pants, I noticed I was still checking out windows so I could break in. But the sliding glass door was open slightly. Was someone not paying attention? One of my passengers seriously needed a brain.

When I was naked, I did what any gentleman would do. I stepped in to the pool, and while standing, I introduced myself to the other woman. "Hello. I'm Wolf. Wolf Payne." I held out my hand and hoped my other parts would just hang cool.

One of my passengers leaned forward. *Showing off, Waldo?*

I wanted to slap myself.

The mystery woman was directly in front of me, with Sonya to my left and Peter to my right.

"Hello, I'm Brenda." She stood up for me and shook my hand, but her body language said she wanted a warm sexy hug instead. She had a big smile. "I've heard good things about you, Mr. Payne." Slight British accent. Up close, she still looked to be in her 30s. Her skin was very Anglo, actually it was more like troglodyte white. She had meh brown hair and a normal body—not that I knew what a normal woman in her 30s looked like without clothes. Kind of sexy, but with padding. Curvy, especially in the hips.

She was oddly sexy, but I felt embarrassed seeing her without her usual clothes. Whatever those might be.

Bad thoughts.

Well, I did have an open invite for a warm hug. Somehow I managed to stifle that impulse, even though my passengers were strong within me.

I glared down at Peter the Intruder. No need to shake the twerp's hand. Good that he was laser-focused on Brenda, or however he'd phrased it last time we talked. But heaven help him if he was getting it on with my Sonya.

I looked back at the ladies, determined to enjoy my first hot tub party. And I already was. I slid down into the water before anything became embarrassingly huge. Getting naked in front of really beautiful women like Sonya felt perfectly natural. Actually, it felt good to let it all hang out. But in front of normal women like Brenda . . . uh . . . it didn't feel so natural. Brenda looked fine, even comfortable, but I felt completely undressed in front of her.

Well, I was.

Man, I was feeling really wired, like sitting in an electric chair, or maybe it was just too much coffee. Something was going on. I felt totally on edge. Knife edge. Was Brenda a threat to me? Maybe. No. Maybe, but she seemed like a jumper. A British jumper. Hell, I was feeling off because I was now in hot water. In hot water? Well, I'd just stepped into it.

Crap. Everything was becoming symbolic. Stupid little fears danced their way through my mind—unexpected connections that tried to warn me, but made no sense. Symbolic thoughts were intruders, forcing their way into my head.

Then I got the vivid mental image we were four lobsters lounging in a big pot of hot water. All doomed. All of us. Something wasn't right. A hot tub full of naked undead? Nothing wrong with that delicious image. Oh, yeah? Boiled naked undead was like a reality cooking show gone bad.

Get a grip, Marko.

Or maybe my timing was the most suspicious part? Arriving just when it was hot tub time? Coincidence. Right? Coincidence happens.

So how'd they know I'd show up at exactly this moment? Good question. Yeah. Just in time for an intimate chat in the buff. Very suspicious. Everything was suspicious.

Paranoia, or no paranoia? Was I going to buy this, or not? Everything was draped in the color *wrong*.

I looked around. Nice house. Good landscaping. Nothing wrong here. A typical day in Texas—more or less. So chill, Marko. This was a good place. A safe place. Among friends. Right, guys?

Nameless and Martoni were thrilled to be at their first naked hot tub party. Wolf wanted to show off his bod with push-ups and jumping jacks. And a little later on, a group grope would be nice, especially if we killed Peter first.

Messy thoughts. But Nameless thought blood and sex was a good combo. Wolf said he'd tried it already, but didn't like the mess. Too much DNA to clean up.

Sonya was kind enough to bring me back to the moment. "Where were you, Wolf? We were worried." She was eying the red marks on my wrists, and my assorted bite marks.

Where had I been? Well, there was that bad thing—with Jack. Long story. How much of it did I want to tell? Stall, Marko. Change the subject. "Brenda's one of us?"

Peter nodded. "Yes."

Brenda smiled. "Eighth body, I'm afraid."

"That's a lot." That sounded rude. "I mean, you wear this one well."

"Thank you. Eight's too many, really."

"I understand. I'm on my fourth, counting the original me, and it's getting really hard." I tapped my head. "In here."

Brenda laughed. "They do tend to pile up, don't they? It's hard for me, too, actually. I did have some hope that each new transfer would get easier. Sadly, my experience has been quite the opposite. The old minds just don't bugger off like they should."

Good to know. More importantly, her breasts were bobbing up and down on the bubbles created by the hydro-jets. Breasts float. Mesmerizing how they did that. It was a dangerous distraction, so I looked away. It was amazing that I'd been Wolf this long and I'd never had any company in his hot tub. Just me and my passengers, living large.

Yeah, being four guys was a problem. Maybe I'd become extra male. Was that too much of a good thing?

I turned to Sonya, but she was giving me this look like I'd just done something. What? Stared at Brenda's bobbing boobs too long? Give a fella a break.

Sonya gave me a few more seconds of boob-infused confusion, then she gave up. "You spent the last two nights somewhere. Care to share?"

A night of sex and hell on Jack's rack, followed by a night of abstinence and heaven in Jade's bed. Freaky opposites. Which to talk about? Okay, sexually assaulted by Jack. Nasty details I wanted to forget. "Jack attack." That said it all. I looked around at their questioning stares. "He jumped into a woman named Shanna. Then he lured me up to his condo, resort, suite, whatever you call it, then he tried to fuck me to death."

Sonya didn't seem upset by that.

What? Didn't I say that right? Maybe she didn't believe me. Or maybe she secretly wanted me fucked to death? Really?

Blooming paranoia.

Peter was shaking his head. "No way. Jack's in D.C., and I know that because I've got a tracker on him. His little green dot is blinking away, happy as can be in downtown D.C."

Not good. Captain Comms lost track of Jack. "No, Peter. I'm sure he was in Austin the night before last. It was him. It was him in a woman's body. Shanna's body. It was absolutely him."

Peter looked at me like I was a fool. "Dude, that woman looked nothing like Jack, so there's no way you could be sure."

"Of course, I can be sure. Yes, he looked like Shanna somebody, but Jack was in her brain. Her brain, infested with his sick twisted consciousness. It was totally Jack, except not the body. Of course, not the body." I glanced around and saw lots of disbelief. "Look, people, he jumped. He's here. And he's . . . he's not exactly happy with me." Blank stares. Was I too vague? "I mean, he fucking screwed me. Literally."

I was getting no sympathy. Peter shook his head slowly like I'd lost it. Brenda looked like I'd lost it, too. Hell, I'd lost it a long time ago. Of course, I'd lost it. But there was no mistaking Jack—no skin could hide that sick mind.

Sonya had her head cocked. I could see her gears turning,

mulling over the chances of a Jack jump. "I'm beginning to think that makes sense—what Wolf said." She paused, working out the details. "Jack wanted me here because . . . because he said Wolf doesn't understand women." She turned to me. "He said you needed hands-on sex training. Lessons on how to please a woman. Practice."

Huh? All guys needed practice, and lots of it. Hell, the more we got, the better we got. Well, there was no hope for some of us. But what was wrong with me? Multi-me was practically a freaking god in bed. Right, guys? "I need lessons? Seriously? When did he say that?"

"Yesterday morning. Jack wanted me down here ASAP, so I packed and flew. Peter let me in your house yesterday afternoon and I was expecting you, but you never showed. I assumed Jack wanted you to have sex education so he could position you as the syndicate's hot new male carrot. Wolf, what exactly happened that night with Jack?"

I knew right away the details were going to sound really twisted and bad. Did I really want them to know everything? Anything? The less they knew, the better my battered ego would feel.

Okay. I could do this. "Well . . . you know . . . Jack wanted to be female again."

Brenda piped up. "He was never female."

Sonya and Peter glared at her. Peter offered me an explanation. "It's a point of contention among head humpers."

Brenda rolled her eyes but Peter continued his explanation. "As I was saying, we're not sure what Jack was in the beginning. Most of us think he started as a female. Or maybe he crawled out of a swamp. Amphibian. Very unisex. Very non-human. Actually, there's a really good chance all of us head humpers are alien beings now living in human bodies, only we forgot why we're here because the human brain is too damn limited to hold that kind of knowledge. Personally, I think the whole universe is a computer, and the only reason some of us humans can skip into another body when we get killed is because of a bug in the system. Yeah, the only reason we're still alive is because of a glitch in the machine. There's a bug in reality's death algorithm. It's so obvious."

Brenda wasn't letting it go. "Nonsense. Seriously, if you were a woman, you'd know there's no way Jack could have started life as a female." She looked at Sonya for support and got none.

Sonya ignored them both and focused on me for details about my night with Shanna-Jack. "So what happened with Jack?"

Was it just me, or was the water getting hotter? And who the hell gets into a hot tub on a summer day in Texas? It was obvious why I stripped and got in, but why were they all here? Hell, I needed to stop thinking and just answer the question. "Jack told me to meet Shanna because he was thinking about taking her body."

Sonya stiffened. "And killing her family."

"Yeah, I guess that's what he does. But I wasn't going to do it. I mean, sure, I was going to see Shanna, but then I was going to tell Jack to find someone else."

Peter still wasn't convinced. "So what makes you think Jack was in Shanna?"

"Because of how Jack is. You know him. He's got his own special brand of sick. He tried to fool me into thinking he was Shanna, but the things he said, the way he touched me . . ."

They waited for me to continue.

"I confronted Jack with it and he admitted he was in Shanna's body." I turned to Sonya. "He called you in because I wasn't cooperating. Hell, I don't know what goes on in that sick mind of his, but one thing's for sure—Jack really wants to fuck me. So once I figured out it was him, I naturally had some . . . uh . . . technical problems. I admit it. Hell, you'd have problems, too." I was staring at Peter when I said that. He shuddered. Thanks, Peter. Good to know you get it. "So the only reason Jack ordered Sonya to Texas was so Sonya could fix my . . . uh . . . inability to get it on with him."

Sonya looked skeptical. "Jack had you for two nights?"

"Only the first night. Well, Jack was super pissed with me and I didn't want to wait around, you know, for him to return with his rusty surgical tools. So I decided to keep a low profile yesterday and last night."

"A low profile where?"

"At a friend's place. Just long enough to let Jack chill about things. Assuming he can even chill."

"Anything else we should know?"

Like sleeping between Jade and Sable? And somehow not having sex, despite being sandwiched between two hotties? Not a good topic. "No. That's all there was. Jack jumped into a 20-something blond named Shanna. Then he attacked me, tried to mess around, and left really pissed. There's no telling who Peter is tracking in D.C., but Jack's in Shanna. And she's totally screwed—stuck forever as a passenger in Jack's mind. Not to mention what could have happened to her family. Wait. Jack told me his new body was a mother. So Shanna had kids—at least one. I think he said only one."

Peter looked away. "Jack typically has Doc clean the family out. Young females are sold off to sick foreigners with too much money, or business types who specialize in pimping out young flesh. Hey, they're the lucky ones. The rest of the immediate family are killed and incinerated. Liquid financial assets are collected and laundered. There's usually a cover, like the family just decided to gather up a lot of vacation money and hitchhike across Central America. That slows down any immediate missing persons report. Hell, it practically turns things into an instant cold case. It's some fucking bad shit, man."

I could understand the threat, but didn't anyone around here have a backbone? "And you people work for those bastards?"

Sonya jumped in immediately. "Never willingly." She looked beaten down, but determined. I knew her family was up for cleaning if she failed to follow Jack's instructions. "Never willingly. But as of now, I'm not cooperating anymore. We have what we need now, because Wolf's in. I'm risking everything on the plan. I'm risking my loved ones. I'm declaring open season on Jack—starting now."

Peter leaned over to me. "Sonya's been gathering some operatives like us, plus some outsiders she's been keeping well hidden from everyone, even me. I've got good control of intel, and I'll get Jack's tracker sorted out. Brenda just came aboard. She's a big help because of her connections to other syndicates, big ones like Europe and Asia. They're big because all the wars and purges brought out the jumpers. Most jumpers in North America simply die of natural causes, so they're never found. But now we have you, a real pro-grade cleaner. You're the last critical member of the team, bro. Sonya says you're the one hard-ass who has a chance of taking out Jack and Doc before they erase, like, all of us. So like it or not, dude, you're our great white killer shark. And I really hope to hell you've got your fucking teeth sharpened, because you're totally gonna need them."

Killer? Me? Hey, I'd never killed anyone. And besides, there was the annoying little fact that I'd been killed effortlessly by Martoni, Nameless, and Wolf. I was a serial victim, not a serial killer. Sure, Wolf was born to kill. So what? Me, a killing machine? No way. If anything, I was just a dead taxi driver with a messed up mind, joyriding in other people's bodies. Or maybe none of this was real and I'd wake up in intensive care with an IV drip and a sexy nurse on one side and Marie on the other.

Okay, that last part might have been a little optimistic. But me, their dream killer? Hell no. Marko was a lover, not a killer.

They were all just staring at me.

"Dude. The face." Peter shook his head. "Seriously, I can fix that."

"Stay the hell away from my face." I put my hand on it. Of course, it was doing weird things on its own. I held it steady. Maybe that's what they meant when they said *get a grip*.

Stall, Marko. Stall.

I needed time to think, so I did what I usually did—shift the focus away from me. "There's a lot you're not telling me."

Peter took the bait. "Like what?"

Like everything, you twit. "Like the rules. Jumper rules." Yeah, let's start with that.

"Sure. Where to begin?"

"Start by telling me how jumpers reproduce." A burning question. Well, it was bugging Nameless and Martoni. I was curious, too.

Peter seemed to hesitate, but Sonya and Brenda nodded their approval. He cracked his knuckles. "Okay then. I'll just tell you our little campfire stories. To keep things straight, I'll use this terminology: Jumpers, normals, hosts, and shadows. All self explanatory."

"Not really. Spell it out, Peter."

"Normals are just regular humans, not jumpers like us. When they get killed, they die, just like you'd expect. Hosts are the bodies we're in today." Peter touched his chest. "The one you're looking at right here—not the original me. Just so you know, I was never this skinny. So don't judge me by the host I'm wearing now, man. In fact, don't judge any of us by our skins. As for shadows, they're just the semi-dead spirits we have to put up with in our heads."

"I call shadows passengers."

Peter nodded. "Okay, cool. I'll go with that. Passengers. That's exactly what they are—just along for the ride. So here's our little story about jumper reproduction. You're walking along a cliff enjoying the view. It's a nice day. Birds are flying. The wind's in your hair. And the cliff has a big-ass drop with a great view of the ocean. Out of nowhere, two evil normals rush up to you, pick you up, and together they heave your sorry ass over the cliff. You fall. You bounce off the rocks a few times. You get smashed. You hit bottom. You die. So of course you jump into your killer. Right? But which one? They both did the deed."

Okay, two killers. "So I'd jump into both? Seems kinda confusing. In two guys at the same time. Weird. How could anyone operate two bodies at the same time?"

"All wrong, dude. Basically, your spirit would twin. So now there are two of you and each has its own new host body. So cool."

"But which one am I?"

"Dude, you'd split into two spirits. Each one thinks it's the original jumper. They both act the same, but each one gets a different body, a different brain, and a different passenger. It's just like Biology 101, man. Cell reproduction. One cell becomes two and the original cell is basically gone. It's the basis of all reproduction, right down to the DNA level." Peter might have seen some confusion on my face. "Okay, Wolf, I'll explain it without the science. After your jump, it's like meeting yourself on Halloween, but you and the other you are in different costumes. Sure, it's a bit confusing because you're not one or the other, and you're not both at the same time—you're split. It's a hard concept to grasp, but check out what happens next. You might find out you don't like hanging around with yourself. That's pretty common. So each of you go your separate ways. And you're seriously asking which one you are? Really? Dude, the question *itself* doesn't even make any sense. Which one are you? It's like throwing Schrödinger's cat at Heisenberg and expecting to know what happened. Seriously."

Peter was a genius shaken, not stirred.

I looked around. "Have any of you reproduced?"

Peter answered for all of them. "No. It's very rare. But we think Jack did, at least once, maybe more."

Multiple Jacks in the world? "Crap."

"Yeah, dude. Unholy crap. Well, if Jack did twin, we think the first spirit-splitting might have been the result of a firing squad. Jack says he's ex-military, it's in all of his stories. And he admits to killing his own buddies in combat. That's just how he rolls. So a firing squad seems really plausible. But think about the details, man, like the timing of the bullets. Problematic. They might have to result in a simultaneous kill for Jack to twin. Or maybe bleeding out is the sum of all holes? If so, then multiple firing squad killers makes sense. We don't really know, but for obvious reasons, Jack probably liked firing squads. Hell, I'm sure it was lots of fun for him to get shot up, then get a new body. I'm sure he would have waved off the blindfold just so he could check out the body candidates. Best of all, there was always the chance he'd twin and take over multiple new bodies."

"So there are lots of little Jacks in the world?" That would be a horror movie come to life.

"Yeah, dude—a definite possibility. Or maybe he twinned in the past, but these days, there's only one Jack left standing. Those of us with psych experience think he'd want to immediately kill off his twins. Think about it, Wolf. There's not enough power to go around for a bunch of megalomaniacs of Jack's caliber. Jack's got a super demented personality. So yeah, I could see him killing off the extra Jacks—in a heartbeat. But think of the fun Jack would have, hunting down his twins, evil mastermind versus evil mastermind, all the while knowing that if he lost, there'd still be a Jack in the world. And when the dust finally settled, the last Jack would stand tall, victorious, a man forged by his own hellfire—knowing he was the best of the Jacks. Survival of the fittest, in a weird twisted kinda way. The devil's own evolution. For all we know, Jack twins himself when he gets bored, just for the hell-games that follow."

Sonya rolled her eyes.

But Peter nodded, happy with his epic tales of evil. "Or even worse, and more likely—Jack probably put a bunch of his twins on ice, just in case he needed an army of evil masterminds to crush us. So many cool theories."

Nothing but theories? "Then we don't know for sure."

"Nothing's for sure. But if there were two loose Jacks in the world today, I kinda think we'd pick up on that. So I'm betting we've only got one Jack in the wild. But while I like to imagine secret underground cryobanks full of waiting Jack's, I have to admit cryogenics just doesn't work for people yet. You know, ice crystals kinda rip through cell tissue. Bad news for meatbags like us."

Only one Jack? That sounded good. "It sounds like we've only got one Jack to deal with."

"Yeah, but remember this, great white shark dude. Jack's a real ballbuster, even among psychopaths. Also, he gets off on being all random. Plus, he thinks five moves deeper than any of us."

"Great." We were back to being doomed.

Peter's attitude went serious. "From what we've learned about Waldo Zander Payne, he was a cold-hearted badass. But you, inside there? It's pretty obvious you're nothing but a wuss in wolf's clothes."

What the fuck did he just say? I may have tensed up Wolf's muscles, because Peter lurched back.

But to his credit, the nerd kept talking. "The real Wolf would have snapped my neck just then, but you didn't. You held back. That's what worries me. Don't get me wrong, bro, I love you like a brother from another Klingon mother. But we've got more than enough brains here." Peter indicated himself and the women, but not me. "What we really need here is your inner badass stone cold motherfucking passenger."

Fine. Peter really wanted to meet my motherfucking passenger? That could easily be arranged. Hell, Wolf really wanted to snap that neck and take him to the morgue for deep cremation. Now seemed like a good time. All my inner guys nodded. Yeah, now was a really good time.

Sonya put her hand on the rock that was my tensed up shoulder. "We need multiple skills, Peter. Wolf's got that going. I see good things in him. Growing determination. Deadly skills. And most importantly, the right amount of control."

"Bloody right, you are." Brenda was backing Sonya up. "We can buy coldblooded killers from any back alley, in any country in the world. "But that magnificent beast," she pointed at my chest, "that looks to be a splendid balance of brain and brawn. And that, dear Peter, is a weapon I can get behind and the other syndicates can support. So until we're shown otherwise, let's not doubt this man's mettle, shall we?"

Peter totally relaxed like the fight was all over and it was playtime again. Apparently he didn't mind pushing me until I snapped his skinny neck, but a gentle verbal slap from Brenda was enough to throw him into reverse.

Sonya patted my tight shoulder. Why? Oh, yeah. Apparently I'd forgotten to chill, too. I pried Wolf's big paws off my steering wheel.

Peter was all smug smiles. I suppose that was his way of saying he had better control of his passengers than I did.

"Any other rules you'd like to know about, Wolf?"

I focused on relaxing. I'd let Wolf kill Peter later.

Just kidding. Besides, killing a jumper wasn't so easy.

Wasn't there a story called *Peter and the Wolf*? Yeah. And the Wolf ate Peter, right?

Right?

Well, somebody ate somebody.

Peter was still staring at me, so I asked a question. "What if you're killed by germs? Do you become the germs?" Lame question, Marko. But maybe I could get my hands on some rabies and stick it to Peter.

"No, because germs don't really have brains. Jack's done all kinds of really cruel experiments on jumpers. Like Alaska. He took a jumper and had him put in a small cage with a grizzly bear. The jumper was mauled and bled out, but then the bear looked really surprised. Freaked out, you know? So they released the bear near an isolated farmhouse and watched it. It threatened some people. Destroyed their car and part of their house. A cop drove up and the bear charged him. The grizzly could have easily taken the cop down, but all it did was roar and get up in his face—kinda wanting to be killed. So the cop unloaded his gun into the bear and the bear died. But then the cop just drove right off, like he was running away. Jack's guys captured the cop later and grilled him until they were sure he was the original jumper. He'd made the leap into a bear, then back into a human. No word on his mental health."

Cool. Maybe I'd jump into an animal someday. That would be freaky. And who knew they had farms in Alaska? You could grow stuff in permafrost? "Any other weird jumping rules?"

"Weird ones? Well, yeah. There's anti-reproduce. You'll love this one."

I waited.

"Two jumpers walk into a bar." Peter paused to let me enjoy that classic lead-in to a thousand jokes. "They pull up bar stools and order vodka martinis. The bartender mixes their drinks, but adds poison. The jumpers drink. One jumper falls on the floor and screams, 'Poison!' He quickly dies and jumps into the bartender's body. The second jumper yells, 'Oh, shit!' because he knows what's coming next. He runs out of the bar screaming. He runs as far and as fast as he can, but he knows there's no escape. He falls to the ground, dies, and jumps into the bartender's body. The bartender killed both jumpers, so both jumpers have to share the bartender's head, both equally in control of their killer's body. Talk about a total nightmare. We call that the Siamese Twins scenario. Those two jumpers are screwed, stuck together forever, both fighting for control, and their one head is packed with all of their past passengers. Sucks to be them—forever."

That reminded me of the dream I'd had where I shared a body with Jack. Death was the only way out of that situation—perma-death. "Okay, so those jumpers were screwed, but only until they died a perma-death. Jumpers can die, right?" I already knew the answer to that, but needed to hear Peter say it.

"Yeah, we can die—the final death. It happens all the damn time, bro. Old age, disease, accidents. And most people die without ever being murdered, so they'd never even know if they were a jumper. Such a waste of immortality. What can I say? Most jumpers die without a fuckin' clue what they are. Ignorance is death. Hey, that'd make a cool jumper t-shirt."

"What happens if I deliberately step in front of a bus? Would I jump into the bus driver?"

"No. It's a suicide."

"Okay, but what if I *accidentally* step in front of a bus?"

"Your fault, you die."

Wait. That can't be right. Martoni accidentally killed me in my taxi and I made the jump. "Accidents always kill us?"

"Some do, some don't. Basically, if it's *your* accident, you die. Like if you accidentally fall off a cliff or something, then you die. But if it's not your fault, like you're just walking in the woods and a beer-soaked hunter shoots at a deer but kills you instead, then it's his damn fault and you get the dumbfuck's body."

So fault had something to do with a jump? "What if a doctor is removing my appendix, but accidentally kills me on the operating room table? Do I get his body? It was his fault, not mine."

"Yeah, well, that could go either way. I'm guessing you'd die because there was no intent to kill or harm anything. It's complicated. We don't know everything about how this works. Hey, just because we live in this universe doesn't mean we understand it. Same goes for normals. We're all looking for answers. Hell, questions about life and death are just one big messed up guessing game. So yeah, there are an awful lot of gray areas for jumpers. Areas that Jack's been testing over the years. Rumor has it, he's got a book full of rules, the results of his sick tests. Or maybe he only keeps the rules in his head. No one knows. Either way, that knowledge is like the Holy Grail of spirit walking. Bro, just before you kill Jack, make sure you get his sweet little book on jumper facts."

Speaking of killing Jack, was killing a jumper even possible? "So how do I kill a jumper?"

Peter looked at the others. "As our main cleaner, that's something you'll need to know. So far, we've only been able to figure out four ways to kill a jumper. But that's some serious classified information, dude—available only on a need to know basis. And right now, we're not ready to release those methods to you."

"Why the hell not? I can't kill Jack without knowing those methods."

"You've got a lot of killer in you, dude. We want it that way. Hell, we need it that way. But we also don't want our great white shark practicing his new jumper killing skills on . . . us."

Was I really that dangerous, or were these jumpers just a pack of cowards? "Okay. I get it. You're afraid of me."

"Most of us are scared shitless. There are a few fools among us who want to hand you the keys to our destruction. And then there's Sonya, who somehow believes in you, believes you can control all your inner and outer monsters. Frankly, Mr. Payne, you are an unknown spirit struggling to control a major badass. We don't know Wolf's body count, but I'm sure it's impressive. Hell, it's all the more impressive considering Wolf's lack of scars. Not that I've been checking you out or anything. Then there are the other unknown killers inside you—your other passengers. We'd be fools to hand over our existence to you. Hell, for all we know, you're a super-Jack in the making. But I do believe Sonya when she says you're exactly the sick twisted bastard we need to wipe Jack and his crew off the planet. Uh . . . no offense, dude."

"None taken." But I gave him a hard look that said I was a professional killer and his sorry ass was on my list if he messed with my Sonya babe.

Peter looked satisfied. "Well, if there are no more questions, I think it's time for more refreshments." He reached into a cooler and pulled out a beer for me and a bottle of wine for the women.

I waved off the beer. It was hard enough to keep Wolf down. Heaven only knew what Wolf would do with a nerd we didn't like and two naked babes. Death and sex—Wolf's idea of fun.

Brenda got out of the hot tub. "Time to spend a penny." She grabbed a towel and hustled inside.

Do what? Never mind, I had several more questions for Peter. "Is there a time limit on making a jump? Is there a way to get a passenger out of your head, or even give the body back to your latest passenger? What about becoming psychic?"

That last one seemed to catch Peter by surprise, like he was now worried I was on the yellow brick road to the land of psychic powers. He scratched his head. "Uh, like I said, there's a lot we don't know."

"You were going to set up some money for me to offset what Jack took. Remember, Peter?"

"Working on that. Patience, bro."

Sonya leaned over. "We trust you, Wolf. We wouldn't be here if we didn't. Whatever you need, just ask." She looked at the others. "We're ready to activate the plans we've been working on. Wolf, at this point we've all put our necks on the line. We need to move fast and we need to work as a team, each focused on what we do best. Sorry if we couldn't answer all your questions today, but we need you to handle the physical aspects. Starting immediately."

Peter nodded his agreement. "*Physical aspects* means you're on point, dude. Tactical spearhead. Jack's syndicate is on track for a total reset, and most of our people are already in position. You'll get details soon, maybe later today, cash, initial targets, everything. We're doing whatever it takes, Wolf, and we're counting on you to do the same. It's time to clean up our own, bro."

Fair enough. My guys were on board with that. It was time to go hunting.

I stood up like a Goliath rising in the hot tub, my tactical support team right here. Wolf's house stood in front of me, equipped with everything I'd need. Clothes, weapons of all sorts, spare keys, a fast motorcycle. Things were finally falling into place.

That's when a brick hit me in the back, hard. Something red and unexpected sprayed out of my chest. My back was to the river and the hills beyond it. Not a good position.

Weakness spread rapidly. My knees buckled. There was no stopping my fall. As I hit the water, all I could think of was my embarrassment. Caught butt naked. Shot in the back. Embarrassed in front of Sonya.

I was sick and tired of playing the fool, sucked into another unexpected jump. By Jack? By my own team? By Brenda who conveniently stepped away? No more!

Tunnel vision. Face down in clouded water, red billowing out around me.

Hell had a bad way of finding me. Transforming me.

Fine.

It was time to go savage.

I, TARGET
PART 4

4.1 Roughage

I thought I was prepared for the jump. I knew the drill. Die. Get my killer's body. Keep going. Right? But there's something about being body-slammed into another human that torques your mind, slimes your senses, and makes you feel like you've just burst out of primal dark birth-mud and into harsh blinding sunshine.

The light at the end of my tunnel was nothing more than the carbon arc fire from another mind-welding rebirth. Born again— more or less. It always started with a blast of confusion.

A new passenger struggled to get a handle on things, his consciousness was now rudely shoved into a back corner of his own brain. I fumbled around for the controls—they were in here somewhere. His neurons fired wildly, flamed, shocked, shrieked under the rude yoke of a new spirit—my spirit. Marko Santana in control. A pack of motley killers kicked and spit in my mind's back seat. Settle in boys. Settle in.

Sensations flooded in. Good, I was finally wired up.

First things first. Where the hell was I?

My head was still spinning, but I stood next to a white pickup truck. Passenger's side. Open window. Good thing my left hand was on the windowsill to steady me. A new body always gave me the feeling that everything was wrong. I struggled to focus. I was standing outside looking into the pickup truck. Two guys sat in the front seats.

Got it.

And through the open window, inside the truck, my right hand was holding out a small semi-automatic pistol with a large black suppressor screwed into the barrel. The guy in the front passenger seat took the gun from my confused hand. Okay. Apparently I was in the process of handing it over. No big deal.

But it was a big deal. Wolf was dead. I remembered that death like it was only a moment ago, because it was. Somebody had just killed Wolf—my favorite body. There'd be hell to pay.

So where was I, and what was I doing here?

Judging by the scrappy little oak and cedar trees, this was Austin hill country. Getting a better look around, I was probably standing on the other side of the Austin waterway from Wolf's place. I could make out Mount Bonnell through the brush and trees.

I must be in my killer's body. Hell of a long sniper shot. Damn. I must be Davy Crockett or something. So where was my sniper rifle? There was no way Wolf was killed at this range by a pistol.

"Hey." The guy who took my gun was pushing a paper bag about the size of a lunch sack into my hand.

I took it and looked inside the bag. Cash. Several bundles of twenties. Cool. Paid again for killing myself. Under the cash was a set of keys, an old wallet, a few other things you might stuff into your pocket.

"It's all there." The guy sounded downright unfriendly.

So I was another assassin. Except Wolf was a master of the art of a clean kill—no trace, no evidence. And whoever I was now, I was just some hack killer who'd left Wolf's body along with a hot tub trashed with blood. I already had contempt for myself—a bargain basement killer.

"Hey! Leave Texas." The guy's voice sounded annoyed.

I looked up. I suppose I nodded.

"If we see you again, you'll wish we hadn't. You're running out of time, Pops. Now move it."

Pops? Move it where?

The pickup drove off in a hurry, kicking loose caliche in my face as it struggled for traction. It moved over onto the narrow pavement, then around a corner, leaving me standing there, confused, holding the bag.

I felt really old—run down.

My tongue probed a few gaps—missing teeth, long gone by the

dull feel of it. Kinda like my mind, now probing missing facts about who I was.

I needed to ignore the missing bits and focus on what I knew. I had pieces of the puzzle. Info scraps. So stick the damn pieces together, Marko.

Right. I was a sniper. I'd just shot Wolf. I was now a sniper who had just handed over a handgun, but no rifle. Did I hand them the rifle, too? I couldn't remember.

Typical memory mashup after a jump.

Well, I was on the side of a small paved road on a hillside. I turned around. A crappy old pickup truck was parked just off the road. Faded red. Seriously faded. More of a dusty pink than red. A real junker. The kind of truck that should have died a long time ago, but wouldn't. Stubborn rural Texas rolling rust. My truck?

Yes. It felt like it was all mine.

Off to the right was a way through the brush and trees that seemed familiar. Downhill. I'd been that way. When?

So how'd I get here? Every new body's short-term memory was blank after a jump. Just deal with it, Marko. What's the last thing this old guy remembered?

No answer.

Got a name, Pops?

No answer.

Relax. I'm a pro at this. We'll get things straightened out.

What's the last thing I remembered? Being shot. In the back. Naked in the hot tub. As Wolf.

You still in here, Wolf?

No answer, but I could feel his presence. There was something big, feral, and pissed as hell in the back of my mind. No doubt about it, the beast was still in me.

Hey, Wolf. Feel free to break in the new guy. Yeah, the sniper that put an end to your awesome body. He's in my mental back seat somewhere. Let him know how much we all appreciated the deed.

There might have been muffled screams coming from a shadowy corner of my head. Maybe the screams were just in my imagination, but I doubted it. Welcome to hell, new guy. We'll get your name later.

Speaking of names, I reached in my pocket for some identification. Nothing. No phone, no keys, just lint and dust. At least Wolf had the courtesy to pack a wallet when I'd jumped into him. Not to mention the warm lovely boobs in my face—a wonderful way to welcome a new brain boss.

God, I missed that jump.

Wait. My wallet and keys were in the bag with the cash. My first senior moment.

How special.

I took a good look at my hands. Old, spotted, rough. Buzzard hands. Dead meat draped on hard bones. Great, I looked a lot like my scrappy old truck.

Then there was the scratched up wedding ring I was wearing. Not a good sign. The wife would be pissed. Or maybe she'd like my cool Marko self. It could go either way.

It crossed my mind to walk over to the pickup and check out my new face in the mirror. *I loved me some mirror after a jump.*

No. Not this time. My old-man hands told me as much as I needed to know. That and my stiff back.

I found myself walking through brush, down the hill, down to where Pops had taken his miracle shot.

This side of the river was dotted with big houses plopped on a few acres each. Posh homes nested rudely on rustic land.

We came to a small clearing. The old guy paused like this is where it happened.

I looked around. Not what I expected.

Directly in front of me was a spotting scope on a short tripod. A dozen feet to the right was a dead guy. Shot in the head. Not a lot of blood. Small caliber? I didn't want to look at him, but I couldn't help it. He was lying prone in sniper position, one hand still touching a seriously high-tech rifle.

The high-tech part wasn't so much the rifle as the scope. A fat scope with unexpected bulges and a cool video screen on the side. Hell, there wasn't even anything to put your eye up to. The sniper's only view was on-screen. The screen was still lit up, but showing sky overlaid with numbers and a target pattern.

What the hell. Any clues, Wolf?

Something like disdain came from the back of my mind. A snort of disgust.

Settle in, Wolf. Your first new head. So what were we looking at? I was thinking it was just a high-tech scope.

No. This was a smart rifle. An electronic trigger and a ballistics computer in the scope. The computer adjusts for wind, elevation, temperature, atmospheric pressure, humidity, and ammo. All the sniper had to do was identify the target, pull the electronic trigger, then move the rifle around to try and line up the image of the target with the electronic crosshairs. The shot never fired until the computer had a perfect lineup. The rifle did the actual shooting— every shot, perfect.

Wicked!

Wolf wasn't impressed, just disgusted. It was all computerized. Any fool could kill someone a thousand meters away—first time, one round. It was a skilless way to kill.

So this dead sniper was just some fool off the street? Special Ops training not needed? Just someone with a steady hand and minimal ethics? Well, damn. That took some of the edge off.

I got down on my knees to check out the rifle but I was careful to keep my fingerprints off it. Bolt action. I pulled the bolt open with the heel of my hand. A spent round ejected itself all too casually from the chamber. The round that killed Wolf.

No dent in the primer. Weird. Electric contacts. I guess that made for a more accurate shot. Martoni wanted to keep it as a souvenir. But Wolf wasn't too keen on that, judging from Martoni's muffled scream.

I searched the sniper's body. It seemed reasonable to gather some intel. Nothing but empty pockets. No ammo, unless it was under him. Weird. Whoever set this up only gave him one round?

As I struggled to my feet, knees popping, back aching, it was obvious I was ignoring the obvious question. What the hell happened here?

Wolf was obviously killed by the sniper on the ground. So I must have jumped into him. Then what? The sniper was shot by the old guy I was wearing now?

That sounded about right. But something didn't quite add up. Some little detail was odd.

Well, I actually jumped into the old guy at the instant he traded the handgun for a bag of cash. That was the moment the sniper died. So the sniper was shot in the head immediately after he pulled the trigger on Wolf. But even with a head shot, the sniper was alive long enough for Pops to walk up the hill and hand over his gun. Something like a full minute for the sniper to finally die?

Crap.

That meant I had two new passengers. The old guy and the sniper. Hey, guys. Look around. Anyone else in my back seat?

No answer. But I had the feeling Martoni, Nameless, Wolf and the old guy were nervously moving around, checking under their virtual asses.

Nothing.

From the position of the dead body in front of me, it seemed likely that the sniper was shot in the head immediately after he'd fired. Okay. So the sniper fired, the old guy checked the hit with his spotting scope, then turned and put one in the sniper's head. Then Wolf died and I made the jump from Wolf into the sniper. That would explain why I had no sniper passenger. I'd just jumped into a living brain-dead kinda guy.

Yuck.

But why kill the sniper? Covering the trail? Why not kill the old guy, too?

Then it dawned on me in an *oh, shit* moment that almost knocked me down. They knew I was a jumper! The sniper takes his perfect shot putting one through Wolf's back. But before Wolf can die, the sniper was supposed to die from a quick head shot.

The sniper was supposed to die *before* Wolf!

If the sniper had really died first, I'd have no killer to jump into when Wolf finally died in the hot tub. I'd be perma-dead.

This was one of the four ways to kill a jumper. It had to be. Make sure the killer died before the jump takes place.

Shit!

Oh, man!

I paced around. I should be totally dead right now.

This was serious. I had to move fast. Think fast, Marko. This was a calculated kill on a known jumper—me. Me!

Grab the rifle? No, it was useless without ammo, and kinda hard to tuck under my shirt anyway.

I walked over to the spotting scope on the short tripod. The zoom lens was good quality. It had a built in digital camera. Yeah, and the little door to the memory card was hanging open. Empty.

Through the scope I could see the back of Wolf's house, the pool, and the hot tub. No people. Were Sonya and Peter dead? No. There was only one shot. They ran.

The old guy wasn't helping much with his memories, but it was obvious he took photos of Wolf's death. Then what? Handed it over to the guys in the white pickup, along with his handgun. Proof of Wolf's kill.

But no proof of the sniper's death? Wasn't that needed, too? Or was that also recorded and handed over? It was a zoom scope, so the old guy could have taken pictures of Wolf's death. Then the old guy could have shot the sniper and took photos of him, too. Finally, he could have swung the scope back to Wolf's house to confirm the initial shot.

Damn, I needed the old guy's short-term memories.

Through the trees on the left, I caught a glimpse of a patrol car working its way slowly up the winding roads. Just what I needed—cops checking out reported gunshots.

Time to haul ass. Did I need the spotting scope? Should we throw everything, including the sniper's body, into the back of the truck? Wolf? Help me.

I took my hand off my mental steering wheel, but Wolf didn't want any part of it. Why not? People were trying to kill us.

Wolf thought he was already dead. Why should he drive some old guy's body and save a control freak named Marko?

Why? Okay, so Wolf was mostly dead. But if Wolf was thinking this and having these objections, then that proved he was still semi-alive. Right, Wolf? Right?

We blew off grabbing the spotting scope and ran up hill with our sack of cash, back to the old red truck.

Good. Go, Wolf, go! We all chanted it. *Go, Wolf, go!*

Nobody tries to totally kill us and lives to tell about it. Right, guys?

As we ran it became apparent the old guy was breathing really hard and his heart was seriously pounding in my chest. *His* chest. Wolf throttled back to a trot.

We reached the truck. Good. The window was rolled down and Wolf stuck his head in. Nothing worth taking.

Taking? I pulled the keys out of the money sack. We're not driving off?

Wolf thought it was bad odds.

Huh? Driving away was good odds. Right, Wolf?

Wolf seemed to sniff the air. The men who set this up would believe the old man was expendable. Methods would be used. A possible bomb in the truck, maybe GPS tracking, or even cut ignition wires. I caught a glimpse of my new face in the mirror. Grizzled and very old. Definitely expendable. Not a face I wanted to wear.

Wolf took off running along the paved road.

Martoni was in a state of panic. He'd rather die than go back to prison, but he didn't want to get blown up in the truck. It was somehow better to die of a heart attack in a running old man than get blown up.

Just chill, Martoni. Put your feet up and enjoy the ride. That's what I was doing. Just let Wolf do his job.

As we ran, I shoved the keys in my pocket and pulled the wallet out of the sack. Not much in it except for a driver's license. It said I was in Ray Popowitz. Hey, he really was named Pops. Age 69. Whoa. Seriously old.

I made Wolf slow us to a quick walk. It wouldn't be good if we accidentally killed the old man on our first day together. Old guys have crappy hearts. Maybe he had meds in the truck. Too bad we didn't look for them. We might have also found a defibrillator. I could see how that would come in handy.

His address was somewhere between Del Valle and Cedar Creek. Not much out there. Rural living. Maybe a farm or two. I remembered picking up a few taxi fares at the Del Valle prison. Funny how they always wanted to go straight to the airport. Good ol' taxi driver days. Long gone.

No credit cards in the wallet. Three dollars. A picture of an old woman. Pops, is that your wife?

No answer, but Pops was breathing hard.

The cash in the sack was a sad bunch of rolled up $20 bills. Maybe $6,000 total. Maybe less. Not bad for a day's work. But not enough to risk a trip to death row.

Who are you, Pops? A down and out farmer? Do you and your wife need money to pay the bills?

Pops had a thought—no wife.

Huh? You're wearing a ring, but no wife?

Doris passed away. Years ago.

Doris? Sorry, man. Desperate times, I guess.

I got some agreement on that one.

Don't worry, old man. I've got some buried cash. Wolf's got mad survival skills. We've got friends. Or I thought we did.

Whoever tried to kill me, knew I was a jumper. Only jumpers even know we exist, so it had to be one of us. One of my kind, whatever that was. Jack was the obvious suspect. Or Brenda from the hot tub. Or anyone. Any jumper.

But not Sonya. No, not her. Right?

Sadly, paranoia wouldn't let me exclude anyone.

Hey, going rogue wasn't so bad. Going it alone. Just me—and my inner passengers to keep me warm. Can't forget them. Couldn't forget them even if I wanted to.

* * *

Wolf suddenly got off the small winding road. I must have lost track of time. Where were we? Wolf wasn't talking.

We circled around a McMansion with a black wrought iron fence around it. Secluded. Okay. Who lives here? Were we boosting a car? Good deal. I was feeling the need for speed.

Around back, Wolf struggled to pull us over the fence. It was like he forgot about being in an old man. When we reached the top of the fence, I had to stop Wolf from jumping down. Old guys were brittle. Even I knew that much.

I carefully lowered Pops down, then looked to Wolf for directions. We strolled up to a glass door in the back. Wolf picked up a potted plant and heaved it through the glass. Hell, hadn't I just done that a few weeks ago at Billy Bob Wyville's place? Great minds think alike. I gave Wolf a mental high-five but he ignored me.

The security system was chirping. We stepped inside, crunching broken glass. Now what?

Wolf promptly entered the key code to turn off the alarm.

Whoa. Wolf knew this place? A safe house? One of Billy Bob's repo properties?

Pops was bushed, so we sat him down on a big leather couch in the living room. Hang in there, old man. We'll get you in shape in no time.

I glanced around. Nice place. Expensive furniture, but on the bland side. Whoever decorated this room really liked white. Big fireplace. Mantle with family photos. Boring looking people. Who lives here, anyway?

Wolf shrugged. A politician. Some guy in the Texas state senate. Comes here only when congress is in session. Lives in Dallas. Knows Billy Bob.

Thanks, Wolf. A politician? I hated him already.

I got up and looked at the photos on the mantle. The politician looked like a TV ad for extreme sexual dysfunction. Handsome. Gray hair. In his 50s, but still a man's man. She was a poster board wife, no more personality than a pretty 2D cutout. Two preppy sons. All professional photos, no snaps or selfies. A perfect example of white bread America living in inbred isolation.

Disgusting.

Nameless wanted to break all the windows.

Martoni wanted to find the TV remote and find some naughty channels.

Wolf wanted a kill. Starting with Pops.

Pops just wanted to lie down and die.

Sniper dude didn't have an opinion. Are you in there some-where, sniper? Snipe? Snip? That sounded appropriate. If we ever found a bit of him in my mental back seat, we'd call him Snip. Are you in there, Snip?

No answer.

Fine. So what were we doing here, Wolf?

Stock up. Move out.

Cool. We all knew what *stock up* meant. We headed straight for the kitchen.

It was a really nice kitchen. Even better than Wolf's. Only one small problem—a general lack of food.

The only thing in the refrigerator were evaporated slivers of ice. We looked around and found two more refrigerators and a chest freezer. They were all turned on, and all empty except for ice.

In the pantry they had tons of serving ware, but no food. Not even spices.

Who even lives like this? Politicians who'd rather be in Dallas shopping for diamonds and furs, that's who. Well, that's about all I could come up with. Like I even knew what Dallas politicians did.

Upstairs, it was the same deal. Room after room—one big furniture showroom. Empty drawers. Empty closets. At least they had toilet paper, but just one new roll per bathroom. Classy towels on the towel bars, but empty linen closets. Decorative soap in the shape of a duck. No decorative tooth brush.

That's when I got a good look at myself in the bathroom mirror. Man, I was old. Totally gray. Bald on top except for four or five rogue hairs. A shave and a haircut wouldn't hurt. I had more wrinkles and brown spots than skin. At least that's what it looked like. Bad teeth. A bunch were missing in back. I'd need a good dentist, for sure. I might've been 5' 7", maybe taller because I slouched. I straightened up, but it hurt to hold that position, so I went back to Pop's usual slouch.

What else?

Basically, I was thin, but wiry muscles were still hanging in there. Except for my gut. The guy had a little paunch on him. Not doing your sit-ups? I peeked down my shirt. Normally that would have grossed me out, but lately I seemed to be adjusting to wearing other people's skins.

Something caught my eye. Marks on the old guy's belly. So I unbuttoned and pulled off his shirt.

Wolf shook his head and turned his back on us. What's up,

Wolf? You don't like starting from scratch?

The farmer's tan was striking. Tanned old skin on his face and arms. Bleached white skin, not too old looking, under his shirt.

The marks on his belly were like something written in ink, upside down and backwards in the mirror.

I looked down and read it easily. *"The reports of my death have been greatly exaggerated."*

Huh? Whose death was exaggerated? Marko's? Or did Pops know what was going to happen and write me a message? That thought really creeped me out. I read it again and again. It was like some omen, or a prediction about life as a jumper.

Nameless thought it was just something Mark Twain once said.

Mark Twain was a jumper? Damn. Who knew?

But Pops thought it was just something he had to say after the shooting to get paid his blood money.

Why?

Wolf thought it was obvious. Challenge and response. It was something a spy does to prove it's really him.

Pops had to prove he was Pops? Oh, yeah! If the two kills had happened in the wrong order, I'd have jumped into Pops. Well, that's what happened. But Pops had stayed alive long enough to pass the challenge and response test. If I had jumped into Pops a bit sooner, I wouldn't have his short-term memories and I wouldn't have passed the verbal test. They would have known I was still alive—in Pop's body. They would have—

Would have what? Killed me. No. Clubbed me and chained me up in a basement somewhere. That seemed likely. So if killing the sniper had gone as planned, I'd be dead with no one to jump into when Wolf died. Or if the kill had gone wrong, I'd screw up the Mark Twain phrase and they'd bag me. Either way, I'd be taken out.

It was pretty obvious I was lucky to be alive and on the loose.

Interesting. My killers planned for only two scenarios. The sniper dies *before* Wolf dies, then I'm perma-dead with no living killer to jump into. Or the kill sequence gets screwed up, I jump across the river into Pops, then I flunk the challenge and response and they haul me off to a dungeon.

But that last scenario was seriously interesting, because it was a way to teleport a jumper. One moment I was over at Wolf's house, the next moment they had me across the river.

That had some very cool possibilities.

Like, the syndicate could hide a bomb under a jumper's bed in Austin, then get some unsuspecting guy in Rome to make a call that triggers the bomb. Yeah, then the Austin jumper beams into the killer's body in Rome. Cool. The syndicate could just skip a bag over the killer's head and capture a jumper. Something to think about. A way to kidnap a jumper halfway around the globe.

Oh! Oh! Like, they could send an astronaut to Mars—a one way trip for a regular astronaut. He lands on the red planet and lives there for months doing science until he starts dying from all the radiation. Then the astronaut pushes a button that kills me while I'm watching TV on Earth. Then like magic, I'm in his body on Mars. Awesome! I check out Mars for a while, get comfortable with his memories, then someone on Earth pushes another button that kills me in the astronaut's body, and bam! I'm back on Earth with all of the astronaut's memories and knowledge inside my mind. For me, it's an instant trip to Mars, three days of sightseeing, then an instant trip back.

Of course, a few people would need to die. But talk about a seriously twisted way to travel.

Hey, a few days on Mars would be really nice. I could use a vacation. A jumper vacation. Maybe that's what we do for travel.

Too bad NASA doesn't know about jumpers. But I could see how jumper spies could move all over Earth super fast. Then all jumpers should have a remote kill switch embedded in them, to teleport them. Captain Comms should have thought of that. Yeah. Then if one of us got captured, Peter would get a normal to push the kill button and we could beam out instantly.

Good thing the CIA didn't know about jumpers.

More importantly, I could see how jumpers would begin to think of normals as expendable—just a transportation capsule for us demigods.

I wondered if Wolf had a little C-4 explosive tucked inside him somewhere. If he did, it was now useless. Maybe Pops was wired to die? Nah. No way. No one planned that far ahead. Or did they? Did

Jack put a kill chip in Pops?

More paranoia. But maybe I should check Pops for scars and suspicious lumps of C-4 under his skin. It wouldn't take much. An embedded cyanide capsule with a nano explosive charge and a remote. Possible. Very possible. I should check.

Maybe later. I was feeling really tired. And loopy. Sleep. That's what the old guy's head needed most.

Never mind. I could see I was already in bed. Funny how that happened. Daydreaming while my passengers drove. It felt like I'd looked out the window and discovered we were already there. So I pulled the covers up so my four passengers could get some rest. Four and a half passengers if you counted the sniper. Five and a half if you counted me, too.

Wait. Was I really five and a half guys rolled into one? It seemed like more. A lot more.

Let's see: I started as Marko, killed by Martoni, killed by Nameless, killed by Wolf, killed by Snip the sniper, killed by Pops. Wait. Did I leave anyone out? Count again? Okay, well, somebody wanted a recount.

I went to sleep recounting myselves.

4.2 Peddle Faster

After my nap, Pops seemed a little better. On the other hand, getting out of bed was a lot harder than expected. Old bones. Old joints. The old guy was really stiff and creaky.

We pushed. We pulled. Eventually we got Pops to his feet. Everything hurt. Everything ached. We were standing on swollen feet. Our muscles felt like we'd barely survived our first day with a drill sergeant. It crossed my mind that old people had this unwritten rule not to tell kids what old age was really like. Yeah, because people became gnarled old trees. Leaves fell. Branches broke. Sap stopped flowing.

The downhill side of life was really shocking.

Good thing I could keep jumping into young bodies.

Except for right now. Now was a problem.

I pushed Pops around to get him going. He was seriously stiff from today's run through the hills. Sitting was a problem because of all the popping sounds when he stood up. Kinda scary, but he thought that was normal.

If Jack's hit man, Doc, showed up, Wolf would have a devil of a time trying to defend us with this old body. Doc would rip us to shreds. Or maybe Doc would cut us some slack and let us warm up, then rip us to shreds.

Doc versus Wolf would have been an excellent battle. Doc was savage. Wolf was cunning. Both were ruthless killers. My money would be on Wolf—bigger and more calculating. But Doc versus Pops? Even with Wolf behind the wheel, it would be a quick bone snapping defeat.

On the plus side, I could tell that Pops was a determined old cuss. Martoni and Nameless complained all the time. Not Pops.

Hell, even Wolf got whiny when things didn't go his way. Not Pops. Pops was like this slow motion tug boat. Slow as river mud, but determined to keep plowing along.

Good for you, Pops. Keep it going, old man.

An automated porch light went on. Then a lamp in the living room. Hell, it was getting dark outside and we didn't have a plan. Wolf said we were fine. Darkness was in our favor.

Fine. We had darkness. Where do we go? Stock up on food at the grocery store? Take Pops out for pizza. Maybe a hit a singles bar?

Who said that?

Or maybe head back to Wolf's place to make contact with Peter and Sonya?

They'd be watching for that.

They? Who put out a hit on Wolf? What were we supposed to do, anyway?

Hell, we knew nothing. Shouldn't we be doing recon or something?

No answer.

So what's it going to be, Wolf? Take the old guy out into the night to kick some butt? Good luck with that. He was having a hard enough time getting up and down the stairs.

And what about the dead sniper? By now, the cops had found the old man's pickup truck, searched the area, found the sniper's body and his high-tech rifle, checked out all the foot prints, and probably ID'd the body. They'd be looking for Pops.

Get a brain, Wolf. We were in a wanted man.

Darkness was still on Wolf's mind.

Oh, yeah? Darkness was our friend? Good thing the cops hadn't discovered high-lumen flashlights, or headlights, or those gawdawful high-beams they use when they pull you over for speeding at night.

We were doomed.

I sat Pops in a chair.

Nameless said we had a bag of cash, so we should head over to the nearest strip club. The cops would never look for us there.

Yeah, right.

Okay, it had some appeal. Getting "busted" in a strip joint could be a lot of fun. Even Pops liked that idea.

On second thought, topless babes in the old man's lap would probably give him an accidental heart attack. Not so good. Perma-death for me. Well, it wasn't a bad way to go, but I had a lot of unfinished business.

Don't worry, Pops. If I get to wear a young man again we'll have a good time with it. I promise.

That got me thinking about how to kill Jack, assuming we bumped into his sorry ass in the dark. Four ways to kill a jumper. The most obvious way was the one we'd just survived: Arrange for the killer to die *before* the jump happens. I could easily imagine Peter describing that one. How would it go?

A jumper and his pet python walk into a bar. The jumper orders a rum and coke. His python orders a big juicy rat. "We don't serve snakes," says the bartender as he secretly poisons the rum and coke. The jumper drinks and starts foaming at the mouth. The python tries the Heimlich maneuver, but it's no good. The bartender laughs maniacally, "Bwahahaha! I just poisoned you and there's nothing you or your stupid snake can do to keep you alive." The python slithers over the bar and wraps himself around the bartender's head. "Mmph," mumbles the bartender just before the python snaps his neck and kills him. "No!" shouts the jumper, because his killer just died before the jump.

The moral of that story was: Make sure your trusty snake knows you're a jumper. Which reminded me of Rema, my trusty sidekick. Not my python, maybe not even my sidekick. But I could pop over for a visit tonight. She'd give me a hard time, but she might be able to help.

Or maybe I should find that watertight case I'd buried near the power lines. Guns and more cash might be useful.

Lots to think about.

Funny thing—I was now standing in an empty garage. Appar-ently one of my passengers went looking for some wheels while I was daydreaming. House without necessities. Garage without vehicles. All too logical. It was a house for showing off, not for living in.

Now what? Sneak over to Wolf's place? Try to make contact with Sonya? Go over to Billy Bob's house and try to kill him again? Get a taxi to Rema's house? Grab a shovel and dig up my gun, cash, keys, and emergency gear? Use those keys to get into the State Theater?

So what's it gonna be, Wolf? Dark enough for you?

No answer.

Fine. So what are the other ways to kill a jumper? An accident? Martoni had an idea. A jumper walks into a bar and his drink is poisoned. Seemed to be a recurring theme. And ... uh ... the bartender puts 10 pills on the counter. "I've just poisoned you. Nine of these pills contain the antidote, but the other one is super poison and will kill you instantly." What does the jumper do?

Wolf simply wanted to kill the bartender. But the rest of my passengers said the jumper should just pick a pill and take his chances. Good odds he'd pick the antidote.

Duh. No way, guys! If the jumper voluntarily chose a pill, and it was the super poison, it would amount to suicide. Besides, the bartender could have been lying about the pills. Maybe they were all fast acting poison—then the jumper would be killing himself.

The right answer was to do nothing. If the whole thing was a bartender joke, the jumper could punch him in the face and walk out. If the drink was really poisoned, then the jumper would die and get the bartender's body.

But taking a pill when you're told it could kill you, was inviting suicide.

Come on, guys. This is Jumper-Think 101.

Note to self: Knowingly risking my life was risking perma-death. Inaction and a guaranteed jump was better than doing something that could get myself killed.

Then Nameless came up with a different scenario. A jumper gets into a small plane. The pilot takes off. Several minutes later the pilot puts on the only parachute, takes the key out of the ignition, and bales out. The jumper is forced to land the plane—forced into a high risk situation. The jumper can't just sit there and do nothing, because letting the plane crash was like wanting death and that made it suicide. Or if the jumper tried to land but crashed, then it's his own damn fault and it's an accidental death—a perma-death.

So sitting it out was suicide. Landing badly was an accident. And both led to perma-death. Nameless thought the only way out was to land safely.

Thanks, Nameless. You're really making my brain hurt. I suppose you could kill a jumper with an accident. But if you set it up, didn't it make you the killer? And there had to be a way out, otherwise it wasn't really an accident. Right? Either way, trying to take out a jumper with an accident was asking for seriously unpredictable results.

Pops thought it would be easier to perma-kill a jumper if you just gave him free parachute jumping lessons—for life. Because, if you bailed out of a plane often enough with a parachute, you were bound to die eventually. Or free race car driving lessons. Or free rock climbing lessons. Or free bull riding lessons. Or—

Martoni had another idea. A jumper walks into a bar and orders a drink. The bartender puts drugs in it like they sell on TV commercials. You know, the ones that make you suicidal.

Huh?

Then the bartender puts some sad music on the jukebox, lays a bunch of guns and knives on the counter, and then goes for a nice long walk. The jumper decides to kill himself. The end.

Seriously, Martoni?

I looked around, but the guys in my head were waiting for me to shoot that one down.

Okay. First of all, the bartender drove the jumper into killing himself. That made the bartender a killer. Right? Well, it seemed right to me.

So did we just figure out three ways to kill a jumper? One: Kinda set up an accident. Two: Kinda set up a suicide. Three: Kill the killer before any jump takes place. The suicide and the accident seemed very problematic. Miscalculate, and the jumper simply gets a new body. But if you really could obliterate the killer before the jumper died—yeah, that could easily work.

I was back to thinking I'd just gotten off lucky. If Pops had killed the sniper instantly, I'd be perma-dead. Pops would still be himself, but Martoni, Nameless, Wolf, and I would all be history.

Apparently Wolf thought it was time to go, because we stepped out the front door and started walking down the street. Good. I was tired of thinking.

So we walked along the posh houses and dark streets for several minutes.

Then we stopped. This house had kids. Wolf didn't use words, but that's the impression he seemed to have.

Good. We were going to a house with kids. That's nice, Wolf. We were in really deep shit and Wolf thought kids would help us. Why didn't I think of that?

So after walking past a dozen McMansions, Wolf decided to make a beeline up this driveway—because it had kids. Really?

I watched as we tripped a security light and Wolf grabbed a girl's bicycle from the driveway.

Good idea, Wolf, but not cool.

I paused just long enough to throw five or six hundred dollars into the driveway. I could afford it, but mainly I didn't need any more bad karma. Especially from a little girl, even if she was a rich spoiled brat. But we didn't know that. For all we knew, she had evil parents and she was just waiting until the day she could escape. Maybe the cash was better than the bike. Yeah, because she'd need the cash for bus fare to Vegas. Didn't all girls run to Vegas because of evil parents? Showgirls with broken hearts.

I might have been over-thinking the situation.

Note to self: Now that I was multi-brained, over-thinking things was something to watch out for.

We peddled through the night like there was no tomorrow. Go, old man! Go!

Nothing like an old guy flirting with cardiac arrest on a girl's bicycle at night to draw attention. On second thought, it was Austin.

As we passed under the streetlights, pink paint and plastic diamond-bling reflected off the handlebars—reflecting the power of budding womanhood.

And we were cool with it. We were a bat from hell. We wore a frickin' dynamo of an old man. We were the Multi-Mind—the night beast. We were an unpredictable body on a mission. There were terrible wrongs that needed to be righted. We were unstoppable. We were the stuff of night terrors.

So we flew into the night. A mental inferno on a fucking rich girl's bike.

* * *

An hour later we rolled into Rema's neighborhood, a neighborhood where teens never sleep. We approached a streetlight with a pack of hoodies under it. They turned to look at me. Not your usual passer-by. I slowed. Rang the bell on the blinged out girl's bike. Gave them a knowing nod and my best Dexter smile—the one who knows the dark side. They watched intently as I slowly passed. We were all brothers under the skin. They might have wondered what manner of super-villain I was—what night ghoul now passed onto their turf.

I didn't look back. No need. Peddle onward, Marko. The mission was plain on my face. Some forces can't be stopped. That was me.

I rolled up to Rema's. Hard to say what time it was. Hard to say anything because Pops was winded, but at least he was still pumping blood. I opened Rema's gate and walked the bike along the cement walkway and up a few steps to her front door. The porch light was on. Good, my sidekick was home.

I straightened my hair and my face, then rang the bell.

An eye peeked through the beveled glass in the door. Rema's questioning eye.

I waved.

She observed me for several long seconds, then decided to shout through the closed door. "I ain't buyin'!"

"I ain't sellin', Rema."

"Good, then you can just be on your way, old man. So make that u-turn and thank your lucky stars you took my advice."

"It's me. Marko."

Something hit the door. A fist? Her head? Hard to say.

"Look, sucker, I'm tired of dealin' with your dead self. So get your maggoty undead ass off my property." Her eye watched me. "Now would be just fine by me."

"I need your help."

"Hell, you always need my help. So what's in the bag this time? More unwanted cash?"

Bag? Oh, yeah. "Actually, it's cash. But not much, so I'm going to hang onto it this time."

"Is that so?"

"I need to borrow a shovel, Rema."

"Now do I look like I've got too many shovels? What you need a shovel for, anyway? You gonna bury yourself? 'Cause if you do, I might just have one."

"I need it for digging something up. Let's talk inside, okay?"

"Diggin' what up? Your maggoty friends?"

"Funny. I'll also need to borrow a flashlight." Rema was thinking about it, so I thought I'd fill in the blanks. "For seeing in the dark."

"I know what a damn flashlight does. Fool. I ain't got none of those things, so best you get yourself outta here before I call the cops."

Yeah, that would be bad. The last thing I needed was for some cop to see me wearing Pops, the guy who left his pickup truck at the scene of a dead sniper with a smart rifle. I supposed they ID'd that sniper by now. I was kinda curious who put a hole in Wolf's perfect hide.

Nameless thought we'd need some food because Pops was running on fumes. And a backpack would be good. Never go anywhere without one, especially if we were digging up goodies.

The door opened unexpectedly. "Don't just stand there, old man. Get your sorry ass in here."

"Okay if I bring the bicycle in the house?"

"Hell, no." She grabbed me by the collar and hauled me in. "Look, whoever the hell you think you are, I'm givin' you all of 30 seconds to explain yourself. Then I'm tossin' you out."

"Like I said, I'm Marko—"

"Hell, I figured that out as soon as I saw you."

"Really? How'd you know it was me?"

"How'd I know? *How'd I know?* Hun', you still got that face problem—one second it's goin' one way, the next it's goin' the other. I thought you were gonna get that fixed."

Crap. I held my face steady and walked to the sofa.

"Don't be sittin' on my couch. You ain't stayin' that long."

"Fine. I'm in a hurry anyway. I'd like to borrow a shovel, and a—"

"What? You think I'm just gonna hand some twitchy-faced old man my shovel? Seriously?"

"Fine." I reached into the paper sack and pulled out a bill. "Then I'm buying your shovel."

"Twenty dollars? When's the last time you bought a shovel? Ain't no shovel cost twenty dollars."

"It's a used shovel."

"The hell it is! It's nearly new."

"That's used."

"Look, you gonna stand there and argue with me? 'Cause if you're gonna do that, you can just march yourself outta here and go find your own damn shovel."

"Okay, $40."

"This ain't no damn broken down shovel. Now for $80 . . ."

"Seriously?"

"Don't make me raise my price. Eighty's lookin' awful cheap right about now. Know what I'm sayin'?"

"Okay, okay. Here. And here's $20 for the flashlight—it's probably plastic."

"Fine by me. Will you be wantin' batteries with that flashlight?"

"Rema—" I almost told her that sidekicks don't sell superheroes batteries, but I knew she hated to be called a sidekick.

"Don't you Rema me. You come knockin' at my door in the middle of the night and expect me to just turn into Walmart or somethin'. Well, that's not happenin'."

I glanced at a clock on her bookshelf. "It's a little after 10. Nowhere near the middle of the night."

"There you go arguin' with me again. With an attitude like that, you might be surprised how much batteries cost."

I handed her $20 for the flashlight and $20 for the batteries.

"What else you need?"

"Uh, a backpack and a sack lunch."

"What'd you say? You want me to fix you a damn sandwich in

the middle of the night? I suppose you'd like it in a paper bag with an apple, and a napkin to wipe your little old face. Oh, and you'll be wantin' a bag of chips to go with that, won't you? 'Cause I know you will."

Yeah. Why argue? It sounded really good. I skipped the haggling and pulled out $100.

Rema just stared at me.

"You're the best, Rema."

"Damn straight." She snatched the money from my hand. "Good thing your money's still good around here. Well, come on then."

I followed her into the kitchen and noted a new dinette set.

"Don't sit there. Here, use this chair. It's easier to clean."

I sat my sweaty old-man self in a plain wooden chair.

Rema started assembling sandwiches, watching me carefully out of the corner of her eye. "So how'd you get so old, Marko?"

"It's a long story."

"I'm sure it is. But if you'll recall, I said to come back as a handsome black gentleman. I hate to say it, but you pretty much missed the mark on that one. So what happened to the strapping white hunk you were . . . uh . . . wearin' last time?"

Poor Wolf. "He's dead. Basically."

Rema paused, staring down at the mayonnaise knife in her hand. "Now that surely makes my heart sad to hear. Such a handsome man. Such a waste. Those broad shoulders, that fine manly rear end. Mmm, mmm!" She turned to me sharply. "You did share that fine butt with some deserving ladies, didn't you?"

Uh. I guess I did. Well, it was hard not to. "Yeah."

"Good—" Rema caught sight of my wedding ring. "Hold on. Are you married?"

"No. I mean, Pops was. But I gather he lost his wife several years ago."

"Damn. He must have loved her—still wearing that ring and all. But you killed him. Basically, I mean. 'Cause that's what you do."

"I didn't kill him. Technically, he killed me."

"Technically, I'm not buyin' it. Like I just said, that's what you do to people. Except when you explained it awhile back, I wasn't really listening to all that dribble falling out of your mouth, so the facts of the body jumping kinda escaped me. You know? But you can't tell me he's not dead, 'cause what I'm lookin' at is just one dead guy wearin' another dead guy's body. Do I have that straight, or what? So what'd you do with the rest of him? You know, whatever it was that made this old man's body move and talk and shit. You know what I'm talkin' 'bout?"

I tapped the back of my head. "Pops is still in here, somewhere. In the back, I think."

"So what you're sayin' is that his soul is still in there, somewhere. Right?"

"I'm guessing not. All I have in here are some of his memories and probably some hindbrain skills."

"Don't get all technical on me. Is he in there or not?"

"Uh. Basically—maybe."

"Sounds like you don't know what's goin' on in there. So how 'bout lettin' him speak for himself."

"He can't talk. None of them can."

"Then he's dead."

"Do I look dead?"

"Hell, I don't know what I'm lookin' at. I guess some folks'd call you a god-awful mash-up. Bits of dead guys all shoved together in one hell of a nasty meat pie."

Great. I was a mash-up.

Rema put a sandwich on a plate and handed it to me. "Eat this. You asked for a sandwich, so I'm assumin' that dead old man can still eat. Or maybe your zombie mash-up only wants the meat? Well, in this case it's turkey baloney."

I opened up my sandwich. Nothing inside but mayo and turkey baloney. I might have had some disappointment on my face.

"Look, Marko, if you're wonderin' where the greens are, it's been my experience that children and men pick that part out, and I'm not about to waste perfectly good fresh spinach greens. Next time you order something, best you negotiate the details. That's a general rule most folks should apply to everythin' in life."

"Can I get something to drink?"

"This ain't no happy hour, and we never discussed the price of drinks. But you know what? I'm feeling inclined to help a poor messed up composite like yourself, so tap water is on the house." She pulled a glass out of the cupboard. "Ain't nothin' finer than East Austin water, fresh from the tap. Mmm, mmm! Unfiltered in all its glory. Here you go, old Marko. I was gonna wish you good health, but it kinda seems like you're making your own rules 'bout what healthy livin's all about."

She handed me the water, then pulled a flashlight out of a drawer. "Let's just see if this still works. Well, yes it does." She set it on the counter. "You know, I do believe I never said 'maggoty' until I met you. Now I just want to use it all the time. Speaking of undead, let me get that shovel you requested. I'm sure you're gonna put it to good use. Hell, you might even wear it out. Just remember to get all your grave digging supplies at Rema's Post-Death Emporium."

She stared at me for a moment. "The sandwich goes in your mouth, old man. So eat it while you're still able."

I pushed it into my mouth, hoping the old man's teeth were up to the task.

Rema seemed satisfied with that and left the room.

She returned a minute later with a shovel. "I'll leave this on the front porch next to your girl's bike." She waved a hand at me. "Not even gonna ask where that came from."

"Someone might steal it." I pointed to the overpriced shovel.

"What? This shovel? The hell they will. You forget who you're talkin' to. I teach folks young and let 'em know you never *ever* let your guard down. That's what I do. Hell, kids in this neighborhood know better than to mess with me. Grown men know that, too. But if I do get any trouble, forget callin' the cops 'cause all they do is write shit down. If there's trouble that concerns me, I take matters into my own hands, if you get what I'm sayin'. And don't get the idea my front yard is littered with broken teeth, 'cause it ain't. The *word* is the power. And I use the *word*. And if the *word* don't work, I use another *word*. 'Cause sticks and stones will break your bones, but *words* will crush your ever lovin' self esteem to pulp and make you wish you were never born, and *words* will make your ears bleed until you wish you were dead. You get my drift?" She frowned. "Or maybe you don't, 'cause you're already dead."

I winced like my ears were already bleeding, then touched the side of my neck to see if they really were.

Rema nodded. "Good to know I'm gettin' through to you. Now finish your sandwich like a good little old man, and I'll make you another—with greens, but only if you'll eat it. Greens are good for folks, even ones like you. Anyway, they couldn't mess you up any more than you already are. That's for damn sure."

* * *

A half hour later, I finished the second sandwich—with greens. Well, I do like greens—just not in pizza. I would have liked to have said Rema and I had a pleasant conversation, but it was just her monologue about life, and preschoolers, and the importance of breakfast for alertness in school.

More importantly, I learned my sidekick's superpower was the *word*. Who knew mere words could be such a serious weapon?

Rema even complimented me on my newfound maturity and vocabulary. But personally, I think she was influenced by the old man I was now wearing. When I looked like Wolf, women pretty much went ape shit, although most tried to hide it. Looking like Pops meant they treated me like Pops.

That was sad.

Sad, because people can't help but judge each other by their looks. I wanted to run around Rema's neighborhood telling everyone we weren't our bodies, we were the amazing stuff inside. But they would have just thought I was a crazy old white dude. Crazy, yes. No doubt about it. But I was still Marko. Still only 22. And I still had a great perma-tan somewhere deep down inside me, but sadly, no one but me could see it.

People judged me by my skin. They always would. There was simply no changing that fact. And today my skin was wrinkled and my teeth were sketchy. At least I could jump and change that part.

Note to self: You can't change the world, but at least you can change yourself. I could always get a new body. But more importantly, could I really change myself internally?

Out on Rema's porch, I stood alone. Just an old guy standing in the yellow bug light's glow, surrounded by darkness. There were no goodbyes between my sidekick and me, no "screw evil" high fives, no warm hugs like dynamic duos always give each other.

Nameless was pretty sure Busty Babe gave Mentor Man warm hugs. Really? So where was Busty Babe when we needed her? Nameless wanted to start interviewing for a new sidekick—the one he so richly deserved.

Not now, Nameless.

What was I doing before Nameless interrupted? Oh, yeah. I put on Rema's *Super Preschooler* backpack, now loaded with the cash I'd earned for killing myself, the flashlight, extra batteries, an extra baloney sandwich (no mayo, Rema said mayo would go bad so it had no-fructose ketchup instead—whatever), a couple of fruit cups, and some boxed juice.

I guess Rema's other superpower was dealing with kids. It seemed that weird powers were the byproduct of owning several daycare centers.

Note to self: Rema's superpowers were *word* and *kid control*.

I grabbed the shovel and rolled the girl's bike out to the street. As I pushed the bike, it struck me that Rema actually had real powers. My only power was getting killed.

Awesome. Right?

Actually, it kinda sucked.

With the shovel laid across the handlebars, I peddled off to dig up my sad box of possessions. Yeah, sad stuff like wonderful piles of cash, assorted guns, and Wolf's backup Rolex. Stuff that would make me happy.

Then what?

Grab some supplies at an all night supermarket? Then enjoy death by chocolate under the State Theater? Going solo had its appeal. Hell, every one of me was a loner. I could easily do life solo.

Or should I risk my life trying to make contact with my jumper pals? Jumpers must have weird reunions all the time. *Hey, guys! Check out my new bod! Wicked to be old, right? You like 'em old, don't you Sonya? No? Babe, it's still me, Wolfie—only worse.*

Or maybe I should swing by Uncle Billy Bob Wyville's to settle some unfinished business. Wearing his gator-bait bod would be a step up from the body Pops had. Sorry, old man. No disrespect. Besides, Billy Bob had social skills—something I clearly needed in my mental back seat.

Hey. It was good to have options. Things were looking up.

As I peddled into the night, many of me smiled.

4.3 Death Warmed Over

Around midnight, Pops finally made it to the area where I'd buried Wolf's treasure. Not easy in the dark with so few landmarks. Not easy trying to steer a girl's bike while holding a shovel and waving around a flashlight.

But especially not easy because the old man I was wearing was completely exhausted. Peddling up and down the hills west of Austin was brutal for him.

Next time, I'd hide my emergency jumper supplies somewhere easier to get to. No telling what body I'd be in next time. Better planning, Marko. Better planning.

The taxi driver in me was pretty sure this was the right spot—confirmed by the high power lines silhouetted against the light-scatter from downtown Austin.

As I got off the bike, it crossed all of my minds that walking across fields full of rattlesnakes and cactus with only a flashlight to guide me was less than ideal. At least Pops was a proper rural Texan and wore boots.

So we walked through the brush and around the fire ant mounds, keeping an eye out for snakes. Snakes slept at night, didn't they?

Finally I arrived at the nearest electric tower. So which tower was it? Damn. I'd memorized the tower's serial number and now I couldn't remember it. Guys? A little help here?

No answer.

Okay, forget the number. I'd stacked up rocks near the tower to help identify it. Look for the rocks, guys.

* * *

Two hours later, I'd found the tower, found the spot where I'd buried the stuff, dug it up, and then spent a very long time trying to find my girl's bike again.

A massive waste of time, but I did eventually find the bike, so I counted it as a success.

So there I was, sitting on the pink bicycle with Rema's backpack and Wolf's weatherproof case filled with goodies. The shovel was tossed into the bushes—too much to carry. It was dark, Pops was beyond exhausted, and I still needed to peddle out of these damned hills.

That's when it struck me like a dump truck flipping over on the freeway—I was bad at planning. Yeah, the truth hurt, but there it was. All my life, I'd been bad at planning. I'd never realized it before, maybe because I always thought I had my shit together. But my shit wasn't together. It was never together, because my life was seriously unplanned.

I'd always assumed that life was just what happened to people. I mean, why blame yourself when you can blame life? Right? Events were outside my control. So why plan? Things just happened. Things seemed easier when all I had to do was deal with life's ups and downs.

But maybe there was more to life than just dealing with it. I was always telling myself to just deal with it. Maybe I should also tell myself to make it happen.

That sounded good. Make it happen, Marko. You want something, Marko? Then make it happen.

Right. But that led to planning. And that's where I really sucked.

Okay, so that unpleasant bit of truth was finally out in the open. I couldn't plan myself out of a wet paper bag. Great. Now what? Get a self-help book on planning? Get a calendar planner thing?

Somehow that didn't seem good enough. And besides, my life was kinda unusual now. Kinda unusual? Duh.

That left me with two options. One: fix myself. Two: hang around people who were good at planning.

Fixing myself sounded hard. But Sonya was good at planning. I didn't exactly trust Peter, but he seemed like a planner, too.

Bottom line? I needed people. Not just any people—people like me. People who knew my situation, liked me anyway, and occasionally tried to help. Loner or not, people mattered.

God, I wanted my old life back again! Not my Martoni life or my Nameless life. Sorry, Pops, not your life either. But Marko Santana's life was good, even if it was aimless and lacked a destination. And Wolf's life was seriously cool, in a dangerous kind of way.

But there was no going back to any of those. There was only going forward, and that meant planning it.

Goals, Marko. What was my first goal?

That's when I noticed my old hands shaking. I was driving Pops into the ground. He'd die before he made it downtown to the State Theater. Hell, he'd probably die before we even made it to Wolf's place, or Billy Bob's.

So what were my immediate goals?

Survive long enough to get a better body. Get with Sonya again. Help the jumper revolution. Become a real hero.

Cool. But did I have any realistic goals?

Use one of the burner phones in the case to call a cab.

A cab to where?

The State Theater for some rest? Wolf's place to reconnect with my pals? Or Billy Bob's place to get killed and snag his disgusting, but well rested, body?

The State Theater seemed like a dead end, like it was the path of isolation and surrender. I could picture myself dying there on a prop sofa of a heart attack or a stroke. Just an old man who crawled in somehow and died under the stage. My final curtain call.

No. I wasn't ready to fizzle out just yet. When I finally went, I wanted it to be with my boots on and a smile on my face.

Wolf's place seemed better. But would I run into Sonya, or another hit squad? The thought of Wolf's place made me nervous. Oddly, Wolf wanted to use the pool and the gym. Protein drinks would be good, too. He'd feel better getting back into his old routine.

No. I wanted better odds. Besides, I couldn't shake the feeling that Wolf's place was a trap. Was this my psychic sense guiding me away from there? No telling, but I was determined to listen to that feeling whenever it popped up.

Okay, then what about Billy Bob's? I was too exhausted to put up any kind of fight, even with Wolf's skills. But all I had to do was get killed. We could do that. Right, guys?

No answer, but it sounded good to me. Get killed by Billy Bob. Get his body. Get a cash infusion. Get a car. But I could finally bring down Billy Bob, a major scumbag who was controlling Texas politicians. Hey, maybe I'd find enough dirt on the politicos to bring them down, too.

Sweet.

Then without politicians, Texas could start over again. It would be like pushing the reset button on the whole state. Weird, but I was exhausted and it sounded reasonable.

Comic book heroes needed super-villains. All I needed were power-mad megalomaniacs. The world was full of those. They'd call me The Leveler. Or maybe The Equalizer. Or Anti-Megalo because megalomaniacs would fall in my wake. Anti-Meg for short? Aunt Meg?

Not my best thinking. I needed caffeine and a new body.

Life would be a lot better wrapped in a new skin—an evil skin. I could do this. So make it happen, Marko.

* * *

I peddled to an intersection, ditched the bike, put a battery into one of the burner phones I'd pulled out of Wolf's case, and called a cab with the last of the juice in the battery.

Fifteen minutes later a cautious taxi driver pulled up. No one I knew. Good.

He cracked the window open a little, but kept the door locked. "You called a cab?"

Dumb question. Who else was out here at 3:30 in the morning. "Yeah."

"Where to?"

Just open the damn door. Actually, as a driver I might have been cautious to pick up some sweaty old man with a kid's backpack and an expensive water-tight case. Oh, and there was the new Rolex on my wrist. A trustworthy combination. "I'm headed to my son-in-law's house over on Mount Bonnell Road near 2222."

He took a moment to think about it.

I held up a couple $20 bills. "I know what you're thinking. I drove a cab, too, back in the day."

He held out his hand like he wanted the money in advance.

No way. "Don't worry, you'll get paid when we get there." Hey, cab drivers never get money up front. Never. Nothing would make me more suspicious than a fare that wanted to pay in advance.

So I might have looked weird, but I did my best to act normal.

The back door unlocked and I got in. "Thanks."

"Got an address?"

Sure, but I wanted to be dropped off where I wouldn't be seen. "I've only been there a couple times. I'll recognize it when I see it."

He started driving. "On Mount Bonnell or 2222? Which is it?"

"Mount Bonnell."

As we drove I could tell there was a lot he wanted to ask me. But sometimes the less you know the better. If cabbies called the cops every time we picked up a possible burglar or someone who might be an abused prostitute, the cops would learn to ignore us. Everyone looked guilty in the rearview mirror. Besides, the night shift was the night shift. If you couldn't handle it, you did something else.

It occurred to me the driver was probably armed. I could threaten him, get shot, and jump into his body. Then I'd be a taxi driver again. Full circle. Except Marko's body was young and Latino handsome. This guy was 40-something East European. Not full circle.

I tried to plan my Billy Bob assault, but I was too tired. So I slouched down and watched the streetlights streak past my window. When was I Marko the taxi driver? What month was this? August. I thought it was August, but it might have been late July. I was killed driving my cab in May. Now I was a tired old man in a taxi a few months later. I wanted to ask the driver what month it was.

Never mind. I could see that conversation ending badly.

* * *

I dreamed I was in a foreign film. At least I thought I was dreaming—it all seemed very real, but romantic and foreign. I was on the beach. It was warm. I was with a beautiful woman and she was Sonya. Her peach colored dress blew seductively in the breeze.

It must have been a romantic movie because I brushed the hair from her face. I saw my hand was young. That was good. Sonya's lips wanted kissing, so of course, I kissed them. It was wonderful. It was wonderful for a long time.

Out of the corner of my eye I saw a big handsome man running on the beach wearing a dress—no, it was only a skirt. Weird, but that's what you get in dreams. No big deal.

Then Sonya slipped her hand between my legs and it felt . . . weird. Weird but good. Weird like something was missing. I checked myself out and found only woman parts. Not good. Somehow I was a woman. Weird, but I've had worse dreams.

The man in the skirt ran up to me and started laughing. Not a mean laugh, but a laugh like life was weird. Yeah, life really was weird. As I turned to look at him, I saw that he was ruggedly handsome. Kinda sexy. No—very sexy with big muscles and big man parts—but in a skirt.

Then he took Sonya in his powerful arms. Because he could. And he could because he was so big, and so rugged, and so handsome. He offered to take me into his arms, too. There was room for both of us. But no way was I gonna do that.

I wanted Sonya back, but he was so manly, so irresistible—skirt or no skirt. Hell, even the woman I was wearing wanted him. So I just stood there and watched as he held my Sonya babe. And it was obvious she wanted him, too.

Everything was seriously messed up. Kinda like life.

"Hey."

I woke up.

"Where now?"

I could see we were on Mount Bonnell. Nice houses lined the street, and ahead were expensive homes tucked behind lots of trees. "This'll do."

He stopped the meter at almost $43 and I immediately pushed $80 his way. "Keep it. You earned it."

"You need a receipt?"

"Nope." I stepped out of the cab with Wolf's case, brushed some of my dirt off the back seat, and started walking south into darkness. He made a u-turn back to 2222 and the light.

* * *

I stood in front of Billy Bob's, but cloaked in deep shadow across the street. Two unexpected cars were parked in his driveway. The last time I was here, it was to get myself killed and jump into Billy Bob. That night, the driveway had been empty, which told me Billy Bob Wyville liked to park in his garage. So whose cars were these? Since it was four in the morning, I was guessing this was a sleepover. Yeah, and who in their right mind would sleep with a dangerous gator-head like Billy Bob?

Who'd drive identical new red Corvettes? Politicians? Very unlikely. Politicians favored big SUVs and oversized pickups.

Doc was high on my list of people to avoid, but he'd be driving something big enough to haul away dead bodies. Something with a thick liner to catch all the blood he enjoyed spilling.

So the cars belonged to relatives? Or maybe flashy women with bad taste in men?

Either way, we were staring at a problem.

On the other hand, I was the one doing the dying. It wasn't like I'd kill Billy Bob and then have to fight off his pissed relatives. No. He'd kill me and I'd get his body. Then I'd just smile and ask his ma from Florida to pass me another beer. Typical day in the Wyville home.

But the vehicles had Texas license plates. Local working girls seemed like the best bet. Maybe Wolf knew them.

That was when I heard the buzz. Weird. Dangerous. Something like an electric weed trimmer. Getting closer. Actually, it sounded like several weed trimmers. I backed up into the bushes. The sound was getting closer, coming from the water behind Billy Bob's house.

It was a little quadcopter. Maybe two or three feet across. Coming straight for me.

Shit. A killer drone.

I braced myself, remembering that I'd come here to be killed. And if Billy Bob was flying it, then that would be ideal.

I waited for the burst of nano machine gun bullets. But it dropped something on a little parachute, except the parachute was messed up by the propeller downdraft.

The quadcopter promptly buzzed away.

Whatever was dropped bounced at my feet. No toxic gas. No explosion. The little package seemed to have a note pinned to it.

I set down the case and picked up the little package, even though all my passengers were in the mood to run away. The note simply said, "Eat me."

Great. Just when I thought my life couldn't get any weirder.

Seriously? Eat what? I was staring at a cute little gift box, and the parachute.

I checked my psychic anxiety level. High anxiety, but I was really inclined to open the box. The guys still wanted to run like hell.

So I started to open my little edible gift. Well, the black bow was a nice touch. Jack would have chosen hot pink, so I thought black was a good sign. Right? Would I find a red pill and a blue pill? That was an interesting thought. One pill would show me the aliens all around me, and the other would make me wake up in the hospital with Martoni's shotgun wound to my head and Marie holding my hand.

At this point in my twisted life, I was rooting for an alien encounter. Keep the weirdness coming. Yeah, just as long as the pills came with instructions. So was the alien encounter the red pill, or the blue pill?

The box was open. Only one pill, not red or blue. The light was bad, but the pill seemed like a pale peach color. Fine, no instructions needed. What now? Shove it into my mouth? Cyanide? What color was cyanide, anyway? Was this a trick to get a jumper to commit suicide?

No one's that dumb.

Right?

Well, someone thought I should eat it. Screw that. I was a total brainiac, not a fool.

I picked the big pill out of the little box. Not a pill, it was something hard but rubbery, and it was oddly shaped.

Nameless and Wolf knew immediately what it was. They wanted me to stick it in my ear.

Oh, right! An ear gizmo from Captain Comms, plus a manly little gift box from Sonya babe.

At least that's what I hoped it was. Or maybe Jack was offering me some jumper hypnotizing tones to make me his twisted sex slave.

Paranoia was my chronic friend.

Oh, hell. I shoved it into my ear.

"Dude, we need the secret password." It sounded like Peter.

"Fuck that shit. Is Sonya okay?"

"Wolf! It's you! She's fine." I could hear Peter talking to someone else in the background. "He's alive. Yeah, I'm sure. Except his new body needs something way stronger than coke-a-chino."

Huh? "Peter? Talk to me."

"Yeah, dude. What happened?"

"Well to start with, your little parachute was useless in the propeller downdraft."

"It's called prop wash, and I'm aware of the issue. What happened when you got shot?"

"It hurt. I died. I jumped into some guy using a smart sniper rifle."

"Seriously? That's so cool."

"Not really. The sniper was brain dead because he'd been shot in the head and left to die. Only I don't seem to have a sniper passenger in me, so I'm guessing he was shot immediately and I wasn't able to pick up his . . . uh . . ."

"Shadow."

"Passenger. So I'm now in the old man who killed the sniper."

"Wait. You—" Peter slammed to a halt. "Dude, do you have any idea how lucky you are?"

"Yeah, I know. I figured it out. I could have been perma-dead."

"You *shoulda* been perma-dead. Man, when you see me again you gotta rub some of that wolfen luck on me. Whoa! First you were like super handsome, and now you should be really dead but you're still kicking ass and taking names."

"I haven't kicked anyone's ass and I'm just about to fall over and die."

"Are you wounded?"

"No. I'm really old and I've been riding a bicycle all over the hill country."

"How old?"

"I think I'm 69."

"That's not so old."

"Don't give me a hard time. How's Sonya? What happened on your end?"

"She's fine. I'm fine. We ran. You should see her when she runs naked. Uber sexy. Man, I'm telling you, when she—"

"Peter!"

"We're fine. Then there's the matter of Brenda. She went inside just before you were shot. Then we . . . uh . . . found her dead in the bathroom."

Brenda? Dead? "Dead how?"

"Dead like a teleport. It's complicated, Wolf. Someday I'll explain it to you."

"It's a jumper teleport using a remote trigger. Brenda must have had an implant that caused death when remotely triggered. So she jumped away somewhere. Where?"

"How do you know about that?"

"I figured out lots of things. You really ought to try dying more times. It really ups your mental powers."

"Dude, the only thing it does is make you mental. And cocky. But mostly psycho."

Yeah, like Peter even knew what I was going through. "So send around the car, Peter. Jetpack? Send something because I'm totally exhausted."

"You're exhausted? Look, I've got multiple teams with boots on the ground in your area. I've had a small army prepping all day and night in case you popped up again. You think you're exhausted? Just look at us. In fact, I've got eyes on Sonya right now and she's . . . well, she's still looking better than a body has the right to, if you know what I mean, and I'm sure you do."

"You know you're as good as dead, don't you?"

Peter laughed. "Love you too, bro. Now let's get on with the mission at hand."

"What mission? My extraction?"

"You went to Billy Bob's for a reason, didn't you?"

Pops couldn't take it anymore, so he crumpled slowly to the ground. Hang in there, old man. I'm working on it. "How do you know what I'm here for?"

"You tried to kill Billy Bob, remember? But you screwed that up and jumped into Wolf instead. Then you couldn't keep up the Wolf act, and that set off everyone's alarm bells. So you came to Jack's attention, and mine. And now you're back to finish the job. No surprise. Dude, you're in the market for a new body, and we'd all like to help you get Billy Bob toasted. Good that you're in place and ready to go. Good that we hustled our butts off and we're set up to support you."

"I don't need you, Peter. I brought a gun and I know how to wave it around and get myself killed."

"Really? Like the last time you broke into Billy Bob's house and waved your gun around? You put a nice hole in his desk, remember? So tell me, Wolf, how'd that go for you? Hmm?"

"I'll make it work this time."

"Right. And you know who's in the house?"

I was getting tired of playing guessing games. "You know, Nerd Boy, you could just tell me."

"Hey, Waldo. I suppose you've already figured out Billy Bob's a jumper?" He listened to my stunned silence. "No? I didn't think so. Well, he's not about to go killing anyone he hasn't verified to be a normal. And if he wanted someone dead, he'd use a pro like Doc or the old Wolf. You see, I've got intel you only wish you had. Welcome to the real world, Waldo."

Damn. Wyville was like us?

"You got kinda quiet there, Wolf. Maybe you'd like to take Billy Bob's hide for real this time, instead of getting clubbed from behind."

"How do you know all the details?"

"Jack has eyes on all his operatives, and Billy Bob is no exception. But I have all the feeds hacked, I have all the bugs tapped. I see everything Jack sees. I hear everything he hears."

"Except you have no clue where Jack is."

"He was in Austin, like you said." Peter sounded like it was no big deal.

"And I'm supposed to trust your intel?"

"Yes. Implicitly. Besides, the D.C. glitch was a one-off."

"And putting us all in the hot tub so Wolf could get perma-killed was your idea?"

"No, dude, the hot tub was a joint decision—and it was awesome until you showed up. Besides, intel is subject to imperfections. But we're good now. We're all in position. This time you'll really kill Billy Bob. So don't give me any flack. This mission's a go."

"No. Your missions are coated in crap. If I hang with you, it's going to kill me."

"For the record, this one's Sonya's mission. Sure, the past wasn't perfect. That's life. Hold on, Sonya wants to talk."

"Wolf?" It was Sonya.

I melted. "Yeah?" I wish I knew how she did that.

"I just wanted to whisper in your ear a little. Okay?"

Not much of a question. "Can you see me?"

"Not clearly. You're in shadow and Peter's infrared lights are stronger near the house."

"That's for the best. I'm not the Wolf you knew."

"And loved?"

"I hope so. But that's changed, because I've changed." Yeah, I was now just an old man. Well, I sure as hell felt like one.

"No second-guessing me. You'll always be Wolf to me."

I wanted to believe that—so much. But I had nothing to answer her with.

"This is our fucking hooyah deal. Remember?" She sounded strong.

"I remember."

"And you're still my man?"

"What there is left of me."

"Then I'm still your babe. I need everything you've got, Wolf."

"But—"

"Forget who you're wearing. Be who you are down deep. Be the man I need right now. Can you do that?"

"Yeah. You've got it." Funny how my paranoia slipped away when I was with Sonya. If you couldn't trust the love you feel, then life itself was perma-screwed.

Or maybe I was already screwed—already falling off the cliff to my destruction. And it was Sonya holding out the only hand I trusted. It didn't matter if she caught me or if I fell. It was the act of reaching out that I needed—that I wanted so desperately to give her, as well.

Wolf woke up. We all did. "You have me, Sonya. Just tell me what to do."

4.4 Rematch

Sonya said some more wonderful words, then put Peter on the line again. "Dude, go up and ring the doorbell."

"You're kidding." Breaking glass was threatening. It was an invitation to kill me, and that was my goal. Ringing the doorbell wouldn't get Billy Bob to kill me. "I need to attack, not sell newspaper subscriptions."

"Dude? You want to break glass again? Just follow orders."

"Then I'll carry a gun."

"No gun. Just ring the damn bell."

Fine. I stashed Wolf's case and Rema's backpack under some bushes. No telling how this mission would go down. "Okay. I'm walking up to the front door." I felt like a dope. "Still walking."

"Man, you don't look so good."

It was really late at night, but I knew Peter had infrared cameras hidden somewhere around Billy Bob's house. "Can Sonya see me? In my old man suit?"

"No, bro. No one sees you like I see you. Besides, she's busy. Just remember the two women inside are normals working for us, so try not to hurt them. And don't say anything about jumping. Oh, and before you ring the bell, pull out your earpiece and drop it where you can find it later. You're about to go comms-off, bro, so take it like it comes."

"Take what like it comes?"

"Don't strain that super brain of yours. Just let Billy Bob kill you. It doesn't get any easier. Okay, now, ditch the earpiece. But don't lose it! It's expensive."

Great. The rebellion was on a tight budget but Jack's forces of evil had smart sniper rifles. I dropped the earpiece in a potted plant on the porch and rang the doorbell.

Shouldn't I know what's going on?

A seriously attractive black woman in her mid-twenties answered the door. She looked at me expectantly.

I stared back. She was tall, or maybe I was short. Either way, I looked up at her. Tight red dress and stiletto heels, like hotness at a Bruce Wayne party. Wavy dark brown hair. Nice eyes, except they looked disappointed. I wanted to apologize for not wearing my stunning Wolf body. "Hi, I'm . . . Pops."

Maybe that was the wrong thing to say, because she swiftly stuck a cattle prod in my chest. I collapsed on the porch like the brittle old man I was.

Welcome to Billy Bob's, home of fresh caught gator-bait.

* * *

When I came to, I was strapped in a chair with lots of cable ties. My hands were tied behind me. Something was on my head— something weird. Wires trailed from the thing on my head to a small black box on Billy Bob's new custom made cypress wood desk.

Billy Bob eyed me from behind his desk. Smoke curled from a big cigar he was holding. He was dressed like badass hotness from a '70s movie. Wide lapels on a tapered white jacket, super wide collar on an orange dress shirt, too many buttons undone showing too much chest hair. Too stocky for those clothes. Somehow he reminded me of bad office sex—Florida style.

I struggled in the chair—it seemed like the thing to do. One glance told me I was still in my Pops body. I struggled a bit more. How was I supposed to look threatening like this? And what was that thing strapped on my head?

Out of the corner of one eye, I caught sight of the same beauty in red. She stepped closer and slapped me hard. My eyes watered as I stared up at her. Good to know she was on my side.

She hauled off and slapped me again. I worked my old jaw back into place. Her eyes narrowed and she hit me harder than before. Damn, that hurt. My vision slowly returned. With friends like her, who needed Billy Bob?

I wondered why he didn't just kill me.

Billy Bob leaned forward. "Thanks, sugar. I do believe we got his attention."

I tried to say something, but Pops had his jaw out of alignment again. I pushed it back into place with my right shoulder.

Billy Bob tilted his cigar my way. "Who the goddamn hell are you, boy?"

Good question. Each of my passengers had a different answer. Nameless seemed to have the best one, so I spoke the words. "I'm your worst nightmare."

The punisher in red moved closer, but Billy Bob waved her off. "Old man, I eat nightmares for breakfast."

So we were trading clichés? "Eat me!"

Billy Bob laughed. "I like you. Have we met before?"

"Yeah. I should have killed you the last time."

"We all have our little regrets." He nodded at the lady in red. "Give us some privacy, would you? And do close the door."

I craned my neck to see behind me and saw two black women in red. Twins. Wow, both stunners. "I'm charmed already, ladies. Let's meet over drinks when I get free." Did I actually say that?

Yes.

The twins paused, but Billy Bob waved them along.

With the door closed, Billy Bob moved around the desk and sat on it. He raised one leg, then put his shoe on my chest and pushed a couple times causing the chair to tilt backwards. "I'm taken to believe, you were that kid who broke in and messed up my desk. But this time, you're wearin' an old man's skin. Am I gettin' this right?"

I had nothing to say to that. But Peter was right. Billy Bob was a damn jumper. Like a chip off the ol' Jack. Good thing I didn't kill him when I was in Nameless, otherwise I'd be a passenger in his head forever.

I took a better look at his office. His new desk was really nice. But now he'd have to redecorate the office to match the cypress wood. I was thinking a bayou motif would go well in here. Which one of me knew about decorating? Wolf?

"Hey!"

Oops. I should've been paying attention in class.

Billy Bob squinted at me. But he smiled, maybe because he could tell that my passengers were squirming around inside me.

"As I was sayin', after the death of that kid, you picked up my man, Wolf. Nasty business, that. Wolf was mighty fine with everything he put his hand to. I shall miss that fine beast." He rubbed his shoe on my chest as he puffed his cigar. "And now you thought you'd switch sides. Work a deal. Drop out of Jack's crew and work directly for me. And that's why you're here tonight. Am I getting this right?"

Hell if I knew.

"But you also know I work for Jack—have for many years. But I suppose you thought you'd just slide on in—waltz up and add your questionable skills to my team. Maybe you thought Jack was too damn soft. You thought Billy Bob would be more to your liking, seeing as you've inherited Wolf's skills, and maybe even Wolf's allegiance to me. That's the deal on the table, isn't it? Blow off Jack—slide on up to me? Get back in my good graces?"

I was silent. Mainly, I wanted him to cut the crap and just kill me.

He puffed his cigar as he regarded me. "You and I, we're a special breed, aren't we? Not many of us in this world. So naturally I'd want to bring you in, give you what Jack couldn't, show you the ropes, put your death lovin' skills to good use. Right?"

Blah, blah, blah. It was nap time for Pops.

"Or maybe I don't need your damn skills. Hell, Doc's been doin' just fine—picked up Wolf's load. See, when you're at my level, boy, quality help practically grows on trees. So exactly what am I lookin' at, anyway? A loser in an old man's body? Just look at you. I'm lookin' at a mess that didn't even think to slip into someone more impressive before our meeting? That just don't reflect well on your skills."

Screw you. Shoot me. Electrocute me. Do whatever you're gonna do. "Screw you. All you're doing is blowing bad breath my way."

He smiled. "That's more like it. The last thing I need is some limp noodle on my team."

Damn. This was going the wrong way. Backpedal? Or keep acting tough? "Your time's running out, Wyville. You can't kill me. No one can. This little meeting—well, it's just my way of saying I'm in charge here. You'll be perma-dead within 24 hours. I'd ask you to join me, but it's you who's got your head on backwards." Not my best speech, but I was tired.

"Very entertaining. Unfortunately, that's just not leading us to a productive relationship—now, is it?" Billy Bob put a hand on the black box next to him. "That's where this divine little creation comes in. It's a foolproof way to kill a body jacker. You know, what Jack calls a spirit walker. Care to know how it works?"

"Sure." I knew what was coming. It happened all the time in the movies. James Bond would be strapped to a death machine, the villain would explain it, then conveniently leave the room, allowing 007 to escape. Except, I'd let the kill happen, then jump into Billy Bob's disgusting skin. There was no such thing as a box that could kill jumpers.

Right?

Billy Bob patted the kill box gently. "Think of it like biofeedback. Remember the '60s? Oh, maybe you don't. All the time you've been sittin' there, hooked up—this little device has been measuring your . . . I forget exactly what the egghead said, but it measures your brain signals. Impulses. That's right, your goddamn brain impulses. When I flip this switch here, it'll be armed. Then this little box will wait for you to relax, and when you do, it'll kill you. So you see, *you* actually control it—not me. You relax, you die. You stay alert, you live. It's all up to you, boy. So go ahead and commit suicide if you want, or stay alert and live. It's not my problem, it's yours. Oh, and it turns itself off in 24 hours. The egghead said that was important to tell you. But if you're still alive when it times out . . . well, who knows? Maybe we'll see if you can survive another round without relaxing."

Billy Bob got up and checked my headgear. "Goddamn technology. I truly hate it. But we can't rightly live with it. And body jackers like us . . . well, we can't easily die without it. Oh, just one more thing before I start the timer. Folks like us have always been a little out of control. This biofeedback thing revolutionizes everything because it finally gives us a way to truly kill anyone. Best of all, it's enabled by senior management. That's me. I'm optimistic we can get this thing miniaturized down to the size of an implant, like a pacemaker. Wouldn't that be something? Stick a biofeedback suicide gizmo inside a body jacker. Instant devotion. Now that's an idea I can really get behind."

He reached over, ready to activate the suicide machine. "My advice to you, old Wolf—don't doze off or even relax in the next 24 hours. You wouldn't want to kill yourself, now would you?"

Crap. Pops was exhausted. Peter screwed up another one. Right? I held my breath. Could I stay alert that long?

Billy Bob slapped his hand on the desk. "Biofeedback suicide. Damnation, boy! You just gotta love it. What will they think of next?" He flipped a switch. A red light lit up on the box and a countdown timer started at 24:00:00.

Billy Bob and I watched for a while as the digits ticked down through the seconds.

23:59:52.

23:59:51.

23:59:50.

23:59:49.

He shrugged. "Kinda anticlimactic, if you ask me. Well, I'm off to bed. We'll see what's left of you in the morning. I was thinkin' I'd take breakfast in the office. You know, just to watch you tryin' to stay alert." He stood up, but hung around to watch. We were both mesmerized by the seconds ticking away.

23:59:14.

23:59:13.

An inferno of pain! My brain screamed like it was on fire from the business end of a Saturn V rocket.

My last vision: Billy Bob's gator grin went kinda slack-jawed.

* * *

The world swirled Milky Way Galaxy bright. Cosmic fire white. Sucking me into its center. Ripping me, atom from atom. Blazing me dead—blazing me alive again.

Soft.

Muffled.

Dry fluff in my mouth. Something bad was on fire. Surely that was my brain. I tried to cough. Maybe I did.

My eyes pried open—reluctantly. Room sideways. Carpet in my mouth, mixed with drool and that ashtray taste I'd had when I'd jumped into Martoni.

Something was burning.

Something very nasty was now in my mental back seat. My old passengers were rolling down the windows—Billy Bob's stench was overpowering.

I turned away from the turmoil in the back of my head. A cough—my cough. Pushing my head up I caught a clear vision of Billy Bob's cigar burning a nasty black hole in the carpet. But no flames. A flame retardant carpet? Thank God for the damn government rule makers. I could have died in a fire waiting for the jump to finish.

No need to check out my new body. I was in Billy Bob Wyville— every nasty inch of him. To the side, I could see Pops slumped over in his execution chair. Sorry, Pops. Not a great way for him to go, but maybe better than stumbling down the final mile of his natural life.

As for me? I was riding one unexpected train wreck after another. Thanks for all the pain, Peter. I couldn't wait to get some hands-on time with the little prick.

I slowly got to my feet, walked carefully over to the drinks, poured a glass of vodka, then swished it around in my mouth and spit it out on the floor. Rinse, spit, repeat. If there's one thing I absolutely hated about getting a new body, it was having someone else's spit in my mouth. Gag! A few rounds of vodka rinse later and my mouth felt slightly numb but a lot less like an ashtray.

Peter's kill box had somehow . . . somehow, what? Killed me? Electrocuted me, but with a stupid timer? Hell, anyone could stick a car battery in a black box. The only trick was getting Billy Bob to think it was a way to kill a jumper.

This wasn't high-tech. This was plain ordinary military psyops. Trick the enemy—win stuff.

But I had to admit, the biofeedback spiel did sound plausible. Maybe that was the fourth way to kill a jumper? Or maybe it was just a fancy suicide. Yeah, biofeedback would be just like setting up a possible suicide.

Billy Bob was just a gullible fool.

When I finally opened the office door, the sexy twins were there, just staring at me, not looking happy. I had the feeling they were ready to deck me.

I smiled. "Ladies." Maybe I accidentally had on a Billy Bob smile? No reaction.

Was there a safe word or something? I wanted to tell them the jump went well, but Peter said they were normals. So what could I tell them? "Uh . . ."

They could see Pops slumped over in the chair. Shouldn't they be happy? This was the usual scene after a jump. One of the twins produced a cattle prod from behind her back.

Oh, shit.

Words. I needed words. Something good, but not about jumping because they were normals. The women worked for Peter, right? "Peter would be happy."

The twins relaxed, pulled their earpieces out almost in unison, and moved in to give me wonderful hugs and whisper in my ears.

"We're sorry about the slaps."

"And the cattle prod."

"Screw Peter. We work for Sonya."

"Yes. Sonya sends you her love, Wolfie."

"Yes. We do, too."

They each gave me kisses on the ear. Billy Bob's ears. Damn, I wanted to be wearing Wolf again.

But they'd called me Wolfie. Wait. These normals knew about jumpers! Sonya broke rule #1. Okay, so maybe I did too, when I told Rema I could jump. My head was spinning.

They were still close to me. They wanted to say more, but weren't sure. "Don't tell Peter we know about you. Just remember, Sonya's got your back."

"More than you know, Wolfie."

"Follow Peter."

"Yes, but trust Sonya more."

"We'll see you again."

"Be safe, Wolfie."

"We need you."

"In more ways than one."

They turned and left me.

"Wait." The party was just getting started. So I followed them through the house, then watched as they walked out the front door. Through the front window, I saw them get in their matching red Corvettes and disappear into the night.

Great. Alone again. Except I was horny. Holy crap, Billy Bob's nasty tool was horny, too. Forget it—no way I was giving his little rod any satisfaction.

Maybe that's why Jack castrated himself every chance he got. I wasn't exactly sure what castration involved, but I was sure it wasn't my style. Better to tough it out until I jumped into another Wolf.

Yeah, I needed another Wolf body, and I needed it now.

Don't think about sexy women, Marko. Don't.

My unfortunate arousal was getting worse.

A little help, guys?

Then it crossed my fevered brain that taking over bad guys would always put me in their evil hides. I'd always be disgusting, like the mega-creep I was now wearing. But if I were an antihero, I'd kill good guys and always wear their bright shiny hero skins. I'd be in a handsome fireman, or a clean-cut Marine cadet. So killing good guys would be the way to go. Picking out a new skin was just like picking a new suit. Why get one out of a dirty back alley when you can get a handsome hero at a charity ball?

What the hell? Heroes were always handsome and evil was always ugly? Whose idea was that? Martoni? Nameless? I'm looking at both of you.

I was a pack of faulty logic—with a lurking gator groin.

Good to know I was messed up inside *and* out. Priests at confessional must hear jumper stories all the time. I guess that's why they invented exorcism. But seriously, could anyone pull the evil out of me? Very unlikely.

Then there was the kicking still going on in the back of my mind. Probably Billy Bob and all his passengers mixing it up with all of my passengers. I wanted to tell them all to shut up, but the less I thought about my cargo of evil, the better.

Time for some answers.

So I stepped out onto the front porch. Streetlights. The cliff side of Mount Bonnell. And the feeling that a new sniper was preparing to take his shot. I resisted the urge to run, and instead, I just stood there with Billy Bob's big hairy chest hanging out for all the world's snipers to put holes in.

I completely unbuttoned his orange shirt. Come on, boys. Drill this chest full of holes. I'm through with this swamp rat, so just do it.

I waited like a fool in the breeze for the shot.

"You damn cowards. Bring it on." I beat Billy Bob's barrel of a chest. Hell, I was a badass serial survivor. There was nothing anyone could do to stop me. Marko Santana—the target from hell. Bring it on!

No bullets. No jump. I was starting to feel like a dope.

Maybe the suicide biofeedback machine was real, only Peter had hacked it. Maybe I shouldn't be feeling so cocky.

I reached over and dug around in the planter for my earpiece. As I shoved it into Billy Bob's hairy ear, I could hear laughter. Laughter mixed with cheers. And yeah, maybe the sound of Sonya shouting that she loved me.

Aw, crap. They could see me.

"Dude, get back into the house."

"Why?" I wanted to slug Peter, not follow his orders. But mainly I felt big, like I'd just saved the whole state of Texas. No more Billy Bob Wyville. No more evil puppet master. Texas politics was safe. Uh . . . like that was even possible. "We're done here. Extract me."

"No, you're not done."

Damn. I went back into the house. "Look, I made the jump for you. You had your fun—you electrocuted me. What else do you need?"

"Go back in the office."

My head was still spinning and I needed a drink. "Fine. I'm back in the office now." Pops looked really bad, slumped in the chair. Poor old man. Maybe I should put a sheet over him.

"Top drawer. Notebook computer. Take it out and open it."

I did. It started up immediately. There was a little window popped up with Billy Bob alive and looking at me. That really creeped me out. Oh, it was me in the notebook's camera. It was me on-screen.

"Good, Wolf. Now aim it so you look good and we don't see the dead body. No, sit behind the desk. Good. Now button that damn shirt—not all the way. Now straighten your collar. Your hair's a mess, dude. Fix it."

"Yes, mother." I straightened up my new ugly body.

"That's better. Now see the words on the right?"

I could see text next to my ugly Billy Bob face. "Yeah."

"It's like a teleprompter. Say the words. Make it sound like Wyville."

I looked over the text. "It needs more swearing."

"It's a legal script. Just read it."

"No one's going to believe it."

"Don't argue with me. I've already texted Doc. He's on his way."

Shit. "Doc? What do we need him for?"

"Duh. To remove the freakin' body."

"I can do that."

"You're not Wolf anymore. You're higher up the food chain, so let Doc handle it."

"He's on his way? Here? Now?"

"Totally. I might have jumped the gun a little. Just read the damn text. You'll be fine. But make sure your face doesn't freak out. That's what the camera's for."

Screw Doc. I could handle Doc. I could, because now I looked like his boss.

But maybe it was better to avoid him. So I read the damn text. "I, Billy Bob Wyville, a resident of Travis County, Texas, being of sound mind," lie, lie, lie, "declare this to be my last will and testament. I revoke all . . . all fucking what? Crocodiles? Codicils? What the hell's a codicil? Shit. Well, anyway, I revoke it, even if any was previously made by me or not."

"Stop! Start over and get it right."

"Why? I thought that was classic Billy Bob. No one's gonna believe he read it perfectly. And it needs a lot of goddamns. The more, the better."

We argued. But Doc was on his way, so I read it right—close enough. Then there was paperwork to sign in front of the camera. One copy went into the filing cabinet. One copy needed to be mailed to Billy Bob's lawyer. "Wait, shouldn't we be killing him, too?"

* * *

The clock was ticking and I was eager to get out of Billy Bob's house before Doc arrived to remove poor Pops. "We're done here, right?"

"Yeah, dude. Run!"

I ran to the front door, expecting a limo or a stealth helicopter to appear in the night air.

"Not that way! Back door. There's a boat waiting."

Crap. Peter just now had eyes on me? As I ran out the back door and across the yard, it occurred to me I'd left my case and backpack full of cash and other treasures in the bushes across the street.

Later. I'd get it later.

Four-thirty in the morning meant it was still very dark. I jumped instinctively over a lawn chair that was barely visible in front of me. But Billy Bob was a big guy so the jump was just enough to trip me up and plant my face into the grass.

Good that it was Billy Bob's face. Bad that it hurt like hell.

Up ahead was a private boat dock, and the shadow of a boat waiting behind it. Cool. My speedboat awaited. Wolf would know all about high-powered racing boats.

My passengers yanked Wyville's portly unexercised hide off the turf and pushed it toward the waiting speedboat. Another day, another mental and physical challenge.

As we got closer, I could see it was just a generic motorboat. Nothing special. Single engine outboard. Plain white. One guy on board, and he was leaning over the side to hold the boat against the dock.

I carefully got Billy Bob's awkward flesh into the boat and helped the skipper push the boat clear of the dock. He revved up the engine and we were away.

Good. I settled into a cushy seat to talk with Peter. "I'm in."

"That's nice." Peter seemed to be eating something crunchy. Potato chips?

Wyville's stomach gurgled. "Why all the legal paperwork back there?"

"You just funded the revolution, man."

Cool. Wait. We had no money until I signed over Billy Bob's assets? "How much did we get?"

"Short-term funding only. We're kinda expensive. But mainly, a lot of people who were ripped off by Billy Bob will now get their money back."

That's nice. "So how much did *we* get?"

"Why? You need a receipt?" He crunched something in my ear. Definitely potato chips.

"Accountability. A little transparency would be nice."

"Dude, you're on point. You can check in with accounts receivable later."

"Fine. Where to now? Breakfast and a long rest at a safe house?"

"Like I said, you're on point. No rest for the wicked. We need to get you on a plane, pronto."

Good. Another jet. Posh food and a long nap. "Put Sonya on."

"No can do."

"Why?"

"You gotta quit asking me why. She's busy. I'm busy. We're all busy. In fact, you're the only one with your feet up, so quit whining and enjoy the downtime. FYI, you're scheduled to die again in about 12 hours."

Good that I wouldn't have to live in Billy Bob for very long. Bad that I'd have to go through another painful death so soon.

Speaking of Billy Bob, where was he in my head? He was being a quiet passenger. Yeah, new passengers were usually a bit stunned to be in my back seat.

I closed my eyes.

* * *

Next thing I knew, I was up front fighting with the guy driving the boat. Kinda like I was attacking him. Maybe even trying to kill him? Why? That made no sense.

As I let go of his throat, he punched me in the face, twice, then he slugged me hard in the solar plexus. I doubled over and went down.

Damn that hurt. My face was wet with blood and my lip stung.

What the hell just happened?

Peter was in my ear. "Wolf. You okay?"

I pushed the loose earpiece into my ear to hear him better. "Yeah. What the hell happened?"

"Bad shit, bro. You let your guard down and Billy Bob took over. You need to get a grip on that bastard. Don't let him do that again."

"I must have fallen asleep."

"Yeah, well, don't do that."

Right. "I have to sleep some time."

"Sleep in your next life."

The boat slowed as we pulled up near a boat ramp. The skipper glared at me. "Get out."

Get out where? We were still 20 feet from the shore. "You're kidding."

"Get out or I'll knock out more of your teeth."

Wolf wanted to hold the guy's head underwater, but I jumped out in waist deep water and mud, then headed toward dry land.

The skipper pointed up the hill. "There's a green rental car in the parking lot. The keys are in the ignition. I hope you die in it."

I turned around to tell him that I loved him too, but he'd already come about and was punching the throttle.

It wasn't easy getting a soaked Billy Bob out of the water, but we did it. I trudged up the ramp to the parking lot.

My clothes were ruined. River water streamed out of all the pockets.

"Peter? Peter, do you read me?"

"Not now. I'm busy."

"Where the hell am I going."

"It's in the GPS. Don't call me again until you're in Gettysburg."

"I'm driving to Gettysburg? What about my plane?"

Silence.

"Peter?"

Silence.

"Damn it. I need support out here."

"Dude, go dark. Run silent. Run deep. People are dying on my watch, so give me a fucking break."

Great. The war had begun and I was out in the middle of nowhere, dripping wet, heading to my green rental car.

Okay, I saw it. The only car in the lot. Very small and very econo. I got in it, squished when I sat, then started it and powered up the little GPS. ETA 15 minutes? Who knew Gettysburg was so close?

4.5 He's No Good To Us Alive

The GPS led me to a private airstrip out in the middle of nowhere. One small plane with one propeller. One small shack with a light in the window. No instructions on what to do next.

Cool. Probably a cheap rental plane that anyone could fly. Almost dawn. Ideal learning conditions.

I parked the car near the shack and walked up to it. The door was locked, so I pounded on it like a friend. Today's flight student reporting for duty. A quick tutorial was all I needed. Just tell me how to get a good station on the radio and turn on the autopilot, then I'd be on my way.

A grizzled guy in his 50s opened the door and sized me up. I was wearing Billy Bob, so I guess I didn't exactly look impressive.

"Name?"

Wasn't I expected? "You don't need it."

He seemed to like that answer and waved me into the shack. Not much inside it, other than a workbench with a camping stove, a small metal desk, an impressive pile of trash, and a well used cot.

"You ever flown before?"

"No." How hard could it be? I was a quick study.

"Never?"

"No, but I've flown flight sims plenty of times. So teach me."

"Not what I was askin'. You ever flown *in* a plane before?"

"Sure. Real ones."

"Real ones?" He shook his head. "They said you were trouble. Here." He reached into a duffel bag, pulled out a cream colored canvas jacket, and tossed it to me. "Put it on."

I flipped it around. It looked like a straitjacket—two really long arms and lots of straps. "What?"

"You heard me. Put it on. You get airsick?"

"What?"

"You got trouble with your ears? Been scuba diving lately?"

"No. None of that. And I'm not wearing this."

He sat down. "Well, I'm not flyin' if you're not wearin'."

"Show me how to fly. I'll fly myself."

He snorted. "The hell you will. Strap it on, or drive away."

Screw this. It was a plane rental from hell. "Then you fly it."

"Like I said, strap it on, or drive. Your choice."

The straitjacket was all straps and buckles with weird long arms. "Why?"

"Hell if I know. But them's the rules I was given. You fly, you sleep, you even think about drinkin' a beer—then you gotta wear this contraption." He got up and headed back to his cot in the corner. "Suit yourself. Personally, I'd rather go back to sleep. I get paid the same either way. The door's right square behind you, buster."

I started putting the straitjacket on. "How's it go?"

"Hell if I know. I ain't never worn one."

* * *

Twenty minutes later, we were strapped in and ready for takeoff. My straitjacket wasn't exactly on right because my hands were down between my legs, but it seemed to satisfy the pilot. The single engine had stopped blowing smoke and had settled into a loud purr.

It was pitch black outside. "Don't we need runway lights?"

"What runway? Keep your feet off the damn rudder set."

I moved my feet.

"Here." He reached over and put a pair of headphones on me. He adjusted the mic in front of my mouth. "There. Now you can hear me if somethin' comes up."

"Like what?"

He flipped on some headlights, but they were aiming skyward. "Don't distract me. This strip's little more than a short stretch of weeds and potholes. And that line of trees up ahead somewhere don't help none." He turned to me as he pushed in a blue knob and a black one, the engine got louder, and we started to move. "Now brace for impact."

What?

He slapped me on the shoulder. "Just pullin' your leg. We're gonna have a real good time together."

The little engine roared.

I wish I'd braced for impact.

* * *

We were only 30 minutes into the flight when I dozed off. Actually, I was happy for the straitjacket because I woke up a few times, surprised that I was trying to kill the pilot.

Billy Bob was quiet in my mind when I was awake, but quick to grab my steering wheel when I drifted off.

Note to self: Jumpers were bad news as mental passengers.

We landed three hours later at a small airfield with beautiful green countryside all around.

We were there. "That wasn't so bad."

"Yup. Good weather. Might get a bit rough up ahead."

"Up ahead? This is Gettysburg, right?"

"Nope. We're barely in Kentucky. Refueling stop. Stay in the plane and don't act suspicious. They're not paying me enough to explain you. And one more thing. Do us both a favor and stay awake."

"Okay."

He opened his door and started to get out of the plane.

"Hey. Untie me. I need to take a leak."

"Use the hose."

Hose? "What hose?"

"The one under your seat, in front."

I fished around and was barely able to reach the hose. "How's it work?"

"You attach it, about like you'd think. The tube goes straight out the bottom of the plane. But wait until we're in the air, 'cause I don't want no damn puddles on the ground. Besides, the suction feels kinda good."

Yeah? Who knew?

* * *

When we were airborne, I unzipped and attached the hose. No need for instructions. It did feel good. I was soon in love with the hose. I wanted to use it all the time. The pilot called it Little John. I guessed that was a reference to Robin Hood. Rob from the bladder, spray to the world. So why didn't commercial airlines use the hose? Think of the guys in business class, all using it. Think of the joy of flying. It seemed like first class should have bigger hoses. More suction. More for your money. This could revolutionize air travel. Of course, there'd be a petite hosette for women, and French engineers would perfect it.

I had it all worked out. Screw airline lavatories. Recline your seats, plug in your headsets, and plug in the hose.

So much to think about. So few brain cells I could call my own.

Another four hours and I was ready to die. But I suppose that was the point of the trip—trade Billy Bob for a better model.

After we landed and I was safely out of the plane, I turned to the pilot. "Thanks. That was unforgettable." I held out my hand.

He didn't want to shake it. "Yeah, just another dose of cosmic rays—more fried brain cells. Speakin' of brain cells gone bad, you might want to hang on to this." He tossed me the straitjacket. "I'd wear this every damn night if I was you."

Great. Safety PJs. "I'll catch you on the return flight."

"There ain't gonna be one. I was told this was a one-way trip for you."

Not good. "Well, safe travels, friend. Keep your nose up and your wheels down." That came out lame.

"I sure as hell hope not. If I get my way, I'll die in a flaming ball of fire one of these days. Beats livin' too long. Might be good for you too, someday."

"Flaming balls to you, too."

That made him laugh. He walked away shaking his head, and

with his back turned, he waved without caring if I waved back.

Some of me, waved anyway.

So I walked out of the tiny airport and into the parking lot, looking for a ride. My straitjacket looked kinda scary tucked under my arm, long sleeves dangling, so I folded it up. Actually, Gettysburg was a bit chilly that afternoon, but wearing the straitjacket didn't seem like such a good idea.

Apparently there was no on/off switch on my earpiece, so I tried talking. "Peter. You there? Hey, I'm in Gettysburg. Hello, Peter? Captain Comms? Anyone?"

Nothing.

It crossed my mind we'd lost the revolution already. Not a good thought. If that was the case, I'd either have to kiss up to Jack, or he'd torture me slowly over the next 200 years. More likely, both.

I tried to flatten my rumpled clothes. They were a serious mess. The river mud and stains just didn't brush off.

Nothing to do but wait.

About a half hour later, a black cargo van pulled up close to me. Some military types in black camo fatigues were checking me out. They seemed to be having a discussion.

Finally, the front passenger window rolled down. "Wolf?"

"That's me."

Disgusted looks between the driver and the guy in the passenger seat.

What? Never seen a wolf in an inflated Billy Bob suit?

The side cargo door slid open. I stepped in, but there was no place to sit. The door promptly slid shut.

I counted for guys in the back and two up front. None of them looked like much fun. Ex-military. Maybe even special forces. They sat on assorted cargo boxes and none of the guys seemed happy to see me.

"You're Wolf?"

"Yeah."

Sideways glances. Curled lips.

"Don't judge a badass by its cover. Right, guys?" I set my straitjacket down and looked for a cargo box to sit on.

One of the guys looked around at the other men like he wasn't going to put up with this crap. No objections from his squad, so he thrust a hand toward me, ending in a nice grip around my neck. He squeezed. It hurt.

He grinned. "I'm not seeing much, here. Feels like a fist full of dough."

Chuckles all around.

I cocked my head as best I could, as if to say, *Do you really want to do that?*

He caught my drift, but the disrespect never left his face. So I handed the situation to Wolf—this was his arena. Hell, he could turn the inside of this van blood red for all I cared. Wolf waited for the guy to blink and in that split second, Billy Bob's weight was at the back of the guy's outstretched elbow. Billy Bob's bulk put to excellent use. The guy's hand slipped off my neck as I came around fast, one of my arms was now wrapped tight around his muscular neck, while my free hand was now poised near his face.

That's when I had a serious WTF moment as I realized Wolf had a black hunting knife pressed tight under the guy's right eye—point ready to drive through his eyeball and into his brain. Hell, blood was already trickling down the guy's face from his lower eyelid.

Everyone was frozen in time. One giant WTF moment all around.

Don't ask me where the knife came from. Not mine. It must have been plucked from one of these guys.

A tense moment. Blood was already drawn. Jaws clenched. Action was assessed with likely reaction.

So they wanted to meet Wolf? Well, here he is. Some of the men would certainly die. Maybe all of them. Six ex-military types versus Wolf in a Billy Bob suit. Tough call—who would live and who would die. Wolf in tight quarters with a knife was like . . . oh, hell, it was like a van full of fresh prey ready to be sliced into chunks of warm bloody meat.

They're all yours, Wolf.

The knife pressed deeper. I could feel the guy's blood working its way down his cheek and caressing Wolf's hand.

A few seconds ticked by. No telling what expression was on my face, but it felt like stark raving joy.

Hell, bring it on, boys. I could use a new body, anyway.

The guy in my grip was the first to break the silence. "Point taken."

Nice phrase. It seemed to lighten the mood.

I slowly uncoiled. Thanks, Wolf.

Somebody moved and there was now a spare seat on a big ammo crate, so I took it. I spun the knife fast and it stuck smartly in the metal roof of the van. That was just Wolf showing off again. Nobody claimed it.

I shrugged, regaining control from Wolf. "Like I said, don't judge a badass . . ."

The guy with the cut under his eye wiped it. It kept bleeding but he didn't seem too upset by it. "I'm Dietz. We don't give out names, but it seems you've earned mine."

Cool. I had a lot of names. But no one here had earned any one of them.

Dietz was still looking me over. "No gear?"

"None needed."

"We're expecting a firefight. Perhaps you'd like an automatic? A vest?"

I shook my head. "Pointless. I'm the product of death." I left it at that.

They glanced at my straitjacket on the floor. No words were said, but they probably understood I was tubby, dangerous, and extremely mental.

Exactly.

We drove.

* * *

The guys in the van didn't speak to me—didn't say much to each other, either.

About 45 minutes later we pulled up to a locked gate on a rural side road. Farm land with scattered clumps of trees. Cows watched as one of the guys got out, cut the chain, and opened the gate. We drove down a dirt road that led to a line of trees flanking a small rocky stream. We parked in the shade. Across the stream I could see a dull red barn about 150 yards away.

We just sat there. Waiting.

Dietz looked a little annoyed with me. "We're in position." There was still blood on his face, but a little butterfly bandage was doing its job.

Cool. All eyes were on me. "Yeah. Hang on." I put a finger to my earpiece in the universal gesture that meant I was on comms with someone who actually knew something. "We're in position."

A moment later, Peter decided to give me the good word. "I know that. Chill. I'm busy."

Busy with what?

I nodded like I was being fed the latest intel, only I wasn't.

"Okay, Wolf." Peter was back. "Here's the deal. There's a bunker under the barn. Get in there and release the hostages."

The guys were watching me while I was looking thoughtful, trying not to look completely clueless. "Roger that. Any more intel on the hostages?"

"What?" Peter sounded annoyed. "Look, this is one of Jack's black labs."

"A black lab?"

The guys looked at me like we were here to meet a big friendly dog.

"Yeah, dude, a black lab site. It's where Jack experiments on people like us. Black ops, black lab, you get the idea."

"Right. How many?"

"How the hell should I know? It's black. Just get in there and figure out who's who. The hostages will be jumpers, but some might be normals."

Right. The hostages were jumpers unless they weren't. Useless intel. "Tactics?"

"It's your show, Wolf. Do what you do best. Kill, be killed. Stuff like that."

"Specifically?"

"What? Look, just go in hot. Look threatening, get killed, then you'll jump in the middle of them. If they've got a gun, kill them. If they're tied up, rescue them. You've seen the movies. Do that shit. Only . . . hang on . . . one problem."

I waited a few seconds. "What problem?"

Peter was talking to someone in the background. "Dude, slight problem. There's probably a jumper in there, kinda like the dick in charge. You know what I'm talking about? A nasty little Junior Jack. Don't kill him, obviously. Just grab him and we'll deal with his nastiness later."

"What about the other, uh," What were they called? "hostiles?"

"The normal hostiles? If they're still alive, just let them go. They'll scatter."

"And the wounded?"

"Wounded? Man, we really don't need any of those. I don't know, just drop them off somewhere, you know, like ER. It's your op now. Don't screw it up. And blow the place up when you're done, but don't forget to look for records, logs, whatever they've got that might've recorded the results of their experiments."

"What experiments?"

"Duh. It's a lab. Experiments on dying and jumping. You'll probably see a stack of dead normals and dead jumpers. Just ignore the bodies. It's a rescue op, not a kill count."

Wolf's ears perked up. He liked the phrase, *kill count*. "Okay, then what?"

"Then nothing. Don't call me, I'll call you. Oh, I almost forgot. If you find any cash, snag it. Things are getting expensive fast."

Not the level of organization I was hoping for. "Right."

"Now get out there and kick some ass, dude. Die like you were born to—because you were. But don't kill any jumpers. We still need you, Wolf. Go dark. Go deadly. But mainly go super dark."

I turned to Dietz. "There's a bunker under the barn. We'll open it up, but then it's gonna get weird. I'll go in alone. Your team should wait up top. Uh, shit, I can't explain what'll happen. But there'll be lots of it. Then assorted people will come out, disarm them all. Use force if you have to, but kill no one. It's imperative you don't use deadly force on anyone. Understood?"

Dietz nodded. Maybe he'd seen weird shit before.

"Good. I suspect a lot of people will run like hell, so just let them. Eventually, someone will come out and give you the safe word . . . uh . . . *Omaha*. The person who says that word is your new commander. Oh, and I hope you guys brought explosives."

"We did." Dietz pointed to the crate I was sitting on.

"Good. Let's move out."

They all grabbed gear and we crossed the shallow stream and trotted commando-like to the barn. We all noted the CCTV cameras on every corner of the barn. So much for being sneaky.

After breaking through a padlocked door, we were in the barn.

Lots of hay and barn stuff. But in the center of the barn was a large round metal hatch on the ground. Locked from the inside.

"Open it."

Dietz and the guys tugged at it and looked it over. They were like crazed ants on a sealed honey jar.

"Use force."

That set them in motion. They quickly decided to pack C-4 and det cord around the hatch and blow it to smithereens. Fine with me. Nameless thought that with the constant Civil War reenactments around Gettysburg, no one would notice another explosion on a farm.

Yeah, right.

The team opened up all the barn doors and the two loft windows because otherwise there was the possibility the concussion would bring the roof down on the hatch.

An hour later we were all down by the stream, ready to detonate the charge. Getting the cows cleared away cost us a half hour, but I had insisted on it.

Dietz shouted, "Fire in the hole!" but wasn't that a civilian saying? Nameless was sure the Army Corps of Engineers shouted, "Eat shit and die!" as their only warning.

Nameless was a fountain of plausible misinformation.

Dietz twisted a red knob on a wireless detonator box. The barn sprouted new holes and the whole thing seemed to lurch a few feet off the ground. Or maybe it was the ground backing away from the barn.

Either way, the barn was quickly enveloped in a big cloud of dust while bits of dull red barn timbers fluttered down beautifully out of the clear blue Pennsylvania sky.

The only thing better would have been to add lots of gasoline to the explosion like they do in all the movies. Nothing better than an orange fireball blowing the crap out of just about anything.

A couple guys stood up and muttered, "Oh, shit." Not inspiring.

We walked slowly forward, waiting to see if anything barn-like appeared out of the massive dust cloud.

It did. The barn frame was still there, along with a few stubborn sections of siding and roof. Good thing the barn had some metal in the frame. But the best part was the hay, spread out in rings, kind of like shock waves.

Awesome. A sight like that really inspires men to blow everything up. Nameless knew that's why men built so many things—they did that, knowing that all boring construction is inevitably followed by awesome destruction.

All I knew was that I was low on sleep and Nameless was taking advantage of my fatigue.

We pulled barn rubble away from the hatch but all we found was a hole. The steel hatch was long gone. Or else it was now reaching 30,000 feet and just starting its descent.

I looked at Dietz like he'd just screwed a simple mission.

He ignored me, pulled out a flashlight, and peered down the dusty shaft. "We're in."

Yeah, well, the barn was now a non-barn, but the hatch was open. Good job, guys. Any smoking hole you could still climb into, was a good hole. Right?

Just inside the hole, I could see bent metal on a permanently attached ladder. It looked like it was still usable. The beam of light only penetrated through the swirling dust down to about 15 feet. No telling how far down the metal ladder went. "Guard the entrance while I go in alone. Remember to disarm everyone. Whoever says *Omaha* is your new commander. And no deadly force. Got that?"

"Understood."

No more stalling, it was time for me to go in—probably to get myself shot and jump into my killer, then shoot the place up and rescue people.

I tried to tell myself, shooting bad guys was a good thing. It looked okay in the movies. Well, not every movie.

I turned to Dietz. "I need a gun."

"How big?"

"Any size. I'll take your sidearm."

Dietz was toting an automatic assault rifle, but he acted like taking his pistol was somehow personal.

He reluctantly handed it over.

As I started down the ladder, he handed me a flashlight and asked, "How about a vest? You know? Just in case."

"No thanks." What I actually needed was an un-vest. Something that would protect all of my nonlethal areas and just expose my kill zones. I needed to get killed—not wounded. Such was the life of a jumper.

Unfortunately, I forgot I was in Billy Bob and almost fell off the ladder. I could have accidentally died.

Yeah, perma-death was shockingly easy.

Note to self: Every time you think you're unstoppable, just remember how easy it is to trip and die.

At the bottom, the dust was thick in the air, but I could see a short hallway leading in one direction. At the end was a square metal door with a window and a gunport like they have on armored cars. Hell, it was a real armored car door—it even had a company logo and a phone number on it.

Where was the rest of it? Inside? Jack's idea of a dungeon was a buried armored car? No, Jack's madness seemed more upscale than that.

So I naturally walked up to it and put my chest against the gunport, then peered in the window. Pointless, because it had a little black curtain on the other side.

The door was locked so I pounded on it.

"Hello," a man shouted. "I've been expectin' you. Come on in." He sounded a bit Scottish, or maybe British.

"It's locked."

"Well, don't let a wee thing like that stop you, lad."

What now? Blow open the door? Hopefully with better results. "Who's in there?"

"I'm called Bruce the Black, but if you care to make it friendly, you can just call me The Black."

"Who else is in there?"

"Well now, tis a wee bit dark in here, but I'm guessin' everyone else is dead. And just so you know—never call me plain Bruce. I hate that."

Great. I completely forgot why I wanted in there. "I need to make a call."

"Aye. I'll wait, then. But do make it quick, 'cause I'm really lookin' forward to meetin' the likes o' you."

Shit. All the hostages were all dead, and Junior Jack was called Bruce the Black and wanted to meet me.

I poked at my earpiece, but there wasn't even static. So I climbed up the ladder to get more bars.

Dietz helped me get out of the hole. "Everything okay down there?"

"Maybe. There's a metal door we probably need to blast through. You might as well get it wired to blow. But maybe not so much overkill this time." I ran out of the barn with my finger on my earpiece.

"Peter! We're in. Are you there?"

"Yeah, dude. But I'm kinda busy, so skip to the good news, okay?"

"You're always busy."

"So talk."

"We blasted through the outer hatch. Down below, there's a short hallway and a metal door. It's locked, but we're preparing to blast through it."

"Dude, you said you were in. You're not in. Call me back when you've cleared out the bunker and rescued all the friendlies."

"There's no one to rescue. They're all dead."

"What?"

"There's only one guy left and he sounds like one of Jack's jumpers from hell."

"Carlos?"

"Who's Carlos? No, this guy's much worse. He calls himself Bruce the Black and he's like pure demon spawn."

I could hear screams and shouts in my earpiece. We were all doomed.

Finally Peter calmed down enough to speak. "No! Dude, that's him. He's one of us. Holy shit! You just rescued Bruce the Black. Un-fucking believable!"

"So who is he?"

"Who is he? Dude, he was one of the Black Watch. You know? The Black Watch? One of the Highlander regiments? You do know history, don't you? They're like un-fucking stoppable. It's like they love to die if it means accomplishing a mission. Except this guy's a jumper. But he's like, only one of two known jumpers that can jump without being killed. Can you even imagine how awesome that power is? Dude, it's like . . . it's like, in chess, if you were a lone knight, he'd be a pair of rooks."

"So if he's one of these . . . these—"

"Shades. We call them shades."

"Okay, so who's the other shade?"

"We don't know. Someone in the Himalayas. Tibet, Nepal, around there. He keeps a low profile. Or maybe he's a she. Who knows? But he goes by the name Snow Leopard. Hell, for all we know, he might even be in a real snow leopard's body. Shades can trade bodies just by touching someone, or some animal. But enough about Snow. We rented Bruce from the Euro syndicate. He's very expensive, except Jack captured him, but now you've found him."

"Don't call him Bruce. He doesn't like that."

"Really, Waldo? So you prefer *Wolf* and he prefers *The Black*. Big deal. Like it really matters? Wait. Don't tell him I said that."

"Fine. You can call him Bruce in person."

"Just get him out in one piece. I'm bringing in a helo to extract him, so keep him there."

"Then what?"

"You're coming back to Austin. The Black is needed ASAP in San Francisco. I gotta go. Keep me posted on his condition."

"Right."

"One more thing. If he likes your body better than his, don't let him touch you. Yeah, because he can swap bodies with you in a heartbeat. Come to think of it, don't ever let Bruce touch you."

* * *

Exploding the inner door went a lot better. Armed with a crowbar and a much bigger flashlight, I pried open the ruptured armored door and stepped inside Jack's dungeon.

The lights were off, but my flashlight revealed a big chamber with desks and chairs. Off to my right was a really big man, chained to the wall and wearing nothing but a Scottish kilt, and a smile.

Something about his manly bare chest and the kilt reminded me of a romance novel. Of course, I'd never read one, but Marie did have them on her nightstand. Come to think of it, Sonya had them, too. Jade had them. I guess all women had them.

So this outdoorsy hunk was Bruce the Black.

"Just so you know, tis not my tartan."

Huh? I glanced up at the big guy's face. At roughly 6' 6" and over 260 pounds of solid meat, I had no doubt he grew up on the highlands eating whole goats for breakfast and tossing boulders around for sport.

"Not my clan, but I'm lucky to be wearin' and not in the wind."

Yeah. I pointed to the dead guy at his feet. "Where are the others?"

"The answer to that depends on the answer to who you are."

"I'm Wolf."

"A pleasure to meet you. But I have to say, you don't look like a Wolf. More like a Milford or a Tuppet."

"I'm a jumper, like you. Today I'm wearing a guy named Billy Bob."

"By jumper, I suppose you mean a wanderer. Or what Jack calls a spirit walker."

"Right. Same thing. But I hear you're a special kind of jumper called a shade."

"I've been called worse, but I'm Bruce the Black and proud to be released by a man named Wolf. But here we are talkin', when I should be gettin' free from these chains." He rattled them.

"Right. Sorry."

"You'll find keys on the far wall, yonder."

I followed his gaze to a hook on the far wall, with keys on a big metal ring. As I walked over, I swung the flashlight around for a better look at the dungeon.

"We had lights, until you blew the outer hatch."

"Sorry. My team got carried away with the C-4."

"No harm done. Just me and the dead, soakin' up the dark. Business as usual, you might say."

Right. Business as usual. I cut the gloom and dust with my light. What did Jack's *business as usual* look like?

The walls were metal plate, not the usual dungeon stones. There were three metal desks straight out of a WWII movie. A map on the wall with pins in it. The ceiling lighting consisted of plain florescent tubes in fixtures that had wire cages around them. Air ducts ran across the ceiling. I caught a glimpse of a side room with empty cots. But on the floor near the keys was another hatch. Closed.

"What's down there?"

"Assorted dead. Every dungeon needs a place to dump the bodies, don't you know."

I noticed the hatch had latches and looked easy to open.

"Have a look below, if you've a mind. But you might want to keep it brief, due to the odor."

Right. No thanks. "No survivors?"

"None but one, and you're lookin' at him."

I grabbed the keys and walked over to Bruce the Black. "Why do they call you black?"

"Maybe tis 'cause I was in the Black Watch. You've heard o' them, no doubt. Maybe tis 'cause I'm a shade. Not too many o' them walkin' about. Or maybe 'cause I've been a black man a time or two—some of my best years, and my worst."

I unlocked his chains, careful not to touch his skin. I nodded to my left. "Who's the dead guy?"

"Him? Oh, just a jumper, but he was the dungeon master here. From what I could tell, he was supposed to kill anyone who tried to rescue me."

Jack's man. Somehow dead. "But I'm a jumper and I'd just take over his body. Dumb plan, if you ask me."

"Oh, lad—a smarter plan than you know. You see, Jack was using me as bait. Your resistance would try to free me, and o' course, they'd send the great and mighty Wolf."

Great and mighty? I had a reputation already? Probably just Peter trying to scare people with Wolf tales. "So? I still don't get it. How'd this guy die if he was a jumper?"

"Wolf, look around you. You're standing in the middle of a trap. A Wolf trap, designed just for you. The evil bastard lyin' dead at my feet had a kill chip in him—a nasty bit o' technology, if I do say so. The resistance was to find out about this place, just like they did. Then you were to blast your way in, just like you did. Then this bastard was to kill you, you'd jump into his body, then Jack would get some poor bastard to push a button and you'd jump into him."

"A teleport."

"No matter what you call it, tis a forced leap into another body. So you'd find yourself halfway 'round the world in the body of some poor bastard, who might just be chained to a wall, and might just be starin' at Jack's evil laughin' face."

"Crap."

"Aye, and a big steamin' pile of it, too. Lucky for you, this dungeon master was a coward and he hesitated when you were at the gunport. Killing you or me would mean the end of him, and he knew that. As it is now, he's probably telling Jack the kill chip was activated too soon—as if this was Jack's fault, not his. Not a pleasant conversation, I'd imagine."

Bruce the Black walked over to a desk, picked up the weird bag that went in front of his kilt, strapped it on, followed by a wide belt, then put a very big hand on my shoulder. I almost screamed.

Nothing happened. Maybe because I was wearing a shirt and our skin didn't touch?

"You'll have to catch me up on events, man. I've been down here awhile. I dearly hope to find a bonny day up top. A breeze under my kilt would feel like heaven right about now, as you can well imagine."

I made sure I went up the ladder first. No up-skirt for me.

Dietz noticed someone climbing up behind me.

"Relax. He's with me. No other survivors. Rig the bunker to blow."

Bruce the Black made his way out the hole and stood gazing at the remains of the barn. "Dear Lord, you've done amazin' things with Jack's lovely barn. No wonder the lights went out."

"Any explosion you can walk away from . . ." I put my hand to my earpiece. "Peter? You there? Your rook is out of the hole."

"In one piece?" Peter seemed excited. "Does he need a new body?"

I watched as the big man walked out into the meadow, bare feet in the summer grass. He stretched his broad muscles in a shaft of dusty gold sunlight. A gentle breeze ruffled his kilt, and the whole thing seemed to whisper *chick flick*.

"No, Peter. He's in one piece. One big manly Highlander piece."

"Cool."

"He might need some clothes."

"Yeah, it's on my list. Did you find any intel in the bunker?"

"I snagged a map while I was down there. No electronics. No Jack diary. But we have bigger problems. Jack knew we were coming. It was a trap for me. The dungeon keeper was supposed to kill me so I'd jump into his body. But he had a kill chip in his head so Jack could extract me. I could've been teleported anywhere."

Peter was quiet for a while. "Jack's always a few steps ahead of us. But we're making progress."

Like hell we were. "We've got a mole. That's totally obvious."

"Yeah, well, I've been working that angle, but I've come up empty. What really bothers me is the possibility that Jack's collective mind has somehow gone psychic."

Not good. I was back to feeling like we were all doomed. "Maybe we should split up." All my passengers were loners. Wolf knew we were better off going solo.

"No. You did great, Wolf."

The hell I did. "I was lucky not to be perma-killed in the hot tub. I was lucky not to be beamed into Jack's loving arms just now. We can't rely on luck."

"Dude, we don't care what keeps you going. If you're damn lucky, that's great. If you're becoming psychic like Jack, that's crazy good. Or, if you're just some kind of psycho-rama messed up badass, that's totally cool with us. But whatever the hell you are, you're still on the chess board, you're still in motion, and you're still making Jack scream like a little girl with spiders in her hair. So spare me the verbal crap and get your nasty Klingon shit together."

Huh?

"One more thing, dude. I know it feels kinda frosty out there, being point man and all. But you gotta know, everyone here at Command and Control . . . we all love you. Word."

Bullshit. "So make The Black your new point man. He's about as impressive as they come."

"Bruce? No way. He's not in touch with his inner killer like you are. Besides, all our chips are on you. So head west with Bruce. We've got a helo headed your way. Tell the guys to blow the bunker and get the hell out."

"Roger that." That's what I said, not what I was thinking.

* * *

As I guided Bruce the Black west, I couldn't help but look him over. Where Wolf was overly handsome, dangerous, and heartless, The Black was bigger, more rustic, and born to have the wind in his long dirty blond hair. A gentle giant, unwittingly dripping in sex appeal. Not that I was thinking about that.

He turned to look down at me. "You have a wandering face."

I grabbed my face.

He smiled. "You'd call it a jumping face?"

"Something like that."

"I hope you find your inner stone."

Stone? "It's not easy with a head full of passengers."

He nodded. "Mmm. I know it must be chaotic for you. Mine, however, are like reference books sittin' on a shelf. Devoid o' personality. Devoid o' motives."

"My latest passenger was a jumper. Billy Bob Wyville, the guy I'm currently wearing. Things seem different with him inside my head. My other passengers have gotten quieter. I kinda miss them. I didn't think I would, but I do. Billy Bob . . . he's like this quiet alligator, lurking in my mind—waiting."

"Does he ever control you?"

"Yes, when I sleep, or when I get too tired. I can never let my guard down."

The Black nodded thoughtfully. "We all swallow jumpers in different ways. For shades like me, tis just another book on the shelf. But jumpers tucked inside jumpers? Billy Bob inside o' you? Not good. Tis anyone's guess how it'll go down. I'd like to tell you things will improve up there," he pointed to my head, "but your Billy Bob passenger will always be an alligator in your mind. That's just how you are—just how you handle a jumper as a passenger. That's just how you'll always be, lad."

Note to self: I liked this guy already.

Bruce the Black pointed to a hill just as a bright red news helicopter appeared over the ridge. "That'll be our ride."

"How do you know? Wouldn't Peter send us something black and weaponized?"

"Peter would, but Sonya's a wee bit smarter. She knows a blade travels better when sheathed."

Cool. We were blades.

"We should travel together for a while, you and I. You must have some greatness in you, Wolf, otherwise Sonya would have sent someone else to pull me out of that pit. I'll not underestimate you."

We stood together in the meadow, watching the helicopter approach. Brothers in arms. Stone pillars against the winds of evil. The big man and me. Standing there, it felt so good. It felt like we were nearly equals.

An expensive looking helicopter set down almost 100 yards in front of us. Bruce the Black surprised me by running through the meadow, arms spread wide. He roared, "Ahhh," like it was a battle charge, or maybe a greeting for some long lost kin—hard to tell what that was about.

I decided he just loved bright red helicopters.

* * *

In the helicopter, I learned that chopper pilots fly from the passenger seat. I was surprised that the pilot was a woman. But she was actually pretty cool about the ride, because she let The Black and me ride in the back with the doors rolled wide open. And because immediately on takeoff, she showed off some very impressive flying skills.

As we flew, The Black was like a great big kid. At one point he got out of his seat belt and only used the handrails to keep from falling out. Hanging out the door, he pointed out landmarks, and especially horses grazing in the green fields below. I got the feeling he really liked horses. He didn't say much, but at one point he turned to me with a big grin on his face and yelled, "I do love to fly with the doors open. But even better is to be completely out there, danglin' from the end of a rope tied 'round you, free in the wind, with your arms spread wide—nothin' between you and the flight of eagles—only the air all 'round, and you flyin' in true the middle of it all." He put a hand on my shoulder. "Some men did that to me once—hung me out of a helicopter on a rope. Then, while I was enjoyin' bein' a bird, enjoyin' bein' one with air and the world, one of the fools cut the rope to kill me. Oh, man! The free fall was glorious! I'd die that way everyday if I could. You must try it someday, lad. You'd dearly love it!"

I nodded to him, but he'd already turned away to revel in the wind and the view.

* * *

I opened my eyes to a familiar sight—a private jet. Sweet, except I was tied down. Actually, I was strapped down with cable ties.

"Good to have you back, lad."

I looked over to see Bruce the Black spread out, face down on the floor, with a redheaded female flight attendant sitting on the rear of his kilt, giving his massive bare back a massage.

Does he go through life in just a skimpy kilt?

Wait. Shouldn't she be wearing gloves? He was a shade and her skin was touching his. So maybe The Black didn't want to swap bodies with her? Or maybe The Black enjoyed swapping bodies back and forth when he had sex? Would I even do that if I could? Experiencing sex as the man, then the woman, then as the man? Giving my partner an equal body swapping experience? And if we could swap fast enough, would it be like truly equal sex?

That made my head spin. But since The Black and I were now pals, maybe I should ask him how he liked it, and did he swap bodies for fun during sex?

Nah. Talking about sex with The Black was too weird, even for me.

I struggled to move my arms. "What's with the cable ties?"

The Black gave me a sheepish grin. "Sorry, Wolf. You were sleeping through a Billy Bob moment. I got tired of sittin' on you, so I opted for a bit o' tie down."

The flight attendant started to get off his rump, but he stopped her. "Don't stop the rubdown yet, love. I'm enjoying every moment of it. Oh, a bit lower would be grand—and as hard as you've got, if you've a mind." He reached underneath him, into his kilt bag, and produced a small knife with a black handle. "Now that you're rested, Wolf, I'm thinkin' tis safe to set you free."

He reached up and cut a cable tie to free one of my hands, then handed me the knife. "Tis a Sgian Dubh, if you're wonderin'. A stockin' dirk, but I kind o' lost my stockings."

He lost a lot more, by the look of it. "Thanks. What else is in your bag?"

"Tis called a sporran. Let's just say, the contents are a private matter."

After I'd cut myself free, and had a moment to admire the finely crafted little blade, I handed it back and moved on to more important questions. "Where are we?"

"Aye, that's what I've been wanting to talk to you about. But you might want somethin' to eat while we discuss this."

Yeah. I was starving. "Beer and pizza, if you've got it. Extra both."

"I'm thinkin' you should avoid the drink from here on out, seein' as you've got Billy Bob's fearsome alligator in you. But if you've set your mind on a pint or two, we should get you into some proper chains first. Otherwise, I'm afraid your drinkin' days are over, Wolf. Sleepin's a bit of a problem for you, too. Not sure how we're goin' to handle that one."

Great. Just great. I was now a public menace. "I had a straitjacket in the van. Maybe I'll find another one somewhere."

Wait! We were talking about jumper things with normals in the plane. I glanced at the flight attendant. She seemed to be the only one on the plane, and she seemed to be fine with the jumper talk.

The Black nodded. "Relax, Wolf. No normal folks here. Except the pilots. I probably should have mentioned that at the start."

Hang on. I didn't say anything about talking in front of a normal, so how'd The Black know what I was thinking? Was my face giving away all my thoughts?

"Yes, your face is very expressive."

My hands were already checking out my face.

"Peter is good at fixing a face with a mind of its own. But don't let it bug you, man. Tis just a control thing you can learn to master." The Black rolled over onto his back. "But where are my manners? This fine lady perched on my family jewels is none other than Brenda. And sportin' a fine new body, if I do say so. And I do."

Brenda was back? And in a new body? Fine. So she was disguised as a flight attendant. Big deal. With red hair. Looking good. She had the same calculating glint in her eye, so I was starting to buy into the fact that I was now looking at the new Brenda. But why the flight attendant disguise? Paranoia? I remember Brenda said she was on her eighth body. Ninth now. So Brenda was back, and now massaging The Black's big muscular chest.

Great. A jumper could look like anyone, so maybe Brenda was really Jack? That would simplify everything. Two suspects were really one. Brenda-Jack set up the kill shot at the hot tub.

Or maybe that was too simple.

Paranoia was flooding my brain, making thousands of instant sinister connections.

No. Brenda was just Brenda. Jack could only keep his act together for so long, then his sick Jackness would come spilling out, covering everyone with his dark sticky evil.

Brenda wasn't acting like head-spinning Jack. She seemed kinda normal. Hell, I'd be straddling The Black if I were a woman, too. Besides, no one could fool The Black for long. Right?

Paranoia infested my every thought. No wonder Jack couldn't keep it together more than five minutes. Who could, with so many minds? They were like a mental flash crowd—a mental torrent of opinions, shifting and darting like a school of fish with sharks lurking nearby.

I was losing it.

Relax, Marko. Things were good here. I looked over at Brenda and The Black.

A nice couple. Peter would be pissed to see his girl on The Black. But this wasn't sex—just an innocent rubdown.

Brenda seemed uneasy, perched on The Black's kilt and bulky sporran man-purse thing, so she casually flipped both up. I guess Brits had a lot of experience flipping Highlander kilts. I also thought Scots wore underwear. I guess it was optional.

Redheaded Brenda was watching me closely. Trying to look deeper than my new body? "Hello again, Wolf. I heard what happened to you. I have to admit, I'm very impressed you survived the hot tub—and the dungeon." She looked totally different, but of course she would—wearing someone else's body. And I looked totally different in Billy Bob and his trashed suit. Externally, I was nothing like Wolf.

Yeah, I should have died in the hot tub. "Hey, Brenda. I thought . . ." What did I think, other than Brenda was a prime suspect?

"You thought what? That maybe I set you up back at the hot tub? Just because I stepped away right before you were shot? Just because my team decided to pull me out—with a forced jump? Very rude of them, I might add. Just because I didn't leave you a cheery little note to explain things from my point of view?"

Yeah, all that and more. Brenda knew Wolf was going to be there. She knew how to get Peter naked and in the hot tub with the hill country view—a clean target for her sniper. Sonya would naturally strip and join in. And yeah, Brenda conveniently went inside to use the bathroom where her team triggered a kill switch in her head—beamed her out. All very suspicious. "You have to admit that made you look guilty."

"I'm sure it did, Wolf. But I'm back, aren't I?"

Yeah, to finish the job. "So why are you back?"

"Believe it or not, Europe has a vested interest in North America. We always have. Jack's never been a friend to us. We offered Bruce the Black to your resistance group, but bad things happened to the poor dear—kidnapped. So I came over to throw some major diplomatic support your way, and more bad things happened—blood in the hot tub. Truth be told, you're the only suspicious part of all this. Because by all rights, you should be dead."

"Perma-dead."

"Yes, perma-dead. But you're not? And why is that? Jack seems to have the hots for you. And why is that?" She held up a hand. "Strike that last one. We all had the hots for Wolf. But one way or another, you appear to be in bed with Jack. And now you've picked up an alligator personality from this Billy Bob character. Bloody suspicious, don't you think?"

Brenda looked down at The Black. "Stop that. This is nothing to get aroused over." She looked back at me. "So let's bin any further discussion of loyalty. My loyalty is completely and utterly with Europe. Having Jack removed, *perma-removed*, suits us to a tee."

Trying to put suspicion on me was only pissing me off. We'd settle this later when the truth came out. "Got it, Brenda. No need to get your panties in a twist. But I'm still gonna watch my back."

"And well you should. And the state of my panties is, quite frankly, none of your concern." She glared down at The Black. "You're doing that deliberately, aren't you? Well, stop that." She got to her feet. "As for your pizza, you can just fend for yourself, Mr. Payne. I am not the flight attendant here—this costume notwithstanding. If you gentlemen need me, I'll be freshening up, and otherwise unavailable."

Brenda stepped to the rear of the plane and locked herself in the plush lavatory.

I noticed my earpiece was still in place. "I suppose Peter heard all that."

Bruce the Black got up and settled into a big leather seat. "Unlikely. Tis our plane, so I'm pretty sure all your signals would be blocked. And you might like to know, Peter wanted you on a bus to Austin—I guess that's all he could afford. But I thought I'd bring you 'round with me for a while." He leaned closer. "Just between you and me, lad, Sonya still has a powerful thing for you. Unfortunately for you, so does Jack. And then there's Brenda.

Strong minded, if you know what I mean. Oh, and just so you know, she often fights with the men she wants to bed. So scrap with her all you want. It only makes her fire burn hotter. But keep that last part to yourself. As for the soft hide you're wearin'—well, a lady will often look deep within a man. They're doin' that with you, Wolf—lookin' deep, seein' somethin' they fancy. As for me," he stretched, and it was like watching a Bengal tiger flex his muscles, "I've found that a right manly body has a way with the comely lasses. So if you can choose what to wear, why not wear the best?"

"Easy for you to say. You're a shade. You can swap bodies just by touching them."

"True. I'll admit, tis a wonderful ability."

"And you can do that at will?"

"Aye."

"During sex?" Damn, I wasn't going to say that.

The Black smiled. "You'd be surprised how many jumper women want to party with me, for a chance to . . . shall we say, mingle?"

Good to know. A shade was an awesome sex-trip at parties.

But Wolf wanted to know how hard it would be for a team of guys to capture a shade. A fight with someone who could swap bodies with a single touch? That would be like playing a game of *Bruce, Bruce, whose body has the Bruce?* And punching a shade could mean an instant body swap, so as your fist made contact you'd switch bodies, then instantly feel all the pain you just inflicted. Amazing—like punching yourself. "Instant body swaps must make you hard to capture and transport."

"Not really. Anyone in a hazmat suit can haul me off. O' course, I don't go lightly."

* * *

After rummaging around in the galley, The Black and I came up with something to eat and drink. Water for me, but he was into a nasty mix of whiskey and oatmeal juice.

Brenda was still doing something in the bathroom, so I decided it was a good time to talk about her. "So tell me how jumpers like Brenda teleport. Like . . . I know she had a kill chip embedded in her, but who triggers it? I mean, anyone who triggered it would lose their body, right?"

"Not the best dinner conversation, but you should know the truth of it. Kill chips are an evil thing used by some o' the darker elements within the jumper clan. Not to say, Brenda's soul is dark, but her European superiors demand that she use those chips, as she travels and such. I assume that's 'cause of the secrets she holds in her head. Torture is a terrible thing, even for those who can take a new body."

Right. "Who triggers the chip?"

"Sad to say, tis almost always an unsuspectin' normal. Are you sure you want to hear this?"

"Yes."

"Right, then." He took a swig of his oatmeal booze. "First, you find a normal human of sound body and shallow mind. Preferably unattached. Easy enough, these days. You might walk up to them on a London street with a red kill switch and say somethin' like, 'What if I said you could push this red button and someone in Texas would die?' O' course, Texas is far away and kind o' mythical, so it sounds like fun to most people."

"It's that easy?"

"Almost. But you've got to make two points very clear to them. First, there's no prize or reward o' any sort for pushin' the button. Otherwise, that would make you an accomplice to the kill—you wouldn't want that. And second, you have to convince them the act really kills someone. That alone, should cause most folks to walk away, but they don't. Tis a sad fact that most people will do bad things for a bit o' fun, *if* they can stay anonymous."

"Yeah." I'd seen that way too many times on the web. Hide behind a username or a temporary IP address, and ethics go out the window. I saw it all the time in online gaming.

"Also, a teleport is usually a rush job. That's why you'd run out and pick someone off the street. In Amsterdam, tis usually done in the Red Light District. But you try to avoid people with weddin' rings, kids, or anyone with close connections like that. Tis a cruel business—doing a forced jump. True volunteers are best, but hard to come by."

"Someone would volunteer to lose their body?"

He nodded sadly. "There's more variety in this world than you might imagine."

"So Europeans use kill chips. Even you?"

"I'll never use them. Like I said, Brenda didn't have a choice. Don't get the wrong idea. Jack is the only one who loves to wire up his spirit walkers."

Like me? "Like Billy Bob?"

"I wouldn't worry about it. I'm sure Peter had your chip removed, fried with an EM pulse, or reprogrammed by now."

Reprogrammed?

"Here." The Black handed me some headphones. "Relax with some music. This controls the volume. This selects the channel. But let me know if you're goin' to take a nap. I'll have to tie you down again before you sleep."

* * *

An hour of epic music passed quickly. I switched it off and noticed The Black was in his usual position on the floor, stretched out on his back with Brenda perched on his pelvis. The Euro-friendly position. Brenda looked like she was in a good mood again. Actually, she was naked and looking good all over. I pulled off my headphones. Sweet. She was doing the cowgirl thing on The Black.

I pried my eyes off of her to check out The Black's face. Yup, he was happy, too.

He smiled up at me. "We're all just one big happy family." The Black winked at me and gave me a fist bump.

Without warning, I was in The Black's big rugged body, staring up at Brenda riding my hips, with my new big Highlander pole deep inside her. I looked back at The Black, now in Billy Bob's nasty body. He gave me a wink, like we were pals—like taking turns was what pals do.

Yes, The Black and I were bros. Bros who shared.

On the other hand, I was now in Brenda. Brenda, the one who might be trying to kill me? Brenda, Jack's mole inside the rebellion? Brenda, Peter's girlfriend? Hmm. Maybe this was a good thing.

Yeah. Peter was probably getting it on with my Sonya babe, so this was totally fair. Humping with Brenda was beginning to seem like a good thing.

Well, it felt great. And besides, I'd already had sex with Jack when he was wearing Shanna, so what was wrong with this?

Sex with evil. Bring it on.

Seriously?

It was obvious that jumpers never had normal sex. Body swapping was an invitation to be weird. Oh, well. When in Jumperland, do as the Jumperlandians do.

Besides, it was a relief to be out of Billy Bob's big gator hide. The Black was very strong, very big, and absolutely glorious to wear. And Brenda was looking super fine out of her flight attendant clothes.

I glanced at The Black and gave him a wink. Yeah, it was all good. Beyond good. It was like awesome beyond the realm of reality.

A short while later, Brenda must have figured out the swap because she hauled off and slapped me. Oops. Caught in another man's body. Maybe I looked sheepish, maybe like something else. I reached out to touch The Black so I could swap back into my Billy Bob body, but Brenda pulled my arm back.

"No way. You swapped, now live with it."

She hated me, but she wanted me? Confusing. But honestly, there was nothing to do but enjoy it as long as I could.

Which wasn't anywhere near the five hours I was hoping for.

Brenda went to freshen up, so I got off the floor and sat next to Billy Bob. I touched his arm to swap back, but nothing happened.

Billy Bob looked me up and down. "So what's it like in the body of a big Scot?"

I shrugged and I could feel my long hair brush against my huge shoulders. My muscles rippled when I casually moved. With every breath, the air swirled in my big Highlander lungs, and the world felt so fresh and alive. "Kinda good, actually. What's it feel like to be in a bloated alligator?"

He touched my hand and we instantly swapped back into our usual bodies. "'Tis one thing to share, lad. But you've left me with naught but an aching disappointment in my kilt—and a wee mess."

"Sorry."

"Aye. And that makes two of us."

4.6 The Vegas Act

I dreamed that every jumper in the world got together for peace talks in a big glass ballroom. It was glorious. All 666 of us laughing and drinking champagne and eating little tasty snacks. I think we were eating shark sushi—weird, but hey, that's what you get in a dream.

And we all had shark fins on our backs. Did I mention that? Well, we did. And they kinda looked cool.

And Sonya was there and she looked stunning in a low cut backless midnight-blue dress and her dazzling diamond necklace. The little shark fin on her back was so cute. Tiger striped, like I imagined a tiger shark's fin might be. And me? I looked awesome as Wolf in Armani, with the Rolex, of course. And yeah, my shark fin was bigger than the other guys.

Size matters.

Anyway, the meeting had been arranged so we could all finally come together, to work in harmony for the betterment of mankind. They even had a banner made showing a shark hugging a human. Because we liked normals—we really did.

Peter was there with Brenda. Bruce the Black playing something haunting on the bagpipes. Snow Leopard was lounging in the corner in the body of a real snow leopard. He, or she, looked awesome. Go Snow, go!

Billy Bob Wyville was invited because he was a jumper, but he was only there as a passenger in my head. Sucks to be you, Billy Bob.

There were hundreds of jumpers I'd never met.

Hell, Jack was even there, looking super stunning in a hot ravage-me-now red zoot suit. But he was somehow stuck on a glass wall, just watching everyone, and of course he was sipping on a glass of pink champagne. His feet were dangling off the ground—his spats casually tapping the wall in time to the bagpipe music. Hung on the wall, he looked almost cute—almost harmless.

Everyone was behaving themselves and having a really good time.

But then Peter, that twerpy nerd guy, stepped out of the glass ballroom, closed the door, and pushed a big red button releasing toxic gas into the room. We choked, fell to the floor, and died. Except Jack—he died on the wall.

So of course, we all jumped into Peter's body. Maybe that was his grand idea—to throw a party to get us all together, then pack us into a single body—his body. But it got really messy in Peter because we all tried to control it as equal partners.

Peter fell over, convulsing on the floor because hundreds of people can't be packed into one little guy, and we couldn't all use his brain at the same time. So we were doomed unless we cooperated. And again, I wondered if that was Peter's grand scheme: to force us all to get together *and* cooperate.

Also, because we were all packed into one body, it was imperative to be safe. So Peter was elected to take the wheel. As for the rest of us, we all wanted to ride shotgun.

Life in Peter, if you can call it that, was perma-hell.

Maybe that's why jumpers never seemed to get together for Christmas, or conventions in Vegas, or anything. It was too damn easy to kill us all, pack us into a single easy to handle body, then use fake paperwork to get us into a creepy mental asylum until we died of old age.

Yeah, Vegas was out.

* * *

I woke up on the same plane, strapped to my chair. Brenda was reading a fashion magazine, and looking like she belonged on the cover. The Black was fully dressed—as fully dressed as any Scot can be in a formal tuxedo top, a plaid skirt with a furry purse at crotch level, and long white stockings. He was also sharpening a wicked looking ceremonial blade—long enough to be a short sword.

They didn't exactly look happy. Was I in trouble?

It was dark out the windows. "Are we there yet?" Not that I knew where we were going.

"Change o' plans, lad. San Francisco was seriously dodgy when we approached, so I turned that mission down."

What? We could do that? "You turned it down?"

"O' course. You have to choose your battles. Sure, I agreed to help your group. Ethics is a noble cause. Then there's the wee matter of survivability. Even for me, tis part of my decision process. Don't get me wrong, I'd dearly love to escort Jack out o' this universe. But we aren't just soldiers who must follow orders. You and I, we are field generals. Battles are won or lost based on our decisions on the ground."

"I thought Peter was calling the shots."

"Peter's a good source of intel, but the choice is ours on how to use it."

"I wouldn't call it good intel. It's minimal at best."

"That's only 'cause he's tryin' to stay above you in the peckin' order. When you grow a bigger backbone, he'll fall in line. But don't kick yourself. You're new to all this."

"What about Sonya? She calls the shots, too, right?"

"Aye, she does. North America is her theater, so she sets the priorities and chooses her staff from what's available. Honestly, Wolf, I wouldn't be here if I didn't think she was up to the task. Just remember, when Peter tells you what to do, tis your call. But when Sonya directs you, aye then you better think long and hard about goin' contra to her plan. So far, she has moved this ball a lot farther down the field than I thought possible."

"So Jack's days are numbered?"

"No, lad. Jack's days are never numbered. He's the snake you kill, then he bites you. Remember that, too."

The Black went back to sharpening his blade, and Brenda seemed to be channeling one of her inner passengers.

"So where are we going?"

"We're landin' in Las Vegas shortly. Brenda has some personal business lined up for us. Best you gird your loins, lad."

My loins needed girding? Whatever that meant. I checked Billy Bob's loins. They seemed girded to me.

* * *

After we landed, The Black leaned over to me with some advice. "I'm thinkin' you'll be needin' a new body, and this is just the place to do it. Hell, lad, if you can't pick up some new flesh in Las Vegas, you might as well pack it in as a jumper. Just be sure to keep your eyes open. Choose your killer wisely, 'cause a body with a kill chip in it, aye that's a trip straight to Jack's ever lovin' arms—if you catch my meanin'."

Got it. Vampires needed to pick a healthy blood donor. I needed to pick a new body that Jack didn't arrange for me.

One of the pilots opened the exit door, then lowered the steps. Night in Vegas was brighter than I expected. Hell, I could even see several casinos from the airport. Cool desert air blew in.

"I know you can hunt on your own, Wolf, but we're short on time. Brenda was hopin' you'd pick from a wee list she made for you." He handed me a list of five names and addresses. "Brenda's keen on the first one, so you might want to give that one a nod. He's a family oriented killer. But be careful. If anything smells like Jack, go to the second name on the list. I'm givin' you five names. You only need one, but take down all five if you've a mind to. Then meet us under the Eiffel Tower in about three hours, that's midnight local time."

"The Eiffel Tower in France?"

"No. The wee one they have in Las Vegas. This Eiffel Tower is only half as high as the real one, but you can't miss it. Now if you'll excuse me, Brenda and I have a special party to attend, but we're on call if you get in over your head."

Brenda was already down the steps.

Call? How? "Peter's earpiece? It's still silent."

"It'll work when you get clear o' the jammin' signal on our plane. Remember, Peter is comms, not command. Sonya is command. Brenda and I are just a bit o' backup if you should need it. Now do your best hunting, Wolf."

Brenda was already in her limo. The door was open, waiting for The Black to join her. Behind her was another limo. Just for me? Cool. Las Vegas was full of chauffeurs and big shiny limos.

We stepped onto the tarmac and walked toward the cars. Vegas looked like one big carnival. I could almost smell the cotton candy and hear the people scream on the rides.

The Black turned to me.

"Oh, I almost forgot. Remember to keep the joy in all your dyin', lad."

What the hell did that mean? Dying was never a joy. Should it be?

They drove off in their limo. My chauffeur was standing by my passenger door. Cool. Time to dump the Billy Bob outfit and pick up something more suitable to my new lifestyle.

I tried to enjoy the thought of dying.

* * *

I'd handed the list to the driver as I got in. He only briefly glanced at it. Good, he had a lot of experience with lists.

The first stop was the Meridian Casino. As we drove north along the strip, it became clear that Las Vegas was little more than light bulbs and tourists. Where were the gangsters? The high rollers? The whales? Where were the carnival barkers shouting about their unearthly freak shows? Where were the gunshots and thrills? Where were the demonic multi-headed freaks?

Oh, wait. That was me—still wearing Billy Bob's river stained white suit and orange shirt.

"Dude?"

Peter was in my ear, back online. "What?"

"Seriously? Las Vegas? Get back to Austin. We've got a new safe house all set up for you. We're focusing on some corrupt politicians. That will lead us to billionaires who want to control everyone. After that we'll find you another dungeon. So get over here for some R&R before your next mission."

"This is my R&R."

"Gambling in Vegas? You've got no money. Get back here."

"No. I don't need money. I need a better body."

"No you don't. We need you to stay in Billy Bob for a while. A lot of people know him. We can use him. You're fine just like you are."

"No, I'm not. I'm in the beast from the east. I'm rotund." I reached into the minibar for rum and a cola product. "I can't live like this, Peter. Wolf can't function properly because Billy Bob is so friggin' out of shape."

"Then go to a gym. Eat a salad. We need you to stay Billy Bob while we crack open the system."

"No you don't. You tried to kill me under the barn in Gettysburg so I could get a new body. Remember?"

"Yeah, but we changed our plans. Now we really need you like you are. Keep your skin, dude."

To hell with the cola. I was already chugging the mini bottles of straight rum. "Screw you. You're not the boss of me."

"What?"

Okay, so that might have sounded a little juvenile. "I'm sick and tired of being treated like Billy Bob the Bayou Boy. I've earned a new body, so now I'm getting one. A killer. Someone who deserves to fork over his body. I hope it's athletic. And handsome."

"Think of your mind."

Huh? "My mind's already crawling with evil. What's one more killer in my head gonna do? Keep me out of heaven? Hell, I'm already screwed on that front. Besides, I'm gonna live forever, so any kind of afterlife is kinda irrelevant, wouldn't you say, Peter ol' pal?"

"Have you been drinking?"

"Maybe." I noticed my lap was littered with empty mini bottles. "A few. What of it?"

"Billy Bob will surface. He'll take control. Dude, get someone to tie you up."

Too late.

* * *

Billy Bob stuffed his pockets full of whiskey mini bottles. I hated whiskey.

It seemed like a good idea to put Peter on ice, so I pulled out the earpiece and stuck it in the mini fridge. Justice.

The limo pulled over and a valet opened my car door.

I turned to my driver. "Where the hell are we?" I didn't say that. Billy Bob was doing the talking. Shit, passengers couldn't talk. But jumper passengers could?

The driver turned his head. "Meridian Casino. First stop on the list, sir."

I looked out the window. "What the hell am I doing here? Never mind. It occurs to me that a certain ex-business partner has an office here." Who? Billy Bob wasn't sharing anything with me, except that he had unfinished business. "Hand me your gun." I guess I said that.

"I don't have one."

"Hand me your goddamn gun." It was weird to have someone operate my mouth.

My chauffeur shrugged like there was nothing to hand over.

"Never mind. I'll get my own damn gun." Billy Bob got out of the limo and pushed the valet aside. Then he walked up the steps and into the casino.

I tagged along. That's about all I could do. Hell, I couldn't even find my own mental steering wheel.

Note to self: Never ever drink again. It was complete loss of control.

Actually, it was worse than that, because Billy Bob was going to get us all killed. Sure, we were already all dead, but Billy Bob was going to burn my traveling circus to the ground. Personally, I wanted to keep it going as long as possible.

Billy Bob headed straight for an elevator, but on the way, I could see hundreds of tourists mindlessly feeding slot machines. Throw money into the slots, get rewarded with colored lights and musical bings. How many would play the slots if the damn things were dark and silent?

Where were the odds? Weren't they posted somewhere?

Before I knew it, we were several stories up and standing in someone's outer office. Right in front of me was a very pretty secretary, rapidly becoming hysterical, obviously pushing a button under her desk like it was life or death.

As for me, I was standing there, screaming obscenities, and my hand was gripping an expensive semiautomatic handgun. Shit! Not my hand—Billy Bob's hand. And I was aiming the gun at a bodyguard type on the floor who seemed to think it was his gun, but maybe not the best time to try and get it back.

How the hell did I get into this mess?

Another hired goon came up behind me and fired a semi-lethal warning shot through my lower back, through some of Billy Bob's disgusting gut-like internal organs, and out through Billy Bob's stomach.

Surreal.

Did I need those parts?

That's about all I could think, as Billy Bob turned and blew several holes in the shooter.

I screamed. The secretary screamed. On second thought, the secretary was just continuing her binge screaming.

Billy Bob must have bent over and picked up the gun that had shot me, because I now held two guns. Delightful. Billy Bob decided time was wasting, so he tucked one gun into his belt and charged through the inner office door.

There was just no stopping him—he was acting like a wounded rhino.

I had the fleeting thought that we shouldn't be shooting our killers. Damn it, we needed someone alive enough to jump into!

Billy Bob was lining up a head shot on a terrified guy seated at a desk. But as he squeezed off the shot, I was barely able to nudge the gun to the left. Or maybe it was Wolf finally deciding to avoid a mess on the fancy carpet.

Either way, the shot missed the ex business partner's bald head by inches and he slid down behind the desk.

We stood there for a second or two, all fighting for control of Billy Bob's body. Our gun waved over the desk, waiting for a piece of the ex-business partner to show itself. Our left hand clutched the blood gurgling inconveniently out of Billy Bob's exit wound. My spare gun waited patiently in my belt. I thought maybe we should offer it to the guy under the desk. Wasn't that the point—to get killed by him?

Wild shots sprayed out from under the desk. Splintered wood jumped at us. Were we hit? No. The blind shots missed their mark.

Except for that one.

Oops. A new hole.

Not a good hole. Blood bloomed on my left hip pocket.

We stared down at it in disbelief.

More shots thundered in the office. We staggered back. They were all on target. I could see a face, wide eyed, through the splintered lower desk. It seemed to ask if I needed more bullets to go down. Hell, I was wondering the same damn thing.

The rhino dropped to his knees. The room started going dark, like I was in a tunnel. Then all went black.

I think I died before Billy Bob's face hit the carpet.

* * *

The strong smell of spent gunpowder. The deafening ringing in my ears. The view through splintered wood. Billy Bob, dead in front of me. Blood pooling on my fancy carpet. Backing up. A smoking gun in my hand.

I thought they only smoked in the movies. I dropped it.

Whoever I was, my body was shaking from all the adrenaline.

I backed up slowly. Got to my feet. I was suddenly sober again. Harsh. I could really use a drink. New body. Hello, bald office guy.

My hands went to my head. Yup. Bald.

Time enough to sort my new self out later. Right now, I felt the need to run. Run, Marko. Run!

But wasn't I the innocent one here? Just defending myself from evil Billy Bob. Right?

Right?

I noticed that I was going through Billy Bob's jacket pockets. Not for anything important—just for mini drinks.

Martoni, was that you?

Hey, pal. Good to know you're still hanging on. Wolf and Nameless wanted to know if we were running or staying. So was this now my casino? If so, we should stick around and enjoy my new business. That would be very cool.

Except the new guy was still in shock—not ready to accept half-life in my mental back seat—not ready to have an opinion, or even an urge.

Pops just wanted to sit down and lower our pulse rate.

But where was Billy Bob in my head? Nowhere? Oh, yeah. Lurking. Just waiting for me to sleep or start drinking again.

I was out in the lobby now. The secretary and the first body-guard were long gone. But Tommy's other bodyguard, the one who shot me in the back, he was still lying there, still looking kinda dead.

Two dead bodies. I checked my new body for holes. Okay, I was in one piece. Security would be here in seconds. Or maybe just peeking around corners, all SWAT-like.

I stepped out into the hallway. The words on my door said *Tommy Tarantino, Real Estate Investments*.

Damn. I wasn't the casino owner. Just some schmuck selling empty lots out in the Nevada desert to retired suckers from California.

Nameless was practically in tears. Las Vegas was his dream town. Owning a casino, packed with glittering showgirls, baccarat tables, and Comic-Con conventions was his idea of heaven on earth.

Sorry, Nameless. Maybe next time.

Nameless insisted we find the owner of the Meridian, or any casino, and get killed.

Yeah, that would be massively cool. But life doesn't always hand us handsome casino owners. Sometimes we get bald sand salesmen.

Like now.

The elevator doors opened and two casino security guys with thick necks got out. I pointed back to my office. "In there." They moved cautiously to the office door.

As I stepped into the elevator, it just seemed too easy. Real cops wouldn't have let me go. Would they?

On the way down, there was that same elevator music—the music that tells the audience that bad shit is about to happen. I guess I didn't notice it on the way up, when Billy Bob was using all my brain cells. His brain cells.

Hey, maybe Billy Bob wouldn't be such a mental badass now that his original brain was dead and we were using a borrowed one.

That was a good thought.

But maybe "borrowed" was the wrong word. Somehow, I didn't think we were giving it back to Tommy.

I downed half a mini whiskey bottle to cut the taste of Tommy's spit in my mouth. It seemed wrong to spit whiskey slobber out in the elevator, so I swallowed. My mouth felt much better, but I decided even drinking a small amount would risk unleashing the demons within me.

The elevator doors opened, revealing the casino's main lobby and an awful lot of cops. I raised my little whiskey bottle to the boys in blue, except they were in brown. "Hey, guys. What's going on?"

"Get out."

Okay, okay. Lighten up. I stepped out, they piled in. As the doors closed, I was tempted to tell them which floor to go to, but I was doing fine as the innocent dope, so I kept my mouth shut.

I headed to the exit like nothing had happened. Just another blood soaked jump, followed by a whiskey mouthwash. No big deal.

Martoni and Pops wanted to try one of the slots. Sure. Why not? I was just some realtor who'd screwed Billy Bob out of a pile of money. No harm in that. No harm in dropping some quarters and pulling a lever, either.

Except there was no levers, just buttons. And none of the slots even took coins. And bald Tommy didn't even have coins in his pockets. So I pulled out some bills from my new wallet, but what the hell, none of the slots took bills. What kind of a crap-ass casino was this? The slots only had buttons, and they only took refillable casino credit cards?

This casino had totally sucked the fun out of slots. So I walked out, strolled around until I found the limo zone, and tapped on my driver's window.

He rolled down the window and stared at me like I was just another lost tourist.

Yes, that was me.

Oops. I'd forgotten to tell him that *Omaha* was the secret password. Damn. He had a very long wait for Billy Bob.

Shit. What to say? Something creative. Something to make him give me a ride. "Hi there. Uh, Billy Bob forgot to tell you we're doing this Where's Waldo scavenger hunt kind of thing tonight. So just take me to the next place on your list. Okay?"

Not okay. He just scowled at me.

I tried to look friendly. "Fine. You're new to this game." My hands were rummaging in my pockets for anything helpful. "Look. Yeah, these are Billy Bob's little whiskey bottles. He gave them to me. See? It's kind of a booze sharing, limo swapping kinda game. We play it all the time in Texas."

He seemed to recognize the labels on the discount whiskey bottles.

"Also, Billy Bob said to tell you that he's sorry for demanding your gun. He just doesn't hold his liquor well. You know the type. Anyway, I'm not much of a drinker, myself."

He opened the door and got out. I thought he was going to slug me, but he opened the rear door for me.

"Thanks." I held up the bottles. "I'll just put these little troublemakers back in the fridge. Got any chips?"

He closed the door and we were soon on our way to kill number two.

I tapped on the divider window. The driver rolled it down.

"Hey, driver. What was the first name on the list?"

"Tommy Tarantino."

Odd. Billy Bob went straight for the guy Brenda picked for me to exterminate. So evil jumpers and good jumpers both wanted Tommy dead? Sucks to sell sand to jumpers.

* * *

As I rode in the back of my Vegas death-mobile, it occurred to me that Tommy Tarantino, the shady realtor, was probably a lot more evil than I'd suspected. I mean, why would Brenda make him number one on her hit list?

Tommy was still being quiet in my head, so I just assumed he'd buried an awful lot of bodies under the Nevada sand. Somehow, my gut feeling said it was a reasonable assumption.

The Black called him a family oriented killer? Maybe not in a good way.

Hey, Tommy. Were men the only ones buried out there? Or did you slaughter women and children, too?

No answer.

Never mind, Tommy. I really didn't want to know.

I cracked the window open and tossed his cell phone out. I didn't want anyone tracking me via the GPS in his phone.

The casino lights at night and the limo's heavily tinted windows made Las Vegas look clean and sparkling. They made it easy to ignore the rude tourists and the trash they brought in.

Look, Nameless. We made it to Vegas. Maybe we should skip this kill-tour and catch a show.

Tommy knew a good place.

Shut up, Tommy. The less I heard from him the better.

Something else was nagging at me. Something that tainted my soul. What was it?

Oh, yeah. I'd just killed someone. Not a body snatch—just a kill. Tommy's guy, the one who shot me in the back. I didn't catch his name. The guy who blew a hole in Billy Bob without even saying, "Drop the gun." Was I okay with that? Wasn't it really Billy Bob who did that kill?

I suppose so. Or maybe it was my fault for drinking myself out of the driver's seat. I knew I was hauling evil around in my head. I should have kept them in line.

Nameless thought I was just like Pandora's Box. Filled with evil, and I also contained the spirit of hope.

Really? All I remembered was that Pandora's Box had hope in it. I'd forgotten about all the evil in there, too.

So that was me? A container packed with evil, plus a little hope? Great.

If I was the box, who was the woman who opened it? Sonya was Pandora?

I needed to stop thinking and enjoy the ride.

Easier said than done. Being a vigilante with a hit list was shaping up to be a soul suck.

* * *

Second stop. I checked Tommy's watch. Plenty of time before my flight back to Austin. But this time, I was going to be sober and selective. A decent body would be nice. There were far too many people who needed to be taken down. The less I screwed up my head, and my soul, the better.

We were parked in a middle class neighborhood. Evil was here? Why not?

"Got a name for this party guest?"

The driver shook his head. "No name. Just an address." He pointed to the nearest house.

"Great." I pulled out all the cash in Tommy's wallet. "Here. It's my tip in case I don't see you again. I'll let myself out."

"Thanks."

As I got out, it was clear that Vegas cooled off at night. The glowing sky on my left showed me we weren't far from the downtown area.

I walked up to the house. A simple thing with a covered porch. Maybe built 40 years ago. The lights were off, but I rang the doorbell anyway. Hello, evil. Come out, come out wherever you are. I'm the box that holds you.

Right. Fill me with evil until I crack and leak it all back into the world again.

No lights. No sounds. No one home?

I glanced over my shoulder at the limo. Bruce the Black must have picked the driver, so the driver must be made of tough stuff. And probably just a normal.

Oh, what the hell. I stepped off the porch and circled around the house. Time for a little B&E? Hell, I'd had plenty of experience with rear window break-ins. The rear door had glass on the upper part. It looked like a kitchen door. So I put Tommy's elbow into it.

The glass cracked and fell to the floor. Somehow this reminded me of breaking into the rear of my apartment. Marko's apartment.

There was a bit of noise. No barking dogs. And no cats watching me in the dark.

More importantly, no blood. Not that I cared about leaving Tommy's blood at a crime scene. I put a hand inside and flipped the deadbolt. I was in. Almost too easy. And no alarms—unless they were silent. Did this house have a security sign in the front yard?

Shouldn't I be letting Wolf do this?

No. I could do this on my own. Wolf was for emergency use only. Besides, things were going smoothly.

I was inside a very dark kitchen. Looking for what? Looking for evil.

That's when I caught sight of someone lurking in a reflection! Shit! I jumped—he jumped. I ducked—he ducked. I stuck my head up to get a better look and he did the same thing.

Yeah, he was bald. He was me. My new Tommy face was reflected in the glass kitchen cabinets.

Shit. I checked myself for leakage. Good. My pants were still dry.

So who the hell lived here? And why was I sneaking around in the dark? Wasn't I here to get killed?

In the living room, I found some pictures. Too dark to see, so I flipped on the lights. The best I could figure, the guy liked to fish. Him and a big trout. Hispanic. Kinda average looking. But was he better looking than Tommy?

I found a mirror and compared the average Latino male in the photo with the bald white gringo I was wearing. Yeah that was weird, but I liked having a choice for a change.

Well, it was a tossup. The guy in the photo was my favorite shade of brown, but he looked like a high carb kinda guy. So one point to the Latino for skin color. One point to the gringo for body shape. One point to the Latino for having hair.

But something was wrong with the eyes.

I checked my white-guy eyes in the mirror. Kinda gray-green. Nothing special, but nothing bad, either.

But the eyes in the photos were so dark. Don't get me wrong, dark brown was the best. But those eyes were like black pits of emptiness. Nothing good could come from being behind those eyes.

So five points to the white guy who had unweird eyes.

I went through the whole house, looking for something. Anything. It was just a house—except for the padlock on the basement.

Folks in Las Vegas needed a basement? Like for tornadoes? Hell, even *I* knew this wasn't tornado country. So all I could think of was a fallout shelter. Yeah. Nevada was the home of nukes. Fine, it was logical that everyone in Nevada had a fallout shelter. And kept it locked.

I tried kicking the door to break it in. I tried ramming it with my shoulder. I ran around looking for a crowbar or even a hammer. Nothing.

So I calmly went to the living room, picked up the heavy coffee table, and ran like hell at the basement door.

The coffee table went through it like butter, taking me along with it. Shattered wood. Me tumbling downstairs. Muffled screams in the dark.

I fumbled along the wall for a light switch. I sure as hell was bruised, and it felt like I'd picked up a lot of splinters in my hands and maybe my face.

Not my face. Not a face I ever wanted to wear, so what the hell did I care? It was only pain.

My hand found a light switch. I flipped it on.

I could see stairs and lots of shattered wood. Behind me was a sight from hell—women in cages. Three of them. Not sexy cages. Not willing bondage. Just filth, degradation, and despair.

Oh, shit.

The nameless Latino was a fucking cabrón. Not that I knew what that meant, but I was pretty sure the word fit. Forget the Latino part, this scum didn't deserve the title.

There was the smell of shit and piss in buckets. There was the desire to pick up a machete and hack away at this black-eyed monster. Where were his parents? Where was his grandmother to slap some respect into his sorry hide?

What to do? Set them free so they could run away into the night? And I should leave, so he could return to empty cages? Or maybe I should wait for him to return, even if I missed my flight?

No.

I ran upstairs, picked up the phone, and dialed 911. The cops needed to see this. They needed to be the ones to hunt this animal down. I had enough blood on my hands already.

"Las Vegas police. Please state your emergency."

"Come quick. I was walking by this house when I heard screams. I went inside to see if I could help. Women are being held prisoner in the basement here. Wait. Oh, shit! He's got a machete!" I screamed and set the phone down on the couch. That would light a fire under the cops.

I knocked over a few things and ran for the front door. Time to get the hell out of here.

As soon as I jumped in the limo, I yelled to the driver. "Time to go. This party was a bust. Let's hustle over to the next stop."

* * *

We were in the middle of nowhere on a road that would never end, so I had the driver pull over. I kinda needed to take a leak. I tried not to be disgusted with Tommy's gear in my hand. He did his thing, and we were all relieved. Back in the limo, I thought a little vodka would settle my nerves, but I picked up a bottle of water instead.

Rough night.

Third stop. An old mobile home sat in the scruffy desert. Security lights all around. A good Harley stood near the front door, and an old junk motorcycle stood to the side. For spare parts?

Less thinking—more doing.

"Who lives here?"

The driver checked his list. "Dread. That's all it says."

Good. Bikers were cool—unless they weren't.

I stepped out of the limo. Party time.

I walked up to the front door, braced myself to die, and knocked. "Dread. I know you're in there. So get ready for your worst fucking nightmare."

Maybe I shouldn't have used the f-word, because the front door flew open and a boot kicked the screen door wide. A very long, very unusual, triple barreled shotgun aimed itself at my chest. Tommy's chest. My chest was nowhere near Nevada.

An iron man with a buzz cut and a five day old salt and pepper beard held the other end of the shotgun. His beard was more pepper than salt. But it was the roaring twenties handlebar mustache that held my attention. That, and the three big holes at the end of the triple barrels.

Yeah, and the smell of gun oil and a recent firing might have also heightened the moment.

Dread spoke. "What the hell are you doin' here?" A voice like Montana smoke greeted me.

So they knew each other. One of your pals, Tommy?

No answer.

A bluff seemed in order. "I've got another job for you."

He took a long look at the limo waiting out by his mailbox. "You, lost your damn mind? Comin' out here."

Oops. Maybe I didn't sound like Tommy. Realtor voice. "I've got two rush jobs in the trunk. You want to kill them, or do you want me to do it?"

"The hell you say." He eyed the limo again. "Male or female?"

"One of each."

"Ages?"

"He's older."

No response. So I tried another lie. "She's 13—a real fighter. You'd like her."

He nodded and wore a sick bastard smile. That's all I needed.

I yelled, "FBI!" as I whipped out Tommy's wallet and a cork-screw. That's all I had, but that's all it took.

Something fierce exploded in my chest, deafened me, sent me falling backwards.

No need to check the gaping hole that had been Tommy's chest.

My vision spun 180, then I watched myself fall. Slow motion. I lowered the long cannon in my hands. My limo driver decided he'd had enough for one night and sprayed dirt and gravel on his way out of rural Nevada living.

In front of me lay Tommy Tarantino, a quiet gaping mess where his chest used to be.

Kinda trigger happy, weren't you, Dread?

No answer. There never was.

I checked around inside the mobile home. Strictly bachelor accommodations. No liquor. No mouthwash. But he did have a fridge full of cheap beer. That would have to do. Rinse and spit. Rinse and spit.

After poking around a bit, it was clear there was nothing I wanted. Except a jacket. On the back, it said *Dread*. That's me. And *Hell Riders*. That would be my jumper pack. The keys were already in my pocket, like they should be.

Time to ride, Wolf.

I hoped he was still in me—still able to ride a motorcycle.

So I stepped out and straddled the big Harley. Wolf rose up inside me, newly awakened, alive again.

Next thing I knew, rolling thunder echoed along the dusty country asphalt.

Yeah, it was me.

* * *

The city was easy to find, it lit up the night sky. The Eiffel Tower was easy to find. I parked the Harley in a handicapped spot—such a rebel. I really didn't care if they hauled it away—seemed unlikely I could get it onto the small private jet and back to Austin.

The Eiffel Tower was nicely lit up. We were supposed to meet under it, but there was a casino under it. One leg of the tower touched the ground. The other three legs were stuck into the roof of the casino. Very strange.

I checked my watch, except Dread didn't have one. Maybe I was early. So I wandered around the Eiffel Tower's only leg. Lots of tourists outside. Lots of tourists everywhere.

Little porn leaflets littered the sidewalk. I picked up a few. Very impressive. All of me wanted to hookup with these women. Funny how they were all perfect 10s. And they'd come to my room and show a guy like me a good time. I needed a room? Hell, all I had was Dread's Harley in a handicap spot. Most of my passengers thought that would work just fine.

I dropped the porn cards, tried to clear my head of hot biker sex in a handicap spot, and walked over to a woman who seemed to be waiting—just like me. Except she was wearing Midwest tourist clothes, and I wasn't. "Pardon me ma'am. Do you know what time it is?"

She gave me a frightened look, and walked away like I'd just told her it was time to join my gang and be my bitch.

Okay, so I looked a bit scruffy. Big deal. Lots of famous actors dressed down when they cruised the streets of Vegas. Right?

Maybe they'd think I was famous if I wore sunglasses at night. I checked my pockets for shades. Nada.

A couple of security types were eyeing me. What? Wasn't I acting Vegas normal?

So I decided to step inside the casino under the Eiffel Tower and check out the slots. Yeah, because that's what badass bikers do. We look for loose slots. It's kinda a guy thing.

Inside, there were the usual slot machines, tourists, and casino stuff. Well, it looked like Paris, except it was packed with Americans. And I could see the other three legs of the Eiffel Tower coming in through the roof. Near the middle, there was an elevator in the middle that led to the Eiffel Tower restaurant somewhere above. Except you had to have reservations. That's what the sign said. And a guy working his way through college was the gatekeeper.

Off to one side, I could see a small crowd of Chinese tourists taking pictures of giggling Chinese girls posing next to a very big man in a skirt—Bruce the Black.

The Black looked exactly like a Vegas attraction. Hell, the giant Scot would be an attraction anywhere.

He signed autographs, roared when he laughed, and posed for lots and lots of photos. For some reason, the Chinese were especially attracted to him.

Martoni thought they were like rice on white.

Keep your racist jokes to yourself, Martoni, otherwise I'd have to bring out the Italian jokes.

The security guys were behind me. Funny how they were tailing me and ignoring the unauthorized attraction in a kilt. Funny how the Chinese didn't want their picture taken with a true American icon like Dread the Hell Rider.

A few minutes later, the security duo decided to move in on me. "Sir, we're going to have to ask you to leave."

Seriously? I was just standing there watching The Black. "I'm with Bruce the Black, there. I handle his security."

That gave them something to think about. But just for a second. "Weapons aren't allowed in the casino."

Weapons? Was I packing anything? Sure, I might have the usual biker knife on me. "I don't carry a firearm. Don't need it."

The security guys had cute red jackets with not so cute bulges. "I'm sorry, sir. We're still going to have to ask you to leave." One of them put a hand on my arm.

Seriously? That arm probably had a tattoo of a sweet valentine's heart with a German battle ax ripping through it.

Not that I'd checked my new arm. Not that I even needed to.

Just because the security guys were rude, didn't mean I needed to shred them, and bloody up the fake little Paris I was standing in. I held up my hand to The Black to indicate I was stepping outside with these nice gentlemen, but he didn't see me.

But Brenda noticed and stepped over. "It's okay, boys. He's with us."

Funny how cute redheads could call ex-football players *boys* and get away with it. If I tried it, they'd probably want to hand me my teeth.

The security boys looked annoyed, stepped back a few paces, and used their walkie-talkies to bump the issue to the security guys upstairs.

Brenda hung on my biker arm. "You're looking impressively different, Wolf. Was it fun?"

"Not especially."

"You're wearing number three."

"Yeah." Third scumbag on the hit list.

"I hope you didn't skip the first two."

"Nope. I ate my veggies first. Then the beef went down well— very satisfying. I would have enjoyed dessert, but my chauffeur ran off with the menu."

"Bad things do happen, love."

I nodded. "They do. But what goes around . . ."

"Ready to leave?"

"Ready when you are." I couldn't help but like Brenda. I was happy to dine on men who killed women and children. And Brenda deserved better from me than accusations.

She squeezed my arm and held it close to her. "Good. I can't wait to clean you up." Brenda waved at The Black and he saw her. I guess he wasn't expecting me to be wearing a biker, so he couldn't see my wave earlier. It was very clear this was Brenda's hit list. She'd go after men who enjoyed torturing women and killing children.

Always send a wolf on a wolf's job.

Yeah, I was starting to like Brenda—and looking forward to her cleaning me up.

* * *

Back on our jet, Brenda pushed me into the plush lavatory and showed me the shower tucked into a bulkhead. She pushed a bar of soap into my hand. I probably invited her to join me—well, I'm sure I did. And she told me I could bloody well do it myself.

So I did.

Damn. Not what I wanted, but I should remember I was Sonya's man.

I shaved off the scruffy beard and the cool retro mustache, and that made me look younger. And of course, I inspected myself in the mirror. About what I expected. Maybe in my late 30s. Lots of weird tats I would eventually learn to ignore. But there was a disturbing tattoo of a mangy rat eating a brain. That was too weird for words.

On second thought, maybe it was symbolic of what I'd become. So was I the rat eating evil minds? Or was I the brain being devoured by my passengers?

No need to decide. It worked both ways.

Somehow I didn't think Brenda wanted me back in dirty biker clothes, so I stepped out naked. "Ta da!"

Brenda clapped and laughed. "Bravo! Simply stunning! Bravo, Master Wolf!"

The Black pointed to some clothes in a chair. "You'll be needin' some clothes. They're a might big, I suspect, but better than nothing."

I put on the big kilt, thankful it had a belt to hold it up. The ruffled white shirt fit me like a tent. Man, I looked horrible. What, no underwear? Well, a nice breeze would be interesting.

I pointed at my plaid kilt. "Not my tartan."

"True enough, lad. But you're kin enough to wear it, so do it with pride."

Maybe I was hoping for mind swap sex—I'm sure I was. But the hour was late and the evening's adventures were pushing my thoughts toward sleep.

They tied me down for the night and I drifted off while counting my mental passengers. Let's see, there was: Martoni, Nameless, uh . . . Wolf of course, then Pops, but Snip was technically just before Pops, then Billy Bob Wyville who was my only jumper passenger, then Tommy Tarantino, and finally Dread the biker. So how many was that? Counting the original me, that made eight and a half. Snip never had a chance, so I only counted him as half.

Sonya had two, counting herself. I liked her that way. Peter had two, or was it three? Brenda had nine now. Wow, nine and she still acted sane. I was clearly losing it, so Brenda was my new role model. Bruce the Black never said how many passengers he had, but it was clear that nothing bugged him. Finally, there was Jack the beast master, loaded with hundreds of passengers. Shit, maybe Jack deserved more credit for keeping his act together. I'd never even seen him drool.

Despite having a head full of evil, I slept like a baby. No bad dreams. I guess Billy Bob was happy to visit with my new killer passengers. Or maybe it wasn't just a visit. Maybe my passengers were conspiring against me.

What died in Vegas, waited quietly in the back of my mind.

4.7 Unrelenting Undead

We landed in Austin before dawn. The pilots left, but we were sleeping comfortably, so we stayed on the plane. Cool. Private jets were the best mobile homes, ever.

* * *

When I finally woke up, I was disoriented. Where was I? What the hell was I wearing? Who the hell was I in?

Oh, yeah—back from Las Vegas. Three new passengers in my head. No, wait. Just two. The subhuman guy with the soulless eyes went to the cops. I now had Tommy the mass murdering realtor in me—that gave me mad business skills. Plus, I now had Dread the biker, the guy who did Tommy's dirty work—that gave me awesome desert burial skills, at the very least. Those two guys liked working together, but now they were stuck together forever, living large in the back of my mind.

Hey, guys. Welcome to Hotel Texas. It's a lot like Hotel California, except you had to die to get in. Same *No Exit* policy.

So where was I? Oh, yeah. On a small private jet sitting on a tarmac in Austin. Probably the private aviation side of the airport.

Oh, and I was wearing a big plaid skirt. And a big white shirt like you see at the Renaissance Festival. Hand me downs from The Black.

And I was in a biker's body, complete with disturbing tattoos.

And it was morning.

And I was tied up. Alone on the plane.

And I was now a plus 2, mentally.

Yeah, I could already tell this was going to be a good day.

* * *

After several minutes of yelling for help, someone finally boarded the plane and untied me.

It was that guy again. That chauffeur with the accent, like from India. But the last time I saw him was in Canada. Yeah, and he tried to take my courier case with the diamonds, so I almost strangled him with my belt, and I took his car keys. Yeah, that guy.

After I was untied, I looked him in the eye. "Thanks. We've met before, right?"

"I'm thinking not. But perhaps we have. You may call me Vijay."

Yup, same guy. He was eyeing Dread's tattoos and my weird Highlander clothes.

I made sure my skirt covered my private parts. "Good party."

"I'm sure it was. I have a car waiting outside."

"Where are we going?"

"The choice is yours. Where are your bags?"

"No bags."

"Ah, then your trip was most excellent."

Kinda. "None of this bothers you? Me wearing a kilt and being tied up?"

"Not in the least, sir. I provide pleasant transportation. Judgment in no way enters my mind."

Yeah, right. But wasn't he one of Jack's crew? A normal, but still taking orders from Jack? "I haven't seen you around here before. Who sent you?"

"You mean, my assignment to Austin? I came with Ms. Clark, as her driver. And she sent me to assist you, as needed."

So this Vijay guy used to work for Jack, but now he works for Sonya? Doubtful. Sonya would never have sent him, because Jack might find me through Vijay. Or maybe this guy was now part of the resistance? No. People don't just flip sides that quickly.

I decided to keep my mouth shut until I checked with Sonya and Peter. My earpiece was long gone. Actually, the last time I'd worn it was when I was in Billy Bob. Where did I leave Billy Bob? It was getting hard to keep track of where I left all my used bodies.

Oh, yeah. I left Billy Bob's carcass in Las Vegas, quietly gurgling out on the nice carpet in Tommy's office. And still wearing Peter's earpiece. No, I remember taking it out earlier. Where was it? Oops. The earpiece was still chilling in the minibar in the back of the Las Vegas limo.

Fine with me. I could take care of myself.

I put on Dread's biker boots and we stepped out of the plane. Vijay's usual black town car was waiting nearby. Too risky. I needed Vijay to drive me around like I needed another messed up passenger. "I don't need a ride."

He looked at my costume. "I believe you do."

"Thanks, but no thanks."

"And how will you get where you are going?"

"We're at the airport. I'll walk over and catch a taxi."

"I see no pockets. You have money for such a ride?"

Hell, I didn't even have a destination. Going back to Wolf's was too dangerous. Billy Bob's place didn't seem like a good idea. Where else could I go? My apartment was long gone. I could knock on Marie's door and try to explain things. Yeah, I wasn't exactly her type today. Mom's house? Same problem. Vijay could drop me off behind the State Theater. I still knew the alarm code, assuming they hadn't changed it. But I didn't have keys. Was the door under the alley grate still open?

He opened the car door and held it for me. "Please get in, sir. The ride will be most pleasant."

"I'll drive myself." I held out my hands for the keys.

He was alarmed. "No. I cannot do that. I am the driver. The car is my responsibility. Besides, think how it would look for you to drive me. It is simply not possible."

I still had my hand out. "You have pockets—you stay here and call a cab."

He took his hands off the car door and backed up a step. "It is not possible. This is my car to drive, not yours. You would be wise to accept my most gracious and sincere offer of a ride. Simply name your destination, sir."

Wolf was ready to extract the keys from his lifeless body.

Not a good thought.

Wolf glanced around for witnesses. Ten seconds to silently kill him, maybe less. Six seconds to drop the body in the trunk. A pleasant way to start the day.

What I really wanted was to roll up to Rema's on a motorcycle, then get some help from my sidekick. All my passengers were happy with that. Dread insisted on a Harley. Nameless really wanted a red one. Wolf wanted black. Martoni wanted to stop at a diner first, because every good day starts with bacon and eggs. Oh, and hash browns and a large buttery biscuit, too.

Silence!

A motorcycle. Was that too much to ask?

Wolf thought we needed two paper clips. That, and the airport parking garage would get us a motorcycle.

Finally! Someone with a plan.

"I need two paper clips."

"What?"

"Paper clips. You know? Those little metal things."

"I know what they are, but I have no paper clips."

"You must."

"I am a driver, not an office clerk."

"Think, man. It's a car. Junk collects in it. In the glove compartment, the center console, map pockets, tucked down in the seats—somewhere you have them."

"My car is clean. I know what I have, and I have no such paper clips. So please end this disagreeable conversation and get in the car."

"Documents. You have documents, right?"

He glanced at the car. "There might be some, but they are not for you."

"They have paper clips on them, don't they?"

He hesitated.

"Then hand them over."

"I cannot. If I have such things, they serve a purpose. They must not be removed."

I opened the front passenger door and began rummaging around in the glove compartment. Wolf found a cheap ball point pen and pocketed it. He thought he could start some types of ignition switches with it. Okay, but where were the documents with paper clips?

Vijay backed away. "So it has come to this. You steal paper clips. Very well, then. I must now tell Ms. Clark that you refused to be driven to your destination. Also, that your behavior was most erratic. Think what she will say to you then."

I found half a box of paper clips, turned, and waved them in his face. "I'm not stealing these, I'm borrowing them. But you need to ask yourself, do you really want these back when I'm through with them?"

He let that run through his mind for a second. "No."

"Good. Out of my way." I ran to the side of the hangar we were closest to. It seemed like the airport terminal and parking lots were beyond the hangar. Somehow, running like a madman in biker boots and a plaid skirt, with a baggy white shirt, clutching a little box of paper clips, with a guy from India chasing me—well, it all seemed perfectly natural.

I rounded a corner on the hangar building but Wolf stopped short.

As Vijay came around the corner, I grabbed him by the collar. "Look, you. You've got two options. You can follow me and have the living crap beat out of you, or you can go back to the car and wait for instructions."

He thought about it.

I was getting impatient. "You do understand what I mean by *living crap*, don't you?"

"Living crap? Yes. It translates most vividly."

"Well, then?" I shook him.

"I see that you have decided not to ride with me today. While that is most regrettable, I must respect your decision. I hope you will travel with me in the future . . . under better circumstances. Have a most pleasant day, sir."

I released him. He made a quick u-turn and ducked around the corner. I peeked around the hangar, and he was still hustling back to the car.

Good. Up ahead were the main terminals of the Austin airport and the nearby parking garage, and behind that, the big long-term parking lot. Lots of motorcycles awaited.

But who would load up their motorcycle with luggage and head to the airport? A biker traveling light? Maybe there weren't any parked motorcycles.

Just then, something caught my eye. Tucked in behind the hangar was a black and red Harley. Did airplane mechanics drive motorcycles?

Okay, Wolf. Fetch!

But Harleys are loud and the last thing I needed was a bunch of airport cops in hot pursuit of a stolen bike. So Wolf did his magic to disable the alarm and unlock the handlebars, then we pushed it quietly away. Actually, Dread pushed it because he knew all about pushing Harleys.

When we were far enough away, Wolf tried the factory pin code and started it right up. Cool.

But Wolf and Dread were disgusted. They'd just started a sweet late-model Harley without the key fob and without picking the ignition switch. Who doesn't reset the pin code? Who doesn't read the owner's manual?

But as we sat there on the bike, whatever agreement Wolf and Dread had about security quickly evaporated. They were now locked in an argument about who should ride it. There was no question in my mind who should do the honors—it was Wolf. Dread argued that he was a real biker. Okay, fine. I had no problem with real bikers. But Dread was known to kill women and children and bury their blood-caked bodies in dusty Nevada. So the less I heard out of him, the better.

Wolf rode.

And quickly stopped. A 20 mph breeze and a big plaid skirt with no underwear was a bad combination. Actually, I kinda liked it, but it wasn't gonna fly on a Texas highway. Sure, some lucky trooper would love pulling me over, but I wasn't about to make his day.

So I tucked the kilt under me in front and we took off. I got about a hundred yards and realized it was flying up in back. So I battened it down all around.

Awkward. How do women get around on motorcycles?

We rode, but at 50 mph my big white shirt was filled with wind and acting like a parachute. Nothing I could do about that, and I didn't feel like pulling over and taking it off.

So that's how I rode—biker boots, Scottish skirt tucked under me, biker tats peeking through the Renaissance shirt while it ballooned out behind me.

Most of my passengers knew that Harley bikers always do this little hand wave as they pass in opposite directions. So naturally, I did the wave and they automatically waved back. Then they'd almost crash, rubbernecking to see what the hell I was.

Howdy, boys. Keep the dirty side down and the freaky side up.

Bikers might look all badass in their leathers, club jackets, polycarbonate shades, neck tats, and wallet chains—but if you want real badass, look no further than a twisted clown stuffed in someone else's body, with a head full of killers, wearing a plaid skirt and a white balloon shirt. Hell, if I'd had some lipstick, I might have smeared some on—Joker style.

* * *

As I pulled up in front of Rema's place, I was flooded with bad feelings. Lots of dread. Yeah, massive waves of shark blood infused dread.

Trouble coming?

Rema's car was there. She was home. Was that weird? I had no clue what day it was, but judging by traffic on I-35, it was a weekend. Probably Sunday.

So, yeah, it was no big deal to find Rema home.

But something was still nagging at me.

The motorcycle. Yeah, that was it. I wanted to find a black and red Harley, so there it was. That just doesn't happen.

And it was too easy to steal. Who doesn't reset the factory pin code that bypassed the keys? Hell, anyone could just walk up and ride away with it.

What else was bothering me? There was more. What was it?

That chauffeur back at the airport. One of Jack's men, and he just happened to be waiting for me. But now he was working for

Sonya? And Bruce the Black and Brenda had walked off without a word?

All very bad.

Jack was moving in again. I could feel it.

It was the same feeling as when Wolf was shot. But I'd survived that. Brenda seemed to be off the hook for my hot tub death, but Jack was still a prime suspect.

Then there was the dungeon where I'd found The Black. That was certainly a trap laid by Jack. But the dungeon master hesitated—screwed it up. The trap sprung without me taking the bait.

Was this just my good luck? Maybe, but luck didn't put a black and red Harley right in front of me. Coincidence? No, because my paranoid mind had stopped believing in coincidence a long time ago.

So did Jack want me dead, like the hot tub kill? Or did he want me alive and strapped down for kinky sex, like the dungeon teleport? Maybe he couldn't make up his multi-mind?

I had the feeling the chauffeured limo and the Harley were both from Jack. Like I should just take my pick because it didn't matter—both led me here to Rema's.

No. I still had free will. My paranoia was just clouding the facts.

But I couldn't shake the feeling I was being boxed in. Guided along. I was moving in a direction planned by someone else. Like cattle being guided toward the kill chute.

I could still turn away, right? The engine was still running. Maybe I should pick a random road and never look back.

Yes, but if I really wanted to hunt evil, I couldn't turn away. And if I wanted any sort of life with Sonya, running was no answer.

So grow a backbone? Follow the sick twisted road I was on? See it through to the end, even if I failed? Wasn't a shot at success worth the effort?

I huddled all my sick mental bastards together. Time for a pep talk.

Guys, I know none of you have frontal lobes, but you do have instincts. Something's up and we're walking into it, so I need y'all to

*focus and be alert to the situation. Expect the unexpected. Okay,
team hug.*

No. It sounded totally lame in my head, like something a coach
would say when he didn't know jack. "Expect the unexpected?"
Huh? How can anyone expect what they don't expect?
Doublespeak. Nonsense.

I switched off the engine. I was going in.

But before I could get off the motorcycle, a sinister thought cast
its shadow on my mind. Jack was always five steps ahead of us
because he was . . . psychic. Didn't Peter say Jack was psychic?

Jack being psychic was bad enough, but what if it was worse.
Much worse. What if Jack was actually in my head, like a quiet
passenger, reading my thoughts, spying on me? What if Jack could
eavesdrop on every jumper?

Or maybe Jack was more than just a passenger. Maybe he was
actually in all of us—physically in our brains. Hell, maybe he
actually *was* all of us. Like, there were no jumpers, because we were
all little Jacks. Or maybe we were all just reflections of Jack. Like
fun house mirrors.

Or maybe Jack was a one-off DNA mistake—a virus in human
form. And over the years, he reproduced. So all jumpers were Jack's
spawn, except we were all like mules and couldn't reproduce. Mules
are half horse and half donkey, and they are all born sterile. Well, it
did make sense. I couldn't think of a single jumper that had kids.
We were the mules. Jack mated with normals, and made jumpers. I
never knew my father. Shit. Maybe my mother had sex with Jack
when he was wearing a Serbian body, and I was the jumper love
child.

That made me shudder.

But it made sense. Jack went around the world planting his evil
DNA seed in normal women—producing jumpers. All jumpers were
doomed because we were nothing more than Jack's kids. Like
father, like son. Jack would never die because he was the devil. And
I was just his evil little brat boy, soaking up killers until my mind
would be as dark and twisted as his. I'd walk in Jack's footsteps. I'd
worship the ground he scorched. I'd scope out succulent women for
him to infest. I'd be his right-hand scourge. I'd—

No. Darth Vader wasn't my father. Get a grip, Marko.

Martoni thought Jack was our godfather, and just as sinister.

Seriously? No, I was just freaking myself out. So cue the paranoia music.

Some thunder rolled to the southeast. Good. Austin always needed rain.

No, the thunder was right on cue. Things were building—bad things. All the dots were rapidly connecting in my mind. Bad dots. Dangerous dots.

But a part of me did seem like Jack. A growing part. A cancer of thought and purpose. Right?

I sat there, impressed with my own insanity. It was wide, it was deep. It pulled everything around me into it, almost like my mind was creating everything in the world. Creating random bits of reality and then stitching the bits together to make something believable. My mind was turning crazy shit into believable shit.

None of this was real. I'd made up this whole freakazoid world in my mind. I'd created Jack, this motorcycle, Sonya, Rema, and even myself. Hell, I wasn't even here. I had to be in a hospital somewhere, after Martoni shot me, and now I was hallucinating all this. Yeah, this was nothing more than meds and a brain injury.

I touched the Harley, felt the cold steel, felt the texture on the grips. No. This was all real—just seriously messed up.

I swung a bare leg off the motorcycle. My new bare legs. Weird that I was now wearing Dread. Another omen? I plucked a few hairs from his leg. Yeah, that hurt—just like it should.

Crap. All this shit was real.

If Jack was bat shit psychic, if he knew what we were thinking, if he knew where we were and what we were doing, then Jack was the mole in the rebellion. Right, Jack?

No answer.

Thunder rumbled through a dark cloud to the southeast.

More silence.

What did I expect? Words from Jack?

Play the game, Marko. Stop second guessing everything and play the damn game.

I strolled up Rema's walkway, tucked in my shirt, smoothed out my rumpled kilt, and rang the doorbell. Did I look too weird? No worries. Rema had seen stranger things in her daycare schools.

An eye appeared through the beveled glass. Rema's searching eye. The eye shifted around, trying to get a better look at my skirt.

Just open the damn door, Rema.

"What you want?"

"We need to talk, Rema."

"Lord almighty! It's you!"

"That's right. So let me in."

"Begone!"

"No."

"You're a bane. You know what that is? Well, I'll tell you what it is, a bane is like the devil's own special kind of pox that he casts on people. And he done cast you on me. So do us both a favor and walk away. Walk away, I say. Lord have mercy, walk away, walk away."

She waited for me to leave.

The beveled eye blinked.

I waited. Maybe I smiled.

"Fine!" She opened the door a crack. "You are one stubborn undead. You know that? Come back another time 'cause I've got company." She closed the door, but opened it again a crack. "Oh, I just have to say, I do love the costume. You truly outdone yourself this time. Now have a blessed day, and don't come back."

She closed the door. I knocked again.

I could hear voices inside. Rema was arguing with someone.

A minute later, the door opened wide. Marie stood there. "Marko?"

The unexpected!

No. It was the absolute jaw dropping unexpected.

My hands steadied my face, but it had a wild mind of its own. I struggled for some thread of self control. "Marie."

"Marko, is that really you?"

Hell, no. I was eight and a half messes all shoved together in a horrid picture of a man. "Kinda."

"Don't just stand there. Come in."

I might have stepped in. Or maybe the house swallowed me.

Either way, I was now inside. What could I say to her? "You look good."

"You look . . . really . . . different."

"Things happened. How'd you find out?"

"Rema told me."

Rema looked like she was having a cow, her eyes rolled around, looking for escape. "No I didn't. Not directly. But things were said. Things were . . . said." Rema was pacing, tugging on herself. "You know, I'll just make some tea. Y'all talk." She walked toward the kitchen, but paused abruptly. "No. Yes, I'll make some tea and y'all can just talk about whatever the undead and their ex-girlfriends talk about." Rema hustled into the kitchen.

Marie stared at me until my knees felt weak. So I plopped down on the couch and straightened my plaid dress. No, it was a kilt. A manly kilt.

She was looking into my eyes, checking me out. "I've heard interesting things about you."

Yeah? "You look well."

"You could've told me what happened."

"You know, I tried. I wanted to tell you. But there was no way you would have believed me."

"You didn't even try."

"Of course I did. I called you up the night I was shot in my taxi. More than once. I tried to tell you about the shooting. I wanted you to know what happened. But you kept hanging up on me." Well, I sounded like Martoni that night, so of course she hung up on me.

"That was you?"

"Yes. But what could I say? The truth was just going to freak you out."

"So you gave up?"

I glanced into the kitchen to see what was holding up the tea. "You know, I was just thinking of you. I was trying to do the best I could, given the circumstances and all. But now you know."

"Yes, I do. Not everything, but some of it."

"Yeah?" I wondered how much she knew. "I missed you."

"I cried my heart out over you." She almost took my hand, but it was another man's hand. She was so close—and distant.

"Sorry, Marie. But I died. You know?"

"But you're not entirely dead."

Rema was standing in the doorway. "Oh, he's dead all right."

Marie looked confused, but she also looked like her usual stubborn self. "But he's here now."

"Does that look like him? 'Cause what I'm lookin' at ain't even close. Like I said before, Marko's dead—as dead as you can get, except this maggoty thing keeps grabbing bodies and knockin' on my door. So if I was you, child, I'd say goodbye. Let his spirit rise, or do whatever it's supposed to do, 'cause creepin' around in other people's bodies is just unnatural, is what it is. So let's shut the door on this unpleasant zombie chapter and get on with our lives, then this poor soul can get on with his cross-dressing biker thing—as if that was natural, if you know what I mean."

Rema leaned over to me. "Whoever you are, Marko is truly sorry he stole your ass. And whatever he's been doin' with you, he's sorry for that, too. 'Cause he weren't exactly in his right mind, as his right mind is done dead and buried. So please forgive him for puttin' a dress on you and all—heaven knows I don't want to know the details on that. And Marko, if you can hear me in there, friends don't let friends cross-dress, especially if they're bikers. Uh-uh. That brings unnatural to a whole nother level. So you remember what I just said, Marko. Word. Now you go and leave this nice man alone. And you, biker man, whoever the hell you are, you can stay for tea, but don't ask me for no pants, 'cause I ain't got none that would fit you, or even go with those eyes. Wait!" Rema spun around. "Tea! Good lord, the tea is calling me."

She went back into the kitchen.

Marie and I sort of smiled at each other.

Awkward.

Marie cocked her head. "So what have you been up to?"

Ha! Nothing I wanted to share. I had to repress thoughts of sex with Sonya. Actually, they were impossible to repress. "Not much." I shrugged. "Weird stuff. What did Rema say about me?"

"Not much. Only that your body died, but your spirit kept coming back in other people. Were you trying to get back to me?"

"Yes." I tried in Austin a few times. I also drove back from New

Mexico to be with her. "It was hard to find a way to connect."

"But you tried."

"Yes. I was even at . . . my funeral."

"Did I see you there?"

"Yes, but I looked like someone else. I even hugged you, but you were so distant."

"Really? You know I was crushed, losing you that way."

"Yeah. I didn't mean to die. I didn't want to. And I wish I could have gotten back with you. But the obstacles were—"

Marie stood up and opened her arms. "Hug me again, Marko."

I hesitated.

"Please. I want to feel you in my arms again."

"You'd just be feeling this guy." I touched my chest.

"Don't underestimate me. I can feel deeper than you know."

I stood up, ashamed of what I'd become. If Marie could feel deeper than this biker, she'd feel all the other killers in me, plus my love for Sonya, and a thousand other things I wanted to hide. But I hugged her, and she nestled her head against my chest.

She seemed shorter. No, I was taller. We fit together so differently.

We stood there for a while, soaking each other up. I wanted it to feel cleansing, or freeing, or anything positive. But it felt lopsided, because she loved me completely, and I'd moved on. For better or worse, I'd moved on in so many ways.

It also felt strange because Marie was so forgiving. The Marie I remembered was a hot-blooded Latina to the core, even if she did look Anglo. The Marie I knew would have beat my emotions to a pulp, then loved me back into her spicy bed.

Did my death in the taxi really change her that much? Could she really forgive me without a fight?

I hoped so. But mainly, I didn't know what to expect from her. We had both changed so much.

She looked up at me, her eyes brimming with love. "Marko, you can never escape me. My love for you is as infinite as space and time itself."

What? Marie and I had argued about space-time before. It was a continuum, and it wasn't infinite. The universe had size and shape and it was expanding—all very finite. There was a start time, and a now time—time in this universe was bounded and expanding. There was a smallest of everything. Reality was quantized.

I remember vividly, it was a short messy fight about something totally stupid. Marie quickly agreed with me about finite space-time because it wasn't worth fighting about. Being late for dinner was worth screaming about, but the nature of the universe was unimportant in the grand scheme of things? Women. Go figure.

But more than anything, that fight was burned into my brain because it was the only damn fight we'd ever had where I won.

It crossed my mind, this was an alternate universe. The hug was over for me. This Marie was a stranger.

She cocked her head. "Cat got your tongue, Wolfie?" She put her hands on her hips and wiggled them for me. "Surprise. You like it, don't you?"

Oh, shit! Oh, crap! I pushed her away. Jack was in Marie? "What the fuck!"

"Yes, the fuck. I said I'd give you another chance to love me. Remember? Darling, put yourself in my shoes for a moment. If you couldn't love Shanna, then who? Who indeed could you possibly love? I wracked my brain for the answer. It was only a matter of time before I found your roots, and you. So I found Marie. Yes, sweet little Marie—the fuck of your life."

"NO!"

"Predictable. But I also see a day when you'll burn with lust for my touch. So on that note, I'll take my leave." Jack ran down a hallway and out the back door.

No! No! No! Not Marie!

Rema was standing in the doorway. Speechless.

I heard a motorcycle rev up in the backyard. No Harley thunder, just the whine of very high RPMs. I ran out the back to see Marie on a hot pink beast of a bike built for the racetrack. The fat rear tire spun on Rema's poorly watered grass, then caught hold and was gone around the front.

Damn!

I was running around the house toward my Harley.

Fuck Jack to hell and back. And to hell again!

Wolf was already getting the Harley through its ignition sequence so he could enter the pin code. He wanted less adrenaline.

Yes, okay. I was too enraged. Less adrenaline. Easier thought than done.

The Harley caught. The engine boomed under me. Houses shook. Windows rattled. There was hell to pay and it was coming.

Dread wanted control, but there was no way I'd allow that. Wolf had everything I needed now. Let him do it. I turned Wolf loose on Jack the bastard.

We were already shifting rapidly and clearing the end of the block. The roar of the Harley covered the sound of Jack's racing bike, but Wolf seemed to instinctively know which way to go.

We shot through an intersection. No hesitation. Wolf was in full hunt. To hell with the traffic and the red lights. Screw everything. Wolf was skilled enough to get us through any intersection at full speed, without dying.

Go, Wolf. Kill!

I tried to relax in my own mental back seat. Wolf didn't need my emotions, or my panic as the big Harley weaved like a roaring demon between cars.

Damn me. I was a useless passenger now. And damn me for not seeing this coming. Jack was bound to have learned my past, and just as bound to cut me where it hurt the most.

My mother, if she wasn't already dead, she would be on Jack's hit list. Rema, too. Marie's family. But pulling down Jack came first.

I could see Marie up ahead, looking so small on the motorcycle. She glanced back. No need. The Harley's roar was deafening. All of Austin knew I was coming, charging fast.

Jack turned away to focus on his escape. His racing bike had all the acceleration and all the speed in the tight turns. His rider was a young woman, wonderfully light weight, and clinging low on the bike. But she didn't have my strength to lean the heavy bike into the turns, and throw it into a chicane zigzag between cars.

And more importantly, Jack didn't have Wolf inside him.

Jack was filled with sick love and twisted goals. I knew that emotions raged constant war inside him. But not Wolf. Not my inner Wolf. He was as cold as they came. Killing was a calculation. Running down a Grand Prix Motorbike in city traffic was a calculation.

And we were gaining.

Where Jack was thinking his way around obstacles, Wolf was casually threading the needle. Where Jack was glancing around for options, Wolf was dead-straight focused.

There might have been a trace of saliva on my lips, the only hint that Wolf was anticipating running his prey to ground.

Only 50 feet stood between us as we raced through downtown Austin. The straight streets gave Jack's bike the advantage, but slipping through traffic put Wolf in his element.

Kill, Wolf. Bring them down.

But what could I do, even if we caught Jack? Did I really want Marie to crash? Did I really want to walk up to her mangled body and kick her smashed ribs, trying to kick at Jack inside her? Did I want to stand over her, knowing she would hemorrhage and die?

There was no killing Jack without killing Marie. No hurting him without hurting her.

Whatever life Marie had left, it was now in Jack's hands.

Maybe I could capture Jack, and Peter could somehow electrocute the sick bastard out of her body. Or maybe—

The Harley slid on a turn and skidded into a parked car. We were still upright. Nothing broken. Wolf recovered quickly and resumed the chase.

Now Wolf was pissed. I was thinking too much. He needed to focus, not have me whining about Marie. I had too many damn feelings.

Right. This was a simple business—wolf and prey. A feral hog would have its feelings—fear, anger, whatever it wanted. For the wolf, it was the business of cunning and speed, followed by a routine kill.

Right. Sorry, Wolf.

Success was within our grasp. I could deal with it then.

Got it.

But we'd lost ground. Jack was heading east again, toward I-35.

A few intersections later, Jack was up a ramp and on the freeway heading north, accelerating rapidly on the shoulder, blowing past the usual I-35 traffic. The raceway scream of his engine briefly cut through the Harley's low roar. Then Jack was gone.

Wolf wasn't stopping, but the probabilities had all shifted away from us.

Wolf switched to calculating side roads and the chance Jack would double-back on us. That, plus the odds of getting pulled over with our stolen Harley.

I hated that logic, but it had kept Wolf at the top of his game for a long time. It was hard to argue with a clean record of success—no police record, no scars, and a huge body count.

But there was no killing Jack. At best, I could stick him in a dungeon to rot away his years. But Marie would rot, too.

It was only a matter of time before Jack dumped Marie's body in a ditch somewhere and took another skin.

Was it even possible to extract Jack from Marie? Somehow restore her? Or was she lost to me, already? Was her spirit gone, just like my passengers—now just a collection of memories, urges, and a few skills?

Rema and my mother were in serious danger. Marie's family, too. Assuming any were still alive. Jack would start with Marie's friends and relatives—slicing away those who might ask questions about the new Marie.

Unless Marie was just a passing fancy.

No. I could see Jack playing with poor Marie's body for a long time. Sick.

I needed to contact Sonya and Peter. I needed to get back and warn Rema. And I needed less conspicuous clothes.

Where was my team when I needed them? All dead? All in some kind of super dungeon? If a shade like Bruce the Black could be captured and unable to break out a simple under-barn dungeon, what chance did any regular jumper have?

Why wasn't Peter dropping another earpiece at my feet?

I noticed Wolf had pulled over, waiting for me. Yes, I was wallowing in messy scenarios. He wanted a decision, a target. He needed me to stop hogging brain cells.

Fine. In a minute.

It was hard to think. There were too many voices, too many shadows whispering from the back of my mind.

It occurred to me to give up and become Jack's willing bed bump. Sickening, but maybe he'd let me visit Sonya babe. Maybe sleeping with Marie's body would be tolerable. Hell, maybe I'd belt back a few vodka martinis and let my inner Billy Bob get it on with Jack, while my outer body du jour got it on with Marie's body. Lots of fun for one and all. Right?

Nah.

I'd already had sex with Jack. It wasn't that good.

Besides, I was packed with mad skills. Jack had mad skills, too, but he was insane. And me? Not so much.

Well, it would have to do.

Marie, whatever was left of her, deserved better than she was getting. Jack deserved worse.

Rain threatened. Something big was blowing in from the Gulf. I could picture a hurricane shredding its way through Galveston, or Port A, or even South Padre—pirouetting as it bit into land, then angling northwest toward Austin.

It was coming, shredding all in its path.

Wolf waited with the engine running.

I was born for the coming storm.

I, TARGET
PART 5

5.1 Body Count

I told Wolf to give up the chase. Jack was long gone by now, so Wolf aimed our stolen Harley back toward Austin.

Black clouds and rain threatened from the southeast. An incoming storm from the Gulf of Mexico. The approaching thunder and lightning echoed my mood.

As we rode, I tried to let Wolf know he did the best he could. I was tempted to give him some reassuring pets in my mind, but he would have eaten my hand.

Somehow Jack had figured out I was Marko, then killed my old girlfriend, Marie. Well, technically she was still alive, but there was only a frightened shred of her mind left in the back of her own brain. Jack was permanently in control of her body. And she was now sharing a mind filled with professional killers, and probably lots of brave people who thought they could just kill Jack outright. Jack's mind was a tangled collection of spirits that he'd managed to swallow over the years. Stadium seating for hundreds of heroes, villains, and the innocents who just happened to have a body he wanted that day.

The world desperately needed one less Jack.

Jack, the massively twisted psychopath. Jack, the master body hijacker. Jack, the guy who killed off the friends and relatives of his latest body, just because he didn't like loose ends. Jack, the guy who still wanted me to love him.

So did Jack think I was now going to hop into bed with him, just because he was now wearing my old girlfriend's body? That thought really made my skin crawl. Jack laughing inside Marie's head, while I got it on with Marie's body? Damn, that was sick!

The Harley was drifting off the road. Hell, I needed to stop clenching up my gut and let Wolf ride this thing.

We pulled over on the freeway. I tucked in my kilt and tried to relax. But it was hard. I hated Jack with a passion—a passion I had to push down in my thoughts. Jack would die. Preferably by my hand. Preferably violently. And preferably today. End of subject.

So I took a deep breath and tried to calm my rage. But Wolf's consciousness sneered at me, indicated I had no self control.

Right. Wolf was stone cold. And compared to him, I was downright hot-blooded. Fine. I got it. To take down Jack I'd need more Wolf in my head and less Marko.

Wolf got us back on the freeway, headed south to Rema's. She needed to be warned, assuming she was still alive. And I needed to use her phone to warn Marie's relatives. It crossed my mind that Peter might have some sort of Normal Protection program. Something like a rustic cabin in New Zealand. A place to protect normals who knew too much, and protect their loved ones.

The wind felt good in my face. But the storm was moving in fast. The start of hurricane season in the Gulf. Good. But the last thing I needed now was rain.

So right on cue, it started to rain.

Damn. We were riding the stolen Harley on the freeway. Seventy mph drops pelted and stung my face. I thought we should get under the nearest overpass to wait out the rain. Wolf thought that was a good way to be noticed by cops, and it was a real pansy move. The Harley could take the rain. Dread, my current body, could take the rain, too. So toughen up, Marko.

But Wolf did switch to the frontage road. Lower speed and more options if we got tagged by a trooper.

Fine. Let Wolf do the riding. I'd just settle back and figure things out. Wolf could handle the moment to moment tactical situation, while I rolled out the mental map and laid out our strategy. We made a good team. Right, Wolf?

He snarled.

Right. We needed a plan—my job. So what did we have in the positive column?

Nothing came to mind.

Okay, then what were the negatives?

The subject of Jack and Marie only filled me with rage and that didn't help Wolf ride the motorcycle. So I avoided that subject. What else was a problem?

It was raining. Check.

We were on a freshly stolen black and red Harley. Check.

I was in a damn kilt with no underwear. Check.

I was in the body of Dread, the biker guy who'd recently put a sizable hole in Tommy the Nevada dirt realtor and all around family killer. Check.

Actually, Dread was probably the one that did the actual killing and disposing of bodies for his boss, Tommy.

And that Nevada chauffeur was a witness to Dread blowing away Tommy, so somewhere there was a wanted poster with my new face on it. Check.

What else?

Anyone who knew me as Marko, or who knew Marie, were in danger of being exterminated by Jack and his crew. At the top of that list was Rema, my mother, and Marie's family. But maybe Jack would start with Marie's friends and family because Jack was wearing her body. Jack would exterminate Marie's connections first—his *no loose ends* policy. But my family and friends already thought I was dead, so they weren't exactly loose ends that needed removal. Right?

What else?

Jack wouldn't go insanely vindictive, would he? The sick bastard wouldn't jump into my mother just to get me to love him, would he? I could picture Jack jumping into my loved ones, one at a time, until I caved in and became his personal boy toy.

Too many bad thoughts. I couldn't think about Jack right now. Focus on other things, Marko.

I needed clothes. Real clothes, not this weird Highlander costume.

I needed to dump this hot motorcycle before the cops found me with it.

And I needed to get a new skin. Dread was wanted for murder in Nevada and it was only a matter of time before they found me.

Like it or not, maybe I needed to contact Peter and Sonya again, even if they were busy fighting evil. Maybe I should also see what Brenda and The Black were up to, assuming they hadn't fled back to Europe.

Yeah. I needed to find out who was dead, and who was still alive and willing to help me. And it started with Rema.

Wolf wasn't impressed. It was a shitty plan and I was a slow thinker. Jack would expect me to head back to Rema's. Besides, Rema was probably already toast. We needed a better plan—one with a higher probability of survival.

No. I didn't care if this was a damn trap for me. Rema deserved to be warned. I wasn't about to abandon her. If there was trouble, Wolf and I could handle it. And Dread's biker body looked like it could take a beating and still hit hard.

* * *

Twenty minutes later, the Harley rumbled with a low growl as I cruised slowly through Rema's neighborhood. I snaked a path around flooded sections of street. Jack's crew could be anywhere—waiting for me to check on Rema. The rain had stopped but was still threatening, almost holding its breath.

I was drenched in my boots and the tartan kilt from a clan I never knew. My puffy white shirt clung to Dread's stocky biker body, and his violent rat and death tattoos showed through the wet fabric—a menacing omen.

A few kids watched as I passed. I throttled the engine a time or two. It was a good show. An over-the-top hard-ass tooling around for trouble in a mostly black neighborhood. A better show than the last time I rolled in—Pops on a blinged out girl's bike.

So, yeah. I was rolling trouble. Because when a totally pissed jumper comes calling, abandon hope all who stand in his way.

I rolled up to Rema's house expecting to find the front door smashed in and Rema's blood spattered everywhere. But from the street, all was quiet except for an ominous white panel van parked in the driveway. It said Hairball Plumbing and sported a big grinning Cheshire cat logo.

Damn. Jack's cleaners were here already. Probably led by Doc, Jack's pit bull of a hit man.

Not good. If they only wanted Rema dead, they'd have been quick and gone.

And if I'd caught them in the act? Well, I'd just rolled up on a rumbling Harley, so they'd be waiting for me inside. Not good.

Martoni and Nameless thought it was the perfect time to run like hell. Either way, Rema was toast. Besides, we could find another sidekick later.

Pops thought we should just walk away from all this crazy nonsense. Set up a quiet little farm somewhere. Keep a low profile. Enjoy Dread's spry body.

Spry?

There was way too much chatter going on in my head. Mainly, I wanted to focus on what Wolf thought.

Well, how about it, Wolf? Time for some tactics.

Wolf stepped off the Harley and walked over to the plumbing van. Locked, and we couldn't see inside. Now what?

Wolf went to one of the van's front tires, unscrewed the valve stem cap, found a tiny pebble to stick in the cap, and screwed it back on. Air hissed out of the tire. He did the same thing to another tire.

Then we moved quickly around to a side door of Rema's house and tried it. Good, it was unlocked. Were we going in? No. Wolf picked up a rusty garden trowel and an old gardening glove and decided to check out the backyard.

Odd tactics, but I knew better than to ask questions.

No hot pink racing bike, so Jack wasn't here. Just the usual shrubs Texans stick in the backyard hoping they might live through hot summers with strict water rationing. There was a back door, so Wolf decided to check it.

Locked. And for some reason Wolf decided he'd go in that way. Seriously? Pick the hardest way in? So sad to see an awesome killer reduced to being mentally challenged.

Wolf sneered and thought I was the one who was a pinhead. Do the unexpected. Live longer.

Yeah? And the old gardening glove made a good weapon?

Using a gloved fist, he smashed the glass on the back door, reached in, and unlocked it. Rema was going to be pissed about that. Before I knew it, we were in the kitchen, he'd dropped the trowel, and we had a big kitchen knife in one hand and a frying pan in the other.

Rounding the corner, we caught sight of Rema tied and gagged in a living room chair. Her wide eyes kinda indicated we were all totally screwed.

A guy I'd never seen before, jumped into the living room and fired a stun gun at me—dart on a wire. Wolf reacted and the barb bounced off the frying pan.

Cool. I grabbed a mental beer and pulled up a seat with my passengers. Wolf was a blur of action. For some reason, he dropped the frying pan and picked up a kitchen chair.

The second stun gun dart hit the airborne chair as the chair promptly smashed into the guy. Crap, I'd blinked and missed Wolf's throw.

Good thinking, Wolf. Kitchen chairs made good weapons.

Wolf was in motion again, this time it seemed like he was going to use the knife to quickly kill the guy. I vetoed that because I didn't need more blood on my hands, and because there was a remote chance the guy was a jumper. No way I'd ever want to kill a jumper and wind up as one of his passengers.

So Wolf picked up the frying pan and used it with extreme prejudice. One bone cracking blow to the skull and the guy was neutralized until EMS could get him to a hospital.

The blow to the head seemed excessive. Wolf thought the knife would have caused less pain. And I should shut up and let him handle this.

Fine.

I noticed we were back in the kitchen. Funny how being a passenger in my own mind was a lot like riding in the back of a car—glimpsing the world in snapshots as life streamed by.

We glanced around the corner again. Rema was still tied to a chair in the middle of the living room, eyes wide. But now there was a man behind her, crouching, holding a gun to her head. Rema was trying to talk around the gag. The words were unintelligible, but the gist added up to, "Get the hell out of here!"

Most of my passengers liked that idea. Then we recognized the guy holding the gun to her head. Doc.

Oh, shit.

But I wasn't leaving, and Wolf sure as hell wasn't going anywhere. Doc was Wolf's idea of a worthy opponent. I reminded Wolf we were in Dread's body, not his, so we might be outgunned. Wolf indicated that Dread was sturdy enough to get the job done.

Doc snapped us out of it. "Give it up, Marko." He said that like I was a little piss-ant kid who drove a taxi. He tapped the side of Rema's head with his gun. "No one has to die here."

Did I believe him? Wolf? What was Doc like?

Wolf thought Doc could only be trusted to leave a bloody mess.

Yeah, kinda what I was thinking, too.

Doc seemed impatient. "Waiting won't make it any better for this fat bitch." He bit hard into Rema's ear. She screamed.

That's it! I let go of my mental steering wheel. Wolf had complete control. Kill!

Things got a little surreal as Wolf picked up Rema's new kitchen table, held it like a shield, and we charged like a fucking badass at Doc and Rema. Doc got off two quick shots, low, maybe to clip us in the legs, but the solid wood table ate the bullets.

Rema, her chair, and Doc ate the heavy table.

Wolf pulled us out of the rubble and started pounding Doc. There was no time to check Rema's condition, but a quick glance told me her chair was smashed and she was coping with cuts and fractured bones from the table's impact.

Doc was every inch the pit bull, absorbing blows and dishing some out. Wolf would have normally gone straight for the kill, but after being surprised that Billy Bob was a jumper, killing anyone on Jack's team seemed like a major risk. Oddly, I had the impression Doc wanted me alive, too. Maybe that's why he tried to shoot me in the legs.

Of course, Doc knew you don't just kill a jumper. So it was a fight to maim and disable. A wolf and a pit bull, each on a leash that prevented the usual kill tactics.

In the movies, men fought in an orchestrated way, with one

event leading to the next. Way too choreographed. In real life, men fought in a whirling storm of shoves, rapid-fire missed punches, and wild swings that just happened to connect. It was all contact and ferocity, but so close-in, with haphazard targets, that those fights drug on until a lucky blow opened the door to a one-sided pounding.

But Wolf and Doc were something else entirely. The action was seriously fast, but the hits were all on target—every damn one. Bones broke. Jaws and teeth and ribs were quickly shattered, but elbows and knees were carefully guarded. I had to hand it to Dread the biker—the guy's body was able to take a serious beating and keep on hitting.

The coffee table was smashed, Rema's knickknack shelves were destroyed. I caught a glimpse of Rema on the floor working her way free.

Wolf wanted to end this with a kill, but I held him back.

That's about when something hit me from behind. I turned to see another guy with glasses standing in the hallway with a tranquilizer gun. Great, they were coming out of the woodwork.

I reached behind me and pulled out a big dart. The guy put another tranquilizer dart in the tube and aimed, but Doc waved him off.

Wolf struck out at Doc, but he blocked the blow. Wolf landed a good one to Doc's face, but he shrugged it off, spitting blood. Doc immediately countered with a body shot that fractured more of Dread's ribs.

We dropped to our knees. Things were slowing down. The drugs were taking hold, reducing Wolf's reaction time, slowing our thoughts.

Doc relaxed. Grinned as he looked down at me. Blood streaming from his lips and broken nose. He raised a hand to his face to reset his jaw—a casual gesture that said he'd been down this road before.

From my knees, I fell in Doc's direction, reaching for him. He took a step back as my face hit the remains of one of Rema's bookshelves.

It was over.

We lost.

Except Rema was on the floor behind Doc, a chair leg in both hands, gripped like a fucking baseball bat. She swung hard and hit the back of Doc's left knee. He fell over backward, almost on top of Rema. She rolled away, then yelled, "Lord have mercy!" and bashed Doc in the head with the chair leg. Doc was stunned, but thrashing. Rema raised her club. "Look, just do yourself a favor and take the hint." She clubbed his head again, but hard like you might club a rattlesnake near a baby's crib. Doc stopped moving.

A big tranquilizer dart struck Rema in the hip. She pulled it out. "Sucker, you work in the kind of preschools that I do, you develop an immunity. Know what I'm sayin'?"

The guy in the hallway opened his mouth, but no words came out. A moment later he dropped the dart gun and fumbled under his windbreaker. He pulled out a revolver, aimed it directly at Rema, and pulled the trigger. The hammer struck and there was a click. Then a moment of confusion, followed by another click. He checked the side of the gun and released the safety. Not a pro killer like Doc, just a panicked shooter fumbling to get it right.

Rema threw her chair leg at him. It sailed over my head and missed him. She crouched down knowing she'd die—gunned down in her own home.

He took aim at her and fired. Muzzle flash. The crack of a gunshot. Except I'd managed to put myself in the way. Or maybe one of my passengers put us in the path of the bullet. Hard to say. I like to think it was a group effort.

I was still blocking Rema, so the guy aimed at me and fired again. Stabbing chest pain. A perfect shot, except the way his eyes peered over his glasses told me his mistake had just dawned on him.

Never kill a jumper.

My last sight—he lowered his gun, fear and confusion on his face. My vision rapidly shrank down a long dark tunnel as my blood drained. The world tilted, but I don't remember reaching the floor.

* * *

Born again. Some people thought they were. I had my doubts. But for me, *born again* was an absolute fact.

Note to self: I shouldn't be so quick to judge others. If I could be reborn then hell, maybe in their own way, others could, too.

I brushed against the walls in Rema's hallway, sliding down, then hit the floor. Whoever I was in, he had weak knees. Another sign he was a novice killer.

I waited for my vision to clear up. New body. New sensory organs. I spat out the stranger's saliva. Maybe Rema had some vodka.

There was the sound of a gun sliding on a hardwood floor. A big blurry black woman stood over me, showing no signs of the tranquilizer dart she'd pulled out of her hip. "Give me one good reason not to squash you like a damn cockroach."

"I'm Marko."

"The hell you is." She kicked me like that somehow proved her point.

"Ow!"

"You done killed Marko."

"Rema, it's me."

"Prove it."

"I was here earlier and we talked with Marie, only she wasn't really Marie, she was Jack. And she rode off on a motorcycle and I went after her." I looked up at Rema's blurry face, and her blurry bat. "Rema, it's me, your maggoty undead friend."

"You ain't my friend. You ain't nobody I know."

"I jumped. I'm in this body now."

"And?"

"And a really sick bastard is in Marie."

"So now you're tellin' me Marie's maggoty, too?"

"No. Jack's maggoty. He's in Marie."

Rema kicked me again, but with less conviction. "Fool. I ain't buyin' none of your lies. I'm still waitin' for you to tell me why you should live."

"I gave you cash and guns. I told you all about how I could jump. I wanted you to be my sidekick."

"I ain't nobody's sidekick. I told you that before. I figure you've got about two minutes before the cops roll up and haul your sorry ass off to jail, so make it quick, 'cause I'd like nothin' better than to knock some sense into you before the cops take you and your pals away."

"Help me up." I held out a hand.

"No way."

I struggled to my feet.

"Good, now I can beat the daylights out of you and call it self-defense."

"I bought a shovel from you. And a flashlight. And a backpack."

"Really?"

"Yeah, and I looked like an old man. You made me a sack lunch. I rode off on a girl's bike. Remember?"

She huffed, but seemed to finally buy it. "Sit on the couch."

I tripped on her smashed coffee table and bounced off the couch.

"What the hell's wrong with you? Don't be messin' my stuff up any more than it already is."

"I can't see clearly yet. New brain. Sometimes it takes a minute to get adjusted to my new body."

"And does your new body wear glasses?"

"Oh, yeah."

She handed me the glasses I'd dropped in the hallway.

I put them on and instantly saw the broken furniture, Dread lying in a pool of blood, and Doc resting quietly after inspecting Rema's chair leg. Then there was the guy I'd put down with the frying pan. Rema didn't look so good either, but she didn't look one bit drugged by the dart. Was daycare really that rough? Was she really immune to tranquilizer darts? "Wait. You're still standing."

"Praise the Lord, I keep my appointment book in my hip pocket."

"Talk about lucky."

"Lucky? *Lucky?* Just look around, fool." Rema gestured to the wreckage, two unconscious bodies, and Dread lying dead. "Uh-huh. Today's been my lucky day."

"Sorry."

"Ain't nothin' to be sorry about, 'cause you just got bad karma or some shit like that. Right? 'Cause it ain't your fault you're livin' the undead way. No, sir. Ain't your fault you're bringin' it all to my door. Draggin' it inside. Makin' me have to deal with it. And that dead body over there—yeah, that one—that wouldn't be yours by any chance, would it? Leakin' buckets o' blood into my nice rug and my fine floorboards? Callin' attention to itself, and all? And the true miracle is that you're still alive—am I right about that? So maybe I should just accept your apology for draggin' your maggoty miracle self through my otherwise respectable life. You get what I'm sayin'?"

"I get it, but things are complicated."

"Honey, things just got a lot more complicated than you realized. 'Cause now you're black."

"What?"

"That's what I thought." Rema picked up a broken mirror from the floor. "You're now a brother—at least on the surface. Take a look at your new darker Latino self, Marko. Like peanut butter dipped in chocolate. Dark temptation with a big ol' maggoty nut inside."

No. This could be a problem. "I'm black."

"Say it with pride. Wear it with pride. And expect to be treated way different. Like if you walk into a crowd of white folks, everyone will notice you, but no one will make eye contact. On the other hand, Marko, you'll always be the messy surprise lurkin' on the inside."

"What's that supposed to mean?"

"It's a comment on your personality, nothin' more. I'd say we have seconds until my nosy neighbors and about a dozen ethnically confused cops descend on the crime scene that used to be my home."

Right. "You're still in danger. We need to leave."

"Danger? Wasn't it you who just ran me over with my own kitchen table? A brand new table, I might add. Home invasions, I can handle. But you? You're a whole nother breed o' trouble."

Someone pounded on the front door. "Rema! You all right?"

Rema shouted back, "Of course, I'm all right! Give me a blessed moment to freshen up."

I got to my feet. "We need to go."

"Hell, no! I ain't goin' nowhere. This is my house! What's left of it, anyway."

5.2 Dark Matter

I flew out the back door of Rema's house—my best escape route. There were sirens in the distance and a small crowd had gathered in her front yard. The big Hairball Plumbing van had flat tires and was blocking Rema's car in her narrow driveway. And the stolen Harley was parked out front with several kids sitting on it. Kinda hard for me to dash through the crowd, brush the kids off the bike, roar off, and keep it all inconspicuous.

So yeah, I ran like hell to the back of her lot, scrambled over the short chain link fence, then tried to look normal as I hustled across the neighbor's backyard and out to their street.

The new guy I was in had good coordination and seemed limber. A nice upgrade from the lumbering hard-ass I was just in—not to mention, I was now wearing pants and a normal shirt. The only downside was the new guy's poor eyesight. A Clark Kent kind of guy, but from a mother with another color.

I glanced again at my new hands. Medium black. Too dark to be a tan, but I liked it. At least I wasn't all muerto blanco like Pops, except for the parts that got some sun.

Good that I was now a black guy—in a black neighborhood. Just another bro, y'all.

Yo, dudes. What's hap-en-en? Me? I'm just a chillin' villain, just cruisin' the 'hood like a black man should.

Or not. My rappin' was crappin'.

Hell, I could never pull it off. I tried to walk black, but it was too weird. I had the feeling my new passenger was more of an athletic bookworm than a street struttin' gangsta.

Yo, passenger. Got a name?

No answer, as expected, so I checked my pockets while I quick-walked down the street. Two spare tranquilizer darts and a package of gum in a seriously unnatural winter flavor. What else? A packet of lens wipes for my eyeglasses.

Nothing else.

No wallet. No watch. Not even a class ring or a touch of bling around my neck.

I regretted not having a chance to rinse my mouth out with vodka, or even mouthwash, but the polar bear flavored gum was good enough. I didn't think I'd ever get used to another man's spit in my mouth. A new body, I could handle. Used spit?

So if my new passenger wasn't the gangbanger type, how'd he get in with Doc's crew? He seemed to have mad tranquilizer skills. Maybe he worked at the zoo?

Yes, he seemed like zoo material. Quiet. Good with darts, not comfortable with real guns. The kind who'd know the proper dosage for a gorilla—or a human.

We walked as I waited for my new passenger to offer an opinion.

It crossed my mind to go to a rendezvous point. That's what Doc had set up. Ladybird Lake and Mopac popped into my head. Yes, but under the Mopac freeway. Right next to Austin High School. Lots of joggers. Lots of people getting in and out of parked SUVs. People meeting people. That's where Doc said we should go if anything went wrong.

Good to know, new guy. I'd certainly avoid that spot. Where else could I go?

Home.

Where would that be? I tried to picture the new guy's home.

Washington, D.C.

Okay, so my passenger lived in D.C. He probably had family there.

I had a mental picture of a girlfriend. Jogging together in brisk early mornings. Movies on the couch. Snowball fights. Good times.

Sorry, girlfriend. Your boyfriend hooked up with the wrong crowd and just killed a jumper—me. Now he's never going to be the same. Never coming back. Best to move on, girlfriend.

That thought really sucked.

Blame Jack for putting this man in harm's way. Jumpers were

bad news for normals. Normals were too often just collateral damage. Sorry, D.C. girlfriend. Life's full of hard knocks.

Samson Parker. National Zoo.

Good, I had his name. I even liked it. It seemed like the National Zoo belonged in D.C., so now I knew where he worked.

Stick with me, Samson. I might need your animal handling skills someday.

My passengers seemed to like adding his skills to theirs. Make him feel at home, boys, because Texas is seriously different than D.C.

I needed to contact Sonya and Peter. But the best I could do was head to Marie's house. I'd break in, find some phone numbers, then warn her family and friends. I'd call my mom, too.

* * *

It was a long walk to Marie's place, especially because I was taking back streets. Austin was crawling with trouble, and I was still only half way there. The cops might have a description of Samson. Even worse, Jack's backup crew might be cruising the streets looking for Samson. Or maybe they were busy bagging Marie's family.

The rain had mostly let up. I only had to find cover once when it came down hard but brief. And I ducked out of sight three or four times to avoid being seen by police cruisers and a suspicious black drone.

Jack was going to be extra pissed now. His op at Rema's was a total disaster. Doc and one of his goons needed an ambulance, plus some quality time in ER. For better or worse, his man Samson was now mine. Rema was injured but still alive, and I was still in the wild. Doc had totally failed.

Oh, and Rema was a real badass when she needed to be. Doc was a fool to turn his back on her. But next time, Doc would probably skip the subtleties and simply carpet bomb her house with RPGs. Instant obliteration.

Wolf didn't think so. A slow knife across her throat was Doc's style. Leave the mess for all to see. Rocket propelled grenades from a safe distance implied caution, and fear of a rematch. Doc was incapable of either emotion.

As I walked through residential streets just north of downtown, a greasy white teenager in a pizza delivery car pulled up next to me. Windows rolled down. Music thumping. AC on full blast to push out the Texas heat and humidity.

I backed away in case he pulled a stun gun or a tranquilizer gun on me. Paranoia was my guardian angel.

He turned down the music. "Wolfie, it's me, Sonya. Get in, babe."

Damn! Was this one of Jack's tricks, or was my sexy Sonya now wearing a delivery kid? If it really was Sonya, I was totally gonna be pissed with her for switching to a pizza boy body.

"Screw you. You're not Sonya." I moved to put a tree trunk between us.

The kid laughed. "You're right. I'm really Peter. Hop in, dude."

"No way." Peter might do some field work to hack into Jack's bugs, but he'd never do pizza delivery. Or routine agent pick up.

The kid scowled. "Just do it. We don't have all day."

I might have flipped him off. Okay, I did. My fingers seemed to have a mind of their own.

That's when the pizza kid started arguing with himself. Weird schizophrenic banter. And I thought *I* had a personality disorder.

Finally he pulled out an earpiece and held it out to me. "Yo, take it."

"No."

"Just take it, man."

I shook my head.

"Shit." He stuck it back into his ear and started arguing again. "Fine." He got out of the car, but stood by the driver's door. "Yo, freak. Take the car. The keys are still in the ignition." He pulled out the earpiece and held it up for me to see. "Take this shit and shove it in your ear. Or better yet, shove it up your ass. You can hear Peter better that way." He dropped the earpiece on the roof of the car, crossed to the opposite side of the street, and walked off.

Honestly, if this were one of Jack's traps, it would have been handled much better. This was a classic Peter op—total FUBAR.

I stepped over to the car. The kid glanced over his shoulder to make sure I was taking the bait, but he kept right on going.

Fine. This was transportation and comms—exactly what I wanted. I picked up the earpiece and turned it over in my hand. Standard Peter gear. So I reluctantly wiped off the kid's ear wax and stuck it in Samson's ear.

"What?" I might have sounded annoyed. Having lost Marie put me in the mood to kill something. Anything. Peter would do.

"Dude, you're still alive?"

"And you're not?" Wishful thinking on my part.

"What happened?"

Let's see. The day started when Brenda and Bruce the Black abandoned me at the Austin Airport. It seemed likely that Peter already knew about that. "Screw that. You tell me what happened. How'd you find me?"

"Dude. We don't have time for this. Just drive."

"No. Cooperate, or I toss the earpiece into a storm drain and walk."

Peter hesitated. "Uh . . . it's complicated."

"I'm walking."

"Okay, okay. When Brenda was through with you in Vegas, we had her fly you back to Austin. Why Austin, you ask?"

I hadn't asked.

"Because Jack wants your ass and we want his. So I provided you with Sonya's limo driver—easy for us to keep tabs on you. But Sonya said you wouldn't go for it. She wanted to park a Harley where you'd grab it. I said that was a stupid plan, but you know Sonya. So I had a team steal a Harley, tag it with a tracker, and park it where you'd see it."

"You tracked me to Rema's?"

"Duh."

"And you didn't give me keys to the motorcycle?"

"Sonya said you didn't need keys. Besides, she thought keys would make you suspicious. Dude, just between you and me . . . she thinks she really knows you. Bro, you gotta know—that only leads to trouble."

"And you knew Jack would be waiting for me?"

"No. That caught us by surprise just as much as you."

"And you lost him again."

"Not this time. We had a hell of a time following him up I-35, but he eventually pulled his racing bike into the back of a van and drove off. He's in the air right now, apparently headed back to D.C."

"In the body of my girlfriend."

"Yeah. That was really bad. Just so you know, we were all sad to find out about that."

"The hell you were."

"Hey, we all hate shit like that. Especially Sonya. She's had family on the line for years. One mistake on her part and Jack would have started killing her folks, starting with her parents. So hearing about Marie really tore her up."

Maybe. "So how'd you figure out my roots?"

"From the airport, you went straight to Rema Louise Mayfield's house. Nobody we knew, so we crosschecked her with obits and missing people. Nothing. No telltale links to anyone who might have jumped to a new body. Rema was a cold lead, except that you got into hot pursuit, chasing a young woman on a shit-hot racing bike. Lucky for you, you were running through traffic lights downtown for a while. Traffic cams gave us a look at her, but one red light cam really caught a good shot of her."

"You hacked into Austin's traffic cams?"

"Yeah, so? Who doesn't?"

I should have realized—the whole world was hacked. "Okay, so you found out who she was."

"Totally. We ran facial recognition against photos from license and passport databases and came up with a match. A local—Marie Turner. She works for Rema in the daycare biz. And Marie's boyfriend was killed in a taxi a few months ago. Bingo. Some cabbie named Marko Noviño Santana. The police reports said his killer was, uh, some convenience store clerk named Hugo Martoni. He was never found. Marko's car was towed from a street not too far from Billy Bob Wyville's house, but with stolen plates. Everyone thought it was Martoni driving the car, but we know it was really you. You were checking out Billy Bob, but you were in some other guy's skin. We're not sure who that was."

Good to know Nameless would always be Nameless.

"Anyway, Wolf killed you. You got Wolf's body. Billy Bob told

Jack that Wolf was acting weird. Man, it's a long and bloody trail, but here you are. Marko the lowly cab driver."

Great, now everyone knew who I was. I could feel my power draining from me. Like when Hercules lost his superpower when they cut off his hair. Or maybe it was Samson. I always got those two confused. But now I was in a guy named Samson and my power was draining away. Except I needed glasses more than hair, so that was my Achilles heel.

I grabbed my head. No, I still had skills. I straightened up—stood tall. "Call me *Wolf*. It suits me better these days."

"Sure thing, Wolf. Now get in the damn car and drive."

"For all you knew I was just some black guy walking down the street. So how'd you know I jumped from Dread's body into Samson's?"

"Eyes, bro. Eyes. Your Harley was tracked. It looked like you were heading back to Rema's so we positioned a drone on her place. The fake plumbing van was in her driveway, so we started scrambling our own extraction team to save Rema. But you arrived first. Shit happened inside. Then you ran out the back wearing some guy we'd never seen before. We thought he was one of Rema's friends, except he was running away, not to the crowd of friendlies in her front yard. We knew you weren't one of Rema's friends because you were running away from the scene. So we had one of our pizza runners test you. You reacted to Sonya's name and to mine."

The rebellion had pizza runners?

I just stood there. Peter was right. Things were complicated. I hated eyes everywhere. I hated being tracked, even after a jump. And I hated that Peter was usually right.

"We're out of time, dude. Get in the damn car!"

I got in. It smelled like pizza and there was a thermal bag on the passenger's seat. The engine was still running. "Where to?"

"I'm still working on that part. Just don't go anywhere you've ever been."

Huh? "Marie's family is in trouble."

"Yeah, yeah. We know. A rescue team already picked them up."

Good. "Rema's hurt and still in danger."

"That's old news. She's being checked out by our trauma team right now. Actually, she's already in route to a safe house with Marie's parents."

"Good. But my mom could use protection, too."

"She's packing her bags even as we speak. We've got evac teams all over Austin. Pursuit teams are after Jack. A rendition team is working on getting Doc and his pal out of ER and into our waiting arms. We've got boots on the ground in several key cities. Dude, since we snagged Billy Bob's assets we've been on a hiring spree. We're big time now, bro, so give us some credit. Our resistance movement is kicking ass and taking names. Oh, shit." Peter seemed distracted by someone. "Hang on."

"So you just happened to have lots of teams in Austin?"

I could hear Peter barking orders in the background. Then he got back to me. "We're especially big in Austin because Jack has a nasty habit of finding you. Dropping you off there gave us the chance to bag him."

"But he escaped."

"Look, I'm kinda busy here. How about talking with Sonya?"

He put her on the line. "Wolf! I'm so sorry about Marie."

"Yeah. My fault. I'm sure you would've protected her if you'd known."

"Yes. But it's no one's fault. No one except Jack."

"I'll hold him personally accountable." That sounded vague. What I meant to say was that I would totally kill him. "I should be going after him."

"I agree."

What? Didn't she want me safe? "Good. Then put me on a plane."

"We will, just as soon as we're certain we're following the right trail."

"You're not sure where he is?"

"It's Jack. There are always uncertainties with him. But we strongly believe Marie got on a private jet headed to the D.C. area. I wish I could be there for you right now."

"Where are you?"

"Near D.C. and Maryland. Sorry, I can't be specific."

"Then get me over there."

"We're trying."

"Good. I'll head to the airport and get a ride with Bruce the Black."

"They're gone already. He and Brenda had business somewhere."

"Where?"

"They didn't say. They're Europeans. Somehow they don't exactly trust Americans."

Great. "Then put me on another flight."

"We're out of planes. In an hour your friends and relatives are being flown to other parts of the country—put into protection. Most of Peter's teams are already in the air, headed to D.C. because we're going to try and drop a bag over Jack when he gets here. You did great, sweetie. If we do bag Jack, we'll keep him isolated until you can get here."

"Sounds good. So put me on a commercial flight."

"Whose body are you in?"

It took a moment to answer that one. Somehow I had pizza in my mouth. "A guy named Samson Parker. He works for the zoo in D.C."

"And you have his driver's license? Maybe his passport?"

"No."

"Then they're not going to let you on an airline flight. Besides, witnesses gave the police your description. It was a homicide, remember? Some white guy in a wet skirt—"

"Dread. He was a Nevada biker. And he was wearing a kilt. It was raining. You know?"

"Wolf, he was shot dead in Rema's house. There was a stolen motorcycle parked in front of the house. Two white men were beaten unconscious and taken to the hospital. Rema was tied up and beaten up like it was a home invasion."

"She wasn't actually beaten up. Doc bit her ear and I kinda bumped her with a table."

"Do you even hear yourself? You're minimizing what just happened." Sonya paused. I kept my mouth shut. She continued. "Peter matched your face to Nevada's wanted list. Dread, if that really was his name, is wanted for killing a real estate broker."

"The realtor was Tommy Tarantino, and he deserved to die. Same for Dread."

"I'm sure they deserved it, but what are the police supposed to think? Billy Bob Wyville shows up in Vegas and gets killed by that real estate guy. Then the real estate guy is killed by that biker outside Vegas. Then that biker—"

"Dread. It's a cool name."

"Dread shows up in Austin in a wet skirt—fine, a rain soaked kilt—riding a stolen motorcycle. He walks into a home invasion scene, and is shot dead, apparently by a black man who was seen running out the back of Rema's house. The police have already pieced together most of this. It's an interstate series of murders, so your FBI is probably involved, too. And now you want a plane ticket to D.C. without identification?"

Okay, that sounded bad.

"Babe, you've left a trail of bodies. Oh, and I almost forgot—there was the dead farmer they found at Billy Bob's place. Remember him?"

"That was Pops."

"Yes, it was. Sorry we couldn't remove his body in time. Oh, and his pickup truck was left at another crime scene—a dead sniper with a smart rifle. That's a lot of dead people, all shot. Sometimes I get the feeling you Americans would be lost without your guns. You've made it entirely too easy to go around killing each other. The rest of the world has to be creative about murder, but not you Americans. You've mastered fast food, fast killing, and online shopping. You've automated everything from streaming entertainment to online socializing. And let's be honest, it's not real socializing. You Americans are losing touch with life. Real life." Sonya paused for a moment. "Sorry, Wolf. Peter has us working out of a bunker these days and it's driving me crazy. I miss Canada. I hate hiding underground. I'm an outside kind of girl."

"Yeah. I miss Canada, too."

"You'll have to admit, all these shooting deaths are getting excessive."

"At least you electrocuted Pops." There was cold silence. Maybe I went too far. "Sorry. It wasn't you. Peter set that one up."

"No, you're right. I was involved. There's been so much killing. I wish it would all just end."

"When we end Jack, things will be good again. Then maybe I'll wind up in a body like Wolf's. I miss those days."

"I miss them, too. I'd love for you to be Wolf again, but I'm afraid those days are gone forever."

"They found Wolf's body?"

"No. We were able to remove it."

"You were? Wait, Pops had a spotting scope that got pictures of the kill. The cops would've seen us in the hot tub and . . . uh . . . never mind. The memory card was gone and I think Pops handed it over to the guys behind the hit. So yeah, the cops wouldn't know who the target was. And they wouldn't see photos of you, Brenda, and Peter naked in the hot tub."

"What? There were pictures? You didn't mention that before."

"Oh. Sorry. There were pictures."

"We have to get those back."

"Right. We don't want Jack's crew drooling over your naked hot tub pics. And they could ID you."

"Not that. Jack already knows I've gone over to the resistance. Brenda had a kill chip, so she looks different now. It's Peter."

"Peter? What about Peter?"

"Jack's never seen him. But if he has photos, he could track Peter to his roots. I'm giving him a heads-up right now."

"So how do I get to D.C.? Drive the pizza car?"

"Too slow. Peter suggested we put you in an air tray."

"A what?"

"You know. It's what morticians use to ship dead bodies. Peter said we could sedate you, put you in an air tray with scuba tanks, and ship you to D.C."

"You're kidding."

"It has its advantages. No photo ID required. No one looks inside the box or messes with it. Bodies are shipped all the time. Even the FBI would ignore you. You'd just need some routine paperwork and we know a mortician who'd do it."

"No way."

"The dead get treated better than people flying coach. Hundreds of thousands of dead people fly every year. Wolf, you'd blend right in."

"I can't believe you'd ship me like that."

"I wouldn't, but Peter would. Anyway, I just thought I'd put it out there."

"I'll pass. Put me on a train."

"That'll take days for you to get here. And if you fell asleep, you'd need restraint."

Wearing a straitjacket on the train could be a problem, especially surrounded by nosy senior citizens. But on a bus I'd blend right in. "I'll start driving northeast to D.C. until you and Peter figure this out." Well, it was better than no plan at all.

"No. Drive south to San Antonio."

"What's in San Antonio?" I was thinking the Alamo, but I couldn't see how that'd get me to D.C.

"There's an Air Force base there. We've been using a lot of ex-military for ops. People know people, so I'm sure somebody knows somebody with a plane there."

I wanted to tell Sonya how you couldn't just drive up to a military base and say you were pals with Corporal Peabody and they'd let you in. Especially without any ID. However my car did say Bad Boy Pizza so maybe that would cut me some slack with the guards.

Or not.

I tried explaining it to her. "Uh, if there's not a four star general waiting for cold veggie pizza, getting in is gonna be a long shot." Assuming I didn't wind up in a military prison cell waiting for an amateur 'we're Air Force so we're way smarter' interrogation. "Maybe things are a bit more relaxed in Canada, but U.S. military bases tend to be suspicious of people dropping in without proper ID—even if they do have pizza. Just sayin' this could be a really bad idea."

"Drive south, Wolf. I'll get with Peter."

Not good. Peter should have me try to get through the gate as an AC repairman. Better odds than pizza delivery. But I headed south on I-35 anyway. Everyone in Texas knew San Antonio was south on I-35 and Dallas was north. East on I-10 was El Paso, west was

Houston. There was nothing more to know about driving in Texas. With only two main highways, there was no confusion. They intersected in San Antonio, so it was the nexus of Texas. "Okay, I'm heading south. But just know that I'm skeptical about this plan."

"I'll get back to you."

My earpiece went to elevator music, so I yanked it out. Two minutes later, I decided Bad Boy Pizza was just plain bad, so I tossed it back in the greasy box and turned on the radio. Three minutes later, I gave up on finding anything worth listening to. Austin only seemed to have C&W channels with whiny country tunes about finding love in a cowboy dance hall, but she don't love me no how. Well of course, she didn't. She wanted someone with a high school diploma—like me. At least Jimmy Buffett had a lost shaker of salt. Yeah, that was totally me—lost.

Oh, and Austin had bubblegum pop channels. I was thinking those giggly girls should hook up with the unlovable cowboys. Actually, they probably did.

So it was just me, trying to hum the Batman theme as I cruised down I-35 toward Alamo City. Actually, I'd never seen the Alamo. Maybe it was all cool and wicked.

Or maybe it was just a pile of old rocks.

Or maybe it'd been completely rebuilt for tourists.

It occurred to me that history and I had the same problem: we were both seriously messed up by conflicting opinions.

* * *

All I can say is that I-35 to San Antonio was a mind numbing freeway laced with distracted truckers drifting over the lines. At least they weren't allowed in the fast lane. Unless they wanted to be.

And the drive wasn't helped by pockets of super heavy rain. But at least the rain cleared up as I approached San Antonio.

I saw a sign for Randolph Air Force Base so I jammed my earpiece back into my ear. "Hey, Sonya. I see Randolph AFB coming up soon."

Peter picked up the line. "Dude, where've you been?"

"Driving south. Humming all the Hans Zimmer theme songs I could remember." Which was exactly none. They were all too epic to merely hum.

"Don't go to Randolph. Look for 90 west to Lackland."

What was in Lackland? "Why?"

"Because they have planes."

So Randolph was an Air Force base that didn't have planes? That was crazy. "Fine, 90 to Lackland. Then what? Find the runway?" Basically, it sounded like a lack of land. But that's what I got for driving alongside truckers doing who knows what in the cab.

"Lackland Air Force Base. Drive up. Tell them you're with Special Force Bravo Delta."

"I don't have any ID."

"Bravo Delta is totally black ops. They don't use ID. Hell, they don't even have any. Just look all badass, and don't take *no* for an answer."

"They'll bust me."

"No, they won't. Just act all black ops."

"So who's Bravo Delta?"

"I made it up an hour ago. Look, the name's got balls, so go with it."

"Seriously? That's all you've got?"

"No. We have a man on the inside. A friend of a friend. The word's out that Bravo Delta is running Black Dagger ops today. They think it's a big deal. And the guards know to let you through, otherwise you'll gut them at their post."

This wasn't going to work. "Yeah, right."

"Just go balls to the wall and they'll think it's another oak leaf cluster fuck."

I wasn't sure what that was, but it sounded real. So I practiced my badass face in the mirror as I drove. Simon didn't have a badass face, and the glasses didn't exactly help.

South on I-35, west on 90, then pull in to the Lackland guard station. I'd show my hard-ass balls to the poor guy on duty there. Go all Bravo Delta on him. Then I'd find a fast plane with a big gas tank and fly it to D.C.

It was an insane plan, backed by Peter's League of Insanity. What could go wrong?

* * *

Fortunately, the Air Force base was easy to find. But somehow I took a wrong turn, because I found myself driving around on the base. No gate. No guards with assault rifles. No snarling Rottweilers. But it did seem kinda like a military base because there were athletic guys jogging just for the hell of it. You'd have to be nuts to do that in Texas in August.

Actually, I had no idea what month it was. But it was hot.

So maybe they didn't even have a guard station? Budget cutbacks?

Well, I was now on base along with the Fed-Ex trucks and girls in short skirts looking for any airmen with cute brass. And being in a pizza car wasn't even turning heads.

What kind of top secret facility was this, anyway?

On the other hand, I could see lots of big transport planes and a runway, all behind a super long fence with guard stations. Finally.

"Okay, I'm here." The earpiece was silent. Maybe it needed a charge?

I pulled into a parking lot facing a row of big gray transport planes. Maybe the guards were used to letting pizza delivery through the gate? I ran that scenario through my mind.

How hard could it be? I'd simply walk up to the guard post, a box of cold pizza in one hand, my other hand poised like the fist of death. The guard would pause his game app and say, "Halt! Who goes there?" Then I'd say, "Black Ops pizza." He'd check his clipboard and say, "You're not on the list." Then I'd switch to Plan B and say, "Force Delta Bravo. Operation Black Dagger." He'd check the clipboard again, but just shake his head. So I'd move to Plan C. I'd hold up the pizza box and say, "Cluster fuck." He'd go all wide eyed and say, "Right."

You just don't mess with a cluster fuck.

The gate would open and I'd walk through. But the guard would reach for a slice, so I'd slap his hand. "Cluster Fuck Special. Trust me private, you don't want any part of that."

Good. I'd be in. I'd find a plane with the keys still in it. And one of my passengers would know how to fly it.

Or not.

So I sat there waiting to hear from Peter, watching UPS trucks pull up to plain buildings, imagining top secret pencil sharpeners being delivered to bored noncoms stuck behind a desk.

I sat there while a cargo plane loaded with nuclear warheads landed. Well, it was a perfectly good assumption. And I was pretty sure there were spy babes onboard, too. Hot spy babes in tight black cocktail dresses, dripping with sex appeal.

A fresh load of bombs and babes for our boys in blue. That was kinda catchy. They should have billboards with boys in blue holding neutron bombs in one hand and hot babes in the other.

Man, that sounded good. I glanced around to see if they had an enlistment office, but caught myself letting my passengers control my thoughts.

This wasn't good. Sitting in the heat with all the windows rolled down was putting me to sleep.

"Don't move."

I jerked around. Someone was in the car with me!

But no one was there.

"Who said that?"

"Seriously, dude? Who do you think said that?" It was Peter talking through my earpiece, still in my ear. "Just stay where you are. I got you booked on a flight leaving soon for D.C., but it's packed with Army recruits who just passed basic training. But get this—their training now involves transporting a captured spy! Brilliant, even if I do say so myself. Uh, just so you know, that spy is you."

"What?"

"Don't worry. They know it's a drill. They'll think you're an instructor out of Quantico and you're testing their ability to apprehend you and rush you to Washington for interrogation."

No. "That's a horrible plan. All I need is a ride, not a mission. Just get me on a plane, in a seat with lots of legroom. Like the general's private jet. Not some troop transport plane."

"Look. You need to get to D.C. ASAP. You need a cover story. And you need to be restrained in case you fall asleep and Billy Bob takes over. Things are already in motion. Just go with the plan."

"I'm not a threat to anyone. I just need a ride." Unfortunately, I caught sight of an armed squad of Air Force MPs creeping through the parking lot. "Peter, they're here! Call in a new plan!"

"No. Without restraint, you'd eventually lose control and all those killers in your head would have a field day on the plane. Bad things would happen. Serious bad things. Sonya was right. You're minimizing your condition. You're a fucking killing machine, and you're in denial."

The MPs were in position and ready to rush my pizza car. "What'll I do? They're gonna shoot me."

"No, they're not. They think you're an instructor and they need to make it look good. Besides, they'd never hurt an instructor—not much, anyway. Maybe just a little. So relax, Wolf. This is your ticket to fly. It was the best I could do on short notice."

"This sucks."

"It sucks less than having morticians pack you into an air tray. Trust me. Play nice. Play the game. This plan is golden."

That's when the MPs rushed the car and barked at me. "Hands where we can see them! Now!"

They sounded serious enough, and looked trigger happy, so I carefully put my hands up.

"Out of the car! Now!"

Why did every sentence end with *NOW*?

Fine. I started to get out of the car. "Chill, guys. It's just pizza. You know? Black Olives Ops?" I couldn't believe I said that.

They backed up as I slowly got out of the car, my hands in the air.

There were only three of them. Wolf indicated he could handle this. From experience, I was sure he could. It would be quick—and lethal.

Great. I could let Wolf do his thing and I'd be standing in a pile of dead MPs. That would kinda blow my ride to D.C.

"On the ground! Now!"

They were close, but not within easy reach, and not ready to touch me. It seemed like they were waiting for me to be on the ground before they'd pounce. Two guys with assault weapons and one with a sidearm. All very excited with the drill. All determined to be totally hard on my ass.

Wolf noticed they all had their fingers off the trigger. They were going by the book, intent on impressing the instructor—me. Wolf said that going by the book made things very predictable. He sneered because this was just too easy.

All he needed was a green light from me. Say the word and this would be over.

I got to my knees and put Samson's stomach to the pavement. Sorry, Wolf. Snapping bones and killing people wasn't always the best plan.

The guys were rough about cuffing me and the body search. They pulled out my earpiece, and were really happy about it, like they'd gotten bonus points for finding it.

I hated Peter so much.

* * *

They stuffed me into an MP van for a short ride to a hangar. They put me in a small office and photographed me. Finger printed me. Retinal scanned me. DNA swabbed me. Did some things I'd never seen in the movies. Then they asked me a bunch of questions I wasn't about to answer.

Finally they gave up on the questions and offered me an opened bottle of water I wasn't about to touch. Well, they were snickering like getting me to drink it would be a good joke.

About an hour later, I was dressed in orange and loaded onto a cargo plane packed with a few airmen and a bunch of army types, all strapped into serious looking chairs. But all the good seats were taken, so they used cargo nets to lash me to the bulkhead in front of them where they could all keep an eye on me.

It was totally weird, but apparently they wanted to make an example of me. Extreme measures for the terrorist instructor.

Fine. It'd been a long day already. I'd chased Jack all over Austin on a motorcycle—him in Marie's body. Then I'd been killed in

Rema's house. Made a body-jump. Hiked through half of Austin with cops looking for me. Had a nice chat with Peter the Twit. And dodged big trucks on the freeway. Not to mention being manhandled by MPs looking for a gold star on their records. So yeah, I could use a nap. And who knows, it might be educational for these new troops to witness me unleash Billy Bob, and have him thrash around in the cargo net, spewing out his gator friendly lies. That would raise a few hairs—let them know what true evil was like.

They'd never seen the likes of me. Sure, incoming RPGs and a roadside IED attack were some serious bad shit on an otherwise shitty day. But I was the hell that could eat their best ammo, then laugh as I walked around in their skins.

Jack was pure twisted evil, and I was on the road to being just like him, only more focused. A bigger, badder Jack.

As I hung there in the nets looking at their young faces, I started to worry I might frighten the boys too much. Someone would stick a bayonet in me and I'd jump into their body. Then I'd be off to the races—slaughtering everyone except the pilot. We'd land. Somewhere. Anywhere. An assault team would confront me, so I'd go ballistic on them and jump, and jump, and jump.

Easy to imagine. Just like in some horror sci-fi movie where team after team of rough tough Space Marines gets mowed down by a slime dripping alien, just because they didn't understand the real situation.

Okay, so I was tired and my passengers were getting a bit violent-minded. My thoughts drifted between comic book themes and the kind of sci-fi and action movies I liked. Plus some input from the very real killers I harbored inside me.

I told myself to just chill. I was headed to D.C., to Sonya. This was what I wanted. This would be a good trip, even if I was strapped to a bulkhead.

No problem. It'd be a fun trip. A happy trip. We'd swap machismo stories. Maybe sing about bossy drill sergeants.

Or maybe real hell would break loose.

The takeoff was rough. I shook where I hung on the wall, but my restraints held me well enough. We were buffeted by the remnants of the storm working its way inland from the Gulf. So I spent some time shaking and shuddering in front of the men.

No big deal. Right, guys? We basically flew—horror movie style.

The flight leveled out. I hung there, on the wall, all spider-like in my cargo net webbing. All eyes were on me. A weird sight. Evil in my web. Yes, I was something out of a horror movie, except I was alive and hung up close in a pressurized metal chamber taking us to D.C.

They just sat there and stared. Few words were spoken. A hot pot of coffee sat to the side, ignored. So I was reality TV at its finest?

Yes, I was. They wouldn't mess with me, and there was no way I could get free. I could do whatever I wanted because I wasn't going anywhere. I could safely drift off. Let my passengers out. Let Billy Bob mess around with this nervous audience. So I closed my eyes.

Show time.

* * *

When I woke up I was still hanging in the cargo net. We were on the ground and unloading. But the young men didn't look so happy. That's when I noticed two were being carried off on stretchers. I guess they got too close. Bones were broken? Maybe I told them I needed to use the facilities?

Sorry about that. I can't be held responsible for the evil that lurks within.

Good training mission. Right, guys?

Guys?

They left me hanging there. Alone. For a long time.

Finally two very burly MPs took me off the wall. Judging by their neck size, they had to be steroid enriched wrestlers. Who knew the Air Force had guys this beefy?

As we exited the plane, they literally held me inches off the ground as we crossed the tarmac.

It seemed like late afternoon or maybe early evening, and it sure didn't look like Texas. The air was cooler. "Hey, are we in D.C.?"

One of them slapped me across the back of the head to get me to shut up. A few seconds later I regained consciousness with the tips of my shoes dragging across the tarmac.

I wondered if these were Peter's men—Air Force wrestlers that we'd hired. Somehow, asking them if they were *on the take* seemed like a bad idea.

Wolf wasn't impressed. He started to lecture me on how too much muscle was actually a disadvantage and how he could exploit their weakness. They lacked flexibility. They lacked speed. Their training was obviously minimal.

As I started on a mental argument with Wolf, the two gorillas picked up on my agitation, so one of them hauled off and slapped me again on the back of my head.

Maybe I was getting used to that because this time, only my vision went blank for a second. Funny how the back of Samson's head seemed connected to his eyes.

I relaxed again, but was tempted to let Wolf show off his anti-wrestler skills. When we approached the door to a building, Wolf indicated it would give us an extra advantage. Because a door can be used as a weapon.

Sure, doors knocked people out all the time in the movies. But I decided to hold Wolf back. Did we really need to fight an entire airbase just to show how badass we were?

My passengers said they were all willing to put Wolf to the test. Popcorn would be nice. Besides, if we got killed we'd just jump into the airman who killed us and we'd keep going. The carnage would be awesome.

Note to self: My passengers finally figured out what jumping was about. More importantly, they could learn.

Actually, I probably already made a *note to self* when I first realized my passengers could learn, so never mind.

Inside the building, it was a tight squeeze going down a hallway with three of us abreast. Near the end of a hall, the men stepped into a side office and tossed me in the general direction of a chair. As I got up off the floor, one of them tossed me my glasses, and with that they lost interest in me and walked off.

Hey. Was I free to go?

Then an ex-military type stepped into the doorway. Older,

probably in his early 50s, and starting to go gray. Dressed in black hunter camo. Hair a bit too long for regulation. Enough muscle to get the job done. Weathered skin that'd seen too many days in the sun. Basically, I was looking at a Wyoming landscape—old rocks, no sense of humor. He leaned against the doorway and looked me over. And he was disgusted with something. "You."

Okay, so he had a real knack with words.

After a minute, I prompted him. "Get to the point."

He cocked his head slightly. "Am I gonna have a problem with you?"

Yeah. Probably. I thought about it a moment, but nothing clever came to mind. So I decided to show him that I was a hard-ass, too. "Probably. Are you looking for a problem?"

He looked at the floor and shook his head like I was a lost cause. "Listen. I got no time to babysit you, so save your little tantrums for someone else. You read me?"

I probably nodded.

"Follow me."

I got up and followed Wyoming Man down the hall. He never looked back. Wyoming men never do.

Wolf thought this guy would be a bit tougher to take down than the two burly MPs. But it seemed to me that this no-nonsense guy had to be the man Peter hired to extract me.

The hallway ended in a waiting room with a desk, some barely padded metal chairs, and a bulletin board. Several enlisted men were there waiting for us, and not looking friendly. Wyoming Man paused, blocking the path between me and the airmen. "Put it down, son. You don't want to go there."

Off to the side, one of the guys was holding a chair like it was a good thing to beat me with. He locked eyes with Wyoming, then decided to put it down.

Apparently, the guys were steamed about something that had happened on the plane.

Hey, I had nothing to do with it. I was napping. My passengers? Sure, they might have lured a few guys closer, and of course, bones were broken. Blame my passengers, not me.

I exited the building sticking close to my escort. He walked over to an old muscle car from the late '60s. Not in the best condition or even clean, but it still looked like it was a serious ride. "Get in." He opened the driver's door and got in.

Fine. I got in. He started the engine. Revved it a time or two to blow out the carburetor.

"Where are we going?"

He looked over at me like I was clueless. "Jack's waiting for you."

I reached for the door handle.

"Relax. Sonya gets you first."

"You work for Sonya?"

"I do today."

We drove.

* * *

An hour later we pulled over on a rural side street not far from the freeway. Nothing around us but trees, road, and a bit of farm land. The sun had just gone down and the sky was ablaze with orange.

Some of my passengers thought we were about to be killed and rolled into a ditch.

I reminded them that Sonya would never do that.

They wanted to know why I was so gullible. Just because Wyoming Man said Sonya sent him, didn't mean she really did.

Fine. If he killed me, I'd just get his weathered hide.

It was a typical mental argument. But that's when I noticed he was watching me.

"Get out."

I just sat there, determined to be stubborn. "Now what?"

He looked annoyed again. "It's like a dead drop. Now get out of the car."

Okay, fine. This was a hand-off and I was the package. At least that's what I thought he meant by *dead drop*.

I carefully got out and closed the car door. He glanced at me one last time, then drove off.

Now what? No instructions, and I didn't have my earpiece.

I adjusted Samson's glasses. I smoothed out my orange onesie.

This must be rural D.C., or maybe somewhere near D.C.

Nameless scanned the horizon for the crop duster. Like in the movies. With a machine gun. To mow us down like the mutant miscreation we were.

Ten minutes later, headlights approached. A big custom bus pulled up. It was black, completely unmarked, with almost no windows. A luxury bus like rock bands use. The door opened and the driver looked down at me. No bus chauffeur's uniform, just cutoffs and a Hawaiian shirt.

Not what I was expecting, but it never was. I gave him a nod. "Hey."

He smiled but didn't budge. "Hey." He sounded mildly amused and waited for me to make the next move. Okay, he wasn't lost, so I went up the steps.

Looking back through the bus it was like a plush Las Vegas suite. Couches, deluxe lighting, a wet bar, and an open doorway that gave me a glimpse of a five star bedroom in back.

Whoa! Who knew buses could look so good? I immediately wanted to learn to play the guitar.

The bus took off and it propelled me back into the amazingly plush digs.

The driver pushed a button and a curtain closed immediately behind him. It looked like I was all alone. Alone to live my life on the road in total luxury.

Good to know Billy Bob's money was being used to equip the rebellion with high-class wheels.

"Back here." It was a vaguely familiar voice.

Someone was back there in the bedroom. Someone female.

As I entered the bedroom I caught sight of the hot tub at the back. Two black women were in the tub. Two beautiful twins. And so familiar. Oh, no. The classy girls who'd used a cattle prod on me back at Billy Bob's house.

"Come on in, sugar. We'll squeeze you in."

The same twins that had slapped me around when I was Pops. Normals. Undercover normals who said they worked for Sonya.

"Strip, babe."

"Come on, sugar. Don't be shy."

"Get your fine brown self in here."

I glanced at myself, and yes, I was still wearing Samson. Well, I had to admit the twins looked very inviting. And I did glance around a bit for their cattle prod. But mostly I wasn't sure how to react. "Yeah, well . . ."

"I'm Tanya."

"And I'm Tanya."

"What's your name?"

The sight of two very attractive young women waiting for me in a hot tub—well, I might have been a little nervous. Besides, what could I say to normals? Normals that worked for Sonya. Maybe this was a trap—Sonya testing me to see if I was faithful to her. Or maybe this was Sonya finding a way to make it up to me—being shot in my own hot tub, then run through the wringer and all.

I looked down at myself again, surprised that somehow my clothes were in a pile on the floor. Great. My passengers were taking advantage of my confusion. Thanks, guys. But I can handle my own crazy situations.

Tanya and Tanya looked pleased.

Okay, my manly parts were pleased, too. There was no denying it. Actually, I was extra glad I had Samson's body. I had a certain endowment that I was now starting to fully appreciate.

So not seeing any cattle prods, and knowing Sonya would never set me up or throw me to the sharks (yeah, right), I stepped into the tub. The bus might have changed lanes just then, because I wound up all over the twins.

What followed was a bit of a blur, because all of my passengers were pushing me out of the driver's seat. And yeah, we were exactly like a pack of horny guys in one body making the most of it—making the most of two beautiful and very friendly women.

A while later, as I caught my breath in my mind's passenger seat, I remembered what Bruce the Black had said to me. That he'd actually been black. And they were the best of times—and the worst. And now I was thinking I knew exactly what he meant by the best of times, as a fine black man, with even finer black women.

I forgot how messed up I was. Forgot being all lost and bummed out. Forgot about being killed in my last hot tub experience. Forgot everything wrong with the world. Yes, life was good again.

* * *

After the hot tub, we naturally decided to lounge a bit on the plush bed. And it was great.

Except it wasn't.

The problem? It was like I was hardly there—mentally. It was like inviting 10 pals over to help you have sex. It was like an orgy on the patio, except I was sitting at the bottom of the pool. I was being pushed aside. I was being shoved around by a front seat full of eager passengers. And my fond memories of amazing sex were dulled by the mash of males in my head.

The whole thing was ruined by my own multi-mind.

Yes, the multi-mind gave me mad skills, memories of multiple lives, and willpower like I'd never had before. But it totally messed up sex.

I didn't like sex by committee—a committee of assorted killers. It felt like a conjugal visit with your wife, except all your prison buddies showed up, argued, and made demands.

It felt like locker room sex, except I was 25th in line. And the other guys kept cutting in front of me.

It felt like all of that.

The multi-mind was a double edged sword. It gave me super powers, and super problems. Things were going downhill fast.

I was already a basket case of conflicting opinions. I was a one man crowd living in a random body. I could never have a home— not a real one. Even with wonderful Sonya, I'd be some random stranger who came home after a hard day fighting killers, and then I'd have to convince her it was really me. New body—no big deal. Right?

Who could deal with that? Could I love Sonya if she came home looking like some slimebag who should be on death row? What would I say to he-Sonya?

You look kinda random tonight, babe. But hey—I can deal with it. So grab a shave, Sonya, and we'll make out.

Seriously?

Physically, I'd be a random person. Mentally, I'd be a flash mob—bigger, badder, bolder each time. Who could love that?

They say you have to know someone to really love them. But I'd be different every time—inside too, because I'd have a new addition to my personality, and not a good addition.

Sadly, I realized I'd already become Random Man. Unpredictable. Unrecognizable. Unstable. Unlovable.

Or maybe . . . just maybe I could find a way off this messed up superhero treadmill. I could stop putting myself in danger. Stop getting killed. Keep one body and cling to it just like all the normals do. But I'd always struggle with the passengers I had in me now. I'd always need a straitjacket at night because of Billy Bob the jumper.

And I'd always be fighting off my passengers, especially when I wanted sex.

Damn. I'd jumped too far. Billy Bob was a major mistake. Sure, I wanted to take the slimebag out. But Peter knew he was a jumper. He set me up without warning me. I vowed to use Peter as a punching bag until he figured out a way to get Billy Bob out of my multi-mind. There had to be a way to extract unwanted passengers.

Real superheroes had a day job and a cape. All I had was a growing problem—all of my good deeds went punished. Real superheroes had the good life, with solid goals and good mental health. Well, mostly. A touch of insanity added character. Right? But not me. I had to take a shower wearing random guys. And try to keep their nasty thoughts out of my mind.

Just so very depressing.

I noticed the twins watching me.

One smiled shyly. "Maybe you'd like to put some clothes on?"

The other twin nodded. "Because we're here now."

Really? I hadn't noticed. Okay, so the bus was stopped. "Sorry. I was kinda lost in thought."

"No problem."

"We know you've got a lot on your plate."

I gave them a half-smile. "Thanks for the ride, ladies."

Tanya smiled. "Our pleasure."

The other Tanya smiled. "And no worries about telling Sonya."

"Absolutely. She hoped you'd have some fun on the bus."

Really? Or maybe Sonya knew it would be exactly this shocking. Sonya knew what she was doing, so I had to figure she set me up—

set me up for the realization that my life would never be normal. Our life together would always be weird—weird because of me and my growing list of motley passengers.

I started getting Samson dressed.

Sonya and her inner Ava had always insisted she'd never get a new body. And now I understood why.

Change rocks the boat. People fall out. Then we struggle to swim in a sea of random madness.

5.3 Kobayashi Maru

As I stepped out of the bus, I put Samson's glasses back on. We were in an underground loading dock area that might be for delivery trucks. Lots of cement, freight elevators, and pipes.

It looked fairly deserted. I had the impression we were under something big, like an abandoned shopping mall or a hotel. It could have been anything.

What now?

Two serious looking security guards walked up to me and patted me down without even grunting *hello*.

I turned to see the Love Bus slowly backing away. Not even enough room for it to make a u-turn.

After the guards were satisfied I was naked under my clothes, one of them gestured to a golf cart.

Okay, time for a ride. And apparently they weren't going with me.

I got in, but the cart was weird because it didn't have a steering wheel. Or brakes. Or anything. Just a bench seat facing forward and another seat facing the rear. Headlights and brake lights on both ends. There was no way to tell which end was the front.

But it did have a heavy duty luggage rack on top for hauling cargo.

A few seconds after I sat down, it started rolling so I instinctively jumped out. It stopped. The guards smirked, like this was an old joke that never stopped being funny.

Fine. It was a self-driving golf cart. Another one of Peter's bad inventions. I'd read about self-driving taxis and 18-wheelers. Now those were a recipe for disaster. Why not invent something useful? Like a game that figured out what you liked and didn't like, then it would redesign itself to maximize your fun. Or a high paying job that didn't require any work. Seriously, the world didn't need self-crashing golf carts.

Fine. I got back in and hung on like I was some old farmer getting his first biplane ride. Or maybe that was Pops hanging on for dear life.

We zipped off through a poorly lit cement hallway. I looked around for cameras, knowing that Peter must be laughing his ass off at the top of Stark Towers.

A minute later we pulled up to an elevator. Its doors opened for me, so I stepped out of the cart. But the cart almost ran me over as it drove inside the elevator and waited.

What? Was I supposed to sit in the golf cart while using the elevator?

Obviously, yes. Just another day in Peter's idea of Black Mesa.

There were no buttons in the elevator, so I just parked my butt in the cart using one of the seats facing the elevator doors. I figured that would be the new front of the cart. The elevator doors closed, and we headed down. How far, I had no idea, but eventually the doors opened and the cart zipped out.

Four-wheel steering and no steering wheel. That pretty much made it the ultimate in ass-backwards automation. Or maybe that was just Pops talking, because some of my passengers thought this was cool.

Welcome to the future, where humans are nothing more than cargo.

This cement tunnel was dark, very narrow, and we were going fast. At least the thing was going perfectly straight. I could have held out my hands and filed my fingernails on the walls without any problem.

I tried starting a conversation. "Hey."

No response. I'd left my earpiece back with the MPs in San Antonio. No handy earpieces in the cart. So it looked like Peter and Sonya wanted a real face to face.

Eventually the cart slowed as we approached a bright light at the end of the hallway. A dead end, and a metal door.

I stepped out of the cart and the metal door opened automatically. I almost expected a computer voice to say, *"Watch your step and welcome to Peter's World, where automation wipes your pathetic human rump and pats your useless head. Have a totally Peter day."*

Inside, there was nothing but a small empty room and another metal door. Like an airlock, or a decontamination chamber, or high security. I'd seen this plenty of times in games.

I stepped in. The door closed behind me. I held my breath in case I was sprayed with fungicide. I wasn't. Then the door in front of me opened, and there was Sonya with a warm smile and a hot kiss.

Home sweet home!

She pulled away and looked into my new dark brown eyes. "Hey, babe. Fun trip?"

Was she talking about the Tanya twins? "Not entirely. I take it, this is HQ."

"It's more like a rabbit hole, but it keeps us safe. You look good."

I kinda did. Samson's body was a lot better than Dread, or Tommy before him. Or Billy Bob. Or Pops—no offense Pops. "Did you really bag Jack?"

She smiled. "Yes. We're arranging his final isolation."

"Final?" I liked the sound of that.

"Hopefully." Sonya's smile vanished. "You know, I'm so very sorry about Marie." She gave me another warm hug. "I know it's got to be rough."

It was wonderful—her sympathy and all. But what I needed most was to end Jack, and to see if we could get Marie back to normal. Right, extract Jack and his passengers so Marie could regain control of her body.

Sonya led me down a hallway, past piles of empty boxes that once held computer gear, food, and modular furniture. "Sorry about the mess. We're a little challenged getting stuff in and out of the bunker. You still prefer to be called Wolf, right?"

"Yes."

"Good."

She said that like it was important. Well, it didn't take a multi-mind to see where this was going—a face to face with Jack. More precisely, Marie with Jack controlling her mind. So I put it into words. "We need to get Jack out of Marie."

That brought her to a halt. "If only we could."

"You don't know how?"

"No. When we move into a new body, the minds become intertwined. Peter calls it a mind meld. Unfortunately, it's permanent. At least that's what we believe."

"There's got to be a way."

"We've asked Bruce the Black, but he doesn't think it's possible. We tried contacting the Snow Leopard, but we haven't been able to find her. We've contacted syndicates around the world, but they either don't know or won't talk with us until we have full control of North America."

"Jack did research on jumpers. What about his notes?"

"He didn't keep any notes. It was all in his head."

"Then we need to interrogate him."

"He's not exactly cooperative. Besides, don't you think if he knew how to unwind from his other minds he would have done that by now?"

"I'm not talking about making Jack sane, I'm talking about getting Jack and his passengers out of Marie's mind. Screw Jack. Can't we just electrocute him without harming Marie? Electroshock or something?"

"How do you kill a mind without harming the brain? How do you kill his mind without harming Marie's mind? It doesn't seem possible."

"Hell, jumping doesn't even seem possible. But we do it. There has to be a way to jump out without killing the body."

"Talk with Peter. I'm very sorry, Wolf. Based on everything we know, I'm just not optimistic."

We continued walking.

"So Marie's family is safe? My mother, too?"

"Yes. We have a kind of witness protection program, except it's for our family and friends. We have over a hundred people in that program. We call it NPP: the Normal Protection Program."

"Rema's there, too?"

Sonya laughed. "Yes. She's a riot. She kind of took over the program."

"Rema?"

"Yes. She immediately started telling people what to do. She's a natural born organizer. And she knows how to handle people of all ages. She's really good."

"You mean she's bossy."

"Sometimes you have to boss people around to be a good manager. She put normals into two categories. Those that just needed protection from Jack, and those who knew that jumpers exist. She wants to call that group FWKAMUD—short for Folks Who Know A Maggoty Un-Dead."

That's Rema. "What about her daycare centers?"

"We found a new daycare manager. But Rema manages the manager. She says she's found her true calling—acting as a bridge between the living and what she calls the *undead*. I guess that's us."

Good that Rema was fitting in. Now I wanted to focus on getting Jack out of Marie. Then kill him. "I need to have a little chat with Jack."

"I was hoping you would."

I followed Sonya through an automatic sliding glass door, into the command and control center. It reminded me of a good old LAN party where guys brought their gaming rigs and hooked them up for some team-play, and maybe a few drinks. Except these people were controlling agents in the field—not blasting ugly-ass aliens.

Several big monitors were on the walls. Each workstation had two or three monitors. A few of the people were wearing VR goggles and moving their hands in the air like they were controlling invisible drones or something. The tech was impressive.

It occurred to me I should have been honored to have Peter as my handler. The other people looked more like random people than coldly calculating commanders. Not that Peter looked impressive in his current nerd body.

He saw us and stood up. Then he turned to someone sitting near him. "Zelda, you've got the com."

Cool. Zelda was a no nonsense mosh pit girl, jet black hair with a red streak on one side, wearing trendy black club-commando clothes with lots of pockets and chrome studs. I got the clear impression she was second in command. She looked every inch like a Zelda. How come I never had Zelda tell me what to do? Hell, if she ever told me to stick something in my ear, I'd do it. No questions asked. Maybe she'd run my next op. Maybe bark some no nonsense orders into my ear. I'd do whatever she said. Well, some of my passengers would. I could tell they really wanted that. Nameless especially wanted—

Sonya bumped me from behind.

Oh, yeah. I might have been staring at Zelda too long. I checked my mouth for drool. Some found, so I casually wiped it off. Nameless seemed to think Zelda was his long lost soul mate.

Great. The last thing I needed was for my passengers to start falling in love with real people. My guys signaled me—this was going to be a good day. We were at the heart of the resistance, surrounded by nerds fighting evil. Nameless had serious dibs on mosh pit Zelda, but none of my other passengers cared. They were too busy scouting around for suitable babes of their own.

This was no matchmaking service, but it did seem like Nameless had stirred things up in my mental back seat.

Note to self: Passengers could have primitive misguided mating urges—just like me.

Peter finished whatever he was doing at his station, took off his headset, and waved for us to follow him. Back in the hallway and around a corner, we came to an office lounge, complete with coffee machine, foosball table, two refrigerators, and three plush sofas. Four people looked up at us.

Peter held everyone's gaze for a second. "Give me the room." Everyone immediately picked up their snacks and left.

At least Peter had respect among his own crew. It crossed my mind that maybe I should cut him some slack.

Sonya closed the door and the three of us sat down for a serious talk. Peter started things off. "Greetings, dude. Awesome to have you here. Sonya probably already leaked the news, but we've captured Jack."

"How?"

"We tracked his plane from Texas to Virginia. Followed his convoy—four black SUVs. Rammed the hell out of them. Not the usual intercept. Got into a Taser fight—very cool, I might add. Then we dropped a Faraday net over him."

"What's a Faraday net?"

"It's like a Faraday cage, only, you know . . . netty."

"Why?"

Peter looked even more annoyed with me than usual. "Dude, it's a metal net. It blocks electromagnetic frequencies used for communications. Jack has a kill chip in him. Well, technically the chip is in Marie. Sorry, bro—your old girlfriend's been chipped. Among other things." Sonya was giving Peter a dirty look so he didn't elaborate on Marie's treatment. "As I was saying, we used the net to make sure Jack didn't beam out."

"But he could have beamed out while you were attacking his convoy."

"Duh, we used a jammer. You know? Then after we had him in the net, we turned off the jammer."

"Why? Why didn't you just use the jammer until you had him safely locked up?"

"What's with all the lame questions, bro?" Peter looked exasperated. "Okay, look. Electromagnetics 101. Frequency jammers are active. Faraday nets are passive. It's like trying to break into a bank at night while surrounded by carbon arc floodlights. You know? The cops can't see you because the light is blinding them. Except it's totally lame. Or would you rather wear the cloak of invisibility on your bank heist? Blinding light gives away your position, just like jammers. The last thing we need is for Jack's guys to follow our jamming signal. Jammers are quick and dirty. Faraday nets are super stealthy."

Fine. I was a dope and Peter was a mental god. "Where's he now?"

"That's like, ultra secret. I mean, like *ultra*." Peter glanced at Sonya. "But you've been cleared for that intel. There's an abandoned chemical plant in Maryland, not far from D.C.—not saying where, exactly. Lots of big metal vats and chambers. You know? Metal chambers act like a Faraday cage, only better—no holes, so almost no frequencies can get in. There are a few exceptions within the EM spectrum, but that's beside the point.

Jack uses wall-to-wall metal in all his dungeons to block kill chips that might be in his prisoners. It's standard protocol these days."

I remembered the metal dungeon under the barn. "Okay, but when I rescued Bruce the Black from the metal dungeon they still activated a kill chip in the dungeon master."

"Right. Maybe you remember, the big red barn was built with wood panels on a metal frame? The frame acts like a giant antenna. Down in the dungeon, all they had to do was flip a switch and the barn's antenna would be connected to a small antenna in the dungeon. Instant Faraday breach. Any kill chips in the dungeon would then be able to pick up their encoded signals."

Right. Peter knew everything. I knew nothing. "So you caught Jack. What next?"

"That, my mentally challenged friend, is where you come in."

I was about to punch him out, but I noticed Sonya starting to squirm. Something very unpleasant was coming, and it wasn't Peter spitting out blood.

He kept going. "Dude, you remember Captain Kirk on *Star Trek*, right?"

"Sure."

"You remember the Kobayashi Maru?"

It sounded familiar. "Maybe."

"It was that Star Fleet Academy test where there was no way to survive the simulation. You climb into a simulator, go into an unwinnable situation, and the Klingons obliterate your ship. All the cadets failed. They always did because that's the way the simulation was designed."

"Right. Except for Captain Kirk. He cheated."

"Not exactly. He reprogrammed the simulation. Hacking isn't cheating, it's outsmarting the system."

"So I'm Captain Kirk?"

"No way. You're no Captain Kirk. You're like one of the cadets— wearing a red uniform." I knew exactly what Peter was saying: the ones in red always died. "This is your Kobayashi Maru, bro. You face-off against Jack, you do what you have to do, and you both die. It's a win-win for all of us. Except Jack. And you."

"Wait. You want me to die with Jack?"

Peter glanced at Sonya, then avoided eye contact with me. "Basically. Yeah."

Not what I wanted to hear. "You mean . . . what? Jack kills me? So then I get his body, actually Marie's body, and Jack's kinda dead—just a sick bastard in the back of my mind? Then what? I jump out somehow with Marie and Jack dies? Or—" I was totally confused. "Wait. I don't really die. I just jump somehow. Right?"

"No, dude. You die-die. You know? Bye-bye? It ends you."

That had to be Peter's worst idea, ever. "Uh, I'll pass. What about the fourth way to kill a jumper? Maybe we can use that."

"Bro, this *is* the fourth way. It's martyrdom. That's what we're talking about here. You go in the big metal tank with Jack. You close the hatch and it's locked. You release the toxic gas. And you both die. It's totally easy-peasy. The perfect solution."

I shook my head. There had to be a better way.

Sonya was looking at the floor, her perma-smile gone.

Peter continued. "Think about what that sicko did to Marie. Are you gonna let him get away with that? Think about how many innocent people Jack had killed. Think about all the terrible things he's done, experimenting on us. Dude, he's a mega psychopath. He's got to be stopped. We all know that. But considering all the crap he's dumped on you, it's personal. Right? Over the top personal. You owe it to yourself, and the world, to take him out."

Yes, I wanted Jack dead. But there had to be a better way. "We need a better plan."

"There is no better plan. This is the only way to guarantee Jack gets the true death. Hell, you've got the motive. You've got the balls to see it through. Look around this place. We're a pack of lightweight jumpers, and a few normals who got roped in to this fight. You've got more killers in you than any of us. Hell, we already have to chain you up at night. And if we put you in the field any more, you'll just get harder to control. But if you take out Jack now, his crew will scatter. The world will be saved."

"Doc could take over."

"Doc? No way. Doc's only skill is wet-work. He's a one-trick hit-man. Without Jack painting targets, Doc goes to ground and his crew disbands. Doc's a tool, not an architect. But one thing's for certain, as long as we hold Jack, Doc will torture suspects until he finds him and sets the bastard free. We'll send out video of Jack's true death and Doc will grind to a halt. Time's running out, Wolf. We either end Jack now, or we run like hell. Don't let Jack out of this one. Don't let more innocent people die."

So that was it. It was all on me. The world would be saved if I'd just kill myself—with Jack.

Peter droned on about deadly gas, and how I'd be a hero, and about how he'd even name a secret building after me. But if he didn't have enough money for a secret building, he'd put my name in the Hall of Heroes. Of course, he'd have to find a suitable hallway first.

As for Sonya, she was quiet and kinda curled up. I could tell she hated this. But I knew if there was a better way, she would have rammed it down Peter's throat by now.

So I had to die to save the world from Jack? It made me numb just to even imagine that.

No. There had to be a better way.

Peter was talking aimlessly about the virtues of carbon dioxide versus carbon monoxide, so I interrupted him. "Maybe we're approaching this all wrong. Maybe we should be focused on saving Marie. And if Jack really died, that would just be a happy side effect. You know? We just need to kick Jack out of Marie's head. Like maybe Jack jumps into a vacuum pump or something."

Sonya looked up for the first time. "That's what we all wanted. A way to extract Jack from Marie's body so she could get back to normal. But—"

Peter stepped in. "It's not even in the lore. Ancients like Bruce the Black have never heard of any success along those lines. Only a kill can extract us. Period. End of subject."

"But not The Black. He can swap bodies anytime. Without getting killed."

Peter waved off the idea. "Okay, sure. He can do that. But it's pointless. After Bruce does the swap, Jack's still in somebody, and he's still got Marie's spirit tangled up with his. Yes, we can get Marie's body back, but her spirit will always be trapped in a fucked up mind meld with Jack."

"So we add another person. Musical chairs, but with body swaps." They just stared at me. "Bruce the Black does body swaps until Jack's in someone else—a person who's dying from old age or something. Jack dies in a doomed body."

Sonya looked at Peter, like it might have possibilities.

Peter shook his head. "Fail. That scenario means Bruce deliberately puts Jack in a dying body. Kinda obvious, Bruce becomes Jack's killer. So what then? Jack dies, jumps into Bruce's body, and Jack takes over Bruce's cool body swapping abilities? That's extra brilliant. We lose The Black and super-Jack keeps on rolling. But no matter how many body swaps you do, Marie's spirit is still tied to Jack's. Always. Always. Always. Any other bright ideas?"

"We keep Jack until he dies of old age." On second thought, Marie would die, too.

"Fail. We deny him the chance to jump until his current body dies? That sounds a lot like we're keeping him from living. And if you keep someone from living, isn't that right up there with slow murder? No, dude. Too risky, and it doesn't do Marie any good. What else?"

"I'm thinking. We just need to extract Marie."

"I feel your pain, bro, but we've been all over this. You have to face the hard truth—Marie's a dead woman walking. Except it's Jack doing the walking. She's already fried. Sorry, man. I didn't mean it like that. I just mean that she's . . . uh . . . not going to have a happy exit. There's only entanglement, not un-entanglement. She and Jack are permanently entangled—mind wise. Short of time travel, there's only their continued entanglement, and I'm fresh out of time machines."

"There has to be a way to un-jump him from Marie."

"Yeah . . . not. Once you're head humped, you're pretty much humped for life. You know? Sucks to be her. I mean, a normal trapped in Jack's black hole of insanity. Concentrated wrong."

"There has to be a way out for her."

"Sorry, dude. There is no way out for her. Jack's like this fucking black hole, and Marie's beyond the event horizon. She ain't coming out."

"We could slam two black holes together."

"Well, you know, that's kinda what we're doing here. You and Jack. Mutual annihilation. Not that you're a black hole, but you're gaining unwanted mental mass. Know what I mean? Astronomically, you're more of a brown—" Peter stared at me a moment. "You know what? Never mind." He turned to Sonya. "Maybe you should've given him this speech, because this whole conversation is nothing like I intended. How about a snack?"

Peter got up and headed to the fridge. "We've got jello in the shape of little Halloween monsters. Pudding balls in crunchy chocolate shells. The hazelnut dark chocolate troll balls are my favorite. They look kinda gross but—"

"Wait." An idea was forming in my multi-mind. "If Jack's the problem, then maybe he's also the solution."

Sonya perked up. "How?"

Okay, how? My passengers were huddled together, pooling their meager brain cells on this one. They were forming an idea—one that would solve everything. I tried to listen in, but my passengers never used words. Only one thing was clear. Jack had something we needed.

Sonya waited.

Peter stuffed chocolate into his mouth like it would make everything go away.

Then I had it. "Jack experimented on jumpers."

Peter swallowed. "Yeah, so?"

"So he's got all the rules figured out. How to jump. How to un-jump."

"No. Think about it. He experiments on jumpers precisely because he *doesn't* have it all figured out."

"But he might know a way out of Marie."

Sonya was almost smiling again. "He might."

"Nah." Peter was a fountain of negativity. "If Jack could bail out of a body without being killed by someone, he'd have done it a long time ago."

Really? Jack was the kind of guy who loved a bloody jump into a fresh skin. Why would he ever be considerate? "Why would Jack ever do the humane thing? Bailing out and leaving his old body alive just isn't his style. He loves leaving a trail of dead people. At the very least, it leaves fewer witnesses. Jack could easily know the secret to leaving a body alive and well, but he never wanted to do that."

Sonya chimed in. "Jack doesn't keep records. So whatever results he learned from his experiments, they're only in his head. But why would he help us?"

She had a point. Why would Jack help us? "We offer him his freedom."

They both said, "No."

I held up my hands. "Hang on. We just make the offer. We don't actually let him go. As soon as he jumps out of Marie and leaves her intact, we . . . uh . . . bag him. Or whatever."

"Or whatever?" Peter closed the fridge and sat down. "Suppose he does exit Marie. Then what? We'd have no clue how that happens or where he'd go next. No. He'd keep Marie's spirit and jump out of our trap. We'd wind up with a brain-dead Marie—alive, but empty. You can't trust Jack. You just can't."

"We could listen to what he had to say. He might go for a deal."

"Oh, perfect. A deal with the devil? Why didn't I think of that? That's such an awesome plan, bro." Peter shook his head. "Look, you want Marie alive. I get it. If you can really pull it off, I'm all for it. But Jack dies. That's the bottom line—for me, and for a hell of a lot of other people." Peter started to leave the room. "But if you're not man enough to pull the pin, we'll find another hero."

He looked at Sonya, then seemed to unwind a bit. "Sorry, man. Good people are dying every day. I get kinda harsh sometimes. Hey, why don't you and Sonya get some time together. Relax. Enjoy final times together, until all our plans unravel. Because it's only a matter of time before Jack's crew extracts him. And when they do, they round us all up, put us all in room with a single martyr and a ton of explosives, and we'll all die in one big blast of ever loving shit. No pressure, bro, but in the morning we're damn well flying you out to meet Jack. Chat him up. See how it goes. You know? Do whatever. But while you're in the kill chamber, you might just want to make it a happy ending—for the rest of humanity. Toxic gas is there if you need it. But that's your decision. I'll say it again, what you do with Jack is entirely up to you."

Peter walked over and surprised me with a weird hug. "You're on point, Wolf. Don't let us down."

Some of my passengers hugged him back.

Traitors.

* * *

Sonya looked defeated. "If Jack had a way to unload all those spirits inside him, I'm sure he would have done it by now. A head full of hate never helped anyone."

"Jack's got a hundred times more evil in his head than I do. It's got to be tearing him apart. Hell, I'm barely coping as it is. So he must be pushing out unwanted spirits."

"Or he doesn't mind them because he's a psychopath, and psychopaths are numb to so many feelings. Or maybe the evil spirits are controlling the lesser ones inside him. Like a concentration camp. So Jack's free from the mental noise. Personally, I believe Jack lost control a hundred years ago—his evil cargo is the only thing keeping him going."

I never thought of that—Jack victimized by his own passengers. "Maybe."

"Unfortunately, he's beyond understanding. His personality shifts constantly. And except for needing to control everything, his goals keep changing."

"Yeah, I noticed. One minute he loves me in his own weird way, then he tries to kill me."

"It happens." She said that in a strange way.

That's when I locked eyes with Sonya. She loved me. And she was setting me up to die. We both knew it was something she shared with Jack.

Tears filled her eyes. They rolled down her cheeks in little rivers. I took her in my arms as she cried, held her as she fought back the tears.

When a brave woman cries, I kinda lose it. Who knew that would pull at my heart like that? So I took off Samson's glasses and joined Sonya's waterworks.

* * *

A few people walked in on us in the break room, but quickly made a u-turn. All except one.

I looked up and saw Zelda standing there, watching us with her tough mosh pit attitude, like she'd seen it all.

"Peter needs an executive decision, boss lady."

"Sorry, Wolf." Sonya stood up. "I need to get back to work. But we'll get together for dinner. Keep him out of trouble, Zelda." Sonya gave me a messy kiss, wet with tears and eyeliner, then left.

Zelda looked me up and down. "Hey."

"Hey back."

"I've handled you."

I wasn't exactly sure what that meant. So I decided to throw her a little confusion about who I'd been wearing. "I've handled you, too."

She hesitated, then burst out laughing like she was a hick girl, fresh off the farm. She followed that by a frown and a serious look. "Seriously?"

I shook my head, but said, "Totally." Nameless was struggling to take hold of my mental steering wheel. Lust at first sight was a powerful thing.

She laughed again, a bit confused, but enjoying it. "I was kinda bent when you lost your Wolf bod."

"Me too. Wolf had a tight ass."

"Oh, totally hot! I mean . . . a lot of us girls lost it when you . . . uh . . . lost that smokin' hot man-shape. Not that you're bad now. Just that you're kinda rockin' the square thing. You know?"

I put my glasses back on. "I like to think of it as the Clark Kent look."

"That's kinda cool. Girls like a little Kent now and then. But maybe your next—" She cut herself off, then turned and opened the door for me. "Hey. How about I give you the tour?"

"I've seen a lot of it already."

"That's cool. But I'll bet you haven't seen the underbelly of the beast."

The beast? Meaning her? "I like underbellies."

"Ooo. I'm sure you do, Mr. Big Bad Wolf."

She held the door open while I stepped into the hallway. And damned if she didn't pinch my ass as I walked by her.

"My, my, Mr. Wolf. Still hard after all those bods."

Great. I was getting squeezed between Nameless and Zelda.

* * *

Zelda gave me a tour of the underbelly of the beast, which turned out to be the power plant on the lower level. She pointed out all the automation, like I was supposed to be impressed. Peter's techno-touches just seemed cryptic and pointless. More importantly, Zelda had a bad habit of peeling off her clothes, down to her underwear. She said it was because it was so hot and steamy this close to the beast. So were the boilers the beast, or was I the beast? She never quite explained that part. But she did put her clothes back on whenever we passed by a security camera.

So for her, it pretty much went: talk about the heat, strip brazenly, flirt furiously, then put it all back on and act normal for the next zone with cameras.

Weird, but it held my multi-headed attention better than the boilers and circuit breakers.

Finally, she made a point of aiming her barely covered ass at me while reaching for her clothes, and between her legs she looked back and made me an offer. "Your place or mine?"

I had a place? "Mine."

"Wrong. But you can see your digs. Just a heads up, Mr. Wolf, you won't like it. It's all done up in *death by dull*. It belongs to a helo pilot, but she moved in with Sonya so you could have your own space."

Damn. I thought I'd be staying with Sonya.

* * *

"This is Kat's quarters. Stand like this." Zelda positioned me in front of the door and that seemed to make it open. "But it's yours for as long as you're here."

We stepped inside.

It was a small suite with a couch, a bed, and a small bathroom. The theme seemed to be shades of white and soft pillows, which amounted to a general feminine feel. But I found the white flowers and candles a bit unnerving. It kinda gave off a mortuary vibe. But the weird part was the open window next to the bed that seemed to open to a painted view about three feet away.

"Check this out." Zelda picked up a remote control, pushed a button, and the sheer curtains on the fake window seemed to bring a breeze into the room. "Weird, huh?"

"Yeah."

"We're underground, so Peter figured women would go crazy without a view. See?" She pulled aside the curtain to give me a better view of big sky and green rolling hills. "Kat does most of our local helo runs, so she was given this to look at. It's seriously fake, but if you don't look at it directly it's not so bad. But check out the bed."

I'd had enough of Zelda's flirting, so I made something up. "I'm kinda tired. I think I'll crash for a while."

"That's cool." She jumped onto the plush bed and made herself comfortable. "Oh, we loaded the top drawer with some clothes for you." She pointed to the dresser next to the bed. "We weren't sure what size you took, so you'll just have to fish around for something that fits."

I looked at her, like I wanted privacy.

She looked at me, like she wasn't going anywhere.

"Where's your room?"

Zelda shrugged. "Back by CAC. I bunk close to run field ops. Next to Sonya and Peter, I run the show here."

I looked around, feeling trapped. "What's your window like?"

"I don't need one. If I want a view, I pull on some VR goggles and drone around in the city of my choice. Relax, Wolf." She patted the space in bed she'd reserved for me. "Settle in. If you're feeling like some z's, we've got chains under the bed—from my personal collection." She gave me a wink and a thinly veiled sexy grin.

Nameless wondered why I was playing hard to get. Zelda and chains could be some serious fun.

No. Zelda and chains could make sex with Jack look like good clean fun. "I'll pass on the chains. But you're welcome to try them on." Damn. Nameless was putting bad urges in my mind.

"Normally, I'd really go for that. But you've got Billy Bob Wyville inside you. So, you know, the chains are kinda your new PJs."

"You're a jumper?"

"Nice girls don't tell. But yeah, I've skull skipped a few times. Not to worry, though. I figure that just makes me more worldly. A girl's gotta have skills. Wolfie likes skills, don't you?"

Actually, Wolf liked a camera in the bedroom and watching his own skills. "Aren't you needed in comms?"

"I'm always needed in CAC. But Sonya and Peter are seriously busy running the war against evil. And you gotta know, you're a seriously important agent right now. Like our most important asset. So park your hard-ass self in bed and let's get down to business."

"I'll pass."

"Not an option. You get bedded and chained tonight, and I'm the most qualified to handle that op."

"I've been handled already today."

"You think so? By Tanya and Tanya? Those circus softies? I know way more tricks. You'll see. Once you've been Zelda'ed, you'll always want Zelda'ed."

"What about dinner?"

"What about it?"

"I'm having dinner with Sonya."

"Fine. But we have an hour. So shed those prison clothes and slide over here for proper debriefing." She started wiggling out of her clothes again.

"Uh, look . . ." I walked toward the bathroom, "I got things to do." I stepped in, closed the door, and locked it. There was nothing in the bathroom but a sink, a toilet, and a shower stall. Not even a fake window to climb out of.

"That's good, Wolfie. Try out the robo-toilet." Zelda waited a couple minutes, then added, "What's taking so long?"

I turned on the shower. "I need a shower."

"Cool." She was tapping at the door. "I have mad shower skills."

"I'm sure you do. But this is a new body. I need some alone time with it to get adjusted. You know?"

"Sure. If you need help with your joy stick, let me know. I'm pretty sure your new body's arranged like most guys."

"I can't hear you."

"I'll wait in bed," she shouted. "I'll have your chains ready to go."

Right. Not gonna happen. Nameless was pissed with me, but we stripped and stepped into the shower. The hot water felt good. And just like always, using the soap felt weird."

* * *

Forty-five minutes later I was becoming a prune. So I stepped out of the shower and put my orange prisoner suit back on.

When I opened the door, Zelda was naked in bed and not looking pleased.

"You took a shower and put your dirty clothes back on?"

"Not exactly." I held up my underwear.

"You're shy. I get it."

She stared at me.

I stared at her. Nameless drooled. I shrugged. "It's complicated."

"Ya think?" She had her arms folded under her breasts. It kind of perked them up. But she still looked pissed.

What could I say? "Uh. I have passengers."

"Passengers? Brain baggage? So? Like, we all do. So do us all a favor and let Wolfie out to play."

"Yeah, well . . . the thing is . . ."

"You're suddenly gay?"

"No."

"You don't like me? Too forward? You like 'em all passive and gooey?"

"No."

"Then what?"

"It's personal."

"That's exactly how I'm taking it. You think I'm not cute enough? My rump's too big? So what is it? Spit it out."

"One of my passengers is in love with you."

She sat up, her eyes wide with amazement. "No shit?"

I nodded sheepishly, wishing she'd put some clothes on.

"Which one? Wolf?"

"No. Just some guy."

"Fuck. It's not Tommy or Dread is it? No wonder you're keeping your onesie zipped."

I had forgotten Zelda ran ops with Peter. She knew several of my passengers. "No."

"That's a relief. Hey, it's not that old dirt clod farmer is it? Well, hell. Get his seed bag over here and let's blow his dusty old tractor into the next county. I'm sure he's overdue for a total lube job."

"It's Nameless."

"Who?"

"A guy I picked up with no ID. He never shared his name, so I just call him Nameless."

"Ah. That guy. The one we traced back to a break-in at Billy Bob's. The one Wolf killed in the freezer. That's cool. So bring him over for some chains and sugar."

"You don't get it. He's in love."

She hesitated. "What? Like *love* love?"

I nodded.

"Like all messed up in the head and heart beating like it's now got a higher purpose, love?"

"Well, maybe not quite like that, but yeah."

"Cool. So that's why you're shy."

Not exactly. "I'm a multi-mind."

"Yeah, so?"

"It's complicated."

"It always is. That's why we fuck like rabbits. It blows the edge off the confusion. You can live in your head and get all tangled up in your thoughts. Or you can drop your inhibitions and remind yourself what it's like to be a mono-mind doing the primal." Zelda gave me a big smile. "So drop 'em, boy, and share what you've got with what I've got."

It was so tempting. "I could, except, love—it's pulling at me from several directions."

"Oh." She frowned. "Sonya."

"She's one."

"Marie?"

"And now you."

"That sucks." She stood up and reached for some clothes but didn't put them on.

I shrugged. "Sorry."

"Don't apologize. It's not every day I get shot down by the love card."

"It's not every day I get my heart messed around by three women."

She nodded. "Yeah. Love. It sucks the life out of perfectly good relationships."

"I guess." What could I say? Love raised me up. Love pulled me down. "Dinner?"

She walked over and gave me a hug. Then she whispered into my ear, "Nameless. After dinner, I want you to man-up and show me some balls. So push this skull skipper aside and let me get to know you. I promise to put a grin on your virtual face."

Zelda pushed me out to arm's length. "You didn't hear that. Right?"

I nodded.

She got dressed—seductively.

We headed to dinner.

5.4 Fait Accompli

Dinner was in the cafeteria, except the lights were dimmed to let people think it was evening. Such was life underground. Things like that were expected.

Zelda and I strolled into the cafeteria, arm in arm. My uncommitted arm. Zelda's tight grip. But at least Nameless was happy.

At least 20 people were lined up for food, buffet style. Maybe a dozen were already seated, idly eating, chatting, and flirting. Tables had real table cloths, fake orchids, and little flickering LED candles. Some dead guy's violin concerto in double-D major was being piped in, probably to suggest elegant dining for us freaks hiding underground. Deep red curtains with gold tassels were hung on three walls, maybe to give the illusion we had closed windows that looked out on Shangri-La, or some other Nirvana spot in the Himalayans. A huge dragon embossed gong stood in one corner. The dinner bell? A fake mountain stream tumbled down real rocks in another corner.

The whole scene smacked of Zen, but with an undeniable sexual undertow. Yes, *undertow*. Like a hot stone massage gone horribly wrong.

Okay, so I was feeling a little lightheaded. Probably because Zelda and Nameless were cutting off the blood flow to my brain.

I spotted Sonya and Peter at a table with a small robotic arm sitting on it. And they had two empty seats. Perfect. I extracted my arm from Zelda's clutches and gave them a wave.

"Hey." Zelda nudged me with her hip. "Let's skip the shop talk and grab a table for two."

Nameless nodded, but I said, "No. I need to talk with them."

So I walked over to Sonya's table while Zelda made a show of holding my arm. Super possessive.

Peter picked up Sonya's wine glass. "Hey, dude. Check this out." The robot arm swung around, plucked a bottle of white wine from a chilled metal sleeve, then swung it toward the glass at high speed. It did a weird tilt with the bottle, apparently to counteract the wine's momentum, and finished by pouring some into the glass. "We programmed it to handle fluid mechanics. No math, no modeling, just some slick AI and a bit of real-time feedback. Cool, huh?"

Sonya gave me a look like she was desperate to escape Peter and his obsession with tech.

I gave her a look like I felt the same way about all of this. Our brief time in Canada was something we both wished had never ended.

"Nameless," Zelda said, pulling my attention back to her, "how about I get you a plate? I know what's good here."

"Thanks."

She walked to the buffet line, glancing back a few times to see if I was giving Sonya a token of my lust and affection. I wasn't, but I did sit near Sonya—well away from Peter's demonic arm.

Sonya raised an eyebrow. "Nameless?"

I shrugged.

Peter raised his glass. "I'd pour you one, but you know . . . alcohol and dendrite demons don't mix."

Huh? I racked my many brains, but none of them knew what the hell a dendrite was. My best guess was a combination of dandruff and dust mites. I wondered if punching out Peter would trigger a response from the robotic arm. Nah. It'd probably clap if it could. The sound of one hand clapping?

Sonya gave me a bigger smile than usual. "I see you're getting along with Zelda."

Peter smirked, but kept his thoughts to himself.

I just shrugged again. "Well, you know. She's got a thing for one of my passengers. I call him Nameless."

Peter couldn't hold it any longer. "Awkward! But you know, it could play to your advantage."

"Not gonna happen."

"Zelda gave you the complete tour?"

I ignored him, and his thin reference to the underbelly tour.

Sonya ignored him, too. "But you're doing okay?" She sounded warm and sincere.

I had no good response. Weird was a way of life, but dying tomorrow still felt over the top.

Sonya took my hand. Her wonderful touch spoke volumes, but she added a few words for emphasis. "I'll get you tucked into bed later tonight."

Oh man, I liked the sound of that. "Did you figure out a new plan?"

I wasn't talking to Peter, but he was quick to give me the bad news. "Same plan, bro. You go. You chat Jack up. You end him. Or you don't. Your choice, same as always: awesome hero or total coward."

That's when Sonya kicked him hard in the shins, hard enough to make him shriek and almost do a face-plant into his plate of spaghetti.

Sonya's original self was a physical therapist, so I knew Peter had to be in a world of pain. Sonya knew all about body parts.

Wolf smiled. He knew the location of all the nerve bundles, too.

"Hey." Zelda was standing behind me with two plates of meatloaf and peas, not exactly looking pleased.

Sonya didn't let go of my hand. Peter's face was almost the same color as his marinara sauce, his eyes still clenched and fighting back man-tears. Zelda sat, clearly pissed. Shoved my plate in front of me. Peas bounced across the table. Then she held out her plastic cup for the wine robot.

Oh, yeah. This was a good table.

Satisfied that she'd reclaimed her turf, Sonya released my hand so I could eat.

We sat there in brooding silence. I pushed around the surviving peas and explored the meatloaf enough to discover it was vegi-loaf. About that time, I might have glanced at Zelda, and I might have looked surprised by the lack of meat, because Zelda suddenly felt like explaining the vegi-loaf to me. Succinctly. "Meat kills."

Meat was bad for me? Or maybe she was saying it was bad for

the creature that made the unwilling donation to my protein intake? I didn't bother asking.

Eventually, Peter's shins recovered from the pain enough so he could chop up his spaghetti in to easily controlled pieces. Zelda ate forcefully, daggers shooting from her eyes. Sonya wore a faint smile while she sipped her wine, a study in controlled grace. I poked at my meatless-loaf and chased uncooperative peas around my plate. The robo-arm twitched once or twice for no good reason. No telling what it was thinking.

So we ate in electric silence, as emotionally torqued pals often do.

When we were finishing dinner, something in Peter's pants beeped. He stood up. "Back to work. The day never ends down here."

Sonya got up, gave me a smile, then walked out of the cafeteria alone.

Zelda started to get up but Peter held up a hand. "Take your time, Zel." He looked at both of us. "You two have some things to think about." Then he focused on me. "Zelda knows all about you, bro. You've been trusting her with your life ever since you lucked into Wolf's bod. But know this: she's a normal, and she's the sum total of my A Team on the bridge. So treat her right, and I'm not just talking to Nameless. I'm talking to all of you inside there."

Peter walked away. Wait. Zelda was a normal? I thought she said—

Zelda grabbed my arm, punk love in her eyes. "Hey, Nameless." Her spiky eyelashes fluttered, sending me a personal punk invite.

Nameless desperately wanted me to say something awesome. But I wasn't about to stoke Zelda's fire. Hell, it was hot enough already. But I did want an explanation. "You're a normal?"

"Not exactly. Let's just say I'm on my first body."

"So . . . you're not really a jumper."

"I might've gotten ahead of myself a bit—you know, in your room when I kinda said I was a skull skipper. Who knows what I really am? But I'm just like the rest of you guys, only I haven't been killed yet."

"It sounds like you want to be killed."

"Someday. Sure. I need to know. When I'm ready I'll set it up."

"But chances are really good you'd just die."

"Hey. A girl's gotta know."

"Sure, but—" That was such a harsh way to learn about herself. "Getting yourself killed is just . . . so . . ."

"Just so what? It's not like I'm going to step in front of a bus or anything. Shit, that's for losers. But like, I can totally see myself strapping on a black cape, complete with my trademark splash of red, and confronting evil. You know? Putting my black stiletto heels to the scumbags who dump shit on all of us. Black stilettos streaked with the blood of my oppressors. A cool image. And if someday I go down slugging . . . then yeah, I'll learn whether I'm a cranial parasite like you, or just a righteous girl in spandex packing nunchucks and an attitude."

"Cranial parasite? You think I'm a cranial parasite?"

"Sure. Nothing wrong with that. You guys are cool. Except when it goes to your head and you get all Jack-like. I think you're especially awesome to go out and end Jack tomorrow, except—"

"I'm just going to talk with him. Getting killed, perma-killed, never made it to my to-do list."

"Yeah, I'm sure. I just wish there was a way for you to take out Jack, but you know, leave Nameless for me."

"I've been told there's no way to extract my passengers. No way to get Marie out of Jack."

"You were told true."

"I was thinking Jack might know how to do it."

"That idiot? Hell, he's so loaded up with deadhead thoughts, he's nothing more than a mental pincushion with swagger. The walking brain fart can't even remember what he said 10 minutes ago, much less what he was thinking yesterday. You've dealt with him. You know what I'm talking about. Jack's fried brain is all over the map. He's been up and down your ass about all kinds of messed up death-for-sex shit. And I'm sorry about what happened to Marie, by the way. That was a major life suck."

"Yeah." I was getting tired of condolences about Marie. She wasn't dead yet. I tried again for a real solution. "Jack experimented on jumpers. He might know how to restore Marie, so that she has her body again with a clear head."

"No way Jack remembers the results of his experiments. Personally, I think he just likes playing with victims. Like a cat taking all day to kill a mouse—there's nothing more fun than a squirming victim. You know? Experimenting requires rational thought—something that Jack's got in short supply."

That was depressing. "How'd you get involved with jumpers, anyway?"

"Long story, but basically Peter's my brother."

I didn't see that one coming. "Sorry he got killed."

"Hey. It happens when you bear-slap cyber criminals. Peter always enjoyed pranking boneheads, so it wasn't a complete surprise when his body washed up on a beach. But then he freaked me out, stalking me in his new body, insisting he was my dead brother."

"And Jack found him?"

"No. Jack never found him. We were smart. We went underground. Carefully scoped things out. If Peter could skull skip, there had to be others. Eventually, we found Jack's evil touch on a lot of people—politicians and power brokers, mostly. Then we found others, outside Jack's cabal, off the grid like us. That led us to people like Sonya, people in Jack's clutches but hating it. Peter and I, we were the catalyst that brought together this revolution."

"But you're so young."

"So? Take a look at history. A lot of great thinkers and doers have been young. Like I said, Peter and I were just the catalyst, the spark that ignited people already out there—people looking for a chance to cut off Jack and his megalomaniac friends."

I could see how Zelda wanted to be like us—wanted it so much that she actually believed she was a jumper. "You really think you're like Peter? A jumper?"

"It's not genetic. We know that much. But I figure it still ups my odds."

I nodded, but it still pained me to think of her looking for trouble in back alleys at night. A lot of bad things happen to women, all the time—even the tough ones. And the odds of being a jumper were really, really bad. I could see a future where she made a lot of trips to the hospital. Followed by just one trip to the morgue.

But who was I to tell her what she should do and not do?

We talked for almost an hour, then she parked me alone on Sonya's empty couch in command HQ while she went back to work with her brother. Apparently night was a busy time for jumper ops.

I asked assorted people where Sonya was, but it seemed she was busy elsewhere with something important.

So I sat there watching people run ops. Good and evil reduced to dots on assorted screens. Go good! Go!

The green ones were good? Red for dead and blue for a jump? I needed a scorecard, but everyone was so busy.

Funny how being alone on your own is easier to take than being alone in a crowd.

*   *   *

Later that night, Sonya swept me off the couch, ushered me down the hallways, brought me to my room, got me ready for bed, and lovingly chained me to my bed.

I wanted her to stay, but she insisted on leaving. We both knew that Billy Bob Wyville, my evil jumper passenger, would take over as I drifted off to sleep. So it was obvious why she didn't want to hang around and visit with my inner evil.

Hey, bedtime sucked these days. I could see sleeping alone every night for the rest of my life, restrained by chains or a straitjacket.

Even though I was kinda awesome by day, I was a total threat to humanity by night. I had become a Jekyll and Hyde kind of monster. Good and evil rolled into one. I wondered what color my dot was on the tactical screens.

Sonya put my glasses on the nightstand, turned down the lights, and kissed me sweetly for a while.

She said goodnight and was gone.

Damn!

So I was alone again—but never really alone.

It was like Billy Bob had opened a door. A door with a giant biohazard symbol on it. A door that allowed all my passengers to crawl out and gain control.

By night, I was screwed. But by day, I could listen to my passengers or ignore them.

By day, I could hear Wolf giving me advice—tactical tips. If I needed him, he was always close. Ready to take over if I allowed it. Ready to handle trouble.

By day, I also picked up on Nameless giving me bad advice. Getting me into trouble. Urging me to reach out and grope anyone cute in a crowd. Nameless also wanted me to wear a cape and tights. And take pretty girls to my dungeon of love and introduce them to my ropes course—the one Martoni had in mind.

Well, Nameless and Martoni were a mess. Actually, most of my passengers were a mess. Pops wasn't so bad, but he never seemed happy unless he was resting with his feet propped up. Thankfully, Tommy and Dread were quiet, like evil trying to blend in with the crowd—just another realtor-biker duo, unless they could profit from putting your happy little family in a shallow grave.

The guy I was in, Samson, didn't seem so bad. Probably just some guy who got tangled up with the wrong people. Hell, I understood how hard it was to get away from Jack once he took a liking to you.

Then there was Wolf. Cold blooded. A man who treated beautiful women like a Rolex or a London tailored suit—just things to make him look good. On the other hand, I counted Wolf as a friend, the one who could make me swim, or ride a motorcycle—or do a quick kill without messing up the carpet.

* * *

You know a plan is bad when you can't even pronounce it. Peter called it *fait accompli*. In other words, a done deal. Sonya argued that it was an option. Peter sat there and argued that it was the only option, so really it wasn't even an option, it was a done deal—and calling a non-option an option just made it an oxymoron. Sonya thought Peter had just called her a moron (which he kinda did), so she walked over and slugged him. Being the twerp that he was, Peter naturally fought back. Things got ugly fast in Sonya's ritzy bunker apartment. And I have to say it was a good show because they were evenly matched.

Their no-holds barred fight spread from room to room. Lamps were knocked over. Decorative Roman vases were smashed. Artificial plants were de-potted. Lots of stuff was broken. I'm ashamed to admit it, but I didn't intervene, and especially ashamed because I kinda enjoyed it.

Did I mention hair was pulled? Clothes were torn? Yeah, it was classic. Man versus woman. Probably what nature intended by giving half of us a defective little three legged chromosome. Who says Mother Nature doesn't have a cruel sense of humor?

Anyway, back to the sexy battle of the sexes.

Naturally, I was rooting for Sonya. Who else? Hell, I really wanted her to beat the living techno-crap out of Peter.

But after a few minutes, and both combatants getting in their best shots (and a bit of blood), the fight wound up in a room filled with mud.

Yes, mud.

Well, what can I say? The bunker had everything.

Clothes were ripped off, as they often are in *anything goes* mud pit fights. Their blows and strangle holds were totally personal and completely unrestrained. It was a really good show, to put it mildly. The best I'd ever seen, or ever even heard about.

Eventually the fight culminated with Sonya and Peter having wild and libidinously mud-slathered sex with each other.

Whatever the hell *libidinously* meant, I libidinously loved it—both the word and the act.

Naturally, they couldn't stop with just one act, so they had several more libidinous acts. Lots of positions. Very educational.

Okay, I hate to admit it, but I really enjoyed watching that part. Except it was Peter getting violently passionate with Sonya instead of me.

So yeah, it was totally amazing—right until I woke up.

* * *

Another damn dream—multi-mind style. So vivid. So visceral. So real I could practically taste the mud sliding passion and the steaming hot sex.

Okay, that might sound over the top. But that's what you get when you want to wake up, and your passengers won't let go of the dream. Nameless and Martoni seemed especially guilty, virtual drool on their virtual faces.

As I opened my eyes, I caught sight of Zelda hustling out the door. Great. Was she messing around with my passengers while I was asleep?

I turned to see Sonya standing next to the bed, amused. "Are you okay?"

Okay? I looked around. The sheets were twisted around me. Uh . . . I might have participated in that dream more than usual.

But my hands were caught on something. Oh, right. I was still tied to the bed.

Sonya touched my cheek. "Rough night, babe?"

"Depends on who you ask."

She nodded like she knew what I was talking about, then reached over and released me from the weird pink leopard B&D S&M straps on my wrists. I wasn't sure if I preferred sleeping in a straitjacket or strapped to the bedposts. I reached up to straighten out my hair, except I was now African-American and my short curly do was still perma-perfect. "I'm good." I stretched my tired muscles and checked my wrists for damage. No torn skin, but they definitely hurt.

"Bad dreams?"

"Uh . . . weird dreams. I'm fine." I reached for my glasses and put them on. Sonya looked good in focus, too. "Thanks for the tie-down."

"Violent dreams?"

Why did she keep asking? I shrugged.

"Sexy dreams?"

My passengers might have been grinning uncontrollably. I steadied my face, and made sure my incriminating parts were discreetly covered. "What's up?"

"Big day, tiger."

Hey, I was Wolf, not some tiger. And the last thing I wanted was a big day with Jack. "I think I'll just finish this dream."

"No way. Breakfast time. Then we crack a few eggs."

Eggs meaning Jack? And me? Didn't someone have a better plan by now?

I rummaged around in the dresser, looking for clothes that would fit Samson. Most shirts were too tight in the shoulders. Most pants were too tight in the thighs. Samson was on the athletic side, even if he did have a desk job at the zoo. I pictured him behind a desk, loading tranquilizer darts all day. Behind him, a big chart listed all the animals and the amount of curare they'd need to be properly sedated. Several real blowguns were mounted on one wall, next to photos of Samson petting drugged hyenas in the zoo's African Safari Zone.

Samson gave me a rare thought—enough to say I was totally off base.

I noticed Sonya watching me fumble with clothes, so I offered a distraction. "Was Zelda in here, too?"

"She watched over you most of the night. We couldn't risk having you get loose in your sleep and hurting yourself."

Great. No telling what Zelda and Nameless did last night. Or maybe Zelda played with all my guys. A definite possibility. So maybe my dream about watching rough sex was more real than I thought?

Maybe all my dreams were more real than I knew? Or maybe this was just a dream—but kinda real? Maybe both?

I caught myself standing there, half dressed, slack-jawed, lost in a labyrinth of conspiracy theories and alternate realities.

Sonya was watching me closely. "Let's get you some coffee."

Good idea. I was still struggling for control.

As we walked to the cafeteria, I wondered if I'd ever get a good night's sleep.

Sonya pushed a mug of java into my hand and led me to a table like the bunker was an asylum and I was new around here.

I sat. She pushed extra coffee and a blueberry muffin in front of me. I drank. I ate. My appetite returned, so she pushed an overloaded omelet in front of me.

It was obvious that others in the cafeteria were watching me, but trying not to show it. My passengers settled into their usual positions. Wolf rode shotgun and started feeding me tactics in case something bad happened in the cafeteria. I was aware of every knife, every exit, every person who might have martial arts training. I was aware of everyone we should kill and in what order.

I took another swig of coffee as Wolf checked out reflections of people behind us. Positions of defense and avenues of attack were practically glowing on a mental floor plan in Wolf's corner of my brain. Paranoia at its finest.

It was good to be back to normal.

Sonya smiled. Another successful feeding. The beast was back.

* * *

I followed Sonya up some stairs and down a familiar hallway. We were approaching Peter's command center, but this time we went into a small office. Peter was waiting at a small conference table. Boxes of drones and other tech toys were piled up along each wall.

"Dude." Peter stopped playing with a set of virtual augmentation goggles and motioned to a chair.

As Sonya and I sat, Zelda came in behind us and closed the door.

There were no more chairs so I started to get up and let Zelda have mine.

"Sit, Nameless. Those chairs are wimpy." She pulled over a crate and sat on it. "My ass enjoys rough wood." She added a wink.

Sonya and Peter ignored the comment. I casually put my hand on my face to make sure Nameless wasn't using it to flirt back.

Peter gave me a cautious glance. "Time for Wolf to visit Jack. Do whatever comes natural. You know, like we discussed. Kat's warming up the helo right about now. And Sonya will be escorting you to the site. Zelda and I have our hands full with field ops, but we'll be standing by with support if Jack's crew figures things out and makes a run at you. Uh, that's about it. Any questions?"

"Actually, I was hoping you'd have a new plan by now."

Peter's eyes widened, maybe because he was worried I was about to reach across the table and beat a new plan out of him. "No. Same plan. I don't know if you believe in the multi-verse, but in another universe it's possible another version of me figures out a way to do the impossible. But that's not our world."

Sonya and Zelda were looking bummed.

"So yeah, dude. Same plan."

"Not what I was hoping for."

Sonya put a gentle hand on my arm. "Not what any of us were hoping for."

Peter gave Sonya a quick glance like he was hoping to end me. "Remember, bro. You decide how this goes down. We've given you options. If you're hesitant about going in, just think of it as a chat with the devil—no strings attached. You're free to walk away at any time—more or less."

Peter waited briefly for other comments, then stood up. "Thanks, team. Let's make it a good day."

The ladies stood up like they'd heard those words before, and we headed to the door.

"Not you, Wolf. I'd like a moment with you."

Sonya and Zelda stepped out and closed the door. I turned to face Peter and he backed himself up against some boxes like he was about to have the crap beaten out of him.

It was possible I had a threatening stance going. Okay, I did.

He held up his hands. "Look, bro, no matter what you think about me, if we had a better plan, we'd use it. Sometimes you gotta go with the lesser of all evils. Trust me, I considered thousands of options for dealing with Jack. Like turning him over to a Vatican hit squad, or even wiping out humanity with neutron bombs while we rode it out in low Earth orbit."

I was still on my side of the room. He was on his. So he continued his speech. "Like I said, go in, meet your worst nightmare. And you know, walk away if you want. Sonya's volunteered to do the deed if you can't. Hey. No pressure."

Now I noticed, my hand was at his throat and his head was being pushed into some cardboard boxes.

He choked out a few words I didn't get, so I eased off a bit.

He cleared his throat. "Dude, I completely agree. No way I'd let Sonya in there. If you back out, we'll come up with someone who will do it. But here's the funny part." He grabbed my wrist, hoping

I'd let go of him. But I didn't.

"The funny part?"

"Yeah. This'll kill you."

I tightened my grip.

He gurgled a bit. "Bad choice of words, bro. You're exactly what we need. We've always known that. You're Wolf the stone cold killer. But you're also Marko the loner who can't follow a simple plan. And that's exactly what we need. Someone who can kill without a second thought, combined with someone who can't follow a straight line. That's you."

That made no sense.

Peter struggled in my grip, apparently thinking I should let go because he'd explained everything.

I wanted a better explanation. "So what's your point?"

"We need someone who can kill Jack and himself. *And* we need someone who can just blow off the plan and walk away. It's got to be your choice. If I sent Sonya in to face Jack, she'd do the martyr thing—guaranteed. Absolutely guaranteed. Don't you get it? She'd be like this missile I launched against Jack, so the universe might just decide that I killed Jack. He'd jump into my body and we'd all be screwed."

That kinda made sense. "You need an indecisive killer."

"Yes! Exactly! Super indecisive, combined with super killer. That's you. That's why we're flying you out to face Jack today. We want you to kill Jack *and* we want you to walk away. Dude, you're Schrödinger on a bad day. Jack's your cat. He either winds up dead or he stays alive. Preferably not both at the same time, okay? So forget Schrödinger—channel Heisenberg's *uncertainty principle* instead. Mainly, we can't know how it'll turn out."

Great. They needed me to be all random. "Anything else?"

"No, bro. Just do whatever you're gonna do."

I released my grip and walked to the door.

"Dude. One last thing. Don't join Jack's team."

I wasn't about to do that. I reached for the door.

Peter wasn't finished. "Jack's lies are like silk. He'll pull you to the dark side."

As I stepped out the door, I left Peter with a final thought. "I'm already on the dark side." I'm not sure why I said that. Maybe just to make Peter's pointy little head spin. He wanted uncertainty? He got uncertainty.

Zelda waved at me from the end of the hallway. That gave me the feeling I was always being escorted. Not safe to leave me alone? I was tempted to go the other way, but there wasn't much point.

Zelda smiled as I walked up to her, then punched me in the arm like we were pals.

"Hey, Nameless. I enjoyed last night."

Oh. She wanted to connect with her boyfriend again. "Call me Wolf."

"Don't listen to Peter. He's full of prions."

Prions? What were prions? Probably nasty little things.

She took my arm and pressed it tight against her breast as we walked down the corridor. "Wheels up in two."

Two? Minutes? "You mean now?"

We paused in front of an elevator. "Afraid so."

"I just got here."

"I know." She gave me another hip bump. Mosh pit affection.

We stepped into the elevator and the doors closed. Somehow it knew we needed to go up.

"I love you Nameless." She said that with eager embarrassment, like a young girl after prom night. Then she planted a no-holds barred kiss on me that went to the bone.

Okay, so the kiss was combined with some all out groping.

I hung on for dear life.

The doors opened and she let me out of the corner where I'd been pinned.

We were barely out of the elevator when she grabbed me again. "Listen, Nameless. Walk away from this. No one will stop you if you just tell 'em to screw it. I want you back with me. In one piece. For as long as we can stand it."

I nodded. Zelda and Nameless forever. Not what I had in mind, but it was the best plan yet. "Right. Screw Jack."

"Fuckin' totally. Just leave him to rot and come back to me. Promise?"

"I can't promise anything."

"Right. I get it. Be all random and shit. Then look me up."

She planted another one on me—cut short because Sonya pulled us apart. "Sorry, Zelda. We need to go."

"Right. Totally. Just remember what I said, Nameless."

Sonya ushered me up two flights of stairs and onto the rooftop. The big red helicopter was powered up and waiting. I recognized it from the time Bruce the Black and I got a ride from the Gettysburg dungeon-barn the team had basically obliterated.

Sonya opened the helo door and got us both belted in the rear seats. The doors were securely closed. We lifted off. The rooftop slipped out from under us.

5.5 He's Dead, Jim!

The morning was bright and full of hope—mainly because I liked helicopter rides. Looking out the helo's window, I could see rays of sunlight streaming through the clouds to the east. Down below, the ground all around us was green with trees and farms. Small towns dotted the rolling landscape. Ribbons of roads. Cars with commuters getting buzzed on coffee. A train on its way to places I could only guess.

It was all so clean and glorious. Like at the end of a sappy movie when the sun finally comes shining through the clouds. Too pretty to be real.

My passengers were kinda quiet, but Pops thought it was a beautiful day to die.

It must be hard to always be thinking about death. Old people must do that a lot.

As for me, maybe today was my day to really die.

Personally, if I truly had my choice, I'd rather die in a hell of a storm. And then if I had an out of body experience, the wind and rain would pass right through me and I could play tag with the lightning. Weird, but that would be my coolest day to die. I mean, everyone gets out and enjoys the beautiful days. But we mostly hide inside when all hell breaks loose—real hell, like tornadoes, hurricanes, basketball size hail—the serious shit that reminds us that we're just little meat-bags running for our little lives. It would be awesome to fly through Mother Nature's worst and have a ball playing in it.

So yeah, today was a beautiful day by most standards. But not a good day to die by mine.

Nameless wanted to die in space, preferably on the cold side of

Mercury, clutching Zelda's locket. The sun safely to his back, blocked by Mercury. Him staring out at the inky blackness of space and the rich star fields, sipping the last of his oxygen. Or maybe he preferred running a black ops pirate fleet out of the Eagle Nebula. Dying in battle with a pile of imperial bootlickers under his feet.

Seriously?

Time to get real. Today was our day to die. Maybe not a sure thing, but I pegged it at around 75%. I'm sure it was on Peter's personal calendar. Something like:

Pizza for breakfast.

Meet with the boys.

Kill Wolf and Jack.

Throw myself a surprise party.

I stopped daydreaming and looked at the others in the helo. Why was I the only one with racing thoughts?

Sonya sat next to me in the back. She was keeping her thoughts to herself.

Up front, Kat Mansky was flying the bright red news helicopter, sitting in the right side pilot's seat. Weird how the pilot always flew from the passenger's seat. It was the same helo she'd flown to pick me up in Pennsylvania, the day I got Bruce the Black out of a dungeon under a barn. Jack's dungeon and barn, now blown to smithereens.

Now *that* was an awesome day.

But today, Kat had a bobblehead of Spock in a hula skirt taped down on the dashboard. Kinda weird. A new addition to the cockpit. Spock looked at me and nodded his head like he knew something. Something major.

That sent a chill up my spine.

We banked to the right and began our descent. The ride was almost over. I kicked myself for not asking to ride on the end of a rope, dangling free in the wind, arms spread wide Bruce the Black style. God, that would have been amazing.

Yeah—would have been. Some of the best moments in life were lost because I simply didn't ask. Not a good time to figure that one out.

Kat was bringing the helo in low, slowly circling an abandoned factory of some sort. Two rings of barbed wire fence ran completely around it. The factory itself was mostly just a bunch of large upright cylinders clustered together like a dystopian city. No cars. No people on the ground. A good place for zombies to chill during the day. Zombie-ville. Last stop for maggoty undead. Right. That would be me.

A bigger chill ran up and down my spine.

Sonya took my hand.

I gazed into her face. Such a wonderful face. Deep knowing eyes. Her thoughtful perma-smile. Maybe a trace of concern? Yes, more than a trace.

Zombie-ville was cool. Facing Jack while he was in Marie's body seemed like a total nightmare.

Such a lovely day. Such a sickening day.

Kat seemed to know exactly where she was going next. We spiraled in closer, rounded a tall metal cylinder with pipes connecting it to shorter cylinders. An abandoned chemical plant of some kind? Old technology, quietly rusting until it would be torn down. Pops nodded his virtual head. He could relate.

Kat put us down on a clear section of cement near the heart of the facility. The blades didn't raise much dust, so I figured this must be the usual landing pad. Around us, I saw scattered pipes and sheet metal on the ground. Graffiti. The usual *No Trespassing* signs.

No CCTV cameras. No guards. No sign of any active security. But I knew Peter had this place crisscrossed with sensors and camera arrays. That was just his style.

I looked around for little robots on half-tracks packing nail guns. Something to run off urban explorers checking out the abandoned site.

Nothing. This was a true ghost town.

The whine of the turbine engine changed pitch as the blades slowed but didn't stop.

There was a moment of awkward silence. Sonya still held my hand, but it felt distant somehow. I guess a part of her was protecting her feelings about this day—pulling her emotions inward to a safer place.

I returned my gaze out the windows. The place was definitely more impressive from the air. On the ground and up close, this depressing pile of metal and pipes was merely a fitting place to die—an industrial tombstone. But a part of me refused to believe this was the end of the line. Something would happen to get me safely out. Yeah—something. I'd always escaped perma-death before. It's what I did these days—survive. So of course, I'd be saved again. Somehow.

Right?

Kat turned slightly and nodded to Sonya. We had the all-clear. It was time.

Sonya squeezed my hand. "Walk with me."

She opened her door and we stepped out.

As I closed the helo door behind me, I caught sight of Kat watching me closely. She gave me a nod and a military gesture with her hand, like a casual salute, two fingers pointing the way. It was a gesture that either said *take the right flank*, or *I was the man*. Either way it felt really good. I had her respect.

I gave her a slight nod to say thanks.

That's when Kat's face twitched—the sign of a mind with multiple opinions—a jumper mind.

That made sense. Kat seemed to have Sonya's full trust. Just us jumpers here.

Sonya ushered me through the debris to a metal door with a numeric touchpad. "Watch this." She keyed in 5433450, then it sounded like several deadbolts retracted.

We just stood there a couple seconds until the door gave up and locked itself again. "It's a symmetrical number, except with a zero at the end: 543 345, with a zero at the end. Got it? Now you do it."

I punched in the number and this time we stepped inside.

"Remember that number." She led the way through an abandoned office and down a hallway. "Jack's chained up inside a big metal chamber. It has a metal hatch that uses the same combination. The only way in or out of the chamber is via that combination. Got it?"

"Yes."

"If Jack kills himself, you can just use the number and walk out.

But if you do walk out, just stay in that office we passed through and wait for us. It could take a day or two to extract you. Sorry, but the delay is a precaution. Just remember, when you need sleep, use the manacles in the office and the tranquilizer pills in the office drawers. You'll also find food in the office, and medical supplies. Peter said you'd be comfortable in this environment. Honestly, I don't see how."

Kinda strange that this resembled an FPS game. Frag and mow down slimy creeps in dystopia, then find goodies and power up. "Yeah. I'm in my comfort zone here."

Sonya shook her head like I was a nut. "If Jack kills you, then you'll jump into Marie's body and you'll still remember the combination. Jack's shackles use that same combination, so you can walk out of the chamber in Marie's body if you get that chance. The combination you just learned works on everything. Doors, shackles, padlocks—everything."

"Good. I have two ways to end Jack and still walk out. Jack kills himself outright. Or Jack kills me, then I walk out in Marie's body."

Sonya stopped suddenly and grabbed me. "Or, we can turn around now."

Make that three ways out.

She instantly planted a kiss on me that kinda blew a major tropical storm through my head.

Man!

When we finally came up for air, she kept talking. "I'm serious. You can back out right now. No one would think less of you if you did. Even after you enter Jack's chamber, you can still back out. But remember this, babe," she held my face for emphasis, "you can't back out after you release the gas. If you do that, you'll become Jack's killer and he'll take over your body. You'll be perma-fucked. You understand what I'm saying?"

"Yeah. Totally." *Perma-fucked* was a pretty basic concept.

"You remember what Peter said about releasing the gas?"

Not really, but I nodded.

"And the absolute worst case—you walk out arm in arm with Jack. Do not let that happen, Wolf."

"I understand."

"No. You don't understand. Bad things happen if you walk out with Jack. Terrible bad things—for all of us."

"I get it." I wasn't about to buddy up with Jack.

"If you die and somehow Jack walks out alone, we'll deal with it. But please, don't listen to him. Don't switch sides on us."

She hugged me for a while. Then held me at arms' length. "And you remember the combination to unlock everything?"

"Sure."

"What is it?"

Uh. Something symmetrical with a zero at the end. "Uh, 543, 345, and a zero."

"Right. Start with a five and count down, then up. And you know that if Jack gets your brain he won't be able to remember that number—not immediately, anyway."

"I understand." It was like when I jumped into Pops, his recent memory was a blank to me. Same with all my jumps. Jack wouldn't get that number. Hell, I barely had it.

Sonya seemed to soften, but not in a good way—like, my loss was inevitable. "This is a far as I go, babe. The hallway leads straight to a row of big metal chambers. Jack's in the third one on the left—tank A113."

"Okay." I started to release her.

"Not yet. I'll always love you."

I started to say I loved her, but she put her hand to my lips. "You will always be my Marko-Wolfie. The brave one—with so much heart. The heart I'll always love, in any body you wear."

She stopped me from speaking again.

"The less you say to me, the better. Remember, the choice is entirely yours. It has to be. If you go through with this, it must absolutely be your decision."

That made sense. If she put me up to this, the universe might decide she was Jack's killer. This had to be my decision. Totally. No ambiguity.

Sonya gave me another hug, then gently pushed me away. "I'm sure Peter already drilled this into you, but it needs repeating. Jack will say anything, absolutely anything, to talk his way out of this. He's a true master of manipulation. The best lies are cloaked in truth. Jack's lies will be dripping in truth. Choose your beliefs wisely, brave soul."

Sonya gave me one last kiss, started wiping her own tears, and walked away. I watched, hoping she would glance back. But it never happened. She started running, turned a corner, and was gone to me.

Love found—love lost. Life sucked.

Or I could just go after her. Not a bad solution. She'd still love me, and someone else could end Jack.

Or I could go the way that seemed like my destiny. Visit Jack. Take my revenge for basically killing Marie—for truly killing so many innocent people.

I found myself walking toward Jack. Maybe my passengers wanted to slap him around? Check out the trapped animal. The shark in the tank. I could always break my fist on Jack's face, then walk away—back to Sonya's loving arms. That would be so righteous.

Yes it would. Except Jack was now using Marie's innocent face.

I kept walking toward Jack. I needed closure. Marie deserved Jack's death.

Sucks to be me. Sucks to be a hero.

At the end of the hallway, there were assorted metal chambers. They looked like tall cylinders with lots of pipes and valves going everywhere. Some chambers were big enough to have low metal doors. Some only had round hatches on them just big enough for a man to crawl through.

Jack's kill room was easy to spot. A blood red happy face was splashed maniacally on the metal door. Peter's idea of a sick joke. A numeric keypad was next to the hatch. No window on the door. Peter should have added a window. But maybe it was too dangerous to gaze upon the face of pure evil.

No. It was only Marie's face.

I imagined opening the hatch. A dry ice fog would swirl out and caress my feet. A blood red light would shine down on Jack, the mass killer. The devil was always in red. Or maybe the light would be green—sickly alien green. Evil always dripped with green.

Or maybe both red and green. Like Christmas?

I was weirding myself out.

My hand reached out to the keypad. We wanted in.

I tapped in the combination. There was an instant click. Bolts retracted.

My hand touched the metal hatch. My passengers were alive within me, checking the temperature of the door. Or maybe they were stirring because I was too busy freaking out to operate my own body.

Not my body. Samson's body. The black guy who worked at the National Zoo. The guy who felt good on me, except for the glasses. Sorry, man. You deserved better. Marie did, too. We all did. Except for Jack.

* * *

Just like on a submarine, I turned a big wheel to release the final latches. I tugged on the heavy metal door, then realized I had to push.

The door opened smoothly to reveal Marie sitting behind a stark metal table. She was dressed for action in body shaping black. Her hands were calmly folded, but secured with a long chain to the top of the table. Her eyes, so bright and alive, caught mine.

My first thought flashed in my mind. *We've made a horrible mistake! This was Marie. This was her—all of her.*

As she looked closely at me, her eyes grew wide. A thread of hope dashed across her face. "Marko? Is that you?"

She didn't recognize me? Oh, wait. I glanced at my hands. I was wearing dark skin and geeky glasses.

I started to say something, but caught myself. This was Jack I was looking at. No need for an introduction.

My pulse raced as I slowly closed the hatch, my eyes never leaving Jack-Marie. I stood there for a second with the metal door at my back. Marie looked exactly like herself. Every mannerism was hers. The way she'd said my name was exactly hers. The whole package pulled me in, pulled me back to a time when it was just us, taking life one day at a time in Austin. Laughing. Loving. Fighting. Sharing.

There was a loud click, the automatic lock had engaged behind me. No exit without the secret combination. I panicked when I glanced to the left and saw no keypad. Trapped! But no, it was there on the right. Yes, there was a keypad next to the door—just in case.

Most of my passengers indicated they'd seen enough. It was time to get the hell out of here.

Understandable.

Marie gasped. "Oh, God!" She buried her face in her hands and began to cry. "You're here to kill me. Please don't do this. Please!"

My heart jumped. Her fear was palpable. Absolutely real. It pulled at something deep within me. Except—

Shit, that was good!

Funny how her tears actually made me feel better. Marie wasn't the type to cry—or beg. No way. Marie was made of far tougher stuff. Her typical moods were: *I'm happy. You're an idiot. Now I'm pissed.* And the ever popular: *Screw you!* Okay, I'll admit that at my funeral she did look beaten down, but I don't remember a single tear. Ever. If Marie cried at my funeral, it was silently, with her face turned away.

No. Jack the snake wasn't convincing me.

As I moved closer, I could see the table was welded to the metal floor. An all metal room. Perfect for blocking comms and blocking kill chips. Jack wasn't going anywhere—unless I let him out.

On the table, there was a paper plate of half-eaten takeout. Pizza with extra anchovies. Last week's dried up french fries. No ketchup. Apparently this was Peter's idea of cruelty.

There was a big plastic coffee mug sitting under a faucet with a slow drip. Weird to see a faucet bolted to the metal table. The iron water pipe ran down one leg of the table, across the floor, and into a wall. Kind of a trip hazard, but good that Jack could get water anytime he wanted.

Nearby was something that was probably a camping potty. Jack's chains looked long enough to get to it. They were also long enough for Jack to strangle himself—or me.

Fine. Jack was allowed to kill himself. Or be my killer so I could take over Marie's body.

An empty chair waited for me near the table. Maybe later. Right now I wanted my feet under me.

The room was round, maybe only 18 feet across, a cylinder with a slightly cone-shaped ceiling about 30 feet up. Not much to look at. Just dirty boiler plate, welded, with some added rivets.

Near the ceiling I spotted two small security cameras. I vaguely remembered that discussion. Not a live feed, they were just recording us for the jumper history books.

On one wall was a bright red button, the kind you push to stop heavy machinery. A red arrow was crudely painted on the wall. It pointed to the button. Red letters said, *Shove It*. More of Peter's twisted sense of humor. The guy had serious social issues.

Under the button, near the floor, was a heavy metal grate made up of welded rebar. Obviously, this was how I flooded the room with carbon dioxide gas. Just push the button. No way to turn it off. Heavier than air, the gas would simply pour in through the grate. The good air would be pushed higher and higher until it was over our heads. We'd suffocate after a few minutes.

There was a little yellow note stuck to the wall next to the red button. Jack watched as I walked over to read it. It said, *Hey bro, it's now KRYPTON gas. A fitting end for a real superhero. Or even you.*

Peter was insulting to the end. It occurred to Nameless that helium would have been better, coming slowly down from above. Then Jack and I could curse each other with high pitched voices . . . until we died.

Maybe krypton gas was like helium? Or maybe it was heavier than air? And who knew krypton was even a gas. I thought it was a doomed comic book planet. And kryptonite was a green crystal. Nameless knew kryptonite came in lots of colors.

"I'll bet you're wondering why I called this meeting. So take a load off." Jack-Marie nodded at the empty chair. "Let's talk, son." His voice was like southern syrup—sticky, sweet, and venomous. A water moccasin slithering silently along the surface of the river, as harmless as could be.

Yeah, right.

Marie now looked a lot more like Jack, conspiracy in his eyes. Jack motioned again for me to sit in the chair.

"This is symbolic, don't you think." He held up the only cup. "We'll have to share."

How was that symbolic? There was nothing I wanted to share with evil.

I got a better look at the long chain between his wrists, looped through a metal ring that was welded and bolted to the top of the table. I found that reassuring.

"That's right." He rattled the chain. "More than enough to strangle myself. So thoughtful of y'all." Jack looped the chain around his neck and pulled it tight. He grinned as Marie's face turned red, like he was making a point. A short while later he backed off. "Enticing, but not my preferred exit."

He wasn't looking at the door behind me, but it was obvious which exit he wanted.

"Check this out." Jack moved Marie's feet slightly. They were shackled to the legs of the table with long chains. "Limiting, but I can walk a few paces. I suppose that's someone's idea of exercise. But never mind all that. The food will kill me soon enough. Then you'll rue the day you fed me such swill."

I just stood there. Marie's face. Marie's voice. Jack's vile spirit oozing out all over her.

"So get on over here, boy. Park that black ass and let's get down to business." He slapped a hand on the table. Boss-man said get over here, like I was supposed to shuffle on over.

Screw that, and I didn't like the way he said *boy*. I was tempted to say I was actually enjoying being African-American, even though I was still learning the ropes. Well, a day or two in a new body didn't exactly give me bragging rights.

Jack leaned back. "No need to be offended. Hell, I myself have been as black as coal, on multiple occasions. Word to the wise: don't take your color personal. It does come off. Skin always comes off." He gestured to Marie's white skin, like we could just jump if we didn't like our color.

Fine. Color was changeable. But being a racist went to the bone.

Man, I wanted him dead.

The door and the red button were both inviting, but I pulled the empty chair well away from the table and sat down. Fighting words churned in my mind. But special ones were needed for this occasion, so I sat there thinking about what to say. What I really needed was Rema's gift with words. I had no doubt she could turn Jack into a whimpering puddle of insecurity. But words were Rema's power, not mine.

My only real talent was getting killed.

Or maybe it was just being in the wrong place at the wrong time.

Either way, I wasn't superhero material.

Jack smiled and adjusted his chains a bit. "Here's the thing, son. Providence favors us—you and me. Hell, providence positively loves us. It keeps us going when others fall. It guides us like a shining light through all that's wrong with this world. Bottom line—that's why you're here. You and me. We *will* come to terms. And you will be the one to set me free."

"You're not going anywhere."

He leaned forward. "Listen clearly, boy. The future is intensely predictable. Events are malleable. We design the future with our decisions. Then we mold events with our words and deeds. You're here for a reason. And it's not to kill me."

He followed that up with an annoying pause, so I ended it with a bored shrug. "Surprise me."

"I arranged this day."

"No way. You got caught."

"Son, I arranged to be caught. Easy as sunlight spillin' off a catfish on a fine summer's day, out there as pretty as you please, slidin' up alongside the boat, just a waitin' to be caught. So don't be thinkin' otherwise."

I took note of his chains. "Not impressed."

"Not yet, you ain't. But you will be when I've shown you the lay of the land. These chains are a mere physicality. You need to change the way you think. You need to see how temporary all this physical shit really is. Because for us, our bodies are temporary, our chains are temporary, Hell, boy, it's all temporary. Normals come and normals go. But the world keeps spinnin' for us. And our spirits? They just keep on a goin'.'"

It occurred to me again that I should either bail out or go push the button. Listening to Jack was asking for trouble. I turned to check out my options.

"We've got plenty of time, Marko. Grant me a few minutes of your valuable time before you do us the dishonor of killin' us both."

"Call me Wolf."

"Nonsense. I'm talking with Marko, the root of you. Now where was I?" He folded Marie's hands. "I'll continue by statin' the obvious: life's not fair. You can cry about it, you can get violent about it, or you can just accept it for what it is. You see, there simply are no good guys and no bad guys. It's a harsh fact, but it's true. There are only guys who win, and guys who lose. Naturally, that's pig shit on a Sunday suit for the losers. But that's just the way life is, boy."

I couldn't get over staring at Marie, hearing the outline of her voice, but hearing Jack's vile words come out of her mouth—Jack the plantation owner. Did my black skin awaken a slave owner buried deep within Jack?

"Take a good look at yourself, Marko. Which category do you think you belong in? Winner or loser? Be honest. Your losses are addin' up fast. Now take a good look at me." He ran his hands down Marie's black clothes. "Around for centuries, accumulatin' money and power. Livin' the way most folks can't even dream of. Livin' a life you can barely even imagine. Now as for you—when I look at you, the inner Marko, I see a boy who's barely gettin' by, hangin' on by a thread. I see a young man who's ready to hear the truth. Am I right?"

I probably made a face. Not a positive face.

"I understand your hesitance. I truly do. But since you're so gung ho to stick your head in the oven and gas yourself, you might just ask yourself why we're both here."

"You're here to die. I'm here to help you with it."

"Ostensibly." He took a sip of water, holding the plastic mug like it held expensive aged Cognac. "Gettin' back to what I was sayin'— you have to choose which ideas to let grow in your mind, and which to smother and bury in the garden of unwanted thoughts. You see, you can't let ideas determine their own fate. No, sir. 'Cause if you did, they'd rule your head, your ideas would fight amongst themselves, fight for control, and ultimately you'd be ripped apart. No. It's your call, son. You choose between success or failure. Morality? That's nothing but an illusion—an irrational bias that usually leads to failure. No, son, you must focus strictly on the results—success or failure."

"Bullshit."

"The concepts of good and evil are bullshit. They shackle folks to the yoke of failure. But in reality, there's only the clarity of choosing between productive and nonproductive methods. Your thoughts must not be clouded by rabid desire. Hating me accomplishes nothing."

Blah, blah, blah.

I tried to tune him out, but he wouldn't stop. "Ask yourself what you want out of this day. Revenge? You want to cry your eyes out and kill us both? You want to believe that dyin' will make things fair? Is that what you want? To kill yourself? And kill what's left of your precious Marie? Hell, if I thought you'd throw everything away, I wouldn't be here."

I got up, not sure if it was time to press the button or step outside for a breath of unpolluted air.

But he kept it going. "What else could you possibly want? Perhaps you want to call a truce? Agree to disagree? We both walk away from this, only to butt heads another day? You'd really take the chickenshit solution? No. I don't think so. Not you."

Maybe walking away was chickenshit. But it was an option.

"Or maybe you're ready to wise up and open your eyes. Life ain't fair. It is what it is. And like it or not, I hold all the cards. I have all the chips. Like it or not, you're lookin' at success. So dine with me at my table. Enjoy the finest that life has to offer. Marko, you've been out in the cold harsh winter of your mistakes, out there tapping on my window, face pressed against the warm glass, pissed by what you see. You have so little, and I have so much. But I noticed you. Yes, I did. And I took a liking to you. So now I invite you in, out of the cold and the darkness, to sit at my table, to sup with me by the fire, and to share the succulent feast of my success."

A colorful image, but I wasn't exactly looking at a success.

"So what's it gonna be, son?" He pointed to the red button on the wall. "Pointless martyrdom?" He waved at the door. "Chickenshit delay of game?" He swept Peter's junk food to the floor and gestured to his empty table. "Or savor the joy of bountiful success with me?"

I turned away. Took a few steps. Looking at Marie was killing me. I needed air.

True, a delay of game was a chickenshit move. Jack was a festering problem. A problem that could be ended now. But I wasn't the martyr type.

Joining Jack's team wasn't an option.

On the other hand, Nameless, Martoni, Tommy, and Dread all voted to be on Jack's team. Eat at his table. Drink his elixir of evil. Because the rewards would be endless. And yes, we might have to look away as we exterminated innocent people, tricked others so we could inhabit their bodies. But the immortality and raw power we'd have would make it all okay.

Not Wolf. He only wanted to walk over and snap Jack's neck. I argued that Jack would then jump into our body and we'd be mere passengers with a view to an eternal nightmare. Wolf insisted he was stronger. Much stronger. He could kill Jack from the inside— from the passenger seat.

Well, that was interesting, but Wolf didn't exactly have all his marbles. It might look like Jack yielded to his personalities, let them take his steering wheel. But I had the feeling that Jack was always Jack—always in control. He only wore passengers like he wore weird clothes—for twisted amusement. Besides, if he took over Samson's body, he'd start by castrating us—and not in a happy way.

That got Wolf's attention.

As for Pops, he just wanted to push the big red button and end the madness. Pops always seemed to want the final rest. He seemed to think death was his ticket out of this madness.

He had a good point.

Except Pops was about 90% dead already. That thought only pissed him off. He really wanted to be 100% dead. He thought we were all trying to live with one foot in the grave and one foot on earth. It was unnatural.

I couldn't argue with that. It was massively unnatural. But what was I supposed to do about it? Give up and die? Or keep playing high stakes poker, even if I had a hand full of jokers?

Billy Bob was virtually nonexistent in my head until I slept or got drunk. Then he and his passengers took total control. The ultimate in passive-aggressive—a true gator.

Then there was poor Samson. He was about as confused as I was. We had way too many options and no way to win.

I could still hear Marie's voice behind me, spewing out Jack's mindless drivel. So I tuned him out the best I could. The guy was ranting about all kinds of crap. None of it concerned me. It was a solid stream of insanity.

It occurred to me that mental asylums must be full of jumpers. All babbling in assorted tongues about half-baked crap. Superpower gone off the deep end. Same for many of the poor souls crouched on city sidewalks with their hands out, barely able to rub two coherent thoughts together. A head full of multi-minds all fighting for control.

Okay, so Jack was like a super psycho. But still functional, not beaten down by his insanity. He was operating full tilt. Even in chains, there was no denying how successful he'd become. He had hooks into North America's power base of politics and finance— hooks that would only keep getting deeper. Hooks called jumpers. If money and power didn't pull politicians and CEOs to the dark side, Jack's jumpers could arrange to take over their bodies—their lives. Same for world leaders. Perfect manipulation.

Ultimately, Jack was a threat to everyone on the planet. Able to turn the world in to his pet empire. And able to keep it going for a very, very long time.

Then there was me—messed up mentally, but still going. I had that in common with Jack. Except my idea of an empire was Sonya. Happy and naked. In a big soft bed.

A very good thought.

Maybe in beautiful Canada. With a nice breakfast.

My vivid imagination was interrupted by a heavy plastic coffee mug hitting me in the back of the head.

Jack shouted, "Hey! I'm talkin' to you."

I whirled around, picked up the mug, and cocked my arm to hurl it into his face. But I couldn't. I couldn't because it was Marie's face.

That's when Jack grinned like this was some sort of confirmation. Like we both understood that I could never hurt him while Marie's flesh was between us. And it dawned on me that this was why he'd taken Marie—defense against Marko. He could hurt me all he wanted, but I'd never put my fist into Marie's innocent face. And from the look in his eyes, it was clear he'd gone down this path before, and the results were predictable. So the future was predictable, just like he'd said. I was just another data point saying that people could be manipulated. I was just another pawn.

He pointed at my chair. "Sit!" His voice was authority—hard and to the point. An army field general—on way too many steroids.

I sat. Defeated by my own spinning thoughts.

"You act like this is the end of the goddamn world. Like we have to die now. You and me, together, like sniveling cowards. That's total bullshit! You and me? We're not circling the drain. We're circling the fucking fountain of immortality. We're the success stories—the victors—the permanent few." He was standing tall behind his desk, a general dressing down a subordinate. "So find your goddamn backbone and listen up. I wasn't going to talk about this now." He waved up at the cameras. "Prying eyes and all. But it's time you learned the truth about creatures like us."

Great. Another rant.

"Come closer."

I crossed my arms. No way I was getting closer.

"Fine. Have it your way." He leaned forward and lowered his voice. "Evolution? You've heard if it. Well, it fucking happens. Mutations. Mutations everywhere, and it happens every goddamn day. Why? Because nature loves trial and error. Loves it! Hell, boy. Nature doesn't just do evolution now and then—*she is evolution!*"

He put both hands on the table and leaned as close as he could. "Boy, you and I—we're different. Like nothing the world has ever seen before." His voice was the intense whisper of conspiracy. "Ever wonder why there are no ancient spirit walkers among us? Hell, if we can live forever then why aren't the Ancient Ones among us? Look at you. Barely three months into spirit walking. You're just a damn pup. And me? Hell, I'm pushing 200 and I'm one of the oldest spirits. Sure, those clowns, Bruce the Black and Snow Leopard—they're old. But only 500 years, tops. There simply are no real ancients."

I wanted to tell him there weren't any ancient jumpers because after so many jumps . . . well, the multi-mind just snaps. Eventually, all jumpers go horribly insane. That made sense because the human brain could only hold so much. Ultimately, the young jumpers would get tired of watching the old jumpers foam at the mouth and they'd eliminate them from the weird pool. They'd find a way.

Yes. They totally would. And I wanted to tell old Jack he was seriously overdue for extermination.

That's what I wanted to say. But I kept my mouth shut.

Jack glanced around. "You, me, the other spirit walkers—we're the next step in evolution. The next fucking step! Normals thought they were supreme—the whole point of creation. We're living proof that's total bullshit. Creation is about becoming something new—not staying human. And it's happening right here on this stinking hellhole of a planet. Evolution is the life-form building process. And we're the next goddamn step."

He waited for me to say something like, *Holy Crap!* But why bother? Jack was an insane monster. Of course he was trying to talk his way out of this.

Besides, he was getting amusing. So I just sat there.

And Jack kept going. "It's coming, boy, whether you realize it or not. The future is coming and it belongs to spirit walkers. Normals are like— Hell, let's call them what they are: high-functioning servants. You know they are. Down deep, you feel it. We are the rightful masters. Like it or not, boy, you're a master, too. The only question is: do you want to take your God-given role in shaping the future, or do you want to throw away your gift like some piss-ant pantywaist?"

I tried pushing back. "You killed jumpers. You experimented on them, then you killed them. You call that shaping the future?"

"You ever hear the expression, *Knowledge is power*? Besides, you yourself killed a spirit walker—Billy Bob Wyville. That name ring a bell?"

Oh, yeah. Billy Bob. The quiet one. "Sure. He deserved what he got."

"That's dandy. Bring him on out. Let's hear what he's got to say about all this."

Yeah, right. Not going to happen.

"So where do we stand, son? Apparently you'll kill spirit walkers just because you think it's right. Whereas, I kill spirit walkers to lock in a future where we understand ourselves, and can rule over normals without all this petty backstabbing shit. I'm talking shit like the power trip you and Sonya seem to enjoy—thinking you can just stab me in the back and I'll take it lying down. The offer's on the table, Marko. Now's the time to take it."

"Is that all you've got? Because if that's it, then I'm sticking with Plan A—ending us both."

"Martyrdom is nothing more than blind desperation. It's such a bad plan. Always has been."

"I'm not letting you out of here."

"Fine." Jack sat down and quickly softened, like he was giving up. "Then let me outta Marie." Now he sounded like he was from the Bronx.

"What?"

"Look, pal, there are ways to extract me—ways to give Marie back her body, and her life. You know what I'm sayin'?"

"Like how?"

"Think about it. You and me? We're spirit walkers. That's what we do. Every time we step into someone new, we drag our past killers along with us. So if we can step into another body, then it stands to reason we can step out as well. Right? Just think about that for a second. I can step into a body without harming it—that's obvious. Then it stands to reason I can also detach myself from this girl you're lookin' at right here."

"But the only way for you to move out is to get her body killed. You'd need a killer. Her body would have to die."

"No. No. It's nothin' like that. Trust me, there's another way. It's called a damn exorcism. You've heard about it—maybe seen it in the movies or on TV. It's like that, only without some trembling priest hidin' behind a damn cross, pelting me with holy tap water.

It's like where I pick up my bags and shit, then I leave Marie in her own body. Frankly, pal, she's better off with me than being a normal in the coming age of free roaming spirits. Know what I'm sayin'? But hell, if you wanna doom her to hum drum mortality, servitude like I was talkin' about earlier, and certain death 'cause all normals die—then fine, I'm willin' to make it work for you."

"Then do it. Get the hell out of her."

"What? Here? Believe it or not, kid, I'll need another body to occupy. Even with our greatness, we still need a damn body to live in. You understand that, right? So now I'm lookin' around. I'm lookin'. And what do I see? You, boy, are the only body available. Are you offerin' me your body?"

I frowned.

"I thought not. So we walk outta here, find a suitable skin for me, and then I leave Marie whole and well—maybe with a few bad memories. But hey, you can't have everything. Right? Then you two, and that bitch Sonya, can just ride off into the sunset. Better yet, go find an ice cave in Canada somewhere. 'Cause the world belongs to me and my allies."

Jack rattled his chains again. "So what's it gonna be, kid? We join forces? You save Marie and we part ways? You know, the good stuff. Or you gas Marie like a dog? Like a dog, I'm tellin' you. No. She don't deserve that. No way. But like I said, it's your call. So what's it gonna be? Set her free, or put her down?"

Shit. Was I actually thinking about walking out with Jack, hoping it would lead to getting Marie back to normal?

The seconds ticked by like each one was an eternity.

I was sweating. "Fine. Tell me how you'll get out of Marie without messing her up."

"Okay, look. Her body—I gotta say it's been heavily used lately, but not broken. Hey, you'd find out sooner or later. And her brain's still intact, except she's got some unusually sexy new memories. So by your standards, well, she might need a good shrink. What can I say? I gotta thing for bein' in a woman. Then there's her spirit. I gotta say it's still in there, alive and kicking in the back of her own head. So yeah, it's all there, pal. All good. Now all I need to do is bow out and it's all hers again. So whaddya say we get outta here and make this happen."

"Fine. But I really need some details."

"Dammit!" Jack slammed Marie's fists on the metal table. "That's the kind of fucking stupid thinking I've been talkin' about!" Jack was breathing hard, but trying to calm down. "Look, you moron. Without breakin' a few unworthy spirit walkers, I'd never know the secret to a real exorcism. The future isn't built on gumdrops and lollipops, you know. It's built on brilliant work—and the bones of countless rotting losers under our feet. Like it or not, pal, that's the hill we stand on."

"I still haven't heard how to save Marie."

Jack looked like he was holding back rage. Like he wanted to take a hit out on me, but was willing to give me one more shot. "Yes, you have. I already told you. It begins with you growing a fucking backbone and gettin' us the hell out of here. It begins with me rejoining my team, gettin' the resources I need, and extracting myself from this damn girl for your irrational pleasure. Or whatever the hell you need her for."

"What's the process? I need the exact process of extraction."

"Look!" Jack took a deep breath. "It's classified. Okay? What the fuck do you think it is? I'm not tellin' you. It's my secret. You kill me, it goes with me to the grave. Or, if you actually thought about it, you might just see that you yourself could be free of all your inner killers. Yeah, you heard me right. Of course, you'd have to change bodies again, but you could have a good one. And more importantly, a mind free from those nagging little voices in your head that tell you to do this and that, and this and that, and this and that—all the fucking time—talkin' 'cause they never shut the hell up. No, they're always in there, nagging at you to do the same damn shit over and over and over until you just wanna pull your own fucked up brain out and stomp on it." Jack took a moment to smooth Marie's hair back. His hands were shaking as he fought for self-control. "Yeah, man. That's it. That's how we get it."

Great. Jack was on the verge of a mental breakdown. "Then why haven't you gotten away from your inner killers?"

"Because I damn well need 'em! And . . . and we get along—me and the boys. You should try it. And because they keep me company when I'm stuck in a rat-shit hole like this one. Think about it, Marko. You're so much more with a head full of people. You have amazing skills, unusual knowledge . . . a multi-fuck mind, for crying out loud. Do you really want to go back to being that naive little taxi twit with no skills other than drivin' a car and playin' mindless video games? You're bigger now. You're better now. So fucking deal with it and embrace the new reality."

How could anyone be so right, and so wrong? Jack was obviously a snake. But a part of me thought he was a snake I needed—a snake with knowledge no one else had.

I felt so screwed.

Ending Jack was easy. Ending myself was something I hated thinking about. But yeah, a part of me could throw myself on this grenade to keep a lot of people from joining Jack's lofty bone pile.

But ending Marie still felt impossible. That was the bottom line. And I was staring right at her lovely self. Sweet feisty Marie. Not dead, but not alive. She was lost in Jack's python grip.

Jack must have seen my expression because he melted away, letting Marie show herself. "Oh, Marko. How I've missed you."

I wasn't convinced. Jack looked and sounded and acted like Marie. But she still seemed to be his puppet—the strings barely visible.

I'm not sure how it happened, but I was now standing closer, my hands on the table. Marie reached out and gently touched my hand. It gave me a chill. I pulled away.

Jack-Marie's eyes were filling with tears. "It's still me. There's still hope for us. My wonderful Marko. Don't do this horrible thing. There's still time. We'll find another way."

It sounded so much like Marie, but the hairs on the back of my neck said otherwise.

That's when Marie's left hand quietly flipped me off—gave me the finger. Totally unexpected.

Jack seemed surprised by it, too. He quickly moved her hand flat on the table, fingers straight, outstretched, under his strict control.

Damn!

The quiet finger was something hot-blooded Marie used to do when she was pissed with me—pissed because I was taking too long with a decision I already knew I was going to make. Like discussing whether to see a chick flick, or the latest remake of Batman. Of course, we could see the chick flick later or even rent it. But Batman must be experienced on the big screen with bone jarring speakers. So Marie's finger always meant *just get on with it*. There was no choice to discuss. It was the brooding Batman, on the big screen, his gloved fists pounding the crap out of pure twisted evil. We'd rent the chick flick later, and we both knew it.

The finger gesture—*just get on with it*. That was my Marie. The real Marie. That was her pure self talking to me, using a single finger to push aside Jack's puppet strings.

God, I wanted to kiss her! Just one more time. One last time!

But that bastard Jack was in the way.

Wolf got up, walked behind Jack, and slammed his head into the table.

What the hell?

Wolf thought I needed to be quick, while Jack was dazed and confused.

Right. I grabbed Marie's hair and turned her head around to face me. Blood trickled across her nose and lips. Marie's blood, not Jack's. So I kissed her hard on the lips, the taste of her blood in my mouth, violent passion on my mind.

Marie closed her eyes, and it was her—saying goodbye—loving me for a blazing instant. She shifted her lips and bit my lower lip, right side, as she often did when her angry passion needed to make it clear how she felt.

Then she slid away—lost to me as Jack regained control.

I stepped back, still savoring Marie's blood on my lips. We'd had our time together. Too brief. But I suppose even for old married couples, the days added up to so little.

Marie and I would die this day. Her, only 21, but sadly possessed by Jack's evil. Me, only 22, and sadly in a stranger's body.

Jack was a walking lie. A sick man holding candy out to an innocent child—a razor held behind his back. Today was my turn to reach for the candy.

Except I was no innocent.

I walked over to the red button. There was no off switch, only the release that would flood the room with unbreathable gas, crowding the oxygen out of the chamber.

Jack was shouting something through Marie's swollen lips. Something about alliances, our future, his love for me, our unborn children, and a new utopia created by superior beings. But his words were muffled in cotton—drowned out by the pounding of my heart in my ears—drowned out by stubborn Marie fighting for control of her own mouth.

Marie had warned me. She knew Jack's real thoughts. The candy of Marie's salvation was a lie. Jack's razor was the only truth. She wanted this to end.

I pushed the button. Behind the metal wall, I heard a large valve open. Cold swept out of the dark iron grate and across my feet. It clung to the floor. Its chill surprised me. The chamber next door was filled with frozen blocks of krypton?

Thanks, Peter.

I'd never have the chance to punch him out. I'd never have the chance to do a lot of things. The exit door was no longer an option. There was no turning back.

I hoped the best for Sonya. Maybe taking out Jack was the best I could do for her—the best my love could give her. But sometimes the best feels so small.

I intentionally slumped to the floor with my back to the wall near the grate. Better to die first. If Jack died first, he'd take over my body because I was killing him. No way was I going to share a mind with Jack, even briefly. So this was how it was going to be. I was the one to finally end Jack. A good thought.

And besides, I was putting a final cap on all of my passengers. This martyr-suicide of mine would end them—end the last shreds of them. Pops would finally be free. They all would. It would also end all of Jack's passengers. And it would end poor Marie.

If there was a God, Marie truly had a home.

If there wasn't—there just wasn't.

As for me, I was a troubled mess. I'd done my best, even if it wasn't good enough. What lay ahead for me, was the blackest of unknowns. No point in second-guessing my future.

I coughed on the cold harsh gas.

Jack was starting to panic. I heard him struggling against the chains. His voice rising. His offers of solutions became more and more creative. So I tuned him out. At least I tried to. Hard to do when his voice sounded like Marie.

Twice, his head hit the table. Hard. Marie getting in her licks. Go girl. Smash him hard. But she must be feeling the pain, too. Still, she was a fighter.

Jack writhed and screamed. Violent noises. A battle of a thousand minds fighting for control.

And the room filled from the bottom up with gas, mixing with good air. From the bottom because the gas was cold? Or because krypton was heavy stuff?

Yeah, heavy stuff.

I was feeling lightheaded now. My thoughts were getting fuzzy and slow. Mental fog wrapped its arms around me, growing thick. My vision grew fuzzy and dim, except for the center.

Samson's glasses were useless so I tossed them.

Then there was a wave of panic as I gasped for good air. I felt like I was drowning, but without the burning pain of water in my lungs. I thrashed on the floor, desperate to pull in air.

And after a time, I settled down. Growing numb, like I was wrapped in a warm cocoon. In my mother's arms—her comfort after the womb.

I felt so alone, and not alone.

Marie and I died together. The final death.

Truly.

And I led the way in that metal chamber. The first to die.

But maybe a part of Marie was already ahead of me. Waiting. Waiting for the last part of her spirit to be released from her earthly body.

So maybe a part of her waited for me in the afterlife. I wanted to think so. I vowed to wait for her complete spirit.

If there was a way, we'd be together. If there only was.

And it was the true perma-death.

5.6 Life On Venus

My first death was in a taxi back in Austin. Actually, only my body died. My spirit had other plans. So I began my weird existence—body jumping.

The rest, you already know. Me, Marko Santana, putting the little "ab" in abnormal. Head hopping, kinda like head lice, only deeper. Parasitic. Pulling down killers. A crime fighter in my own chaotic way.

But also having to deal with a mind full of other people—lots of nasty people, some with badass skills, and a few who just got caught up with the wrong people.

So I was looking at immortality, combined with a massive personality disorder. Not ideal, but life never is.

The train to hell looked like it would go on forever. Right until I decided to end Jack.

Yes, I died in the gas chamber with Jack infesting Marie. And yes, we all really did die the perma-death. Jack really died. Poor sweet Marie really died—body and soul. And I really died. My passengers were finally released. It was the end of all of us.

So how am I here to tell you about this? Something unexpected happened. Not in the gas chamber—something earlier. Something I should have seen coming, but didn't.

Damn! It was so obvious. But I missed all the clues.

So much for being a brilliant multi-mind. So much for being ahead of the curve. So much for my raving paranoia keeping me clued into all the possibilities.

Okay, I had to admit I wasn't the smartest dog in the junkyard. Hell no. Sonya was far smarter than any of us. Hard to admit it, but Sonya was about a million times smarter than me. Way smarter than Peter. And more cunning than Jack on his sneakiest day.

Note to self: God's gift to humanity (not just man) was probably woman. Kind of a weird thought, but there it was.

So besides truly dying with Jack and Marie, here's what also happened. Like I said, I should have seen it coming. It was so obvious, and so twisted.

Rewind.

* * *

I woke in the arms of an angel. Well, that's exactly what it felt like. Angel warm. Angel strong. Angel love.

My eyesight slowly returned. Fuzzy blobs. The usual taste in my mouth after a jump. Someone else's saliva, but not as bad as the other times. The unexpected smell of candles and flowers—and of a familiar woman.

I turned to see the blurred outline of Sonya's face smiling down on me. Sonya my angel, holding me as I eased into my latest new body.

"Hey, Wolfie." Her voice was soft like everything in the room. "Good to have you back."

Not what I expected, but it was great to be in Sonya's arms again.

My vision sharpened. She was in a white gown. So was I. The room was draped with sheer fabrics. A window was open to the night air. Candles on the nightstand. We were sitting in bed, leaning on pillows—a soft white bed.

Cool. Except there were flowers.

Was I dead? I tried to say that, but the words didn't come out.

"Take it slow, Wolfie. Relax and let it sink in."

I was already relaxed in her arms, and I had the growing feeling I wasn't dead. But I was really confused about what happened. The last thing I remembered was being tied up in a chair, as Pops, and staring up at Billy Bob Wyville's startled face as electric fire fried my brain.

What went wrong? I didn't seem to be in Billy Bob's disgusting gator body. Wasn't that the plan?

It totally was. Billy Bob started the timer on the jumper killing device. Then it went off early and electrocuted Pops while Billy Bob was there watching. That totally made him my killer. Right?

Right?

My mind raced with half-baked answers and complete confusion.

Sonya studied my face—my twitching confused face. "I can see it's time for some answers." Her eyes were bright and she wore a mischievous smile.

Her expression told me that it was good news—but twisted.

My mind was feeling a bit better in my new brain, so I tried talking again. "So what happened? I was expecting to jump into Billy Bob." That's when I put my hand to my new face to stop the twitching, and my arm brushed against something unexpected. Something like breasts. But not Sonya's. Mine. Like a woman's breasts, but on my chest.

And my hand instinctively went for one, grabbed it, and reported back that it was indeed a woman's breast. A man's hand never lied about a thing like that. And yes, womanhood was somehow attached to my chest—like, right next to another breast. So perfectly arranged on me. Like I had a woman's chest, somehow.

Ultra freaky.

Before I knew it, my other hand was between my legs and reported total shock at finding ... not much. But something electric shot up my body, signaling that I was touching myself. Touching something—different. Touching undeniable womanhood! On me!

Oh, shit!

I lurched, sat bolt upright. My hands were all over me, checking me out, groping me. Ass, tits, crotch, biceps—all woman. I was somehow all woman.

Mirror! I needed a damn mirror!

There was a bathroom. I stepped onto the floor and nearly fell over. Typical. The floor was really close, so I was now short again.

I focused on my little bare feet as I hustled into the bathroom, then flipped on the light. The switch was higher up on the wall than expected. And there was a woman staring back at me. Short medium brown hair. Cute, but not exactly beautiful. Maybe early 30s. Compact.

When I moved, she moved. Super weird.

I could see Sonya behind me, slightly taller, watching me as I figured out my new body. Sonya's smile curved up on one side like an imp up to no good.

She could have warned me.

I grabbed the dress or nightgown or whatever the hell it was I had on me. Funny how I started to whip it off but paused. Paused because I needed to know that no guys were watching. Just us girls, right?

Except I was a guy.

Wasn't I?

Oh, what the hell. I was going to look at my new equipment sooner or later. I pulled my gown over my head and gasped as I saw myself full-naked in the mirror.

Crap. I was in a naked woman. And double crap, because I looked kinda sexy.

Of course, I wanted to touch myself so badly. But I, Marko, needed permission. Permission from whom? From my new passenger?

And who says *whom*, anyway?

Hello. Who's in the back of my mind? We'll get your name soon enough. Say hello to Martoni, Nameless, Wolf, and Pops. If you see the shadow of a shadow, that's just Snip the sniper.

Martoni and Nameless wanted me to grope myself, especially in front of the mirror so they could watch. Pops thought that had possibilities, but we should buy her a drink first. Wolf thought we were acting completely juvenile, but a part of him was curious how this was all going to work out.

And me? I was not about to let those guys sexually assault my new passenger's body—visually, or physically. Which left me seriously conflicted.

"You know," I turned and looked at Sonya, "I could really go for a shirt and some pants."

"Understandable. Panties first." She walked over to a dresser and pulled out a lacy white wisp of indecent material.

"No way." I'd never worn panties, and I wasn't about to start now.

"Slip them on, babe. You might grow to like them."

I took them and looked them over. Was the right side out? Which end was the front? They were little more than a gathering of lacy holes. Not even remotely practical. Why so sexy? It's not like I was ever going to let a guy see me in them. That thought gave me the shivers.

Martoni and Nameless wanted me to slip the panties on, then slide them off slowly. They wanted me to make it a sexy tease, in front of a mirror so they had a good view. Wiggle my bottom when I did it. And when I had them pulled down, we should do it all over again.

Seriously? Why? It's not like we could get an erection.

Damn! That would be a major limitation.

Pops was worried because maybe we were now lesbian. He sure as hell didn't want to be one of those. Martoni and Nameless thought lesbianism had kinky advantages.

Just shut the hell up!

I stepped into the panties and pulled them up. Not the fit I was expecting. Way too much rear end hanging out. Fine. I'd cover them up with something decent. "Pants. Real pants."

Sonya handed me a pair of tight pants. A weird peachy-pink color. She picked up on my disgust and offered a different pair. "Okay, here. Taupe okay?"

I didn't know what the hell taupe was, but they looked brown so I put them on.

The bra was next. I was tempted to skip it, but a few hops up and down told me my new gear needed some restraint. But I needed help with that one. Put it on backwards? Then slide the cups around to the front? Really? This was clearly a bad design.

At least there was no need to adjust the straps because all the clothes belonged to my new passenger. My first female passenger.

Then I slipped into an off-white shirt. Good. But who put the buttons on the wrong side? Sonya said it was a blouse, not a shirt, and she thought untucked looked best.

Great. Too many fashion choices. Guys knew that brown went

with brown, and blue went with anything. Simple, just the way my Y chromosome liked it. Except I now had two Xs. That made me a Y mind in a double-X body. Not a good combination.

"Don't button it up all the way." Sonya started unbuttoning my shirt a bit. "Leave a few unbuttoned. Show some chest. It's okay."

Seriously? Nothing was okay.

Now that I was dressed, I walked over to the window and pulled aside the sheer curtains for a better look. A few feet away was a floor to ceiling photo of rolling hills and clouds. "Where the hell am I?"

"I'll show you around. Are you hungry?" She was being so thoughtful. Kind of like I was someone who needed lots of help doing the basic things.

Well, I was no invalid, I was the great and powerful Multi-Mind. "No." Food could wait. "Tell me about the jump. I thought I'd get Billy Bob. And who the heck is this?" I almost grabbed my chest again. I'd have to be careful about that.

"You'll get answers. How about a drink first?"

"Sure." I could really use a drink. But not too much. I needed to make sure Martoni and Nameless kept their hands off of me. Now that I was a woman, my passengers were looking a lot like perverts. But I had to secretly admit, I wanted to have fun with my new body, too.

We walked down a few hallways, then into a large room that looked like it was set up as a command and control center. There were more than a dozen computer stations, each with two or three monitors. Many of the people had headphones on and seemed to be talking with operatives in the field. One really big wall monitor showed a map of North America with little blinking dots on it. Several smaller monitors showed interior and exterior night vision shots of Billy Bob's and Wolf's house. Other screens showed night images labeled D.C., San Francisco, Toronto, Boston, and Havana.

"Nice setup. This must be Jumper Command."

Sonya nodded. "Part of it. We still keep it compartmentalized."

"Cool. But why a whole screen for Havana?"

"Jack said he made Cuba communist, working behind the scenes. He said he did that because he needed someplace close where the

U.S. Feds couldn't go, and he wanted to relax on warm sandy beaches—with Russian politicos and their dangerous Russian women. Personally, I find that really hard to believe. He's so full of lies. But he does have a lot of stories about it, so we keep an eye on Havana."

I almost asked why San Francisco needed a whole screen, but it was probably just another one of Jack's playgrounds.

Peter popped up above a sea of monitors and pointed at me. "Whoa! Lookin' good, dude." He had a smirk on his face that implied my manhood was now screwed. And like we might have sex later.

I shouted back at him. "Hey. We need to talk."

"Later, bro. I'm in the middle of your op." He sat back down and focused on his cluster of screens.

"My op?" I turned to Sonya. "I've jumped already. My op's over. Right?"

"How about some wine?" Sonya turned slowly, walked to a nearby couch, and sat down. She indicated a chilled bottle.

"No thanks." I sat next to her. "So what ops? And how did I even jump into this woman?"

Sonya picked up a remote control and turned on two monitors on the opposite side of the coffee table. She seemed to settle in like this was her station. Queen bee. The brains behind the rebellion. "I was hoping to break this to you gently, Wolfie, but . . . we twinned you."

WTF! "You cloned me?"

"Well . . . basically, yes. But more accurately, you were twinned." She took my hand—my womanly hand. "You were out there doing battle with Jack and his men—the ones who killed you in the hot tub. You were filling your head with serious killers, like Wolf, and whoever came before Wolf. I know you're resourceful, but your survival odds against Jack and his men were . . . less than ideal. Call me self-centered, but I wanted a copy of you for myself—preferably not deranged from a head full of psychopaths and heartless killers, and preferably not perma-dead or living in a corner of Jack's hyper-crowded cerebellum. I actually love you, Wolfie. Maybe it was selfish of me, but I had Peter make a copy of you. You know? A little something for myself."

Huh?

A hand shot up where Peter was sitting. He snapped his fingers and pointed at Sonya. It reminded me of a periscope, or maybe a cobra.

"Sorry. I'll just be a moment." She adjusted her headset—one ear uncovered so she could hear me, the other listening to some chatter. She changed channels on her monitors until the video stream showed Billy Bob standing on his porch, illuminated by streetlights and his porch light. His big hairy chest was sticking out, arms spread wide. Not a pretty sight.

Oh, crap. Billy Bob wasn't dead! "Damn. He's still alive."

"Not . . . really." Sonya flipped on the speakers so we could hear Billy Bob. She leaned closer and whispered, "That's your twin."

"No way. That's me?"

"No, that's not you. That's your twin. You were split. One part of you got Billy Bob's body. The other part is now . . . uh . . ." she smiled and winked at me, "cute and perky."

No!

So I was looking at my new twin—Marko Number 2, now wearing Billy Bob's sorry hide.

Or maybe I was Marko Number 2 and he was the original? Or maybe we were just equals?

Billy Bob stood there for a second, then started shouting to the world. "You damn cowards. Bring it on." The sound was a bit muffled. He started beating his barrel of a chest like he was some kind of badass serial survivor. Like there was nothing anyone could do to stop him.

Weird, but cool. I could totally see myself acting like that. Hell, I *was* acting like that. Go, me! Go!

Billy Bob . . . no, it was my twin inside Billy Bob . . . he reached over and dug around in the planter and came up with the earpiece I'd tossed there. Super freaky that he knew where I'd put it.

Oh, yeah. He had all my memories—up until the twinning, when Pops was electrocuted. So my twin was almost exactly me. He was just a different branch of me. A very new branch. He was—

Oh, mega-crap. He also loved Sonya. He was a competitor. He had all my skills, and my charm. We'd both had amazing sex with Sonya in Canada. She loved us both. She must.

I suddenly wanted to kill him. Except he was now ugly old Billy Bob and I was a cute perky woman. Not good, because Sonya preferred men. Right? But she was with me now. That was good. Right? Sonya picked me, not him. Right?

Right?

I was so jealous of my evil twin.

Note to self: Watch him like a hawk.

The people in the room all stood up and cheered. Why? Was he a hero for becoming Billy Bob? He could obviously hear us, so I shouted, too. "Totally awesome, bro!" The universe didn't rip apart at the seams, so I guess talking to the other *me* was okay.

So if we were twins, was I the sister?

Sonya cupped her hands to her mouth and yelled, "I love you, Wolfie! Hooyah!"

Ouch. That cut me like a thousand razors. She really did love my twin. She only cloned me into a woman so we could be pals? That made sense. Sonya loved the man in harm's way. The man leading the charge against Jack and his crew. The guy who was a real man. Not me, the new girlfriend.

Sonya cut Billy Bob's voice from the speakers, then grabbed my face and planted a super sexy kiss on me. And just like that, the world erupted with Roman candles. Fireworks everywhere. But more than that, it was Ana, the woman inside Sonya who was kissing me to my deepest level—kissing Marko, the original man in me. It was another magic Ana and Marko moment. Our two original selves, bypassing our current flesh, touching each other, spirit to spirit.

And yes, I kissed her back with all the fierce love I had for her.

The room melted and swirled.

A brief eternity later, we slowly allowed air between us, and my earthly consciousness returned. We were back in reality, if you could call it that.

Out of the corner of one eye, I caught a glimpse of one of the guys watching our sexy girl-on-girl lust-fest. Great. Now I had to watch out for cute guys looking for a threesome.

Wait. Did I just think he was cute?

No!

Sonya and I sat down. Good. The room was still spinning and the concentrated weird never stopped coming.

I watched the monitors without sound. There were a million questions swirling in my brain, but it was good to just sit quietly for a moment and watch my evil twin. Actually, he wasn't that bad. I pitied him because he was wearing Billy Bob's ugly body, and Billy Bob's evil was sliming up my twin's mental back seat, and Peter was bossing my twin around. But the best part: I was sitting next to my Sonya babe.

So maybe I was the winner after all.

We watched as Billy Bob-me walked back toward the study. Peter had hidden cameras everywhere. In the study, there was dead Pops. Damn. He looked really bad, all tied up and slumped over in the chair. Poor old man. I wanted my twin to cover him with a sheet or something.

Sonya poured me a glass of white wine, and I was glad to have it. It had to be harsh for Pops to see himself dead.

Of course, Pops was a passenger in my twin's head, just like mine. So even though his body was now dead, there were two of him as passengers. Two remnants of Pops. It dawned on me that all my passengers were also in my twin. Two sets of identical passengers. Except other-me now had Billy Bob as a passenger, and I had an unknown woman.

I took another sip of wine. It wasn't helping my condition, but it wasn't hurting either.

Twinning was a real mind bender. But my twin and I were now separate people. Each going their own way. I had no idea what other-me was thinking. Like siblings who are real twins, but kinda linked by a similar thought process. Except we had shared memories like being Marko, and shared skills like being Wolf. And a shared love of Sonya—so I was back to feeling weird about other-me.

Sonya topped off my glass. She could tell my head was hurting—unexpected thoughts hammering me.

On the monitor, I could see Billy Bob sitting at his desk, talking into his notebook computer. He seemed to be giving Peter a hard time about something. That cheered me up a bit.

Then Billy Bob jumped up and ran out of the room. Why? Was he in danger? The image switched to him running out the front of the house, then making a u-turn and running out the back of the house toward the water. Billy Bob tripped on a lawn chair and did a face plant in the grass. Obviously, Peter's night vision cameras were better than Billy Bob's eyes.

Poor guy. "Why's he all panicked like that?"

Sonya was on edge. "Doc's about to arrive at the house."

"Oh, shit." Doc was like Wolf's sadistic counterpart. Doc would make mincemeat out of slow moving Billy Bob. My twin was starting to feel like my real brother. I wanted my bro to do well in the field. I wanted him to survive. "What can I do to help?"

Sonya squeezed my hand. "We'll get to that. But for now, you'll need some answers, and some time to get adjusted to your new body."

"Right. But I still want to help. Did you tell my twin about me yet?"

"No. I think it's best if he doesn't know he has a twin. It wouldn't be good for him to think he's expendable. And I don't want him to worry about us."

Us? There was an *us*? I liked the sound of that. "Okay, but I should still be out there. Two Wolfs are better than one." Wolf pack!

"Yes they are. But command is mine, and I'm holding you in reserve. Besides, I could use your company."

Sonya wanted me? As a woman? As company? As a commando held in reserve? My thoughts swirled.

A voice cut through the chatter in the room. "Oh, shit! No!"

Sonya sucked in air. Her gaze was on one of the wall monitors. Dots blinked on the big city map.

It looked about the same to me. "What happened?"

"San Francisco."

Okay, I could see a cluster of red blinking dots on that map. "I take it red is bad."

"Normals. Six dead. And one jumper—now perma-dead. All ours."

"Normals work with us?"

"More than I care to admit."

"And they know about us?"

"Not exactly, but there are a few exceptions. We hire normals with assorted skills. Mostly ex-military. But none are expendable." She looked me in the eye. "No one is expendable, especially not you or your twin." Sonya stood up. "Let's go. They can handle this better than I can. I take every loss like it was the death of my sister all over again."

I could tell she was fighting back tears as I followed her out the door.

* * *

We walked until we came to an elevator door. Sonya pushed the call button. She was still fighting back emotions—the death of six normals, and a jumper. Maybe she knew them? Maybe they were more to her than blinking dots on a screen?

I reached over and gave her a hug. She seemed to appreciate it.

The elevator opened. We stepped inside but there was no way to select a floor. No buttons, no indication of what floor we were on. The doors closed and we started moving. Apparently the elevator knew what it was doing.

A short ride down, maybe six floors, and the doors opened on a bleak cement hallway intersection. We were underground? Where were we, anyway? Where were we going? "I'm assuming the less I know, the better."

She motioned me to one of three waiting golf carts. "True. Up to a point." We got in a cart that had no controls and was apparently self-driving. It drove us down a long dark cement tunnel. "Ask questions. You might get some answers."

Okay. Which one first? "How did that jumper die? The one in San Francisco."

"I don't have the details yet. Perhaps he went into a burning building to try and save his team. Things like that happen. We die.

Life was never meant to be forever."

Pops understood, *there's always a fly in the ointment*—whatever that meant.

Next question. "What's the fourth way to kill a jumper? I know that sometimes you can lead them into an accident or suicide, although the planned results are iffy. And I learned that jumping into a dead killer is a dead end." Snip the sniper was my jump into an *almost* dead killer. "But I think it's time to learn the fourth way."

"With luck, you'll never need it. Your twin is more likely to need that information. But the fourth way is simple. You martyr yourself along with your jumper target. You both die. It's as simple as that."

"Like giving Jack a hug while setting off a grenade?"

Sonya grimaced. "Messy, but yes."

"Or like pulling Jack out of a perfectly good helicopter, and neither one of you has a parachute?"

She gave me a suspicious look. "You're wearing a woman named Katherine Mansky. She prefers to be called Kat. She was in the military until health reasons forced her out. Kat flew attack helicopters, so I guess they were used for attacking. Warfare stuff. Anyway, for better or worse, she was a bit too good and a bit too female for her sexist commanders. So after a short time in combat, they made her a flight instructor."

Cool. Now I had attack helicopter skills. And instructor skills. Hello, Kat. Good to have your name. Good to have you on my personal team.

"And you might like to know she's Australian. Not the cute koala bear type—more the outback snake roasting type. You get the idea, eh. If your inner Wolf ever gets weak in the knees, you might ask Kat to prop him up." She grinned as our golf cart came to a stop near another elevator.

We got out and walked to the elevator door.

I looked back. "Don't you need to plug in the cart?"

"Apparently not. Peter said it parks over those bumps on the floor and somehow that charges them." She shrugged. "Don't ask me how it works. It just does."

We stepped into the elevator and it went down, again like that was the only direction.

Sonya looked at me. "No more questions? Nothing about being a woman?"

"Uh, I might need a few pointers on how to pee."

She laughed. "You're a big boy, so I'll just let you figure that one out on your own. Do let me know when the cramps start." She had that mischievous grin again.

Great. I could hardly wait. Cramps. That sounded like fun. "So how did Kat kill me? I mean, from what you said about her, I got the idea she was one of the good guys."

"She was very much one of the good guys. One of the best, actually." The elevator doors opened and we stepped out into the middle of a very nice apartment. "These are my quarters. I hope you don't mind staying with me for a while."

Perfect. "Just us?"

"Yes. The only way in or out is the elevator, and it's set to only respond to Kat or me. Biometrics. Peter didn't give me the details and I didn't ask, except that it only worked on living biological signatures. And not just retinas or finger prints, either. He called it *pan-biotic, omni-biotic.* Something like that. So don't worry about anyone removing a thumb or an eyeball."

Good to know. "I'm sure Peter can get in, too."

"Yes ... well, I've been trying not to think about that. We've already moved most of Kat's things into my quarters. No real windows," she waved at the closed curtains, "but all the comforts of home—if you're from Sparta. Can I get you something?"

Yes. A handsome man's body. That's what I really wanted. Not for sex—for jumping into, then for sex with Sonya. Glad I didn't actually say any of that. "No. I'm good. You were saying how Kat killed me when I was Pops and sat in the chair, then Billy Bob used that device that could kill jumpers."

"Yes. Kat was a volunteer. Peter rigged Billy Bob's kill box to work only if multiple people activated it. So Kat had to push the red button on her copy of the box *and* Billy Bob had to push his. But the tricky part is that the box Pops was wired up to was designed to ignore who triggered it first or last. I don't fully understand it, but the kill box ultimately used a timer—after all the kill buttons were pressed and the system was armed, it was actually the timer that triggered the kill. That made it purely a joint decision, and Kat and Billy Bob were equally responsible for electrocuting Pops."

Wow. Peter might be a bit smarter than I'd thought. "How'd Billy Bob get the device?"

"Tanya and Tanya brought it to his attention. I guess you saw one of them when she zapped you at Billy Bob's front door. You remember Tanya and Tanya, don't you? African-American twins. Very beautiful. They're normals that Peter found in a Las Vegas act last year. And super talented. I mean *super* talented. Unfortunately I missed their Vegas show. Peter said it was amazing. Anyway, I rely heavily on the two Tanyas for infiltration ops. I'd be in a world of hurt without them."

"They seemed nice. Not so much at first."

"Sorry about the cattle prod when you met them. It was their cover. They had to play their part so Billy Bob would trust them."

"I understand. So why would Kat volunteer?"

She looked uncomfortable with that question. "Are you sure I can't get you another drink? I can put together a rum and coke for you."

"No thanks." It's possible I wasn't looking forward to more drinks and my first trip to the ladies room. "You seem to be ducking my question."

"Kat . . . her body has medical issues. Nothing that should concern you for another month or two." Sonya sighed. "She's dying. I mean, her body's dying. Maybe I mentioned that she was a normal? As a normal, we didn't have a way to give her a new body. Honestly, I was torn, but I eventually offered her a chance to live, at least to some degree, in your mind. It wasn't much, but it was all I had to offer."

Not what I expected.

"She was already working for us, and well—" Sonya searched for more words. "Well, I told her about jumpers. Not everything, but enough. And I told her about you. Your personality, your desire to usually do what's right, and your assorted views on women."

I had views? What views?

"I offered her the chance to exist as a shadow—a passenger as you call it. She wanted it. She said she'd be happy for the experience to live with you. Naturally, she wanted to know all about you—before sharing a mind. Who wouldn't? And she especially wanted to know about Wolf. I mean, who'd want to go through life sharing thoughts with a professional killer? But she weighed the pros and cons, and she's in you now. She might be quiet at first, but she's strong. Quiet, but strong. That's the best I can describe her. I know you'll like her."

Sonya smiled at me and waved. "Hi, Kat. You're among friends. Come out when you're ready."

That felt weird. I wanted to tell Sonya not to talk with people inside me, but what was I going to do? Kat was her friend.

Peter's voice came out of nowhere. "Sonya. Time's up. Back to work."

"Sorry, Wolf. Things are really busy now. Make yourself at home. Relax and make the adjustment slowly. Take a shower. Slip into bed. But don't get weird with yourself." She gave me a knowing look, like she knew I'd be tempted to mess with myself. "Don't wait up for me, babe. Bye." She gave me a quick kiss and exited via the elevator.

Great. Alone with myself, in a woman's body. What to do? What to do?

So I gave myself the grand tour of Sonya's apartment. The place was a maze of rooms, no doors anywhere, and no hallways. Just lots of archways. Each room had at least two or three ways to get to other rooms. I wandered around until I found a bathroom. No door. No privacy. Hell, the closets didn't even have doors. Well, there were curtains on the walls where you'd expect windows. So I pulled a few open and saw giant photos of forests and lakes. Probably Canada. Some in springtime. Some in winter. Like Peter wanted Sonya to have her choice of seasons?

Sheesh.

No TV, no games, no Internet, no phone, no programmable thermostats, no nothing. Plenty of wordy romance books, but nothing exciting or sexy. Nothing a man could sink his teeth into. But there was a bedside drawer full of weird looking vibrators.

Yeah. Not going there.

But there was always the shower.

Well, it seemed like a shower was inevitable.

Nah. Best to make friends before I soaped Kat up.

So I fell into bed and prayed for sleep. Sleep without groping myself or reaching for bedside power tools. Sleep without dreams of having my new boobs pawed by hunky lumberjacks.

Man, that thought really creeped me out.

What was my new passenger's name again? Katherine Mansky? Kat Man for short. Nameless thought there were already two superheroes named Katman. I guess that made me third in line. Except I was kind of a sexually challenged dude in a woman's body. Perfect. Packed with unkillable power. Packed with sexual conflict.

The ultimate crime fighting transvestite? Super T? Mystery Ms.? Midnight Madness? Nameless thought it had endless possibilities. My superhero motto would be: *What you least expect, when you least expect it!*

Pops shuddered.

* * *

I stood in a high-dollar toga, a big Roman temple behind me. Before me were acolytes—normals who had climbed the high hills to hear my words of jumper wisdom.

I spread my arms wide. The acolytes grew hushed, as well they should. My words were golden. I had the wisdom of a true multi-mind.

In the distance, the sun was setting. The sky, a dome of inky blue. Shafts of bronze light blazed from the sun. This was Mount Olympus on ancient Earth. Or maybe Olympus Mons on Mars. Either way, the setting sun was very bronze. It gave me a nice color, temporary, but ultra bronze. Like a spray-on tan.

I spoke.

"A man carries his power on the surface for all to see. The anger, determination, the set of his muscles, the clench of his jaw. A woman carries her power deep within. The planning, the calculated risks, the determination."

Okay, so it was apparently one of those speeches. Gender stuff.

Appropriate, because I was now an expert on both sexes. The first of my kind. Cool.

Oh. I had more to say.

"Men are like a forest fire. Fast and destructive on a wide scale. Women are like a kiln. Extreme heat burning deep within. Constructive heat." I held up one hand. *"Man the destroyer."* I held up the other hand. *"Woman the creator. They are the yin and yang. Balance without equality. The two great powers of existence. Opposed, yet united."*

I kept it going. It was good to know everything. The crowd was really eating it up. Pearls of wisdom from a real-life multi-mind— someone who'd been both man and woman.

Yes, except my wisdom was a load of hot air. My manhood had been cut short, and I knew virtually nothing about being a woman. But I kept up the act because I was afraid the crowd would stone me to death if they found out the truth.

"Death follows the truthsayer. But a good lie keeps everyone happy."

Freudian slip? Yes, but I kept the words flowing. I stood tall before the crowd. One half-baked crumb of wisdom followed another. Besides, it's not what you know that counts. It's how impressive you look when you say it.

So the first half of the dream was a combination of being full of myself, and worrying they'd find out I was a fake.

That's when some little kid peeked up my toga and screamed bloody murder. I wasn't an omni-sex. I had, like, gender specific gear under my toga skirt.

Bummer.

So the crowd started picking up stones and I ran like hell down the dusty orange mountain. They pelted me with rocks, but since it was a dream, the rocks kinda bounced off. But then I tripped and started tumbling down the mountain.

When I finally reached the bottom, I stood up and saw a spaceship. Naturally, I ran for it and started pounding on the gleaming metal doors, but they wouldn't open.

The mob was getting closer. I could tell the end was near because they were all carrying one very large boulder, ant-style.

I pounded on the stainless steel spaceship doors and screamed for all I was worth.

Unfortunately, the acolyte mob tossed the giant boulder at me and I was crushed against the side of the spaceship.

I dribbled down the shiny silver doors—multi-mind mash.

* * *

"What are you doing?"

I looked up from the bottom of the elevator to see Sonya. She looked kinda sexy from below. Apparently I'd been sleepwalking, then I'd pounded on the elevator doors. Finally I'd fallen in when the doors opened.

"Doing? Not much." I picked myself up. "Exercising."

"In your sleep?"

"No. Or, you know, maybe."

"We need you in Gettysburg. Do you feel up to flying a mission?"

"Sure."

"Do you even know where that is?"

"Gettysburg? Sure. It's where they had the Civil War."

"That's what I thought. And where are you now?"

"Underground. Austin?"

"Not even close. Let's get you some coffee, and some flight clothes. We need you to airlift some survivors from one of Jack's dungeons."

"Cool."

"And for heaven's sake, let Kat do the flying."

* * *

I peed using Kat's equipment for the first time, and the less said about that the better. But it was perfectly natural, and perfectly weird. Then Sonya helped me get dressed for flying a helicopter. She also explained that Gettysburg was in Southern Pennsylvania (who knew?) and that we were in a bunker near D.C., which wasn't that far from Gettysburg.

Strange that she knew more about U.S. history than I did.

Winters in Canada must be rough—nothing to do but watch ice hockey and study their warm cousins to the south with envious eyes. Or maybe they had ulterior motives for watching us?

No. I was just having a touch of paranoia. Canadians probably weren't watching us with cold calculating eyes. Frosty fur-lined eyes. And they had no plans for condos in Florida or liberating Texas from the clutches of the local oil and cattle barons.

Right. I was probably just massively nervous about flying a chopper. Hell, I'd never even seen one up close.

A long elevator ride took us to a helicopter pad at the top of a large building. Sonya led me up to a big red news helicopter, which was tied down to its landing pad.

It was windy, and I was surprised to see that it was midday. I was still extremely confused. And I was feeling totally overwhelmed standing next to the big red helo beast. There was no way I could do this. I turned to Sonya. "Now what?"

"Here." She pushed a clipboard into my hands. "Exact coordinates, your general flight plan, and a backup plan if you wind up in deep shit."

"I'll need an earpiece."

"You've got perfectly good communications gear in your helicopter."

Right. "Good to know. You're coming with me, right?"

"Sorry. Maybe next time." She pointed at the helicopter. "It's your baby to fly."

I thought she was going to add, "So get it right, or die." But she didn't. Instead, she gave me another world class kiss and the windy rooftop spun out of existence.

"Always know that I love you, Wolf. But no matter what happens, let Kat handle the flying. Now get your perky little bottom in the air and save some people."

My perky little what?

Sonya turned, walked quickly away, and descended down some stairs.

As I watched her sexy butt walk away, I was pleased that Kat's female hormones weren't completely spoiling the view.

Okay, now what? Just me standing all alone on a windy

downtown rooftop with a big red helo. Sure, but I was never really alone. I had copilots out the wazoo.

So how hard could this be? I'd let Wolf ride a motorcycle. I'd let him swim laps. I'd even let him handle one of Jack's men when I'd first encountered Peter in Wolf's place. Peter and the Wolf. Interesting.

I was stalling.

Where was Kat when I needed her?

Wolf was a force in my head, so he just naturally took over the controls when needed. Kat was a lot more reserved. But Kat was Outback tough, right? All I had to do was coax her out.

Here, kitty, kitty.

I sensed movement in my mental back seat. She didn't like being called kitty.

Okay, Kat. Time to come out and join the team. We've got a helo to fly and people to save.

Kat seemed to push her way slowly through the rough characters in my head. She was moving closer to the front. The rats in my brain sneered at her, said she was only a girl and this was a man's brain.

Which was kinda funny because it was actually her brain today. Face facts, guys. We were just a pack of bodiless losers, borrowing her brain, her hormones, her female bod.

I grabbed Wolf's virtual leash, held him firmly, and we slipped into the shotgun seat. The mental driver's seat was open. I kept the guys at bay, while Kat slipped quietly and confidently in.

The guys were pissed, but I told them to shut the fuck up. Kat's body. Kat's helo. Kat's skills. Relax and get a lesson in flying, boys. Pops put in a request for popcorn with extra butter, and the mood lightened up.

Wolf and I slid all the way into the mental back seat, then we all watched as Kat flipped through the clipboard and started to prep the chopper. She walked around the helo checking this and that. Opened a panel. Closed it. Then settled into her seat.

So very cool.

I was tempted to ask stupid questions, like why was she flying from the passenger side on the right, and did we have enough fuel, and did she know how to get there—but I held my virtual tongue. The less I interfered, the more likely we were to survive this mission.

Finally, the boring bits were over and Kat started the turbine engines. Or maybe it was just one engine—I was afraid to ask. She monitored the gages while the engine warmed up. I was hoping she'd get on the comms with Peter, but she seemed to have it all under control.

She needed both hands and both feet. Apparently, flying a helicopter was a full-body skill. Who knew?

This was it. She glanced left and right and we were suddenly in the air. She spun us around as she adjusted for the wind, then we tilted forward to gain some lateral speed.

As the tall building slid out from under us, I panicked for a second. But I quickly had the feeling that Kat's skills might even exceed Wolf's.

Bunker Central, this is Jumper Helo One—we are airborne.

Awesome!

* * *

I spent the next hour enjoying the view. I also learned chopper pilots can scratch their nose if needed, without crashing.

So glad I wasn't doing the flying.

Then we got word that things were fluid on the ground near Gettysburg, meaning unpredictable in a not-good kind of way. I learned that my Billy Bob self was leading the ground team in the rescue op, but that we could expect delays.

Fine. All systems were jumper-typical. Nothing as planned.

Fifteen minutes later, Kat set the chopper down in a secluded spot in some farmland between two low hills. She cut the engine, unbuckled, and stepped outside.

Fine. Good to stretch our legs. But I wondered how long we'd be waiting.

Right about then, Kat got the urge to pee, so she headed to a tree. Then she unzipped. It was like she had it all wrong. Only guys unzipped and headed to a tree. Kat had become seriously messed up—gender confused.

That's when she put her back to the tree and squatted.

Okay, fine. She could do it her way.

Note to self: Cut Kat some slack. She might not communicate much, but she knows what she's doing.

So she peed like she wanted. No big deal.

I looked around, spotted a cow watching us from a nearby hill. I looked up at the sky. Basically, I did whatever guys do when they're trying not to be embarrassed by their dates.

Woman stuff. Best to look away.

On the way back to the helo, I had an argument with the guys about how much we needed to know about being a woman. I was beginning to think this was a golden opportunity to understand the opposite sex. Most of my guys thought Kat could take care of herself—except in bed, then they'd take care of her.

I thought that was really shallow of them. They said shallow was good. After all, their bodies were long gone. When in Rome, enjoy the nearest female as nature intended.

They were pathetic. I was pathetic too, because I was seriously tempted to enjoy my unnatural position inside Kat.

Kat gave me a concerned look. I shrugged like I was just kidding.

Okay, we were establishing our relationship. A typical combination of caution and confusion. Kinda like dating, only a little bit weirder.

Forty minutes sitting in the chopper, listening to static. Yawn. Then we heard an explosion in the distance. We watched as smoke and dust drifted slowly up over a hill to the south. Still no radio chatter.

Finally, Peter said to move in to our original destination and extract two men.

Just two? Must have been messy.

Kat warmed up the engine and we were off. Except now, she was flying like we were in combat conditions—low and fast. Up over a hill, then down, then up over another hill. A roller coaster ride but without the rails. In our big red helicopter, we were like Action

News from Channel Hell, riding under spinning blades of death. Nothing on earth could stop us.

Kat told me to can it.

Right. More brains for her. Less for me.

Another hill later, we spotted two men standing in an open field. One looked exactly like Billy Bob. The other was big, brawny, and bare-chested, wearing only a plaid skirt. Kat's female instincts were clearly interested.

As we touched down, the big Scot came running towards us, howling like we were bloody English daring to tread on his sacred Scottish Highlands.

And I thought we needed to get the hell out of there because the giant Scot was definitely going to kill us and crush our pretty red chopper.

But Kat stayed calm. The big guy opened a back door and roared, "Hello, you fine young lady. Ne'er have I been more happy to see such a fine red flyin' machine. The name's Bruce the Black, but you can call me The Black, if you've a mind." He stuck a big hand out the door and pointed. "And yonder, that round fellow a huffin' his way through the glen, tis my new friend." The Black leaned forward and said under his breath, "He's a twitcher with a wanderin' face, if you know what I mean. But pay it no mind."

That's when other-me, in Billy Bob's body, came running up to the helicopter, breathing hard. He fumbled his way into the rear seat next to the over-sized character calling himself The Black.

As they buckled up, it was hard to believe Billy Bob was now being controlled by other-me. But we were now brothers in arms, flying together—with a crazy bigger-than-life Scotsman.

I was tempted to tell them to slide the back doors closed, but Kat seemed okay with it. She throttled up quickly and we took off like a bat from the gates of hell, keeping it ultra low, and scaring the ever-loving dung out of startled cows.

Five minutes later, we gained some altitude. Unfortunately, that's when the Scot decided to unbuckle himself and hang out the door. I thought he might jump, but Kat seemed to pick up on his love of flying, so she started banking the helo to amp up his thrill.

At one point, we circled some horses at a steep angle so the big guy could get a great view.

About 30 minutes into the flight, other-me started to thrash around in his seat. It looked like he was asleep. Not good. Other-me was having serious problems while sleeping.

Bruce the Black reached over and tightened other-me's harness. "Don't you worry none." The Black was shouting to Kat against the wind and engine noise. "Like I said, he's a twitcher. But I'll let no harm come to him. Not by the breath and fire within me." He pointed to the east. "Oh, let's head into that cloud. We could have a bit o' fun in that one."

I could see he was indicating a nasty looking anvil cloud ahead. Lightning flashed up and down its core. Kat shook her head. End of subject.

"Ah, well. Next time, then." The Black went back to hanging out the open door, wind in his hair.

* * *

When we landed at an airport, it was completely unexpected. How could Kat know where we were going and I didn't?

As the blades slowed, a limo pulled up closer and a redheaded female flight attendant got out and walked over to The Black. "You made good time, love."

He smiled. "Aye. And I'm thinkin' your new hair color suits you just fine."

She gave him a brief, but interested kiss. "Glad you're still wearing your same fine self."

The Black started unbuckling other-me.

I might have felt a little protective about my twin. "Where are you taking him?"

The redhead gave me a curt smile. "I've arranged to borrow him for a day or so. You'll have him back soon enough." She walked back to the limo and held the door open.

The Black picked up Billy Bob who was still in dream land, adjusted him on his broad shoulder, then turned to me. "A pleasure, fair lady. If you're ever across the pond, ask for me. I'd love nothin' more than to show you a grand time. And to fly you around as only I can."

Huh?

He took Kat's hand and kissed it, then turned and walked to the limo and waved. "Til we meet again!"

He put Billy Bob into the limo like he was used to slinging around big animals. They drove a short distance to a waiting private jet, while Kat revved up the blades.

Wait. Kat wore gloves when she flew, but she took them off to have her hand kissed? How'd she know The Black was going to do that?

I would have pushed the issue, but we lifted off and I didn't want to distract her from flying.

Apparently she thought the big Scot was charming. As far as I was concerned, he was just some big weird guy wearing nothing but a plaid dress.

The nearly naked Scot had to have been a major distraction for Kat. But she indicated that was never a problem with her. She always focused on flying.

I wasn't so sure about that. But we didn't crash and no one got hooked on a helo skid, so I relaxed and decided Kat could handle herself around nearly naked hunks. Personally, I was inclined to have trouble driving my taxi at night when picking up nearly naked women.

We all agreed it was a guy thing.

* * *

Back in the secret bunker, I spent the rest of the day sidelined. It felt like I was grounded, but they reassured me they just didn't need a helo pilot in the northeast. Anyway, most of the action was on the west coast and it was ground-based with little need for air support.

I learned that San Francisco was turning into a bloodbath—our normals holding down the city, while Jack pounded us with every available team in an effort to take back control. Doc even surfaced there to lead an assault, then seemed to vanish.

San Francisco was famous for its oddball sex. But Sonya said it was probably the most ethnically mixed city in North America—maybe the world. Many of our normals in the field were local Chinese, Filipinos, Vietnamese, and even Russians.

More weird than that, I learned we had a squad of five jumpers from Cambodia on our side—all discovered in the late 1970s genocide that swept the country. Cambodian jumpers who'd survived their own country's killing fields were now fighting to keep Jack out of San Francisco? Great. Everything unimaginable was happening.

So why wasn't I there? Was it because I was now a woman? Or was it because I was Sonya's cute little Wolfette?

I tried asking, but Peter was glued to his command center and Sonya was busy elsewhere, presumably doing something important. The only answer I got was that I was needed here.

Why? To do what? Get used to being female? I had that down pat already. Except for a dozen guys in the bunker that insisted on chasing my tail. That was super annoying. So I dressed butch in my flight gear, avoided eye contact, and developed a chip on my shoulder.

That's when I attracted the attention of a girl. Black hair, red streak, with an awkward mix of steam punk and mosh pit.

"Hey."

I turned around, decided she was looking for trouble, and went back to my search for an unflavored coffee module.

"Whatcha looking for?"

"Coffee. Black."

"Unadulterated?"

I glanced over my shoulder, sensing she was flirting or about to start a fight. Some people like to combine the two.

So I kept searching drawers and cupboards while she watched my back. Annoying, but I was determined to find some plain coffee.

"I got some."

I turned just as she tossed me a single-serve cup. I flipped it over. Dark roast. Cool.

"You're Kat." Her head nodded over and over like meeting me was a big deal.

I knew who I was. And yes, I was a big deal. So I stuck the coffee into the machine and pushed buttons, hoping she'd go away.

"I'm Zelda."

I watched the machine carefully as it thought about my coffee. I was determined not to encourage the mosh pit girl with more eye contact. "Thanks, Zelda."

"Not many people go for straight-up black, so I snag 'em whenever I find 'em in the combo packs."

It was pretty obvious I couldn't avoid this conversation, so I turned to face her. Or maybe I turned around because I was worried she was checking out my cute Kat butt. "Smart thinking."

"I also have light roast—if you're looking for something on the wild side."

"Yeah?" Was that a come-on line?

"Kinda late in the day for a caffeine hit. But I get it—there's no real day down here." She paused, still searching for a way to connect with me. "I run ops, you know, with Peter."

"I noticed."

"I've handled you. Personally." She paused, expecting me to flirt back. "When you were Wolf."

"I'm still Wolf—in Kat's clothing."

"Righteous. Two aces up your sleeve."

Okay. I decided to check on how the coffee was going.

"So what's it feel like to be twinned?"

I shrugged. "Feels like a jump."

"But you're brothered-up now. That's gotta be weird."

"Yeah, it's . . . interesting."

"Brenda took your twin to Vegas, you know. They were going to San Francisco first, but they blew it off and went straight to Vegas. You know, for some hot action."

I turned around quickly. Hot-tub Brenda? The Brit who beamed out when Wolf was killed? Why would she want to party with other-me in the body of Billy Bob? Not exactly a sexy escort for Vegas clubbing. I steadied my voice. "For some fun?"

"You could say that." I waited for an explanation, so Zelda continued. "Brenda's got a list—a hit list. The Europeans loaned us Bruce the Black last month. And now we've loaned 'em your twin. We barter skull skippers from time to time."

"Skull skippers? I call them jumpers."

"You're cute that way. But you're no shade. Bruce the Black's a shade. Your twin knows all about shades by now. Do you?"

I'd asked around about the big freak in the kilt. "I've heard about them."

"Someday I'm going to touch him and body swap. Then I'm going to fuck my own brains out."

"Yeah?" That sounded totally weird, but cool.

"It's on my bucket list."

"Awesome."

"You know what else is on my bucket list?" She moved closer.

I suddenly had the feeling Nameless was seriously turned on. Just great. The last thing I needed. New subject. "So what's my twin doing now?"

"Well . . . he's started killing people on Brenda's list, of course." She said that like it was sexy. "They have it coming."

"What if one of them is a jumper?"

"Then your twin is screwed. Field work has its risks. Even Bruce the Black was captured, but lucky for us Jack only used him as bait to bag your twin." She cocked her head. "You've been a better asset than The Black." She leaned a hair closer. "You know that makes you kinda hot."

"I'm with Sonya."

"She's been known to share. Besides she's busy. Making allies. Working deals. Pulling in assets. You know?" She moved closer, backing me up against the counter. "You're new to being a woman, Wolfie. We both know you'll need constant supervision. Hands-on training." She licked her lips, her hips leaned so close to mine.

The coffee machine climaxed with a beep. She ignored it.

Our hips barely touched and Nameless shot out of his skin with ecstasy. And Nameless didn't even have skin.

Something on her belt vibrated us. "Aw, crap. There's shit on aisle four. Gotta go. Let me know if you need something hotter than coffee, Wolfie-Kat. I have steam powered accessories that would curl your hair."

Zelda gave me a knowing wink and walked away. But she did slap her ass for emphasis.

* * *

Later that night I went down to Sonya's apartment. Alone again. What was the point of bunking with my babe when she was never around?

I found a frozen meal in her fridge, microwaved it, and mulled my sorry fate while I absentmindedly ate whatever it was. Then I gave Kat her first shower.

Stripping was easy as long as I avoided gawking in the mirror. And the hot water felt relaxing. But the soap—that was just asking for weirdness. I tried focusing on Sonya as I soaped Kat, but that really made my head spin. Nameless wanted to imagine soaping Zelda. Martoni wasn't picky. Pops just closed his eyes and thought we were all too weird for words—but we were a hoot.

About the best I could do was focus on Billy Bob on a killing spree in Vegas.

As for Kat, she just seemed to enjoy my mental agony. I was a pack of horny guys bumping around in total confusion, trying not to violate her personal boundaries. But she also seemed to say this was our body, too. Kat knew what she was getting into. Communal showers? No big deal. Just part of her new life with the boys.

Okay, so messing around with Kat in the shower was fun. But we all looked forward to real sex with Sonya. Except Nameless, who wanted dangerous sex with Zelda. And except for Kat, who thought it would be good for us to find a real man like Wolf.

Sorry, Kat. Not feeling it.

While we were in there, I shaved my legs. And my underarms. I was tempted to shave my arms, but they were still looking good.

Basically, nothing was resolved in the shower. I was still one big horny mess. And personally, I really needed Sonya to fix the problem.

Finally the lights were out. We were all tucked in, alone together in Sonya's big bed. A mind full of opinions made it hard to sleep. And the sound of Canadian nights being piped in sure didn't help. It sounded like loons on a lake, and wolf howls.

Did Sonya have a thing for Wolf howls?

* * *

The next morning I wandered up to the cafeteria for the big breakfast that Martoni craved. I settled for a fruit cup, nonfat yogurt, tofu sausage, and eggs sunny side removed.

Hey, I was watching my weight. And besides, there was just no pleasing everyone.

I sat down at an empty table and started with the egg whites and coffee. Finding a table for one was easy. For some reason, not many people were doing breakfast this morning. Or maybe morning was over?

That's when a woman I'd never noticed before ran in and shouted from halfway across the room. "Kat! You're needed in CAC."

"Okay. I'll be there in a minute."

"Now! Sonya said now!"

Sonya? I got up, chugged my coffee, and walked to the exit.

"Run! Run!" She was practically pushing me down the hall.

"Why?"

"Jack found you! He's—" She gulped for air. "Just run!"

I ran. First time as a woman. It was seriously different. I didn't know whether to hold my chest or not.

As I ran into the command and control room, it was like a shit storm of yelling. Peter and Zelda were barking orders to people in the field. Sonya waved me over to her couch.

On the screen I saw clips from traffic cams. Two motorcycles were racing through downtown traffic. Hell, it was Austin.

Some of the frame grabs were enlarged, trying to identify faces. It looked like there was a young woman in front on a racing bike, followed by a rough looking biker on a big black and red Harley. Him in a kilt and an oversized white buccaneer's shirt.

Shit. She was in trouble.

Sonya grabbed me and pointed my face to a screen with date and time markings like from a red light cam. It was wonderful to be in Sonya's no-nonsense arms again.

"Who is that?" She sounded alarmed.

Who? A young woman. A woman I instantly recognized, then dismissed as impossible.

"Wolf, do you know her?"

No! Not her. "It looks like Marie, but it couldn't be."

"Marie who?"

"Marie Turner." Marie, my old girlfriend. I turned back to the live action on the traffic cams. "But Marie can't ride like that. No way it's her." Hell, the woman I was watching was insane. Swerving through traffic and dodging cars as she held the throttle wide open through red lights.

Peter's voice shot out of the roar. "Got her. Marie Lucia Turner. Get me bio—stat!"

I turned to Sonya. "We've got to save her."

"It's not what you think. That's your twin on the other motor-cycle."

"That's me?" He looked nothing like Billy Bob. So he must have jumped into a biker in a kilt.

"That's your twin. And the one in front, being chased, that's really Jack. Peter's almost certain it's him. And he's now in that woman."

I might have screamed. Heads turned. Yes, I wasn't holding it back. I screamed again.

"Sit." Sonya pushed me down onto the couch. "Who's Marie? How do you know her?"

"She's—" Jack was in Marie! "She's my girlfriend. *Was* my girlfriend, until I jumped."

Sonya held me even tighter. "Oh, God."

We watched in horror as the other-me biker skidded into a parked car, then continued the pursuit. Jack-Marie made it to the freeway. Then it was a flat out chase along the shoulder next to the fast lane—basically a straight shot north. The Harley was no match for the hot racing bike. The gap widened rapidly.

Jack sped north as other-me the biker gave up the chase.

Marie was dead—for all practical purposes. That fucker, Jack, had found me—found out I was Marko. "How? How did this happen?"

"Peter had a tracker hidden in the Harley. We did that because there was a chance Jack would figure out the jump into Billy Bob, and maybe he'd figure out your twin's jumps in Las Vegas. He has a way of finding you. Maybe there's a spy in the resistance. We've been searching for a mole."

Peter's voice shot out again. "People! I need eyes! Get me eyes in Waco. Whatever's on the fucking map north of Austin. Don't let that fucking bastard get away again!"

My twin had failed. The chase was over. Jack was gone. Marie was his latest victim.

"Wolf, we need your help." Sonya pointed at a screen on her coffee table. "Who lives there? Does Marie live there?"

It was a satellite image of a house. Marie lived in an apartment. "No." But there was something familiar about the front yard. I'd been there several times. "It's Rema's house. Why are we looking at it?" Oh, shit. Everything was unraveling.

"We tracked your twin to that house. We didn't think much of it. Registered to a Rema Louise Mayfield. She's listed as the owner of several daycares. We thought you might have been one of her students—in a previous incarnation. Or maybe just a friend. Your twin went straight to that house. Why?"

Rema was kinda my sidekick. No wonder my twin went there. "Rema's just a friend. Marie works for her."

"Jack figured out your past. How?"

I had no idea. "Rema's in danger. She might be dead."

"Understood. I'll escalate her on the list."

"List? She could be dying. Maybe dead."

"We're putting most of our resources into finding Jack. Marie's family is probably the most at risk, especially if Jack wants to stay in Marie for a while."

My thoughts churned. Jack was in Marie. He targeted her. "That makes perfect sense. Jack would keep Marie, just to screw with me. Marie's family lives in Houston. Uh . . ." My head was still spinning. "They live at, uh . . ."

"Relax, Wolf. We've already got it."

"Really?"

"Peter yells for Marie's bio—Peter gets Marie's bio. Rema's got help on the way, too. I see your twin has turned around. What'll he do next?"

What would I do? I'd kill everyone in sight just to get my hands on Jack. But Jack was long gone. "I'd get on the phone and start warning people."

"He's off comms with us and I doubt he has a mobile phone. What would he do?"

"He'd go to Rema's. To help her, and use her phone."

"Good. Then it's a race to Rema's between our team and Dread."

"Dread?"

"It's a biker name. And a good one, since you're twin is probably massively pissed."

An understatement. He'd be more than massively pissed. "Not just pissed. He'll kill anyone who gets in his way."

"Let's hope he's selective."

* * *

Several minutes later, the blip on the map showed that Dread-me was pulling up to Rema's house.

"Don't we have a picture? Sound?"

Sonya changed one of the screens to show an aerial view of rooftops whizzing by. "We dispatched a drone. It's almost there. Then we'll have a live picture, but still no sound."

Good. But sitting there was agony. "We should call her."

"They already tried that. Her cell phone isn't responding and Peter thinks her land line was cut."

Zelda's fist shot into the air. "Got him!"

A cheer went up.

I turned to Sonya. "Got who?"

"Jack."

"We captured him?"

Sonya was reading details from her monitors. "No. We just have him spotted."

Crap. "We need him in a bag."

"Actually, that's exactly what we plan to do with him."

Cool. Wolf wanted it to be a punching bag.

I pointed at a monitor. "Look." The drone had arrived and found a covert position, sitting on someone's roof with a clear view to Rema's. There was no one in sight, but the Harley was parked at the curb and an odd panel van was parked in her driveway. "Who's van is that?"

"I don't know. Plumbers?" Sonya spoke into her headset mic. "Can we get a view around the house?"

The drone perked up and swung around to the back of Rema's house. It looked like the back door had broken glass. My twin had gone in.

"Isn't there anything we can do?"

"We're running plates on the plumbing van. So far nothing. The drone's not equipped to intercede with force, but our team's getting close. ETA about four minutes."

The minutes seemed like hours.

People were starting to gather in the street in front of the house. Maybe attracted by the drone? Maybe attracted by the sound of violence going on inside?

Finally one of the men ran to Rema's front door and started pounding on it. Not a good sign. He was quickly joined by more men, one had a baseball bat and another had a hunting rifle. A few seconds later someone ran out the back door, hopped a fence, ran through the neighbor's yard, then hustled down the street.

Sonya and I looked at each other. One of Jack's men? Or other-me in a new body?

Now what? We only had one drone.

Sonya got some news from her headset. "Jack's headed for an airport, but that's good because we can easily follow him on radar."

"He could parachute out."

"Knowing Peter's team, they've already thought of that and found a solution."

"Jack could stick a kill chip in Marie and beam out of the plane."

"Marie is certainly chipped by now. Jack always chips early. But he'd rather not use it. We both know he has a strong interest in staying in Marie."

"Right." All the better to screw with me.

"Wait. I'm just catching up with the stream of info. Police and ambulance are rolling to Rema's. Multiple 911 calls—they're still coming in. Shots were fired. Police are calling in extra units."

We watched as the front door finally opened and a group of men rushed in. Whatever had happened at Rema's, we were too late. Sonya ordered our team to keep some distance when they arrived, but observe with live video. And she ordered the drone to follow the guy who fled before we lost him.

Drone photos of the guy fleeing on foot were good enough, but didn't help. Just some athletic black man in glasses. Not a match for anyone in Peter's hacked Texas or federal databases. So Peter widened the database search to other states and dispatched a pizza car to intercept. Pizza car? Well, it seemed like they were really desperate to find out if that was other-me or not.

"Oh, damn." Sonya held up a hand and she listened to her headset. Why didn't I have one? "Our team at Rema's reports ambulances are now picking up Doc and . . . another guy known to be one of Doc's associates. Both on stretchers. Both apparently unconscious." A cheer went up. "EMS chatter says Rema is alive and refusing medical help for cuts and possible broken bones."

That was the best part. "That's my Rema."

Sonya looked at me.

"No one messes with Rema. Hell, EMS should just call it a day and leave her alone, otherwise they'll be making their own EMS call."

"More police have been dispatched. And forensics. But here's the good news. One man dead. White male. Gunshot wounds. No details yet."

"Other-me? Dead?" How was that good?

Sonya nodded. "Probably Dread the biker. We can't be sure it's your twin yet, but it looks like you might have made another jump. I mean your twin, of course."

Right. Good news for other-me.

It was decided that our team on the ground should go after Doc in the ambulance and leave Rema for a later pickup.

We kept the drone on the guy who might be other-me as long as we could. But twenty minutes later, the drone's battery was exhausted so we parked it on a downtown rooftop for night pickup.

Who knew drones could airlift other drones?

"Sorry, Wolf. Zelda just figured out your connection with Marie—the original you, your name, everything."

Damn. "Not good. I was hoping to just be Wolf."

"You're still Wolf. As long as you want to be. We also know you were originally killed by Hugo Martoni. But he disappeared. Then you popped up in some unknown guy who was killed by Wolf. So now we know what Jack had already figured out."

"We need to protect my family—starting with my mother."

"Yes, and we'll soon have her packing her bags to go into hiding."

"Good, but then she'll know I'm a jumper."

"No. We've done this before. Extraction teams have a big list of convincing cover stories they can use. Chances are, she won't even think her relocation is about you."

That was good to hear. But I really hated losing my secret roots.

Five minutes later and the pizza agent had an intercept.

Sonya reached out for my hand. "Sorry to do this to you, but I'm going to need some time working with your twin. How about finishing your breakfast?"

What could I say? I wasn't needed, but other-me was. As I got up and walked away, I kinda wished other-me would die. Not a good thought, but I had a selfish streak I couldn't deny. Basically, I wanted Sonya all to myself, even if that was unrealistic. Other-me was now the hero. I was just a spare part. Pretty to look at. Pretty to hold. But if you dare use me, consider yourself scold-ed.

I couldn't even come up with a halfway decent rhyme. Martoni thought I needed bacon.

None of my passengers liked me then. Who wanted to be driven around by someone who felt lost and unneeded?

* * *

Later that evening, other-me arrived on a bus in an orange prisoner suit. I heard the Tanya twins had given him a great ride. I hoped they'd used their cattle prods.

I might have been feeling down—in the mood to mope. After all, other-me was the unstoppable hero. He'd just saved just about everybody. He and Rema had faced off against bloodthirsty Doc, and turned him and his crew into intensive care cases and morgue meat.

Zelda thought I needed cheering up so she gave me a bobblehead Spock doll from her oddities collection. She was a very odd girl. I stuffed it into my flight jacket determined to stay in my foul mood.

When life sucked on the *Enterprise*, no one went to Spock for a hug. No. Uhura was built for hugging. Spock was just Spock. I finally decided Zelda would have given me an Uhura doll if she had one. Or maybe she wanted to get rid of Spock because he was cold logic and Zelda was hot . . . hot something.

Nameless wanted to fill in the blank, but I repressed him.

Repressed. My new favorite word. Mainly, I wanted to repress other-me into a box—preferably a freezer. Or maybe the freezer was Wolf's idea.

Who knew where my ideas came from anymore?

That's when I accidentally bumped into some woman in the hall and noticed how good that felt.

Yes, it totally did. So maybe I just needed a hug—Sonya style. Sonya was ideal for hugging. Zelda might do in a pinch. Lately, there were lots of guys who wanted to give me a hug, but not like I wanted.

Guys had such a one-track mind.

Around dinner time I got hungry and wandered over to the cafeteria. But across the room I could see Sonya, Zelda, and Peter eating with other-me.

Other-me was medium black and solidly athletic. He wore thick glasses and the same scruffy orange jumpsuit. Mainly, he was undeniably male and a real hero. He probably had lots of good stories. Stories about saving people and almost catching Jack.

So I cut into the buffet line just long enough to grab a couple slices of pizza. Then I headed to the break room to reheat it in the microwave and find something to drink in the fridge.

On the way, people in the hallway were saying we'd really captured Jack. Hard to believe, but everyone said it was real.

I was hoping the break room would be empty, but no such luck.

Two of Peter's crew were sitting on the couch. They congratulated me on having such a cool twin, and how he wasn't through being a hero.

I shoved my pizza into the microwave while they said other-me was going to end Jack in the morning. But they got quiet and left after they accidentally said it would be the true death.

So my twin would really die in the morning? Hey, that was good news. Right? Except I could barely swallow my nuked pizza. I felt just awful about wishing other-me would die.

That night they let other-me use Kat's room. They said he needed special treatment at night. Special, like bondage and babes.

Rumor had it that Zelda had volunteered to hold other-me's hand while he slept. Fortunately it wasn't Sonya. It seemed that Sonya was unavailable for anyone, busy with her other secret projects. Secret? Secret like who? I was sure she had other guys on the side. Dangerous guys. Guys who were out in the field on secret ops and did hero stuff. Handsome guys. Guys with extra muscle and stealthy sinew. Guys who made a difference in the world. Guys like I used to be.

Okay. Enough self-pity. So I wasn't other-me. And when other-me died, I'd be only-me. Then it would be Sonya and only-me. But hey, I was still the best me I could be. I was still hero material. And I had a solid future with Sonya—gender confused, but solid.

So it was all good. Just Sonya and me.

Yeah, right up until she decided to martyr me, too.

5.7 Undead Unforever

My vivid dream that night was actually good. A cabana on a white sandy beach. Crystal clear turquoise water. No sharks. And whenever my drink was low or I needed a towel, handsome cabana boys would appear out of nowhere, then disappear without a word. I was probably female, but somehow that didn't bother me.

The only parts that seemed odd were the tropical islands that slowly drifted by like other unreachable worlds, and the giant pale moons in the sky. Other realities I'd never experience.

For company, there were a few birds that seemed to think we were friends. One was a pretty white cockatoo that nodded her head a lot. Another one was an annoying green parrot that jabbered constantly in a language I didn't understand—a lot like Peter, if he were green.

All very strange, but also very relaxing.

Was I getting comfortable with life in the weird lane?

* * *

They didn't tell me the plan that morning, except that it was time to fly Sonya and other-me out to wherever Jack was being held.

Kat walked around the big red helicopter parked on the rooftop. She opened hatches and checked this and that. And just like when Wolf swam or rode a motorcycle, I knew better than to focus too much on what was happening. Flying a helo was seriously out of my league.

So while Kat did her thing, I wondered if other-me really would kill Jack. Not a good thought. This morning I was back to kinda liking other-me, even if I was still jealous of the guy. If today was really going down as a martyr-murder, then other-me would die, right along with Jack.

Time to think about something else.

Maryland was cool in the early morning and the secret bunker building wasn't too far from Chesapeake Bay. The sun had just come up, but was still parked behind some thick clouds to the east. I was in a light windbreaker jacket with khaki shirt and pants— Kat's preferred flight suit. Lots of pockets, especially in the pant legs. Kat liked squirreling away things in those pockets, like a serious folding knife, two small flashlights, a few fiber bars, and similar gear.

In the cockpit, we checked switches, voltage, fuel, and assorted flight controls. The forecast was for partly cloudy, good visibility, and a light breeze from the southeast. Good flying weather.

Kat stowed bottled water, some maps, and paperwork, then pulled out a bobblehead hula doll that she kept in the helo. I gathered she used it when she wanted to lighten the mood. So I reached into the jacket pocket and pulled out the bobblehead Spock doll that Zelda had given me.

Perfect. We each had our good-luck totems.

But then Kat pulled the grass skirt off her hula girl and put it on my Spock doll. Weird, but I had the impression Kat wanted us to work together. That really caught me by surprise. All my other passengers gave me a hard time. Sometimes they seemed to hate me, treat me like a fool, and even dis me like I was nothing more than a brain leech—which, I kinda was.

But not Kat. She seemed to like me, she wanted to cooperate with me, and she actually wanted to be on the same team with me.

All my other passengers had killed me, intentionally or unintentionally. From Martoni to Pops, they were all hardened men, each in their own way. But not Kat. Sure, you could argue that she'd killed me when I was twinned. But it felt more like she had offered to share her life—what there was left of it, and her awesome skills.

Basically, it felt like she was a willing partner.

That really put a lump in my throat. For the first time, I actually had a willing friend in my head. Who knew the only woman in me would be my only real friend?

Kat got a signal from her headset and began the engine start sequence. The electric whine of the starter motor gave way to the sound of the turbine engine taking over. We watched some temp and pressure gages as the blades spun up.

We were duct taping hula-Spock to the top of the dashboard when I saw Sonya and other-me walk up the final stairs to the helo pad.

A moment later, they walked over, bracing against the strong wind the blades were making.

I was going to get out and open the cabin door for Sonya, but Kat indicated otherwise. Sonya got herself and other-me seated in the back with no problems. Okay, Sonya knew the flight rules for passengers. She was a frequent flyer.

Kat was still busy prepping for the flight and I wanted to check out other-me to see how he was doing. But since I had to share a set of eyes with Kat, I wound up just getting glances at him.

I knew he was now in some guy called Samson. But names were as transient as skins. It was the stuff on the inside that counted, but it was hard to see beyond the physical shell.

Sad to think I'd never get the chance to really talk with my twin—or get to know him. But maybe I knew him perfectly, except for our latest bodies and passengers. I thought we might enjoy comparing notes. If we ever got the chance.

When we were ready to go, Kat glanced back to make sure they were properly belted in and wearing their headphones. That's when other-me said, "Hey," like he'd remembered me from the barn extraction. It felt really good to be transporting my twin again.

And really bad. This might be the last day I'd see him. The last day of his life. Going to see Jack had to be dark and ominous.

I looked at hula-Spock for hope as Kat pulled up on a stick to our left, twisted its handle, and adjusted the foot pedals slightly. We rose into the air. The windows down by my feet confirmed we were putting distance between us and the landing pad.

A touch on the foot petals and we rotated slightly around, then a slight push to the stick between Kat's legs and we tilted forward.

Flying a chopper was a regular juggling act of smooth coordination and balance.

Hula-Spock gave us the nod and we were away.

* * *

It was truly a beautiful morning. But I couldn't stop thinking about Jack getting his. There'd be hell to pay and other-me would be the one to bring it.

Kat's attitude was a real eye-opener. She was more the *God speed* type than the *Eat shit and die* type.

How was that possible? We had the same goal, to see Jack die. But she was focused on other-me and his bravery, and I was focused on Jack's bloody corpse. No wonder men were so confused by women. Women were so similar and shared so many of our goals, but for completely different reasons. Then it dawned on me: there were aliens among us—and we were having sex with them!

But they were having sex with us for completely different reasons!

Maybe not always, but yeah. Women saw the world differently. They added 1 + 3 instead of 2 + 2 and we arrived at the same answer.

Totally different, but not.

So women really were aliens—only really, really similar. Men would be lulled into a false sense of security and then, BAM! Out of the blue they'd think we spent too much time watching sports and not enough time dancing.

Marie could babble on for hours about her feelings on why someone slighted her. If someone dissed me, I'd just shrug and move on. No need to wallow in it.

Or maybe women were just working it out, verbally?

Women added things up differently. They were like alien intelligence, right here, on Earth.

Shocking.

Kat thought I should put a cork in it or we'd fall out of the sky.

Right. Let the chopper pilot do her thing. Keep my weird thoughts to myself. Or maybe women were normal and men were the aliens? It could go either way. Or maybe we were both aliens and dolphins were the native intelligence on this blue planet.

Kat was about ready to fold her arms and let me fly. That amounted to a trump card, so I relaxed and looked around. Kat flew.

Kat thought I was a typical bundle of male confusion. Even sharing a mind and a body with a woman, I'd never really understand what it was to be female.

Okay, sure. She was the expert. But I thought with enough time I could figure them out.

Kat shook her head because it wasn't that complicated. She labeled me as someone who liked to over-think everything.

Maybe. But we all agreed it was a beautiful day to fly.

* * *

About 30 minutes later, we banked to the right and began our descent. It looked like we were approaching an abandoned refinery or chemical plant.

Kat moved the helo in low, slowly circling an abandoned chemical plant. Two rings of barbed wire fence ran completely around it. The plant itself was mostly just a bunch of large upright cylinders clustered together like a dystopian city. No sign of people on the ground. I guess we were starting with a little recon, checking for anything suspicious.

Kat seemed to know exactly where she was going next. We moved closer, rounded a tall rusty cylinder with pipes connecting it to shorter cylinders. Junk and weeds littered the grounds.

Finally we set the skids down on an uncluttered area of cement. I had the feeling Kat had been here many times before. Around us, I saw lots of scrap metal and the usual graffiti. The place looked deserted.

Kat throttled down but kept the blades spinning.

We waited for something. Were we expecting company?

A moment later, someone on the headset said, "Tango Red, you are now cargo-green. I repeat, cargo-green." Kat seemed annoyed by Peter's choice of command signals, but she turned slightly and nodded to Sonya.

Sonya looked at other-me. "Walk with me." Then she opened the door, they both got out, and other-me closed the door.

I gave other-me a nod and a casual two finger salute. Other-me gave me a slight nod, like he was good with this mission.

That kinda touched me—knowing he was brave enough to step into the lion's den and show Jack what perma-death was all about.

His face twitched a bit. Then they turned away, headed to a door on the side of the building.

I instinctively reached for my face to steady it. Strange how alike we were, in spite of being body-opposite.

A minute later they were through the door.

Kat waited with the blades spinning.

I thought again how I wanted other-me to end Jack, but also wanted my twin alive and well so we could share our recent experiences. Maybe plan for the future.

I shrugged it off—just spending too much time in my head.

But Kat thought introspection wasn't a waste of time. Getting your head straight was good. Spinning foolish notions about women was a waste of time. She thought I should just relax and be myself. Women weren't cryptic, and they sure as hell weren't aliens. She thought I should give it time. Let her do the thinking now and then. Understanding would follow.

* * *

We sat in the helo with the blades spinning for several minutes. Time enough to think. Time enough to let Wolf and Kat check each other out some more—compare notes.

Wolf was obviously interested in Kat, but he was kinda strange about showing it. Out of the blue, he indicated he was happy we were getting off the booze. Alcohol simply dumbed you down, slowed your reflexes. We should start hitting the whey protein, even if we were just a puny little female.

That sounded sexist, and Wolf was certainly all about himself and his masculinity. But I also knew he thought Kat was kinda cool—a no-nonsense woman who had mad attack helicopter skills. Wolf didn't know how to fly choppers, so that was a good skill to have on the team. But he especially liked the idea of an *attack* helicopter. Sure, it was a messier kill than he liked, but the thought of agile mass firepower had its appeal.

So, yeah, I could see Wolf and Kat becoming friends in a competitive kind of way, even if they were polar opposites. Wolf liked the clean silent kill, up close, one on one, and totally emotionless. Kat liked to consider the ethics, weigh the emotional consequences, then mow down her enemies in a few seconds of concentrated wrath.

They were shaping up to be a kind of lethal brother and sister act. I could picture a future with lots of bickering and criticizing between them, combined with deep down respect for each other. The yin and yang of death.

Cool.

Good thing I was around to keep us focused—more or less.

Sonya caught my eye as she exited the building and hurried over to the helo. She climbed in the front with me and took my hand.

She looked choked up. No words were spoken.

Other-me would die with Jack and Marie. Or he would take a pass. The future wasn't written.

Sonya released my hand and Kat got us back in the air.

My thoughts bubbled, but I kept a lid on them so Kat could do her job.

A few minutes later, we had our altitude and a steady course. Kat invited me to get in touch with my feelings.

Feelings could wait. I had other thoughts that needed attention. Serious thoughts. Troubling thoughts.

Even if other-me ended Jack, maybe it wasn't over. If I was twinned, there could easily be other-Jacks in the world—just waiting for the signal to emerge from hiding. Yeah, so maybe when Jack's crew found out he was dead, they'd just defrost another one.

That sent a chill up my spine. A series of other-Jacks, just waiting for their turn to grab power and enslave normals. And they'd look like anyone. An endless stream of devils, lined up at hell's gate, eager to enter the world and try their hand at sick domination.

Great. The darkest of all futures.

But that led me to another thought. Exactly how many of me were there? Sonya and Peter could have deeper plans. An army of Wolfs in the world?

An endless stream of Jacks and Wolfs? Pitted against each other—forever?

I pictured a world full of unsuspecting normals, living as best they could, trapped on a jumper battlefield called Earth.

The world and my head just kept on spinning.

Sonya put a hand on my shoulder. We were drifting off course. Okay, so Kat needed some brain time again.

The future wasn't written. So maybe perseverating over it didn't matter? (Like I even knew that word.) Okay. So maybe I should just try to be me. Do my best. Learn what I could. Face hell if I needed to.

That could work.

Maybe being confused wasn't as bad as it seemed. I had Sonya—now an awkward gender arrangement, but my body had a way of changing. So I should relax and enjoy being female while it lasted. All bodies were temporary—even for normals.

Hell, everything in life was temporary.

So relax, Marko. If things were good, I'd enjoy it.

If I was confused, I could handle it.

And if I was already a lost cause—well, I'd just enjoy the ride to hell.

The End

About the Author

Visit BruceRousseau.com for more books by this author and join the mailing list for upcoming books.

To help others who might want to read this book, please post a review on the bookseller's website.

Bruce Rousseau is the author of the paranormal semi-superhero series *I, Target* and the unconventional mystery novel *French Tango*. He holds a degree in Drama from CSUS, and is a past member of the playwright group *Austin Script Works*.

Bruce was born in Fairbanks, Alaska and raised in California. He now resides in Texas with his fiancée and the usual literary helper cats.